S M Harrison was born in Manc[...] involved in mediaeval re-enactme[...] firstly as a founding member and [...] more recently as a member of the *Towton Battlefield Society* and its re-enactment arm *The Frei Compagnie,* re-creating both mediaeval combat and civilian life. In *A Rose of England* that experience is brought vividly to the page, bringing palpable realism to the towns, castles and battlefields of fifteenth century England during what is now known as *The Wars of the Roses*.

Also by S M Harrison:

Prequel to *A Rose Of England*
THE COLOUR OF TREASON

Featuring Jack de Laverton:
FOR KING AND COUNTRY

www.smharrisonwiter.com

S. M. HARRISON

A ROSE

OF

ENGLAND

A NOVEL OF THE WARS

OF THE ROSES.

First published in 2013 by *Kingmaker Press*.

A catalogue record for this book is available at the British Library.
ISBN-13: 978-1482646955

ISBN-10: 1482646951

W for Warwick, good with shield and other defence,
The boldest under banner in battle to abide;
For the right of England he doth his diligence,
Both by land and water, god be his guide!

Twelve Letters to Save England (1462)

Dedicated to the memory of Michael McNama.

ONE

FRANCE, JULY 1470

Elizabeth Hardacre snatched an urgent breath into her lungs. 'What if we are seen, Master Higgins?' she asked.

Higgins raised his thick grey brows. 'Seen, Elizabeth? Of course we shall be seen!'

Higgins had misunderstood her, but then he hadn't noticed the man follow them onto the boat at Dover; the man she knew she did not want as a witness.

Higgins leaned into her with the sway of the carriage. 'All will be well, Elizabeth,' he lisped. 'What could be more natural than offering your condolences and the condolences of your king?' He laid a gnarled hand on hers.

Elizabeth drew back from him into the close darkness of the carriage, still unwilling to tell him about the man she instinctively knew followed them to Valognes; the repulsive Higgins could not offer her comfort, only one man could do that and because of Higgins, her family and her own stupidity, she was about to betray him!

As the chariot took them through the curling cobbled streets to the exiled Duke and Duchess of Clarence's lodgings, an uneasy feeling began to grow within her, and Elizabeth knew it was not just from the closeness of Higgins; only a few days ago she had told Lord Wenlock, the Captain of Calais, that she was here only to comfort the Duchess of Clarence on the loss of her child and because of Elizabeth's past, Lord Wenlock had believed her! Elizabeth shuddered despite the summer heat; how many more lies and deceptions would there be before she could return home?

As soon as the chariot stopped Higgins opened the door, momentarily blinding Elizabeth with white sunlight. He hurried to confer with a slim man Elizabeth recognized: the Duke of Clarence's steward. She reached for the package concealed beneath her cloak, suddenly feeling its weight as though it would draw her down into Hell.

Higgins returned to the carriage and helped her down from it. The warm summer air was tempered by the smell of damp stone and the thick rich smell of roasting meat, which wafted down from the kitchens.

'Come, Elizabeth,' Higgins said brightly and offered her his arm.

Reluctantly Elizabeth took it, knowing that as they walked across the courtyard each step she took brought her closer to the dénouement of other people's plans she now wished to be no part of.

'We are fortunate, Elizabeth. The Duke of Clarence is at home.' Higgins smiled a lupine smile.

'Fortunate, indeed, Master Higgins,' she said without enthusiasm.

Higgins turned to her quickly. 'How else could your father's death be avenged, Elizabeth?' he asked sharply. Elizabeth sucked in her breath at the mention of her father; it was her promise, made to her father in his final hours, which had set her on this course.

'Elizabeth, answer me!' Higgins pushed. 'You know Warwick was to blame!'

'Does every death need to be avenged, Master Higgins?' she asked. She had once been as sure as Higgins and her family that the Earl of Warwick was culpable, but now, as the moment drew near, she was not so certain.

Higgins stopped walking and Elizabeth stood on the hem of her long gown.

'Christ's wounds, Elizabeth, how can you say such a thing? Your family all spoke as one! You know in this you have their blessing!'

'I know but...' she could not give voice to the doubts that were growing.

Higgins gripped her hand. 'Child, all will be well,' he said with surprising softness. 'I will be near. No harm shall befall you, I swear it!'

Elizabeth wasn't thinking of herself; she was thinking what the consequences might be for others. She drew her gaze up to his. 'Hasn't there been enough death, Master Higgins?'

'Exactly so, Elizabeth, and the only way to end this is to support King Edward. Only he can bring peace to England.'

Elizabeth fixed Higgins's eyes; for once he was speaking what he believed to be true.

'Come, no more of this,' he said gruffly. 'Let us go in.'

They turned towards a dark doorway over which the Duke of Clarence's banner hung, barely tugged by the breeze.

Once they were safely inside, beneath the glow of sooty lanterns, Higgins paused. 'Let me see the letter,' he said.

Elizabeth reached under her cloak and tore the flimsy pocket that had weighed on her so heavily. She pulled out the parchment. It was cold in her hand as she studied the large smear of blood-red wax that bore King Edward's mark. She handed it to Higgins. As she did so she noticed that there was something else there too. She frowned and Higgins marked her look of concern.

'What is it, Elizabeth?' he asked.

'Another letter for Clarence, from his mother perhaps,' she said, though the thumping of her heart told her she believed it was something very different. She took out the other letter and turned it over in her hand.

'Santa Maria!' she gasped, 'it is for the Earl of Warwick!'

* * *

'Please forgive the intrusion, mademoiselle,' the stranger breathed as he swept an elegant bow in the young servant girl's direction.

Cheeks flushing, she dropped a swift curtsey. 'You must be lost, my lord, for the Duke of Clarence's quarters are across the courtyard.'

The stranger followed the gaze of her wide blue eyes, noting the man and woman as they entered the Duke of Clarence's apartments, then he turned back to her. He smiled, held her gaze and then brushed a dark curl of hair away from his face slowly. 'It seems His Grace has enough company, and I would not wish to intrude,' he said smoothly. He bowed again to her as though she was the Queen of France. 'Enchanté, mademoiselle. Perhaps we shall meet again? I truly hope so.' Then he turned and strode away from her. After a few paces he paused and smiled at the girl over his shoulder and her cheeks flamed again.

* * *

'Why would King Edward write to the Earl of Warwick? Unless...unless he means to offer a pardon?' Elizabeth asked, staring at the letters as if they were apparitions. 'Surely he cannot believe Warwick would accept terms so given?' Elizabeth remembered King Edward at their parting. He had said 'letters' but she thought he had meant more than one for Clarence; it had never entered her head that he might write to Warwick too! Yet his seal was unmistakable, as was the name written in a scribe's clear hand.

Higgins frowned; evidently he was as puzzled as she was by the discovery. 'What you say would make sense,' he said solemnly. 'A pardon. I cannot think what else it might be.'

Elizabeth studied his face. This letter was Higgins's nightmare too – the last thing he wanted was for Warwick to be pardoned!

'He must never see it!' Higgins growled.

'But what if the letter contains something else – something we cannot discern? Then to not give the letter to Warwick, to deny King Edward the opportunity to score whatever points were intended, well that is... treason.'

'No!' Higgins replied. 'He must not see it!'

Yet the letter gave Elizabeth no less trouble. If she was brave or stupid enough to give Warwick the letter then he would ask her questions she would not want to answer. In short, he would learn of her meeting with King Edward and would he not guess what then had followed? But yet the letter bore Warwick's name, and it was right and proper that he received whatever King Edward might send, only then would he have the full picture of the situation. She killed the thoughts in her mind. How could she ever see Warwick again? How could she look at his face, knowing that he had failed both her and her father as Higgins had pointed out so eloquently?

But now Higgins was silent and Elizabeth thought it unusual that he offered no further guidance. King Edward had set them both a riddle that had no easy answer.

'Come,' Higgins said, suddenly animated, 'let us finish this.'

* * *

Elizabeth's mouth was dry. Would she be able to speak? Would she be expected to do so, or would Higgins deal with everything? Perhaps she could just curtsey, hand over the letter to the Duke of Clarence and then leave. But one glance at King Edward's spymaster told her that Master Higgins had no intention of letting her off so lightly. She was about to seek his reassurance when the large doors opened and the steward addressed them.

'His Grace will see you now,' he said.

Sweat trickled down Elizabeth's back; there was no returning to England now!

They were shown into a damask-curtained anteroom and then ushered closer, just beyond the threshold to the Duke of Clarence's rooms and Elizabeth wished that she was anywhere but here. She looked round nervously; servants slipped into the shadows and for a heartbeat she wondered whether one of them could be their pursuer.

Seeing her concern, Higgins nodded a warning and it brought to mind Elizabeth's purpose here with sharp clarity: this was a dangerous game and Elizabeth knew the consequences of playing the wrong card! Any one of these people could be the ears of the King of France, or the Earl of Warwick or even the King of England!

Shutters blocked out the fierce whiteness of the day. Heavy crimson tapestries cloaked the walls and Elizabeth wondered how many secret doors and passageways they concealed. How many clandestine trysts and covert meetings had occurred in this chamber? How many secrets had passed between friends and enemies? She could only guess at what this room had seen and now, like a theatre, it was to bear witness to another intrigue: her betrayal of the Earl of Warwick.

When they finally entered his apartments the Duke of Clarence had his back to them. He was talking with his manservant; he was cognizant of their presence yet he did not turn. Elizabeth had not really studied him before. He did not quite have his brother's stature, Elizabeth thought, and his hair was slightly fairer and more curly.

Suddenly he spun round on his heels; his fashionable short cloak swirled around him, glittering with gold and gems. A broad smile stretched his lips, his teeth showing like pearls. His blue eyes danced between Higgins and Elizabeth for a moment and then they alighted on Elizabeth and stayed there.

She curtseyed low and Higgins stepped back to bow beside her.

Clarence held out his jewelled hand to each of them in turn to kiss and as they did so they looked to each other questioningly.

'Well, what do we have here?' Clarence exclaimed, still studying Elizabeth. 'Visitors from England?'

5

'Your Grace,' Higgins began, but Clarence waved his ringed hand to silence him. 'Mistress?' he said enthusiastically.

His countenance might have reminded Elizabeth of his elder sibling, but there was wildness about his eyes that was different, a skittishness like that of a young colt, and it made Elizabeth wonder how Warwick could ever have trusted him. But then if she had not heard it spoken at court would she ever have believed that Warwick would have allied himself with Lancaster either? The truth seemed stranger than the Mysteries of York. Yet who was she to judge?

'Your Grace,' she began as she rose, 'I am Elizabeth Hardacre. I have come to seek your permission to visit the duchess; we are old acquaintances from Yorkshire and I served her also at Queenborough.' She almost added The Erber, Warwick's London home to the list, but to do so brought her too close to dangerous ground.

Clarence paused for a moment. 'You came via Calais?' he asked.

'Yes, Your Grace,' Elizabeth answered.

'Lord Wenlock agreed even though you came from my brother?'

'Yes, Your Grace,' Elizabeth said, trying not to choke on her guilt at the deceiving of Lord Wenlock.

Clarence continued to study her. 'You are the one who carried the letter from Middleham?' he asked slowly.

'Yes, Your Grace and I wish now to visit Her Grace at this sad time,' she added gently, mindful of the anonymous servants around them. She remembered the letter Clarence spoke of: a link in the chain that had arranged Isabel Neville's and Clarence's secret wedding. Part of her wished she had never seen the damned letter, let alone have delivered it, for that letter had been the start of everything!

Clarence's face became solemn. 'Indeed, you rightly remind me of the loss of our son,' he said sadly. 'I do believe the duchess would be glad of your company. Exile is not a pleasant estate.'

'Your Grace, I bring you something else...' Elizabeth said tentatively.

'Yes?' Clarence asked. He read the plea for privacy in her eyes. He dismissed the servants with a commanding nod.

Elizabeth reached into her cloak. 'It is from your brother, the king,' she said in a hushed tone that would not have been out of place at Ellerton Nunnery. She held out the sealed letter. She looked at her trembling hand as it met his, not daring to look at

6

his face. She wanted Clarence to be angry with her, to rebuke her, saying that he would have none of Edward or his letters, for he was Warwick's loyal son-in-law – but he did not; he was no more loyal to Warwick than she. Instead he reached out and snatched the letter from her. Then he turned his back to them again as he broke the seal, reading quickly.

Elizabeth and Higgins looked at each other. Higgins smiled reassuringly, but at that moment nothing in the world could comfort her, least of all Higgins's lupine grin; she was playing a part in the dismembering of Warwick's coalition and she loathed herself for it. She had wanted to do the right thing: make the right choice for once in her young life, but this did not feel right and she knew she would regret this always! Higgins's look of satisfaction was the twist of the knife in the wound; he had spent months planning for this, knowing that Clarence was teetering on the edge of loyalty and that this letter would bring him back to Edward, slaying Warwick's alliance as he did so. And Elizabeth was the instrument of it; gaining them swift entry past Lord Wenlock, for who would suspect Elizabeth of bringing harm to Warwick, her lover? Who here knew of the hurt that had been done to her; of the death of her father at Middleham and the promise she had given him as he lay dying? Her throat tightened: it was not easy to betray those she had once loved so dearly, whatever promise had been made and however much one's family and one's king wished it so.

Clarence finished reading and he turned again to face them. His face was stern but his eyes flashed with a fire that revealed his thoughts before he spoke them.

Clarence turned to Elizabeth. Taking her aside he whispered: 'My lady, you may say to my brother that I do love him well and that it would please me to come home as he begs me to do. But it cannot be now. I am vulnerable at present. My wife cannot travel and her father is close by. But when the moment is right – and it shall be right – then I shall come to him. You must tell him this yourself for I fear to write it. My lord of Warwick has spies too.' Then he stepped away from Elizabeth. She shuddered at Clarence's words of warning and the man on the boat came to her mind again.

Higgins looked relieved, but Elizabeth wanted to strike Clarence's untrustworthy face. How could he change sides so easily? Was he not of noble birth? Would he not still have power and status under a Lancastrian regime? Had he not become the heir to much of Warwick's estates and fortune when he had married his daughter Isabel? And did he take King Edward for a complete fool? Did he think Edward would ever favour him with any real power after his desertion to Lancaster with Warwick? Elizabeth did not think so, even though she was sure Clarence would blame everything on Warwick. But then wasn't she betraying Warwick for her family too?

Abruptly Clarence looked at her. 'Will you do this, Mistress Hardacre?' he asked, fixing her face intently. 'Will you speak to my brother?'

She bowed her head, which he took as a sign of respect but which was in truth because she could not bear to look on him any longer. 'I shall, Your Grace,' she said. The words almost stole her breath.

As she walked slowly from the room Elizabeth hated Clarence for his weakness, she hated Higgins for his cunning, but most of all she hated herself. How could obeying one's dying father and grieving mother bring such pain?

Her stomach twisted into knots as she walked blindly beside Higgins. All she could think of was Warwick. Right at the core of her, right at the centre of her being there was something that would not let go of him, something that was holding tightly to the memory of what had passed between them; of what they had meant to each other. As if she was riding a wild horse, this part of her held on more tightly the more impossible the journey became, clinging to some unseen hope. And as she slipped closer to the moment of Warwick's demise, that small grain of hope was her only comfort.

Higgins smiled wolfishly as they entered the hallway. 'That was elegantly done, Elizabeth,' he said.

Elizabeth spun round. 'I hope you are satisfied,' she hissed, 'for that is the last thing I will do for you or King Edward! I have done as you wished; now you will take me home to Lazenby as you promised.' Tears stung her eyes. She hoped her family would be happy now that she had fulfilled her oath; hoped that she could forget the terrible deed she had just done and return to some kind of peace in England.

'Oh, no Elizabeth,' Higgins said, taking hold of her' arm and turning her to face him.

'No?' Elizabeth jumped at the word.

'You will do whatever I ask of you in the king's name. I must learn as much as I can about Warwick's invasion plans, and you will ensure we have a reason for being here! There are men I must meet and letters I must send, but be assured, Elizabeth, I shall not be far away.'

For a moment Elizabeth gaped at him. Why had she ever expected Higgins to keep his word?

He said nothing, a smirk claiming his weather-beaten face.

Eventually she found her voice. 'You should remember, Master Higgins, that I still have the king's other letter!' She saw him flinch.

'Do whatever you must,' he said sourly. He tried to sound nonchalant, but Elizabeth knew he was torn almost as much as she was. The possibility of a pardon for Warwick was more than Higgins could face.

'For now, I shall do nothing,' she said, 'but remember that it is still a card I can play, and for us not to deliver it goes against the king's wishes, something I would like to see you explain to him. If you do not take me to Lazenby then I will have no choice but to surrender the letter to my lord of Warwick!'

ANGERS CATHEDRAL JULY 1470

The carriages left them at the foot of the Montée St-Maurice. Richard Neville, Earl of Warwick looked up and saw the grand façade. Bathed in warm sunshine, two elegant gothic towers of cream stone with tops as pointed as sharpened swords completed the impressive visage. Gold glittered at their pinnacles and Warwick had to blink and turn away from the blinding reflections. Beneath the towers the tympanum showed the brightly painted figures of St John's vision in the Book of Revelation: Christ in Majesty holding the Book of Life, flanked by the symbols of each of the four Apostles. Warwick looked down, unsettled by the gravity of the symbolism above him.

Crowds had gathered to cheer their progress and Warwick's heart quickened as the noise grew louder with the royal party's approach. Banners bearing the fleur-de-lys of France and the swan of Anjou had been hung from every half-timbered jetty.

9

Smiling faces peered from every window and waved from each newly swept street. Warwick kissed the hand of a little girl who was sitting on her father's shoulders and touched his hat to every woman he saw. He walked slowly at the side of the countess. He was conscious that she was struggling to maintain her dignity because of the voluminous brocade of her gown and the slipperiness of the red woollen cloth that carpeted the whole length of the street up to the cathedral. She held the black damask of her gown with one hand, revealing a flicker of red silk kirtle as she walked. Her other hand reached for the crook of his arm to steady herself. How he wished it were Elizabeth who was by his side now. He swallowed against a tight throat; he must not show any weakness. Not today. He smiled broadly to the cheering onlookers as he followed King Louis and his brother Charles up the hill. Both were wearing the ceremonial vestments of bishops of France. Immediately behind them was the slender silhouette of Marguerite d'Anjou and at her side the portly Edouard, as dark as she was fair.

And still the crowds cheered. Warwick knew why – these were Marguerite's people and they wanted her once again to be Queen of England. He wondered whether they also cheered for the recent betrothal between their prince and his daughter; the surety on the bargain he was about to make.

He looked at Marguerite again; a small black and ermine clad figure not ten paces ahead of him. By Christ she was proud! These might be her people but she did not acknowledge them as Warwick and his countess did. She walked confidently ahead, her eyes fixed firmly on the church's façade, her neck and back stiff and straight. She had not changed, he concluded, and that was what worried him. Throughout all their negotiations he had not seen one flicker of good humour or compassion. There had not been one sign of any remorse or regret, not for anything. King Louis had of course been at his flattering best and had coaxed and cajoled her as he always did and so she had at last agreed to most of Warwick's terms. But there had not been one smile, not one admission of even perhaps the slightest error on her part. Not only that, there was one condition she would still not agree to – she would not agree to her son, Edouard of Lancaster, accompanying Warwick's campaign. He understood the rationale: if Edouard was lost then so was the Lancastrian cause, but the lack of a royal figurehead was a disadvantage Warwick did not

10

need; King Henry would only be a rallying point for the staunchest Lancastrians. Warwick needed broader appeal if he was to maintain power, and the young prince of Lancaster could provide it. Louis had not completely given up hope, but Warwick doubted if even he could persuade the haughty Marguerite to change her mind.

The congregation was waiting for them as they entered the cathedral, and it reminded Warwick of a wedding, and was this alliance not a wedding of sorts between him and proud Marguerite? But what a congregation this was, too. Bright as peacocks the French nobility stood in gaily-coloured rows. Their jewellery flashed and glittered in the rainbow-tinted sunlight that streamed in through the Norman windows. They bowed and curtseyed as the entourage passed, lowering their heads in obeisance.

Warwick gazed upwards to the remarkable Angevin vaulted ceiling, built, like most of this cathedral, by Marguerite's ancestors. The mark of Anjou was everywhere and Warwick felt it, as though two giant hands were pressing down on his shoulders.

At last Warwick stood before the glittering altar. Above him, at either side of the transept, were two magnificent rose windows of red and blue glass. Delicate dappled patterns of coloured light spread upon the floor like a carpet, so that he stood within the filigreed outline of the rose. How the magic of the rose would bless this union, Warwick thought, making it even more solemn and binding. He noticed the images of the north window in particular – the judgement of Christ. How apt he thought: Christ displaying his wounds surrounded by the catastrophes of the world and he, Warwick, displaying his soul before God and the nobility of France, surrounded by the catastrophe of his Yorkist past!

As they brought the holy relic towards him Warwick closed his eyes in reverence. The smooth wood was warm to his touch and he let his fingers rest on it gently, feeling the softness of its age; just an ordinary piece of wood, yet this was the most important piece of wood in Christendom: a piece of the true cross: 'The Cross de St Laud d'Angers', part of the cross on which Christ had died. He knew of its reputed terrible power: anyone perjuring himself on this cross would die within a year. Watchful eyes weighed upon him like stones; wordlessly they conveyed a thousand thoughts from the onlookers, some of which scorched his mind.

And so, on his knees before the altar he swore. He, Warwick, swore to abandon his Yorkist past and take up the once-hated cause of Lancaster. As he breathed in the pungent incense he thought of his father and his brother, murdered at Wakefield as they fought for York. He thought on his cousin of Brancepath, who had raised the Lancastrian flag only a twelvemonth gone, and whom he had executed for doing so. But most of all his thoughts flew to Anne; sweet Anne who must henceforth be an unwanted guest in Marguerite's household, now that she was formally betrothed. He knew Anne's days would be filled with taunts and jibes and her nights with Edouard of Lancaster... he could not yet think on.

He sighed. Sweat came to his brow and began to trickle down the back of his neck as he spoke the words like a mummer in a play, aware of the illustrious audience eating his words with satisfaction as if they were sweetmeats. The gravity of this oath weighed at his shoulders, like arming himself in new harness for the first time. He let his breath out slowly. This was the most important oath of his life; one he knew he would never break.

As he rose there was a shiver of whispers, which echoed like the murmur of the sea in the cavernous cathedral. He looked up at the painted walls and he saw Christ looking down on him. Would he now be favoured by heaven, he wondered. Or had he committed the act that would eventually lead to his death, and the loss of those who were with him?

As she came forward in a rustle of silk, he saw that Marguerite d'Anjou also felt the importance of the moment. Her eyes, though hostile to him, flickered about the church nervously and he saw her hand tremble as she placed it on the relic. Her once clear voice was indistinct, and even though he was close to her, he could only just discern her promise: to treat Warwick as a true and faithful subject and never to reproach him for past deeds. He wondered if she would keep it. Could she, once England was taken? If ever he wanted to see England again he had to believe it would be so.

As she rose, soaring choral voices proclaimed their union, like a marriage, and there was a palpable flutter of relief amongst the congregation.

King Louis too looked relieved as he swept them out of the cathedral and on to the celebratory banquet.

Warwick looked at the fine red carpet at his feet. He did not want to move; something inside him told him that to leave the comfort of the cathedral was to take the first step of his final journey; the power of the Cross weighed on his mind. He breathed deeply, swallowed down the fear and followed King Louis through the blur of onlookers.

He stepped out into the sunlight, which stabbed at his eyes so that he raised a hand to shield them. He sucked in his breath, grateful for the clean air. Gaudy colours swayed before him like a flock of popinjays and proud French voices cheered them as they made their progress back towards the castle.

Warwick's head swam and he stumbled.

'My lord?' Thomas was at his shoulder. 'My lord are you ill?'

Warwick stopped for a moment. He stared unseeing at Thomas and then the boy's face came into focus: faithful Thomas Conyers who had first brought Elizabeth to Warwick Castle.

'No, Thomas,' he said shakily, 'I am not ill, but I feel like a songbird in a gilded cage. All stare at me, all want me to sing, but no one trusts me to be free to do so! And for my part, Thomas, I am heart sick of staring at the bars of my prison, however beautifully decorated they are.' He smiled at Thomas's concern. 'I am not ill, Thomas,' he said softly, 'but I shall be glad to be away from here.'

Warwick shook his head to waken his senses and then strode after King Louis. Finally the alliance was sealed, Warwick thought, but would it last long enough to put Henry back on the English throne?

* * *

Though it had only been a matter of days, to Warwick his time in Angers had seemed like a lifetime, but at last he was able to feel the girth of his horse beneath him and what gentle breath of breeze there was in this summer heat tugged at his dark hair. King Louis had wanted him to ride in one of the golden carriages 'like the prince he was' but Warwick had told him that he wanted to travel to Carentan 'like the solder he was' for it was as a soldier and not a prince that he would take England! King Louis had frowned but had decided to let Warwick have his way in this,

13

when there were bigger things at stake; not least the fact that the dispensation had still not come. There was no marriage of his daughter Anne and Prince Edouard, only a betrothal; a betrothal Warwick had argued Marguerite could end at any time! King Louis had smiled serenely; 'Richard, I would never allow that to happen!' he had said, as though it was the contract for the purchase of hounds or horses, though he had added: 'and I am certain neither would the church or people of France! The oaths have been given in Angers cathedral; there could not have been more witnesses, Richard!' Warwick had no choice but to trust in King Louis; he could not await the Pope's pleasure in this. He had known it would be difficult – even with King Louis's gold to smooth the way, but England would not wait: even now his brother Fitzhugh was stirring the north, even now Edward would be facing the same dilemma he had faced a year ago and even now he would make the wrong decision, no doubt against Lord Hastings's advice!

Warwick pulled his hat lower on his head to shade his eyes from the sun; he already had the tanned features of a mariner, he thought, and if he looked like a cooked lobster at their journey's end it would only make King Louis right about his riding, and he couldn't have that, though by the amount of dust being thrown up by the horses he was likely to look like a shrouded man when they finally reached their destination. But wasn't that what he already was? He had always been prepared to meet death, whenever it found him; had he not seen often enough how quickly life could be snatched away? But somehow he knew he would know the hour of his passing and he knew it would not be in his sleep! He would not have it any other way; he would go in the midst of life: in the act of living! And who would mourn his passing? His family? His men? His country? He could not be certain; for all these would judge him on his success or failure in this enterprise! Only one person would mourn the man, and God alone knew where she was! As God alone knew if he would reap success or failure against the boy he had loved as his own! He raised his hand to shoo away the buzzing flies; God – he could not think like this; if he doubted himself how would others believe in him? Like his daughter Anne as she joined herself to Edouard of Lancaster, he had to buckle on his Neville war-harness against the world and keep it there, for without Elizabeth there was no one with whom he could share his misgivings, so for the sake of his sanity he must deny their existence!

Carentan was everything Warwick remembered; with its two churches, one recently built by the English, and a castle containing a palace fit for any king, glimmering in the summer sunshine like a large sugar subtlety! It was beautiful, it was luxurious, but Warwick could take no comfort in either fact.

'Everything is to your liking, Richard?' King Louis asked graciously after they had retired to his private chamber after dinner. The casements lay open and a gentle breeze fanned the many candles into glittering dancers and the golden tapestries shimmered as if they were alive.

Warwick smiled; sunburn stung his cheeks and he knew Louis had noticed it. 'Everything is as it should be,' he said smoothly. 'Thank you.'

Louis stroked his hand along his alaunt's silky neck; he loved his dogs more than his people, Warwick thought as he watched the caress.

'But you are not content?' Louis asked.

'You know, I think, what haunts me,' Warwick said. He sipped the cool sweet wine, trying not to be drawn into a debate.

'Failure haunts your mind, my friend,' Louis replied, 'but you have no cause for such thoughts. You are the greatest Earl of Warwick there has been; *you* are the greatest knight, whatever your countess may say and *you* are the greatest man; for although your father-in-law won the hearts of Saracens and Christians alike with his jousting prowess, his honeyed words and rich gifts, he did not make and unmake kings as you do! He did not change the destiny of England, my friend as you shall. History will remember you.'

For a moment Warwick was stunned into silence by his friend's perception. He cleared his throat to speak, but Louis held up his hand.

'Say nothing on this; we both know I am right. You have no cause to doubt yourself, Richard, I know you are the one man who can achieve this; say nothing, it is best.'

Warwick swallowed more wine; in truth it was easier than speaking. Louis gave a small gesture and soft music flowed into the room. Warwick listened in silence to the melody and suddenly realized it was one he knew well! His heart missed a beat for was this not the song of Guillaume de Machaut? Were these not the gentle words he had written to Elizabeth inside the beautiful jewel he had given her? He began to panic at the rising emotion the lovers' words evoked. Not here. Not now. Not in front of Louis!

'Are you well, Richard?' Louis asked perceptively. 'Perhaps too much sun, non? You should have ridden in the carriage with me.'

Warwick met his friend's eyes; could he see more than Warwick wanted him to? 'Perhaps you are right,' Warwick said in a tight voice. 'There will not be so much sun in England!'

King Louis laughed. 'How right you are, Richard. The 'sun in splendour' will be gone!'

Warwick forced a laugh too, still struggling to control the feelings the music had exposed. At this moment Edward, the 'sun in splendour', would be heading north, which was exactly what Warwick wanted him to do. And was that where Elizabeth was also? 'There must be no more delay,' Warwick said, suddenly killing the thought. 'I shall leave in the morning!'

'So soon, Richard? The Pope may yet oblige us! Wait a little longer, I beg you.'

Warwick set his jaw. The task ahead of him was not an easy one, more akin to a labour of Hercules than anything he had yet achieved, but it would be easier to accomplish without the distractions of Louis, Marguerite and their preening courtiers! 'I must ride before the week is out, my liege, with or without the marriage,' he said then added, 'and I must speak with the Duke of Clarence.' He paused, knowing that he should perhaps have used the word 'console'. 'I need to be in England.'

'Ah, Richard, I understand,' Louis answered with a nod. 'Only you can smooth this road the Angels would fear to tread!'

LONDON JULY 1470

William Hastings, the Lord Chamberlain of England bowed low before his sovereign. 'My liege, it is Fitzhugh of Ravensworth,' he said flatly. 'He is in rebellion.' So short a sentence yet such invidious words, he thought.

King Edward's dark blue eyes flamed. 'Fitzhugh? Rebellion? By Christ, Will, how many brothers-in-law does Warwick have?'

Hastings's cheeks began to burn at the insinuation, for he was Warwick's brother-in-law too, but Edward was oblivious to the slur. Hastings was glad that they were alone in Edward's apartments for the revelation that Warwick had raised the north of England against Edward while in exile in France was not something he wanted to discuss with the popinjay courtiers hanging on every word.

'It seems that every part of the north opposes me, but I'll have none of it!' Edward hissed. 'What does our new Earl of Northumberland have to say for himself?' he asked, folding his arms across his broad chest as though he was one of the biblical characters captured in the tapestries that sparkled around them.

'Lord Percy says he cannot quell the insurrection, my liege.'

'Cannot? And do you believe him?'

Hastings knew Edward wasn't really asking for his opinion.

'And Montagu?' Edward continued, unfolding his arms. 'He is in the north recruiting men, can he not finish this?'

Hastings raised an eyebrow at Edward's naivety. Well he remembered John Neville's part in holding the north for Edward, both in the infancy of Edward's reign and latterly as the Earl of Northumberland; but did Edward really expect Montagu to rush to the aid of Percy now – when his precious earldom had been returned to the Lancastrian family who fought against them at bloody Towton?

'We have not heard from Montagu, my liege, but I will send to him if you wish.'

'Do so,' Edward sighed. 'I think Montagu were a better Northumberland!' He turned away from Hastings and began to pace the rich Arabic carpet.

Hastings saw this was a dark road Edward was about to travel; there was no place now for regrets – they had to make the best of everything if they were to hold onto the crown.

'My liege, you had no choice but to return the earldom to Percy!' he offered.

'Oh there is always a choice Will,' Edward said sourly, 'but I have made that choice already. I cannot put Percy back in prison can I?'

'Of course not!' Hastings said. 'But you could not have all the north under Neville command. If John Neville turns against you...'

Edward spun round. Fierce eyes slew the sentence. 'Stop!' he snapped. 'Do not apply a treasonous spirit to my cousin Montagu just because he bears the name of Neville. He could have joined with Warwick long before now. He made his choice, Will, and he chose to stand with me! He is an outcast of his own blood because of that choice, and how did I repay him? By restoring the Earldom of Northumberland to Percy.'

Edward reached for wine and threw it into his throat as if it would wash the Percy name from his lips. 'You know how far back the Percy-Neville hatred goes, Will. Christ God! It's what won us the first battle at St Albans. Do you think Warwick would have been so keen to fight in those narrow streets if he had not known the Percys were the prize?'

Hastings lowered his eyes from the intensity of Edward's. 'I do not know, Sire. I only know that you have rewarded John Neville immensely. By Christ he is now a marquis!'

Edward dragged a deep sigh from his lungs. 'I know you do not trust him, Will. But I still say he would have held the north more strongly for me than does Percy! Aye Percy has his earldom back, but it was I who took it from him in the first place, and he has had nigh on nine years in captivity to reflect upon that!'

Silence as heavy as thunder settled between them. The evening candles guttered in their sconces in the light summer breeze that brought with it the scent of the river.

Hastings knew what Edward was thinking and he was afraid of it.

'I shall go north myself,' Edward said calmly.

Hastings let out a long slow breath through his teeth: it was as he'd feared. He strove to quieten his hammering heart. 'Let Montagu do it, my lord. There is no need for you to dirty your hands. Warwick could land any day,' he said slowly. 'If you go north who will keep the south safe if Warwick returns from France? Who will hold London?' He looked up at Edward and shot him a pleading look.

Edward smiled sardonically. 'Last year, Will, I was slow to react to a northern threat; I hesitated and it almost brought my ruin. I shall not be caught in London with a rebel army advancing to my gates. If we move quickly then we will be back before Warwick comes; he may join this insurrection and shun the Cinque Ports of the south – then what would you say? I think Fitzhugh will not stand long when he realizes he has a Royal army coming for him!'

'My liege you cannot go. You cannot leave London. I know Warwick will come for London; it is the greatest prize. It is like leaving your jewel box open and the door unlocked!'

18

Edward's eyes flashed angrily. 'I *shall* go, my lord chamberlain! I shall show my strength to the people of England and then if Warwick does come perhaps they will be more circumspect about supporting him!' His lips curled as he spoke and Hastings knew that he would not change his king's mind. A cruel light lingered in his eyes and Hastings realized that Edward wanted to prove himself, wanted to banish the demons of the year before when Warwick had all but held him prisoner to his will at Middleham. He wanted the rebels to fracture before *him*, not Percy or Montagu!

'Ned, there is no need...' Hastings began. But Edward trampled his words in a fury that surprised him.

'There is *every* need, Will!' he blazed.

And Hastings saw that the need was Edward's. This was all about his humiliation at Olney following Robin of Redesdale's uprising, when the Nevilles had captured him almost alone; deserted by his men at the threat of Warwick's coming; this was about settling a score: Edward wanted revenge. Edward plainly knew this new threat was Warwick's doing, knew the strategy was as brilliant as before, involving Neville adherents in Yorkshire and Cumbria, but still he would go north in full harness whether the rebels remained or not, to show the restless northerners that they would not catch their king sleeping like a cat before a warm hearth again; this cat had unsheathed his claws.

Hastings bowed apologetically. 'It shall be as you wish,' he said. 'I shall make the arrangements.'

As he left his king a knot constricted his stomach; he hoped that Edward was right and that they could travel to Yorkshire and return before Warwick came from France. The alternative was unthinkable.

VALOGNES AUGUST 1470

Elizabeth closed her eyes and listened. Tentatively she pushed at the door, secretly hoping it would be locked and barred from her. It was not. Sweet incense floated to her in a smoky draught and its effect was instant: memories she had cloaked in grief and hate and simple forgetfulness gathered like revenants in her mind. Her lip trembled. Her hand shook. She wanted to turn and run and now that her letters had been delivered to the Duke of Clarence there was surely no need for this charade - the charade of comforting Isabel! But she knew that was not true; Higgins had made it plain they were going to stay and she knew she had a meagre choice: to play the game by his rules or do the one thing she knew she was incapable of and confess to what they had done. She took a composing breath and stepped into the room.

Though Elizabeth had been in Valognes for almost a week, this was the first time Isabel had agreed to her request to see her; she had apparently been either too tired or too ill to do so but Elizabeth wondered if there was something else, something she dare not think on. She clasped her hands together and walked forward into the half-light.

Isabel lay like a raggedy doll amidst a cloud of pillows, her dark hair lank and her eyes hollow and shadowed.

Elizabeth moved forward slowly, shaken by the change in her friend. She said a silent prayer that her visit might do some good; was it not the way that the women suffered most when their men-folk's pride would allow no compromise?

Isabel looked up. She did not smile or offer other greeting, as if she could not see Elizabeth at all. She stayed as she was, silent and wounded.

'Your Grace,' Elizabeth said as she curtseyed.

Isabel did not move, as though she was not only blind and mute, but deaf also.

Elizabeth swallowed dryly; could grief change someone so completely?

'Your Grace, I am come from England,' she said, still kneeling.

'England?' Isabel queried, as though she was trying to recall the place from a distant dream.

'Yes, Your Grace. It is I, Elizabeth. Do you remember me, Your Grace?'

Isabel moved against her pillows, trying to sit up.

Elizabeth hurried to help her and at last their eyes met. Quickly Elizabeth lowered hers; the power of dark Neville eyes was something she did not seek.

'You?' Isabel said. 'You - dare to come here?' The tone of her voice was as flat and dark as shadow.

Elizabeth looked down while she gathered her thoughts; she had never imagined how difficult this would be. And if this was hard, how before God would she ever face Warwick again? She swallowed dryly. 'I heard of your loss, Isabel and came from England to do whatever I can for you.' If she could offer some comfort, would that not make some amends for the hurt that would so surely follow?

'How did you hear?' Isabel asked warily. 'Were you at court?'

Elizabeth nodded; she found it impossible to look at Isabel's face. 'I was on an errand for my father.' That much at least was true.

'And did dear brother Edward let you come to me?' Isabel asked sourly.

'He did, Your Grace,' Elizabeth said, still struggling to look at her. 'He sends his condolences and his good wishes for your return to good health.' Part of her wanted to tell Isabel everything Edward had said, but she knew that was impossible; one did not divulge the secrets of a king!

'So, you think him not such a bad brother after all?' Isabel asked brusquely.

Elizabeth shrugged. What could she say about the loathsome Edward who had offered her himself as reward? He was no more wretched than she was, perhaps less so! 'I do not think my opinion of him matters; it is what your father and husband think that is important.'

Isabel sighed. 'My father no longer holds him dear, though in truth Elizabeth, I no longer care what they think. I am heartsick of politics. It is true that I once wished to be a queen, who would not? But I have paid the ultimate price for my ambition, Elizabeth, the loss of my son!' Isabel's voice cracked and tears came to her eyes.

Elizabeth's heart squeezed; she too understood loss. 'Oh Isabel, I am so sorry,' she said and placed her hand on Isabel's arm.

Isabel began to sob.

Elizabeth pulled her closer. 'You cannot easily withdraw, Your Grace,' Elizabeth said softly, 'your father and husband will need your support.' The irony struck Elizabeth like a slap! She had chosen her family over Warwick, yet she was urging Isabel to support him! No, it was not hypocrisy, for there was still something deep within her that had never let go of Warwick; part of her still wanted Warwick to win and the revelation stunned her.

Isabel drew back from her, her tears momentarily controlled. Her dark eyes fixed Elizabeth's. 'Is that what you really bring, Elizabeth? Support for my father?' A smile twitched the corner of Isabel's mouth. 'I doubt that came from Edward!'

Elizabeth studied the counterpane. 'No Your Grace, it did not.'

Isabel shifted her weight on the bed. She leaned forward, locking on to Elizabeth's gaze. 'You love my father do you not?' she asked.

Elizabeth swallowed hard and tried desperately to read Isabel's face, but just as Warwick did, Isabel had rendered it inscrutable.

Elizabeth bowed her head. 'I never meant to hurt anyone; you must believe me, Isabel. I never set out to love him, I swear it.'

'And for all that time I thought it was someone in his household who held your heart. You must have thought me a complete fool, railing against your lover and all the while it was the earl!'

Elizabeth looked up. 'Never, Isabel. But I meant no harm...I could not help it.' Elizabeth wanted to explain, but how did one explain what had happened? Or what had happened since? 'I wanted to tell you, Isabel, truly I did. But somehow I could not find the right words...the right moment.'

'There are no right words,' Isabel said. 'And before God it cannot ever be right.'

Elizabeth's heart thumped at her throat.

'But it was his choice to make,' she continued 'and I cannot judge him in that.'

Elizabeth stared at Isabel. What did she mean?

'For all his ambition, wealth and power Elizabeth, the one thing my father never attained before was love.'

Elizabeth's heart stopped. What was Isabel saying? What of Higgins's revelation that had broken her heart?

'But your half-sister?' Elizabeth stammered.

Isabel wrinkled her nose. 'Margaret?'

'Yes.'

Isabel shook her head. 'You know what men are, Elizabeth! He cannot have been above fifteen when she was conceived for he was in the wild county of Cumbria. It is a mistake many men make in their growth to manhood; though for some it is not such a mistake, it is a habit – how many bastards does the king have now? Three? And how many men come to their marriages as innocent as they expect their brides to be?'

Elizabeth could hardly take in her words. Speech certainly would not come to her. So it had not been a love to be jealous of as Higgins had said: Warwick had not lied to her!

Elizabeth stared at Isabel through tear-filled eyes.

'You have brought my father happiness in a time of trouble,' Isabel said. 'I think he never truly knew it before he found you.'

'But – but the countess?' Elizabeth stammered.

'The Beauchamps were very proud, Elizabeth,' Isabel continued. 'My Grandfather, Richard Beauchamp, was called 'The Greatest Knight' in his time. He was known from Jerusalem to Constantinople for his chivalrous deeds and his jousting prowess; his chapel at Warwick is the finest in the land; how could the Nevilles ever be the Beauchamps' equals? How dare they set their ambition so high? And did my mother not often tell my father so? She even plans to proclaim her father's deeds in manuscript so his heirs will be proud of their Beauchamp lineage! My father can never live up to my grandsire's name in her eyes. Perhaps even now this is why he strives ever harder to advance the Neville's cause and will not bow to fickle Edward! He dare not fail the Warwick legend, you see?'

Elizabeth put her hand to her face in disbelief. Why had she not trusted the soft words Warwick had spoken to her, why had she not believed in his sincerity? No, she had believed perfidious Higgins instead! Oh what a fool she had been!

'Will you not go to him?' Isabel asked. 'There has been enough grief, enough loss,' she said wearily. 'Let there be some joy for once!'

'He – he is here?' A sudden surge of emotion tightened Elizabeth's chest and she fought to push it down, down into her stomach so that it might not engulf her. Santa Maria, how could she face him? 'I – I cannot. For we cannot be seen together Isabel; it is impossible.'

Isabel frowned. 'No Elizabeth you are wrong, so very wrong,' she said.

Elizabeth looked down, trying to pull her scattered wits together.

The silence that fell seemed infinite, but Elizabeth did not have the strength to break it; she was using all her resolve to hold back the tears still stinging her eyes.

'Elizabeth you must see him,' Isabel said. 'You should trust in him. Only he can return us to England and the land to peace.'

Wasn't that what Higgins had said about Edward - that he was the only man who could bring peace to England?

Elizabeth looked at her friend; Elizabeth admired her – in spite of her everything she still believed in her father, when she could so easily have held him responsible for all her woes, as Elizabeth had done!

Elizabeth rose from the bed. 'I do believe in him, Isabel,' she said. 'It is myself I doubt.'

Isabel said nothing but gently shook her head and sighed.

'Adieu, Isabel,' Elizabeth said and kissed her cheek, 'you must get some sleep. It was I who was supposed to bring you comfort!'

'Adieu,' Isabel replied. 'Seek love while you still may,' she advised with a gentle smile.

Elizabeth smiled thinly and then returned to the hallway.

Tears welled in her eyes again. Blindly she walked back towards the entrance. It was all she could do to stop herself from running, though she wasn't entirely sure from whom she was running! Warwick? Higgins? She sniffed back the tears; it would not do to let Higgins see her like this. But what did that matter now? Her hands balled into white fists. A plague on Higgins! Why had she ever listened to him? Why had she done as he and the king asked? She knew she had done so to appease her family, but here in France, the revenge they craved no longer seemed a good enough reason for what she had done.

'Have you forgotten me so soon, Elizabeth?' The soft, deep resonance of the voice stopped Elizabeth in her tracks. Her breathing quickened. She closed her eyes and swallowed hard. Not now, she thought, please God, not now!

She had dreaded this possibility from the moment she had agreed to leave England with Higgins but now, with Isabel's revelations scorching her mind, this was the last thing she needed. How could she face him after what she had done? God's breath, how little faith she had had in him! She heard his footsteps coming closer.

'Can you not look at me, sweeting?' his voice wavered a little as he spoke. 'Are we strangers to each other?'

Elizabeth smelled his familiar scent and her heart squeezed. God in heaven! Her shoulder warmed under his hand and she felt a gentle pressure as he turned her round to face him. One more step and she would be in his arms. Slowly she opened her eyes and looked up to meet his face. There was grief in his eyes but she saw also a longing that she could only have dreamed of. And there inside her was the flame. He had lit it; re-kindled what she had thought was dead – but how?

'Richard,' she whispered. Blood rushed to her cheeks. She had no time to say or do anything; he pulled her to him fiercely and his mouth came down on hers. She leant against his body and for

24

the first time since her father's death she knew comfort and love, and for a perfect moment, there was nothing else, just the bliss of their reunion. Then gently, reluctantly, he drew back from her a little. His eyes met hers. It took all Elizabeth's strength to stay there, to meet those dark eyes and not shatter like glass in front of him.

'How do you come to be here?' he asked her at last.

Elizabeth bowed her head; the guilt of her meeting with Clarence stabbed her, a blow that caught the pit of her stomach. She knew she should tell him the truth, but how could she explain? She tried to remember why she was here: her family had set her on this path. As Higgins had pointed out, this was the only way to return to them.

'I came...' she staggered clumsily over the words, 'for Isabel. I could not...' she swallowed as the sentence tried to strangle her, 'let you know of it.'

'No, of course not,' he said. He lifted her chin gently and Elizabeth's stomach curled at the perfection of the smile he gave her. 'I am glad that you are here,' he breathed.

Elizabeth wanted to confess to what she had done, but how could she? How could she hurt him when he was so vulnerable to such an attack? He was an exile, a fugitive, a man with a price on his head! She choked it all down. She could not make this right between them. If she loved him at all she would end it now!

'I cannot stay,' she said sharply, 'it would not be right.'

'It would be right for you to stay with Isabel would it not?' he asked. He looked puzzled.

'Perhaps,' she said curtly. 'But the countess made it clear I should not be here – with your family.' She looked at him defiantly, almost daring him to make her stay. But how could she stay, much as she wanted to, how could she even face him when she knew she had failed him so completely?

'Ah the countess,' he said. 'Ellerton Nunnery?'

Elizabeth nodded; her dry throat prevented her from saying anything more about how she almost died at Ellerton Nunnery, a sojourn arranged for her by Warwick's countess.

'I cannot imagine you in a nunnery.' He smiled. 'Well, we must not displease the countess!' Warwick gave a throaty laugh that made Elizabeth shiver with pleasure in spite of her despair.

25

Warwick saw it. 'I have missed you so much,' he whispered and then kissed her gently. 'I always hoped I would see you again before...' He left the sentence hanging.

'Before you invade England?' Elizabeth ventured. 'It is no secret, Richard; London is full of talk of it. You are expected.'

'Expected am I?' he asked. 'Well, they had better expect the worst, for I am in no mood to play games with Edward this time!'

Elizabeth saw the passion in his eyes: he would stop at nothing to bring Edward down; but without Clarence, was it possible? And Edward's pardon, if that was what it was, would surely be best left unopened? Perhaps she was right to keep that from him also.

Warwick recovered himself. 'I am sorry, Elizabeth,' he said more softly. 'I am sorry we have been apart for so long.' He looked into her eyes. 'When I have taken England you must come to me. I shall send for you and you will live like a queen.'

For a blissful heartbeat Elizabeth considered the impossible picture he painted for her; the perfect existence she knew could never be theirs. Then she killed it in her mind as she should have done long ago. She had to end this now, for both their sakes!

'I have no wish to live so,' Elizabeth said with forced conviction. 'I shall be glad when this is all over and I can return to Yorkshire and what is left of my family!' she said.

Warwick frowned. 'What do you mean sweeting? What has happened?'

Elizabeth drew her eyes up to his. Could he really be ignorant of what had befallen her father?

His eyes were wide with questions.

She took a deep breath. 'My father is dead,' she said in a toneless voice that cost much effort.

'Dead? But he was...'

'At Middleham!' she hissed. 'Your promise was worth nothing! You keep no one safe! I want nothing more to do with you. I am here for Isabel and Isabel alone!'

She saw a look of horror cover Warwick's face. She tried to block out the pain it caused her; if she could just shut out the pain then she would be able to leave him and one day he would thank her for it.

'Tell me Elizabeth, are you in earnest?' he asked. 'About Sir Robert?' His eyes searched her face frantically. 'How?'

Elizabeth almost sighed at the sound of voices approaching. 'I must go,' she said and lowered her gaze quickly.

'Tonight,' Warwick said anxiously. 'Elizabeth please, come to me tonight, for I must return to Carentan on the morrow. We must settle this. I must know what happened.'

Elizabeth said nothing. How could she talk of her father with him? For if she once began the tale would she not tell him all – that it was her promise to her father that had brought her here? That she was damned Edward's spy? She ached to have Warwick love her as before, but the shame of her betrayal scythed into her. Warwick must never come near her again; he must never know what she had done.

'My lord,' she said and dropped into a curtsey just as the Earl of Oxford came into view.

'Warwick!' Oxford greeted him enthusiastically and Elizabeth took the opportunity to escape. She heard them strike up a conversation as she rushed from their company. It was as if a weight was pressing down on her chest, threatening to crush her black heart.

'What have I done?' she sobbed. 'Oh Santa Maria please forgive me!' But she knew it was not the Holy Virgin's forgiveness she needed: it was Warwick's.

* * *

Perhaps Elizabeth should have trusted Brother William of Jervaulx for he had been right: there was some relief in confession - even if that confession was only to Sarah of Warwick and not to the man of the cloth who had tried to help her.

'You are not to blame, mistress,' Sarah said softly, masking from her voice the astonishment evident in her eyes.

Elizabeth looked up. 'Not to blame?' she asked in a choked voice.

'To refuse the wishes of the King of England is impossible,' Sarah said wisely. 'Look how many lords bow to him and how many ladies fall willingly into his bed. You did neither of these things. I think you were very brave.'

It sounded so sensible coming from Sarah, but Elizabeth was beyond comforting. She did not feel brave. She felt completely wretched. 'I can blame my father, for it was his choice in the beginning, I can blame King Edward and I can blame Master Higgins, Sarah, but that would be wrong. *I* took my father's letters to King Edward and *I* brought King Edward's letters to the Duke of Clarence!'

'I think you had no choice,' Sarah answered.

'There is always a choice, Sarah,' Elizabeth said, 'and somehow I always seem to make the wrong one! I thought following my family's wishes was the right thing to do and Master Higgins made me believe that it was, but in the end I have betrayed Warwick.' Tears stung her eyes.

'No, you must not think so,' Sarah said. 'My lord of Warwick loves you, I know he does. He will understand that you were sick with grief; that it was what your family wished, but you have to trust him.'

Elizabeth shook her head. 'Will he understand when Clarence and his men desert him? He will hate me for my part in it and he will be right to do so, though it will be no more then I hate myself!' Tears flowed onto Elizabeth's cheeks.

'My lord is no fool!' Sarah said sternly. 'Why do you take him for one?'

Elizabeth looked up at her again.

'Do you not think he watches the Duke of Clarence's every move? And he will know how hard it was for you – to have to choose between him and your family. He will understand. Remember, mistress, he has chosen the Neville family before his king.'

Elizabeth smiled thinly. 'That is hardly the same, Sarah. He must never know what I have done; he must never know that I failed him.'

'You think he does not know already?' Sarah asked.

Elizabeth gasped. Her eyes flew to Sarah's face. 'How could he know?' she demanded. Had Higgins played a double game with her? Had he been so cruel as to reveal her treachery to Warwick?

'He has his spies,' Sarah said calmly.

Elizabeth sighed with relief. Of course Warwick had spies; Elizabeth knew that all too well. Jack de Laverton, the spy she had killed, sprang into her mind and she shivered. Could someone really have been there at Edward's court? And what about the man she had seen on the boat from Dover? She felt sick.

'I cannot trust in that, Sarah. I cannot tell him,' Elizabeth said flatly. 'He leaves for Carentin tomorrow. All I have to do is keep away from him until then.'

Sarah arched her brows. 'You would not see him?'

Elizabeth shook her head.

'Even though he asked you to go to him?'

Elizabeth knew what would happen if she saw him alone: she would dissolve like sugar in water; there would be no way to resist him. 'No, Sarah I will not see him,' she said with forced resolution. 'It is best for both of us.' It was certainly best for him, she thought, and did she not owe him this release?

'And when he has gone, mistress what will you do? Return to England with Master Higgins?'

There was no judgement in Sarah's voice, yet it stung Elizabeth like a slap. What would she do? Her stomach twisted in knots at the thought of returning to Edward's court. Yes Higgins had said they would return to Lazenby, her family home, but now she knew he would not honour that promise. He would take her to London and King Edward and the reward she did not want: to be Edward's mistress!

'I do not know, Sarah,' she said truthfully.

All she knew was that she had to find a way to escape from Higgins and that would not be an easy thing to do. In the meantime she hoped she would not have to meet the Earl of Warwick again, for that would be her undoing.

~TWO~

VALOGNES AUGUST 1470

The night candle flickered in the sultry breeze that brought the smell of summer meadows into Elizabeth's chamber. The gauzy silk of the bed curtains fluttered like sails beside her as she lay there. With Sarah gone to the Duchess of Clarence, Elizabeth was alone. She had lost all track of time staring blindly at the embroidered canopy above her, her mind ebbing and flowing like the sea as she relived the events that had brought her here.

Though she had forbidden her mind to think of Warwick, it disobeyed her. He had asked her to come to him. 'Tonight,' he had breathed in a voice that made her skin tingle. She had heard his longing, a longing she shared, but which she did not dare satisfy.

She turned onto her side with a sigh. Would it be so wrong to love him now? Would that not make amends for what she had done? Her mind worked on a twisted logic; if he never found out, her deceit could never hurt him and she could bring him comfort as before. Fickle Clarence would perhaps have deserted him anyway and as Sarah had said, would Warwick not have him watched!

But had she not often thought that when Warwick looked at her he saw directly into her soul? If she let him come closer he would see the blackness there for himself!

The sound of the door latch stole her breath. She closed her eyes against the sudden burning of tears, for instinctively she knew he had come.

She heard his footsteps hush along the rushes and she bit her lip to stop herself from crying out.

The bed creaked softly as it took his weight. Warwick leaned over gently and Elizabeth's resolve to resist him began to fail her.

'Are you asleep, sweeting?' he whispered.

Elizabeth knew her fluttering eyes had betrayed her. Slowly she opened them and turned to face him.

He smiled down at her. 'Were you tired, Elizabeth? So tired that you could not come to me?'

Elizabeth returned his smile instinctively; delighting in the way his dark eyes caressed her. Then she remembered her father and the promise she had made him; she killed the look. 'Go!' she said. 'Go, before I scream!'

Warwick's eyes widened. 'Please sweeting, at least let me know your accusation against me.'

Elizabeth manufactured a glare; he looked so beautiful, she wanted nothing more than to curl her fingers in his thick dark hair and pull him to her, but she knew she must not weaken. This was for both of them, she told herself.

Warwick held up his hands and tilted his head in submission. 'I am your prisoner,' he said softly. 'Call the guards if you wish to, but I humbly ask that you tell me what happened. Your father was my dearest friend, Elizabeth. Please, for that reason alone, can you not speak to me?'

Elizabeth nodded her head for him to move away from the bed and he did so without complaint, his hands still held up in surrender.

Elizabeth swallowed with difficulty. Why did he have to come? She wanted him so much, but she must not show it!

Warwick moved to the table. He lit more candles from the nightlight and then poured two cups of wine. He turned slowly and held one out to Elizabeth. His eyes captured the candlelight like the night holding stars. Elizabeth looked away quickly; she could not let herself be undone!

'Tell me, sweeting,' Warwick said gently. 'Tell me what happened.'

Elizabeth took the wine and gulped it down, hoping it would give her courage. She knew she should call out and have him taken from the chamber, but there was alchemy in his eyes and she could not refuse his request; he at least deserved the truth of that.

'You know of Ellerton Nunnery?' she asked.

Warwick watched her over the gold rim of his cup, his eyes never faltering in their gaze. 'I do and I am sorry for it,' he said in a voice that caressed her wounds.

'I did not blame you,' Elizabeth said. 'How could you have known? How could you have helped me? And was it not something I utterly deserved?'

Warwick moved to speak but Elizabeth silenced him with another glare. 'My father's man John Higgins rescued me, and I returned to my family.' She paused, waiting for Warwick to ask her about Higgins, or give her some clue that he knew more, but he did not. She breathed deeply, knowing that she had to choose her words carefully; she had to give him enough of the tale to be

31

credible, but not too much so that she divulged her invidious position! Santa Maria, she hated this deception!

'I travelled to Middleham to see my father and I hoped to ask Sir John Conyers to let him come home.'

'Elizabeth,' Warwick admonished gently. 'You should have known my steward would not have agreed to that.'

Elizabeth shrugged.

'My father could not have come home, even if he had wanted to for he was dying! He was caged like a common prisoner and he was dying!' Her voice rose in a note of anger; too well she remembered the sad sights of Middleham.

'What?' Warwick started towards her. 'What was he doing there? I gave no order...'

'No direct order, I'm certain, my lord,' Elizabeth said sourly, 'but my father had tried to ride to the king. Sir John locked him away for he would give no assurance that he would not do so again...' Tears began to clot her throat as the memory swamped her. 'And then came Losecote Field and your exile and Sir John was summoned into the king's presence and no one bothered about my father!' She caught her breath. 'He was left in the dark and dirt and filth of that place!'

'My love, I am so sorry!' Warwick said.

'Sorry?' Elizabeth had expected Warwick to be as angry as Sir John Conyers had been at her father's anticipated betrayal of them to King Edward. But Warwick's eyes were soft. He put down his cup. He came closer.

'No!' Elizabeth said. 'You failed him, Richard! You failed me!' The grief rose now in an uncontrollable tide; she had not intended to go so far; she had wanted to be calm and stern and cold, but she couldn't do it.

In a heartbeat Warwick's arms were about her and she pressed her head against his shoulder, seeking the comfort she had often craved but dare not dream of.

Warwick stroked her head gently. 'I am so sorry, sweeting,' he breathed against her hair. 'I am so sorry, my love.' He said the words over and over like the calming rhythm of the sea and Elizabeth became lost to it until there was only the sound of their breathing. It seemed as though the world had ended and they were completely alone.

When Elizabeth woke she was still in Warwick's arms. She did not know for how long she had slept, but the candles were low in their stands and for all that time Warwick had not stirred. She looked up.

Warwick sighed; a sound laced with both sorrow and regret. 'Elizabeth?'

For the first time in her hearing his voice was uncertain.

'Can you forgive me?' he asked gently.

Elizabeth knew what her answer should be; had she not said she would end this for both their sakes?

'Can you forgive me?' he pushed softly. 'Forgive that which is truly unpardonable?'

Elizabeth swallowed hard. How could she withhold forgiveness from him when it was his forgiveness that she desired most of all? Not that she was brave enough to seek it.

'Sweeting, I will do whatever you may ask of me,' he said. 'For your family. For you. Please, say I am forgiven.'

Could her forgiveness mean so much to him? She more than anyone should understand that it did! She disobeyed her head. 'Yes,' she murmured. 'Yes you are forgiven, Richard.' He finished her sentence with his lips on hers and it was as though she had been frozen by the winter cold and here he was – the warm spring sunshine come to thaw her.

'Richard,' she said, her voice thick with emotions she could barely control, 'we should not...' She was too late to stop what she had known would happen at this meeting. Now he was here she did not wish him to be anywhere else.

'God alone knows how much I have missed you, sweeting,' he said.

Elizabeth wound her fingers in his hair, drew him down to her; this was not the time for talking, even though there was so much she wanted to say to him, if only she had the courage to do so. But as she slid her arms about his neck, none of it mattered, for her arms held all that was important to her.

Elizabeth felt like a shot bowstring – pulled to the tension of breaking point and then released so rapidly that she was still dizzy with bliss. Slowly she began to connect with the world again.

Warwick lay heavily upon her, his breath hot against her cheek, his body slick with sweat. He looked as though he would not be able to move even if Edward himself walked through the door.

With the faintest of movements he snuggled beside her and began to drift into sleep.

Elizabeth's eyes were heavy-lidded too, but the nagging wound of her betrayal still goaded her, as if an arrow had pierced her and only the shaft of it had been cut off.

She whispered a prayer to the Virgin for guidance, for in spite of the danger it had brought, she could not regret loving Warwick tonight.

* * *

Warwick woke to the sound of hushed voices; Elizabeth was hurriedly dismissing her astonished ladies from the room as quietly as she could. Pale light glimmered in from the new morning. It sparkled red and gold in Elizabeth's unbound hair which wrapped around her like that of the fabled mermaids. As he watched her, the heat of desire stirred once again within him. Yet as he thought on last night, he knew things had changed between them. Elizabeth had matched his passion with a ferocious energy, desired him more than ever before; had wanted to possess him and be possessed by him; yet something was wrong. He cursed inwardly at his witch-like second sight and then thought himself a complete fool if he imagined that the months they had spent apart would not have touched her. She had lost her father, an act for which he knew he must atone, and had been sent to a nunnery, another event for which he blamed himself. How could she still be the same? Guilt knotted his stomach and he swore to make amends. But yet there was something else, he knew there was.

'Elizabeth,' he said huskily as he untangled an arm from the rich coverlet and held it out to her. 'Come back to bed.'

Elizabeth turned like an angel; a whisper of silk barely concealed her curves from his gaze. Her face was flushed, he guessed from the embarrassment of discovery by her women, but her eyes flashed like the finest green glass as she looked on him and he saw in them the mirror of his own lust.

'I am sorry, my lord,' she breathed softly as she came towards him. 'I did not want to waken you. I know you have a difficult journey; I thought you needed the rest.'

Her fingers linked into his and he pulled her gently towards him. 'Carentan is not so far,' he said.

''Tis not the ride I was thinking of,' she answered perceptively. How right she was. She smiled at him and his heart fluttered; how could he have ever let her be parted from him? Her moist lips came down onto his and she slipped her free hand inside the covers, stroking the line of dark hair that rippled down his body. He could bear it no longer. He threw the covers aside and snatched her towards him, as though the Devil himself was trying to steal her away from him; then he rolled her over swiftly so that she was underneath him. He had never seen her like this, as hungry for him as he was for her. Perhaps it was just the long absence; perhaps it was something else, something he dismissed for now. God's breath, how his memory of their love-making had failed him!

Slowly they began to settle to normality, like the sea after a storm surge. Yet there could no longer be any normality, he told himself; he was preparing an invasion – the battle to end all battles, he hoped. How could he pull her into this? How could he put her into such danger that she could lose her life? If he loved her enough he would send her away from him, make sure she was safe. And yet his need for her was stronger than ever before and it seemed that she also knew the same yearning.

'I want to come with you, Richard,' she said, as if she had read his thoughts.

He exhaled slowly, clearing the ground for battle. He rolled onto his side and drew her into his shoulder. Her eyes were still dilated with lust and they appealed to all of his senses, plucked at his heart like a lute string.

'Elizabeth, I –'

'Richard, do not shut me out again,' she said. 'Though I have enjoyed the reunion, I do not want to endure the parting!'

She kissed his neck, and his resolve began to waver.

'Isabel needs you,' he said. He knew it was a lame excuse and she stiffened at it.

'Not as much as I need you,' she retorted. 'May God forgive me for my sins!' she teased.

He smiled. 'I want you safe, my love that is all. I failed you before; I shall not do so again!'

'You will love me and abandon me in the same hour?' she asked crossly.

He sighed. 'Yes,' he said reluctantly, pulling her to his chest more tightly, 'but I do not want to. Leave you, that is.'

'Then at least let me come to Carentan, if not to England,' she said. 'Let me see those to whom you swear allegiance.'

Warwick closed his eyes and breathed deeply. To refuse her was to hurt her again and he did not want to do that. But he could not take her to the heart of Marguerite's entourage, could not show her off as he wanted to, or give her the attention she deserved. 'Please, my love. Do not make this more difficult than it has to be. I need you to stay here with Isabel. Here you will be safe. The countess is in Marguerite's company; I would not wish you to feel her malice again.'

Elizabeth shuddered against him and he knew that he had wounded her.

'And when shall you return?' she asked stiffly.

He stroked her hair. 'A few days, no more. Then I must oversee the preparation of the fleet myself; I must go to the coast.'

She raised her head expectantly. 'The coast?' she purred.

The softness of her voice spoke to his heart, but he should be strong, he told himself. 'It is not as comfortable as here, Elizabeth. Barfleur is overfull of bad-tempered Englishmen. You would be bored.'

'Bored?' She gave an ironic laugh. 'There would be more to see there than there is here!' She stroked his cheek. 'And I would be with you, Richard.'

He did not answer.

Her eyes fixed his gaze. They were wide and beautiful and pleading. She blinked very slowly and brought her hand up to his face again. One finger delicately traced the line of his jaw. 'Please, Richard,' she murmured.

His heart squeezed. He could not shut her out again, for to deny her was to deny himself. And for all the pain she had suffered because of him, did he not owe her this much at least?

'Very well,' he said gently, 'but remember Elizabeth, Barfleur is a soldiers' town.'

'And I will be a soldier's woman!' she said triumphantly.

He laughed at her delight and then drew her mouth to his, tasting her sweetness. But part of his mind told him that to take her with him was a mistake. He had said it was a soldiers' town to make it sound better than it was, for in reality it was a stinking, overcrowded cesspit of a place. Battle hardened men did what unoccupied soldiers did best – they got into trouble. Already he had hanged two of them for raping a young woman, and as the money became tighter and the food stores ran low, he knew they were going to become harder to control. Yet how could he leave her behind? Truly Isabel had brightened with Elizabeth's arrival, but his own need for Elizabeth was greater and he had to make amends for the wounds he knew she had already suffered because of him. Silently he prayed that he did not regret it.

* * *

Elizabeth looked along the corridor before closing the door to her room. Thank God it was Compline and most of the household were at prayer; hopefully no one had seen her visitor enter. How she could even stand to be in the same room as him she did not know. No, that was not true; she did know – she did so because she had no choice!

'Tis well done, Elizabeth!' Higgins's voice showed more emotion than his face.

'Well done?' Elizabeth snapped.

'Aye.' Higgins raised an eyebrow; he evidently knew she and Warwick were lovers again. 'Now you can stay with him. Who knows what we can learn.'

'Stay?' Elizabeth's stomach lurched. She had thought that now Warwick had gone to Carentan she and Higgins would be able to escape to England. 'I do not want to stay!' She tried not to sound as desperate as she felt. If she stayed then it was only a matter of time before Warwick learned the truth! 'But I thought...'

'Elizabeth,' Higgins's tongue lisped over her name. 'Do you not see how useful you are?'

Elizabeth knew exactly what he meant, but she wanted no further part of this treachery. 'He has gone to Carentan, and I have no intention of being here when he comes back. By then I shall be on a boat to England and you shall be with me!'

Higgins's laugh was like someone walking on gravel. His head rocked back and Elizabeth could see his uneven teeth. She clenched her fists at her sides. 'Even if I went with Warwick, you could not come with me!' she hissed. Not that she had any intention of going with Warwick to Barfleur.

'Not come? Do you think I am a milksop? You think I would let you out of my sight?'

Elizabeth's cheeks burned with anger. 'But Warwick cannot see you!' The pitch of her voice rose in panic. 'He knows of your involvement with my father at the very least. He may also know that you work for King Edward! The risk is too great.' But evidently Higgins did not see the impossibility of the situation.

Cold fingers slid around her wrist. 'I am almost family,' he said. 'And I have come this far. I will not draw any attention, Elizabeth.'

Elizabeth met his gaze as firmly as she could. 'No,' she said.

Higgins growled and his lips drew back into a snarl. 'If you do not accommodate my wishes then I shall have to let Warwick know what I know about you! I am sure he would find that very interesting!' He tightened his grip further.

Elizabeth's wrist grew hot under his twisted fingers; the ones broken during his torture on his fateful mission for Warwick.

'You would not dare!' she hissed.

'Would I not? There is so much I could tell him; perhaps I should mention your private meetings with King Edward too?'

'Nothing happened as you well know!' Elizabeth snapped.

'I know nothing of the sort, Elizabeth,' Higgins snarled. 'I have seen how you behave at court – your dance with Lord Hastings showed me how wanton you can be. I only have your word that nothing lewd occurred between you and the king, and as we both know, you can be less than forthcoming with the truth!'

Elizabeth snatched her hand from his grasp and glared at him fiercely. She had enjoyed her dance with Lord Hastings before they left court and did she not owe him something for his timely intervention? She rubbed at her burning wrist with her other hand while she struggled to staunch the rising anger.

'I cannot go with Warwick!' she pleaded, hoping Higgins would see the pain he was causing her.

But Higgins shook his head. 'I need to see his fleet,' he said flatly.

'You do not need me to do that!' Elizabeth said. 'I am sure once you get to Barfleur it will be obvious!'

'I'm sure it will. But I will not be able to see what is planned; what he asks King Louis for. But you can know this. Perhaps he talks in his sleep?' Higgins laughed darkly at his taunt. 'If you help me then he will not learn of your part in it from me, Elizabeth, I swear it.'

'I cannot trust your word! It means nothing!' Elizabeth snapped.

Higgins caught her arm again and fixed her eyes with his. 'You can,' he hissed. 'But if you do not help me then the knowledge of your betrayal will only add to his troubles!'

Elizabeth did not know what to do. She had based her strategy on Warwick never learning of her visit to Clarence, or of Edward's letters. Higgins was now threatening to reveal her for the liar she was; Warwick would never forgive her!

'Then I will give him Edward's letter – would you like Warwick to have the king's pardon?'

Higgins growled. 'And will he not want to know how you came by such a letter?'

She looked at Higgins. His eyes narrowed wolfishly and a stiff smile twisted his mouth into a sneer. Could she really trust him not to reveal her secret? She stared into his face, trying to read him.

'Your bright eyes might bewitch most men, Elizabeth,' he said sharply, 'but they will not work on me. I have sought Warwick's ruin and you will help me accomplish it. You know what I suffered in his cause!' He held up his broken hands again, to emphasize the point. 'Nothing and no one can stand in my way Elizabeth, not even you.'

Elizabeth snapped her gaze away from him. What could she do now? She thought for a few moments, her mind hurtling from one mad idea to another, each as impossible as the next. The only thing she was clear about was that Warwick must never know she had taken her father's letters to King Edward or that she had spoken to Clarence on Edward's behalf. Perhaps if they went to Barfleur there would be some way to rid herself of Higgins's winter shadow? Some other path might reveal itself; it was a port after all! But the longer she spent in Warwick's company the closer she came to revealing all. Santa Maria, there was no way out of this!

Warwick should have found the entertainment enjoyable, well if not entirely enjoyable at least a distraction from the conflict assaulting his mind. After all the festivities were meant to celebrate the alliance between himself and Queen Marguerite and Anne's betrothal to Edouard of Lancaster which sealed the bond, but the doubts about this Lancastrian alliance and the veracity of Marguerite's oath were still with him and no amount of dancing and jesting could brush them aside. There were also the details to settle, but to Warwick they did not really matter; King Louis could deal with those, Warwick need to focus on what was to come.

He loosened the collar of his shirt to try and obtain some relief from the heat, but this was summer and this was France, not Yorkshire! His head began to throb to the rhythm of the drums and he knew he should try to clear his mind of these troubles. He could yet see no other way than the course he had chosen and had Louis not offered the reassurance of land on this side of the Narrow Sea if all failed? The word caused a shiver to lick at his spine; had that word not haunted him since he took the mantle of Warwick? Failure was not an option he could contemplate; the illustrious legend of his forbears would not allow it!

He drank some of the cooled wine, but even from the golden cup it didn't taste sweet; there was still too much to think on, for on God's earth only death was a certainty.

'Richard, you are solemn on a happy day!' Louis's voice showed gentle concern. He mopped at his brow with a silken kerchief.

Warwick smiled ruefully.

'That is better, my friend,' Louis said, brightening. 'It is not every day one betroths one's daughter to the future King of England! You should celebrate what we have achieved!'

Warwick looked about him; neither his countess nor Marguerite looked any happier than he did, though Anne, God bless her, was smiling at the sullen prince at her side.

'Celebrate?' Warwick asked. ''Tis but a job half done, my liege. I shall celebrate when all is won.'

'Ah, Richard, it is the dispensation that worries you? It will come, I am certain of it. Christ knows we have paid enough gold and silver for it, non?'

Warwick nodded. He knew from Archbishop Neville's experience of obtaining a dispensation for Isabel and Clarence's wedding that these things could not be hurried, that they took months rather than weeks, even when their gold had been given. Louis had been over optimistic to think this could all have been settled before Warwick left for England.

'Richard, clear your mind of this worry. I will see all done as you would wish it. Lady Anne as you see is in Marguerite's household; she has accepted all.'

'Not all, my liege. Still Lancaster will not sail with me.'

'You are right, Richard, but I will see that the marriage holds. As to him sailing with you, I fear I cannot change her mind.'

Warwick sighed. 'Loose ends have a habit of unravelling.'

'Indeed Richard, but what of my lose ends, hmm?'

Warwick met Louis's keen gaze. He smiled; Louis never missed an opportunity to push his own cause. 'England alone holds my thoughts, my liege. Burgundy will have to wait.'

Louis's face clouded briefly and he mopped at his brow again. 'It cannot wait long, Richard. I need a solution and you are the man to bring it about.'

Warwick almost sighed again; it seemed that he was the only man who could bring anything about; must he do everything himself? He restrained the urge to speak his mind. 'I have given my word to serve you in this. It will be done.' He gave a slight inflection to the words which Louis understood.

'I value your word above that of other men,' Louis said smoothly.

Warwick raised his goblet again. 'Good,' he said and then drank deeply.

Louis said nothing but gave a sagacious nod; he was clever enough to know when to push a point and when enough had been said. 'All will be well, Richard,' he said again. 'A promise is a promise.'

'In these few days there have been enough promises made here to keep the world in thrall, if all hold,' Warwick said.

Louis met his eyes. He knew that it was Marguerite's word Warwick doubted, but he offered no further reassurance. 'God's will be done, Richard,' he said.

Warwick wondered if even God could hold Marguerite to her oath.

Later, as Warwick sat in his apartments, the doubts rose again. He ran his fingers through the damp hair at his brow. Servants shifted in the shadows like ghosts and in the silence his thoughts drifted dangerously close to disaster and he knew he had to do something if he were not to go mad. Anne and his countess were no longer with him, they were committed to Marguerite's household until success in England had been achieved, and he knew that the sooner he left, the sooner they would kiss England's shores again. God's blood, he needed some comfort and there was only one person who could give it!

Without a word he gathered up his cloak, draping the heavy brocade over his shoulders as he walked. His spurs echoed on the stone as he took the steps two at a time, calling loudly for his horse and sending a servant scurrying to the stables ahead of him.

He strode quickly across the courtyard. The sun was low in the western sky, casting long shadows, which chased him across the cobbles. Everything was gilded with a warm orange glow and the air was thick and humid, as if thunder were only heartbeats away. And he knew what people would say: that a thunderstorm was a bad omen for the alliances made that day.

'My lord,' Thomas Conyers called breathlessly, trying to keep up with him, 'King Louis is asking for you!'

Warwick raised a hand to halt Thomas's conversation, but he did not stop walking. His throat was tight – he'd had enough of the French for one day, perhaps even for a lifetime. He reached his horse and mounted quickly.

There was a crack of thunder in the distance.

As he was about to turn the mount away Thomas caught at the reins. 'My lord, what shall I say?'

Warwick's eyes flashed down to Thomas.

'Say that I have gone to break the great news to the Duke of Clarence personally!' Warwick could not keep the sarcasm from his voice; Clarence of all people would not think today's agreement great news. It was true that Warwick had accomplished much in his negotiations; Clarence would keep many of his lands and, in the unlikely event that Prince Edouard and Anne had no issue then Clarence would be the heir to the crown. But the reality was that Clarence had lost the greatest prize and gained little. Though Warwick knew the crown had already fallen from Clarence's reach when they fled England; he wasn't sure if Clarence realized it yet. Warwick had gained little too; he was able to keep his great estates of Warwick and Middleham, but his greatest prize was that Anne would one day be Queen of England, though a thousand obstacles lay in her way, not least his taking of England.

'My lord? Your answer?'

'Thomas, are you deaf?' Warwick growled. He was desperate for some respite from this attention; he needed some time to lick his wounds and prepare for the invasion. And he needed Elizabeth. He had promised an absence of only a few days, but the stalling of the haughty Marguerite and the futile wait for the dispensation had lengthened his absence to almost a week and something deep inside him now demanded that he honour his promise to her to return.

'But, my lord you cannot ride without an escort, it is too dangerous!'

Lightning cut across the smouldering sky and something inside Warwick snapped. 'Then saddle up!' he yelled as he dug his spurs into his courser. He turned the horse on its hocks as he watched Thomas scramble for the stable, then he sprang for the gates, eager to be away from the stifling formality of the French court and the peevish gazes of Marguerite and her entourage.

The lush pasture lay like velvet beside the crumpled ribbon of road. Warwick was glad that he had his courser so that he could set a decent pace. Villagers scattered before him like frightened rabbits as he thundered along, casting a cloud of stones and dust up from the road like a raging wind.

Sweat stood out on his horse's neck like sea foam on the shore, but Warwick did not spare the spur. The sultry air burned his lungs. There was a feeling almost like panic within him, which tightened his chest as he rode, and he knew he had to reach Elizabeth as quickly as possible. What if he lost her again? The months apart had seemed like years and he doubted his own ability to stand the pain of another separation.

* * *

Sparks flew from the horses' hooves as they danced onto the cobbles of the courtyard. They skidded to a shuddering halt in a cloud of hot white breath. Above his head the brooding sky crackled again.

Warwick's heart was pounding almost as quickly as that of his sweating horse as he dismounted. He threw the reins to a startled groom without a word and then ran up the steps, his sword slapping on his thigh as he did so. As he marched along the smoky passageway he shrugged off servants as a horse shakes off flies. His determined footsteps echoed back to him, and it was as if that was the only sound in the world, that and his hammering heart.

He flung open the chamber door without knocking and heard a girl scream in surprise. Ignoring her protests he marched through the antechamber and up to Elizabeth's door.

He paused to catch his breath, rubbing the dirt and sweat from his brow on his velvet sleeve. Then he opened the door. The storm broke overhead. Rain hit the windows like stones.

'Richard?'

He heard the alarm in Elizabeth's voice as she called to him.

'What is wrong?' She rose like an angel before him, her eyes widened by fear. Her full red lips were slightly parted and she held her breath, waiting on his words.

But none came; the sight of her had rendered him speechless.

Instead he strode to the bed and reached for her.

Her cool slender arms wrapped around his burning body and she tangled her fingers in his hair.

'What is it, Richard?' she murmured.

He answered her only with reckless kisses and then rolled Elizabeth back on the bed.

Rain hissed in the courtyard and the night splintered around them.

Elizabeth had ceased to question him and from the way she pressed against him he knew that she desired him as much as he desired her.

At that moment he wanted nothing else in the world – kings, continents and countries were all a meaningless blur in his mind; only loving the woman beneath him could assuage his desperate physical need.

The air was hot, laced with the scent of man and woman and heavy from the quickening storm. Warwick did not want to move; he was at ease in the closeness of Elizabeth and slowly his body began to find its equilibrium.

After some moments she wriggled beneath him and, conscious that he must now be hurting her, he rolled onto his side.

She turned to look at him. A pink flush coloured her cheeks and chest and the lust was still bright in her eyes. Her lips parted in a smile.

He did not want to speak, to spoil the perfection of the moment. He reached out and stroked her damp autumn-coloured curls from her brow. But he saw something in her face that demanded reassurance from him.

'You cannot know what you are to me,' he said huskily. 'Elizabeth you are my lifeblood, I swear it. *Soulement une.*'

It can have been for no more than a heartbeat, but he thought he saw the ghost of a frown at his words. Then she smiled and reached her fingers to his lips. He kissed each one in turn.

Her eyes met his. 'What is wrong, Richard? Why did you ride back so late when the darkness and the storm were looming?' she asked gently.

He did not want to think on today, but he heard the anxiety in her voice.

'I had to,' he said softly. 'I needed you.'

Elizabeth smiled again and linked her fingers into his.

'I gave my word, sweeting,' his voice was thick in his throat, 'I gave my word to honour those I once thought had no honour and to win for them the sweetest prize, the prize of the English throne. And,' his voice grew thicker, 'and I gave my daughter to them.'

Elizabeth must have sensed his pain at the loss of Lady Anne for her hand caressed his cheek. Her eyes glittered with sudden tears that matched his own. She blinked and like small pearls they trickled down her face. 'Oh Richard,' she whispered and pulled him to her.

He buried his face in the sweetly scented silk of her hair.

'It must have been so hard for you,' she said.

She could not know how hard, he thought. How could she know what it felt like to lie with those he had spent half a lifetime hating? How could she know what it was like to lose a child?

'It is over now,' she said, 'at least until you are the master of England.'

He smiled; she had pulled the sunlight from beyond the storm cloud – he would not have to set eyes on Marguerite again until she was once again Queen of England.

'You are right, Elizabeth,' he said and hugged her to him. But what nightmares must he yet face before then? He shuddered. As long as she was with him, he could face it.

He wound an arm around her possessively; he had so feared the loss of her that he had ridden like the Devil today and he reflected that she had seemed to share the terrible thought that they might again be parted.

She turned to face him, but did not shrug off his arm. She studied his face for a long moment and he could see that something was troubling her still. Was it what he had sensed earlier?

'Richard,' her eyes fixed on his. The sudden seriousness of her tone was unnerving. 'There is something I must tell you,' she said. Her voice wavered. She caught her breath.

'Hush,' he whispered, he did not want to hear her, wanted nothing to intrude upon this fragment of happiness.

'Please, Richard, I must...'

'Not now my sweet one,' he said gently. He saw her chew at her lip. He flicked a thumb across her cheek in a caress. 'Can it wait until morning?'

Her eyes searched his face and he saw her lip tremble a little.

He leaned forward and kissed her. She weakened under him and circled his neck with her arms. He coaxed her lips to respond and they parted allowing him in; that sent a fire to his loins he would not have thought possible after his earlier exertion. But he had awoken her too. Her questing hands slid down his back and drew him towards her. Spent though he was, he was aroused by her eagerness and for the second time that night they broke together like the sea upon rocks.

* * *

Elizabeth stared at her reflection in the beautiful gilded mirror in Isabel's chamber. Isabel lay sleeping, resting from the heat of the day. The other women had been dismissed and Elizabeth was alone. She concentrated hard on the image. It was as though she was staring at another creature; someone who looked like her, stared from an ivory mask with wild green eyes like her, but who was merely playing a part like an actor upon the stage.

She had tried so hard to confess to Warwick, to tell him not to trust Clarence; not to trust anyone, even her. Especially her. But his urgent need for her had stopped her speaking the hurtful truths, for if he could trust her no longer, then whom did he have left? And she could not bear to think of him alone; he had needed her support and that had eased her sense of guilt a little. Like a gentle breeze from the dales on a hot day, it had tempered the heat that burned constantly in her belly: her fire of self-loathing. For the first time she had seen Warwick wavering and uncertain, touched by self-doubt, and she was glad she had been able to steady him, strengthen his resolve, for the only way either of them would see England again was as part of this Lancastrian alliance, she knew that now. She knew he was the only man who could do it, accomplish that which she had heard Londoners say was impossible: the deposition of King Edward. Only Warwick had the charisma and strength to lead men in such an uneasy alliance; to take them where they did not want to go and to keep them together as brothers in arms if not brothers in love. And so she had held her tongue and hated herself again for not facing the truth. She had promised herself that she would leave him, but when it had come down to it that was easier said than done, not only because it was so easy to love Warwick's company, but also because she knew if she had not complied, Higgins would have told him everything. Though she couldn't bear the thought of Warwick hating her, it was the thought of the pain the revelations would cause him that had made her stay; did he not have the weight of the world resting on his shoulders as it was? And perhaps, just perhaps, she could be of some use; bring some comfort, even mayhap go some way towards making amends? She smiled mockingly to herself and the creature smiled back: there was no way to make amends for what she had done.

The door clicked as Sarah returned. She gave Elizabeth a puzzled look and Elizabeth wondered what Sarah must think of it all! What must she truly think of her?

'I will sit with her, mistress,' Sarah said. 'You look as though some fresh air will do you good.'

'Thank you,' Elizabeth said, glad of the opportunity to free herself from the claustrophobia of the house. She smiled thinly; did her cares lie so heavily upon her? Quietly she left the room, taking care that the sound of her leaving did not wake Isabel.

She moved quickly through the house; the air was close and heavy and she began to feel as if it were choking her, or was that just the guilt?

Eventually she reached the entrance and stopped suddenly, as if she had seen a ghost; only this ghost wasn't Jack, this was a living, breathing ghost she recognized!

'Thomas?' Elizabeth hardly knew the man in front of her in the doorway. His tousled hair was bleached like driftwood beneath his cap, his face was as tanned as a sailor and he seemed somehow taller. 'Thomas Conyers, it is you!' she laughed.

'Elizabeth?' He dropped his look to her feet and bowed graciously.

She remembered the heat of their last angry encounter and she now regretted her part in it. 'Thomas,' she said as she reached him, 'please Thomas.' She could not let him go again without healing the wound; God alone knew what danger they yet had to face.

His eyes found hers and his face broke into a lopsided smile, showing his white teeth. It was a smile to break hearts. 'I am sorry, Elizabeth,' he said softly, 'for what I said in London...I had no right to say those things.' He dropped his eyes meekly. So he too had thought on that day at Warwick's London home; the day when he had seen her and Warwick together and told her that she was just a distraction for Warwick.

Elizabeth reached up and kissed his cheek. 'We must always be friends you and I,' she said and then smiled at the pink blush that came to his face. 'Are we agreed?' she asked.

'I have thought on it often,' he said. 'I was such a fool.'

Elizabeth began to interrupt him, but he shook his head. 'No, Elizabeth, let me speak.'

This was a different Thomas, Elizabeth thought, but then he too had seen many things in the last few months. Neither of them were the same person who had left The Erber in the spring.

'I now know my lord Warwick better,' he said, 'I know that he is above all men I have known, and I know what it means to be in his favour: it is to walk in the sun; it is to be blessed.'

Elizabeth took hold of his hands in hers. 'Oh, Thomas,' she breathed, glad that they were friends again and that he shared her opinion of Warwick.

'Do you forgive my stupidity?' he asked softly.

Elizabeth's throat constricted. She nodded. 'If you also forgive me,' she said huskily, 'for I know I did not spare you my tongue!'

Thomas laughed then, showing creases at his eyes she had not seen before. Indeed he was no longer the boy she had thought of

48

as a brother. She let go of his hands and looked at him for a moment. As he stood there in Warwick's scarlet livery, she knew he had become a man, and better than that, a man trusted by Warwick.

'You are right, Elizabeth,' he said, 'you did not spare me, and I deserved all you said. I had no right to say such things...to judge what I did not know. But at least now we can part as friends,' he said.

'Part?' Elizabeth asked. She had only just found him again.

'Aye. I am to go to the coast and help to prepare the fleet.'

Elizabeth gaped; his words had brought her back to reality – the only way back to England was by war.

'Do you not trust me to make a good job of it?' Thomas laughed at her consternation.

Elizabeth shook her head. 'No, Thomas, of course I trust you and more importantly, so does Warwick. It is just that it makes me think on the dangers to come.'

'War is never pleasant,' Thomas said sadly.

Elizabeth saw a mist in his eyes and she shivered at the nightmares he must have seen.

'But we have no choice now, Elizabeth. My lord Warwick does not undertake this lightly, as I am sure you know.'

She knew all too well. She nodded.

'But, I tell you, Elizabeth, I have seen none braver. When we fought for our lives against Lord Howard's ships, he would have boarded them with only a handful of men! And what prizes we won!' Thomas had a gleam in his eye like a veteran.

'You were pirates?' she asked.

'Aye, some call us so! But we had to live, Elizabeth. We had to eat!'

Elizabeth smiled at the animation in Thomas's voice and the brightness in his eyes as he spoke of battles, piracy and treasure.

'But let me tell you, Elizabeth,' he continued, 'that without that sting in my lord Warwick's tail, King Louis would not have been so accommodating!'

Elizabeth frowned. 'I do not understand, Thomas.'

'Louis wanted my lord to hide his ships,' Thomas said. 'The Burgundians had complained that he had taken valuable prizes and that by harbouring him and Clarence, King Louis was breaking the Treaty of Peronne. So again and again Warwick sent the fleet out. Each success added more pressure on King Louis to meet with him, to help him. Eventually King Louis gave in; he held jousts in Warwick's honour, fêted us, and gave us gifts of gold, jewels and silk. Eventually, to lessen Louis's embarrassment, my lord Warwick did move his ships and in return King Louis has funded our cause.'

'So you are now a rich pirate?' Elizabeth teased.

For a brief moment there was a cloud in Thomas's eyes, but as quickly as it came, it passed.

'I have some money, yes,' he said quietly. 'But I think we shall spend most of it preparing for war.'

'Oh!' Elizabeth laughed, 'I thought you would use most of it to buy a French bride!'

Thomas did not laugh. Wounded blue eyes met hers. 'Mayhap,' he said curtly, 'if I survive.'

Elizabeth saw that she had somehow hurt him, but before she could say anything, Warwick's voice echoed in the hallway.

'You have not left yet, Master Conyers?'

His voice sounded stern, but Elizabeth saw that he was smiling.

'At this rate it will be Michaelmas before we are in England!'

'My lord,' Thomas bowed to his earl. 'Elizabeth.' He nodded his head to her politely.

Elizabeth smiled at him and he returned it as he turned away from her.

Warwick joined her as they watched Thomas leave.

'He is a good lad,' Warwick said, 'but I forget, you knew that already.'

Elizabeth smiled up at him. 'Without Thomas, I would never have made it to Warwick Castle,' she said. 'And I would never have met you!'

'Then indeed I have much to thank him for,' Warwick said as he bent and kissed her forehead.

Elizabeth wondered what would have happened if she had not ventured to Warwick to petition for her father; but it was beyond regret.

'Do we follow to the coast?' she asked, trying to shake the thought from her mind.

'Aye, sweeting,' Warwick said, 'just as soon as Louis's six hundred crowns arrive!'

Hastings knew it was a bad idea to disturb Edward now, but he also knew he had no choice; Edward would want to know his news. Hastings gripped Higgins's letter tightly in his hand, crumpling the parchment.

Edward's expression was one of puzzlement as his eyes flicked between the tattered paper in Hastings's fist and Hastings's serious countenance.

Hastings cleared his throat before speaking. As he said the words Edward's expression did not change. Then, incongruously, his lips widened into a broad smile.

'Hastings, you jest!' Edward laughed huskily. He swaggered closer, a half-empty goblet swaying at his fingertips. 'Tell me that you do! And then come and join us! The ladies of York are just dying to meet you!' He cast a quick look back over his shoulder which was met by a peal of squeaky giggles.

Hastings noticed Edward's doublet was open to the waist and half of his points were already undone.

Hastings stood perfectly still, trying to retain his composure. 'I do not jest, my liege,' he said calmly. 'Lady Anne Neville *is* betrothed to Lancaster,' he repeated. He waited for the inevitable onslaught.

Edward's face darkened like a thundercloud. Within two heartbeats the goblet hit the tapestry, the wine staining it like blood. The cup landed with a loud clang on the tiled floor, its jewelled rim dented beyond repair.

'God's blood!' Edward roared. 'Warwick shall not be forgiven for this!'

Hastings nodded, but he said nothing; it was best not to.

'Get out!' Edward screamed at the half-dressed ladies who were still giggling together at the board. 'Get out, all of you!'

Hastings held out an arm as Edward staggered with the effort of shouting. Edward's weight sagged against him as his legs refused to bear the burden any longer.

The women skittered around the room like chickens, grabbing whatever clothing of theirs they could lay hands to.

Hastings steered Edward towards the bed. He sat heavily on the silk coverlet, and brought a hand up to his head, as if to ease a sudden pain.

'How could he, Will?' he asked tearfully. 'How could he marry her off to *him*?'

Hastings raised an eyebrow, but curbed the desire to remind Edward of what he had almost done to Lady Anne last Christmas in these very apartments; the final breach in the break with Warwick. 'My liege it is politics, that is all,' he said flatly.

'Politics!' Edward scowled. 'A plague on his politics, Will! Get me wine!'

'Ned, perhaps not now,' Hastings said, trying to keep his voice even.

Edward turned fierce eyes up to him. 'Do not nursemaid me, Will!' he bellowed. 'Bring me more wine!'

Hastings bowed his head and moved over to the table. As he poured the wine, Edward said nothing. His eyes searched the vacant space in front of him as he thought on this latest development.

'So he really means to kill me?' he asked almost plaintively as he took the wine Hastings offered.

'It would seem so,' Hastings said, 'for I do not see how you can remain alive and yet not be King of England.' Had Burgundy not sent letters warning him of just such a threat as this? Higgins too had suggested a Neville-Lancastrian alliance was imminent and that the marriage would be the seal to the uneasy pact.

Edward nodded and then threw the wine into his throat savagely. 'And Clarence?' he growled. 'What does my errant brother think of this?'

'He is to be their heir if they have no issue,' Hastings said.

'Ha! Well that is not likely,' Edward hissed, 'even if they beget an heir as Lancaster was begotten!'

Hastings smiled; many suspected Lancaster was not Henry's son, not when he was the image of the late Duke of Somerset and Henry prone to bouts of madness when he didn't even know who he was, let alone be capable of fathering an heir, though he had honoured the child as his own. And Hastings knew Edward was right: in reality Clarence had no hope of ever attaining the crown. 'As to Clarence's thoughts, Ned, I cannot say,' Hastings said. 'Though Higgins did say that your letter has been delivered to him and that he keeps close by your brother and Warwick too.'

Edward looked up at him suddenly. 'She did it?' Edward cried. 'Warwick's little mistress did it!' Edward brayed with laughter.

Hastings gave a rueful smile; he wondered if Elizabeth knew how important Clarence's defection could be. 'She did, my liege, as Higgins promised,' he said softly.

'Then the game's afoot, Will,' Edward said more brightly. 'The trap is set for Warwick and I swear he shall fall into it!'

Hastings nodded. 'As you say, Ned.'

'And,' Edward continued with a lascivious grin, 'I shall have to devise a suitable reward for Mistress Hardacre!'

Hastings lowered his eyes; he knew what sort of reward Edward meant.

VALOGNES AUGUST 1470

Elizabeth's breathing came in short gasps that she could barely control. Her throat tightened with panic. Of all the things that could have gone wrong, this was probably the worst!

Higgins stared at her impassively; had he not heard her?

'I tell you, it has been taken!' she almost screamed at him.

Higgins furrowed his brow. 'You have asked your maid?' he asked in an untroubled voice, as though she had mentioned what was for supper.

'Of course!' Elizabeth cried in exasperation. 'But I know she would not have taken it.'

Higgins was suddenly animated. He gripped her wrist. He drew her close; his eyes fixed her face fully. 'You cannot *know* anything!' he hissed. 'You can trust *no one*, do you hear me?'

Elizabeth forced herself to meet Higgins's unyielding look. 'There is worse,' she stammered.

Higgins narrowed his eyes. He did not loosen his hold.

'Edward's necklace is also missing!' Elizabeth's heart was racing now. The necklace, so obviously a Royal gift, and the letter, still bearing Edward's seal would prove her treachery to Warwick. 'What are we to do? We must get them back!'

Tears stung Elizabeth's eyes, but she forced them back; she knew she should not show any weakness in front of Higgins. God in heaven, how she regretted this whole adventure! If she had confessed to Warwick then this nightmare would not be happening.

Higgins nodded. 'I will talk to the servants,' he said darkly. 'Warwick keeps a close guard; one of them must have seen something. See if you can frighten your maid into telling you the truth!'

Elizabeth snatched her hand from his grip. 'Sarah will have had nothing to do with this!' she snapped.

Higgins smiled and shook his head. 'You can trust no one, Elizabeth, least of all a servant. We play for high stakes you and I, the very highest, and that means we are in constant danger. Speak to her soon, Elizabeth,' he growled. 'Or else I will have to!'

YORK AUGUST 1470

'Aaahh!' The pain in Edward's eyes was excruciating. 'God's blood, Will!' he cursed as Hastings pulled back the shutters and allowed the harsh white sunlight to spill into the room. He turned his head away from the blinding light, but that too was a mistake, for the sudden movement caused a pain in his skull like a kick from a horse.

'I did say, Ned that I thought more wine inadvisable.'

Edward could tell by his voice that his chamberlain was smiling. 'You did, Will,' he said wearily. 'You did. And I hope you are pleased with yourself!' he growled. Suddenly a strange scent tweaked his nostrils. 'Sweet Jesu, Will. What is that smell?'

'You know what it is, Ned,' Hastings said impassively.

Edward groaned. 'Oh Will, no!'

Hastings laughed. 'Eel and almonds. Your physician swears by it as the best cure there is for the consequences of too much drink!'

Edward's stomach began to heave as Hastings brought the platter closer and the smell of the raw eels seemed to reach down his throat and twist his uneasy guts.

Edward turned to look at him pleadingly, but Hastings's face was set.

'I have already spread the paste onto the bread for you,' he said wickedly.

'I thank you, Lord Chamberlain, you are kindness itself! A true angel of mercy!' Edward said sarcastically as he struggled to sit up. He wrinkled his nose as Hastings placed the platter on his knees. 'I do not suppose you wish to eat it for me too?' he growled.

'No thank you, my liege,' Hastings replied. 'But I could always send for your physician if there is a problem! I'm sure he could suggest a stronger remedy if needs be!'

Edward almost laughed, but his throbbing head prevented him from doing so; he knew Hastings was trying to teach him a lesson, and it had nothing to do with eel and almond paste! He met Hastings's amused expression seriously. 'As always Will, you are right,' he said evenly. 'But there is no easy cure for the cancer that will come.'

'No easy cure, Ned,' Hastings said, 'but a cure does exist!'

Edward knew what his chamberlain was going to say, knew that he'd been right about leaving London, that it was like leaving the doors and windows open and inviting in the thieves. And like a thief Warwick was coming! 'I know, Will,' he said, answering the unspoken question. 'We shall leave soon, I promise. But 'tis not yet certain where he will land.'

Hastings frowned. 'Ned, you know as well as I where that will be.'

VALOGNES AUGUST 1470

At the sound of the door, Elizabeth looked away from the window.

'You sent for me, mistress?' Sarah asked quietly. She stared at the rushes as she dropped into a curtsey.

Elizabeth breathed deeply, trying to steady her nerves. 'Yes Sarah. You know I asked you about a letter and a necklace I cannot find?'

'Yes, mistress.' Sarah's eyes did not leave the rushes and she knotted her hands together in front of her stomach.

Elizabeth wondered if Higgins could be right after all; it was not like Sarah to be so demure. She gritted her teeth. She could not believe Sarah had played any part in this; Santa Maria, she had told Sarah *everything*! Both Lord Hastings and Master Higgins had told her to trust no one, but in her despair over Warwick she had divulged the whole tale to Sarah! Not so much 'the perfect spy' after all, she thought ruefully. She closed her eyes briefly, focusing her mind.

'Sarah,' Elizabeth said more firmly. 'It is very important that I find them, do you understand?'

Sarah looked up at her for a moment before contemplating the floor again. A thin strand of blonde hair escaped from her cap and for some reason it made her look younger. Still she said nothing.

Elizabeth rose from the settle. She tried to quieten her drumming heart. Surely Sarah could not be responsible for this? Elizabeth had to know the truth. She reached out and took hold of Sarah's hands. They trembled at her touch as if Elizabeth had scalded her.

'Sarah,' she said, trying to keep her voice even. 'Sarah, I must get them back. Do you hear me?'

Sarah still did not respond. Why did she not defend herself?

Elizabeth tightened her grip. 'Sarah! I *must* get them back. Do you understand? My life could depend on it!'

Sarah looked up at her, her blue eyes wide in panic. 'I swear I did not take them, mistress!'

Elizabeth felt some relief at that; she could see Sarah was telling her the truth. But the alarm in her servant's face told her there was more to this. 'Sarah? What is it?'

Tears began to run down Sarah's cheeks. 'Oh, mistress!' she wailed. 'Please forgive me!'

'Sarah?' Elizabeth asked. 'What has happened?'

'I'm sorry, mistress,' Sarah sobbed.

Santa Maria, what had she done? 'You must tell me everything,' Elizabeth demanded, maintaining her grip on her distraught servant. 'Do you understand? *Everything!*'

Sarah nodded.

Elizabeth led Sarah back to the window seat.

Outside the oblivious world rushed by in a dizzy haze of preparation. Out there Warwick was amongst them, his energy burning him like fire, using every part of his being to draw them all together against Edward. And inside this room Elizabeth was part of the ruin of all his plans. But he must never know of it.

'I meant no harm, mistress,' Sarah sobbed as she sat down. 'I should have thought more on Master Atherstone and then none of this would have happened.'

Elizabeth was puzzled; what did John Atherstone of Warwick, Sarah's beau, have to do with this? 'Sarah, you must tell me all,' she said more gently.

Sarah took a deep breath. 'He had such lovely dark eyes, mistress and he was so handsome with a wide smile and black hair

56

which curled at his collar. A proper gentleman he was. Oh not so grand as my lord of Warwick, but as fine a man as ever I did have conversation with...' Sarah clamped her mouth shut, suddenly aware of what she had said.

Elizabeth's eyes widened. 'Who was he, Sarah?' she asked.

Sarah shrugged. 'Guy de Burgoyne,' she stammered. 'He seemed so kind, mistress. He said such lovely things to me. He brought me flowers and sweetmeats, and he looked so fine too; his clothes were of the best black velvet trimmed with silver! Did I say how handsome he was?'

'He *spoke* with you?' Elizabeth asked, amazed that Sarah would not question the motives of such a gentleman's attention to her.

Sarah nodded. Tears welled again. 'Oh, worse than that, mistress,' she said and began to cry again.

Elizabeth gripped her hand reassuringly.

'We – we came in here, mistress. I swear it was his suggestion, but I did not refuse.' She hung her head in shame. 'We – we only kissed, mistress,' she muttered into her chest.

Elizabeth's throat tightened with anger. Sarah had brought a man into Elizabeth's chamber! But she needed to know the whole tale, so she bit back her anger and nodded for her to continue.

'Then he wanted wine, mistress,' Sarah continued. 'And when I returned with it he had gone. I have not seen him since.' Sarah began to cry bitterly now. 'I was such a fool, mistress! I thought he liked me, but I was just the way in to steal your things!'

Elizabeth pulled her to her shoulder. The anger waned; Sarah would not be the last woman to be undone by a bright smile and beautiful eyes, Elizabeth thought. At least it showed that this Guy de Burgoyne was no common thief; this man had known what he was after. A common thief would not have taken the letter; he would have grabbed candlesticks, or Elizabeth's Book of Hours, things that were portable and saleable. This man had risked much in wooing Sarah and then entering Elizabeth's chamber with her; he was certainly daring. Suddenly a thought sprang into her mind and it sent a cold shiver down her spine. Could Guy de Burgoyne have been the man she had seen on the ship and the man she sensed rather than saw at the harbour?

* * *

Elizabeth knew telling Higgins of the dark stranger was going to be difficult and her tongue stumbled over the words as she confessed. She braced herself for his anger. She held her breath.

'You should have told me of your suspicions,' Higgins hissed. 'I expect the man *is* one and the same.'

Elizabeth hung her head. Instinctively she had known the man was avoiding Higgins, but she had somehow assumed that the man was acting on her behalf, not against her. She had no way of knowing that, and it now seemed that she had misjudged the situation badly.

'I should have been more attentive,' Higgins said, evidently seeing her anguish. 'I have been so busy lately with gathering details of Warwick's force for King Edward that I have left you all but unguarded.'

Elizabeth shuddered. She did not want more attention from Higgins, but if her treachery was discovered he might be her only hope of salvation.

'That is past,' she said. 'We cannot change that. But who is this man, Master Higgins and more importantly, what does he want? If it was simply to expose me, then he could have taken the necklace and the letter to Warwick straightaway.'

'You are right, Elizabeth,' Higgins sighed, 'which makes me think he too plays for higher stakes.'

'What do you mean?' Elizabeth asked. Fear began to cloud her vision.

'He could simply be one of Warwick's men, but that is the best scenario. He could be a man of Burgundy, but worst of all he could be a man in King Louis's employ.'

Elizabeth gasped.

'Indeed,' Higgins said, 'for King Louis to have knowledge of us within Warwick's household is dangerous indeed. Who knows when he would break that news to the earl?'

'Or why,' Elizabeth added, 'for it could strengthen or weaken their cause.'

'It would strengthen the bond between King Louis and Warwick, would it not?' Higgins said grimly. 'If he could prove King Edward had spies here and that he, Louis, had uncovered them! We must hope that is not the state of affairs. There are many possibilities but as yet few answers. My own enquiries have confirmed your servant's story. He has been here as long as we have, this Guy de Burgoyne and it seems that straightaway he singled

Sarah out for special attention. I am sure the name is false, and I am equally sure that she will not see him again.'

'Then what do we do, Master Higgins? Now can we leave?' The word 'leave' had a haunting quality to it, because in her soul the last thing she wanted to do was leave Warwick, and the longer she spent in his company the harder leaving him would be. She looked at Higgins pleadingly.

'We do nothing,' Higgins said flatly.

'Nothing?' Elizabeth asked in disbelief. 'But what if he reveals us?'

Higgins shrugged. 'We have to act as if nothing has happened. We may be fortunate in that he may simply want money for the items, but I doubt it. As you say, he has had time to pass them over to Warwick, or whoever his master is already. Warwick may know all. But we must take the risk; I still have much to accomplish before we can return to England. I need to see the fleet at Barfleur.'

Elizabeth shivered; what if Warwick knew her terrible secret already? What if he had the evidence in his hands? When would he tell her? When would he confront her? And how long could she keep up the appearance of an innocent?

'The only thing I can be certain of Elizabeth,' Higgins said slowly, 'is that we shall know soon enough.'

Elizabeth could not bear the thought that Warwick might know of her treacherous meeting with Clarence on Edward's behalf.

She looked up at Higgins and for a moment his face softened at her distress. 'You have served your king as your father would have wished,' he said softly. 'Sir Robert would be very proud of you.'

Evidently that was Higgins's attempt at comfort; it did not work. Elizabeth's mind was racing through all the possibilities; her stomach turned somersaults as she wondered when exactly she would be called to account.

BARFLEUR AUGUST 1470

'A soldiers' town,' Warwick had called it and it was certainly true. The air was thick with the sound of English voices and the streets were cluttered with livery-jacketed men of all shapes and sizes. But, Elizabeth thought, these were not happy men. They were disgruntled, argumentative and bawdy. It seemed that each

59

twisted alleyway, each dingy tavern and each smoky inn was choked with surly Englishmen. Even now they jostled the men-at-arms sent to clear the way for Warwick and his retinue.

Elizabeth glanced at Warwick. Concern showed in his eyes and she tried to reassure him with a smile; she must be prepared to endure whatever circumstances came their way.

'Thomas will have our lodgings ready,' Warwick called.

She could barely hear him above the noise; she was glad that she did not have to live amongst these coarse and dirty Englishmen all the time.

Warwick had sent word ahead of their arrival and so Thomas was indeed waiting for them.

He smiled and bowed to Warwick and then came round to help Elizabeth down from her palfrey. Stiffly she swung out of the saddle and his strong arms held her while she found her feet.

'Thank you,' she smiled into his eyes. A pink flush coloured Thomas's cheeks and he looked away quickly.

'What news, Thomas?' Warwick was beside them in an instant.

Thomas released Elizabeth and turned to his lord.

'We have almost two hundred brigandines at Rouen, my lord, together with eighty bows and some three hundred quivers.'

Warwick smiled. 'That is well done!'

'I have sent also to Paris, my lord; they hold four hundred bows and a thousand quivers there for us.'

'Excellent, Thomas,' Warwick said brightly.

'But I must speak to you about payment, my lord. Once again King Louis's purse strings seem to have been drawn shut.'

'God's blood!' Warwick growled. 'Does he not see that the longer he stalls on the payment the longer we shall remain in France?'

Thomas looked down. 'I am sorry, my lord, I did all that I could.'

'I am sure that you did, Thomas, thank you. We shall discuss this over supper,' Warwick said as he slipped an arm around Elizabeth's shoulders. He turned to her. 'Do you forgive us, Elizabeth?'

'Of course I forgive you,' she said, 'these are the necessities of war.' And could she perhaps say the same of her own conduct? And would he forgive her as easily? She doubted it.

Warwick began to lead her towards the hall. 'Welcome to Barfleur,' he said brightly, 'our home till we sail for England!'

Elizabeth smiled up at him. She swept her look over his face. She could see no evidence that he knew anything of the necklace and the letter, or what they represented. But she was not reassured. Warwick was the master politician; he could cloak his thoughts behind an inscrutable smile if he wished to, whilst seeing directly into his opponent's unguarded soul, or so it seemed. Elizabeth shivered; whichever way she turned she was trapped in a web of her own weaving! She had only ever sought to do right, but now she had no idea what was right and what was wrong!

The hall glittered with candles but Elizabeth noted there were no expensive tapestries as she would have expected; perhaps they had been sold to buy more provisions or ordnance. She walked further in. The pleasant aroma of cooking filled the room, making her hungry. She smiled as she noted Warwick at the table. He was deep in conversation with Thomas. Lines furrowed his brow, but he dismissed them as he saw her approaching. They both rose and bowed to her as she settled herself between them; this was not the lavish formality of Warwick Castle or Edward's court; first and foremost Warwick was a soldier now. She met Warwick's gaze and he rewarded her with a wide smile. He nodded for grace to be said and Elizabeth stole a look at him as the words of blessing flowed into the room. Elizabeth thought that was another sin she would have to confess! Then the servants brought bowls of rosewater for them to wash their hands and a stream of attendants entered the hall carrying the first dishes.

Elizabeth noticed Thomas watching her. He caught her look and lowered his gaze.

'How are you finding a soldier's life, Thomas?' Elizabeth asked as the first of the dishes were served.

Thomas's cheeks flushed as he fixed her face. 'I did not know this was soldiering!' he said truthfully. 'I had dreamed of wars and battles, banners and lances, but now all I dream about are muster rolls, quittances and bills!'

Elizabeth smiled. 'You cannot have one without the other; an army must be well provided for if it is going to fight well.'

'That is true,' Thomas said, 'but I think that I shall be so exhausted from all this victualling, that I may not be able to fight at all!'

'You had better be able to fight, Master Conyers,' Warwick said, 'or you shall have to answer to me for it! Though I must confess you are almost as good a steward as your uncle, Sir John.'

The smile died on Elizabeth's lips as she thought on Sir John Conyers, the steward of Middleham – the man who had imprisoned her father. Anger tightened her throat.

Warwick must have seen the change come over her, for his hand found hers on the table. 'I am sorry, sweeting,' he said softly. 'I know you hold Sir John and I culpable for your father's death.'

Elizabeth looked up at him. How much she had hated them both! It seemed inconceivable now that Warwick was so near, but in her grief she had believed the untruths of others, to the cost of her soul!

'When we return to England I shall make amends, I promise,' Warwick continued gently. 'He was a good man,' he said huskily. 'I think I never had a better friend. It is that friendship I shall remember, Elizabeth, not our quarrel over fickle Edward.'

Elizabeth's throat tightened further. If she had not been in company she was sure she would have run to some dark corner and cried. But she wanted to show that she too had her pride: she could be like a Neville. She forced a thin smile. 'I confess that I cursed both you and the name of Conyers my lord,' she said coolly. 'And if you ask for your beautiful reliquary you may find it on the path to Jervaulx, for that is where I threw it!'

Warwick's eyes widened and his grip tightened on her hand. Then he drew it to his lips and kissed it. 'I am sorry, Elizabeth,' he murmured.

'Anger and tears will not bring him back, Richard, for if they did then he would be with us today. And is it not a sin to wish him from his place with God?' she said softly.

'You are an angel,' Warwick said.

'Not so,' Elizabeth replied, 'for if God listened to my curses, you will spend at least a thousand years in purgatory, though that is nothing to what I wished for Sir John Conyers!'

'It is understandable that you should have felt so,' Warwick said evenly. 'I do not blame you.'

'And I no longer blame you,' Elizabeth said. 'But I do not think I could go to Middleham again.' Her resolve began to give way as she remembered the circumstances of her father's death. She sucked in her breath to strangle the tears. She had said she had forgiven him, but she had certainly not forgiven Sir John!

Warwick squeezed her hand reassuringly.

Thomas looked puzzled and she saw Warwick flash a dark look to halt his curiosity.

A murmur of approval swept around the hall and Warwick's retainers began to applaud.

'Look, Elizabeth!' Warwick said. 'Here is my acrobat.'

Elizabeth drew her eyes away from Warwick and looked to where the acrobat was performing cartwheels and tumbles faster than a horse's gallop across the centre of the hall. She may have told Warwick she no longer blamed him for her father's death, but had she not paid him back in full measure with her actions? Would he be as understanding about that as he was about the lost reliquary?

'Do you know, sweeting,' Warwick continued, still looking at the whirling man, 'King Louis was so impressed with him that he gave him twenty crowns?'

'He should have spent his money more wisely,' Elizabeth said. 'How many longbows could he have purchased with that?'

Warwick laughed. His breath was warm on her cheek and it distracted her thoughts away from the events at Middleham.

She looked at Thomas. He still looked bewildered. At some point she would have to tell him that she held his uncle responsible for her father's death; that would certainly test their renewed friendship!

* * *

It was apparently the oldest excuse there was, but Elizabeth's claim of a headache had bought her the time she needed for her uneasy rendezvous.

Moonlight washed over the cobbles of the courtyard creating a pattern of soft dappled light, like pale sunshine through trees. Elizabeth smiled; it reminded her of Lazenby, the place she was born, the home of her soul. How many times had she seen candlelight flicker over the courtyard there and heard the warm laughter within as she returned from riding, far later than she should? She remembered the fierceness of her mother's eyes and the soft rebuke of her father – did she know they were worried about her? He would pull her into his chest and hold her gently.

He would whisper in her ear that she owed him much, for he had had to placate her mother!

Master Higgins was in shadow, or at least his face was. Elizabeth could see the glint of his cloak fastening as he breathed. She saw that his hand rested on the hilt of his basilard, and she shivered; she would not like to meet him in the darkness as an enemy.

'What news, mistress?' he asked coolly.

Elizabeth ducked into the shadows beside him. 'I have heard nothing that would interest you,' she lied. She was sure he would be interested to know of Thomas's acquisitions on Warwick's behalf. 'And you?'

Higgins shook his head. 'We leave for England tomorrow,' he said flatly.

The words fell like stones.

Elizabeth reeled with shock. She struggled to speak. 'But Master Higgins...' she stammered.

'Do not argue, Elizabeth,' he said darkly, 'you are in no position to gainsay my wishes! I have seen enough of Warwick's preparations to know that his time in France will now be short. My information is only of use in England.'

Elizabeth breathed deeply, trying to calm her racing heart. 'I do not want to go,' she said, shaking her head. 'I want to stay here.' How she had told herself that she must leave Warwick; that it was what was best for them both, but now Higgins was asking her to, she could not leave Warwick, could not disappear without a word.

Higgins's eyes knifed her in the darkness.

'You shall do as I say, mistress,' he hissed.

'But why would I leave him? What would I say?' Santa Maria, he was all she wanted in the world!

'If you are wise you will say nothing. If you say nothing you will not tell him any more lies,' Higgins said evenly.

Elizabeth bit her lip. God how it would hurt him if she left him now! 'I cannot do it,' Elizabeth said shakily.

Higgins's voice was cold. 'You will leave tomorrow; otherwise you will give me no choice but to tell him of your meeting with Clarence.'

'You would not dare!' Elizabeth said angrily, but she no longer had the counter-threat of King Edward's letter as a safeguard!

'Would I not? That is a great risk for you to take!' Higgins sneered. 'I will leave him a letter,' he said, 'or perhaps I will speak to young Thomas about it instead?'

'No!' Elizabeth cried out; she could not bear the thought of Thomas also knowing what she had done.

'Then you will make yourself ready, Elizabeth. We leave after Mass,' he said coldly. 'I will leave you to decide whether you give him a reason or no.'

She wanted to try to appeal to him, to make him go without her. But with a swirl of dark cloak he was gone from her side and away into the darkness and she knew her position was hopeless.

Elizabeth did not move. Was it the loss of Edward's letter that had forced Higgins to act now, before the truth came out? Did he perhaps know the identity of the thief and fear him? She struggled to make sense of it all. What should she say to Warwick? Or was to disappear without an explanation the best? Then at least he might think she had been abducted against her will. If only she had been stronger and not come to Barfleur!

Slowly she walked back to her apartment. A candle fluttered like a forlorn butterfly beside her bed. Warwick was still closeted away with his commanders; he would not come to her tonight. She kicked off her slippers and rolled back on the bed. If she left now, would she ever see him again?

Her stinging eyes gazed upwards at the rippling silver of the embroidered canopy. As her tears grew fiercer her vision began to blur until she could see nothing clearly. She choked them back as best she could. But she wanted to shout out that it was so unfair! She reached for her rosary and slipped the cold beads gently through her fingers. 'Oh Santa Maria,' she whispered over and over. Was this her punishment for Jack's death? Oh why had she not stayed with Matthew at Scarsdale? Surely Jack would not have dared touch her again? She turned onto her side. She was deceiving herself; Jack de Laverton would never have let her go, of that she was sure. But did that excuse her actions? The dark night of his death had seen her take the first step along this troubled path, and the road did not get any easier. She just wanted to do right, but what was the right thing to do now?

Could she not go to Warwick in all humility and confess what she had done; throw herself at his feet and beg for his forgiveness? Surely he was not beyond such compassion? She wiped her eyes with the back of her hand and sniffed back the tears. She knew the answer. She really had no choice.

* * *

Higgins stared at the letter. It had taken him some time to write; his hands did not cope well with a quill and he no longer saw so well at night. He had to admit there were more blots on the page than he would have liked, but it was legible. He smiled wolfishly; the only bad part in this enterprise was that he would not be there to see Warwick's face when he read it; see the horrified look when he learned that Elizabeth had lost his child, his only son, at Ellerton Nunnery. She had climbed the wall in a bid to escape but had fallen; she did not know of the child for she had been unconscious for a week and the nuns did not want to tell her and as her closest kin, for he had told them he was her kin, he had told them they were right in concealing this from her. He had known then it would be powerful knowledge; that it would allow a vengeful blow to be struck. Higgins wanted to see pain on Warwick's face and know it was the window into his heart. He wanted Warwick to feel what he had felt; to know what he knew: the agony of losing a child. For during that mission, when he lay at his captors' mercy, his wife and child had died and he had not known of it; returning with broken hands to a shattered home.

He folded the parchment over and sealed it with a daub of red wax. Then he sat back; everything was as he had planned it. Soon he and Elizabeth would be back in London with the king. Higgins smiled again, and a grateful king at that!

THREE

BARFLEUR AUGUST 1470

At first light the jetty was as crowded with people as on a market day and without Warwick's retainers to clear a path for them Elizabeth and Higgins struggled to make their way through. There were not as many boats in the harbour as Elizabeth thought there would be and she wondered if many had already sought England's shores. Several boats lay uneasily in the water, their sails flapping in the stiff salty breeze, but eventually Higgins found the boat he had been looking for.

Elizabeth ran her eyes over its sleek chestnut-coloured body; it was already crammed with people. Evidently there were many who wished to leave these shores before Warwick's invasion began.

As Higgins negotiated with the ship's master, Elizabeth looked round the little harbour, taking a last look at France. Sadness weighed on her shoulders like a winter mantle and she wondered if she would ever see Warwick or Thomas again. Her eyes wandered over the crooked buildings, which sagged towards the harbourside in distorted rows.

As she turned to look she saw a figure silhouetted in the tavern doorway, leaning against the frame and staring out. Though she could not see his eyes, it seemed that he was staring at her.

'What is it?' Higgins asked, evidently noticing her anxiety.

'Nothing, Master Higgins,' she said hurriedly, 'a shadow that is all.'

Higgins smiled.

'You do not need to be afraid of shadows, Elizabeth,' he said 'I shall protect you.'

Higgins followed the direction of her stare, but when Elizabeth turned to look back again there was no one there, the figure had disappeared into the crowd and she wondered if she had imagined him after all.

'Come, Elizabeth,' Higgins said, taking hold of her by the arm. 'A few days and we shall be back in England.'

Elizabeth's stomach lurched; she did not want to think about England and what awaited her there; did not want to think on what she was leaving behind or on what Warwick would think when he found her gone. She didn't want to dwell on any of this but her mind disobeyed her and as she walked unsteadily towards the little ship, thoughts whirled in her head like the bright gulls above her and she wondered how this would all end.

YORK AUGUST 1470

William Hastings saw Edward's mood darken like the sky before thunder.

'God's blood!' Edward cried. 'I might be Duke of York by rights, Hastings, but this is a godforsaken part of the world! Fitzhugh might have melted into Scotland at the mere sight of us, but there is such a deal of trouble here that nothing but a commission can settle it!'

'I thought the same, my liege,' Hastings said, 'but can we spare the time?' He knew that they couldn't; but did Edward?

Edward's eyes flashed fiercely. 'It is my duty, Will and if I do not subdue insurrection now, it will only rise again to goad me!'

Hastings cleared his throat, this was not going to be easy, but he had to speak his mind. 'And will Marquis Montagu be called upon as he was in Lincolnshire?'

Edward turned to face him. 'You still do not trust him, do you?'

The wounded look Edward gave him almost made Hastings regret his words. But it was his duty to warn Edward of his fears and he could not get rid of the feeling like sour wine in his stomach; the feeling that eventually John Neville would turn to his brother's cause.

'No, Ned I do not,' he said flatly. He thought of their fierce confrontation in London, when John Neville had all but assaulted him. He shivered at the memory. He and John had never liked each other much and after Hastings had replaced John as Edward's chamberlain the feelings had darkened on both sides. Hastings told himself that this feeling was more than that though.

'He has not wavered, Will,' Edward said brusquely. 'He has recruited more men than I could have hoped for and as you rightly point out, has served on commissions aplenty for me before.'

'I cannot help it, my liege. The feeling will not leave me.'

Edward sighed. 'Perhaps you are right, Will and I should not call on him; even if you are not, it will do no harm for me to guard against it; one must never underestimate the enemy!' he said caustically. 'Besides, I would not wish him to cease his present efforts on my behalf. I will couch it in such terms that he does not feel the exclusion as another slap in the face from me.'

'Aye, my liege,' Hastings agreed. He knew all too well what happened when Neville pride was hurt. 'And do we leave soon?'

'Ah, Will!' Edward sighed. 'These things are never easy to arrange! A full-blown commission could take weeks!'

Hastings sucked in his breath quickly and then realized Edward was smiling.

'You worry too much, Will!' Edward berated him. 'Yes we shall leave soon, just as soon as I have written to Marquis Montagu!'

BARFLEUR AUGST 1470

The little ship rocked gently on the swell as it lay in the harbour. Both the sea and sky were as grey as pewter, as though they reflected Elizabeth's mood. Certainly it was chill for August, Elizabeth thought.

'Hurry, Elizabeth,' Higgins said gruffly, snapping her from her reverie, as he stepped quickly towards the boat.

She followed him across the narrow planking which bridged the gap between the ship and the quay. She had a sudden vivid memory of Calais in the bright sunshine when she had arrived for Isabel's wedding; of Warwick holding her hand, escorting her across such a walkway as she disembarked. How perfect that day had been and the memory of it was a welcome fragment of happiness in her troubled mind.

Reluctantly she followed Higgins onto the crowded deck. She was surprised to see that so many people wanted to leave France for England. She wondered whom they supported – Warwick or ungrateful Edward?

'Elizabeth,' Higgins reached for her hand. 'Stay close by me, for it would be easy to lose you in this crowd.'

Elizabeth's heart jumped. Perhaps she would be able to break away from him somehow and return to Warwick?

The hope died in her mind as she saw Higgins position himself between her and the gangplank, as though he had read her thoughts; and once they were out in the Narrow Sea she knew there would be nowhere to hide from him, and she thought it very unlikely that she could persuade the master to turn the ship about! No, she had to face the fact that Higgins was her jailer until they reached England.

As the ship began to move away from the quay Elizabeth pushed towards the rail. Part of her was expecting to see the dark stranger once again leap the gap and disappear amongst the throng as he had at Dover. Could it have been Guy de Burgoyne? Would he haunt them still? But she saw nothing of interest. Strangely she was disappointed, as though his presence had given her hope, for inexplicably she had always thought that he was one of Warwick's affinity and somehow the loss of her necklace and letter had done nothing to dissuade her illogical mind from that thought.

She watched sadly as the quayside faded from view. As they left the safety of the harbour the wind drove into them and she almost lost her headdress. The little ship began to roll on the swell as they sailed out into the open sea and she saw several passengers cross themselves as the reality of their journey dawned upon them.

Elizabeth stayed at the rail for as long as she could. She tasted the salt on her lips and felt the freshening wind on her cheek. The biting sea spray stung her face as the ship danced on the waves. For these precious moments she was as free as she could ever be and she tried to enjoy it. Higgins however was not enjoying it. He leaned against a post, his moody eyes fixed on her. He refused to let her from his sight and as Elizabeth would not go below deck, he had no choice but to endure the elements as Elizabeth made the most of them. She wondered why he bothered; he could hardly lose her here - unless he thought her capable of dashing herself into the restless sea and saving them all much trouble.

* * *

As the sky began to turn to the deepest blue Elizabeth finally agreed to come away from the bulwark. The firebox cast an orange glow about the deck, illuminating the faces of the travellers, as they huddled together not only for warmth, but for company too.

Elizabeth however craved solitude. After eating her portion of salt fish and pottage she decided to go below. Stealthily she manoeuvred herself between people and around barrels, trying to put some distance between herself and Higgins. He eyed her suspiciously, and for a while he continued to follow her. But his own common sense must have told him that she could not escape from this ship and that wherever she hid from him, he would find her sooner or later.

The large chamber below was also full of people. Their noisy chatter hummed in Elizabeth's ears, like a swarm of bees in summer. She pushed her way through them, to where warmed spiced wine was being served. She swirled the cup in her hands and watched the little whirlpool for a moment, as if she hoped to see her destiny revealed by it. She sipped the soothing liquid and it warmed her throat and belly. The spices reminded her of Christmas; they reminded her of Warwick. They reminded her also of how happy she had been then, but that only served to reinforce her sense of desolation, knowing that she could never return to that blissful time. She had ruined everything!

She moved to the far end of the room, away from the crowd so that at last she could think. She looked back at the noisy gathering and wondered if any of these people had a story as wild as her own. Suddenly Elizabeth became aware of someone close beside her. She sighed resignedly and prepared to meet the unforgiving eyes of Master Higgins.

Without warning a strong hand gripped her arm, pulling her off balance. Before she could cry out the man's other hand covered her mouth. Elizabeth could not breathe. Long fingers pressed on her cheek. She dropped her cup. In an instant she was in the shadows. She stared at the wall, her body pinned between it and her assailant. His hips pressed into her back. His sword hilt dug into her side. His breath was hot on her neck.

'Elizabeth, if you love the Earl of Warwick you will not cry out,' his voice whispered in her ear.

Her heart stopped beating when he spoke. Her head swam but she managed to nod an agreement and he released his hold on her. Slowly she turned round, hardly daring to believe what her senses were telling her. His face was half in shadow from the hood of his cloak, but she would have known him anywhere.

He smiled his errant smile at her as he looked at the shock on her face. 'Good evening, sweetheart,' he said huskily.

His voice was deeper than she remembered it, but the nonchalant way he stood, with his arms folded across his chest, was unmistakeable.

'You must forgive my rough introduction, Elizabeth. I couldn't risk you calling out.'

Elizabeth struggled to speak, struggled to think, and even struggled to breathe.

'J – Jack!' she stammered. 'B – But I thought you were dead!'

'I must thank you sweetheart, for giving me the perfect alibi,' he said. His black eyes flicked to hers and a cold shiver slid down her back.

'How?' She could hardly manage the word.

'But for Brother William, I would have died,' he said evenly.

Elizabeth's eyes widened. 'Brother William?'

Jack nodded.

Brother William of Jervaulx also worked for Warwick; so he had helped Jack as well as Elizabeth. Was that why Brother William had wanted her to seek confession at Jervaulx Abbey and again at Ellerton Nunnery - because he wanted to tell her she was not a killer? Her mind whirled with questions.

'But – there was a funeral?' she stammered.

'Ah, yes,' Jack grinned. 'One of Matthew's best pigs is, I understand, the recipient of my prayers and obits!'

Elizabeth did not smile. 'A pig?' she said icily, 'how appropriate!'

Jack laughed softly.

Red and white points of light floated into Elizabeth's vision as the reality of her situation became clear. She put her hand against the wall to steady herself. She had thought she would never see Jack de Laverton again. Beautiful, dangerous Jack; the very thought of him and what had happened made her feel sick.

'I have been watching you for some time,' Jack said quietly.

Elizabeth met his eyes and her stomach knotted at the thought of him watching her lasciviously, and she remembered the closeness of him at Scarsdale; his hands touching her, his lips hot on hers.

Jack must have seen the fear. Gently he touched her arm.

Elizabeth jumped as if he had burned her.

'I will not harm you, Elizabeth,' he said.

Elizabeth stared at him dumbly.

'I have come to help you. We both know you do not wish to return to London.'

She nodded. Her throat was too dry for her to speak. She tried to collect her thoughts. How could he help her, the man who had changed her life irrevocably? Suddenly her anger found her voice. 'You do not know how many times I have relived that moment,' she snapped, 'the moment when I thought I had sent my soul into hell!'

'And mine?' Jack asked flatly. He held her gaze; waiting for an answer he knew would not come. 'I am glad we are now on the same side,' he said.

'Are we?' Elizabeth hissed. 'I think you serve no man but yourself!'

Jack nodded his head. 'I can see why you might think so, sweetheart, but I swore allegiance to Warwick and I will see my mission through.'

He spoke so calmly that Elizabeth wanted to strike him. It was as if he had done nothing more than blown her an imprudent kiss. 'I cannot forgive you,' she hissed. 'That day in the rose arbour, you would have...' her throat tightened '...if Cousin Matthew had not.... How could you have done such a thing?'

The memories of that day came flooding back to her again: the smell of the stale beer on Jack's breath mixed with the cloying perfume of the roses. She remembered the thorns pricking her as she struggled to break free of him and she remembered her beloved book trampled under their feet. Tears stung her eyes.

Jack lowered his arrogant gaze.

Blood pulsed in Elizabeth's cheeks. How could he answer her accusation with anything honourable?

When Jack looked up at her again his eyes were wider, softer. 'You are right, sweetheart. Forgive me,' he said quietly.

Elizabeth stared at him mutely. How could she ever forgive him? It was too much to contemplate. She shook her head and then looked about the busy cabin, searching for something or someone to help her. But in truth she had little choice – she either allowed Jack to help her return to Warwick, or she returned to Higgins and with that option came the dreadful thought of returning to London.

Jack was staring at her; plainly he understood her dilemma. 'It is your choice, lady. I swear I have changed. You are in no danger from me.'

She met his look with one of suspicion.

'I can help you return to my lord Warwick,' he said, 'or you can return to London with Higgins.' He shrugged his lean shoulders as if her decision didn't matter.

'Or I can ignore both of you!' Elizabeth hissed.

Jack laughed. She watched the ripple of his throat, darkened with the dusky shadow of a day's stubble. His laugh was rich and warm, not as she remembered it.

'I think that would not be wise,' he said. 'A woman travelling alone is vulnerable.'

There was darkness in his voice, which made Elizabeth shiver. How right he was; her encounter with Gervase had made that clear; she had ended up in a nunnery, but it could have been worse! She fought to regain some control. 'Why should I trust you?' she asked indignantly.

'Because you must, sweetheart. I am Warwick's man; you know that. I am your best hope of returning to him.'

Elizabeth let out a long slow breath; she knew that he was right.

'But first of all we must deal with Higgins!' Jack said.

Elizabeth's heart kicked at the sudden malice in his voice. 'Jack no – you cannot kill him!' she said. She knew only too well how killing a man in cold blood felt.

'I should have killed him when he first acted as courier for your father; it would have saved us all much trouble. But I did not, and you have suffered much because of it. He must pay.' He turned away from her.

Elizabeth grabbed his arm fiercely. 'Jack, no!' she pleaded. 'He does not deserve to die.'

Jack looked back at her over his shoulder and she saw his brows pleat questioningly.

'He helped me,' she said. In spite of everything she harboured some sympathy for Higgins. Without him would she ever have escaped from Ellerton Nunnery?

'He helped you because it suited his purpose,' Jack said coldly. 'Do not read anything more into it.'

'No... there was something else...his daughter.'

'You think so?' Jack scoffed. 'I tell you, you are mistaken lady. The man is as cunning as the Devil. For God's sake Elizabeth, he is Edward's spymaster!'

Elizabeth saw his eyes narrow. 'Do not judge others by your own base standards,' she said.

Jack gave an ironic smile. 'He would do anything to bring War-wick down. Do you hear me, Elizabeth? Anything! There will be no room for sentiment; no place for 'daughters'.'

Elizabeth let go of Jack's arm. She knew Jack was right, had Higgins not proved it by making her leave now? 'I had known him for so long as my father's retainer and yet I did not know him at all,' she said sadly.

Jack sighed. 'Very well, sweetheart. Because you ask me to I will leave him for now. But if he crosses our path...' Jack's hand flicked the hilt of his sword warningly.

'Thank you,' she said. But, like Jack, she knew their paths would cross again.

'I almost forgot,' Jack said suddenly. 'I have something of yours.'

Elizabeth gave him a puzzled look.

Jack reached into his doublet. Slowly he drew out something that glittered. It looked like pearls.

Elizabeth gasped. 'My necklace!'

'You should be careful where you leave such things,' Jack said with a laugh.

'You?' Elizabeth cried, her eyes widening. She fixed Jack's face warily. 'Guy de Burgoyne?' she asked him.

Jack nodded his head. 'At your service,' he said with a wry smile.

Elizabeth shivered. Did she have any secrets from Jack? Santa Maria he had been in her bedchamber!

'How long have you been watching me for?' she asked tentatively, trying to control the tremor in her voice.

Jack grinned. 'You saw me at the boat, I think?'

Elizabeth nodded. How could she forget the agile stranger?

'But did you also know I was at Edward's court?'

Elizabeth shook her head.

'Though I did not see him give this to you, I knew of it,' Jack said with a glint in his eye.

Elizabeth's cheeks flushed at the shame of the memory. And did he also know of the letter? Why had he not mentioned that?

'And I also know that this necklace is not the type of reward he has in mind for you when you return. I saw the way he looked at you in the hall.'

'You are not so different then!' Elizabeth said coldly.

Jack turned away from her. 'I regret what happened at Scarsdale,' he said quietly, 'but I cannot change it.'

'No, you cannot,' she agreed.

Jack sighed. 'As I said Elizabeth, the choice is yours.'

Elizabeth shivered as she looked at the shimmering necklace in his hand. She hung her head guiltily, conscious of what it represented.

'And does Warwick know?' she asked uneasily.

Jack reached forward and took her hand in his. She shuddered and tried to withdraw it, but he held it tightly, compelling her attention. His eyes flicked over her face. 'Warwick knows you were there, Elizabeth, but he thinks it was all for Isabel, he knows nothing of your visit to Clarence.'

Elizabeth shivered at the mention of Clarence's name. Then she realized what his words meant: she had no secrets from Jack.

'You... did not tell him?' she asked.

Jack shook his head. 'No, I did not tell him.'

She searched Jack's eyes frantically, trying to see if he was lying to her.

He smiled reassuringly but she knew the respite was only temporary. She wondered why Jack had kept this from Warwick. She almost laughed; she knew why: it gave him power over her. And who knew when Jack would choose to use it? That was why he had not mentioned the letter! They both knew he had it somewhere; both knew he had the power to destroy her if he wished to.

Jack pulled her towards him gently. 'He need never know,' he said smoothly. 'It shall be our secret.'

Elizabeth's stomach twisted at the thought of sharing anything with Jack, least of all such a powerful secret. His breath was warm against her cheek and his eyes were wide and yielding. Was this how he had been with Sarah? No wonder Elizabeth did not recognise him from her maid's description; Elizabeth had never seen Jack like this.

Suddenly Jack looked up. He put his finger to his lips.

Elizabeth turned to see Higgins. He had entered the cabin. He was heading towards them, pushing his way through the other passengers. His eyes flicked frantically over every face, evidently searching for Elizabeth.

Elizabeth's heart quickened.

Jack's face darkened.

'Jack, do not kill him!' she whispered.

Black fire burned in Jack's eyes. 'I take it you do not want him to find you?' he asked as he put the necklace away.

Elizabeth looked at Jack and ran her tongue over her dry lips. She knew she had to make a choice quickly.

'Well, my lady?' Jack asked. 'You must choose.'

Sweat began to trickle down her back. Her palms were damp. She could not face travelling with Higgins again. But how could she agree to be with Jack?

'Answer me,' Jack pushed, casting a quick look towards Higgins.

Elizabeth followed his look; Higgins was drawing clear of the crowd. She could hear his breathing. Panic gripped her throat; there was nowhere to hide; surely he would see her! Frantically she looked back to Jack.

He stood impassively, as though all was well in the world.

'Jack?' she whispered hoarsely.

A smile twitched the corner of his mouth. 'Make your choice, sweetheart,' he whispered. He tightened his grip on his sword hilt.

Elizabeth could hear Higgins's scratchy breathing drawing closer. 'Jack, please!'

Jack's eyes narrowed as he looked back towards Higgins. His jaw tightened. Then he began to slide the sword smoothly from its scabbard.

Elizabeth's heart punched her ribs. 'Jack, please don't!' she whispered.

Suddenly Jack let go of his sword and spun her round.

Elizabeth gasped with shock.

Then Jack pulled her close, wrapping her in the folds of his black cloak. Jack's scent filled her lungs. A shock of his black hair caressed her face. Elizabeth struggled as the memory of Scarsdale began to choke her. But then she heard the wheezing rasp of Higgins's breathing and she shrank away from it, sinking into Jack's embrace. She closed her eyes, trying to forget where she was, trying to blot out the warmth of Jack, the strength of his arms and the thought that they might be discovered. She felt sick. Jack's arms tightened again, pulling her closer.

Higgins came within a foot of where they stood entwined. He stopped. His breathing puffed like a blacksmith's old bellows.

Jack's hands slipped down her back, pulling her hips closer to his. Elizabeth wanted to cry out to him to stop, but the rasping of Higgins breath prevented her. Instead she slid her arms about

Jack's waist and pressed against his chest, desperate to be hidden from view.

Higgins's breathing stayed where it was.

Elizabeth's heart stopped with fear. Her head swam. Her mind still fought to maintain her sense of place, but here, in the warmth of Jack's body, only a whisper from discovery, she was lost. Tears stung her eyes and she could bear it no longer; she would have to tear herself away from Jack, even if it meant Higgins would find her.

Just as her resolve gave way, Jack released her; Higgins was nowhere in sight.

Elizabeth looked up at Jack, startled.

Jack's eyes held her gaze and he began to smile.

Wordlessly they stared at each other for several breathless heartbeats.

Then Jack broke the spell. 'Well, Elizabeth, I could say I am sorry for the necessity of that little deception, but you would know that it was untrue.'

He caught her hand an inch from his face.

Elizabeth dropped her gaze and tried to pull her hand free. But Jack held it tightly, his fingers pressing on her pulse as though he would control her lifeblood. 'Why must you always try to hurt me?' he asked.

'Because you always try to take advantage of me!' Elizabeth snapped.

'I am uncertain who was taking advantage of whom just then,' he laughed. 'Did I not keep you safe, as I promised?'

Elizabeth glared at him and snatched her wrist from his grip. 'And did you not enjoy it?' she growled.

Jack grinned. 'Come, sweetheart,' he said, ignoring her question, 'we must find ourselves a better place than this. Do you have a blanket?'

Elizabeth shook her head. 'Higgins has all our things with him.'

Jack tutted. 'That is a pity, for it will be chill tonight under the stars.' Then the grin claimed Jack's face again. 'Of course you are welcome to share mine if you wish.'

Elizabeth's stomach plummeted. 'I would rather freeze to death!' she snapped.

'Oh no Elizabeth, I cannot allow that to happen. You have put me to much trouble,' he said. 'And I promised my lord I would find you.'

Elizabeth stared at him uncertainly for a moment; she doubted Warwick knew of Jack's quest and she wondered exactly what Warwick knew of their invidious history. Did he know she had wounded Jack? Did he too think Jack was dead?

'Come,' Jack said again, snapping her thoughts. 'You have made your decision.' He reached out his hand to her.

Tentatively she gave him her hand; he was right, she had chosen. Slowly he began to lead her through the crowd of passengers.

'Come, lady, mend your looks,' Jack said softly. 'These people have just seen you in my arms; you cannot now look at me as if you hate me.'

Elizabeth looked up at him and forced a smile.

'Much better!' he grinned.

He led her out onto the deck. The firebox had gone out. The only light was the creaking sway of the watchman's dancing lantern, which threatened to die at any moment. The sky was a diadem of starlight, and the moon was a new thin crescent. The wind screamed across the deck, almost drowning out the roar of the ocean. The planks were wet with sea-foam. The few sails that were still hoisted flapped noisily and it seemed as though summer had abandoned the Narrow Sea as God had abandoned Elizabeth. A few souls huddled close together in their blankets like beggars, oblivious to Elizabeth and Jack.

Jack led her to where several large barrels were lashed together with thick rope.

'These will give us some shelter,' he said.

He shook out his bedroll and then sat down, drawing his knees towards his body.

Elizabeth watched him uneasily. Her face stung with the force of the wind and she wrapped her arms about her, trying to prevent herself from shivering. She knew the answer to her own question as to whether this was necessary, but even in her worst nightmare she had not thought she would have to spend the night with Jack de Laverton. Her skin prickled at the thought of it and her stomach churned like the sea. Her teeth began to chatter.

Jack patted the blanket at his side and Elizabeth sat down reluctantly, leaving as much space between them as she could.

'Sweetheart,' Jack whispered, 'you must come close to me, it is cold and will be colder yet before morning. I promise I will not harm you.'

Elizabeth watched him warily. His eyes were two deep pools of blackness, lit only by the watchman's flickering light. She watched as he blinked slowly; it was like staring into dark water. Her breath caught; she still found him unnervingly handsome, just as she had at their first meeting at Lazenby, when she had delighted in the company of this fine-looking knight! Part of her wanted to believe he would not hurt her, but the episode in the cabin had unsettled her again. So much had happened between them already, she thought. She began to shiver violently.

'Elizabeth,' he said gently, 'I swear it.' He reached out an arm and placed it over her shoulder. He drew her and the blanket into his chest.

Elizabeth did not fight him, but rested her head against his shoulder. The sound of the wild elements dulled as she pressed herself to him. His cloak was warm against her face and Jack's breath caressed her other cheek. He pulled her tightly to him and gradually the heat from his body began to reach her core. The scent of him invaded her senses like incense. The even rise and fall of his chest lulled her. Her eyelids grew heavy. Her breathing began to deepen and in a few more heartbeats she knew she would be asleep. Only God knew if Jack de Laverton's intentions were honourable or not; Elizabeth had no choice but to trust him.

BARFLEUR AUGUST 1470

'What do you mean she has gone?' Warwick growled.

'I have searched everywhere, my lord,' Thomas said apologetically. 'I have spoken with her servants. They did not see her retire last night, and her bed had not been slept in. They have not seen her since the previous evening when she retired early with a headache; they – they assumed she was with you my lord,' he stammered.

Warwick could not comprehend what Thomas was saying. He knew what the words meant, of course, but still he did not understand how Elizabeth could be missing. His mind was a whirlpool of half thoughts; nothing sturdy and nothing sensible would come to him. He thought of a search, but that he knew was ridiculous; he could spare neither the men nor the time to do it properly. And where would they start?

'What do you think, Thomas?' he asked shakily. He could see by Thomas's face that he was as troubled as he was.

'I think someone has taken her,' Thomas said. 'Elizabeth would not leave your side, my lord.'

'Yes, Thomas you are right. She was not happy here I know, but she endured it for my sake; so she could be with me. But who could have taken her Thomas and why would they do such a thing?'

'If we answer the first question I think the last one will answer itself,' Thomas said.

'Can you think of anyone who might harm her?' Warwick asked. The thought began to choke him.

Thomas shook his head. 'No, my lord.'

God's blood what he would do if they hurt her! Then a thought struck Warwick like a sword thrust; perhaps her abduction had been arranged to hurt *him*. Elizabeth was suffering because of him! There was only one person who would wish to hurt him like this.

'Somehow this is Edward's doing,' Warwick said coldly. 'I know that it is.'

'Edward?' Thomas asked in disbelief.

'Aye, one of his agents has no doubt taken her in order to weaken me. If they harm her...' his voice cracked and tears stung at his eyes. Why had he brought her here? If she had stayed with Isabel, as he had wished, then she would be safe still. But that was a lie. He had given in to her request to join him because he had wanted her close. Even though he had somehow sensed the danger, he had been unable to turn her away from him. And now his worst fears were realized: she was gone.

'Where would they take her, Thomas?' he tried to think out loud, to rationalize his chaotic thoughts.

'I do not know my lord, France is a big country.'

'But if it is as I fear and they are Edward's men, then France is not a safe place to hide.' His breath caught at his throat. 'What if they have taken her back to England?'

'But my lord, I doubt if any ships are sailing,' Thomas said. 'Fauconberg reported that the Narrow Sea is full of Burgundians, and Anthony Wydeville too is out there!'

Warwick exhaled slowly. He was almost certain this was the plan; somehow he knew it.

'Go down to the harbour, Thomas,' he said with false firmness. 'See what you can learn. Take a few good men with you, for they might not have sailed yet.'

If he had really thought there was a chance she was still here he would have gone himself, but instinctively he knew she was no longer in France.

'My lord,' Thomas bowed and then hurried from the room.

Warwick turned to the window. He rubbed distractedly at his chin. The day had dawned brightly. There was hardly a cloud to spoil the faultless blue of the sky. The wind whipped in from the sea cooling the sultry air a little, and making the pennants strain against their fittings, but it did not cool Warwick's wrath. It burned within him like an ague and he knew it would not be calmed until he once again had Elizabeth beside him. He let out a long slow breath in a bid to calm the drumming of his heart. He had thought he could not stand another separation from her and now that thought was to be put to the test. Would he be strong enough to invade England, hold the alliance together and win back the crown for Lancaster? Doubt jagged through him like fire. He leant against the windowsill and bowed his head as he prayed to Saint George for courage, and for the resilience to find Elizabeth before Edward did.

NARROW SEA AUGUST 1470

The sky was only just beginning to brighten when Elizabeth woke. For a few heartbeats she did not know where she was. Then it all came flooding back to her like a storm surge and she shuddered. Jack's arms were still about her. She looked up at him and he smiled. She wondered if he had slept at all.

'Good morrow, sweetheart,' he whispered. 'Did you sleep well?'

There was a gleam in his eyes as he spoke which reminded Elizabeth to be on her guard. Did he think he had won her over just because she let him keep her warm?

She began to wriggle free of him and his blanket.

'You are right,' he said 'we shall be easily seen on this deck come daylight.' He struggled to his feet and then held out his hand for her.

She looked up at him and he met her gaze evenly. She hesitated and then took his offer of help.

'Are you hungry?' he asked.

Elizabeth nodded. She smoothed out her gown as best she could with her hands and adjusted her headdress. She presumed she looked like she had been tumbled by him and she could tell from his face that he was thinking exactly the same thing.

'Do you never give up?' she asked hotly.

'Not I, sweetheart,' he laughed. 'Come, let us find some break-fast.'

He stayed close beside her as they made their way along the deck. The wind had died to a low moan and the sea too seemed to be at ease. They stepped carefully round and over some people who had braved the chill of the cloudless night and who were still soundly asleep. A small group of travellers had gathered towards the stern. Jack walked over to them. 'Wait here,' he said to Elizabeth, 'and keep watch for our friend. I will get you something to eat.' Conscious of the attention of the travellers he added 'my love,' and gave her a peck on the cheek that made them look away and made Elizabeth wince. He winked as he turned from her.

Elizabeth pulled her cloak about her; the sun was not yet risen fully and there was still a chill in the air, though the sky was now a bright clear blue. She gazed beyond the ship to the ocean and watched the white-topped waves gallop beside them as they raced for England's shores. She closed her eyes and breathed in the fresh salty air. Just one more day, she thought, then she would be rid of Jack de Laverton! Then a horrible thought struck her: what if he would not let her go? At Scarsdale she'd had to resort to stabbing him to get away from him! Would she be able to do so again? She shivered at the memory.

'Are you cold, sweetheart?'

Jack's concern sounded genuine and Elizabeth shook her head quickly, anxious not to receive any more of his attention than was necessary; the sooner she could be rid of him, the better. But for now he did serve as protection from Higgins, if they encountered him again.

Jack had returned with some cold meat and cheese and a large brown loaf, which he split into two. Elizabeth's stomach growled as she smelled the bread. They moved behind some large cases and sat down to share their food. Elizabeth had not realized how hungry she was, or how good day-old bread and cheese could taste. She was aware that Jack was watching her, but she tried to avoid looking at him.

'It was the best I could find,' he said apologetically.

Elizabeth knew the conversation was only so she would meet his eyes. Reluctantly she did so. 'Thank you, it is good,' she said warily.

Jack smiled at her.

'Jack,' she said softly.

'Yes?' He held her gaze.

'What will you do with me when we reach England?' she asked.

She saw his eyes cloud over.

'That rather depends,' he said.

'Depends?' Elizabeth asked. She did not like his evasiveness. Why could he not say what his plans were? Was it because he knew she would not agree to them?

'We are not in England yet, sweetheart,' he said darkly.

'Do not play games with me!'

He smiled again. 'You do not need to worry, I would not hurt you, Elizabeth,' he said gently. 'I would never do that again.'

Elizabeth fixed his eyes. Anger tightened within her. 'That does not really answer my question! And why should I believe you? You certainly intended to hurt me before!'

Jack lowered his eyes for a moment, considering his response. 'Elizabeth,' he said softly, 'all I can say in my defence is that you do not understand. One day mayhap I will explain. But you must believe me; I regret that day as much as you do. If there were any way I could change what happened, then I would do so. But I cannot. It is past.'

Elizabeth clenched her teeth.

'I beg your forgiveness,' he said.

Elizabeth's eyes widened. 'Forgiveness?' she hissed. This man was impossible! His eyes seemed honest, yielding even, but Elizabeth was not interested. 'Do you know what it feels like to believe that you are damned?' she snapped. 'To think that your soul will endure indefinite torment?'

Jack said nothing. He contemplated his bread.

'No!' Elizabeth said. 'I thought you did not. From that day to this I have believed that I was beyond salvation, believed that whatever I did would not matter. And I was wrong, Jack, I was not damned.' And would she have ever gone to Warwick's chamber that night if she had not believed that she was beyond redemption? She did not know. She put the thought aside.

Jack looked surprised by her passion. 'Would you wish me dead, then?' he asked.

Elizabeth shrugged; the question was rhetorical anyway seeing as he was here.

'Elizabeth, do you wish you were heading to England and Edward with Higgins?'

Elizabeth shrank from the sudden venom in his voice.

'Well, do you?' Jack gripped her arm, compelling her to look into his face. 'Answer me!'

'No – no,' Elizabeth stammered, 'of course not.' That part at least was true.

'Then there must be peace between us,' Jack said solemnly. 'You must forgive me as I have forgiven you.'

'Forgiven me?' Elizabeth asked in disbelief.

'Yes,' Jack said still holding her tightly. 'Do you think it did not hurt? You stabbed me, Elizabeth, remember? I had lost a lot of blood too by the time they found me. I was close to death; I was choking on my own blood. Do you know how that feels?' he asked indignantly.

Elizabeth lowered her eyes from his face. She remembered the dark liquid pooling beside him on the cobbles. She remembered the fear and panic, knew again the wave of nausea as the magnitude of what she had done struck her. She had not meant to kill him and part of her had screamed at her to stay and help him after the knife struck home, but she remembered the guilt and fear when she left him in the courtyard as if it had happened last night. She had not wanted to hurt him, but she had. She looked up at him contritely.

'As I said, if it had not been for Brother William I would have died at your hands,' Jack said coldly.

'I am sorry,' she whispered. Suddenly tears stung her eyes; she never wanted to hurt anyone, part of her had wanted revenge for the hurt Jack had done her and she was desperate to go to her father, something Jack would never have allowed; it was Jack's fault – he had brought her to the brink of murder! She began to shiver as she thought on what had so nearly happened; but she was not damned – there was hope for her after all!

Jack saw her pain. He pulled her towards him and she buried her head against his shoulder. How had he managed to reduce her to tears? She swallowed hard, trying to fight them.

'Then you did feel something for me sweetheart – when you thought you had ended my life?' he whispered.

Elizabeth hesitated. In that dark moment she had hated him more than she imagined she ever could hate anyone; but could she tell him that? And afterwards, she had regretted it; that was true, but she could not find words to explain, so she simply shook her head.

That seemed to satisfy Jack, for he tightened his arms about her. She sobbed against his cloak; she would not have thought he would be able to unlock such grief in her. She knew it was not all for him; it was for everything – her soul, her father, her betrayal of Warwick and her separation from him and the uncertainty of her life now. But she did not tell Jack.

'Hush,' Jack said softly. 'It is over. It is past.' He tucked a defiant curl back under her headdress. 'Say nothing more, Elizabeth,' he breathed. 'It is best. We have many dangers yet. We need to be strong. We need to work together. As I said, we are not in England yet.'

YORK AUGUST 1470

It seemed that all William Hastings had done in the last few days was bring Edward bad news. He cleared his throat to continue his reading. 'He also says, that it has been necessary to pull down from the standard in Cheapside, from London Bridge and from the doors of divers churches, a manifesto in which Clarence and Warwick claim they had been driven away by the false means and subtle dissimulative acts of certain covetous and seditious persons! They call upon God and the Virgin, the Saints, the blessed martyr St George and every true Englishman to be ready when they come to punish the aforesaid persons and to see that justice is impartially administered. They will redeem England from thraldom of all outward nations.'

Hastings held his breath, waiting for the thunderstorm.

Incredibly Edward began to laugh. 'Oh Will!' he spluttered. 'Warwick wishes to release us from the alleged thraldom of Burgundy and replace it with the thraldom of France! No wonder he invokes the help of God and all the Saints – he would need it to accomplish that!'

'My liege!' exasperation tightened Hastings's stomach. 'My liege we both know his accusations are false, but we know also that Warwick is all but worshipped in the Cinque Ports. They will not care for the detail; they will rise and follow him if we do nothing to stop it!' Evidently the eel and almonds were all but forgotten, Hastings thought.

Edward's smile died on his lips. His eyes narrowed to strips of stormy sea. 'I am in York, my Lord Chamberlain,' he said flatly. 'What can I do to stop him if he comes now?'

The realization that Hastings was right about travelling so far from London had evidently dawned on Edward, but Hastings resisted the temptation to say something ungallant about Edward ignoring his advice. 'Ned, you must write to Kent; tell them that Warwick and Clarence have joined with France and Lancaster, they might not be so comfortable with that news! Make them understand that you will be there as soon as you can. If they cannot resist Warwick then they must meet you in London. If we hold London, we hold the key to the kingdom.' He almost regretted saying that, for it spoke of a terrible truth; if Warwick got there first he would have the advantage of the capital instead.

Edward nodded and with a quick decisive gesture he signalled for his scribe to take his dictation.

Hastings bowed and made to leave the room, but Edward called him back.

'I must finish this commission Will,' he said determinedly, 'I cannot allow rebels to go unpunished.'

Hastings shook his head. 'Give them reason to love you, Ned,' he said.

'Pardon them?' Edward's jaw slackened. 'Pardon Fitzhugh after what he has done?'

Hastings nodded. 'Issue a general pardon, then we can be on our way to London. Fitzhugh will not trouble you again, my liege. It is more important that we deal with Warwick when he comes.'

Edward nodded his assent and Hastings bowed as he left him.

Hastings walked out into the white summer's day. The pungent smells of the city came to him on the hot breeze, which blew up from the Ouse. He caught the sounds of the city too; bells clanging, the sounds of horses, carts and animals and merchants and fishwives shouting in the deep throaty tongue of Yorkshire which he was still struggling to understand, all oblivious to the fate hanging over their king. Above it all he heard the great bell of Archbishop Neville's Minster, and for a moment he had the notion that he was laughing at them still pinioned in his northern Diocese whilst Warwick was about to land on England's south coast.

NARROW SEA AUGUST 1470

'Ships!'

The cry sent a wave of panic throughout the little vessel.

Elizabeth lifted her head from Jack's shoulder.

'Burgundians,' Jack said.

Elizabeth looked to his face and saw it had darkened. Her fear grew. 'Will they let us through, Jack?' she asked.

Jack's hand moved to the hilt of his sword. 'I do not know,' he said flatly. 'We are in a French ship and the Burgundians are still smarting from the wounds Warwick inflicted upon them; they blame the French for allowing him to stay there. Come sweetheart, let us keep out of the way. Higgins could be anywhere and the last thing we want now is an encounter with him.'

They rose and moved to the bulwark, from where they could gain a better view. The ship that came alongside was indeed Burgundian. It was a large three-master with huge taut sails curving into the wind. Elizabeth noted also that both fore and aft it was well provisioned with cannon, undoubtedly another legacy of Warwick's adventures.

'We have no chance,' Jack said, following the direction of her look. 'We cannot outrun her and we certainly cannot fight her. Whatever they ask for they will get.'

'But what will they want?' Elizabeth asked him. She could not keep the fear from her voice.

Jack put an arm across her shoulder and pulled her close. 'I do not know, but I suspect they will ask us to follow them into port.'

'Back to France?' Elizabeth asked hopefully.

'No, sweetheart. They will take us to Bruges.'

Elizabeth met his look with alarm; they would have no compassion for any of Warwick's household there. 'Jack, what shall we do?' Her heart was racing now. 'What if they know who we are?'

Jack smiled reassuringly. 'I am certain they will not. These are sailors, not spies. We must not panic, Elizabeth. Stay close to me and everything will be all right, I promise.'

Elizabeth leant against him as she watched the Burgundian ship come about. She did not fight him, she was too concerned with their new situation; Jack was the least of her problems now.

* * *

As the sun rose to kiss the sea with gold, Elizabeth saw that Jack was right; the Burgundians were making their little vessel follow them back towards the French coast, but she knew they would not be returning to where Warwick was waiting.

Many of the passengers had fallen to their knees and were frantically invoking all the saints they knew, making promises to go on pilgrimages and donate their wealth to the church, if only they would protect them now.

Jack drew her aside. 'What story shall we tell them, Elizabeth?' he asked.

Elizabeth looked at him blankly. Her mind was in such a panic that she could not think.

'I suggest that we are no longer Elizabeth Hardacre and Jack de Laverton!' he said wisely.

Elizabeth sought in her mind for an answer.

Jack was looking at her intently. He had probably got a thousand names to use, she thought; there was Guy de Burgoyne for a start!

'Elizabeth,' he said gently. The tone of his voice demanded her attention. 'It would be best to say we are married. That way they will not part us.'

Elizabeth sucked in her breath. 'How well that will suit you,' she said coolly, unwrapping Jack's arm from about her shoulder. Of course he would say such a thing, but she could not agree. She could not be left alone with him for long – one night had been enough!

Jack shrugged as if it did not matter. 'It is your choice, sweetheart. But I think it best. If you have another plan I would love to hear it.'

Elizabeth wrestled with the thought. In one sense he was right; no one could part them if they were married; it would be improper even for a brother and sister to share quarters. But then did she want to stay with Jack anyway? Perhaps this was an opportunity to break free of all her shackles and for once make her way on her own. But that was a hard choice, especially when Jack had so much experience and he offered his assistance. And so far as she knew he was working to Warwick's orders - she would be a fool to turn him down! And what if Master Higgins found her alone? How would she deal with him? Her memory of her encounter with Gervase and dark thoughts of Higgins's torture of him made her shudder.

Jack's crooked smile came to his lips; he knew she didn't have a plan of her own and knew she had no real choice but to trust him.

She breathed deeply and then fixed his eyes defiantly. 'Very well,' she said, 'but if you try to...'

Jack held up his hands. 'I swear I will not!'

There was still a gleam in his eye that worried her.

'Names, then?' she asked crossly.

'We are John and Elizabeth Thornton of Yorkshire,' he said. 'And you must remember to hang about my neck like a new wife should!' he laughed.

Elizabeth glared at him. Was she making a terrible mistake?

'Leave the talking to me, sweetheart,' he continued. 'Be as demure as you can be...I know that is very difficult for you!' He laughed again.

Elizabeth threatened to thump him as she did her brother Edmund when he was getting out of hand, but she found she could not help smiling. Even with danger courting them, Jack could make her laugh and almost make her forget her fear. 'Jack, please,' she said, 'try to be serious for a moment.'

'Very well my dear *wife*,' he smiled. 'I am here only to do your bidding!'

Elizabeth wished that was true!

'I shall be serious,' he said, smothering his smile as best he could. He met her eyes and held her gaze. Then he reached towards her slowly. 'Give me your hand,' he said quietly. There was suddenly gravity in his voice.

Elizabeth stretched out her palm uncertainly. 'Are you going to tell my fortune?' she asked him, puzzled.

Jack shook his head. 'No, sweetheart,' he said. 'It is something that I almost forgot.'

Jack turned her hand over in his and something cold slipped onto her finger.

'What is it? What have you done?' she gasped.

'It was my mother's,' Jack said softly. 'Please, I beg you, take care of it.'

Elizabeth saw him swallow hard. She looked at her hand. Entwined about her wedding finger was a thin gold band inlaid with red and white enamel. It was a beautiful ring but her first instinct was to pull it off and throw it at him for his audacity, but she met his eyes; they were glassy.

He blinked and looked away from her quickly. 'I will go and see what is happening,' he said brusquely.

Elizabeth turned the ring round gently on her finger as she watched him walk away from her; there was so much she did not know about Jack de Laverton.

* * *

By the time the little ship drew into port, the panic amongst the passengers had settled to a simmering murmur. Elizabeth chewed at her lip as she watched the officials on the quayside. There had been no sign of Higgins, and Elizabeth wondered where he was. He would be desperate to get a passage to England and she wondered whether he would be the first off the ship, demanding to see whoever was in charge so that he could arrange it. She wondered whether he had perhaps forgotten about her in this new scenario, but she knew Higgins better than that!

Jack stood beside her, his hand resting on the hilt of his sword. His eyes too flicked keenly over the passengers.

'What would you do if you saw him?' she asked.

Jack smiled his lopsided grin. 'I think you can guess, sweetheart.'

'But not here, not now, surely?'

Jack laughed softly. 'No, Elizabeth, not here. There are too many witnesses. That is why I did not finish him on the boat, although arranging a little swim for him did cross my mind!'

Elizabeth could see why Warwick relied on Jack.

'Do not worry, sweetheart,' Jack breathed. 'He will not get close to you again. Not now you are mine.'

A shiver slid down her spine at his use of the word 'mine' and she remembered the lust in Jack's eyes at Scarsdale and again in the long cabin. She hoped agreeing to this subterfuge had been the right decision; but if Warwick trusted Jack then she knew she must trust him too. And Warwick had trusted Jack so much that he had let her think she had killed him! Then a thought struck her – did Warwick really know that Jack wasn't dead? She only had Jack's word for it!

* * *

The daylight was fading fast as they were finally allowed to disembark.

Jack looked into her face. 'Now, sweetheart,' he said seriously. 'I will explain our situation to them. Wait here and do not talk to anyone.'

Elizabeth wanted to growl that she wasn't a simpleton or a child – she knew very well what to do, but she heard the serious tone of his voice. 'Very well,' she said.

'Good.' He nodded and then turned away from her.

Elizabeth watched as he moved lithely along the deck; watched as he effortlessly engaged the attention of the Burgundian official ahead of others and then noted how he smiled and nodded, evidently flattering the man's self-esteem with his honeyed words. The official smiled broadly and then shook Jack's hand vigorously and slapped him on the back, obviously congratulating him on his marriage, Elizabeth thought sourly. Elizabeth shrank into her cloak and waited for Jack to finish his performance.

'There, sweetheart,' he grinned as he returned to her. 'It is all settled.'

Elizabeth stared at him blankly. What precisely had he agreed to?

'Do you not want to know where we shall be living?' he asked her.

'No,' she huffed.

'Ah Elizabeth you disappoint me, I thought you would at least have been curious!'

'I just want to go home,' Elizabeth said wearily. She didn't care overly much where they were going to stay; the fact that it would be with Jack was bad enough.

Jack smiled softly and moved closer. 'We shall go home, sweetheart I promise,' he said. 'As soon as possible, I swear it. But they will let no one sail now, not even a newly wedded couple! Not until the Earl of Warwick is caught or drowned or safely in Eng-

land! You must blame him for our current predicament Elizabeth, not me!' he grinned irreverently.

Elizabeth sighed. How long would it be before the Burgundians
lifted their curfew? How long must she endure Jack's company
for?

Suddenly Jack drew her behind him, his hand fastened on hers.

Instinctively Elizabeth knew he had seen Higgins.

Jack's grip tightened almost enough to bruise her and she could
tell by the set of his jaw that he was clenching his teeth.

'What is it?' she whispered. The wool of Jack's cloak was warm
as she pressed her cheek against his back.

'Higgins,' he hissed. 'He is speaking with that pompous official!'
Jack growled.

'Lucky you have already given him our story then,' Elizabeth
observed.

Jack turned and looked at her over his shoulder. 'Luck had
nothing to do with it, sweetheart; everybody loves a wedding!
And thanks to you, Higgins will not be expecting me, will he?' he
asked.

Elizabeth shivered at the thought of Jack's perfect alibi.

'And we will have the best of lodgings!' Jack continued, oblivious to her discomfort.

Elizabeth's eyes widened. What did he mean?

'We go to stay with Senor Gruuthuse, Governor of Holland, no
less! Even Higgins will not be able to disturb us there!'

'Gruuthuse?' Elizabeth asked. She had never heard of him, but
then why would she have? But the Governor of Holland! She
shuddered as she wondered how long she would be able to continue with this deception and in front of a governor and his entire
household! Her throat tightened, but she was determined not to
show Jack her fear.

'We had better let him go first,' Jack said quietly, nodding towards Higgins. 'I would not like to meet him on the gangway!'

Elizabeth heard the dark warning in his voice; if Jack ever met
Higgins again she knew he would kill him.

As they headed towards the gangplank, Jack kept them close to
the other passengers, using them as cover in case Higgins was
still searching for her. Instinctively Elizabeth knew that he would
be, even though she knew his first thought would be how he
could get to Edward as soon as possible.

As they settled into a small carriage that had been provided for them, Jack gave her a reassuring wink. 'It will be all right, sweetheart,' he said softly. 'Senor Gruuthuse is a friend to the English. He hosted them royally when they came over for Edward's sister's marriage to Duke Charles of Burgundy. He is a most particular friend of Lord Hastings as I recall.'

If he was a friend of Hastings, Elizabeth thought, he must be a reasonable man. Elizabeth leant against Jack. She was having difficulty keeping her eyes open now. 'Do you think we shall have a chamber to ourselves?' she asked absently, trying to stifle a yawn.

Jack laughed deep in his throat. 'I certainly hope so,' he said, 'for I would hate you to neglect your wifely duties and we do not need an audience!'

Elizabeth prodded him. 'I meant so that we would have privacy to talk,' she whispered harshly. 'To work out what is to be done!'

Jack sighed.

'Jack?' She looked up at him with sleepy eyes. 'You do want us to go home to England?'

He smiled. 'England is a very long way off, sweetheart,' he said.

~FOUR~

BRUGES AUGUST 1470

It took Elizabeth several moments to realize the situation she was in. She tried to keep calm. She was dressed in a silk shift and lying beside her in bed was Jack de Laverton! The only remotely good part about it was that he still had his shirt and hose on! She counted to ten as she tried to quieten her hammering heart.

Suddenly Jack turned to face her. He propped himself up on one elbow and gazed down at her like some mighty lord! Well she would show him who had the reins of this situation.

'Did you do this?' she growled.

The smile died on Jack's lips.

She turned fierce eyes upon him. 'Did you undress me?'

Jack lowered his gaze. 'No, Elizabeth I did not,' he said quietly.

'Look at me and say it!' Elizabeth snapped.

'Sweetheart, I had nothing to do with it, I swear!' He raised wide eyes to hers.

She heard the contrition in his voice but she ignored it. 'We cannot be like this!' she hissed. 'This is not some cheap tavern where they lay a-bed together! I cannot share my bedchamber with you!'

'For Christ's sake Elizabeth, lower your voice! Or have you forgotten that you are now my 'wife'?' he hissed.

Elizabeth sucked in her breath. How could she forget when he was lying next to her!

'As far as the whole world knows you are mine,' Jack whispered, 'and therefore we have to be together. Or if you would prefer, you are welcome to go and tell them otherwise!'

'I shall!' she snapped as she threw back the coverlet.

'At least think before you do,' Jack said quickly.

She stopped and looked at him.

'They might want to know why you left the ship holding my hand and why you were asleep in my arms when we arrived!' He shrugged. 'But perhaps you will be happy that they think you a wanton who has suddenly had second thoughts about her lover?' The black fire flashed in his eyes.

Damn him, he was right, Elizabeth thought. Her mistake had been to agree to this ridiculous deception! But now that she had, there was no easy way to go back on it. A single woman alone with a man would at best be thought of as a courtesan, and she did not relish the thought of being paraded barefoot through the streets of Bruges like a whore, clad only in her shift and carrying a penitential candle!

'And have you also forgotten that Higgins is out there? And believe me, Elizabeth, he will be looking for you.'

She thought on Jack's words and a sickening shiver slid down her spine.

Jack pulled roughly at the covers and sprang from the bed. Quickly he found his boots and began to pull them on.

Elizabeth watched him mutely as she sought to make sense of her predicament.

He draped his doublet over his shoulders and thrust his arms roughly into his sleeves. He did not bother to fasten the points. Savagely he buckled on his sword.

'Jack, I am sorry,' Elizabeth said quietly. She could see by the colour of his cheeks that he was hurting.

'You still think so very badly of me, don't you?' Jack thundered. 'Am I never to be forgiven? Last night I could have taken you. You could have screamed the place down and no one would have interfered; no one will come between a man and his wife. But I did nothing. Elizabeth, what more do you expect of me? What more could I have done?'

Elizabeth met his gaze indignantly, trying to ignore what he had just said. 'Did you have to come into my bed?' she asked fiercely. She glanced round the room - did she really expect him to sleep on the floor?

Jack moved towards her. He brought his face down close to hers. His eyes narrowed beneath saturnine brows.

'You could at least have placed a bolster between us!' she stammered as she noted his anger.

Jack smiled without mirth. 'The maids can tell how many people have slept in a bed, Elizabeth. And we are newly married, remember?' His voice was a fierce whisper. 'By Christ, you have a lot to learn! Do you want our cover blown on the first morning? Do you know what that would bring?'

Elizabeth shook her head. She bit her lip.

'We are playing for the highest stakes, Elizabeth,' he continued. 'What do you think the Duke of Burgundy does with the Earl of Warwick's spies?'

Elizabeth shuddered as she thought of Higgins and his twisted hands! She forbade her mind to think of it. She shrugged her shoulders.

'Well perhaps you had better think on it! Though of course, *you* could claim to be a spy for Edward!'

The words hurt her like blows and she glared at him.

'Well, sweetheart, why don't you tell them that?' he hissed. 'Go on Elizabeth, turn me in! Betray me as you betrayed Warwick's cause! Or perhaps you do not want my death on your conscience for a second time?'

Elizabeth's heart pounded in her chest. She felt like a silly little girl in a man's world and the fire in Jack's voice reminded her of his roughness at Scarsdale. She backed away from him.

'No?' he said icily. 'Then we work together.' He moved closer to her again. His breath was hot on her cheek and Elizabeth shuddered as she met the fury in his eyes. 'Espionage, as you should know, is a dangerous game, sweetheart! Burgundy is the enemy of France and France is funding Warwick's invasion of England.' He arched an impeccable brow. The implications in his words were clear.

Jack stood up stiffly and walked towards the door. 'I shall enquire about breakfast,' he said coldly. 'I shall send your maid in to help you dress. Come and find me when you are ready, but beware, sweetheart, really I should not let you out of my sight.'

He turned away from her and snatched the door open.

'Jack, wait!' She wanted to tell him that she was not the fool he thought she was! She wanted to say that she did understand the danger they were in and that she knew they had to work together, but he closed the door without looking at her and she heard his footsteps thud angrily along the passageway.

She returned to the bed and sank back against the pillows, tears burning her eyes. The sheets were still warm beside her and Jack's scent lingered tauntingly. Of all the people to be trapped with, she thought! Santa Maria, why did it have to be Jack de Laverton?

Distractedly she pulled the gold ring Jack had given her from her finger. She still had half a mind to fling it at him, but she knew she could not do so. She stared at the delicate lacy pattern of enamel and marvelled at how intricate it was. Suddenly she noticed that inside the band it contained a poesy. Intrigued, she sat up. She wanted to see what message Jack's father had given to his mother on their wedding day. She wiped the tears from her eyes and strained to see what it said. The tiny script had been worn smooth by Jack's mother's finger, but she could just about read it. It was in French. '*Pensez de moi,*' she whispered – 'think of me'. She gasped; this was a ring given by a lover to his lady, not a husband to his wife!

* * *

After a tense breakfast at which Jack had avoided looking at her, they followed the rest of the household across the square to the church of Our Lady for Mass. Elizabeth could not take her eyes off Jack, and she thought at the very least she would look like his new wife in that! She could not imagine what it must feel like to be illegitimate, to be unwanted and unloved! No, she did not know that he was unwanted or unloved, but to be born out of wedlock...poor Jack! Perhaps this explained why her mother had been so rude to him, calling him Jack when she knew he was a knight. 'Someone like you,' she had said to him and Jack's cheeks had flushed in anger. How could her mother have been so cruel? And her nurse Alice had called him a gypsy! Filled with sympathy, Elizabeth tried to catch his look, but he would not hold her gaze. His eyes were dark and brooding; he was lost in inner thoughts and she felt guilty that she had only added to his troubles. She decided that he must not know she knew of his illegitimate birth; it would serve no purpose and might even make things more difficult between them; she could not let it cloud her judgement either. Jack was still Jack.

Although Jack drew her hand into the crook of his arm as they walked together, there was no other sign of familiarity from him. He looked at her so little that Elizabeth could see their fellow guests whispering behind their hands whilst casting disapproving looks in their direction – perhaps their cover would be blown today after all, she thought. 'Jack,' she whispered, 'on the boat, you told me to mend my looks because people were watching us; now I must ask you to mend yours!'

Jack turned to her then. 'Must you?' he asked sourly.

'Jack, you said we had to work together and you were right, I see that now. This morning I was just astonished to find you in my bed, that is all.'

'Oh no, sweetheart,' Jack said dryly, 'I know what this morning was all about.'

'Do you?' Elizabeth tried to hold his gaze, but unusually for Jack, he would not take up the challenge. But she saw him cast a discreet glance at the onlookers and touch his hat to a finely dressed woman who was eyeing them closely.

'You are right,' Jack said. 'We must *both* play our part if we are to come through this unscathed.' He gave Elizabeth an over-sweet smile to placate the watching lady and patted her hand with his free one.

Once in the enormous Cathedral they were shown to Senor Gruuthuse's private seats and for once Elizabeth was grateful for the peace of the church. Perhaps when they returned to England she might return to Ellerton, she thought. There had been something in the ordered existence there that had appealed to her troubled soul; it was as though she had left part of herself behind there. And, she thought, after this latest escapade, there could never be any kind of reconciliation with Warwick. Not only had she left him without a word, how could she tell him she had shared a bedchamber with Jack de Laverton and expect him to believe nothing had happened? As she had said, it wasn't as though they were sharing the room in a cheap tavern - they had chosen to be in each other's company! And how before God could she explain the fact that she was wearing Jack's ring? Warwick must know of Jack's roguish reputation; Santa Maria, he would think the worst!

She lowered her head to hide her stinging eyes. It would always have been difficult to have a future with Warwick, she thought and now it was impossible. She closed her eyes and listened to the soaring choral voices and her skin prickled; they reminded her of the loneliness there had been at Ellerton too. Perhaps returning there was not such a good idea after all.

As though he had sensed something of her troubles, Jack moved closer to her. He reached for her hand.

She looked up at him. Something of the brightness had returned to his dark eyes and she wondered if being in the cloistered space had caused him to reflect also.

'I am sorry, sweetheart,' he whispered. 'Forgive me.'

Elizabeth smiled thinly. 'We must work together, Jack. You were right.'

'I am always right,' Jack said flatly.

Elizabeth gasped at his arrogance and he shot her a roguish smile.

'The sooner you realize that, sweetheart the better for us both,' he said.

'Jack!' Elizabeth was almost speechless.

'If you do as I say then perhaps we will make it to England,' he said. 'If you do not...' He took a deep breath. 'You know as well as I what would happen to us as Warwick's agents.'

Elizabeth shivered as she remembered Higgins's gnarled and twisted hands from the torture the Burgundians had inflicted on him.

When the service finished, Jack led her along the nave. The great doors stood open and Elizabeth had to screw her eyes up at the bright daylight streaming in through them.

Outside the day was becoming hot. The sky was clear and blue with only the faintest whisper of fair-weather cloud to mar its perfection.

'We must talk,' Jack said as he declined the offer of a walk with their fellows. He smiled at Elizabeth so sweetly that there was a murmur of approval from their acquaintances and Elizabeth blushed as they looked at her.

Elizabeth had never seen anything like this city. It was known as the 'Venice of the North' because of its elegant canals, but as she had never seen Venice the comparison was lost on her.

The streets were stone cobbled and much cleaner than either Calais or London. They twisted round fine brick and stone built houses and arched gracefully over hump-backed bridges. Jack took her to gaze over the parapet of one into the glittering water. Light reflected like a thousand jewels beneath her and rippled a dappled dance onto the walls behind her. It was incomparable to any light she had yet experienced; it was as though before now she had always seen everything muted and grey, dulled somehow and only in this light was the world revealed as it should be.

Jack brushed his hand across her cheek and she jumped at his touch.

'Well, sweetheart,' he said gently. 'What are we to do?'

She met his look dreamily, still half immersed in her reverie.

He smiled at the serenity in her face. 'You look wistful, sweet-heart.'

Elizabeth sighed. 'I like it here, Jack,' she said, 'but we both know we cannot carry on like this for long.'

Jack raised an eyebrow questioningly, but said nothing.

Elizabeth ignored the appeal. 'We must make for England as soon as we can,' she said hurriedly.

'England?' He spoke as if it was an enchanted island he had heard of in a legend, rather than his home.

'Yes Jack, England.' Elizabeth hardened her voice.

He nodded. 'If they will let us sail! And even then it might be best to await the outcome – we do not want to be caught in the middle of a war.'

She looked at him quickly. 'Are you in earnest?' she asked. 'We cannot continue this masquerade for long Jack, or at least I cannot.'

'Is it so unpleasant to be here with me?' he asked.

She almost laughed that he dared to ask her. But there was something forlorn about his look that stopped her. And she still did not know the full extent of his connection with her family: what was it they had promised him? She was sailing in dangerous waters so she changed the subject. 'How long can we continue to share a bedchamber when we are not married?

'As long as is necessary,' Jack grinned.

She remembered how he had enjoyed their time together at Scarsdale, why would he not enjoy this? Elizabeth smiled at his audacity. 'You know very well what I mean,' she scolded him.

He sighed. 'Very well,' he said, 'I shall see what I can do.'

'Thank you,' Elizabeth said.

'But it still concerns me that we have not yet encountered Higgins,' Jack said. 'He could yet be our undoing and I would like to deal with him before we leave.'

'How do you know that he has not already left?' Elizabeth asked.

Jack shrugged. 'I don't. He may have been at the harbour at dawn and on the first boat out of here, if any were sailing, but one thing tells me that he did not leave.'

'And what is that?' Elizabeth asked.

'You are still here,' Jack said flatly. 'He will not leave you behind, I know it. Even now he may be watching us.'

Elizabeth looked round quickly, but saw only ordinary citizens going about their business. 'Do you really think so?' she asked, trying to keep the fear from her voice.

'Trust me Elizabeth, I know.'

Elizabeth looked into his face for reassurance.

'Come,' he said.

Jack took her hand and drew her along the canal side. Sunlight sparkled on the water and swans glided beside the bank like lovers courting, honking loudly at the craft that crowded them for space.

'We must face him some time,' Jack said evenly.

'Why can we not just leave? If he is so interested in me he will cross our path whether we seek him or not.'

'That is true,' Jack said, 'but jumping into a boat for England just at this moment might not be the wisest of manoeuvres.'

'Why not?' Elizabeth asked.

'Because Warwick is about to invade, sweetheart. I for one do not wish to become tangled up with an invasion fleet.'

'Would that be so bad?'

'The Burgundians have tried to blockade the French coast, but if Warwick breaks free there will be a battle at sea!'

'But if we move quickly, we can go before then surely?'

Jack shrugged his lean shoulders. 'If we are allowed to sail. But remember, we are guests of Senor Gruuthuse; we cannot simply leave. There is decorum in everything, Elizabeth. And Senor Gruuthuse might prove a useful ally.'

'Jack, I do not believe you,' Elizabeth said, suddenly angry. Jack arched his brows questioningly. 'Don't you?'

'No, I think at this moment you have all that you wish – I am completely at your mercy and you intend to maintain this situation as long as possible! If you were a true friend of Warwick you would take me back to him as quickly as possible, or at the very least take me to England!' She wondered what she would do if he did take her to Warwick.

She saw the colour rise in Jack's cheeks.

'You may think what you like sweetheart,' he growled, 'but the truth is we will leave when I say so and not a moment before!'

Elizabeth stopped walking. How could he turn such a beautiful day into a nightmare?

'I am not your servant, Jack; someone who jumps up to do your bidding!' she said crossly.

Jack pulled her to him so that she was pressed against his chest. 'No, you are not a servant; to the world you are my wife!'

People were staring at them now; even in the noise and bustle of London this argument would not have gone unnoticed, but here in the early morning calmness of Bruges it was nothing short of scandalous.

Elizabeth looked about her. This attention was something neither of them needed.

Jack held her gaze with narrowed eyes. Then, conscious of their audience he leant forward and kissed her lips. 'Forgive me sweetheart,' he said for their audience's benefit.

Elizabeth's first instinct was to fight him off.

But Jack was equal to the situation. 'You must play your part sweetheart, you said so yourself,' he whispered. 'Kiss me.'

'I will not!' she hissed.

'Kiss me,' he whispered fiercely. 'You must.'

Realizing that many pairs of eyes were upon them, she put her arms about his neck where his black curls tangled into his collar and tentatively returned his kiss. Unexpectedly his lips were soft against hers and Elizabeth was astounded by his gentleness. What an actor he was, for his fingers were hard against her back!

After a few moments people began to move away from them, muttering that they did not understand the ways of the English.

Jack released his hold. 'Now walk,' he growled.

Elizabeth did so, but now the light was less perfect that it had been; like a silvered mirror it had cracked and fogged.

'Stop fighting me,' Jack said under his breath, 'it will be best for both of us.'

'Do you think I am like a dog? With a firm hand I will eventually do your bidding?' she asked hotly.

Jack laughed. 'No. I swear I never thought that.'

Elizabeth turned fierce eyes upon him.

Jack pushed his hair from his face. 'I thought you had enough sense to see that I am your best hope, Elizabeth and that if you have to humour me a little, it is a price worth paying!' he said.

Elizabeth did not know if he was jesting with her or not. 'Jack, you are insufferable!' she said.

Jack laughed again. 'Am I? I could always find Higgins myself and negotiate a good price for you!'

Now Elizabeth knew he was teasing her; Jack would not part with her so easily.

'Jack!' she pleaded.

He smiled, recognizing the offer of a truce. 'Oh so there are worse things in the world than being with me?' he said through a broad grin.

'No, returning to Higgins is the only one!'

'What about meeting King Edward again?'

Elizabeth shivered at that thought too.

'So there are at least two things then?'

'Jack, please stop it.' Elizabeth stopped walking and turned to face him. 'We must not fight!'

He smiled. 'Have I not said that? But you must accept that I know best in all of this, sweetheart. We leave when I say so. In the meantime you are supposed to be my new wife! Can you try to give a more convincing performance?'

Elizabeth pressed her lips together defiantly.

He stepped closer. 'If you have something to say to me wait till we are in our chamber,' he said with a wink. 'A wife cannot gainsay her husband in public, you know that as well as I! They will be telling me to beat you!'

Elizabeth shivered. It was true; even her mother would not gainsay Sir Robert in front of anyone. Elizabeth knew that in private things were often very different, but to the outside world Lady Catherine played the part of the obedient wife!

But Elizabeth wasn't Jack's wife! Only God knew how many nights she was going to have to put up with him in her bedchamber and how many days in purgatory she would serve for doing so!

She knew that she had no real choice but to accept the situation; their lives depended upon their co-operation and she had no money with which to purchase a passage to England even if she was brave enough to do so. All she had was Edward's necklace, which offered as many problems as it solved. Then she cursed inwardly; Jack still had Edward's necklace and worse still, he had King Edward's letter too.

'Peace?' Jack asked.

Elizabeth tried to read his face. 'You sound like a cleric,' she scolded him.

'If only I had their money!' Jack laughed.

'Well you would not want to take their vow of chastity!' Elizabeth said caustically. She thought then of Sarah and thought too of the dissolute name he had acquired at Scarsdale. He was nearly as bad as King Edward!

Jack smiled. 'No, sweetheart I would not! A vow like that can damage a man's reputation!'

'How many women have you bedded?' She surprised herself nearly as much as she surprised Jack with the question.

He swallowed quickly. 'Christ's blood! What kind of a question is that?'

Elizabeth's cheeks began to burn. 'Is it not the kind of question a new wife asks of her husband?' she asked dryly.

'No, Elizabeth, it is *not*! Though it is the kind of question *you* might well ask of him!'

'Well?' she fixed his gaze.

Jack furrowed his brow. 'It is none of your concern,' he said gruffly.

'You do not know!' Elizabeth said triumphantly.

Colour touched Jack's cheek.

'And I bet you cannot remember their names! You men are all the same!' she said triumphantly.

'Do you count precious Warwick in that then?' Jack said, rising to the challenge.

'Of course not!' Elizabeth said indignantly. 'I think that he could at least count the women he has slept with!'

Jack lowered his head, letting his hair hide his eyes from her. 'You have me at a disadvantage,' he said coyly, 'I only remember the good ones!'

Elizabeth could not tell if he was serious or not.

'Do you remember Sarah then?' she asked.

'Sarah?' Jack was puzzled. 'Ah, your maid?'

Elizabeth nodded, uncertain why she had taken this tack.

Jack smiled as he looked at her. 'Are you jealous, sweetheart?'

'No!' Elizabeth said quickly. Her cheeks burned.

Jack looked at her and smiled. 'Really? I think there is something there,' he said. 'Something more than you will admit to made you ask that. Remember hiding from Higgins in the cabin? You enjoyed that as much as I did!'

Elizabeth blushed further at the recollection. 'No! I did not!' she exclaimed. Then she remembered how she had sunk into Jack's embrace, but that had been to make certain she avoided Higgins.

Jack laughed. 'You need not be jealous of your maid, Elizabeth; I only did what I had to do. There was not time for more! Anyway she did not stir my blood as you do!'

The old lascivious smile was there. 'Be careful that you do not light a fire you cannot quench, sweetheart!' he said.

BARFLEUR SEPTEMBER 1470

Thomas Conyers woke to the sound of distant thunder. Night was only just fading to grey but already his skin was damp with a soft sheen of sweat. He rolled over on his bunk with a groan. The room echoed with contented breathing and the occasional erratic snore punctuated the rhythm. The pungent smell of his fellow soldiers hung thickly about him. He ran his fingers through his unruly blond hair and then forced himself to get up; he needed some fresh air.

He slipped on his shirt. The linen was cool against his flesh, but as soon as he pulled it down over his body, it stuck to his back. As quietly as he could he pulled on his hose and boots. Then he picked up his sword and livery coat and slipped out into the haze of the morning.

Lightning snaked across the gloom above him and was followed by a heavy boom. To the east where there should have been the scent of morning, there was only leaden cloud and Thomas knew that rain was on the way. He cursed under his breath; a thunderstorm was the last thing he needed. Today of all days!

Reluctantly he threw his livery coat across his shoulders, and stuffed his arms into the sleeves. He buckled on his sword. He smiled and patted the hilt fondly, remembering his father's blessing as he had given it to him. And what work it would have to do for him yet, he thought.

He swallowed against a dry throat; he needed a drink.

He made his way across the courtyard. A dog eyed him from its position by the gate, but did no more than raise its head and follow his progress for a moment, before slumping back down under the weight of the brewing storm.

Thomas followed the smell of baking bread with some eagerness, closing his eyes and letting the scent entice him into the hall.

The heavens growled again.

But before he could make it into the kitchen, Warwick's voice stopped him.

'Thomas!'

'My lord?' Did Warwick never sleep, he wondered.

'It looks as though God has not favoured our enterprise,' Warwick said flatly with a nod towards the glowering sky.

Thomas followed his gaze. Even though he had seen Warwick's skill as a commander and soldier and seen him fight at sea alongside his men, he did not relish what was to come. 'A storm and the Burgundian fleet, my lord!'

Warwick gave an ironic smile. 'It is not of my choosing, Thomas. It will be task enough to beat Edward in battle. We could well do without having to fight the Burgundians at sea first!'

Warwick gestured for Thomas to follow him.

Reluctantly Thomas left the comforting smell of baking and, ignoring his churning stomach, he followed Warwick along the oak beamed passageway to the solar.

Warwick's large desk was covered in maps and charts of the sea and Thomas saw that he had been marking out several routes, Thomas assumed each one dependant upon the elements.

Warwick gestured for wine for them both.

The liquid burned into Thomas's empty belly, but it tasted good.

'Do you think we are ready?' Warwick asked him evenly.

Thomas sucked in his breath as he considered his response. 'I think the men are eager for home – that will give them the advantage they need, my lord.'

Warwick nodded. 'My thoughts also, Thomas,' he said. 'Despite the storm I think we should embark today as we had planned. To delay will seem like a defeat. Call the captains together. We leave after Mass.'

And breakfast, Thomas thought hopefully. 'As you wish, my lord.'

Warwick stopped him at the door. 'Good luck, Thomas,' he said softly.

'And you, my lord,' Thomas replied as he bowed from the room.

And for the first time Thomas was conscious of uncertainty in Warwick's mind and he understood the doubts. If the Burgundian ships were indeed still out there then there would be a fierce battle just to reach the open sea; a battle they could ill afford.

Thomas hurried back to his billet. Now there was no need for silence and he flung the door open with a crash almost as loud as the thunder overhead. Rain began to hiss on the stones behind him; the lazy dog ran for shelter by the stables, its tail between its legs.

'By Christ's holy blood, Thomas!' Will Kennerley called angrily. 'You nearly brought on a seizure. I presume you have a good reason for almost frightening an old man to death?'

Thomas grinned. 'Aye Will,' he said. 'We are to break camp!'

The billet came alive with cheers as men began to rise and collect their clothing together. But Will did not cheer; he did not even smile.

'In this bloody weather?' he grumbled.

'Yes Will. Warwick thought the Burgundians wouldn't like to get wet, but knew that we wouldn't mind!' Thomas laughed.

'Its not easy making old bones move!' Will hissed as he forced himself upright with a groan.

'I'll be sure to tell my lord Warwick to bear that in mind when he is planning his campaign!' Thomas jested.

The billet erupted with laughter.

'I hope you live long enough to experience the pain of it as I do!' Will growled as he swung his legs off his bunk stiffly.

'So do I, Will. So do I!' Thomas said.

'Well don't just stand there Thomas, fetch me some bloody breakfast!'

Thomas grinned at his captain again and then headed back for the kitchen.

Again the sky tore above him and within heartbeats water was dripping from his scarlet coat and his hair was flattened to his head. As he dodged the stream that had suddenly sprung up in the courtyard he cursed the weather again and wondered if their ships really could sail to England in a storm as fierce as this.

* * *

With his friend Robert at his side Thomas walked with the rest of their company towards the quay. Rain trickled off his sallet and ran down his nose and he shook his head to try and stop the irritation. Even before they reached the harbour they could hear the noisy bustle of a town preparing for war; brown and white cows were being driven towards the market, carts loaded with cages of ducks and chickens passed them noisily. All about them was a gaudy tide of colour; red and silver livery coats of Warwick's men; the tawny of Oxford's with their blue and silver stars and several blazons de France.

'Bloody Frenchies joining us!' Robert said with disdain as he eyed them suspiciously.

Thomas followed his look. He shook his head. 'There will be some, but they'll be with the Admiral of France – just keeping an eye on us for King Louis.'

'I hope so,' Robert said. 'I've seen enough Frenchmen to last me a lifetime!'

'And enough French women!' Thomas laughed.

At least Robert had the decency to blush, Thomas thought. Then Robert's usual grin spread over his face. 'Hey, not a word to Martha when we get back!'

'But she knows what you're like!' Thomas protested.

'All the same,' Robert said more softly, 'not a word, eh? And I'll say nought to Lucy!'

'Lucy?' Thomas asked. 'There was nothing there, Rob and you know it!'

'Not on your account, may be,' Robert answered. 'But she liked you well enough, Tom!'

Thomas coughed. 'Do you think Martha will have waited for you?' he asked, trying to ignore the pictures of the pretty blonde Lucy which had sprung into his mind.

Robert gave a nonchalant shrug, as if it didn't matter, but Thomas could see that it did.

'And what of Elizabeth?' Robert asked, as if he'd read Thomas's thoughts.

Thomas shook his head. 'It took a gold angel to find out she'd left with a man called Higgins, but I can't figure out why she would.'

'But what about the blockade?' Robert asked.

'I don't know if they'd let them through or not. They may have taken them to Bruges.'

'How did my lord take the news?' Robert asked.

'Badly.' Thomas found he could not easily sum up either his or Warwick's thoughts without his throat tightening, so he left it at that. He remembered the fury in Warwick's eyes when he told him; the name Higgins was obviously familiar to him.

'She'll be all right, Tom,' Robert said gently. 'She can take care of herself if she has to.'

Thomas found a half-smile from somewhere. 'I know,' he said flatly. But he knew that so far Elizabeth had been lucky, and he whispered a silent prayer to the Virgin that her luck would not run out.

As they approached the wharf they saw the caravel they were to sail in. She swayed in the brisk salty breeze as though she had taken too much wine, but Thomas knew only pride when he saw her: this was the ship he had enabled Warwick to buy by taking the quittance to Jean de Bourée, the treasurer of France. Somehow he felt like he owned her.

'Isn't she beautiful?' he asked Robert.

Robert looked at him as if he'd gone mad. 'It's a boat Thomas!' he said. 'As long as it's seaworthy that's all I care about.'

Thomas smiled.

The dockside around the ship was even busier than the town, with a cacophony of noise from sailors, traders, soldiers and the shrill mewing of the gulls overhead. Accents mingled into a strange unintelligible language, but Thomas didn't really need to understand the words; there was a palpable feeling of excitement as the last barrels and boxes were loaded and the sailors drew up the bear and ragged staff pennant to the top of the mast. Thomas smiled as the bear began to dance in the wind. It reminded him of standing on the quayside at Sandwich waiting for Warwick to return from the Duke and Duchess of Clarence's wedding in Calais. How excited he had been that day – and how naïve! This time he was to be part of Warwick's invasion and his stomach lurched with a mixture of excitement and fear. The sooner they were in England the better, he thought. But there was the small matter of the Burgundian fleet to negotiate and he wondered if they would still be waiting for them. He had fought at sea with Warwick before and he knew it made a battle on land almost a pleasure, for the cramped conditions on deck kept enemy locked to enemy and the only escape was death or the cruel dark sea.

He looked out onto the open water beyond the calm of the harbour swell. He could see the remnants of the thunderstorm in the distance, a glowering gloomy sky punctuated by the occasional flash of light and a booming rumble like cannon fire.

The clatter of horses' hooves and the musical jingle of harness made him turn. Warwick was astride a white destrier. As he reined the mount in, a streak of sunshine came from behind the clouds, and the jewels on its harness and Warwick's cloak glittered like tiny candle flames. The golden collar that hung about

Warwick's shoulders dazzled like a thousand miniature suns and Thomas had to shield his eyes.

'By Christ, he looks like a king!' Robert whispered.

Thomas nodded. Robert was right; if he had not known otherwise he too would have thought Warwick a king, such was his bearing. As soon as his men realized he was amongst them they began to shout out his name.

Warwick smiled broadly and acknowledged them by touching his hat. He waved a salute as the great destrier danced beneath him, splashing in the now steaming puddles. He held the powerful horse on a tight rein, touching his spurs to its flanks to make it circle so that he could survey the crowd.

His eyes found Thomas and he nodded for him to come and take the horse. Thomas gripped the reins and Warwick slipped lightly from the saddle. Thomas handed the reins to a groom and then followed Warwick towards the ship.

The men parted before them, bowing their heads in respect.

Warwick smiled as he passed them, nodding to some he evidently recognized.

'They are with me, Thomas?' Warwick asked.

The dark eyes swept over Thomas in an appraising look.

'Yes, my lord,' he said.

'Aye, now that they have been paid,' Warwick said dryly. 'But are they truly with me, Thomas?'

Thomas was puzzled by Warwick's persistence. 'Yes, my lord.'

'If they are not, then are we all doomed,' Warwick said.

Thomas looked at him quickly, but Warwick's eyes were fixed on the horizon. 'And there our destiny awaits us,' he said, almost wistfully. 'We are the makers of history, Thomas. And God and history will be our judges.'

Before Thomas could form any sort of reply, Warwick strode away from him. The confident smiling face returned as he made his way onto the ship.

Thomas was left behind in the wake of the earl's doubts.

BRUGES SEPTEMBER 1470

Elizabeth watched the evening sky turn the colour of fire as Jack returned. She had spent most of the tedious day with the other ladies and had hated every minute of it. In fact most of the last two weeks had been at best tedious; sewing and embroidery

111

by day and clinging to the edge of the bed at night to avoid turning into Jack's arms! She was still angry with him for his imprudent kiss, but she had to admit that she preferred even his company to needlework!

As he strolled into the solar, the wide grin with which he greeted her had her mind racing with questions. She met his gaze and he gave her a flash of his eyes that made her blush. Immediately the ladies began to whisper amongst themselves about the manners of the English!

'You must excuse me, ladies,' Jack said with an eloquent bow, 'but I have need of my wife!'

Elizabeth's cheeks began to colour further with her embarrassment. Why could he not have simply said he must speak with her? She scowled at him as she took his proffered hand and Jack smiled broadly. He drew her hand to his lips and kissed it lingeringly. 'Come, my love,' he said as he led her from the room.

Once outside in the hallway Elizabeth came close to him. His eyes flickered with tantalizing fire.

'Jack, how could you?' she hissed. 'They think you want to bed me!'

Jack laughed softly and arched his brows. 'How perceptive they are!'

Elizabeth glared at him.

Jack pursed his lips. 'If you sulk with me then I shall not tell you my news!' he said.

Elizabeth's eyes widened. 'What is it?' she whispered. Oh Santa Maria were they to go home at last?

Jack shook his head. 'Not until we are alone, sweetheart. Come!' he said as he pulled her along the hallway. 'You will be so pleased with me!' he laughed.

When they reached their bedchamber they were both out of breath, and any watching servant would have been forgiven for thinking it was nothing more than a newly married couple's eagerness for each other that hurried them.

Once inside, Jack leant against the door for a moment, prolonging Elizabeth's torment.

Her heart kicked her ribs. 'Jack!' she gasped as she stared at him. 'Do not tease me! Tell me what has happened!'

Jack flashed a smile to melt hearts. 'Tonight, sweetheart.' He paused meeting her eyes.

'Yes?' Elizabeth hardly dared to hope her prayers were about to be answered.

'Tonight we leave for England!' he announced.

'Oh Jack!' Without thought Elizabeth flew to him and flung her arms about his neck.

Jack's arms tightened about her, pressing her close to his body. His soft doublet was warm against her cheek as they embraced each other. Thank God, they were finally going home!

'Close after Matins we must be at the harbour side, sweetheart,' he whispered into her ear. 'We must prepare our things and then get some sleep if we can. But if you feel like this...'

Elizabeth drew back from him suddenly and saw the gleam of lust in his eyes. Her heart still thumped with excitement, but she should have known better than to hug Jack; he needed no encouragement.

'I just want to go home,' she said as coolly as she could. She unwound her arms from his neck and then smoothed her dress down with her hands.

'You disappoint me, sweetheart. I had hoped your gratitude would know no bounds!' he said dryly. He turned away from her as he spoke. He gathered his thick cloak and began to examine it thoughtfully, as if it were a new tapestry he had bought.

Elizabeth felt some sympathy for him as she watched his shoulders hunch, but she knew better than to say so.

'Jack,' she said softly.

Wide eyes met hers.

'Thank you,' she said.

'Do not thank me yet, sweetheart,' he said. 'Wait until we reach England.'

* * *

Their footsteps echoed around them. As Elizabeth held Jack's hand she could not see where she was going. There were no cressets to guide them in the narrow streets and as most of the taverns had already closed for the night, there were few pools of brightness to help them either, yet Jack seemed to know his way, as if he could walk it blindfold and Elizabeth assumed he must have been planning their route while she had spent her days on useless embroidery. Mist hung over the water like devils' breath and Elizabeth shivered. She clung tightly to Jack as they walked quickly along the narrow cobbled alleyways and over the bent bridges towards the harbour. With her other hand she clutched her skirts, trying to hold them above her ankles so that she did not slow their pace too much; she felt Jack's need for haste almost as much as she felt her own racing heart. Her throat was tight, partly from the dampness of the night, and partly through fear.

She noticed that Jack did kept his hand on the hilt of his sword and his eyes flicked keenly from one side of the street to the other, leaving no alleyway unchecked, for even though Bruges was a fair city, it still had its share of cutpurses and thieves, Elizabeth thought, for who else would be abroad at this hour? By day Bruges was a pleasant welcoming city, she thought, but now she could not have been more nervous, even if she had been in the darkest streets of Southwark, and Jack's tense alertness did nothing to allay her fears. With her breathing short in her throat she stumbled beside him, wondering why the relatively short distance to the harbour seemed to be taking them an age to cover.

The soft lapping rhythm of the water grew louder as they left the canals behind and came closer to the waterfront. The moon uncloaked itself and Elizabeth could see the rippled ribbon of white silk in the tidal water. In the near distance Elizabeth saw the flicker of soft yellow lantern light and she assumed it must be the boatmen waiting for them. She let out a long slow breath of relief at the sight of them.

'Wait here,' Jack said. 'I shall not be long.' His tone was serious. He slipped something cold into her hand. 'If there is trouble, use this,' he whispered and she realized he had given her his dagger.

She wanted to ask him what trouble he expected and why they could not walk together to where the pale lanterns beckoned them to safety, but already he was moving away from her.

'Be careful,' she whispered.

He flashed a quick smile and then turned towards the harbour.

Elizabeth fingered the jewelled hilt of his dagger with a trembling hand. She saw the cruel glint of metal as she turned it over. A wave of nausea rose to her throat as she remembered the night she thought she had killed Jack. She had never wanted to taste such fear again, but she did so now; it was almost choking her. Her heart punched her ribs as Jack walked away; suddenly she did not want him to leave her.

She tensed her fingers on the knife again and wondered if Jack really thought she would have to use it.

She watched him move cautiously past the first wharf. She could see that he stepped lightly on the balls of his feet, alert as a cat, ready to change direction immediately if he needed to. Then he moved past the warehouse, its large crane silhouetted against the water like a giant hangman's scaffold. She was conscious that she was holding her breath, and that the hilt of Jack's knife was biting into the skin of her palm as she gripped it. Soon Jack would turn sharply and cross the little bridge to where the boat-men stood, she thought. Soon he would beckon her to join him.

The hooded figure leaped out of the darkness behind him.

Elizabeth saw a flash of silver in the moonlight. 'Jack!' she cried and he wheeled round quickly, just in time to feel the bite of steel in his left shoulder. He cried out and then, quick as a fox he turned, drew his sword and in one seamless movement, brought it up hard towards his assailant's belly. Elizabeth held her breath as he drew it up and across, to maximize the damage. It was his attacker's turn to cry out and Elizabeth froze at the sound; there was something familiar in that cry, something that rooted her to the spot.

Jack's sword flashed again and this time it was parried with skill and a deep mirthless laugh came from his assailant's throat.

Elizabeth knew that laugh and it froze her blood: the laugh belonged to Higgins!

Blade sang against blade as the two men circled each other, looking for advantage, probing for weakness. Their breath hung in the air around them like mist. Jack crouched low as he sought perfect balance, trying to evade the onslaught, which suddenly came at him like a storm. Again the metallic song rang out into the darkness and it made Elizabeth feel sick. The blades flashed blue-white in the moonlight. Jack parried Higgins's sword and dagger feverishly and Elizabeth realized with horror that Jack was at a disadvantage because she had his dagger in her hand!

Higgins began to force Jack back towards the quayside.

'Run!' Jack cried to Elizabeth but although she heard him, the word was meaningless, for she was still trying to take in what her senses were telling her. She was snared by indecision; did she try to give him his knife or did she obey him and flee? She breathed deeply, trying to think. No, she thought, she could not abandon him!

With a clatter that stopped her heart Jack's sword landed on the cobbles. Jack sprang forward to negate Higgins's sword and Elizabeth saw the flicker of a knife as it was thrust towards Jack's throat. Jack twisted and turned his assailant's arm, used the strength of his upper body to prevent Higgins from gaining advantage. Higgins dropped his own sword and grasped Jack's collar, trying to pull him off balance and towards the glinting blade.

Elizabeth noticed the cobbles were shiny and wet beneath them. She put her hand to her mouth to prevent herself from screaming as she suddenly realized the dark liquid was blood. Her stomach lurched; she did not know whose it was!

Elizabeth saw the bobbing of the boatmen's lanterns as they hurried across the little bridge.

Higgins must have noticed them too, for his efforts became more frantic as he sought to bury his knife in Jack's throat.

As if she was watching a dream Elizabeth saw Higgins launch himself at Jack, saw Jack stagger under the ferocity of the assault and saw them pitch towards the quay.

'Jack!' she cried helplessly as he stepped onto the edge of the quay, his foot dangerously close to stepping on air.

She thought he must have heard her, for he seemed to gather all his strength together and with one huge effort he pulled himself free of Higgins's grip.

Without Jack's resistance Higgins fell forward, and for one frozen heartbeat he teetered at the water's edge like an acrobat about to perform a somersault, before he plunged over the side and splashed into the water.

Within moments the boatmen were at Jack's side. Frantically they flashed their lanterns out over the water. They peered over the edge, looking for Higgins.

Shivering like a child woken suddenly from a nightmare, Elizabeth walked slowly towards Jack. She saw him leaning recklessly from the harbour wall, his eyes searching the dark water like a madman. His arm was outstretched, pointing to where he thought Higgins might be.

'Jack!' she called to him shakily.

Jack turned quickly and stood up.

'Is – is he...'

'Dead.' Jack finished for her. 'Yes, Elizabeth he is dead,' he said flatly.

She turned away from Jack. A wave of grief rose within her, but she knew that it was not all for Higgins. It was a mixture of grief: for her father, for Warwick and for herself, a kind of self-pity she had been carrying ever since she thought she had killed Jack at Scarsdale and suddenly it threatened to overwhelm her. It tightened her throat, shook at her shoulders and squeezed her chest. But she knew she must keep it down. She did not want Jack of all people to see her vulnerability.

What if she had not called out? Would Higgins have struck more truly? Mayhap he would have killed Jack? Ah, no – there was something invincible about Jack de Laverton and he knew it. It showed in his face; an arrogance that marked him out from other men as much as his olive skin and wild black hair. Jack's hand on her shoulder made her shudder.

'Come, we must go!' he said quietly.

She shrugged him off, knowing she had made the choice of who should live and who should die: she had sent Higgins to his death as surely as if she had struck the blow. But why did she care? It was Higgins after all who had brought her to London and into the presence of the loathsome Edward, Higgins who had orchestrated her betrayal of Warwick and Higgins who was so set on bringing him down. And that was why she had cried out a warning to Jack – for the love of Warwick.

'Elizabeth, please,' Jack said more firmly. 'We need to be away from here. They have called the watch. There will be questions...' He took hold of her elbow firmly and guided her along the tangled web of streets towards safety. And this time she did not resist him. She had no choice now. She had saved Jack at Higgins's expense; she only hoped she had made the right decision.

By the time they reached Senor Gruuthuse's house Jack's doublet sleeve was dark and wet with blood. His face was as pale as a waning moon and he was leaning against her heavily.

It took three of them to carry him up to their bedchamber, whilst another had been dispatched for a physician.

Elizabeth followed them silently. Perhaps she had not saved Jack after all. Without thought she twisted Cousin Matthew's mourning ring on her finger, the one he had given her at her father's funeral; 'Dominus vidit,' she whispered. 'The Lord doth see.' Had He seen their deception and was now punishing them? In her head she asked Him to look down on Jack and to help him, but she was not sure why, for with Higgins gone, Jack's protection was not so necessary, and if Jack died too she was free to do as she pleased.

Jack groaned pitifully as they laid him on the bed, and the sound squeezed Elizabeth's heart. She wondered how he had been on the night she had attacked him. God forgive me for causing him such pain, she thought.

She was suddenly conscious of the servants staring at her, awaiting her instructions. 'We must remove his doublet and shirt,' Elizabeth said hesitantly, not sure if she was doing the right thing, 'and then the wound must be cleaned. Can someone fetch hot water? Do you have Valerian?' she asked through a dry throat.

'Yes, Madame,' the servants chorused.

Elizabeth sat beside Jack as they pushed him forward to remove his clothes. Jack made a soft moan. His eyes were clouded with pain; a deep 'v' sat between his brows.

Elizabeth wanted to avert her eyes, but she had to look; she was supposed to be his wife! Once his fine linen shirt had been removed she stared at his sinuous body without thought, her eyes drawn to the ripple of dark hair that ran from his chest down to his navel and beyond, to where it disappeared into his tight hose. He was not as broad as Warwick, not as muscular, but still she swallowed hard, uneasy at the feelings stirring within her at the sight of him. She had to concentrate on treating his wound; to think of him in any other way – as the handsome knight she had first seen at Lazenby – would be her undoing.

The knife-wound cried at Jack's shoulder like an open mouth and thick dark blood ran down his arm and chest. That was good, Elizabeth thought, trying to focus her mind, it had not damaged a large blood vessel otherwise the blood would be as scarlet as a maiden's cheek, perhaps as hers was now.

A servant appeared with wine, bandages and hot water.

Elizabeth held the liquor to Jack's lips.

'It will dull the pain,' she said.

When Jack signalled that he could drink no more Elizabeth handed the cup to the servant. Jack slumped back against the pillows with a gasp, as weak as a newborn kitten.

A hush fell in the room and everyone looked at Elizabeth. Their expectations lay on her like lead; she was after all his wife to them – this was her responsibility. She sucked in her breath, trying to quieten her hammering heart. If she panicked now she would be no use to Jack and he would bleed to death right here in front of her! She tried to imagine herself back at Lazenby. How many times had she taken the role of her mother when a servant had been hurt or Edmund had taken a tumble from his pony? She told herself this was no different. But the sight of Jack's lithe and bloody half-naked body told her it was different, very different indeed.

Tentatively she began to swab at the wound.

Jack winced beneath her touch and she drew her hand back as if he had scalded her.

'Elizabeth,' he whispered. His voice was thick with pain and it brought stinging tears to Elizabeth's eyes. ''Tis nothing to the wound you gave me,' he said raggedly. 'Do whatever you must.' Then he forced a weak smile.

Elizabeth took a composing breath and then tried again. Blood soaked into the cloth in her hand. It was as dark as Burgundian wine and it made her feel queasy to look at it, knowing it was Jack's blood. She reached for another cloth and then another and each she brought away wet and dripping. Her heart flew to her throat. Oh God in heaven, what if the bleeding would not stop? Tears began to burn her eyes again and she fought not to let them show. She pressed hard on the wound, desperate to staunch the flow of Jack's lifeblood and she found herself whispering to the Virgin to help her.

All the while Jack lay still and grey, and Elizabeth wondered how much blood he still had in him; she prayed it was enough to sustain him. His breathing was shallow but steady, and again she murmured for help from the Queen of Heaven: 'Please do not let him die!'

NARROW SEA SEPTEMBER 1470

Warwick lay on his bed. The constant rhythmic sighing of the sea saturated all his senses. It should have lulled him like a child being rocked in its cradle, but although the hour bell told him it was past two o'clock in the morning, he remained infuriatingly awake.

Thoughts came at him like knights out of the mist. What if the Burgundians were waiting for them after all? What if Edward had managed to raise a significant defence in England? And other thoughts pierced his armour too – what had happened to Elizabeth? The pain of separation was like an old aching knife wound, gnawing at his resolve. Though he knew Higgins had been in Sir Robert's service, he could not quite understand why Elizabeth had left with him. He wondered if it had something to do with the letter Higgins had sent. According to Jack only Higgins had been with Elizabeth at Ellerton, only he could have known what happened there. But could what Higgins had written really be true – that Elizabeth had lost their son at the nunnery, as she tried to follow Brother William and escape? Pain squeezed his chest; why had she not confided in him?

He turned over restlessly. There was still no respite from the noises of the ship – the constant creaking of timbers, the flapping of canvas sail and beneath it all, like some great restless creature, the soft deep moaning of the ocean.

And what had Higgins's motivation been? Why tell him of this now? Why stab him so cruelly? Yes, he was Edward's spy, but this smelled of something more personal. After all, what could be more personal to Warwick than the loss of son? And the knife-twist of the blow was that it came so soon after the loss of his grandson; it cut right to the heart of him. Though he loved his daughters dearly, had he not wished with all his heart for a son? – A boy to carry his name and his bloodline; to ride at his side in battle. He would have been so proud of him, even though he was a natural son, born out of love. Higgins had delivered a blow below the sword belt. He clenched his fists as he thought of him; and to think he had once trusted him to carry important letters across France; trusted him with secrets men could have died for. His blood scorched his veins; no mercy could be shown to the coward, for to also take Elizabeth from him was a crime beyond punishment.

But why had Elizabeth not told him of her loss? It should have been a burden they shared. He shook his head; he knew women found such things difficult to discuss with their men: childbirth was a world in which men were not welcome. But he would have thought... And then he cursed himself for thinking badly of her. Had she not been through enough? She had lost her father and her child; and he had left her alone and vulnerable in England. No wonder she had cursed him! And yet she had found it in her heart to forgive him. No wonder she had wanted to come and comfort Isabel. By Christ, she more than anyone would be able to understand Isabel's pain!

He fingered the coral and gold prayer beads at his waist. He slipped them through his fingers one by one in the darkness, saying a prayer as he did so; each an Ave whispered for Elizabeth and her safe return to him.

The hour bell tolled again.

God it were morning, he thought; at least in the daylight he could keep busy. He could force the melancholy thoughts to the back of his mind and focus on the necessities of his plans. But when the darkness came he was like a child battling with nightmares.

He let out a long slow breath against the claustrophobia of the situation. He wished he could go after Elizabeth himself, but if he did not invade now the weather would mean he had to wait until spring, and that he knew was impossible; neither Louis nor Lancaster would tolerate any further delay, as it was Louis had thought the preparations had taken far too long. Then he thought of Jack: the only man of his company not with him. Jack would find her; he had to believe that. Jack might be a half-gypsy bastard but he was his most trusted man and had always shown him unswerving loyalty. And Warwick knew that somehow Jack would find her. But one thing worried him: Jack seemed to hold a fascination for all womenfolk, as though he exuded alchemy in their presence. They fell into his lap like ripe apples from the trees.

With this thought hot in his mind Warwick knew he would not sleep. He dragged his long gown from its hook and pulled it roughly across his shoulders. He pulled his cabin door open and headed out onto the deck.

He nodded to the watchman and then walked to the rail, to where the roar of the ocean was loudest. Sea spray stung his face and far off in the darkness he heard the solitary cry of a seabird calling to the dawn.

He peered beyond the foaming dark water; he knew his ships were out there, stretching beyond his sight; yet neither could he see the Burgundians or Anthony Wydeville and the 'Trinity'. His hand clenched unconsciously into a fist for he wanted his flagship back; it was yet another thing he had lost!

But where were they, the Burgundians? Had God finally blessed him with some good fortune? Mayhap the storm he and his sailors had followed had scattered them, sent them scurrying for port like rabbits for their burrows when the hounds come. He smiled to himself; Duke Charles would be furious when he realized Warwick had set sail for England at the moment his fleet had turned for refuge! And how furious Edward would be when Warwick once again kissed England's shore.

FIVE

BRUGES SEPTEMBER 1470

As if in answer to her supplication, the flow of blood from Jack's wound began to lessen. Gently Elizabeth cleaned away the clotting blood; surprising herself with her tenderness; she left only enough to protect the wound. She motioned for the servant to bring the candle closer, so that she could see more clearly, then Elizabeth began to dress the wound in clean bandages. The first layer darkened slightly with blood, and she wondered if she had begun too soon, but the second stayed clear. Elizabeth sighed with relief and whispered her thanks to the Virgin. Now she must make Jack more comfortable, she thought, for the pain was still furrowing his brow.

Before she could do any more there was a sudden clattering in the hallway. The chamber door flew open and a man muffled in a long black cloak demanded her attention. He was a large man with hands like a blacksmith's. He was red-faced and sweating. His breathing was short, perhaps from the stairs, and he smelled strongly of wine. He swayed briefly in the doorway before pushing roughly through the waiting servants. He gave Jack a cursory glance through squinting eyes and Elizabeth wondered if he perhaps needed spectacles.

'You have done this?' he asked Elizabeth abruptly as he peered at Jack's shoulder.

'Yes,' she said and lifted her chin to him defiantly.

Jack's eyes flickered open at the sound of her voice, but as though he had no strength left in him to keep them open, he closed them again.

'Hmm,' the doctor said as he scratched at his nose. He glanced over at the bowl of bloody cloths and nodded knowingly. He puffed wine-soaked breath and Elizabeth wondered how much he had drunk. Her heart missed a beat as he turned back to Jack. What was he going to do to him? She had heard stories about physicians giving cures worse than a patient's afflictions. How would she stop this man hurting Jack?

'A knife wound?' he asked curtly.

'Yes,' Elizabeth said hesitantly.

'Deep?'

Elizabeth nodded.

'But you have managed to stop the bleeding.'

'Yes, eventually,' Elizabeth said. She held her breath as the physician stared at Jack closely.

He looked into Jack's eyes and perused his torso as though he were examining a horse he wished to buy.

Elizabeth exchanged looks with Jack as the physician continued to peer at him.

Then the physician rubbed at his chin. 'And his urine?' he asked.

Elizabeth stared at him blankly.

'One must always examine the patient's urine,' he said brusquely.

'For a knife wound?' Elizabeth asked, astounded.

'It tells me whether his humours are in balance! Too much choler, too much spleen!' Then he rose unsteadily. 'Ah, you do not understand! I am surrounded by fools,' he said to himself.

Elizabeth pressed her lips together, folded her arms across her chest and met the physician's rheumy eyes angrily.

'I think there is too much choler in you, madam,' he said tersely, swaying on his feet. 'But that is probably better for your husband!' He nodded towards Jack. 'Saturn is in a good position presently and that bodes well for a wound of the upper arm. I need do nothing else for the moment,' he slurred. 'The muscle may be torn, but there is little we can do about that now.'

Elizabeth let her breath out slowly with relief.

'Change the dressing in three days. If wound fever sets in, send for me again. In the meantime, pray that it does not!'

In a cloud of black cloak, the physician turned away and the servants followed him silently, leaving Elizabeth and Jack alone.

Tentatively Jack reached a hand out towards her. He laced his fingers into hers and then pulled her hand to his lips. They were cold.

'Thank you, sweetheart,' he said hazily.

Elizabeth watched him sink back onto the pillows. Then the tears came. Elizabeth was unsure whether they were tears of relief for Jack, tears of grief for Higgins or tears of desperation that they had missed their boat bound for England. But without thought she leant closer to Jack. 'Santa Maria, thank you,' she whispered. 'Thank you for saving his life.'

Jack fell into an uneasy sleep, hastened no doubt by the wine she had forced into him. He lay helplessly against the pillows.

124

Two vertical lines pleated his brows and Elizabeth knew he was still in pain.

Gently she brushed a dark curl from his damp cheek and tucked it behind his ear. For some moments she watched the steady rise and fall of his chest and was grateful for it. As she shamelessly perused his body she noticed that he bore two further scars of similar size to the wound Higgins had given him and she wondered what had happened to the men who had inflicted them upon him. Had he killed them too? As she watched him she thought that she would never know the real man, doubted if even Jack truly knew himself.

Eventually her eyes became heavy-lidded and she lay down at the side of him to sleep.

In her mind she relived the night's events and she realized that Jack had been right all along; Higgins would never have left without her, and in the end that had been his undoing: she had been the cause of his death.

She wondered if Higgins had been as surprised as she had been, when he realized Jack had not been killed at Scarsdale. What angry bile must have risen in his throat; how he must have cursed. Perhaps it had been his desire for revenge over Jack rather than a wish to have Elizabeth back that had driven him to come after them. For it was not only Warwick he blamed for his past torture; Jack had been with Higgins in France and had completed the mission for Warwick alone.

But no good ever came from the desire for revenge, Elizabeth thought. That was something else Jack had been right about: forgiveness. Was it not much sweeter to forgive than to destroy oneself in the pursuit of revenge?

She turned to look at Jack now. Could she ever really forgive him as he had forgiven her?

DEVONSHIRE COAST SEPTEMBER 1470

The brackish wind whipped along the misty shoreline, ruffling Warwick's hair and stinging his face. He breathed deeply, inhaling the sweet smell of England.

He looked at the faces of his men and saw they shared the same expression: relief. Even though Warwick fought at sea as well as anyone, he too had not wanted a battle with the Burgundians and was glad they had reached England unscathed. But now, as he prepared to disembark, part of him did not want to leave the safety of his ship. For even with the fickleness of winds and tide, at sea he felt more certain.

He stared at the hungry shore, knowing it would take all his strength, maybe even his lifeblood, to complete the task he had set himself. Not that he feared Edward; he didn't, it was just that he appreciated the enormity of what he had to do: to hold Lancastrians tight to former Yorkists, and with such an alliance to defeat Edward, a man who had never lost a battle. He smiled at the thought of Edward; he knew him better than he knew himself, knew that his strategy would have lured him away from London, for Edward's bruised and battered pride would not let him ignore Fitzhugh's rebellion, of that he was certain.

As Warwick placed his feet firmly on the harbour he resisted the sudden urge to kneel and kiss the ground; that he thought would show him too grateful for their untroubled passage.

Suddenly chanting erupted from the crowds of men gathered to meet him.

'A Warwick! A Warwick!'

He nodded his appreciation and the cheers grew louder. He heard nothing for Lancaster or King Henry and knew that winning their supporters over would be more difficult, but it was something he had to do if he was to have any chance of success. He sucked in a deep breath. If only intransigent Marguerite had allowed Edouard to sail with him!

BRUGES SEPTEMBER 1470

Jack leant back against the pillows and sighed. God's breath how Elizabeth had trapped him; just like the unicorn in the tapestries he had seen, he had been snared by a beautiful maiden! And Elizabeth certainly was beautiful, but it was more than that; he admired her spirit, and her courage. How many women would have dared to attack him as she had done at Scarsdale? Or would have even considered making the journey she had made to Warwick to speak for her wayward father? Or would have saved his life as she had just now? She was remarkable; she was perfect, but he knew she could never be his, even though by rights she should be. He tried not to dwell on her father's promise that could never now be fulfilled, yet he wanted her so much. His loins stirred. He almost laughed; even if she were to present herself to him naked, he would not have the strength to act! He looked up at the intricately embroidered fabric on the tester; the spiralled leaves wove a complicated pattern and were dappled with silk roses. It reminded him of the rose arbour at Scarsdale and he sucked in his breath through his teeth; that was the day he regretted most in his life.

The sound of the latch snapped him from his reverie. The door swung open and Elizabeth walked in; she moved as gracefully as a cat, Jack thought as he watched her, and her hair, still unbrushed and unbound from bed, swayed like a silken mantle about her slender waist. He shifted his weight on the bed and tried to swallow down such thoughts of her, but as she came towards the bed she gave him a smile that stirred him again.

A servant followed her into the room. He carried a gilded tray on which were crammed several silver dishes, but even though he was hungry, Jack could not take his eyes from Elizabeth. He could not understand her; there was serenity about her this morning, as though a weight had been lifted from her and he wondered if that was what Higgins's threat had been to her. He had half expected her to scold him for killing Higgins, but so far there had been no sign of rebuke; that would come later when she learned the truth, he thought.

'I will serve him,' Elizabeth said sweetly as the servant brought the food closer.

The servant put the tray down as she bid him, then bowed and left.

'I could find no horses, my lord,' she smiled, in reference to Jack's earlier statement that he was hungry enough to eat one, 'but there is a good chicken broth, some cold beef and salt-fish and I am told the honey cake is the best in the country.'

Jack struggled to sit up. His left arm seemed to have no power in it at all and white pain jagged into his shoulder as he tried to move. 'Thank you,' he said through clenched teeth.

Quickly Elizabeth came to his side. He was annoyed with himself that he had to rely on her help; he was supposed to take care of her. Then her hands pressed against his back and a lock of her hair fell across his chest as she braced herself against him while she moved the pillows. Jack caught the sweet smell of it and the womanly scent of Elizabeth. His loins stirred again, though she seemed oblivious to the effect she was having on him. She had never been so close to him and yet she was more forbidden to him now than she had ever been.

She moved to the tray and Jack watched her pick up a goblet.

'Here, Jack. Drink this,' she said softly.

Jack took the goblet she offered and drank deeply. He was conscious of her eyes on him. It was good wine, but there was something bitter and powdery in it also.

Elizabeth laughed at the face he made. 'It is valerian. It will ease the pain a little I am told.'

She took the goblet from him and then held up the bowl of broth. Jack could see steam rising from the gilded bowl and it smelled appetizingly of chicken and onions. Elizabeth put some on the spoon and then blew on it gently, as if she was feeding a child.

Jack wanted to growl that he could manage, but that would be a foolish thing to do for two reasons. One, he plainly could not manage and two, Elizabeth had never been so attentive towards him. In fact no one had ever looked after him like this.

He sipped the broth from the spoon she offered. He met her eyes. By Christ they were the most beautiful eyes in the world, he thought, and for almost the first time they were not looking at him with any angry fire in them. They were like two clear bright emeralds and they were full of concern and tenderness.

'Is it good?' she asked.

He nodded and smiled. 'Yes. Thank you.' He liked this gentle understanding between them and wished that it could last forever.

She slipped the spoon into his right hand and held the bowl up so that he could feed himself.

She too seemed pleased that there was no tension between them, Jack thought. It was in a woman's constitution to nurture, and it was good that she could nurture even him. That gave him hope.

'Last night,' he said huskily, breaking the companionable silence, 'you could have said nothing.' He had to know why she had saved him.

She looked at him quizzically.

'You could have let him kill me, Elizabeth.' He watched her reaction.

She frowned. 'I did not know for certain that it was Higgins,' she said, 'though I think somehow we both expected him.'

Jack nodded, though she had not really answered his question; had she forgiven him? 'I knew he would not give up on you,' he said. 'He had to try to take you back.'

Elizabeth tipped the bowl for him to drain.

'And the wound,' Jack continued. 'You did not have to help me, though God alone knows what that physician would have done to me if you had not been here!'

She smiled. 'You are still my best hope of going home, Jack.'

She turned to reach for the next platter.

Was that all it was: he was just her best way home; did she feel nothing for him? He moved against the pillows and pain bit down into his shoulder.

'Why on earth would I want to go home now?' he asked. He sounded petulant, when he wanted to sound anything but. But his shoulder was hurting and he truly did not want to go home; did not want to lose her gentle company.

Elizabeth seemed to understand and made a jest of it. 'Why indeed, sir, with me here as your slave?' she asked teasingly.

He half expected her voice to rise in a challenge, but it didn't. She turned her eyes upon him again. 'You promised, Jack, remember?'

'But as Higgins told you, I am a notorious liar!'

Elizabeth shook her head and her hair moved softly about her face. Jack wanted to touch it, wanted to knot his fingers in her curls and pull her to him. He fought the rising passion.

'I think there is more honour in you than you will admit to, Jack,' she said smiling. 'And lazy though you are, even you cannot lie abed forever!'

Jack smiled. 'I can if you lie with me,' he said. Christ's wounds, why had he said that? As soon as she heard the words he saw her frown; he had put her on her guard again.

She handed him a platter of cold beef, which she had already cut for him.

'Here,' she said curtly. She retreated to the end of the bed and watched as he struggled to feed himself with the silver knife. The beef was tough.

'Anyway,' she said coolly, 'I will not wait forever, Jack. If you do not recover quickly I shall leave you here and make my own way to England. With Higgins dead and you on your sickbed, whom do I have to fear?'

Jack met her gaze. The softness had gone, banished by his foolishness.

'Edward has other spies,' he said quickly. But she could see he was clutching at straws and she laughed. He watched the ripple of her throat as she did so and she blushed as she saw his gaze. She turned away.

He wanted to tell her the reason she could not leave without him, but how could he tell her the truth about Higgins now?

'You will have to do better than that, Jack,' she admonished him gently.

He watched as she helped herself to some salt-fish, watched as she chewed it slowly. She met his gaze evenly, daring him to challenge her not to go.

'You are right, sweetheart,' he said, 'but even you are not so heartless as to leave your patient before he is cured!' He cursed himself that he could think of nothing better.

She laughed. 'Am I not? You had better not put that to the test!'

Jack smiled, but there was something in her eyes now that made him uneasy; her confidence was growing. And now she knew she was in command he wondered if she would indeed leave him behind.

DEVONSHIRE SEPTEMBER 1470

Thomas surveyed the countryside. The sky was grey; a misty grey, damp with drizzle in which the distant spire of a church was like a ghost and the forest was a hazy smear on the horizon. He shivered; autumn was definitely here. Soon the September rains would arrive in earnest and that was what worried him. How could Warwick mount a campaign against Edward when the roads would become mud and the fields a sodden stinking marshland?

He was pleasantly surprised that they had received only welcome from the West Country, but Thomas thought they were in danger of being trapped in this corner of England, which Edward could annexe easily; then he could deal with them at his leisure. Thomas thought he would feel easier once he knew exactly where Edward was and where their battle would be. He only hoped it would be soon; provisioning an army was hard enough in the warmth of summer but doing so in the clinging wet of autumn would be near to impossible. He cursed the Burgundians for delaying them; the odds were all stacked in Edward's favour.

Thomas walked back along the walls towards the camp; there must be ten thousand men behind Warwick's streaming banners now. Only Warwick could do this, he thought, only Warwick could call to men's hearts so that they would follow him whatever king he made!

As he drew near to his billet he saw Warwick, laughing with some of the billmen who had arrived this morning. When he saw Thomas he broke away from them and came towards him, smiling.

Thomas bowed. 'My lord,' he said.

'Are they not a magnificent sight, Thomas?' Warwick said brightly. 'And more join us by the hour.'

'Indeed, my lord,' Thomas said.

Warwick frowned. 'Something troubles you, Thomas?'

Thomas sighed; he could never keep anything from Warwick. 'I shall be happier once we know our enemy's position, my lord and know when we shall give battle.'

Warwick nodded. 'We should know by nightfall where Edward is and what his strength is; then can we set our own ambitions, Thomas.'

Thomas nodded.

'You are yet concerned?' Warwick asked.

'It is the seasons I fear more than Edward. It is hard to keep an army on the march in the wet of autumn, my lord.'

'You are right, Thomas,' Warwick said. 'That is why I wanted to be well provisioned from France. Pray God we encounter Edward soon. If he is the monarch he believes he is, then he shall be waiting for us!'

Thomas saw the gleam in Warwick's eye and heard the anticipation in his voice. They didn't match his own feelings. He hoped Edward was waiting for them, for the longer this went on, the more the odds favoured King Edward!

* * *

'So he doesn't even know where the king is!' Robert said sullenly as Thomas joined him in their billet.

'The usurper,' Thomas corrected him.

Robert shrugged.

'No, he doesn't, but he will by tonight,' Thomas answered, hoping Warwick was right. 'We must be prepared to leave early on the morrow.'

'My kit has been ready for nearly two months!' Robert said dryly. 'But I suppose you will need to clean yours again?'

Thomas smiled. 'I shall check it again, of course! My father always taught me that it was the most important thing; your life depends upon it, Rob.'

Robert nodded, but said nothing.

Thomas wondered why Robert was so melancholy; it was usually Robert who cheered Thomas. 'Rob?' he asked.

Robert looked up at him. 'It's just the waiting,' Robert said. He paused.

Thomas knew there was something else troubling him.

'And I'm worried about Will.'

'Will?' Thomas asked. He had been so much in Warwick's company of late he had hardly seen their tutor and captain.

'His age is catching up with him. He grows more bad-tempered every day. I think it's the pain in his legs, though he will not admit to it.'

Robert met Thomas's gaze with worried eyes. 'I fear for his chances in battle, Tom.'

'Then we must try to protect him,' he said.

Robert shook his head. 'I don't think we can; he'd be the death of us too.'

Thomas's heart lurched. 'But we can't just leave him to die!' he said hotly.

'He's a soldier,' Robert said evenly. 'He knows this will be his last campaign.'

Thomas's eyes began to sting and he clenched his hands into tight fists to stop the tears leaching out. The worst thing was he knew Robert was right. Speed was an advantage in battle and that was something their youth gave them and which age had taken away from Will. At Edgecote Will had urged them forward and had forced himself to keep up with them, but the increasing stiffness of age had now robbed him of even that laboured mobility.

'Perhaps Warwick will let him guard the baggage?' Thomas asked hopefully.

Robert snorted. 'You know that he'd refuse. Where's the honour for a soldier in that?'

'In what?'

As if summoned by thought, Will limped in.

Thomas thought the stubble grazing his chin was whiter and that the lines carved into his cheeks were deeper somehow.

'Honour in what?' Will repeated gruffly. His brows seemed permanently furrowed.

Thomas and Robert exchanged glances.

'In guarding the baggage,' Thomas said truthfully.

'Pah!' Will spat as he came closer. 'Is that what you've lined up for me, eh?' he growled at Thomas. 'Putting me out to grass, Thomas?'

'No,' Thomas lied.

'This old warhorse is not for pasture yet, lad, if that's what you're thinking.' Will's face creased like old linen as he sat down.

Thomas looked at him. Fierce eyes met his and he knew it was no use trying to convince him.

'I'll be there with you,' Will croaked. 'That is, if you're planning on fighting!'

'You know we are, Will,' Thomas said quietly.

Will looked from one to the other. 'Then make me proud of you, boys,' he said hoarsely. 'For I do not think we shall fight together again.'

BRUGES SEPTEMBER 1470

The incense stung Elizabeth's eyes as she walked along the dark nave of the church. She shivered; it brought back so many memories of Warwick, memories she had thought were safely locked away at the back of her mind where they could not unravel her; how she had watched him praying, how he had discovered her at Calais. And she wished that he would come unannounced into this church now. Santa Maria, she would not flee from him this time! But she knew it could not be, and sadness encircled her like a wet winter cloak. She shuddered and rebuked herself inwardly; self-pity would not help her now.

The stone was hard and cold on her knees as she knelt to pray and she recalled the hours she had spent in this position at Ellerton Nunnery, saying her daily offices. But today was different. Inexplicably she needed to thank the Virgin for saving Jack and to ask her to help her return to England and Warwick.

As she lit the candle she saw that her hand was shaking. Everything had nearly ended in disaster last night! If Jack had been killed how would she ever have avoided returning to Edward with Higgins? A shiver ran down her spine as though one of Higgins's twisted fingers had touched her. She began to recite her Aves. She slipped the cold rosary beads through her fingers slowly as she chanted and wondered if the Virgin could understand why she was praying for two men, when she barely understood the reasons herself.

Did she have any future with Warwick? How would she explain to him what had happened at Barfleur with Higgins and here in Bruges with Jack? She thought of Warwick's dark unfathomable eyes meeting hers and her stomach knotted. But perhaps she did not have to confess everything, she thought, for the things he did not know could not cause him pain. And he must never know that she had failed him; that she had fallen so far short of what he would have expected from her. His daughters had risen to the challenges put before them, whereas she had wilted; but then she did not have their Neville blood!

'Oh, Richard,' she whispered as tears stung her eyes. 'Can you ever forgive me?' As she placed her rosary in her belt she suddenly remembered the poesy he had given her. The jewel was lost at Middleham, when in temper and grief she had flung it away, but unbelievably she had kept the verse, written in Warwick's own hand. She pulled it from her purse. The parchment was rolled up tightly; its edges tattered and stained, the ink smudged where it had got wet. She could still just make out the words of Guillaume de Machaut's song and she whispered them softly:

'Vous estes le vray saphir
Qui puet tous mes maus garir et terminer.
Esmeraude a resjoir,
Rubis pour cuers esclarcir et conforter.
Vo parler, vo regarder,
Vo maintenir, font fuir et enhair et despiter
Tout vice et tout bien cherir et desirer
Foy porter ...

Seule une,
Richard.'

You are the true sapphire
That can heal and end all my sufferings,
The emerald which brings rejoicing,
The ruby to brighten and comfort the heart.
Your speech, your looks,
Your bearing, make one flee and hate and detest
All vice and cherish and desire all that is good.

I want to stay faithful...

My only one,
Richard.

Tears squeezed through her lashes as she remembered the strength of his arms about her and how he had whispered of his love to her; a love so strong that it was profane, and for which he risked eternal damnation. She remembered too how he had once feared she would be used as a tool against him, but even he had not guessed that she would act as that tool of her own free will! Guilt caught at her throat: *she* had not stayed faithful!

Slowly she returned the parchment to her purse and wiped the tears from her face with her hand. She sniffed and choked down those tears still burning her: she had to regain some self-control if she was ever to get through this. Though she knew facing Warwick would be the most difficult thing she had yet had to do, England was still a very long way off, as Jack kept telling her. She stared through blurred vision at the painted Madonna in front of her. 'Help me,' she whispered, 'for I do not know what to do.'

The bright blue eyes of the Madonna smiled at her infant and Elizabeth too stared at the Christ child. Something flickered within her, something that gave her comfort. She sucked in her breath determinedly and her inner strength grew. There must be no more searching of her conscience; it would change nothing and brought only despair. Only the Virgin was perfect among womankind! What would be would be, whether Elizabeth tortured herself over it or not. She knew that to reach England she needed Jack; he had to be her concern now, even if helping him brought its own risks, for Jack brought more questions than answers.

Thomas waited in the shadows of the room. His eyes flicked from one man to another: Warwick, Clarence, and Oxford; three great lords set to unmake a king. Warwick stood proudly, his arms folded across his deep chest, his head held high. Only the tightness of his lips told Thomas that he harboured any apprehension. Clarence slouched against the wall; his legs crossed, his eyes glowering under sullen brows, his face only brightening if Warwick glanced in his direction.

The scratching of the scribe's quill and the crackle of the fire were a soporific brew and Thomas's eyelids grew heavy, but he could not miss this, the proclamation that would summon the people of England to Warwick's banner.

At length the scribe finished his work and Oxford leaned close to the candle to read it. 'God's blood Warwick, but its good!' he beamed. 'It is as though the Yorkists never benefited from your leadership!'

Thomas saw that Warwick did not smile. Clarence's eyes darkened.

'It is necessary that we are united,' Warwick said calmly as he turned to look at his son-in-law. 'Is that not so, George?'

Clarence lifted his eyes to Warwick and twitched a smile. 'Absolutely,' he said impassively.

'You will sign it first, of course,' Warwick said.

Thomas heard a short gasp as Clarence sucked in his breath, but he recovered well. 'As you wish, father,' he said as he untangled his legs and came away from the wall.

Warwick and Oxford exchanged glances and then all eyes explored Clarence as he took up the quill.

Thomas saw a slight hesitation and a momentary quiver of the pen in Clarence's hand, as though a cold draught had buffeted it; he saw Clarence's throat ripple as he swallowed deeply. Then he signed the paper that proclaimed Henry the sixth as their true sovereign and Edward, late Earl of March, as the treacherous usurper.

When he rose, Clarence smiled the broadest smile Thomas had seen since before their exile from England. Thomas wondered if the hesitation had been nothing more than Clarence's understandable regret at divorcing himself from his family, or if there was something darker there, like tangled weeds beneath the surface of a lake, ready to snare unwitting navigators.

When the letter was sealed Warwick turned to Thomas.

Thomas's heart quickened.

'This must go to London, Thomas,' Warwick said quietly.

'Yes, my lord,' Thomas said, bowing low. He took the letter from Warwick. 'I will send a messenger right away.'

'And Thomas,' Warwick added gravely, 'make sure every captain knows the score: the clauses herein are to be obeyed by everyone. There is to be no looting, no ravishment of women. Any man so caught will hang.'

'Yes, my lord,' Thomas answered.

'And there must be no reprisals,' Warwick continued. 'Sanctuary must be respected, even the sanctuary at Westminster.'

Thomas bowed again as he left them. Something puzzled him; why had Warwick mentioned the sanctuary at Westminster in particular?

BRUGES SEPTEMBER 1470

Elizabeth dismissed the servants but she wondered immediately if she had done the right thing, for that meant the responsibility was once again all hers. As Jack's wife she knew this was what was expected, but she didn't feel old or wise enough and being alone with Jack brought its own danger. But none of the servants said anything or even gave her a questioning look; they curtseyed in mute obedience and then filed out of the chamber.

She turned her attention to Jack and the task the physician had set her.

Jack watched her warily; he knew why she had come.

'How does it feel?' she asked him as she brought the candles closer to the bed.

'Easier,' he said trying to sound unconcerned, but she saw from his frown that his wound was still hurting him.

'I must look at it, Jack,' she said as she sat down beside him on the bed.

He nodded and then shifted his weight against the bolsters nervously.

The silence lengthened as Elizabeth set the candles down nearby. Her heartbeat quickened.

'Let me settle the pillows,' Elizabeth said, trying not to show her anxiety.

She put one arm across Jack's chest while she reached behind him with the other for the bolsters and tried to rearrange them so that he would be comfortable while she carried out her task. His body was warm against hers, and she caught the scent of his sweat. She tried not to look at the honed muscles of his back, defined and tight with tension and pain, but she could not help it. Then she saw something that turned her blood to ice. At the base of his ribs was a thin red scar, not yet old enough to have turned white. Instinctively she knew it was the one she had given him. Without thought she fingered the raised red weal gently, tracing its outline as if it were carved in stone on the sculpture of a martyr. She looked up at Jack. He half turned, his eyes meeting hers over his shoulder.

Elizabeth offered him an apologetic smile.

'Yes, it is the one you gave me, sweetheart,' he said tightly 'And, if you wish to know, it hurt a lot more than this one from Higgins. This is but a bee-sting!'

As though the effort of speaking had drained him, Jack sank back against her. Elizabeth guided him gently onto the pillows. She looked at his face, which was paler than the sheets. She could not check his wound now, not with such a revelation between them and Jack in such pain. She wondered how on earth she could have inflicted such suffering upon him. How could she have hated him so much? Remorse struck at her core.

'I am sorry, Jack,' she murmured as the guilt constricted her stomach.

Jack's eyes flickered open. His gaze was cloudy, but he met her look evenly.

'And I am sorry too,' he said. 'But we must put it behind us. It is past.' His breath rasped in his throat. 'The facts are, sweetheart that I did not rape you and you did not kill me. It is over. We have both paid our debts.' His voice trailed away wearily and he closed his eyes again.

By his words Elizabeth assumed he meant that he had saved her from Higgins by killing him and that she had saved Jack's life by tending his wound. So where did that leave them, she wondered.

Elizabeth sat beside him, and without thinking took hold of his hand. She hardly recognized this Jack as the man who had watched her at Scarsdale. And neither did she recognize herself as the frightened angry girl who had wounded him.

Could she put it all behind her as Jack had? And if she forgave him did that not make her current position all the more vulnerable?

After a while Jack's breathing deepened and she saw he had fallen asleep. She rose carefully so as not to waken him and then moved to the window. She stared out at the misty city as daylight faded to night; autumn had come so soon, she thought. If Higgins hadn't wounded Jack they would be in England by now; but would it be an England they would recognize; one in which she and Warwick could be reunited? Or an England in which to have Neville connections was to admit to treason?

She shivered, suddenly cold. She closed the shutters and then moved back to the bed. She raised the coverlet and slipped in beside Jack. Even though she was gentle he murmured in his sleep. She blew out the candles and then turned to face him. In the half-light she ran her eyes over him brazenly. She watched his chest rise and fall as he breathed. She shivered again and moved closer to him. Then she placed an arm across his warm body. Whatever they yet had to face, they had no choice but to face it together.

* * *

Elizabeth's eyes fluttered open. Light leached in through the shutters, casting white stripes across the counterpane. She felt brighter, stronger and more peaceful than she had been in a long time. Her eyelids began to close dreamily. Jack was warm beside her and without thought, she nuzzled against his shoulder. He stirred. Suddenly she opened her eyes, wakened by his movement and she realized with horror that her arm was still about his body. She looked up at him.

His eyes were wide and smiling. 'Good Morrow, sweetheart,' he whispered.

Elizabeth withdrew her hand quickly. Her cheeks flushed.

'You slept well,' Jack observed with a grin.

Elizabeth blushed further. 'I – I was cold,' she said.

'Of course,' Jack replied softly. His grin broadened; they both knew it was an excuse as flimsy as her veil.

He moved a little closer to her and she noticed that he moved more easily. She noticed his face had more colour about it, though not nearly as much colour as hers must have.

'I will fetch breakfast,' she said hurriedly.

Jack reached out an arm and caught hold of her shoulder. He fixed her eyes with his and Elizabeth hesitated, held by his look. 'Do not rush on my account, sweetheart,' he breathed.

Her heart thumped in her chest. 'But I am hungry,' she said as she wriggled free of him, 'even if you are not!' His eyes appraised her as she dressed. He said nothing. He didn't need to; inside she was like burning fire.

* * *

Jack smiled broadly when she brought him his food. Elizabeth read his look and knew she had been the foolish instigator of those thoughts! His teeth were white against the shadow of two day's growth of dark stubble.

'You look like an Irishman with that black beard,' she teased, trying to distract him from her recklessness. 'I am not sure you would allow me to shave you, though!'

'I think I would prefer the barber,' Jack said with a soft laugh. 'I have seen your handiwork with a blade before!'

Elizabeth smiled, but the guilt twisted again within her.

Jack prodded at the cold beef with his knife and managed to raise the goblet to his lips with his wounded arm, though Elizabeth saw him flinch as he did so. She was pleased that she no longer needed to feed him and it made her more optimistic about what was to come.

As he finished the last piece of bread, Elizabeth decided she could delay no longer. 'Jack,' she said solemnly.

His smile faded.

'I must check your wound.'

He said nothing but his face questioned her.

'It is the only way to be sure there is no wound fever,' Elizabeth said as she cleared away the remains of breakfast.

Jack finished chewing his bread. He nodded slowly and then wriggled against the pillows, trying to get comfortable. He looked up at her and with apprehension in his eyes. 'I trust you, sweetheart,' he whispered.

Elizabeth heard the quiver in his voice. His nervousness matched her own; but if she didn't do this for him, who would? As his wife it was her duty to carry out the physician's instructions and so it must be done. Now. By her.

Gently she untied the bandages and as carefully as she could she began to pull them free. Slowly, layer by layer she removed them until she came to a dark stain. She looked at Jack and saw that he had closed his eyes. His breathing was quick and shallow, almost matching hers.

She hesitated and his eyes flicked open.

'This may hurt,' she said softly.

He smiled thinly. 'It will teach me to get mixed up with you,' he said dryly.

She smiled back at him and then returned her attention to the dressing. Gently she pulled.

Jack sucked in his breath and gave a low moan, but she knew she had to continue. She tugged at the bandage and gradually it began to come away. The stain of dried blood was bigger on the next layer and it was held even more firmly.

She looked at Jack. Beads of sweat stood out on his brow and his mouth was drawn into a thin line.

She bit her lip in concentration as she pulled at the final layer; she knew she must not dislodge the scab protecting the wound.

Jack winced.

'There,' she said, 'it is done.'

She touched the dark scar with the back of her hand.

Jack looked at her anxiously.

She smiled. 'It is cool,' she said. 'No sign of wound fever. And I don't think the muscle is torn, God be thanked.'

Jack sighed. 'You must have prayed devoutly for me then, sweetheart,' he said with a grin.

Elizabeth shook her head. She did not tell him that she had prayed to the Blessed Virgin or that she had made a donation of the last of her money to the church in gratitude. What would he think if he knew she had knelt there in the cold nave and by the light of the flickering candles given thanks for his life?

'I doubt either the Lord or the Blessed Virgin would take much notice of my entreaties,' she said. 'I yet have so many sins to confess,' she said ruefully.

'But murder isn't one of them,' Jack said softly.

'No, not murder. I do not have that on my list. But you do, Jack,' she said. 'You have a murder on your conscience and you should confess it. Everyone accepts that it was committed in self-defence, but you did end Higgins's life.'

Jack shrugged. 'That is for me to decide,' he said defensively. Then he grinned. 'But it is touching that you care for my soul as well as my body!'

Elizabeth flushed. She turned away from his dark eyes and began to renew his dressing. 'I think you should get up today,' she said, changing the subject. 'You need exercise, otherwise your muscles will be wasted, as mine were at Ellerton. When I was eventually fit enough to stand, my legs would not bear my weight.'

Jack's hand squeezed her arm and she realized she had told him far too much.

'The nunnery?' he asked quietly.

Elizabeth nodded and her cheeks grew hot under his look. How did he know about her time at Ellerton?

'I am sorry about the nunnery,' Jack said.

'Sorry?' she asked. 'It was not your fault, Jack.'

'Higgins found you before I did,' he said.

Elizabeth looked at him quickly. 'You were trying to find me?'

Jack nodded. 'Warwick realized the countess knew of you, and after the battle at Empingham he knew he would not be able to reach you himself. I was sent to find you, but Higgins found you first. I failed you, Elizabeth.'

He looked down at the bedcover.

Elizabeth covered his hand with hers. 'It was not your fault,' she said.

Jack looked up at her and smiled. 'Once you were with Higgins I could not make myself known, for I wanted him to believe that I was dead, as I said it was, is, the perfect alibi. And once at Scarsdale even the servants would have remembered me! After all I was the only murder victim they had seen in a long time, I presume. But when you came to London, then following you was easy. There are many places to hide in Edward's court.'

Elizabeth shivered at Jack's knowledge of her; she really didn't have any secrets from him. 'You must believe me that I do now regret what I did for Edward,' she said.

Jack said nothing.

'You must realize that I had no choice,' she continued. Why on earth was she explaining this to Jack, when she knew she could never tell Warwick? God there was so much she could not tell Warwick! She sighed; there was no going back now.

'My father...' She choked on the words.

'Aye, sweetheart, I know. He did not deserve what happened to him,' Jack said.

'No, he did not,' Elizabeth said grittily. 'He should have been safe at Middleham; Warwick promised he would be.' Her throat tightened again as she thought on her dying father. Her eyes began to sting. 'I can never forgive Sir John Conyers, Jack. Never.'

'But if your father had not tried to go to Edward...' Jack said.

Elizabeth scowled at him. 'It should have made no difference. What could those letters have held in them that Edward did not know already? Why did they matter so much?'

Jack shook his head. 'I do not know, sweetheart, but your father thought they were worth dying for.'

Elizabeth sighed. 'And I am here because he did so,' she said sadly. 'For I had to continue what he could not. As he lay dying he made me promise him that I would take the letters. And Higgins and Cousin Matthew and my mother told me that I must.'

Jack looked puzzled.

'They told me that the only way I could come home was if I carried out my father's wishes; but the reality was that it was part of a greater scheme: I was being set up by Higgins to betray Warwick.' Tears fought their way onto her cheek. 'I was 'the perfect spy', Higgins said.'

'The Higgins you begged me not to kill,' Jack reminded her gently.

She nodded. 'I know. You think me foolish,' she said.

'No,' Jack said softly. He reached up and ran his thumb over her cheek, wiping away her tears. 'Not foolish, sweetheart.'

Elizabeth's skin prickled as he touched her.

'We all have regrets,' Jack said sadly. 'We all have things we wish we had not done.'

Elizabeth knew he meant Scarsdale.

'But Warwick will forgive you,' Jack said huskily.

Elizabeth's eyes flew to his like startled birds. 'He must not know, Jack.' Panic gripped her chest.

Jack shook his head. 'If there is one thing I have learned, sweetheart, it is that the truth always comes out...eventually. Is it not better that he hears it from your own lips?'

Elizabeth shrugged. 'I do not know. I cannot think how I could confess it.' Guilt tore her voice to tatters.

'As you have to me,' Jack said gently.

Elizabeth shook her head and the tears began to run down her face again. She wondered why she could confess to Jack what she could not say to Warwick. Was it because Jack already knew everything there was to know about her? Because he had been there from the start of this adventure? 'He must never know, Jack,' she said firmly. 'I could never tell him.'

'Sweetheart...'

'No Jack,' she said sternly. 'You must promise me you will never tell him!'

Jack's lips pressed together in a line. His brows darkened. 'He is my lord,' he said. 'I owe him my allegiance.'

'Jack, please,' Elizabeth begged him. 'Please do not tell him.'

Jack's eyes met hers and Elizabeth's heart began to race. 'Jack?' she whispered.

He held her gaze and the silence lengthened, building between them like the humid air before a storm. But Elizabeth kept her eyes on Jack's, hoping he would feel her anguish.

Eventually Jack sighed. 'Very well,' he said. 'I promise he shall not hear it from me.'

'And the letter?' Elizabeth asked. So far as she knew Jack still had Edward's unopened letter to Warwick.

Jack met her eyes again and for a long moment he held her gaze.

Elizabeth's heartbeat was ragged now. Perhaps he had handed it over already? Why else would he hesitate? Her eyes stung again.

'You ask much of me, Elizabeth,' he said quietly. 'That letter should go to Warwick. It is his by right.'

'But it will not matter now,' Elizabeth said quickly, 'is he not about to invade?'

Jack raised an eyebrow at her. They both knew the letter had wider implications.

'Its only possible use would be to blackmail me!' she snapped. 'Is that why you still have it, Jack; so that I will do what you want?'

Jack looked wounded. 'No!' he said quickly. 'I have never said so!'

'No,' Elizabeth said coolly, 'you have never said so, but you have kept it nevertheless!' Her throat tightened with anger.

'I have said he will not hear of it from me...' Jack winced as he leaned towards her. He narrowed his eyes. 'Unlike you Harda-cres, I know how to keep my word!'

'What do you mean?' Elizabeth asked him.

Jack shook his head and she saw him wince again. He fell back against the pillows.

'Jack?' Elizabeth knew he meant her mother's failure to honour a promise made to him by her father. He had mentioned it at Scarsdale when he haunted her, but she still did not know what the promise was, or why he should dwell on it.

'I have said too much already,' Jack whispered thickly. 'I want to sleep.'

'Jack!' Elizabeth protested, but he turned away from her.

'I swear your secret is safe, Elizabeth,' he said into the pillow. 'Now let me be.'

'Jack?'

He ignored her.

'Jack, please.'

Elizabeth knew she would get nothing further from him. She sat for a moment, letting her heartbeat slow, then she wiped her eyes on the back of her hand and collected up the dirty bandages. She rose and gathering everything together, she made to take them away.

She stopped at the door and looked back at Jack. His breathing had deepened and she knew he was already asleep. Her eyes wandered over his supple body; God he would be easy enough to kill now and no mistake! The difference was, she no longer hated him, but whether she trusted him or his word was another question altogether.

YORKSHIRE SEPTEMBER 1470

Stones flew up from the road as if a whirlwind had hurled itself along the dusty path. Edward dug in his spurs again, sparing neither himself nor his courser. He looked over his shoulder; only Gloucester was keeping up with him, his sweat-streaked roan only a few yards behind, while the rest of his entourage were strung out like beads on an old rosary.

Edward was determined to prove that he had been right and that coming to York had not been the mistake Hastings obviously thought it was, but to do that he had to reach London before Warwick did, and that would be the ride of his life.

At the top of the hill he reined in. His courser was blowing hard, chest and flanks working like a blacksmith's bellows. He reached down and patted the hot wet neck while he waited for Gloucester.

'My liege,' his brother called breathlessly. 'Ned, a few hours will not matter.'

Edward's anger formed into a tight knot in his chest. He nodded tersely at his brother; of course he knew he was right, as was Hastings. Coming to York was a disaster of the first order. But somehow thundering across England at breakneck speed felt better than making a measured progress towards the inevitable: battle with Warwick. Only that morning he had learned that Warwick had landed in the West Country three days ago and the pain of that knowledge was like an open wound. God's blood how brilliant his cousin Warwick was, he thought. He had put him in such a dilemma, knowing Edward would have to exorcise the ghosts of Olney, knowing he would have to deal with the northern rebels himself! And Warwick had outwitted Duke Charles's navy and more infuriatingly Anthony Wydeville and England's too! Only Warwick would sail when others ran for shelter!

A few moments later Hastings drew alongside. His face was flushed and he too spoke breathlessly. 'My liege, we cannot keep up this pace. Our horses will be spent before we make Doncaster and no one will be able to furnish us with enough fresh horses to continue.'

'I take your point, Lord Chamberlain. But I am not a bishop going on pilgrimage!' Edward said brusquely, the anger still tightening his throat. He saw Hastings blench at his words and he felt a little guilty; he was not really angry with his chamberlain, he was angry with himself for not taking his advice.

Hastings lowered his eyes. 'Of course not, Your Grace but...'

'Gloucester has already told me it will make no difference,' Edward growled. Colour rose up Gloucester's neck and burned in his cheeks.

'But to know Warwick will reach London first...' Edward bit his lip as the anger threatened to boil over into uncontrollable rage. He remembered how Hastings had told him London was the key.

'They will not admit him,' Hastings said. 'And Henry is in the Tower. They will not break through.'

'We must not rely on that,' Edward said sharply. Hastings had touched on another mistake: his cousin of Burgundy had advised him to send Henry of Lancaster to him for custody. But he had not listened; neither had he listened to Burgundy's warnings of Warwick's increasing power. And now Henry was almost within Warwick's grasp and he was a sitting target for Warwick's army.

Thinking of Warwick suddenly made him think of Warwick's brother. 'Where is Montagu?' he snapped. He wanted to tell Hastings that at least he had been right about Montagu's loyalty. But this was neither the time nor the place for points scoring: he would probably lose!

'He is but two days behind us, my liege. Perhaps it would be wise to wait on him at Doncaster and then march on Warwick together?' Hastings offered. Edward heard the quiver of Hastings's voice. He admired his chamberlain's courage; Will Hastings would always say what needed to be said, no matter what the consequences were.

'As you wish,' Edward said scathingly.

Hastings nodded his assent and signalled for his messenger.

Then Edward noticed something flicker in Hastings's eyes and he knew what it was; Hastings still did not trust John Neville! Well, he thought, when they all met up at Doncaster he would make them drink a toast together; Hastings would have to trust John Neville then!

BRUGES SEPTEMBER 1470

The candles flickered in their sconces, casting amber patterns around the bedchamber.

Elizabeth settled herself on the bed beside Jack. The remains of their supper lay on the table beside them. Fire crackled in the grate and Elizabeth stared into the flames as they danced up the chimney; gold, yellow, blue and orange and her mind raced far away from her in the smoky warmth.

'What are you thinking, sweetheart?' Jack asked her gently.

Elizabeth started from her thoughts. She sighed. 'You wish to own my mind as well?' she asked.

Jack smiled his lopsided grin, but he did not rise to her challenge. He pushed a lock of untamed black hair from his eyes. 'It was just a question,' he said disarmingly.

Elizabeth looked at him. For once his brows were not lined with pain. His eyes were wide in the half-light. They were beautiful, just as she remembered them from their chess match at Scarsdale.

'You do not have to tell me,' he said softly. 'You can say it is none of my concern.'

Elizabeth smiled. 'It is none of your concern!' she said teasingly.

Why did he have to talk to her and spoil their brief contentment? She knew this would only end in wordplay between them.

Jack laughed.

Elizabeth watched the creases lengthen round his eyes, saw two dimples appear in his cheeks among the shadow of his stubble. She knew she should turn away now. But somehow she could not, not when he was so easy with her company; she did not want to be alone with her dark and troubled thoughts.

'If you must know, I was thinking of my father,' she said sadly. Her throat tightened.

Jack smiled at her. 'He was a good man Elizabeth; a courageous knight and an honourable lord,' he said.

Elizabeth looked at him quickly. 'Did you know him very well, Jack?' she asked, leaning closer.

Jack nodded. 'I fought beside him in the north. I was only eighteen years old. I thought I knew it all, but when the rebels scythed along the valley towards us I realized I knew nothing. Without him I think I would have either died or fled. He taught me so much!'

Elizabeth saw Jack's eyes narrow as he thought on the bloody battle.

'Father would not speak of it much. There were so many killed,' she said sadly.

'Because of your father and Warwick, I was knighted after Towton,' Jack said, sitting a little higher against the pillows. 'He spoke up for me; perhaps made my actions sound more impressive than they were.'

Elizabeth could imagine her father speaking eloquently before Edward, his eyes bright with the excitement of a battle won. He must have thought much of Jack to do so; so why had her mother treated Jack so rudely?

'My father was not given to exaggeration,' Elizabeth said with a rueful smile. 'You must have been very courageous, Jack. He must have thought well of you.'

She heard Jack hesitate and then swallow. 'There is something else...' he paused and looked deep into her eyes. 'I said one day I would tell you; perhaps it should have been sooner, but I cannot change that.'

Elizabeth's heart began to drum in her chest. Had they both been thinking the same thought? Instinctively she knew this concerned the broken promise. She wanted to look away from Jack, knowing this was news she did not want to hear. But like the lamb before the wolf she stayed as she was.

'Do you want to know, sweetheart?' Jack breathed. Still he held her gaze, as if by alchemy.

'Yes,' she whispered even though that was the last word she should have been saying.

Jack's eyes widened. 'Elizabeth, I spoke of a promise not honoured by your mother.'

Elizabeth's throat was so tight she could not speak. She nodded her head. Tears blurred her vision; she knew what he was going to say, knew exactly why her mother hated him.

Jack hesitated, adding weight to the moment, like the calm before a thunderstorm. 'Your father promised you to me,' Jack said slowly.

Elizabeth's chest tightened as though Jack had struck her. Her jaw fell slack and she stared at him dumbly.

'He did, sweetheart, I swear it. I saved his life at Towton, that was why he spoke for me and he chose to repay me with you. I was young; I didn't understand what that meant, though I was told I'd made a good match. It was not until later, when I saw you, that I asked for you; asked him to honour that promise. He agreed, but not Lady Catherine. Not she,' he continued, reaching for Elizabeth's arm as if he feared she would leave him.

'Asked for me?' She mouthed the words as though they were part of a foreign language she was hearing for the first time. She stared into the blackness of Jack's eyes; she saw no sign that he was lying but she did not want to believe this was true.

'No...he cannot... he would have told me!' she stammered, pulling her arm from Jack's grasp.

'I'm sure he intended to do so, sweetheart; you were young and he bade me wait,' Jack said. 'I was content to do so while I fought for my inheritance. But I still have the letter from him, Elizabeth, the letter Lady Catherine refused to acknowledge, even though it bore his seal and was signed by his own hand.'

Elizabeth's stomach rose to her throat and she endeavoured to gather her scattered wits. 'You – you came for me?' she asked.

Jack nodded slowly. His nostrils flared as he breathed deeply. His eyes fell to the counterpane.

So that was why her mother had forbidden him from coming to Lazenby and why Alice, her nurse, had been so distraught when he had: they had thought that Jack had come back for her!

The silence lengthened between them.

Elizabeth struggled to assimilate all Jack had said.

Her father had promised her to Jack as Warwick had promised Isabel to Clarence and Anne to Edouard. It was expected. It was respectable. It was a father's duty to his daughter to do so. Why was she so surprised? Her father had never failed her in anything else, why would he fail in such an important duty? Elizabeth choked back further tears. If it was so acceptable then why did it hurt so much?

Elizabeth met Jack's sad eyes and Elizabeth realized that Jack too was a victim in this.

'I was not good enough,' he said quietly. 'Even as Sir John de Laverton, the knight who saved your father's life, as far as Lady Catherine was concerned, I was nothing.'

The sorrowful look he gave her squeezed Elizabeth's heart in spite of her own pain. She touched his hand. 'Jack,' she said gently, 'I know.' She did not want him to have to say what she had discovered for herself.

Jack looked at her quickly. His brows furrowed. 'You know already? She told you to turn you against me?'

Elizabeth shook her head. 'No one told me.'

'Then how?' Jack asked.

'Your mother's ring,' Elizabeth said, 'its motto: *'Pensez de moi'*. That is not a husband's message to his wife on their wedding day, Jack.'

Jack looked down again. Shame coloured his cheeks. 'No it is not,' he said huskily.

Elizabeth linked her fingers into his. They were both hurting; they both needed comfort. 'It is not your sin, Jack,' she said. 'It is not your fault.'

'My father acknowledged me, Elizabeth,' he said, 'and I loved him.' He looked up at her and she saw his eyes were silvered with tears. 'I too know what it is like to lose a father.'

Elizabeth bit her lip. She blinked her eyes and hot tears squeezed between her lashes. Her chest ached with a sudden overwhelming sense of loss.

Jack smiled sadly. 'The irony is, sweetheart, I should never have asked for you. I needed an heiress with a fortune to help me secure what my father promised me; that which my half-sister keeps from me by court orders and writs: a bastard son cannot inherit, Elizabeth! Perhaps all the more so when he is half gypsy by blood!' He swallowed thickly and Elizabeth watched the ripple of his throat as he fought for composure. 'I should not have asked for you, Elizabeth,' he said softly, 'but I could not help it.'

Elizabeth could contain her grief no longer. 'Jack,' she sobbed.

She saw Jack wince as he leant closer. He put his arms about her and pulled her to him fiercely.

'Sweetheart,' he whispered into her hair. 'I promise you it is true.'

'But why did he not say?' she cried. 'Why did my father not tell me what he wanted?'

'I do not know,' Jack breathed. 'But Lady Catherine would never let you go...even if I had been the King of England I would not have been good enough for you, and for that I cannot blame her.'

'But I would have done anything for him,' Elizabeth protested. Had she not proved that with her betrayal of Warwick?

Jack sighed. 'Would you really have married me if he'd asked you to?'

How could she answer such a question? Yet Isabel had married Clarence; Anne would marry Edouard!

Words would not come to her. Jack's skin was warm against her cheek. She slipped her arms about him and breathed him in as she tried to strangle the tears. Her fingers slid lightly over his warm back. Perhaps if she had never met Warwick, perhaps if Jack had been as she had seen him that first time at Lazenby...'We shall never know,' she murmured, not wanting to relinquish this incongruous comfort.

'No, we never shall,' Jack said ruefully.

Elizabeth heard the sadness in his voice. 'I am sorry, Jack. My family have given you nothing but pain,' she said against his neck.

Jack heaved a sigh. 'That is just the way of things,' he said flatly. 'When you are the bastard child, you learn that very young! You learn that you are nothing.'

Elizabeth shivered. Jack tightened his arms and pressed his face against hers. His stubble grazed softly against her cheek.

'You learn that everything is a fight, Elizabeth,' he whispered. 'You must take what you want, for no one will give you anything; you must be the strongest dog in the pack to survive.'

'And so you tried to take me,' Elizabeth said.

Jack's shoulders sagged. He drew back a little.

'I do regret it,' he whispered, looking down into her eyes, 'but I thought...to restore your honour...we could be married. I know it sounds like madness now, but then I thought it was the only way, sweetheart. I thought that when your father allied himself with Edward and against Warwick he might revoke his blessing because he knew I was Warwick's man. I had waited so long, Elizabeth, I had to do something. You were so close...'

'I have heard of such cases in the courts,' Elizabeth said. 'But I cannot see how you thought it best. How could I love you if you had...' She turned away, too embarrassed to speak the truth.

'I wanted you,' Jack said flatly, 'and by your father's promise you were already mine. Your mother should not have rejected Sir Robert's instructions.'

She looked up at him. 'Mayhap, but you never asked *me*, Jack, never gave me a chance to know you better.'

He smiled his errant smile and caressed her hair from her damp cheek. 'I would have given anything to have the chance to talk with you, but Lady Catherine kept you from me.' He paused and Elizabeth saw his throat working as he swallowed. 'I know now that I was wrong,' he said quietly. 'Can you forgive me, sweetheart?'

Elizabeth searched his eyes; there was contrition there. Dazed into silence, she shrugged. What could she say to the man her father had wanted her to marry; the man with whom she had such an invidious history?

'Can you, Elizabeth? Forgive me?' Jack looked deep into her eyes and Elizabeth's heart fluttered like a caged bird. Then he moved closer, and with a gentleness that surprised her, he touched his lips to her cheek.

It was as though he had caressed her with pure fire. 'Yes,' she whispered.

Jack kissed her again. 'You are mine, sweetheart,' he breathed as he sought her mouth.

They both had wounds that needed salving, but Elizabeth knew this would cause more wounds than it would heal; she fought for control of her body.

'No Jack, please,' she gasped as she pulled away from him. She was suddenly aware of his alchemy and her cheeks flushed scarlet. She had to be honest with him; she owed him that much at least. 'I am not yours, Jack,' she said breathlessly. 'I gave my heart to Warwick.'

Jack drew back from her as if she had burned him.

He uncurled his arms from about her. He pressed his lips together and his eyes darkened beneath a smouldering frown. 'There is no future for you there, Elizabeth,' he said sourly. 'How can there be?' Without waiting for an answer he sank back against the pillows and closed his eyes. 'I need to rest,' he said curtly.

'Jack?' Elizabeth whispered.

He grunted, but did not open his eyes.

'I am sorry,' she said, trying to heal the rift. 'I never knew, I swear it.'

Jack twisted his head against the pillows, tousling his hair into black tangles. Sad eyes met hers. 'Would it have made any difference if you had?' he asked bitterly.

Elizabeth thought for a moment. 'I am not sure,' she said honestly.

'Well, you know now,' he said in a petulant voice that challenged her to make it right between them. But how could she?

Elizabeth's heart ached for him. For years he had kept silent, as her father had asked him, and all that time he yearned for her. It was like something the troubadours might sing about, she thought; it was almost beyond belief. Part of her wanted to reach out to him, to hold him close again, to give him comfort as he had comforted her, but she knew she would give him false hope, and that would be wrong; her father was no longer here to demand her obedience and it was certain that Lady Catherine never would!

As she watched the rise and fall of Jack's chest she wondered what would have happened if she had not met Warwick, if her mother had obeyed Sir Robert's command and if she had followed her father's bidding as Isabel and Anne had followed Warwick's. She knew the answer: this handsome rogue would have become her husband.

* * *

Suddenly Elizabeth was awake. She was alone in the bed. For a few ragged heartbeats panic choked her: Jack had gone! Santa Maria, had she wounded him so much last night?

'Sorry, sweetheart,' Jack's voice found her from across the room. There was no trace of the bitterness of the previous evening in his voice, as though it had evaporated overnight like rain while he slept. He had managed to pull on a clean linen shirt, but had been unable to persuade his weakened arm into his doublet.

Elizabeth tried to calm her breathing. Why was he suddenly so animated, she wondered. 'You will never manage your boots,' she said.

Jack smiled thinly. 'You are right,' he sighed.

Elizabeth heard the frustration in his voice and she felt sorry for him; not only for his current disability, but also for the pain she had caused him last night. She got up from the bed and moved round to him. She took hold of his doublet and stretched it over his injured shoulder and then held the sleeve out for him. She saw a flicker of pain touch his face as he forced his arm into the sleeve slowly.

She smiled at him. 'I suppose I shall have to be your squire?' she teased him.

Jack did not answer and she cursed her insensitivity. How humiliated he must feel, being unable even to dress himself.

'Being wounded has its compensations,' he jested as she leant against him with an arm on either side of his leg while she fought with his long boot.

Elizabeth wanted to rebuke him, but his smile was still thin; she had wounded him enough yesterday, she did not want to hurt him again. 'Remember, as soon as you are well enough to do this for yourself, you are ready to go home!' she said.

Jack laughed softly. 'That is my loss!'

154

'And now you have your boots on, my lord,' Elizabeth said with a mock bow, 'may I ask where you are going?'

'Why to Mass of course!' Jack grinned. 'To give thanks for your assistance!'

Elizabeth shook her head; he was impossible!

'May I come with you?' she asked. She knew what the answer would be, but the truth was she was worried about him. 'Yesterday you almost fainted whilst walking in the yard!'

'I told you, I was hungry!' Jack growled.

'But Jack.'

Jack fixed her gaze. 'No sweetheart,' he said firmly.

'I think I should, Jack,' Elizabeth said. 'I still have your knife.'

Jack laughed. 'I may be wounded, but I am not so helpless that I must rely on a woman to protect me with my own dagger!'

Elizabeth's cheeks burned. 'I shall remember that the next time you are bleeding to death!' she said hotly.

'I did not mean...'

'I know what you meant, Jack. But the truth is you are not well enough to go out alone, you just will not admit it!'

She turned away from him. Why was she so angry that he no longer needed her? Was it not a good thing? She moved towards the armoire and picked up her comb. She tugged at her hair and realized that this was a mistake. Her hair was so tangled that it hurt.

Jack came up behind her.

'Sweetheart, it's not that I am ungrateful,' he said softly.

Elizabeth did not look at him, but continued to pull at her hair. 'Go if you must,' she snapped, 'and while you are out, please arrange our passage to England!'

She heard Jack's boots reach the door and then the latch clicked. She was determined not to look at him, not to show him any of her concerns, but at the last moment she weakened. When she turned he was hanging on the latch, smiling. He gave her a wink.

'Be careful,' she said.

'Sweetheart, I always am,' he said with a grin she found uncomfortably seductive. Then he put the door between them.

* * *

Jack swept up his sword and cloak as he strode down the hallway. Each step brought a dull throb to his shoulder, but he dismissed it as best he could. Though he was touched by Elizabeth's concern and enjoyed the attention that went with it, he had to get on his feet again, even if that brought with it the inevitable spectre of returning to England and the certainty that he would lose her to Warwick unless... But how would he ever convince her of his worth as a husband if a knife-wound kept him bed-bound like a rheumy old man? He found his black velvet chaperon and sat it on his head, tilting the angle until he was happy with it. He wound the liripipe about his throat. Though it was less fashionable than the new velvet bonnets, he still loved it, for it hid the darkness of his skin and eyes from over-curious onlookers.

Jack left the house quickly, knowing he had to cope with the pain that hurrying brought. Though he could never really tire of living here with Elizabeth, he knew he had lain in bed too long. He needed to find out what had happened to Warwick. The last news he had heard said that Warwick was expected to leave France any day and that was now a week ago. For all he knew Warwick could already be in England.

As he walked past the church of Our Lady he crossed himself and made a mental note to confess his lie about going to Mass. He smiled to himself; Elizabeth had not believed him anyway. But what pleased him further was that she had asked him to take care. He put to the back of his mind the thought that her concern may only be because she wanted to go home and that he was her best hope of doing so. Then he thought how her concern would evaporate if she knew he had lied to her about Higgins.

As he slipped beyond the bustle of the merchants he noticed the trees had begun to take on amber hues, the sky was clad in silver-grey and that the wind coming in off the sea was definitely colder. He pulled his cloak about him more tightly. If Warwick wanted to be in England he had better do it quickly, he thought, for the Narrow Sea was no place to be in an autumn gale.

It did not take long to reach the harbour; far less time Jack thought than the night he had encountered Higgins. He paused to catch his breath. He closed his eyes for a moment to stop the world spinning; perhaps Elizabeth had been right to worry about him after all.

Suddenly he realized someone was talking to him. He opened his eyes slowly. It was the harbour master and he evidently recognized Jack.

'You are recovered, monsieur?' the harbour master asked.

Jack nodded, but knew the pain must still show on his face.

'You still wish to make the passage to Angleterre?'

'Yes. My wife is eager to return home,' Jack said.

The man shook his head. 'She may be keen, monsieur but the men will not sail.'

'Will not sail?' Jack asked, knowing that everyone had their price.

'There are still pirates and God knows who else out there, monsieur.'

'But there always are,' Jack said, wondering if he would be able to meet their fee.

'They will not risk it, monsieur. *Certainement,* you would not wish to become one of Le Compte de Warwick's prizes!'

Actually, Jack thought, that would suit them very well, but he could not say so. He had to have some reason for urgency, something that would press them, but which had nothing to do with Warwick. He thought on his feet; 'My wife is expecting our first child – I do not want to leave it too long in case the weather turns.'

The man nodded and he gave Jack a knowing smile. 'You should have said so earlier! That calls for a celebration, monsieur, while we see what we can do for you.'

Jack smiled; so they did have a price after all! He knew that the wine would be more to do with obtaining the right recompense for this hazardous journey than it was about celebrating Elizabeth's pregnancy. Jack knew he had to be careful: the money he had was running low. He still had Edward's necklace however – though that would pay for a hundred passages to England and strictly speaking was not his. Nevertheless he followed the harbour master into his rooms and wondered how he was going to tell Elizabeth she was now with child.

SIX

EXETER SEPTEMBER 1470

Light frosted the windows of the Great Hall and spilled out onto the wet stone of the courtyard. Warwick drew rein and pulled his sweating stallion to a sharp halt. Feet rushed towards him as the grooms came tumbling like children from the stables, their excited babble ringing in his ears like a familiar song – the merry sound of English voices.

He smiled and warmth cloaked his stomach; how good it was to be in England again.

He glanced over at Clarence, waited for his gaze to meet his before smiling. 'Does it feel like home, George?' he asked as he slipped lithely from the wet saddle.

Clarence shrugged. 'Yes, my lord,' he said.

Still the sullenness was there in his voice, Warwick thought, and his look was as dark as night; a look Warwick knew too well of late.

'Ah, George,' Warwick said as he walked round to him. 'I understand. What a choice you had to make. It is never easy to choose away from one's own blood.'

Clarence made a snorting noise; not a laugh, but something he should have controlled but didn't.

'It will become easier,' Warwick said. 'When it is over and Isabel joins you too.' He paused. 'There will be time for more sons,' he murmured.

Clarence slipped down from his horse beside him. His feet thudded onto the stone. His eyes were an icy blaze. 'For me it will never be over,' he hissed. 'I have betrayed my blood forever!' His lip curled angrily. 'And Isabel will not come near me. If I want more children, my lord, I will have to take her by force!'

Warwick felt the words like arrows. 'Time is the best physician, George,' he said softly. 'Isabel will come round. And you are young.' He thought then of Elizabeth; what of her grief at losing her son? – Their son! It was a grief she had chosen not to share with him and he wondered why. He shuddered. His stomach tightened and he was suddenly in danger of becoming maudlin. Yes, he knew how Clarence felt about losing his son, not that he could tell him so! And he wondered if he would have time to try again as Clarence and Isabel would. He shook his head to snap the unwelcome thoughts. 'Come, George,' he said with forced enthusiasm. 'The Courtenays await within; Devonshire is ours, but there is much yet to be done! Tomorrow we head towards London and the Lords of Shrewsbury and Stanley will join us too.'

Clarence mumbled something he could not distinguish and which he thought it was best he did not hear. He knew his own news would further torture Clarence's conscience, but that could wait until after they had supped.

BRUGES SEPTEMBER 1470

'You did what?' Elizabeth snapped. 'Jack, what on earth possessed you? I knew I should not have let you go out on your own!'

He gave her one of his disarming smiles. 'I had to have a reason for urgency, otherwise they would not sail, and what better reason is there than that, sweetheart?'

His eyes were bright and Elizabeth could see that he wished it were all true: that she was his wife and that she was carrying his child. 'And the necklace?'

'Again sweetheart, I had no choice. The jeweller is replacing the best ruby with glass – no one will ever know!' He held out his palms to her. 'I swear it, Elizabeth.'

She sighed at the look he gave her; the one he could always conjure up when necessary and which she was sure had persuaded many a woman to take him into her bed. He was impossible! She moved away from him and looked out of the window over the square. She had grown quite used to the warm stone and the mellow tolling of the bells of Our Lady. She had even thought she was getting used to Jack, if that was ever possible. He was brave and clever and disturbingly handsome, but there was still something deep in his eyes that was dangerous. Though she told herself she had forgiven him and had even said so in church when she had prayed for him, part of her trembled when she met that dark fire. She dragged herself away from her thoughts. She turned back to him, her composure regained. 'So, when do we leave?' she asked sweetly.

'A few days, no more,' he said.

'Was there any news of Warwick?'

A broad smile brightened Jack's face. 'Ah now sweetheart, you will be pleased with me.'

Jack moved to the small table and poured a goblet of wine. Then he came to join her by the window. He offered her the cup, but Elizabeth shook her head; she did not want wine clouding her judgement, especially not where Jack was concerned. She could already smell wine on his breath.

He drank steadily and Elizabeth watched his throat as he swallowed. Her breathing quickened. She tried to ignore it.

'Jack?' She knew he was teasing her.

He lowered the cup and held her gaze. 'Warwick is in England.' He said it slowly, as though Elizabeth was a simpleton, as though she would not understand.

Her heart rose to her throat and she began to smile. 'Oh Jack!' she said excitedly, putting her hands up to her face. Could it really be true?

Jack shrugged nonchalantly. 'We still must wait a few days,' he said coolly.

'Wait?' she asked, puzzled. 'Why do we wait? Why do we not go tonight?'

'All they know here is that he has landed in England,' Jack said seriously. 'They will not sail until they know what has happened. We must await more definite news, otherwise we could find ourselves arriving at the court of a very happy King Edward, and I know you would not wish that!'

Elizabeth's heart sank like a stone in a well. She looked down; Jack was right, she could not face the prospect of returning to Edward's court, especially now that Higgins was dead because of her; there would be questions she could not answer.

Jack came closer. He touched her chin with his finger and thumb and raised her face to meet his. 'We shall go,' he whispered. 'I promise.'

Elizabeth searched his face.

'And if we are to go to England then we need new clothes, sweetheart,' he said more brightly, obviously trying to cheer her. 'You cannot be seen at court in that gown!'

Elizabeth looked at the plain woollen gown she was wearing. It certainly did have a worn look about it. She remembered the opulence of Edward's court, remembered the green damask she had worn for Edward with a shudder; she certainly would need something better if she wanted to visit Warwick in London!

She looked up at Jack. He met her look with an errant grin.

'How would we afford it?' she asked him.

'Sweetheart,' he said as he spread his hands, but he gave no better answer.

Elizabeth wondered if the jeweller was replacing more than just the ruby in her necklace; had Jack de Laverton just become a rich man and her necklace become worthless?

'You shall be the best-dressed Englishwoman in Bruges!' Jack beamed. 'I insist upon it!'

Elizabeth was not sure if it was wise, but if he was spending their money then she had to keep a careful eye on what he bought, otherwise there might not be enough left for their passage to England when the time came!

ENGLAND SEPTEMBER 1470

Even before he limped into their billet, Thomas heard Will Kennerley's faltering approach. He was laughing to himself, a gravely throaty laugh he was trying in vain to subdue.

'What's this, Will?' Thomas asked, smiling at the grin on Will's face.

As he closed the door, Will began to laugh again.

Thomas could not remember the last time he had seen Will laugh.

'You will not believe the story I've just heard from our new recruits, boys,' Will said as he joined them. He sat down on the bench opposite them without a sign of the pain-wracked stiffness they had seen lately. A broad smile still covered his face.

Thomas and Robert leant forward eagerly.

'Well tell us, then!' Robert demanded excitedly.

'Ho, without a drink?' Will asked. 'You should know better than that, Rob! I think some beer will wet my lips and make the story flow a little better!'

Robert filled Will's mug with the aromatic brew and he drank immediately. Then he wiped his hand across his mouth in a gesture of pure pleasure. 'Jesu, that's good, Rob,' he said approvingly.

'Will, your tale!' Robert pleaded.

Will nodded his assent. 'Patience is a high virtue, Rob did you know that?' he teased. 'From Chaucer, that is!'

Rob let out a cry of exasperation.

'Thomas,' Will said, ignoring him. 'You know that Warwick sent John Pike out to Salisbury for men?'

'Aye, Will, he was to request forty armed men from them.'

'Exactly,' Will said. 'Well our earl is the Earl of Warwick *and* Salisbury is he not?' He paused and took another deep draught of his beer.

Thomas and Robert looked at each other, knowing he was making them wait deliberately.

'Salisbury. A beautiful town,' Will said almost wistfully into his mug, prevaricating terribly. 'Lovely cathedral...'

'Will!' Robert protested.

Will grinned and winked at Thomas. 'Well boys, as John Pike is sitting there who should come in, do you think?'

Thomas and Robert shook their heads.

'None other than one of Edward's squires of the body, Thomas St Leger!'

'Ha!' Robert cried. 'I'll bet their faces were a sight!'

'I'm sure they were. He orders them to resist the rebels – that's us – tells them they must not assist these traitors, but should send men to their king immediately!'

'The usurper, you mean!' Thomas said.

'Aye, Tom, but he didn't say that, did he?' Will said.

'True,' Thomas replied.

'Will! What happened?' Robert asked impatiently.

'After some interesting deliberation they come to John Pike and offer him forty marks instead of his men!'

'I'll bet he was none too pleased with that offer,' Thomas said.

'Quite so, Tom. He says Warwick will not accept that and that they had better find the men! So one John Hall, who had already volunteered to serve Edward on horseback, offers to find the men for Warwick if they give him the forty marks!' Will began to chuckle again. 'So we got their men after all!' Will's husky laugh echoed in the quiet of the billet. 'And...and they had to pay the forty marks as well!' Will's laughter was now almost uncontrollable. Tears filled his eyes and he wiped them away with the back of his hand.

Thomas and Robert laughed too.

'It serves them right! They should have given us the men in the first place!' Robert snorted.

'Aye,' Thomas grinned.

But Thomas's smile soon began to fade as he thought more deeply on Will's story. The loyalty of Warwick's household men was not to be questioned, he knew that, but if other men changed

162

sides as easily as this John Hall had done, could these new re-cruits be relied upon when they faced Edward across the battle-field?

DONCASTER SEPTEMBER 1470

William Hastings lowered his eyes from Edward's stare. He knew what the look said – that his judgement had been better than his king's. His mouth was dry. If he could have been wrong about anything in his life he wished it had been about John Neville. But there was no mistake, the serjeant of the minstrels had been clear: Marquis Montagu had declared for Warwick.

Edward glared at him still, as though it was Hastings's persis-tent warnings that had made John Neville remember his Neville blood.

'Ned?' Hastings asked, determined to re-forge the bond be-tween them.

Edward looked away. 'Nothing, Will,' he said. Edward's voice was choked with a mixture of fear and anger, but at least Hast-ings knew the anger was not really for him. This anger had a deeper root: Warwick.

'Why Montagu, Will?' Edward asked still facing away from him. 'Why John, of all people?'

'My liege, I think you know as well as I,' Hastings said softly.

Edward looked at him. His expression had softened but his eyes now glittered and Hastings saw that his king was close to weep-ing.

'He is a Neville,' Hastings said flatly. 'There was always a chance he would one day remember that.'

'But you *knew*,' Edward said. 'You knew he would do this.'

Hastings shrugged. 'I always felt it, Ned. But these things are never certain,' he said softly. The shock of it all was too close for them to analyse what had happened. Mayhap in time they would come to know Montagu's reasons in detail, but now, in the blind-ing aftermath of his declaration, the reasons did not matter.

'I make a poor king if I cannot judge a man as you do, especially a man as close to me as John Neville was,' Edward said shakily. 'Warwick is right.'

'Warwick is not right, Ned!' Hastings protested. 'And it is pre-cisely *because* Montagu was close to you that you could not see it. You thought that kinship alone would seal his oath. I fear it was the loss of his earldom of Northumberland that swayed him. Only he and God know for certain.'

Edward pressed his lips together and nodded. 'So what now, my Lord Chamberlain?' he asked in a torn voice. 'No one will want a king without a kingdom; all will fête Warwick as regent and then Henry as king!' His voice cracked on the last word. 'All is lost, Will,' he whispered.

Hastings placed his hands on Edward's shoulders firmly. He shook him gently so that he raised his downcast eyes. Hastings saw that his bottom lip quivered with the effort of not breaking down completely.

'Ned,' Hastings said steadily, 'I want you to listen to me.'

Edward nodded.

'You can return from this...'

Edward snorted his derision.

'You can!' Hastings said. He had to get Edward to share his belief.

'It is easily said,' Edward murmured, 'but can it be accomplished? Without a miracle, the kingdom is Warwick's!'

'For Christ's sake Ned, if Warwick can come back from exile, then so can you! He does not have Royal blood in his veins as you do!'

Edward pulled free of Hastings's grasp. 'Exile?' he asked as though it was a word from a language he did not know. 'Exile!' The word was as hot as flame.

Hastings saw the burden on Edward's shoulders. How he wished he could lighten it for him. 'Ned, make it happen!' he said, trying to bolster Edward's confidence. 'Just as you came back after Olney, you can come back from this. By Christ it was I who then thought our road had ended. But you were strong then and you must be strong again!'

Edward still said nothing and continued to stare at Hastings as if he was mad to say such things.

Hastings paused and took a deep breath as he thought how else he could encourage him; then he played his trump card. 'Soon, Ned you will have a son to follow you!' He saw Edward's eyes flicker. 'You must not fail *him!*'

Edward raised his hand for silence. 'Leave us,' he said, turning away.

Hastings thought for a moment about disobeying him, but the coldness of the tone told him he had done all he could for now.

He knew they must wait on the news from Edward's outriders, but in his heart Hastings knew that the minstrel's information had been correct: John Neville was coming to give battle and they were too few to face him; too many of their men had vanished into the night, if his steward was to be believed, and even if their numbers matched Montagu's five thousand, it was a battle too bloody to contemplate, for John Neville was the one man Edward feared to fight.

* * *

Hastings interrogated their faces; Richard of Gloucester and Anthony Wydeville shared the same pallid expression: eyes wide as children's, skin bloodless. They said nothing, and for a moment Hastings wondered if their fear had stopped their hearts from beating.

'It's true, my lords,' he repeated. 'Montagu has declared for Warwick.'

Anthony Wydeville spluttered into life. 'The ungrateful bastard!' he cursed. 'After all Ned has done for him! Jesu God, was a marquisate not enough for the grasping Neville?'

'Apparently not,' Hastings said impassively. His heart hammered in his chest as though he had run a mile, yet he knew he had to remain calm; only with a clear head would they get through this – panic and they were lost.

'Where do we go, Will?' Gloucester too had found his voice, though it was thin and quivered uncharacteristically. 'Surely we cannot fight? What does my brother say?'

What could he tell young Gloucester? He could not tell him that Edward had the look of a man without hope, a man who refused to believe the horrible haunting truth. 'He knows we must leave England,' Hastings lied. 'We are too few to make a stand and Warwick, you can be sure, will have cut off our route to London.' He paused, skin cold with sweat, blood thumping in his ears. He breathed deeply. 'We must go to Burgundy,' he said resolutely. 'They are your kin,' he said turning back to Gloucester.

That was true; Edward and Gloucester's sister Margaret was married to Duke Charles of Burgundy. But Hastings knew that Duke Charles had Lancastrian blood in his veins and it was no certainty that he would help them, not even with Margaret's intervention; after all, the exiled Lancastrians Somerset and Devon were living at his court!

'Of course!' Gloucester rallied, his cheeks flushing. 'Of course, Margaret will help us!'

Hastings smiled at the certainty in Gloucester's voice. 'So, we need to get to a port,' Hastings said. 'Gather what you can. Disperse those we cannot take. We make for The Wash and then to Lynn.'

'A good choice. I have connections there,' Anthony Wydeville said approvingly.

Hasting sighed with relief; at this moment he needed Wydeville's support, whatever their differences. 'Good. From there we can make a passage, God willing!'

Gloucester turned on his heel quickly, evidently glad of the necessity of action. Anthony Wydeville nodded his assent and followed Gloucester from the room.

Hastings turned towards the closed door behind him; all he had to do now was persuade Edward that to leave his kingdom was the best course of action, and that would not be an easy thing to do.

LONDON OCTOBER 1470

Pale autumn sunshine flickered rainbows on the Thames as Warwick entered the Tower of London. He strode quickly, eager for his brother's company and to make his obeisance to the king he was about to make.

'Richard!' Archbishop Neville's voice was light with relief.

Warwick smiled. He bounded up the great steps to his brother, and without a second thought, he embraced him. God, how long it seemed since he had seen him!

Archbishop Neville coughed; he seemed a little surprised by the show of affection and as Warwick perused his youngest brother, he thought how much deeper the lines on his brow were and saw a hint of silver at his temples. Sweet Jesu, Edward had much to answer for, keeping him under house arrest! Everyone knew that of the three surviving Neville brothers, George's was the weakest constitution.

'How does Henry?' Warwick asked.

'You shall see for yourself, Richard,' Archbishop Neville said as he turned.

Their boots echoed along the corridors as they walked side by side. 'We had to bath him before we brought him here. You should have seen the fleas! And God alone knows how long he had been wearing that old gown for!'

Warwick shook his head; a small knot of guilt twisted in his stomach at the description of poor witless Henry's condition, for it was he who had first brought him here as a prisoner. 'He is well now?' he asked.

Archbishop Neville stopped. 'I am not sure what you are expecting, Richard,' he said. 'The man is closer to God than to us; his mind cannot yet comprehend what has happened.'

Warwick followed Archbishop Neville into the former king Henry's chamber.

Warwick sucked in his breath in astonishment; the jewelled decoration and the sumptuous draperies, which adorned the room, were as magnificent as any he had ever seen. And to think these rooms had been created for the confinement of Edward's Wydeville queen! Inwardly he smiled at the thought of her leaving this opulence and taking sanctuary in Westminster; there would be no damask covered walls there! Warwick dragged his gaze away from the splendour of the room and sought Henry of Lancaster.

The son of the great Henry the Fifth looked as if a strong gust of wind could carry him from the chamber. The robes he wore must have come from Edward's wardrobe, Warwick thought, for only Edward would order a gown covered with so many gems! It smothered Henry in swathes of velvet, as though a child had put on his father's clothes.

As they approached him, Henry lifted his head from his book of devotions. His eyes swam blindly in hollow sockets. Vacantly he stared at Warwick, met his look dumbly.

'My liege,' Warwick said and knelt at his feet.

As if remembering a lost dream, Henry held out his bony hand and Warwick kissed it. It was cold.

'I do humbly crave your pardon, Your Grace for the injuries wrought upon you,' Warwick said awkwardly. He was about to continue, but Henry cut him off.

'Oh brave Warwick,' Henry said with a smile, 'we do forgive you all these things and more. We know these things are God's will. He tests us daily. We must have patience and forbearance, Warwick! May God graciously teach and illuminate our hearts with the spirit of His wisdom so that we may come closer to Him!'

Warwick cast a sideways look at Archbishop Neville. His brother returned his look with a shrug.

'Good Warwick, now that you have come, may I return to my chamber?' Henry asked quietly. 'The light is too bright in here and,' he leant forward so that only Warwick could hear him, 'and there are too many people. They disturb my prayers.'

'I have a better place for you, my liege,' Warwick said. 'We shall stay with the Bishop of London until your coronation.'

'The Bishop of London?' Henry echoed, as if he half remembered the name. 'I would not like to put him to any trouble.'

'I can assure you, my liege, it will cause him no trouble at all,' Warwick answered. He wondered if all his conversations with Henry would be like this; like talking to a child. 'If you would make yourself ready Your Grace, we shall ride by Cheapside so that the people can see you are once again a free man. Sir Henry Lowys will look after your household.'

Henry's eyes widened. 'My household? Dearest Warwick, I have no need of a household; just my little room and a little peace for worship.'

'Oh but you do, Your Grace, for once again you shall take the throne of England.'

Henry stared at him again blankly. 'And is Marguerite come? Is my Edouard here?'

'They soon will be Your Grace,' Warwick said, startled by this sudden flash of lucidity from Henry.

'Good,' Henry said matter-of-factly, 'for I have missed them.'

BRUGES OCTOBER 1470

The upper jetty of the half-timbered building overhung the shop, keeping the rolls of material on display there out of the sun.

A little bell rang as they entered and the shopkeeper appeared within a heartbeat, smiling eagerly. As one might expect his clothes were well made, better than any shopkeeper Elizabeth had yet seen and as Jack introduced himself in perfect French, Elizabeth tried to ascertain if he had been here before and wondered if this was all part of a prearranged plan designed to unsettle her.

168

Elizabeth looked about her. Never had she seen such a fine array of silks, damasks and velvets. She noted the quickening of her heart; these were going to be very expensive.

'*Monsieur. Mademoiselle,*' the shopkeeper beamed as he gave an obsequious bow.

'*Madame,*' Jack corrected swiftly.

The shopkeeper raised an eyebrow. '*Pardonez-moi, monsieur,*' he said meekly.

'My wife needs a new gown,' Jack said smoothly.

'Of course,' the shopkeeper smiled.

'He does not believe you, he thinks I am your mistress,' Elizabeth whispered with amusement.

Jack cleared his throat gruffly.

The shopkeeper called out to his wife and they heard the rushing of feet on the boards above their heads.

'The best you have,' Jack said determinedly.

Elizabeth frowned at him. 'Jack, what are you doing? We cannot afford it!' she whispered.

Jack gave her his most beautiful smile. 'For you, sweetheart, anything,' he said loudly, with a flourish of his hand that would not have been out of place at court.

Elizabeth groaned inwardly, for within an instant, rolls of exquisite cloth were being laid out before them on the counter by the eager shopkeeper. There was deep claret velvet, honey coloured brocade and a dizzying array of blue damask and cloth-of-gold, from deep midnight blue to one as pale as a winter sky.

'Well, my love?' Jack asked her sweetly.

Elizabeth scowled at him. 'I am not sure...there are so many,' she said, glaring at him. What was he thinking of? They were not rich enough to even be looking at these!

'Ah women, *monsieur*, they have their little ways,' the clothier said, still smiling.

Elizabeth wondered rather uncharitably if he ever got jaw ache!

'Aye,' Jack nodded. 'Come sweetheart. What shall it be? Blue? Gold?' he asked in a voice as smooth as the claret velvet in front of him.

Why was he ignoring her silent protestations? 'Jack they are too expensive!' Elizabeth whispered fiercely.

'Ah, you have married a saint amongst women!' the shopkeeper laughed. 'She is concerned for the price!'

Jack smiled back. 'Then I shall choose, my love,' he said with an arrogant nod of his head that made Elizabeth glare at him even harder.

He began to peruse the fabrics and Elizabeth's eyes fell upon a bolt of green damask and a shiver scratched down her spine.

Jack had noticed too. 'Green damask trimmed with honey-coloured rabbit, sweetheart?' he asked. 'Do not worry, I have not chosen that,' he whispered.

So he had seen her in her green gown at Edward's court! The green gown Lady Fulford had dressed her in for Edward's pleasure!

'Chosen?' Elizabeth asked crossly, suddenly realizing the implications of what Jack had said. He had destroyed her necklace and now he was dictating what she should wear!

'Yes,' Jack said with a flash of his eyes, then he nodded to the mistress of the shop. She laid a hand on Elizabeth's arm, tugging her towards the back of the shop, beyond a thick curtain.

'*Madame, s'il vous plait!*' she said.

'They need to measure you,' Jack called in answer to her puzzlement.

Elizabeth stood indignantly while the mistress of the shop measured what seemed to be every curve of her body. She could just make out the timbre of Jack's voice as he struck a bargain with the clothier, and she wondered if there would be any necklace at all left after this.

As she returned to the shop, Jack looked up at her smiling. 'All done, sweetheart?' he enquired with a charm that could steal hearts. 'Good. Then we can go.'

Elizabeth glared at him; a pox on his arrogance! 'I want to see what you have chosen,' she said petulantly.

'Ah, sweetheart it is a surprise for you,' he said with a wink to the clothier who laughed ingratiatingly.

'Do not worry, *Madame*. He has made a good choice,' he said.

'I want to know,' Elizabeth said hotly, folding her arms across her chest.

Jack's face darkened. 'It is a surprise, my love, do not spoil it.' He took hold of her hand and drew it to his lips. His eyes never left hers and they were bright with mirth.

But Elizabeth wasn't amused. 'If you are going to spend our money, then I would at least like a say in the matter,' Elizabeth hissed.

'If you do not like it then I will send it back!' Jack growled.

The clothier shifted uncomfortably and Elizabeth realized everyone was staring at her; a wife could not argue with her husband like this in public. She took a deep breath and reined in her anger, but made a mental note to continue this when they returned to their lodgings. How could Jack be so arrogant?

'Very well,' she said as graciously as she could, 'but if I look like the court jester then I shall return it.' She smiled a fake smile under furious eyes.

'Excellent!' the clothier said. '*Madame* I promise you, it shall be to your liking.'

Once outside, Jack took hold of her hand again. Elizabeth tried to snatch it away, determined to let him feel her displeasure. The sudden movement must have jarred his shoulder for he grimaced.

'By Christ, Elizabeth! What is wrong with you?' he snapped.

'I am sorry. I did not mean to hurt your shoulder,' she said quickly.

Jack flashed wounded eyes at her. 'Why is it that you must hate me always?' he asked.

Elizabeth did not know what to say; she didn't hate him. Surely he knew what was wrong? She just didn't want him to hold sway over her. 'Jack, I...'

But he cut in fiercely. 'Even when I arrange a present for you – a thank you for looking after me, you have to ruin it, and somehow put me in the wrong!'

He walked away from her, not waiting for a reply.

Elizabeth felt like a naughty child. It reminded her of a rebuke she had received from her nurse Alice, when she had run through the meadow picking the poppies when she had been forbidden to do so, knowing that a thunderstorm would follow. And she had created another thunderstorm here.

Elizabeth watched Jack go. She felt both guilt and anger in equal measure. Had that been all he had meant by the gesture – to thank her? Had it simply been an expression of kindness? Was the choosing of the colour not about control? Or was this whole episode orchestrated to dismantle her defences, to make her think better of him than she should? Jack would like nothing better than to have her believing she was indebted to him, and what better way to achieve this than by charming her with expensive gifts? Is that what other women were like, she wondered, did a new gown buy him a tumble in their beds? Well she would not run after him like a puppy. Mayhap she had misunderstood his intentions, but she couldn't take the risk. She stayed where she was until she could calm herself enough to think more clearly; while she did not have to fall into his arms with gratitude, she realized she did have to make her peace with him, for he had booked their passage to England, or at least he had said he had. Raising her skirts to an indecent height, she hurried after him.

The cobbles were difficult to negotiate in her soft leather shoes and Jack had set an angry pace. But at the corner of the yard before their lodgings he was waiting for her, leaning against the wall with his arms folded across his chest as she had seen him do so many times. His lips were pressed tightly together and his eyes were bright with anger.

'Well mistress,' he said coolly as she reached him. 'Do you go in as my wife or have you finally decided to tell the truth?'

Elizabeth was breathless from running and she didn't answer him straightaway. He mentioned the truth, but she scarcely knew what that was anymore!

He stared at her, his face a study in anger, waiting for her reply.

Had she really upset him so much, or was this all part of his charade? Jack was after all an accomplished actor, she reminded herself.

'We go in as before,' she said sheepishly. Two could play at this game.

'As you wish,' Jack snapped and held out his arm. Elizabeth slipped hers through it.

Jack said nothing as they walked across the courtyard. He did not look at her once, but fixed his eyes in front of him.

Elizabeth wanted to break the silence; wanted to make peace between them, but she was afraid he would read something more into it than she intended, so she too kept silent.

As soon as they entered the house they knew something was wrong: servants were scurrying about like rabbits before dogs.

Jack tensed, and his hand slipped to the hilt of his sword.

'Go up to our bedchamber,' he said sternly. 'Lock the door and let no one in but me.' He looked at her, concern on his face. 'Do you understand? No one.'

Elizabeth nodded.

'Jack,' she touched his arm. She wanted to say 'take care', but he cut in on her.

'Do as I say, quickly,' he barked.

Elizabeth followed his instructions without argument.

* * *

Elizabeth sat on their bed. Then she rose and walked to the window. She watched as daylight faded to brumal grey and the lamps were lit at the corner of the square as the night turned to a deep blue-black. She lit the candles from the embers of the fire and then she returned to the bed. Then she moved to the door; she could hear hurried footsteps on the landing and running up and down the stairs, but none came close to their room. She returned to the bed and lay down; how large it seemed without Jack lying beside her. She placed her hands behind her head and stared up at the canopy, tracing the embroidery with her eyes for what seemed like hours until she gave herself a headache.

When she heard Jack's voice at the door she flew to it as though the Devil was chasing her.

'What has happened?' she asked frantically as she let him in.

A smile softened Jack's frown as he looked at her and she realized how much concern must show on her face.

'Visitors,' he said sombrely, 'and it is someone important, because Senor Gruuthuse has gone to escort them here himself.'

Elizabeth almost wilted with relief; it was just visitors.

Jack's face did not brighten.

'What is wrong?' she asked him. What danger could they be from Senor Gruuthuse's guests?

'It may be nothing,' he said quietly, 'it may just be the Duke of somewhere-or-other.'

Elizabeth sensed there was something he was not saying. 'Or?'

'Or it could be someone we do not wish to see.'

Elizabeth frowned; whom could he mean? Why must he always speak in riddles?

'Who do you fear it is, Jack?' she asked him.

Jack shook his head. 'I shall not worry you with possibilities,' he said. 'When I know more, then so shall you.'

'Jack!' she protested.

'Still,' Jack said curtly, 'at least you will look your best for them, eh sweetheart?'

The sarcasm stung her like a gadfly and Elizabeth hung her head. 'I am not ungrateful, Jack...'

'Really?' He laughed coldly.

His arrogance pricked her again. 'I would have liked to choose for myself, that is all. Especially since I am paying for it! Tell me, are there any precious stones left in Edward's necklace?' she asked haughtily.

'Very clever, sweetheart,' Jack said. 'Since you ask, yes there are. Plenty. But you are right; more than just the ruby have been replaced.'

God's blood, he was shameless! 'So I *am* paying for it all?' Elizabeth asked indignantly.

'Indeed,' Jack said, 'our clothes and our passage home, they all are yours, my lady.' He stepped back from her and bowed almost to the floor. Elizabeth saw him wince as he rose. 'And what would *Madame* like her gypsy servant to do now?' he asked in a tone of iced formality.

Elizabeth sighed; she had won the bout but she had wounded him again. 'Jack we must work together,' she said contritely.

'You thought I had stolen your money didn't you?' Jack growled. 'You thought I had replaced the gems in your necklace and kept the money I got for them and I suspect you even doubted that I had booked our passage home!'

Elizabeth turned away guiltily.

'I thought as much.' There was hurt in his voice.

Elizabeth looked at him. His face was flushed with anger. How did he manage to make her feel culpable? Would he have confessed to replacing the stones in her necklace if she had not asked him?

'I – I am sorry,' she said. 'I never meant to doubt you.'

'But you did anyway!' Jack said testily. He turned away from her, arms wrapped tightly about his body.

'No!' she said. She knew it was a lie, but she needed to repair the damage; they worked better together, she did not want them to fight. She moved closer to him. 'Jack, please.' Whatever this new threat was, she knew they would face it better together.

He turned to face her. His eyes met hers. There was such sadness there that it squeezed her heart. She hated seeing him like this. She wanted to comfort him, wanted to take his pain away. Hesitantly she reached out and touched his arm; she could not have him as her enemy.

'Jack,' she whispered, 'I am sorry...' Her throat was dry; she was stepping into dangerous territory. 'I just want us to be as we were,' she said softly. 'Forgive me, please.'

Jack's face softened and a gentle smile curved his mouth.

Elizabeth stayed where she was, looking into his face; it was as though he had woven a spell.

Slowly he brought his arms about her and pulled her to his chest effortlessly.

'Sweetheart,' he murmured onto her cheek. 'Everything will be all right, I promise.'

Somehow as she breathed him in Elizabeth knew that he spoke the truth. She closed her eyes as she leant against him; it was good not to be fighting with him anymore and he offered her a strange sanctuary against this new danger.

'I am sorry too,' he whispered as he stroked her hair. 'But you will always question me. Why can you not see that I know best?'

Elizabeth shrugged, but she knew the answer: because to give him control made her vulnerable and she was already teetering on the edge of recklessness.

'I will take you to Warwick as I promised,' Jack said gently, 'though it breaks my heart to do so, when I know you should be mine.'

Elizabeth looked up at him quickly and he gifted her a smile she could not help but return.

'You must trust me.' His breath was a whisper on her skin.

Elizabeth's stomach curled. She knew she should pull away now, but the wide darkness of his eyes held her where she was.

He ran a finger lightly over her cheek.

'It will be all right, sweetheart,' he whispered and then lowered his mouth towards hers.

A loud knock at the door snapped them to attention.

LONDON OCTOBER 1470

Warwick watched as Archbishop Neville ate hungrily.

'The roast peacock is particularly fine, Richard,' Archbishop Neville said as he reached for more wine.

Warwick smiled. The food did indeed smell good, but somehow he had no stomach for it.

'Richard?' Archbishop Neville said. 'Starving yourself will not aid you. It will not bring Edward back from the sea.'

'I know, George,' Warwick sighed. 'I just wanted to finish it between us. I thought it would be over before All Saints' Day.'

'You can hardly be surprised that he fled, Richard. John is the best soldier in England and he outnumbered Edward by two to one before Edward's men began to desert him!'

Warwick ran his hands through his thick dark hair. 'I know, George,' he said. The explanation did nothing to relieve his frustration. He picked up his wine and rose from the table. He walked to the window. The casement was ajar and the chill night air prickled the skin on his forearms into gooseflesh. Bells tolled for Compline all across the city and as always in London, he could smell the damp pungent scent of the river.

'But when will he return?' he asked.

'What?' Archbishop Neville asked incredulously. 'He could be drowned for all we know and you are wishing him back to prick us!'

Warwick turned sharply. 'Oh he will return, George. I know he will.'

'I do not see how you can know that. Who will give him succour and, more to the point, who will give him an army? You know how hard that was to achieve and that was from King Louis! Is Burgundy likely to put his hand in his purse to the same degree?'

Warwick sighed. 'I know it sounds impossible, George. But I know I must meet him in battle. Do not ask me how I know this for I cannot explain it. I just know we must meet on the field.'

'Have it your own way,' Archbishop Neville said, reaching for fenberry pie, 'you are determined to secure defeat out of success! You knew he would not be able to resist Fitzhugh's stirrings in the north. The strategy was brilliant, but are you content?'

'There are many obstacles yet, George,' Warwick said returning to the table. 'Past successes are not guarantees of future ones.'

'You have been conciliatory Richard, more so than I would have been!'

'But that is what makes it so hard; returning Lancastrians want their lands and offices back, but how can I remove all Edward's men from their posts without causing a riot? Equally I cannot strip them of their lands; Marguerite and Edouard must do all this!'

'Richard, you are too hard on yourself! You always want perfection and only the Lord can attain that!'

Warwick sighed. 'You are right, brother, but it is such a balancing act that any Fool would be proud of it!'

Archbishop Neville laughed. 'The people support you, Richard; you are more popular with them than Edward ever was!'

'George, you make things sound better than they are!' Warwick said as finally a piece of peacock tempted him.

'No, Richard. Everything is under control. You have your old offices restored as do I, and John is once again the Warden of the East March. God's blood Richard, you are the King's Lieutenant! The country is calm. London is calm. The 'butcher', Lord Worcester is dead. You have reined them all in. And those who are affrighted may go into sanctuary, now that you have issued a proclamation to protect them. No one would dare despoil them! Sanctuary is untouchable, which is as it should be!'

Warwick knew there must be no atrocities carried out in his name or King Henry's; there would be more than enough killing when Edward returned.

BRUGES OCTOBER 1470

For a few ragged heartbeats neither Jack nor Elizabeth moved. They stared at each other breathlessly. Then Jack unwound his arms from about her and swiftly drew his sword. Elizabeth's heart dived to her stomach as he did so; were they really in as much danger as this? And to think she had been foolish enough to fight with him over the colour of gown she should wear! Suddenly Jack pulled her behind him, putting himself between her and the danger. Cautiously he moved towards the door. He tightened his grip on his sword and, hardly breathing, steadied himself to strike.

As quick as thought he snatched the door open.

'God's blood, what are you doing here?' Jack snapped.

'I beg your pardon, my lord but...' The voice descended into a whisper. Jack sheathed his sword.

Elizabeth could not see to whom he spoke. Peering over Jack's shoulder, she could not distinguish the man's features for his face was in shadow. He was dressed in the colours of the night, his cloak shielding him from her gaze.

'I told you never to come here,' Jack hissed. 'Not unless...' He turned quickly to Elizabeth, blocking her view of his visitor.

177

'Sweetheart, I must go out,' he said quietly. He brought his hands up to her face, framing it with his long fingers.

Elizabeth gazed at him askance. 'At this time of night?' she whispered. 'It is already past Compline!'

'Aye,' Jack breathed. 'I must.'

His eyes burned with a dark intensity that told Elizabeth that this was important.

'But your shoulder,' she said and then chastised herself for sounding like his mother. 'What cannot wait until morning?' she asked more determinedly, not really wanting to know the answer.

Jack smiled. 'Do not wait up for me, sweetheart,' he said, ignoring her question.

Elizabeth gripped his arm so that she could make him answer her. 'Jack!' she said indignantly. 'Who is that man? Where must you go? What has happened?' Her voice sounded shaky and Jack smiled again to reassure her.

He leant closer. 'Now you do sound like my wife!' he breathed in her ear.

'Jack!' she said crossly, as he slipped away from her.

She was answered by the slamming of the door. She heard the thud of boots in the hallway and for a moment stood still, frozen with shock. But Jack should have known she would not give up so easily. She tore the door open and ran lightly along the hallway. She peered over the banister.

'Jack!'

Jack and his acquaintance were already at the foot of the stairs. They both looked up at her. She had a better view of his companion now, but she did not recognize him. And if she had seen him before she would have remembered him, for he had a face that sent a shiver through her; he had a nose as sharp as an eagle's beak and eyes that narrowed as he set them on her. The pupils though were large and Elizabeth thought he must be able to see very well in the dark. She turned to look at Jack. He grinned at her and blew a kiss.

'Goodnight, sweetheart!' he called and with a soft laugh disappeared out into the darkness.

Elizabeth was left standing in the hallway like a leper.

She scolded herself for not being wiser – how could she have believed that she was close to unravelling Jack! She should have known that he would have secrets from her and she wondered what plots and schemes he was party to that she had yet to uncover! But was that not what he was supposed to do; after all he was Warwick's spy!

She moved back into their chamber, heavy in thought. She slumped sulkily onto the bed and pillowed her hands behind her head. What had happened to bring such a look of concern to Jack's face and the stranger to their door? She puffed out her lips in a petulant huff. After all they had been through together why had Jack not confided in her? She almost laughed; now she was behaving like a new wife! Jack had dismantled her defences tonight, but the truth was he owed her nothing; the only thing they really shared was their duty to Warwick and a promise her father had made that she wished to forget. Yet Jack's uncovered secret had hurt like a blow and she was reeling from the shock of it; she had thought of them as a kind of partnership, but evidently Jack had other ideas about that. And now she was forced to wait for his return like his anxious wife and ponder on what she would do if he did not come back!

ST PAUL'S CATHEDRAL, LONDON OCTOBER 1470

Warwick looked around him. The sky was bright and cloudless and a northerly wind rushed up from the Thames to ruffle the plumes on the horses' bridles. They tossed their heads nervously, sensing the grandeur of the occasion. Warwick sighed. His own heart thumped against his ribs, for today was almost as important a day as that at Angers, when he had sworn his irrevocable oath to Lancaster; today Henry of Lancaster would once again be crowned King of England.

'My lord?' Thomas's bright voice found him. Warwick heard the quiver of excitement there and smiled.

'Are you ready to see a king made, Thomas?' he asked.

Thomas beamed. 'Yes, my lord.'

He wished he could share Thomas's enthusiasm, but he had made a king once before. Warwick adjusted his jewelled collar about his neck and turned to face him. 'Shall we go?'

'Yes, my lord,' Thomas answered and followed Warwick away from the carriage into the confusion of colour and noise of the crowd gathered in front of the cathedral.

Warwick found his place quickly and suddenly in a blaze of bright trumpets the procession began.

In front of him, Henry of Lancaster drifted along the walkway like a ghost, and as Warwick held the cloth-of-gold train of his robes, it seemed as though it was only his strength that was anchoring Henry to the earth in the brisk breeze.

Crowds cheered, banners rippled. Everywhere the smiling faces of commoners and lords greeted them and gradually Warwick began to brighten.

But one face did not smile. One face was sullen.

'How goes it with you, George?' Warwick asked as he passed by his son-in-law.

Clarence feigned deafness and bowed courteously to prevent the necessity of an answer.

'Do you think he will rally, Richard?' Oxford asked as he carried the great sword of state at his side.

Warwick raised an eyebrow. 'Who can say, John?' he said evenly. 'But Clarence cannot easily return to The House of York!'

Oxford smiled. 'That is true. Not unless he fancies a hazardous trip across the Narrow Sea!'

Warwick laughed softly, but it hid an uneasy feeling within him.

The spires of St Paul's Cathedral speared up to the sky above them. Trumpets sang as they entered; white, gold and red light dappled amongst them like rose petals as they processed to the altar. Jewels glittered, voices soared and Henry shivered like a frightened deer. Wild eyes looked to Warwick for reassurance and Warwick gave him the broadest smile possible. 'My liege,' he said soothingly, as if talking to a jittery mare.

Henry's lips curved into a thin smile, but his eyes remained wide and staring. Incense drifted to them like autumn clouds and Henry gave a cough, which seemed to shake his whole body, and Warwick wondered if he would be able to survive the arduous ceremony. But he showed surprising resilience and as they placed the heavy jewelled crown on Henry's head there was a sweeping susurration as the congregation knelt. For a moment Warwick wondered if Henry's spindly neck would support both his head and the diadem, but when it seemed that it would, and that he would not have to catch the crown, he led the cheers of 'Long live King Henry the Sixth!' and 'God Save the King!'

Warwick felt as though something had ended, as though a door had closed. One chapter of his life, the Yorkist chapter, was now complete and what felt like the final chapter of his sojourn had begun. At forty-one years old he knew he was heading for the eventide of his life and that this achievement, and its defence, would be his epitaph. Now he had stepped upon this path he knew there was no way to turn back from it, for he had given his oath to God.

BRUGES OCTOBER 1470

Elizabeth stared at the bed in disbelief. In the turmoil of the last few days and the worry of Jack's continued absence, she had forgotten completely about the gown Jack had ordered for her. It lay like a woman along the length of their bed, and the sight of it made her eyes well with tears; where was Jack?

Tentatively she reached for the dress. Her fingers hesitated before touching it, as if it were made of cobwebs rather than silk. The pattern was figured in deep rose over bronze, which she knew would compliment her colouring to perfection; her stomach curled at the thought that Jack knew her this well.

As she slipped the cool stiff brocade over her kirtle she wondered what he would have said to her and she shivered as she thought of his eyes coveting her body through the rippling silk. She smoothed her hands over the fabric to flatten the creases and then pulled gently at the satin laces to tighten the bodice over her breasts; perhaps it was as well that he was not here to see her she thought, for even without the jewelled velvet belt that accompanied it, it fitted her perfectly, accentuating her curves alarmingly. Even her mother would not call her a child when she wore this gown, she thought. As she walked along the gallery the servants dropped into deep curtseys, something they didn't usually do and she saw them exchange wide-eyed glances of approval; Jack had chosen well. She descended the stairs carefully, knowing that she had to relearn the art of wearing a ladies' gown if she wasn't to break her neck; how on earth had she managed to dance in one of these? The memories of her illicit dancing came back to her vividly; the colour, the noise, the glittering jewels and bright candles like a thousand tiny suns and the closeness of the men she had danced with, both incurring Higgins's disapproval! She banished the thoughts of Warwick and Lord Hastings quickly; dancing always brought her trouble.

She faced the large oak doors uncertainly. Even though she had Senor Gruuthuse's permission to come here it felt as though she was entering a sacred space. Elizabeth thought the best way to take her troubled mind off Jack was to immerse herself in the illicit magic of Senor Gruuthuse's books. She had obtained his permission to look at them once over supper. He had shown a little surprise that a woman should show an interest in his library and he had congratulated Jack warmly on the fact that his wife was interested in reading, evidently that made her something of a scholar! Jack had smiled broadly and winked at her and Elizabeth had fumed inwardly at his arrogance; as though her intelligence was anything to do with Jack! What she would not give for Jack's arrogance to be with her now! Dismissing the troubling thoughts she pushed at the heavy door. Even before her eyes had taken in the book cabinet, she smelled the rich scents of polished leather and wood and the mustiness of vellum and parchment, which reminded her of Ellerton Nunnery. She remembered how long it had taken Sister Beatrice to create just one perfect page and how much the lapis and gold had cost. But here that cost was replicated thousands of times, for there were more than a dozen volumes, each swollen with illuminated folios and bound in gloriously worked leather.

As she brushed her hand lightly along their arrayed spines she felt humble; she felt privileged to be in this place, remembering how guarded Cousin Matthew had been over his small book collection; she had never been allowed to hold them without his close supervision. What a man Senor Gruuthuse must be, she thought, for neither Warwick nor Edward had a library such as this as far as she knew.

Tentatively she removed one of the books from its place. It was heavy and cold in her hands. She carried it over to the nearest cushioned chair and settled it upon her knee like a small child. With great care she opened it. Inside it had a thick blue folio, then a page bearing the Gruuthuse coat of arms. The next page was of beautiful swirling writing.

At first she thought it was simply the style of the writing that prevented her from reading it, for it was so different from anything she had seen in England. But as she turned the yellow leaves she realized that the writing was in another language.

Held fast as if by a spell, she continued to turn the pages slowly. Interspersed between some of the written texts were lines of music. Elizabeth did not know if they were meant to indicate the song melody to the singer of the text or whether they were for instrumental passages, and she tried to imagine what they must sound like. Perhaps she would ask Senor Gruuthuse.

'Mistress Hardacre?'

The man's voice made Elizabeth start. She jumped up, almost letting the precious book fall from her grasp. Her hand flew to her mouth to stifle a gasp.

'I thought it was you, but at first I did not trust my eyes. I thought you still in France.' William Hastings's brown eyes were wide in astonishment, but his face quickly broke into a broad smile. 'Tell me, how do you come to be here?' he asked.

'My – my lord chamberlain,' Elizabeth stammered. 'I could ask you the same question,' she said. Suddenly she remembered to curtsey to him, though it was probably the most ungainly curtsey of her life. Her mind was galloping ahead of her like a runaway horse; a thousand questions flooded her thoughts. What was Lord Hastings doing here? Did he know Jack de Laverton? Could she continue the lie of her marriage to John Thornton? She thought it best to say as little as possible; wasn't that the way with spies? He had once told her to trust no one – but she had never thought that warning would include himself!

'Indeed you could ask such a thing,' Hastings said sadly. He gave her a clouded look.

She fixed his gaze, trying to encourage him to speak so that she did not have to. What could she say that would not bring her further trouble? No wonder Jack had been wary of being interrogated by the watch after Higgins's death; no wonder he had returned quickly to the sanctuary of Senor Gruuthuse's house; hadn't he once said that the Senor would be a useful ally? If she said the wrong thing now, not only would they be exposed as Warwick's spies, but they would be called to account for Higgins's death!

Hastings smiled weakly, oblivious to her panic. 'You will have mixed feelings about my news, I think.'

Elizabeth tried to concentrate on what he was saying. 'My lord?'

He took a deep breath. 'We are flown into exile, Elizabeth,' he said flatly. 'The king, the Duke of Gloucester and but a few of our host.'

'Warwick?' she breathed. She hardly dare imagine what Hastings was going to say. Could it be the answer to so many of her prayers?

'Yes lady, the Earl of Warwick is the master of England.'

Elizabeth's head swam. She sat down quickly and stared disbelievingly at the tiled floor. She fought hard not to smile at this news – Warwick had won! She had to try and remember that she had once been Edward's agent and that Hastings would expect her loyalty; and then the thought struck her like a blow – Edward was here!

Hastings knelt in front of her. Concern lined his face. He took the book from her and placed it on the little table beside her. 'What a shock this must be,' he said softly, 'you and your father both worked hard for York's cause.'

'Y – Yes,' Elizabeth could barely take in his words. Edward was here in Bruges, in this very house! Her stomach rose to meet her throat. Now perhaps Jack would listen. Now he would have to leave for England! That is if she knew where he was!

'I am sorry, Elizabeth, perhaps I should have prepared you better for the news,' Hastings said, taking hold of her hand.

'No, it is not your fault,' she said shakily, 'this news would have been difficult to bear, no matter how it was told.' Jack had taught her well, she thought; he had pressed upon her the danger they were in, and hadn't that danger increased a thousand fold with Hastings's and King Edward's arrival?

'Come,' Hastings said, 'come and meet the king. At least you will be able to bring him some cheer, for you know he likes your company.'

'No...I cannot, my lord!' Elizabeth was almost frantic. She needed to find Jack, she needed to warn him and she needed time to think. What had Senor Gruuthuse said about them already? She had no way of knowing! Santa Maria, where was Jack? She couldn't do this by herself!

'Please, Elizabeth.' Hastings looked up at her imploringly. 'I shall not leave you alone, I swear. But you will give him some heart.'

Hastings began to raise her to her feet.

'Now?' Elizabeth asked tightly. 'Must we go now?'

Hastings nodded. 'I know you are still a little shaken, but he is in such low spirits, I would be grateful if you would consent to see him now.'

Elizabeth looked at Hastings. His brow was pleated with worry, his eyes wide with concern. How could she refuse him, when he had given her and Lady Anne such good service?

'Very well,' she said hesitantly. 'Though I think there is little I can do.'

The walk back along the gallery seemed to take an age. Hastings held her hand through the crook of his arm, as he had done in London, but the charged excitement of that meeting had gone. Hastings was quiet, solemn and serious – as Elizabeth had never seen him. The silence was intolerable and Elizabeth's curiosity was almost choking her.

'Can you tell me nothing of England, my lord?' she asked softly.

Hastings fixed her face intently. 'There will be time for that later, Elizabeth,' he said in a voice tinged with regret, 'the whole tale is yet too close to recount.'

Elizabeth smiled at him. 'I am sorry,' she said. 'But you can understand that I cannot easily believe it. If I can bring you comfort...' she stopped herself. She recalled with alarm the frisson between them when they had danced in London. What sort of comfort would Hastings think she meant? Did he not keep the king's dissolute company? 'If it gives you ease to talk of it, my lord,' she added quickly.

Hastings smiled gently, noting her embarrassment. 'I promise that I shall talk with you, Elizabeth,' he said smoothly.

Her cheeks flamed scarlet – that was to be avoided at all costs!

He cleared his throat. 'The short tale is that our supporters fled once Montagu declared for Warwick. Edward feels it like a lance wound.'

Elizabeth fought the smile that threatened to come at the news. John Neville had come to his brother's banner at last! 'There was no battle?' Elizabeth asked.

Hastings shook his head. 'I think that is the worst part. Edward has never lost a battle; he would have relished the conflict, I think, even if John Neville was the foe, but in the end his retainers melted away like ice before the sun and there was no other path we could choose.'

Elizabeth looked away to hide her smile; Warwick had won without shedding any blood!

'And I would also like to hear your tale, Elizabeth,' Hastings said. 'I presume Master Higgins brought you here? Were you making for England?'

Elizabeth's stomach lurched; how could she explain about Higgins without implicating Jack and incriminating herself? Thoughts whirled in her head like pennants at a joust and she struggled to find a plausible answer. What should she say? What should she omit? She wished Jack were here – he would know what to do. 'Yes. No. That is...'

Hastings waited patiently. His eyes rested on her gently, as if he understood something of her troubles.

If she did not say something credible soon, Elizabeth thought, he would become suspicious of her.

'My lord, I do not know where to start,' she said, trying to buy more time. And it was true: she was floundering like a fish fresh from the sea. Her pulse thumped at her throat. Could she tell him Higgins was dead? Or missing? Or...

'My lady?' Jack's voice echoed along the corridor.

Elizabeth almost wilted with relief. She turned to face him, her eyes as round as an owl's, warning him to be careful in what he said. That she had no idea where he had been was irrelevant; thank God he had come! And how he had come; of course she knew he had also ordered new clothes, how stupid of her to forget, but the blue and silver damask of his doublet was dazzling and the fine fur trim was as pure and white as virgin snow; even at the brightest court Jack would now draw gazes from more than just the ladies. It took her a moment to realize Jack was speaking. She tried to concentrate on what was happening, on what he was saying, but her thoughts would not be bidden away from him.

'My lord,' Jack swept an elegant bow to Hastings. 'I presume you have a good reason for abducting my wife from the library?' Jack smiled. He cast Elizabeth an irreverent look and his eyes skimmed the curves of her new gown with approval. She wondered if she had given the same impression to him.

Hastings's jaw slackened. 'Your wife, sir?'

'Indeed. I am John Thornton, a gentleman of Yorkshire. Perhaps Elizabeth did not mention it? Perhaps your presence here startled her; you know how women are, my lord.'

Hastings looked at Elizabeth and his eyes widened questioningly.

She lowered her gaze from him and fought the urge not to swipe at Jack for his last comment.

Jack grinned at her.

Elizabeth's heart quickened. She did not want to deceive Lord Hastings, just as she had not wanted to deceive Warwick, but once again she had no choice but to do so. Lies and half-truths seemed to grow like choking vines about her.

Hastings turned an unflinching look to Jack, as though he was determined to see the truth. His brow furrowed and Elizabeth knew he doubted their tale.

The silence stretched into heartbeats with neither man giving ground. Jack held Hastings's gaze confidently, almost arrogantly. It was as though they were locked in combat at the lists, testing each other's strength on the first passes before the veracity of the final joust.

Eventually it was Hastings who spoke. 'I am William Lord Hastings, Lord Chamberlain of England.' His voice was composed and authoritative, but Elizabeth saw a faint twitch about his mouth that told her he was uncomfortable.

Jack nodded courteously.

Elizabeth saw mischief in his eye, as though he was about to point out that Hastings was no longer the Lord Chamberlain of England, but was an exile as they were. But to her relief he did not.

'Your servant, my lord,' Jack said smoothly and offered another elegant bow.

Elizabeth smiled almost proudly; Jack was the consummate actor!

Hastings acknowledged him coolly. 'Your wife,' he hesitated over the word, 'is to be presented to King Edward.' He glanced suddenly at Elizabeth, as though he wondered how much of her past her husband knew. 'She has lately been at court and His Grace wishes to renew their acquaintance,' he added, as if he felt there needed to be some further explanation.

Jack raised an eyebrow, but Hastings offered nothing more.

Elizabeth's heart skipped a beat. Was Jack going to object? Or perhaps insist that he accompanied her?

'As long as I have her back by Nones,' Jack said. 'I have promised to take her to a friend's house for supper.'

Elizabeth tried not to show her surprise – what friends did Jack have in Bruges? She certainly had none, for she knew nothing about the women with whom she shared the solar and mind-numbing embroidery! Was that where Jack had been – with these friends? She wondered if he meant the evil-looking man he had left with, but then she thought he had looked like a man who dealt in corpses not friends! What other secrets had Jack kept from her; she certainly had none from him!

Hastings bowed his head. 'Of course, Master Thornton, you have my word on it.'

'Then I should be honoured for her to be presented to the King of England,' Jack said with an eloquent look. He turned to Elizabeth. 'Sweetheart,' he said as he took hold of her hand. He drew it to his lips and kissed it slowly. He winked again, and his audacity made Elizabeth smile in spite of her fears. 'You look beautiful,' he whispered casting his eyes quickly over her body again. 'Did I not make an excellent choice?'

Her stomach curled. How could Jack be thinking of her new gown now? What if Lord Hastings asked about him? What was she to say? She had heard Jack tell Senor Gruuthuse their marriage had taken place at Amboise when he asked, but the Senor was only making polite conversation. Hastings she knew would be far more inquisitive; he would want to know the details and most especially how Higgins had allowed this to happen. And then there was Edward to face; the last thing she wanted to be in front of Edward was beautiful!

But Jack was a study in calm acceptance. 'Adieu, my love,' he breathed. He bowed to Hastings and then turned swiftly. His cloak billowed round him and the embroidery on its hem glittered like stars as he walked away. Elizabeth watched after him for a moment, wishing with all her heart that he had not left her. Somehow everything seemed all right when Jack was in her presence. But there was nothing she could do about it. She had to face Edward alone.

She took a deep breath, stealing herself for what was to come.

Lord Hastings was looking at her and she fought not to meet his wide brown eyes. Instead she gave him her hand and they continued along the passageway in an uncomfortable silence.

SEVEN

BRUGES OCTOBER 1470

When they entered the salon, Edward was standing by the window. He was staring out into the brightness of the day and dappled sunlight made chestnut highlights in his hair.

At the sound of the door closing, he turned unseeing eyes towards them.

His face was ashen, his cheeks seemed hollow and his brow was furrowed with troubles.

'My liege, I have brought someone to see you,' Hastings said brightly.

Elizabeth curtseyed as Edward's blind gaze swept over her. Then she noticed him raise an eyebrow inquisitively. She smothered a smile: she was a woman after all!

But even the sight of her in her new gown did not overly interest him. 'Not now Will,' he said. His voice was a ghost of its former strength. He turned back to the window.

Elizabeth looked at Hastings and he smiled.

'I think you will see this lady, Ned. Do you not remember her?'

Edward turned back to face them.

Elizabeth rose slowly from her curtsey.

'My liege,' she said, suddenly conscious that he was actually the king of nowhere.

'Elizabeth?' Edward's voice brightened. He strode towards them. 'Thank you, Will,' he said as he took hold of Elizabeth's hands. He searched her face intently and then smiled, but Elizabeth noticed the smile did not fill his eyes as it would have done in London.

Hastings did not leave. 'May I present Mistress *Thornton*, Your Grace?'

Edward looked puzzled. 'Thornton?' he asked. 'Ah, I understand. I have heard it usual for spies to change their names and identities,' he said softly.

'Your Grace, I have met her husband,' Hastings said firmly.

'Is this true, Elizabeth?' Edward's eyes flicked to hers. 'Are you married?'

'Lord Hastings has indeed met Master Thornton,' Elizabeth said guardedly. Perhaps Jack's influence was stronger than she cared to admit, for the half-truths came more easily to her tongue now.

Edward shrugged. 'It is no matter. I am sure he will not object to us having your company.' He drew Elizabeth into the room and settled her on a cushioned seat.

The marital status of his conquests had probably never concerned Edward, Elizabeth thought.

'Hastings. Wine.' Edward maintained his gaze on Elizabeth as he spoke to his chamberlain.

Elizabeth tried not to meet his look; instead she gazed at her hands, which she folded neatly into her lap. She stared at Jack's ring as if it would give her courage.

'What, so demure mistress?' Edward asked. 'Has marriage so changed you?'

She raised her eyes slowly to his and saw they were clouded and dark as lapis.

'We all have changed,' she said. 'None of us are as we were in London.'

'How true that is,' Edward said sourly. 'And I had promised you such a reward!'

Elizabeth shivered as she thought on what might have been.

A servant brought them wine and honey cake.

'It is no matter,' Elizabeth said softly. 'My suffering is slight compared to yours. You have lost England.'

She saw him flinch at her words.

'And none of us may return there until we can mount an invasion as Warwick has,' he growled.

'But my liege, you do not have the support of a king as he did. Would an invasion be possible?'

Edward drew his lips into a thin hard line. 'Do not remind me that my brother Burgundy refuses to acknowledge our plight.'

'Will he not even give you money?' Elizabeth asked.

'He will not allow me to come to court, nor will he acknowledge my claim. Yet he honours the Lancastrian exiles as friends! My sister tells me he wishes to be a friend to England, whoever wears the crown there. Already Senor Gruuthuse says he has sent ambassadors to treat with Warwick.'

'Thank God then for Senor Gruuthuse,' Elizabeth said, 'for he has saved us all.'

'Indeed, we owe him much,' Edward said, 'and may yet require further indulgence from him.'

He reached for the wine and offered Elizabeth some cake. The sweet cinnamon-flavoured pastry melted in her mouth. She chewed it slowly, savouring its richness. She thought how different this meeting was to their last, when Edward's intentions had gone far beyond honey-cake and only the timely intervention of Lord Hastings had prevented her from knowing the king intimately!

Edward did not eat, but poured himself another cup of wine. He watched her intently and Elizabeth wondered what he was thinking. Again the silence lengthened between them.

Edward broke it suddenly. 'Tell me, Elizabeth, did you see much of Warwick during your stay in France?'

Elizabeth choked on her cake. Why would he ask her that? Had Higgins told him of Valognes and Barfleur?

'A little, Your Grace,' she spluttered, 'but mostly I was with the Duchess of Clarence.' More lies, she thought; she was almost as good as Jack now.

'Clarence.' Edward said the name wistfully, as if he had only just remembered his brother was with Warwick. 'Yes, how did my errant brother seem?'

Elizabeth sighed. 'He was not himself; he was much affected by the loss of his son.'

Edward nodded in acknowledgement of his brother's grief. 'Did he seem willing to return to me?' he asked.

'Who can really tell what he is thinking, Your Grace?' Elizabeth answered. 'But he did make me promise to tell you that he would return when the time was right.'

'Why was it not right then?' Edward growled. 'Surely he could have come home.'

'He would have had to leave the duchess behind and he was loathe to do that. She had been very ill.'

'But he has left her now!' Edward snapped. 'Now that he has gone with Warwick!'

Elizabeth lowered her gaze. 'I am sorry, Your Grace, I cannot give better news.' Mayhap she had said too much already.

She heard Hastings move behind them. 'Ned, Mistress Thornton has tried to comfort you,' he said softly, 'she is not responsible for Clarence's conduct. But does she not give you hope that he will join us when we return?'

Edward looked up at his friend. Then he looked to Elizabeth. 'I am sorry, Elizabeth, I am a very poor host.'

Elizabeth looked to Hastings, her eyes pleading to leave.

Hastings shook his head. 'Perhaps when we next meet, you will be more like yourself, Ned,' he said.

'I doubt it,' Edward muttered, 'unless you have a plan to win back my kingdom, Will!'

Elizabeth tried to think like Jack; she should try to gain more information from Edward, if she could take her mind off her own vulnerability. 'And your brother of Gloucester is also here?' she asked tentatively.

Edward smiled. 'That is a subject which does give me hope,' he said more brightly. 'For he has shown much courage, as well as loyalty.'

'Though I have seen him when I was in London, I have not met him,' Elizabeth said.

'We shall remedy that,' Edward said, 'he is as different from Clarence as he can be! You will like him Elizabeth, I promise.'

The door opened quietly and Hastings moved to speak to the steward.

'I shall look forward to it,' Elizabeth said, trying to maintain her attention on Edward while also noting the interruption.

Hastings returned to Edward's side. He spoke softly to him so that Elizabeth could not hear.

'It seems your lord awaits you, Mistress Thornton,' Edward said sadly. 'Though I have done so before, on this occasion I shall not keep a wife from her husband.'

Elizabeth expected a roguish smile to accompany the comment, but there was none.

Elizabeth rose slowly and then curtseyed.

Edward nodded a brief acknowledgement, but did not move to kiss her, as he once would have done.

Hastings escorted her to the door. 'Thank you,' he whispered, 'you have given him heart.'

Elizabeth smiled. 'I think I did very little Lord Hastings,' she said, 'but if you think I did, then I am content.'

Hastings reached for her hand and drew it to his lips. 'It is always a pleasure to see you,' he breathed. 'We must talk further.'

Then he let her go and Elizabeth slipped out into the ante-chamber. Talking to Hastings was something she knew she had to avoid.

Jack came to her quickly. His eyes were dark with concern. He grasped her hands tightly and Elizabeth closed her fingers around his. Santa Maria, dare she admit how much she had missed him?

Elizabeth opened her mouth to speak to him.

'Hush,' Jack whispered, as he drew her to him, 'it is not safe to talk here. Wait until we are in the carriage. Then I shall tell you everything, and you can tell me what passed between you and the wandering king.'

Elizabeth's heart raced as they hurried back along the passageway together; what did he mean when he said he would tell her everything? She tried to contain her excitement; perhaps Jack was going to tell her that they were going home tonight!

* * *

Elizabeth sank into the cushioned sanctuary of the carriage with a deep sigh. As soon as Jack joined her, the carriage moved off with a lurch, forcing them closer together than Elizabeth would have liked. But as they drew in front of the house she saw that William Hastings was watching their departure and Jack put one arm round her shoulder and touched his chaperon with his free hand. Hastings looked away.

She looked up at Jack and a thought struck her like a slap.

'You knew!' she said suddenly. 'By the saints, you knew that night that the visitor was Edward!' Anger tightened her throat, making her voice sound shrill.

Jack smiled ruefully and gave an almost apologetic nod of his head.

'Why did you not tell...?'

He pushed in on her words impatiently. 'I had to be sure of the circumstances. I had to know how he came and why. It would have served no purpose to tell you my suspicions then, and I could give you no reassurance.'

'No purpose!' Elizabeth exclaimed indignantly. 'And I suppose you can reassure me now can you?' She stared at him fiercely, her cheeks as hot as coals. 'Where did you go, hmm?'

Jack lowered his eyes. 'Sweetheart,' he said as he drew her closer, 'do not ask me.'

'I thought you were to tell me all?' Elizabeth broke free from him angrily. So this was how it was going to be, she thought. They were not a partnership of equals; Jack was back in control,

193

for he had answers and all Elizabeth had were questions he would not lay to rest.

'What I did learn last night will please you,' he said somewhat contritely. 'Warwick is the master of all England.'

'I know,' she said flatly, 'I learned as much from Lord Hastings. And do we go to England now?' she asked. 'Or is there something else you have forgotten to tell me?'

Jack hesitated. She saw a muscle twitch in his cheek as the silence lengthened.

'I take it the silence means there is?'

Jack looked back at her. His face was serious. 'I am now in two minds...'

Elizabeth's eyes widened. 'About England? No Jack, it is too dangerous!' She tried to read his expression. 'If they discover the truth...'

Jack smiled. 'It is nice that you are worried for me,' he jested, 'but it is a risk worth the taking.'

Elizabeth stared at him in astonishment. She had hoped this journey was to take them to the harbour but instead it was a journey into a nightmare.

'I swore allegiance to Warwick,' Jack continued evenly, 'and my loyalty stands through thick and thin...'

He hesitated a moment and it was just long enough for Elizabeth to wonder if his remark was a veiled jibe at her.

'All I am saying, sweetheart is that if I can help Warwick by staying here then I must! My only concern was that they may have recognized me from my youth serving Warwick, but I saw no hint of recognition and why would they remember a boy from Yorkshire?'

Elizabeth knew why they might remember him: Jack's handsome gypsy looks.

'And where does that leave me?' Elizabeth asked. 'They certainly remember me!'

Her heart thumped, because she knew what Jack was going to say next.

His eyes widened in a silent plea. 'Stay with me,' he whispered, 'please.'

She turned her head away from him and blinked against the burning of tears. She wanted to go home. She did not want to spend any time here with Edward! It was too dangerous!

'Ah, my pretty one I understand,' Jack said softly.

'Do you?' Elizabeth snapped, her eyes fixing him angrily. 'Do you really? You have no family, no one waiting at a hearthside wondering where you are! How could you know? All you think of is your mission; Higgins was right about you!'

Jack turned away quickly and she knew she had wounded him.

'All I ask is that you think on it,' he said gruffly. 'By staying we can help Warwick with our knowledge of his enemies.' He met her gaze now and she saw pain and anger in his eyes. She had been wrong to lash out at him, however desperate she felt, for she had pushed him away from her and now he would tell her nothing.

A brittle silence settled between them. Elizabeth wanted to break it, wanted to tell him she was sorry for what she had said in anger, but she did not have the courage to do so, fearing she would only make matters worse. Instead she breathed deeply and said, 'I will let you know my decision on the morrow.'

Jack nodded his agreement and then looked away from her again.

They continued their journey in a taut silence and it was some time before Elizabeth suddenly realized that she had no idea where they were going, now that her hopes of heading to the harbour had been dashed like glass.

'Jack,' she said hesitantly, 'where are you taking me?'

Jack honoured her with a scornful smile. 'I have arranged a little surprise for you; something I thought might divert you.'

She knew that wouldn't be completely true, Jack would have some other purpose to this, but she needed to build bridges. 'Please Jack, I did not mean...'

'Do not apologize,' he growled, 'the line is set between us and I shall not cross it again after tonight.'

'After tonight?'

'Tonight you are my wife, Elizabeth,' he said coldly, 'for we are to dine with Jehan de Damas, Senor de Clessy!'

Elizabeth's eyes widened; she felt as though she barely knew Jack. What other connections had he made that she did not know of? Is this where he had been, making connections to the nobility of Burgundy? 'Your friend, Jack?'

'Yes, sweetheart, bastard Jack is well known to the Burgundian court!' He smiled again but with a curl to his lip that Elizabeth hated.

'Jack...'

'Yes?' he answered sullenly.

'I am sorry...I had no right to say those things.'

'No you did not,' he said bluntly, 'but they cannot be unsaid.'

'I know,' she whispered, 'and it is no excuse Jack, but I am just so desperate to go home.'

Jack's face softened. 'Believe me, Elizabeth, I do know what it is like to yearn for home,' he said more gently. There was a wistful look in his eyes as he spoke and Elizabeth knew she had been wrong; someone did wait for Jack's return and she knew it was a woman. Another secret he had.

'You shall go home, I promise,' he said. 'But if we can aid War-wick by remaining here, is it not better to wait just a little longer?'

Elizabeth understood the gravity of his words.

'Elizabeth? Can you do this?' Jack's eyes were wide in supplication.

The look went straight to her core. What choice did she truly have? Were they not in this together?

'It may even make amends...' Jack started but did not finish the sentence, content to let this arrow fall a little short of the butt.

Elizabeth felt it none the less, but on that score he could not tell her anything she had not said to herself already and mayhap he was right. But could she ever really earn Warwick's forgiveness? Her eyes began to sting. She doubted atonement was possible. Would she be doing this for Jack then; because he had asked her?

Suddenly the carriage clattered onto cobbles and Elizabeth saw they were in a large courtyard hung with banners and pennants she did not recognize.

She looked at Jack apprehensively.

'Tonight we are one,' he said as he smudged a tear from her cheek with his thumb. 'Remember that, sweetheart,' he said firmly. 'Tomorrow however is another tale,' he added with a flash of his eyes.

Elizabeth gathered her skirts and made to follow him down from the carriage. She had made her decision, but it would do no harm to let him wait to hear it.

Judging by the amount of gold and silver plate on display, Jehan de Damas, Senor de Clessy was a very rich man and Elizabeth now understood why Jack had insisted on the best clothes they could afford. Could it be that he had planned this all along and that the rich gown she wore had never been meant to be seen by Warwick but by Jack's Burgundian connections instead? Could he not have told her this? Did he really not trust her with anything?

'Jack, how do you know this man?' she asked as they waited to be announced to the glittering hall full of guests.

Jack flashed a mocking smile. 'Why do you not ask me the question as you wanted to? How does the gypsy bastard have such grand acquaintances?'

Elizabeth frowned. 'Jack, I didn't mean that at all!' Did he really think she thought so little of him? She cursed her thoughtless tongue! She touched his arm, but he pulled away from her.

'I just want to know, Jack, truly,' she assured him.

Jack let out a long slow breath. 'Very well, sweetheart,' he said. The black fury in his eyes cooled a little. 'I have been to France and Burgundy many times for Warwick. On my last visit this man who is the lord of Digoine, Clessy and Saint-Amour was newly made a *Chevalier de la Toison d'Or*. Do you know what that means, Elizabeth?'

Elizabeth shook her head. 'A knight of the Golden Fleece,' she said, translating Jack's French. 'But I don't know what that is.'

'It is the highest order of knights in Burgundy,' Jack said, 'the equivalent of our Knights of the Garter. They are created by the Duke of Burgundy himself.'

Elizabeth nodded.

Jack smiled again. 'You cannot know what the court of Burgundy is, Elizabeth. Edward's court is a company of beggars in comparison! And it was at the Burgundian court that I met Jehan. He has been a good friend.'

Elizabeth realized that this was only the surface of a tale as deep as the ocean. She was about to ask him in what way Jehan had helped him, but just at that moment they were announced. Jack reached for her hand and stepped forward proudly. It seemed strange to Elizabeth to hear Jack's full title and his true name announced in French, along with her as his wife! She looked at him quickly. 'Is that wise?' she asked.

Jack shrugged. 'I am known here. I cannot merely be Monsieur Thornton! And Edward and Hastings are unlikely to meet Jehan in their present position are they?' he said. 'And I came here for you, sweetheart; for your amusement, not mine!'

Elizabeth wondered if that was true; surely this was about Jack renewing his acquaintances. She wondered what had happened in the past; if Jack had been Warwick's man how had he made friends at the court of Burgundy when it was well known Warwick and Duke Charles hated each other? She had no more time for thoughts as Jack began to lead her to where Jehan de Damas was seated beneath a golden silk canopy covered in curving red crosses. Jack swept the Burgundian knight one of his elegant bows and for once Elizabeth was able to match it with a curtsey of equal grace. Jack arched a brow in approval and Elizabeth's cheeks flushed.

'Jacques!' Jehan said. 'It is good to see you. It has been too long!'

'Messire,' Jack answered, smiling.

Jehan rose and then hugged Jack to him, kissing him on both cheeks. 'So long that I see you have acquired a beautiful wife!'

Jack smiled again as he looked at Elizabeth. 'Senor de Clessy, may I present Elizabeth, my wife!'

Elizabeth blushed further and lowered her gaze.

'Madame!' Jehan said as he kissed her hand. 'You are most welcome!' There was genuine warmth in his greeting; he must think well of Jack, she thought.

Elizabeth thanked him and then lowered her eyes again, knowing that she should follow the lead of her husband and not make conversation for herself, though she had a hundred questions to ask Jehan if only she could.

'What brings you to Bruges, Jacques? I did not think your connections were to the Yorkist king I hear has landed on our shores?'

Elizabeth's heart thumped in her chest. What would Jack say?

'Messire, we were the guests of Senor Gruuthuse, when suddenly his house became rather crowded!'

Jehan laughed. 'Jacques, you have not changed! It is good to see you. Later we must talk.'

Jack bowed again and Elizabeth curtseyed as they made way for the next guests and then found their places at the long boards. 'That was well done, sweetheart,' Jack said to her as he held the seat for her. 'A pity you cannot always be so well behaved!'

Elizabeth looked up at him quickly. He favoured her with a wide smile.

'Why thank you, my lord. I could say the same of you!'

Jack nodded and then sat close beside her, all trace of his previous anger gone as quickly as a summer thunderstorm.

The servants began to bring food, offering it to Jehan with great ceremony, just as Elizabeth had seen at Warwick Castle when she had shared a place with Warwick himself.

Jack cut everything for her, as would be expected at such a feast, and Elizabeth was impressed by his mastery of etiquette; it was no less than Warwick's had been and she wondered how many ladies he'd had the pleasure of sharing a messe with; perhaps even here in Burgundy.

'What are you thinking?' Jack asked as he offered her the first of the dishes.

She cleared her throat. 'I was thinking of home,' she lied.

Jack widened his eyes.

Did he believe her, or could he tell it was a lie and perhaps guess at the truth? He said nothing but passed the gilded trencher towards her. Elizabeth took a piece of meat and put it into her mouth slowly. Jack's eyes never left her face as she did so.

'Is it good?' he asked.

She nodded that it was.

'As good as at Warwick?'

Elizabeth almost choked.

'I am not a fool, Elizabeth,' he said. 'I know that you dined with Warwick at his board. It caused quite a scandal!'

Elizabeth stared at the embroidered board cloth in front of her, embarrassed that he knew her so well and embarrassed now at her foolish behaviour then.

'Not as much as your dancing with him at Edward's Christmas court, though,' Jack added, 'that really did set the hounds among rabbits!'

Elizabeth's gaze flew to him.

'You see, I have followed you with much interest, sweetheart. Let us hope that tonight you can dance just as well for me, after all, you have danced with Lord Hastings also, 'tis only right and fitting that you dance with your husband too, is it not?'

Elizabeth's pulse was at her throat; she really didn't have any secrets from Jack! Yet it seemed he had so many things he kept from her. She swallowed dryly and reached for wine. She took a long drink and then looked back at Jack. 'Of course, my lord,' she said with as much composure as she could muster. 'How could I refuse to dance with you?'

When the boards were cleared away Jack was almost the first to rise. He offered his hand and when she took it he bowed to her. He led her to the centre of the room and Elizabeth noticed Jehan raise his glass in their direction. He was a good ten years older than Jack, by her reckoning and she wondered what their connection was. She took a steadying breath; the last thing she wanted to do was make a false step and embarrass Jack in doing so. He was an English knight and she was his lady, or at least that was what Jehan believed and for tonight at least she had to believe it too.

The dance was a slow one; one that she knew and Elizabeth wondered how it was that Jack managed to make each moment of contact last longer than it should have done and yet not be out of time or appear to be in the least bit hurried. He turned quickly to meet her, his movements all elegance and charm and she found herself craving the attention of his touch on her skin, on her shoulders and across her back as they met and parted as the dance weaved across the hall and Jack weaved magic all about her. And all the while she basked in his gaze and he was as he had been when she first saw him at Lazenby: the knight who stole her breath from her body and who graced her dreams at night.

It seemed all too soon that they were seated back in their cushioned carriage. Jehan waved to them from the steps of the hall and Elizabeth thought that he must indeed favour Jack by doing so. She was still breathless from the last dance, a lively salterello in which Jack had raised her from the floor with his arms about her waist. Her head swam, whether from too much dancing, too much wine or the intoxication of Jack, she couldn't tell. As the carriage moved off Jack slipped his arm across her shoulders and she leaned into him. She told herself it was for warmth against the chill of the night, but she knew that was only a half-truth. 'Thank you,' she murmured.

Jack smiled down at her and pulled her a little closer.

'You dance very well,' she said, still feeling giddy.

Jack laughed softly. 'I will not ask you who you think is the best dancer. I might not like your answer,' he said.

Elizabeth wasn't sure she could answer him truthfully; had she ever been happier than she was now?

'I am glad you enjoyed yourself, God knows we have seen much trouble and little joy of late.' He reached across and pushed a damp strand of hair from her face.

Elizabeth caught his scent and her stomach curled. She met his eyes; they were as deep and dark as the ocean at midnight and just as unreadable, but she tried none the less, unable to dismiss the feelings he stirred within her. They held each other's gaze for a long moment until Jack leaned forward slowly and met her lips with his.

* * *

'Your husband has abandoned you again?'

Elizabeth immediately stuck the needle into her finger at the sound of Lord Hastings's voice. She let out a sharp squeal and then stuck her injured finger into her mouth to soothe it.

'Forgive me,' Hastings said, 'I did not mean to startle you.'

Elizabeth's heart quickened as he came towards her.

After a short bow he came to sit opposite her on the cushioned high-backed settle.

Elizabeth ignored his question and hoped more like it did not follow.

She removed her finger from her mouth. 'As you see my lord, I am a poor seamstress.'

Hastings looked at her embroidery with admiration.

Elizabeth smiled, for it was progressing better than her usual efforts. 'My mother used to scold me for having the tension too tight on the frame and for my stitches not being even. As you see, it was all in vain.'

'No, it is most impressive,' Hastings said politely. 'You prefer reading I gather?'

'I do, my lord, but I must finish this and today the light is good,' she said casting a wistful look through the open window at the sunlight gilding the rooftops outside.

'It is indeed a lovely day.'

'And the king is hunting?'

Hastings nodded and a sigh escaped through his teeth. 'He loves to hunt,' he said as impassively as he could, but it was clear to Elizabeth that he thought Edward spent far too much time hunting.

'Then already you know where my husband is,' Elizabeth said. She was almost used to calling Jack her husband now, and as she had agreed to his request to stay in Bruges she knew it would yet become more familiar. She tried not to think of the kiss they had shared in the carriage though - that was stepping on dangerous ground and she knew it.

An easy silence settled between them.

'And what are you making?' Hastings asked, returning his gaze to her work.

Elizabeth bit her lip before she answered him. 'It is a coverlet for a cradle, my lord,' she said. It had been Jack's idea to give further credence to their marriage and her pregnancy that he had already announced to the harbourmaster. Elizabeth had to admit that while it might have been a good excuse for risking a passage across the Narrow Sea, it was not such a good idea for keeping them where they were; quite how far she could carry off a fake pregnancy she did not know. Already she had had to keep the maid away from her during her monthly flux for fear of discovery.

'He is a fortunate man, your husband,' Hastings said smoothly.

This was unsafe ground, Elizabeth thought. She saw a flicker of suspicion in Hastings's eyes and wondered how much of their story he believed. She had to concentrate. 'I tell him so every day,' she said trying to keep her voice light, 'and every day he tells me that I am the lucky one.'

Hastings smiled. 'I am glad to see you happy,' he said softly. 'Last time we met in London I think you were much troubled.' His eyes were wide now, drawing her in.

Elizabeth tried to keep control. 'Much has happened, my lord. But I am not the only one for whom fortune's wheel has turned,' she said trying to steer the conversation away from her and Jack and inevitably the spectre of Higgins.

Hastings smiled ruefully. 'How right you are.' His eyes seemed to mist over as he thought on his changed position.

Elizabeth welcomed the silence that followed and picked up her needlework again, hoping he would not question her too closely. She was sure he had doubts about her tale. 'So there was no battle?' she said absently.

'Hmm?'

She stopped sewing and met his face. 'You told me there was no battle with Warwick?' Her voice faltered at the name.

'Warwick came quickly,' Hastings said flatly. 'And we were caught still in Yorkshire. I had thought he would disembark in one of the Cinque Ports but he fooled us all and landed in Devon. We could not get to London before him, but the truth of it Elizabeth is that it was Lord Montagu's defection that was the final blow. All would have been lost had we stayed, for John Neville is the best soldier in England. As it was we had little more than we stood up in. We had to pay for our passage with Edward's rich cloak, with a promise to pay what more we owed when we could. But for Senor Gruuthuse ...'

His voice was husky with sadness and Elizabeth could not help but feel sorry for him.

'I know it does not look like we have much now, and you must think all your effort was in vain,' he continued. 'But we have hope, Elizabeth. And time will be on our side.'

Elizabeth was puzzled. 'Time, my lord?'

'The longer Warwick has to hold his ragtag traitors together without Edouard of Lancaster at his side, the more likely it is that cracks will appear in their union,' he said. 'The bitter Marguerite evidently does not trust Warwick with her son. That could yet be their undoing! And then there is my lord of Clarence...'

Elizabeth's stomach knotted at his words. Jack had told her that Warwick had not yet won and that was why he had to stay here and learn what he could for Warwick. And now Elizabeth saw how right Jack was. And if Clarence turned...

The sudden sounds of horses, hounds and men echoed in the courtyard below. Elizabeth rose quickly and went to the window to look, glad of the distraction. She steadied herself by leaning against the window frame. She hoped Warwick would be able to keep control of England and if staying here with Jack would help him then she knew that was what she must do, even though by staying with Jack she knew she had drifted into hazardous waters.

Judging by the number of bloody deer slung over ponies, the hunt had been successful. The men were certainly garrulous and in high spirits.

'They have had a good morning, my lord,' she said as Hastings came to join her at the window.

Elizabeth looked for Jack. He was seated on a bay hunter, loaned from Senor Gruuthuse, which was streaked with sweat and blowing hard. Jack's cheeks were flushed and he too looked a little breathless. Elizabeth smiled. He was sharing a joke with Edward, who, as if he knew he was being watched, turned to look up towards the chamber. He caught her gaze and gave her a broad smile and a bow of his head. Jack turned and saw her too. Edward said something to him and laughed. Jack dismounted quickly and hurried towards the house.

'I must leave you to your husband,' Hastings said as he saw Jack leave Edward's company. 'There is much I need to discuss with the king. Hopefully he will now be in the mood to listen!'

He bowed and Elizabeth curtseyed.

Hastings smiled at her as he reached the door. 'We must talk again,' he said as he left. 'I think we both have yet much to tell.'

Elizabeth shuddered, for she knew that any conversation with him was a risk. How different it was to when she had shared his easy company in London, but then she had not been working against him as she was now!

Hastings must have almost met Jack, for within two heartbeats Jack came striding into the room. His eyes were bright as stars and he had the healthy colour only a morning's exercise could bring.

'My Lord Chamberlain has gone?' he asked, a note of concern in his voice.

Elizabeth nodded and gave a deep sigh of relief.

Jack came closer. 'What is it?' he asked.

Elizabeth chewed at her lip. 'He suspects us, I am sure of it.'

Jack's brow pleated. 'How do you know?'

'It is something in his manner, in his expression, in his voice. He is not like he was in London.'

Jack laughed. 'I should hope not! You are now a married woman and he is a landless exile!'

'Jack, be serious. I know. Higgins seemed to know him well, perhaps that is the problem.'

Jack sighed. 'Well we know nothing of Higgins and I suspect neither does he.'

Elizabeth's jaw slackened. Her eyes widened. Nausea threatened. Perhaps it was just a turn of phrase.

But Jack dropped his gaze.

'Jack?' she asked.

Jack looked up at her through his lashes. 'I am sorry. I did not wish to worry you,' he said with a note of contrition.

Elizabeth was speechless, all thoughts frozen in her mind, all words strangled in her throat and for several heartbeats she stared at him in disbelief. Eventually words flew like angry birds. 'You said he was dead!'

'I had wounded him badly, sweetheart. The blood on the cobbles was mostly his. No one could have survived the fall into the water. We never found his body, that is all,' Jack replied. 'The boatmen swore it would have been sucked under and then dragged out to sea; that was why we didn't see it.'

Silence smothered them and Elizabeth knew Jack didn't believe what he had just said.

'But if Higgins were to arrive here...' Elizabeth gasped. And if he did return... 'Jack!' It was a cry of fear.

'Hush,' Jack said, wrapping his arms about her. 'If he were about, I would have heard, sweetheart.' He pulled her to him and kissed the top of her head affectionately.

Stunned as if from a battle-blow, Elizabeth did not resist him.

'Jack. It's not safe,' she said into his shoulder. Her voice trembled as she thought on what would happen to them if they were discovered. 'What if Lord Hastings questions me about him?'

'Then tell him the truth. He attacked me. I killed him.'

Elizabeth gasped at Jack's calmness.

'He would not believe it. He would know there was more.'

'You fell in love. Higgins did not approve. Is that so hard to believe?'

'I don't know, Jack. I'm not certain of anything anymore.' Elizabeth pressed herself to him.

Jack tightened his embrace. 'Just a little while longer, sweetheart,' he whispered. 'Please.'

'But if we stay much longer we will be trapped here until the spring,' Elizabeth answered.

'No sweetheart, we can still sail. It is just a little more exciting that is all!' He laughed and Elizabeth watched the soft creases lengthen at the corners of his eyes. Infuriatingly Jack could make light of the darkest of situations.

'Jack, please!' she said as she drew back from him. 'I want to go home!'

'I am listening, sweetheart,' he said. 'I swear it!'

'Good!' The voice startled them. 'A man should always listen to his wife!' Breathless from the stairs, Edward smiled at them. But the smile curved his mouth but a little and did not reach his eyes.

They sprang apart and made hasty obeisance to him. How much had he heard?

He waved them up quickly. 'And no doubt your child is your greatest consideration?' he said, casting a swift look at Elizabeth's belly which made her blush.

'My lord, you are right,' Jack said swiftly, 'but I do not wish to be apart from her at such a time, though I too want him to be born in England.'

Edward raised an eyebrow. 'I know how that feels,' he said sadly. 'The queen too is with child. You must have quickened at the same time.'

Elizabeth felt a dark shudder within her; in the place her child should be. This was another sin she would have to confess and she wondered if Edward saw it.

But Edward's eyes had clouded and Elizabeth could guess his thoughts. Elizabeth Wydeville, Edward's queen, would surely be in sanctuary. Not the most comfortable place to give birth, Elizabeth thought, but perhaps the safest under the circumstances. Yet what did she really have to fear? 'I am sure my lord of Warwick would not harm the queen or the child, my liege,' she said softly.

Jack stroked her hand reassuringly.

'You think so?' Edward growled. 'Then you think more kindly of him than I do!'

'I know he would not hurt her or any woman!' Elizabeth said stiffly.

Jack gripped her hand, warning her to be careful.

Edward turned away and his hands balled into fists at his sides. 'Mayhap you know him better than I,' he said with a caustic edge to his voice.

Elizabeth held her breath; had she said too much? Jack squeezed her hand tightly. They waited.

After a few moments Edward turned to face her. His face had softened and he gave a rueful smile. 'Thank you Mistress Thornton. You have given me much comfort.' He turned to Jack. 'Thornton, you are a most fortunate man, but as to whether you let your wife go home or not, I cannot advise you. You must do as you see fit, but your service in our company is valuable and will

206

not go unrewarded, that I promise. Perhaps you could ask the Earl of Warwick to look after your wife for you? I believe she knows the household well.' Edward shot Elizabeth a sharp look as though he was about to tell Jack that Elizabeth had been Warwick's lover. 'Having served the Duchess of Clarence,' he added.

Elizabeth looked up at him and for a moment they stared at each other, before Elizabeth remembered she was not supposed to do so. She looked down.

Eventually Edward waved his hand to dismiss them. 'I wish to see Lord Hastings,' he said. 'I am informed he has much to tell me and in return I must let him know what good hunting we have had today!'

Somehow Elizabeth knew he was not only talking about the morning's chase for venison.

* * *

They were late for dinner; it had partly been Elizabeth's fault as the lacing in her gown had broken and it had taken an age for the maid to mend it. Jack rushed her along the hallway, his hand clasping hers tightly and Elizabeth feared she would trip on her gown.

'Jack!' she hissed. 'I will be as red and breathless as a messenger if you hurry me so much!'

'They may jump to a conclusion as to why we are late then,' he answered. 'Perhaps that would be an acceptable excuse! More interesting than a broken lacing mayhap!'

Elizabeth flushed further. 'Jack!'

But Jack wasn't listening as he tugged her along the tapestry swathed hallway.

Even with only his household and guests in attendance Senor Gruuthuse had more mouths to feed than had ever dined at Lazenby. Elizabeth had wanted to give an excuse of being ill rather than arriving after everyone else was seated, but Jack wouldn't hear of it.

If they had hoped to enter the room in anonymity their hopes were dashed as soon as they appeared at the threshold, for Senor Gruuthuse's steward announced their names. Elizabeth and Jack exchanged glances; someone new must be here; someone important.

'Senor Gruuthuse, I crave your indulgence,' Jack said with an eloquent bow as they approached the board.'

'Senor, please forgive me,' Elizabeth said plaintively, 'I am the cause of such rudeness, not my husband.'

Senor Gruuthuse smiled. 'It is no matter, Mistress Thornton. Jack. Elizabeth. Please come and meet my guest, Senor de Clessy.'

Elizabeth's stomach knotted and Jack's hand tensed around hers. She saw him take a steadying breath and then turn to where Senor de Clessy was seated.

The look that passed between Jack and Jehan de Damas, Senor de Clessy was unreadable.

Elizabeth's heart fluttered like a wild bird snared in lime! She wanted to be sick.

'Senor,' Jack said as he bowed.

Elizabeth was amazed at the control he had imposed on his voice. Jack tugged her hand and she remembered suddenly to curtsey. She was beyond speech.

The moment before Jehan de Damas spoke lengthened into painful heartbeats. Elizabeth could not swallow, could hardly breathe.

Monsieur Thornton; Madame Thornton,' he said at last.

Elizabeth let out her breath audibly. Then she noticed a gleam in Jehan's eyes. Had Jack known of this all along and not said anything?

'It is good to see you again, Jacques. It has been too long; so long that I see you have gained a wife!'

Elizabeth wanted to faint with relief. She looked at Jack as they turned for their places. He was smiling!

* * *

'How could you do such a thing?' Elizabeth hissed when they returned to their chamber. 'Why could you not tell me that Jehan would be coming here?'

'Because it would only have worried you, sweetheart,' Jack answered smoothly.

She met his eyes. 'You broke that lace deliberately, didn't you? So that you could stage that meeting in front of everyone!'

Jack shrugged disarmingly.

She let out a hot breath. 'Jack!'

208

'Sweetheart,' he said as he sat down on the bed. 'You would have fretted all day, had I told you. As it is, all is well. Edward believes I have made him a new connection with the Burgundian court and Jehan is happy that he has met the exiled King of England! Just in case their duke does remember he has a brother-in-law living in his country!'

It all sounded so easy when Jack spoke of it, as if the drama had been nothing out of the ordinary, and perhaps in Jack's world this was true, but Elizabeth was struggling under the weight of her deceptions.

'No one trusts us, Jack. I can feel it,' Elizabeth said, coming to sit beside him. Jack stretched as languidly as a cat, pillowed his hands behind his head and crossed his ankles as if she had mentioned nothing more significant than what was for dinner.

'Jack, do you not take this seriously?' Elizabeth asked him. 'Must you always walk so close to the edge?'

He grinned. 'Yes,' he said flatly.

Elizabeth let out an exasperated sigh. 'Higgins,' she whispered. 'And now Jehan de Damas! They both know the truth about us and we cannot risk the truth coming out!'

'You are right, sweetheart,' he said untangling his limbs and leaning towards her. 'The stakes are high.'

Elizabeth wished she could be as brave as Jack, but she had no wish to sacrifice herself so far away from home, even if it was in Warwick's cause and this latest episode had pushed her beyond her endurance.

'I want to go, Jack,' she said softly. 'I am sorry.'

He reached for her hand. 'No, I am sorry, sweetheart. Mayhap I should have told you; it was wrong of me.'

'It is not just tonight; it is everything. Higgins; Jehan; Edward, oh and don't forget my baby!' Sudden tears burned her eyes.

Jack sat up and put an arm across her shoulders. 'I am sorry, sweetheart...'

She cut him off. 'I want to go, Jack. Now.'

Jack said nothing. He met her eyes and the silence lengthened as he explored her face.

'I am sorry,' she said. 'I am not as strong as you!'

Jack smiled. 'Do not be sorry, sweetheart, you have helped me more than you know,' he said quietly.

She met his eyes. 'Truly?' she asked him. She never knew when he was being honest with her.

'Aye, and if it had not been for you, sweetheart I would have died that night. I will not forget that, Elizabeth.'

She cuffed her eyes. Why did she still feel like she was failing him?

'You are not angry?' she asked.

Jack shook his head. 'You said you would stay with me for a little while,' he said, 'but I think we both knew you would never stay for the winter and anyway, as you say your child would soon be due and I am not sure even you could get us out of that!'

He tightened his grip on her hand and the cold of his rings pressed against her fingers.

'You are not coming with me, are you?' she asked, though she already knew what his answer would be.

'I cannot,' he said. 'I can serve Warwick better by staying in Edward's household and reporting all I can. And now I am useful to them.'

Elizabeth's throat tightened. How many times had she wished to be free of Jack? But now, when it came to it, she did not want to lose him.

'Say nothing, sweetheart,' he said with an eloquent look, 'it is better.' He let go of her hand and rose from the bed. 'I will make the arrangements.'

'But you will not come with me?' Elizabeth asked him again.

He turned to look at her and she saw sadness in his eyes. He shook his head. 'No sweetheart.'

She saw him swallow thickly.

'Best that I do not, for when you get to London...' He did not finish the sentence, but swept his cloak up quickly and swung it over his shoulder. 'I must speak with Jehan,' he said. 'There are yet more acquaintances I must renew.'

Elizabeth bit her lip to prevent a sob shaking her resolve.

Jack's boots thudded towards the door and she heard the latch click.

Through blurred vision she looked after him.

He hung on the latch as always, waiting for her to look at him. He gave her his disarming smile and then pulled the door between them.

Elizabeth put her face in her hands, glad that he was not here to see her cry. If she had been asked what he was to her, she would have found it difficult to answer; not a lover, not a brother and somehow not even a friend, for there were so many secrets she knew he kept from her still, for what other acquaintances did he have that she did not know of? And yet in a way he was all of these: the man her father had chosen for her. And how could she face the journey to England without him at her side?

BRUGES HARBOUR OCTOBER 1470

Gulls cried out into the bright morning. Elizabeth breathed in the welcome smell of the ocean and her heart thudded with excitement: she was going home.

She watched as Jack spoke at length to the ship's captain. The man nodded as Jack talked and periodically glanced to where she was waiting in breathless silence. It seemed strange to think that she would finally be leaving Jack behind.

She admired the way he moved sinuously towards her. The wind caught the liripipe of his chaperon and ruffled his dark curls at his collar. He smiled as he reached her, but the smile did not brighten his dark eyes as it usually did.

'All is well, sweetheart,' he said with forced cheerfulness. 'They will be loaded soon.'

As she looked into his eyes, Elizabeth's chest tightened. 'Thank you, Jack,' she said through a dry throat. 'I will not forget you.'

Jack gave her a rueful smile and held out his arm for her. 'Come,' he said.

They began to walk slowly to where the little ship was moored.

An uneasy silence settled between them and Elizabeth did not know how to break it. Jack too seemed reluctant to give voice to his thoughts. She smiled inwardly; she already knew what they would be.

As they reached the quayside they stopped. The sea pounded against the wall beneath them and spray splashed in their faces. Elizabeth licked the salt from her lips and as she turned, she met Jack's gaze.

She breathed deeply and shook her head. 'Jack, you must let me go,' she whispered. 'You know it is Warwick I must be with, I have never said otherwise.'

Jack nodded and dropped his gaze for a moment. He swallowed deeply and she watched the seductive ripple of his throat. Then he met her look through his lashes. Elizabeth knew she should look away, but somehow she couldn't force her eyes from his.

Slowly Jack leaned towards her, his eyes flicking from her eyes to her lips and then back again.

Elizabeth's breathing quickened.

Jack brought his hands up to frame her face. 'Adieu, then,' he whispered. He held her gaze for ten wild heartbeats and then gently placed his lips on hers. A shudder rippled through her. There was no challenge, no fight for control of her, just a beautiful deep kiss that melted the marrow in her bones. Tears stung her eyes and she forced herself to draw back from him. They stared at each other and Jack's mouth twitched into a faint smile.

Elizabeth looked down; it would have been so easy to stay; somehow leaving him was now the harder option. She twisted one hand in the other. 'Here,' she said shakily as she held out his mother's ring. 'I have looked after it well, as you bade me.'

Jack shook his head. 'Keep it a little while longer, sweetheart,' he said huskily. 'Our marriage cannot end here.'

Elizabeth reeled as if from a sudden blow. 'What do you mean?' she asked him. 'You know I go to be with Warwick.'

'I know what you wish,' Jack said, 'but you must think before you do.'

Elizabeth furrowed her brows.

'Sweetheart, I need you to still be my wife.'

Elizabeth's stomach lurched. Another of Jack's tricks, she thought angrily, but the look on his face was pleading.

'When you go to London, God alone knows who will be there,' Jack continued seriously. 'Warwick has not destroyed all Edward's men; many will still hold their old offices and run their households as before. And it would only take one of them to learn that our marriage was a sham and to pass that news to Edward...' He held her gaze. 'Elizabeth, I would be uncovered!'

Elizabeth sucked in her breath.

'I am sorry if you thought you would finally be rid of me,' Jack said. 'By all means cuckold me with Warwick if you must, but do not tell anyone you are not my wife.'

'And what do I say to Warwick?' Elizabeth asked shakily, fighting against tears.

Jack shrugged. 'I cannot advise you there, sweetheart. I have said before that I think you should tell him all. He will forgive you anything.'

'Even sharing a bed with his spy?' Elizabeth asked sourly.

Jack looked down. 'Much has passed between us, that is true,' he said quietly. He ran his tongue over his lips. 'Much he does not need to know. You and I both know nothing really happened,' he said raising his gaze to hers. 'No one can say otherwise.'

'But what will he *think*?' Elizabeth asked frantically.

'He will think you are the perfect spy,' Jack said.

Elizabeth huffed. 'Higgins called me that!' she said angrily.

'Then he was right,' Jack said. 'You played your part perfectly. I ask only that you do so still. What you tell Warwick in your bed-chamber is up to you, but make sure you are alone when you speak to him. Remember sweetheart, as long as Edward is unde-feated, our lives are in danger.' He brought his hands up to grip her shoulders, compelling her attention. 'And mine depends on you.' His eyes pleaded his case. 'Please sweetheart, do this for me. Or if not for me, for Warwick, for you know it is he that I serve.'

Elizabeth chewed on her lip. What a fool she had been to think she was putting all this behind her and that she would be free to love Warwick as before!

Jack's eyes were still on her face. How could she refuse him, knowing that she could so easily send him to his death?

'Very well,' she whispered, 'I will do as you ask.'

Jack held her gaze for several heartbeats. 'Thank you,' he said softly.

Elizabeth nodded, but could say no more. Inside she was a mix-ture of emotions, all churning like the sea below them. She lis-tened to its constant pounding rhythm, held as if in a spell.

Jack stroked her cheek gently. 'Come sweetheart, say adieu,' he whispered. He drew her to him fiercely and Elizabeth felt him shiver in her embrace. '*Pensez de moi*,' he whispered against her ear.

She looked up at him. His eyes were silvered with unshed tears.

Elizabeth's throat tightened.

'Go quickly,' Jack said huskily, 'before I change my mind.'

As Elizabeth boarded the ship she turned to look back at him. She saw once more the dark stranger, his arms folded across his chest. Tears stung her eyes as the ship began to move away from the quay and she was forced to admit that part of her did not want to leave him. How hard it was going to be to play the part of his wife when he was so far away. She ran her thumb over the ring on her finger, tracing the delicate pattern of the enamel; she should have known better than to think Jack de Laverton would leave her life so easily. She watched until she could no longer distinguish Jack from the blur of the harbour. Then she turned towards her cabin and wiping her tears away with the back of her hand, she wondered what on earth she was going to tell Warwick.

* * *

Jack watched the little boat until the glare of the horizon stung his eyes to tears; at least that was what he told himself. He turned briskly and walked back towards Senor Gruuthuse's house.

'She has gone, then?'

He hadn't noticed Lord Hastings leaning against the harbour wall; had he trusted them so little that he had come to make sure their departure was genuine; had he hoped to see them as they really were and not playing their parts?

'My lord,' Jack answered. 'She has.' The choked sound of his voice was genuine enough he thought, surely Lord Hastings could see that?

NARROW SEA OCTOBER 1470

The next day dawned brightly and Elizabeth was glad of it, for she had spent a sleepless night thinking about Jack. He still would not be banished from her thoughts as she stood at the rail, letting the wind tug at her headdress and hair and feeling the sting of salt on her cheeks. She felt guilty that she had deserted him when he needed her most. Just as the stakes had risen, with the arrival of Edward and his adherents she had left him to fend for himself. But then she couldn't have kept up the appearance of a growing pregnancy for much longer. Jack knew that; Jack understood. No, Jack understood more than he had said, for didn't he know her better than anyone? She was sorry for the pain she had caused him, but hadn't she always told him it would be so; that she would one day return to Warwick? Yet in some ways Jack had the greater claim on her. What would Warwick say if he learned of Sir Robert's betrothal of her? Would it matter to him? Surely no one could make her honour that promise, could they? But what if they did? Would Jack as a husband be such an unpleasant prospect? Had she not learned enough about marriage to know that even her mother might now approve of Jack with his courtly connections? She didn't know the answers, but the questions kept returning unbidden to her mind; not that any of it mattered now. Jack was in Bruges and she was on her way to England. Mayhap they would not even meet again; for who knew how this war would end?

Elizabeth eyed the blackening sky with trepidation. The sailors had begun to stare at her as though she was somehow responsible for the rising storm and she could hear them muttering unhappily about how having women on board was unlucky, and she suspected that Jack must have paid them handsomely to take her. She stared back at them, but as the wind began to howl like a she-wolf she drew closer to the captain and lowered her gaze.

'I do not hold with such superstitions, Madame,' the captain said in reference to their mutterings. 'But they are ignorant folk,' he paused to catch her eyes; 'ignorant, superstitious folk, but very good sailors.'

Elizabeth forced a smile. 'I am glad to hear the latter captain, for it looks as though we will need all their skill if we are to outrun this storm.'

'Outrun it, Madame?' he asked her with an ironic laugh. 'We cannot outrun *this*!'

Elizabeth shivered, but it was not only the rising wind that made her do so; it was the captain's appraisal of their situation. How could this little ship hope to ride out a storm?

Elizabeth pulled her new cloak about her, and as she did so she thought of Jack, and how he had smiled as he had wrapped it around her shoulders in their chamber. She found herself wishing that he was here with her now. That he had affected her was undeniable, but quite how he had affected her still was not clear to her. He had teased and tormented her, flirted with her outrageously, his eyes bright with a lust he never denied, and yet he had not gone beyond the bounds of honour, and at times the warmth of his arms had been the only thing that had comforted her. Somehow in Jack's presence she had known that everything would be all right, for he had the ability to laugh in the face of danger and had cheated death at least twice that she knew of, as though he tempted and then twisted fate to his own will. But he was not here and she did not know if everything was going to be all right, and Christ's wounds, how she now missed him! She swallowed against the lump forming in her throat. A prayer to the Virgin was the only useful thing she could think of to do, and with still so many sins for which she needed absolution, would the Blessed Virgin heed her?

The captain's voice interrupted her musing. 'I would suggest Madame that you go below, before the weather worsens.' Fear twisted her guts. She followed the captain's glassy stare to where the sky had darkened beyond midnight shadow, even though it was only mid afternoon.

'Sir, I beg your leave to stay awhile,' Elizabeth shouted against the roar of the strengthening wind. 'I do not like the dark... and the cabin is so small.'

The captain shook his head. 'Go below, mistress,' he said firmly, 'and make sure everything in your cabin is tied down. Tightly.' He began to call instructions to his crew.

Elizabeth's eyes widened. Fear rooted her to the place beside the only man on board who did not blame her for the anger of the weather.

'Go *now*, Madame,' he shouted. 'This is a nasty beast of a storm. It is a wounded boar. Anything on deck not lashed down will not survive!' He shouted louder at his men and they called back to him and to each other, knowing that their survival depended on them working together as never before.

Elizabeth did not know which she feared the most, being trapped and sightless in a dark cabin below the water line, or being washed overboard to her death.

Eventually she managed to swallow down her claustrophobia and do as the captain had asked, but not before she had seen something in his eyes: fear!

Rain began to hiss on the deck as she struggled to walk to the cabin. The waves began to deepen, pitching her suddenly forwards as though she was drunk.

The little ship began to roll like a stricken whale and Elizabeth dived ungraciously for the relative safety of her cabin. With a crack like thunder one of the masts snapped under the weight of its own wet sails and as Elizabeth stared in disbelief the untamed canvas took at least two men off their feet and into the wild water.

'Jack, oh God, Jack!' she cried as she threw herself below deck. Was it a prayer, or a wish for him to be with her? She didn't know.

Once in the cabin Elizabeth quickly lashed everything down that she could, though her trembling fingers at first refused to remember any knots. Then, feeling helpless and alone, she searched in her purse for her rosary. As she slipped the icy beads through her fingers she noticed that there was something else there too; it was cold in her hands and at first she could not think what it might be; then her fingers tightened around it and she realized what it was, it was Edward's necklace! Jack must somehow have put it there! Then her heart almost stopped beating as she touched folded parchment; there was only one thing it could be: Edward's letter to Warwick! 'Oh, Jack!' she sobbed, guiltily, knowing that she had doubted him. Burning tears welled up in her eyes. 'Oh Blessed Virgin, please help me!' she cried. But why should the Virgin take note of her? Her only answer was the guttural roaring of wind and sea and she knew that she had been abandoned.

The lurching of the ship was so violent now that even leaning against the cabin wall she could no longer remain upright. She slid to a kneeling position and clutching her rosary tightly, knelt and prayed more fervently than ever before. Her knees ached from the hardness of the planks and she wondered if this was her final punishment for all her sins. Part of her wished for Warwick to be with her, but she was glad that he was not, for if she was to die in this maelstrom, it was better that she did so alone.

As the storm roared about her she found herself praying again; quietly at first but then, as her fear grew, she found herself shouting at the top of her voice. Soon she was on all fours like an animal. Her stomach rose to her throat and she retched until she was sick, but it made her feel no better for it seemed as though her stomach had remained there to choke her. She wiped her mouth on her sleeve and then, crawling like a fallen knight in battle, she wedged herself between her trunk and the hull. She did not know if that was a good thing to do or not, for in the midst of the deafening howl of the storm she could hear the screams and shouts of the sailors and the ominous splintering of wood. But she no longer cared, for she knew she was going to die alone in the darkness. She drew her feet up on the trunk, hugged her knees with her hands and brought her face to rest between her knees. Tears scorched her eyes and her stomach churned with the same turmoil as the sea. A loud crack made the boat shudder from bow to stern and Elizabeth knew that its back was broken. Huddled in her cabin like a beggar in winter, she gave herself to the elements and asked God to forgive her for her many sins and to protect those she would love until the last.

DOVER OCTOBER 1470

The seaweed lay fractured on the shoreline like part of a strange creature's skeleton, its ribs picked clean by scavengers.

'Must have been rough,' Thomas said eyeing the snapped stems and broken roots. 'Dragged up from the seabed that was.'

Robert met his gaze. 'Aye, pity anybody who was at sea last night,' he said. 'They'd have needed Saint Anne's protection and no mistake.'

Thomas flinched at his friend's words. True though they were, he hardly needed a reminder of what Elizabeth must have gone through...if she had come through it. He stared out at the ocean wistfully, as he had once stared out to sea looking for the sails of Warwick's ship; now he scanned the horizon for the sign of any ship at all. There was hardly a cloud in the sky today and he found it hard to believe the scale of the storm that had tortured the coast for the last two days like a howling nightmare. But the throng of wives, sisters and daughters waiting for news of their loved ones told a different story.

'Do you think she was in it, Tom?' Robert asked quietly.

Thomas shrugged. 'Warwick only knew from one of his agents that she was to leave Bruges three days ago.'

'Perhaps she never left, eh, and decided that she liked the usurper's company!' Robert said, evidently trying to lighten Thomas's mood.

'I'm going to speak to the harbour master,' Thomas said, ignoring Robert's attempt at humour.

Robert nodded. 'I'll wait with the men.'

Thomas had to push his way through a crowd of worried faces to reach the man in charge.

The man looked exhausted and was fending off frantic relatives as best as he could. When he saw Thomas he looked up and waved away several anxious womenfolk.

'Well, sir?' he said with a nod of his head. 'You'll not be interested in the small craft we have missing – those that were not wise or quick enough to outrun the storm?'

Thomas shook his head. 'Anything from across the Narrow Sea?' he asked through a husky throat.

The man shook his head. 'Nothing so far today, but with these tides it could be days before things turn up on our beaches.'

Thomas shivered at the thought of Elizabeth being shipwrecked or drowned.

'Are you expecting someone, sir?'

'I am not certain,' Thomas said. 'Anything from Bruges?'

There was a flicker of something in the man's sea-grey eyes.

'Yes?' Thomas asked hopefully as a knot began to form in his stomach.

'I don't know,' the man said evasively.

'But?' Thomas persisted.

The man let out a long sigh, almost like the moaning of wind over water. 'They would have had the worst of it, that is all.'

Thomas sucked in his breath as though he had been punched in the stomach.

'I'm sorry, sir, you'll have to wait and see,' the harbour master said. 'And pray.'

'Well?' Robert asked impatiently as Thomas joined him and the small escort of men. Thomas shrugged. 'No one knows,' he said heavily.

'Great!' Robert said sarcastically.

Thomas flashed him a wounded look. 'Rob,' he said softly, 'she could be dead.' The knot in his stomach tightened further and he thought he was going to be sick.

'Sorry,' Robert said, 'I only meant...well this isn't soldiering is it?'

'I know what you mean,' Thomas said evenly, 'but all soldiers need to learn patience! Didn't Will tell you it was a high virtue?'

Robert hung his head and looked suitably admonished.

'Send a messenger back to Warwick,' Thomas said.

'What?' Robert sounded surprised. 'And what shall we tell him? We don't know anything yet.'

'It tells him something doesn't it?' Thomas said crossly.

Robert still looked puzzled.

'It tells him that the Lancastrians aren't coming either!' That also made Thomas's heart sink, for he knew how much Warwick wanted Queen Marguerite and Prince Edouard to join him.

Robert nodded silently, evidently feeling foolish. Then he turned to go.

'Rob,' Thomas called him back. 'And find us lodgings while you're at it; it may be a couple of days before we know anything more.'

'And what are you going to do?' Robert asked him hesitantly.

'I'm going to do as the harbour master suggests...I'm going to wait.'

'Here?' Robert asked in disbelief. 'Amongst these...these women?'

'Here,' Thomas replied bluntly. Although he knew it wouldn't make any difference whether he was here or not, he thought he understood why the women needed to be at the harbour side. Walking away from the ocean was like abandoning Elizabeth and he couldn't do it.

Though he was a little surprised by his request, the harbour master was more than happy to find Thomas a place by his hearth, especially once he realized he was Warwick's man, or 'our great earl' as he referred to him. Thomas had seen for himself the great affection for Warwick amongst seafaring men and at this moment it was to his advantage too.

'You may wait as long as you like, sir,' he said, 'but I think there will be no ship come to port today.'

'I'll wait all the same,' Thomas said as he settled himself onto a small stool. Flames crackled and spat in the grate and Thomas found himself hypnotized by the smoky dance. His mind wandered as if in some meditation and he remembered the first time he saw Elizabeth, wild as a vixen in Wensley Forest. His stomach came up to his throat. Sweet Jesu, let her live, he thought, blinking his stinging eyes. 'The smoke,' he said hoarsely to the watching harbour master as he rubbed his sleeve over his face, 'just the smoke.'

The man nodded quietly. 'All you can do is watch and pray,' he murmured, 'and hope your prayers are answered.'

Jack lowered his eyes. It would do no good to challenge William Hastings; in fact it would do his cause great harm.

'Alone?' Hastings asked him again, as they stood together in his chamber, his voice pitched high with incredulity. 'When I saw your departure I had not realized there was no one at all with her!'

Jack fought the urge to retaliate. 'I am grateful for your concern, my lord, but my wife is much stronger than you suppose and she has no fear of the sea.' Jack thought of Elizabeth, standing at the rail for as long as they would allow her, sea spray stinging her cheeks to a blush, her eyes bright with excitement as she turned to him and her mouth wide in a laugh which made him want to kiss her. God's blood, he missed her so much already!

Hastings let out a deep sigh. 'I still cannot believe you would send her unaccompanied!'

Jack wanted to say that it was not exactly so; there were people who watched her for him, but that would be to tell Hastings too much. He bridled his tongue. 'My lord, I can see that you have need of good men here in Bruges and my wife and I wish our child to be born in England. You see then that I had no choice. Autumn is a cruel time to put to sea, my lord, but if she had waited any longer she would have been winter's captive. She would not do that.'

Jack saw a smile twitch Hastings's mouth.

'She is uncommonly brave, Master Thornton. You are a most fortunate man. But I would not have allowed my wife to do such a thing, especially not while a child quickened within her.'

Jack smiled. 'She is not your wife, my lord. She is mine.' He said it softly and with a pleasure that stirred his loins. He had seen the way both Hastings and Edward looked at Elizabeth, the way many men did, but he knew her better than all of them and for the moment she was his and he loved it.

'You are right, sir,' Hastings said. 'It is none of my concern.'

But Jack could see that there was concern there; what a pity Elizabeth had gone – there was something she could have exploited in this man.

'And you are right; our household has need of loyal men such as you,' Hastings continued. 'Your knowledge of Bruges and its people will be invaluable to us, and of course you shall be rewarded.'

Jack bowed elegantly. 'I am glad to be in your service,' he said smoothly.

Hastings smiled as he dismissed him, but as Jack left the room, he knew he was treading on dangerous ground. Hastings was no fool; Jack had seen the doubt in his eyes, as had Elizabeth, and already he would be making enquiries into Master Thornton of Yorkshire and his connections. Perhaps he had even sent to Amboise to find out about their marriage. His stomach turned over, danger prickled the hair at his nape. But the exiles' resources were too scarce to waste on such an errand, he thought and without Higgins... if only he had seen the bastard's body in the water! He had told Elizabeth he was dead because he was almost certain that the rogue must be. As he had said to her; no one could have survived the fall into the cold dark harbour; he was sure Higgins had been unconscious when he hit the water, he must have drowned! Now it was not only Elizabeth he was trying to reassure, for if Higgins was to walk through the door he would be undone and there would be no return for him from this; mayhap even Jehan would not be able to help him this time. So if he believed Higgins was dead why had Jack watched every passenger and every member of the crew board Elizabeth's little ship that day? He knew the answer: if Higgins ever got to her again he would never forgive himself.

DOVER OCTOBER 1470

It had been two days since Thomas had arrived in Dover. His fractious company were close to mutiny and even Robert had accused him of being selfish, putting his own feelings for Elizabeth before his duty to his lord.

Somehow Thomas had managed to swallow down the anger. He had expected more sympathy from Robert, but now he was starting to question his own judgement. Perhaps Robert was right and Elizabeth had never left Bruges at all and he was just wasting time.

Robert had never wanted to come on this journey, wanting only to be part of Warwick's personal household guard. But Thomas had asked for him and Warwick had acquiesced, his dark eyes clouded with worry. He had told Thomas to take whatever he needed and Thomas saw that if he had been able to, Warwick would have come himself, would have kept this vigil.

'We leave tomorrow,' Thomas had said sadly in answer to Robert's scowl. 'After Mass.'

Robert had shrugged ungraciously, but had seemed for the moment to be pacified and indeed had not complained to him about another day kicking his heels in the taverns. But now it was time to leave, Thomas wanted to ask for more time.

Robert gave him a stony look. 'It won't do any good, Tom,' he said as if reading Thomas's mind. 'There's no one here. Even the harbour master said they should have been here yesterday if...'

'If they were coming at all!' Thomas finished for him angrily. 'Yes, Rob I heard him!'

He mounted quickly. His sharp tug on the reins made his horse throw up its head, jangling its harness.

He glared at Robert and he looked down, a little ashamedly.

'We shall pass the harbour once more,' Thomas growled as he wheeled his courser round on its hocks.

Robert raised his head and Thomas thought he was going to question him. 'Aye, Tom,' he said impassively, 'one more time won't hurt.'

Thomas nodded his thanks and spurred the restless horse down the slope towards the dock.

The sprawl of women that usually inhabited the harbour master's doorway was gone. The door stood open, but there was no sign of him. A clamour of voices more shrill than the gulls drew Thomas's attention to the quayside where he saw that his small encampment had swelled to more than twice its usual number.

Thomas glanced at Robert who nodded eagerly.

Thomas dismounted quickly and threw the reins to Robert.

As he drew closer he realized that the noise was excited chatter and not the mournful wailing he had been dreading. Beyond the crowd he could see a twisted mast and tangled rigging. His skin tingled with expectation; this was not the fishing boat he had been expecting. It was all he could do not to break into a run. His heart hammered wildly at his throat. 'Please, God!' he whispered.

The harbour master was in the midst of the mêlée, his dark blue bonnet just visible.

'Sir!' Thomas called to him, but it was like shouting at a battle. 'Sir!' he called again and reached out for the man's shoulder.

The harbour master turned, and on seeing Thomas, his face brightened. 'Ah, Master Conyers, thank God!' he said. 'I think we have what you waited for!'

Thomas pushed his way to the front and gazed upon a sad sight.

The merchantman had only one intact mast. Most of her rails had been broken and by the way she was listing in the dock it was clear that she had taken on water.

'From Bruges?' Thomas asked hoarsely.

'Aye,' the harbour master beamed.

Thomas could hear little except his pounding heart. 'Passengers?' he croaked.

The harbour master nodded to where the gangplank had been laid between the battered ship and port.

Thomas fought against sudden tears.

She was limping and her gown was torn at both shoulder and hem. Her untamed hair swayed about her with every unsteady step like knotted rope, thick with seaweed, but it was true; Elizabeth was walking towards him.

Without a single thought to etiquette or protocol he ran down the quayside to meet her.

At first she did not seem to recognize him, and he wondered if the large purple bruise on her cheek was a sign that she had been knocked senseless.

'Elizabeth!' he called. 'Elizabeth!' he called again.

Slowly, as if hearing his voice in a dream, she turned wide eyes up to him.

After a few heartbeats she began to smile and he saw too that her eyes began to fill with tears.

Thomas threw his arms about her and she clung to him like a drowning sailor to a rock.

Her body began to quiver against him and he realized she was crying.

'It's all right, Elizabeth,' he whispered as he held her tightly. 'You are safe now. I've come to take you home.' His eyes stung with tears as he spoke and it was not just because she was crying; it was because he knew that once he reached London he would have to let her go again. He only hoped he did not regret it, for he knew she would find Warwick much changed; the cares of government weighed on him more heavily than new harness. He hoped Warwick would have time for the bright young woman who had risked everything to come to him; the court could be a

224

very cruel place these days, especially for those with Yorkist connections, and as Sir Robert Hardacre's daughter, Elizabeth had Yorkist connections stronger than most.

~EIGHT~

LONDON, WESTMINSTER PALACE OCTOBER 1470

This was not the London Elizabeth remembered. It had always been a noisy crowded place and the thick defining smell of the river had always been there, but it had not been like *this*.

Yellow-green fog choked London's throat, making everything damp and dismal. She brought her hand up quickly to cover her nose and mouth as they past the rotting body of a dog lying in the gutter. Even in the persistent October fug flies hummed about it. Elizabeth turned away. The incessant pulse of the city throbbed as it always did, broken only by the rusty screech of a tattered inn sign above her head.

Thomas turned his horse suddenly avoiding a pile of...of God-knows-what in the street. Elizabeth followed suit.

As they rode in silence she noticed that the people stared at them bleakly. Some even glared at them and she guessed it was the sight of Warwick's livery that made them do so.

She remembered how crowds used to gather at The Erber, eager for a glimpse of Warwick. They used to cheer and throw up their hats at the sight of him and his dazzling household coming home, but now all she saw were harsh eyes and there were no cheers, only muttered curses. She remembered too how they had come in their droves each day at breakfast to eat at Warwick's expense, each carrying away thick slices of meat for their families.

'Thomas,' she called softly, still trying to rid her nostrils of the stench of the dead dog. 'What is wrong? What has happened?'

Thomas turned in his saddle. His eyes met hers and she saw in them such hurt that he almost did not need to answer her.

'Londoners have short memories,' he said bitterly. 'Now they miss their king; the king who did nothing for them!' His voice was a low growl in his throat.

'Then why?' Elizabeth asked.

A wry smile twitched at Thomas's lips. 'Because King Edward owes them money!' he almost spat the words.

Elizabeth furrowed her brows. She did not understand.

'He owes the jewellers, the chandlers, the tailors, the bankers, God's breath he probably owes the whole damned city!'

'And Warwick cannot pay?' Elizabeth asked.

Thomas shook his head sadly. 'How can he? He has given almost all that he has to get this far. King Louis gave money grudgingly and then only after Warwick's smooth persuasion. And how much money do you think the exiled Lancastrians have? Or King Henry for that matter? And the Londoners will lend him no more until Edward's debts are paid.'

Elizabeth bit her lip. Warwick was in trouble. 'When will Queen Marguerite come?' The tone of her voice betrayed her anxiety.

'A good question,' Thomas said. His cheeks flushed pink with anger. 'Why indeed does she not come? Why not send her Prince Edouard to be the figurehead for government?'

Elizabeth knew the answer. 'Because she fears he may have an experience like mine only not come out of it so well,' she said. 'She feared she would lose him.'

Thomas's eyes narrowed. 'Edward would have come.'

Elizabeth could not disguise her shock at the mention of his name.

'Edward would have taken that chance,' he added. He looked away from her, back to the dissenting Londoners and their filthy streets as though he could not bear the thought that was in his mind. 'When he is ready Edward *will* take that chance,' he said through clenched teeth.

A cold shiver licked up Elizabeth's spine, but there was no time to question Thomas further, for the familiar shape of Westminster Palace loomed out of the green gloom.

* * *

Elizabeth had never seen King Henry before and she thought he could not be more different than Edward. Swathed in velvet and ermine he sat on the throne of power, wearing the same jewelled diadem and holding the glittering sceptre, yet he looked less like a king than any man in the room. Suddenly Elizabeth's heart stopped, for she noticed Warwick was by his side. He was animated, introducing the lords and ladies who had come to renew their vows of allegiance. As each bowed at his feet Warwick leant close to Henry, evidently advising him on how to proceed with each. Then he turned and caught Elizabeth's look. He held her gaze, his eyes lingering on her face so that she could not hold in a smile and then, like the sun breaking through clouds, Warwick returned it. Elizabeth's eyes filled with tears. It was the same feeling she had experienced in the Great Hall at Warwick Castle, when she alone had stood before him and his eyes had met hers; she loved him then and she loved him still.

Thomas drew her aside, giving them the opportunity to approach Warwick without the full glare of the court upon them.

Warwick excused himself from Henry's presence and came towards them and Elizabeth thought that she would faint.

Warwick spoke to Thomas, and his voice was like the sweetest music to Elizabeth. 'I thank you Thomas,' he said beaming, 'for bringing her safely to me again!'

Thomas bowed low and without a word withdrew from them.

Elizabeth could scarcely breathe as Warwick turned to face her; how she had prayed for this moment. She wanted to rush into his arms and let him hold her close and never let go of her again. But she could not. He reached forward and wiped a tear from her cheek gently. He traced his finger down to the line of her jaw and it was as if he had stroked her with fire. Yet it had been so gentle, so very gentle that she half thought she had imagined the caress, but the sudden thumping of her heart told her she had not. Then he took hold of her hand and raised it to his lips. His smiling eyes never left hers and she saw in them the same passion and longing that she too felt.

'My sweeting,' he whispered. 'God knows how I have wished for you by my side these past months.' Warwick's voice was low, barely audible, like the hush of a summer breeze in the willow trees. Her heart fluttered wildly.

'And I you, Richard,' she said softly, her voice suddenly tremulous. She curtseyed before him, to perpetuate the formal appearance of their meeting. 'And I must speak with you as soon as ever you can break away,' she added.

'Speak with me? I hope we shall have more than just conversation!' he laughed.

She had almost forgotten his low musical laugh and she smiled at the sudden thought of him naked beside her. But how could that be? She was so unworthy of his love! And what of Jack? 'No, Richard,' she said, trying to gather her thoughts and ignore the effect he was having on her; the effect he always had on her. 'There is something I must tell you.' She needed his forgiveness if they were to have any future together; she had to make him understand. And if she could not...she dared not contemplate it.

He smiled at her again. 'Sweeting, I will hear all you have to tell me tonight and you can say whatever it is as many times as you wish between then and morning, for I swear I shall be yours alone!'

'Richard,' she whispered, 'must you go now?'

He smiled. 'We shall have supper together tonight, sweeting, I swear it.' He gave her an incandescent look that promised much beyond food. He drew her fingers slowly to his lips, prolonging the intimacy between them. They were soft and warm as he kissed each finger in turn and all the while he held her in his molten gaze.

Elizabeth's blood thumped in her ears. God, how she had missed him!

'Until tonight,' he breathed. Then he let go of her hand, gave a sweeping bow and returned to King Henry's side. Henry looked up at him and his pinched and anxious face softened as Warwick spoke to him gently.

Elizabeth turned to Thomas. He was staring at the floor. He shifted his weight from one foot to the other and fidgeted with his gloves.

Elizabeth gave a little cough and he looked up. Seeing that Warwick had returned to Henry he said, 'Come, I shall take you to your lodgings.'

BRUGES OCTOBER 1470

'It shall be done as you wish, my lord,' Jack said as he swept an elegant bow to William Hastings. As he left him he thought it was as though they were at Westminster instead of the exiled court in Senor Gruuthuse's house.

Walking swiftly, Jack sent a man for his things and another to saddle his horse. He slipped Hastings's letter inside his doublet and smiled as it nestled gently next to one of his own – one for Warwick. Not without a little guilt he pinned the gilded livery badge Lord Hastings had given him to his coat; it would serve no purpose to philosophise upon it now, he knew he had no choice but to use the protection it brought him.

Spur pricked flesh as Jack tore through the countryside like a March gale over Wensleydale. He had ridden this road so many times recently that both he and his courser knew the route to

Duke Charles's court as well as they knew the road from Laverton to Ripon and the villagers knew not to get in his way.

More magnificent than anything he had come across in England or France, Duke Charles's court was at last opening its doors tentatively towards Edward and Jack realized that this was the first hesitant step along the road to Edward's invasion of England. Jack knew he had no choice but to comply with Edward's and Hastings's wishes if he was not to give himself away, but yet he felt a twist of guilt at helping Edward ingratiate himself with his erstwhile indifferent brother-in-law and there were also acquaintances here he currently did not wish to renew, though, as he had told Elizabeth, he knew at some point he must.

Rain stung his face and pelted the road like stones as he galloped the last mile and it did nothing to lighten his mood. Cold snatched the strength from his fingers and his knees began to ache and he was glad when finally he clattered into the large courtyard. Cressets burned like tiny suns, banners flew from every turret and lights shone from every glittering window.

The guards eyed him through narrowed stares and barked their salutations. Though they knew him well enough it was evident they would not trust any Englishman, even one so caught up in the business of their duke.

Jack was ushered into a quiet antechamber. The arras glittered in the candlelight and fire snapped in the grate. Jack began to regain some feeling in his hands and steam rose from his clothes as he stood as close to the blaze as he could without burning himself. He sipped the hot, spiced wine and it ran like liquid flame into his belly. He placed the jewelled goblet down onto a table and, chewing at his thumb, paced another turn of the room. Jack's mind should have been working on his mission; on his words to Duke Charles on Edward's behalf for the five hundred crowns a month allowance he was giving him, and on the grateful expression of thanks for agreeing to aid them. But it wasn't. His mind had flown to England where his heart lay with Elizabeth and his fealty lay with Warwick and he wondered what had happened between them. As long as she was happy it didn't matter, he told himself, but his nervous pacing told him that it did.

Quick footsteps in the hallway broke his reverie as a moment later Duke Charles and his entourage spilled into the room in a torrent of coloured silks and furs. Jack dropped to one knee.

Duke Charles was lean and tall and about Jack's age. His hair was as dark and curly as Jack's but he wore it much shorter and his cheeks were as smooth as a woman's, making Jack conscious of the dark growth of beard he always seemed to have these days.

'How fare's my brother of England?' Charles asked. The voice was soft, yet marked with authority.

Jack paused before answering. 'Very well, my liege, I thank you, and he begs leave to know when he may come to discuss his plans with you.' He held out Hastings's letter.

'With me?' Charles gave a slight inclination of his head and one of his richly attired companions took the letter from Jack.

'Yes, my liege, with you. He requests to come into your presence.'

The sigh was almost imperceptible, but Jack caught it. Duke Charles smiled with his mouth alone and Jack saw that it was a smile of cunning.

'*With* me, monsieur?' He repeated. The grey eyes flashed at Jack and the rich collar of the *Toison d'Or* sparkled as Charles circled him.

There was a quiet ripple of laughter amongst the gathering.

Jack's cheeks burned.

'I am so busy with the English that I cannot yet meet with him.'

Jack understood. This meant that Charles was prevaricating; still seeking a diplomatic solution which would ensure that perhaps his cousins of Lancaster had the throne, and which would see Edward lose everything.

'Of course, my liege,' Jack said neutrally, 'I understand.' The Lancastrian Duke of Somerset was still his guest. How could Edward come while he was still here?

Charles smiled a little more broadly. 'You are however right to remind me, as my wife does constantly, that I have not yet received him at court. I shall instruct Senor Gruuthuse accordingly.'

Jack's stomach curled at the thought of the duchess, Edward's sister. He tried to put her from his mind.

Duke Charles turned. Jack bowed his head; he knew this was to be the end of his audience. 'My liege,' he said as Charles and his followers swept from the room. Jack noticed Jehan at the rear of

231

the group; he gave him a solemn nod and then a broad smile. As the door opened Jack heard music and laughter; evidently Charles was not too pressed by the English to forgo his legendary revelry and Jack also noted that even as Edward's ambassador, he was not to be invited to the feast.

After a light supper of cold beef Jack was shown to his lodgings; a dormitory shared by several knights of Charles's mesnie. Mentally he prepared himself for the barracking he would surely get as an exiled English knight at the Burgundian court. But the room was empty; they were evidently partaking of their lord's hospitality and Jack was glad of it. He plumped the straw-filled mattress and seeing no obvious evidence of fleas, he settled himself into the farthest corner to wait for daylight. As he lay there he thought on his own predicament. He liked William Hastings and liked in particular his polite enquiries as to whether Elizabeth was yet delivered of their child, but he could not stay in his service forever. Sooner or later Edward would invade England and then Jack would be forced to declare his hand. He turned on his shoulder testily and heard the scurrying of mice in the corner. He wondered for how much longer he could wear Edward's white rose.

He was still awake when they came for him.

WESTMINSTER PALACE OCTOBER 1470

Elizabeth could not keep still. Her pulse was racing and her skin tingled with expectation.

'Please my lady,' Alyson said with a note of irritation she could not keep from her voice.

Elizabeth took a deep breath.

'You are as nervous as a cat,' Alyson observed, 'and you have not eaten the sweetmeats my lord Warwick sent you,' she added, with a nod to the gilded tray on the table. 'Are you ill my lady? Shall I ask for the physician?'

'No Alyson, thank you. It is nothing any physician can cure,' Elizabeth said truthfully. She bit her lip. She had to remember what she had learned in France and Bruges; she must trust no one. She could not confide her anxiety in Alyson; for once she spoke of it, what other secrets might she let past her lips? And had Alyson's loyalties been wholly transferred from Edward to Henry? How could she know? 'I am not hungry,' she said. She laced her fingers together across her belly to try to keep her hands from twitching. She noticed the cold band of Jack's ring; a reminder of what was at stake.

'But my lady, the cooks have prepared a wonderful supper.'

Elizabeth smiled. Warwick had promised her an intimate supper, yet even this was now the knowledge of the whole household. Jack had been right.

'There my lady,' Alyson said with some pride as she fastened a gold collar about Elizabeth's neck. 'You look like a queen!'

'Certainly it must look better than green damask trimmed with rabbit!' Elizabeth said dryly, reminding Alyson of the last time she had attended her.

Alyson lowered her eyes.

Elizabeth turned to study her own reflection. She barely recognized the woman staring back at her. She seemed so elegant and refined: not a trace of wild hair beneath the hennin and veil, not a crease in the black damask gown. She wondered if this was really how Warwick wanted her to be.

She rose from the seat and Alyson moved to stand behind her.

'You look very beautiful, my lady,' Alyson said.

She spoke very gently, but Elizabeth heard the undertone.

Suddenly Elizabeth realized how stupid she had been! It was only her first day here and already she had almost failed! She had to rescue the situation.

She looked back at Alyson quickly. 'Alyson, can I trust you?' she asked.

'Of course, my lady,' Alyson said, trying to hide the eagerness from her voice.

'I do not know how to tell you this...' Elizabeth said hesitantly.

Alyson laid a hand on Elizabeth's arm.

Elizabeth met her gaze. 'You think I am Warwick's lover, do you not?'

Alyson gasped, but Elizabeth could see that she was not in the least bit surprised at the revelation.

'Why, mistress!' Alyson exclaimed.

Elizabeth fought to keep the smile from her lips provoked by Alyson's acting, which would not have been out of place in a mummers' play!

'I was, Alyson. But whilst I was in France I met someone else,' she hesitated and wrung at her hands, twisting Jack's ring on her finger.

Alyson's eyes widened at the gesture. 'You married him?'

Elizabeth nodded; heat flushed her cheeks.

Alyson gripped her arm, all pretence of decorum abandoned. 'Oh tell me mistress, please!' she said.

Elizabeth flicked her eyes down demurely for a moment.

'I swear I will tell no one,' Alyson promised.

'His – his name is John Thornton,' Elizabeth said. 'Though I call him Jack.' She failed to hide her smile at the thought of Jack, and she thought of Jack as she had first seen him at Lazenby, when just the sight of him had made her breathless. 'We were married at Amboise, but...' she gulped for effect, 'but Warwick does not know of him!'

Alyson gasped again.

'I know Alyson, what a dreadful situation! But I cannot reveal my husband because he... he is with King Edward in Bruges!'

Elizabeth was astonished as Alyson hugged her. 'Oh mistress! You should not have come back,' Alyson said.

'I had no choice; Warwick's men were waiting for me at Dover. And after the storm what else could I do but allow them to escort me here?'

Alyson nodded.

'Alyson, I am at a loss what to do. I cannot refuse Warwick's attentions or tell him of Jack, for what would become of me? I have nowhere else to go.'

'Oh my lady!' Alyson said with genuine sympathy.

'I have no choice...' Elizabeth said, swallowing thickly. She wondered if Jack would be impressed by her acting.

Alyson searched the floor for a moment. 'I can tell my lord Warwick you are ill, my lady; say you have a flux!'

'Thank you Alyson,' Elizabeth said with a thin smile, 'but I cannot hide in my chamber forever. Sooner or later he would come to find me.'

Alyson nodded again.

'You will not give me away, will you?' Elizabeth asked. 'For my husband's sake?'

'No, my lady,' Alyson said. 'I swear it.'

'And there is something else, Alyson,' Elizabeth said, remembering the most difficult part of her charade in Bruges.

'My lady?'

'You must not tell another living soul,' Elizabeth stammered.

'I swear, my lady!'

Elizabeth bit her lip and tears stung her eyes. 'And in that storm I – I lost my unborn child!'

* * *

Elizabeth walked slowly along the passageway to Warwick's apartment. She had little choice, her new shoes were the epitome of fashion, but the toes were so long and pointed that she was terrified of either catching them in her gown or stepping on them. She was grateful she did not have to climb any stairs for she had not mastered that yet. She held her head high, not from any degree of arrogance for she felt quite the reverse, but the exceptionally tall hennin made her tip her chin upwards to balance it.

As she waited outside the door she clasped her hands together and whispered a prayer. There was so much she needed to tell Warwick, including her decision, but so much she did not dare. She took a steadying breath as she heard her name announced. She had to remember what Jack had said: tell him nothing unless you are alone with him.

As she walked into the room she gasped. Everywhere candles glittered like diamonds. Opulent tapestries covered most of the walls and where they did not the wall seemed to be covered in red damask.

Her heart drummed uncontrollably as she was led to where Warwick was seated.

She tried not to look at him, for she was sure if she did her heart would burst. Instead she studied the table. At first it did not seem to be made from wood, for the finely carved and gilded roses about its base twisted with such natural symmetry that Elizabeth thought they could almost have been from the arbour at Scarsdale.

She ran her tongue over her dry lips and, keeping her eyes lowered, she curtseyed as she was introduced to him.

She thought she would faint when he spoke her name.

Only once she was seated beside him did she dare to look at his face.

He smiled.

Elizabeth was hot and cold in the same moment. She wanted to touch him, kiss him, love him, but she knew she could not.

His smile broadened. 'I know what you are thinking,' he said. 'That will come later.'

Elizabeth's cheeks burned and she returned his smile. 'Was it so obvious?' she asked coyly.

'Indeed it was,' he said. 'And I cannot believe we have not been together since Barfleur. It seems like a lifetime ago.'

In many ways it was part of an old existence. 'So much has happened,' she said. 'There is so much I have to tell you.'

He reached for her hand and drew it to his lips.

Elizabeth shivered with pleasure at the touch, as if he had run his finger down her naked spine.

'Richard,' she breathed. It was both an exclamation of her need and an appeal for him not to tease her; she could barely keep her longing under control. Yet underneath, the guilt was there. The fact remained she had betrayed him.

He smiled as he let her hand go and she wanted to cry out in frustration that she could not yet be in his arms.

Two servants waited with bowls of rosewater and at an almost imperceptible nod from Warwick they came and washed their hands for them, wiping them on the softest linen cloths. With equal formality they brought bread and the finest Burgundian wine.

Elizabeth sipped tentatively from the gilded goblet and noticed Warwick was watching her over the rim of his. The look he gave her reached straight to her core. Her cheeks grew hotter still.

Once the fine silver dishes of sweet and savoury delicacies had been brought, the servants withdrew to the edge of the room. Elizabeth released her tense grip on her drink, placing her cup gently back on the white cloth.

She ate tentatively from a dish of venison.

Warwick watched her silently through his lashes.

Her stomach curled with desire and she could not help but smile at him.

She lowered her head, embarrassed that her lust was so transparent. The hennin moved of its own accord and she resolved to try to keep her head still.

'You have had adventures of your own since we were last together,' he said.

Elizabeth's throat tightened. 'I am sorry I left you, Richard,' she said softly. 'That was wrong of me, but you must believe me that I had no choice.'

His hand brushed hers and she looked up at him. His eyes were wide with compassion. He linked his fingers into hers and her skin prickled. 'I know,' he said gently.

Elizabeth saw sadness in his eyes and wondered exactly what it was he knew.

'Master Higgins,' she said hesitantly, 'he...'

'Jack killed him, did he not?'

Elizabeth gasped. How could Warwick know this unless... 'Jack?' she whispered. Even now she was not free of Jack's presence.

Warwick smiled. 'He is good, Elizabeth,' he said and then corrected himself. 'Nay, he is the best. He has sent me word of much that happened, but it is what he did not say that interests me.' His tone was still gentle, still rich with understanding.

'I cannot say anything, Richard,' she said hesitantly. She glanced quickly at the servants. 'Not here. Not now.'

Warwick laughed and Elizabeth watched the smile touch his eyes. 'I see Jack has taught you well!' Then his face darkened. 'You should not have to learn such dark arts,' he whispered. 'I am sorry for it.' Then he raised his voice a little. 'But we should talk now of happier times, and what is to come for us!'

Elizabeth lowered her gaze, knowing any future they had together now looked bleaker than a Wensleydale moor in winter. All hung on what she would tell him tonight.

'I think we cannot speak so,' she said sadly. She met his eyes. 'Not yet. There is much I need to tell you first.'

Warwick's lips tightened. 'I see,' he said. 'Leave us,' he commanded the servants.

Elizabeth perused the tablecloth as if it were a beautiful tapestry worthy of such attention. Her heart pounded; she could hear her pulse in her ears.

'Well, Elizabeth,' Warwick said as the doors closed. 'What is it that you cannot say before anyone else?'

Elizabeth took a composing breath. She looked up. 'I love you, Richard,' she said. 'And I need you to understand that before I tell you anything else. I would give anything for us to be together, to be away from all this,' she raised her hand in a vague gesture, 'from all this!' she repeated. Her eyes began to sting.

Warwick leaned forward. His eyes widened reassuringly.

'I had no choice but to go with Higgins, for he knew a terrible secret about me, one I wanted to tell you, but could never find the right moment to. It is such a secret that I feared it would break your heart and that you would hate me and...' she fought a sob tightening her throat, '...and I could not bear you to hate me!'

'Hush, sweeting,' Warwick said grasping her hand. 'I know already!'

A sudden pain burned in her chest like fire. 'But – but how?' she asked incredulously. Had Jack broken his word?

Warwick looked deep into her eyes. 'Higgins left me a letter when he took you away from me... it told me all,' Warwick said in a voice which slashed Elizabeth to her core. So Higgins had betrayed her as Jack had predicted.

'You know?' she asked. He knew of Clarence! What must he think of her?

'I do.' Tears were bright in his eyes. 'And to lose a child is heartbreaking, you are right, but it is not your fault, my love. How could you think I would hate you, when you are my life-blood?'

Elizabeth heard his voice break with emotion and saw tears moisten his cheeks.

'Which – which child?' she did not understand. How could her imaginary child with Jack cause him so much pain? She drew back from him. 'Richard, what do you mean, it wasn't my fault?'

He cuffed the tears from his face and stared at her with glassy eyes.

'Dear God, you do not know,' he whispered.

Elizabeth knitted her brows. 'Richard!' she pleaded.

'God forgive me!' Pain shredded his voice.

'Richard, what is it? What is wrong?'

'So Higgins has had his revenge!' Warwick said. 'Forgive me, sweeting,' he said as he leant his head against her shoulder. 'Please, Richard, tell me what is wrong.'

Warwick cast his eyes heavenwards for a moment. Then he sucked in his breath as he gathered his strength. Sad eyes met hers. 'At Ellerton, sweeting, when you were ill, do you remember what happened?'

'I – I fell from the wall,' Elizabeth said shakily.

'The nuns did not tell you what they told Higgins, my love,' he said slowly.

Elizabeth began to tremble.

Warwick locked his gaze onto hers. 'They did not tell you that you lost our child, Elizabeth: our son!'

238

Elizabeth's chest constricted as though she was in a vice. Her eyes stared blindly and her mouth fell open in a silent cry.

Warwick gathered her into his arms. The perfect headdress slipped from her head and onto the floor.

'My love, I am so sorry,' he said as he held her. 'I thought you knew.'

Elizabeth could not breathe. Ragged sobs shook her; no wonder she had felt so empty when she left Ellerton. No wonder she had understood Isabel's loss so well! Instinctively she knew this was true.

'He was too small to live,' Warwick whispered as he stroked her hair.

'And...and you thought I had kept this from you?' Elizabeth stammered. She looked up at him through blurred vision.

'At first I thought you had tried to spare me the pain, but I see now that you never knew of him. Forgive me my love for hurting you.'

She pressed her head to his chest and the tears came through her lashes like rain. There was a cold dark emptiness within her, like the deep unfathomable blackness of the longest winter night and she wondered if even Warwick's love could light it for her.

'You were right to tell me, Richard,' she sobbed. 'It was wrong of them to keep it secret.'

Warwick tightened his embrace. 'I never meant this to happen,' he said against her cheek.

'But Higgins did,' she said. She realized it was exactly as Higgins had planned it. How could Higgins have done this to her? She pushed her face against Warwick, brought her arms tightly about his waist as if she would hug him forever.

Warwick breathed deeply. He held her close and planted soft kisses on her head. 'I am sorry, sweeting. How oafish you must think me.'

Elizabeth pressed her head to his chest as though she would listen to his heart for all eternity.

Eventually she spoke. 'I think now I need to sleep.' She doubted sleep would come, so ragged were her thoughts, but she needed to be alone. Christ in Heaven, she had lost their child! 'I must go,' she stammered.

Warwick helped her to her feet. He thumbed her tears from her cheeks gently and then kissed her forehead tenderly. 'You do not want to be with me?' he whispered huskily.

Elizabeth heard the pain in his voice. She shook her head, unable to meet his eyes. 'No, Richard,' she said. 'I – I cannot...tomorrow perhaps...please forgive me.' Her voice failed her. She turned.

'Sweeting, I would forgive you anything,' he said as she walked away from him.

Elizabeth blinked hot tears down her cheeks. She wondered if that was really true. Could he forgive the other secrets she had wanted to confess?

* * *

Elizabeth dismissed Alyson with a wave of her hand. In her current state of mind she could not trust herself to speak to her, in case she said something that would bring disaster; though what could be a greater calamity than this?

She saw concern furrow Alyson's brow. 'But my lady, I can make you a hot bath,' she said, obviously assuming that Warwick had forced himself upon her.

Elizabeth shook her head, unable to speak.

She put the oak door between them. For a moment she stayed there with her back pressed against the hard wood and her fingers curling into the carving. Her chest heaved rapidly as sobs fought to control her. A wave of nausea spiralled up from her core and the room began to spin. Tentatively she walked to her bed and fell upon it, craving solitude, needing its sanctuary. Her eyes burned so fiercely that she thought she would cry, but somehow she was too numb, too cold, too lost. Her hand slipped to her belly, as if to confirm the emptiness of her womb. It should have been the most natural thing in the world, she thought, to become a mother, though from her own mother's experience with Edmund she knew it was not always an easy thing to do. But what sort of a mother would she have made – she hadn't even known she was with child; neither had she felt his loss! But she felt it now: raw pain twisted her insides into a mêlée. She was hollow, like a cored apple. Like Eve she had tasted the forbidden fruit and now had brought herself disaster because of it! Was this not the punishment she deserved? So many things she had done; so many sins and none of them confessed, none of them absolved!

Suddenly she remembered the response for the Office of the Dead:

Peccantem me quotidie et non poenitentem, timor mortis conturbat me. Quia in inferno nulla est redemption, Miserere mei, Deus, et salva me.

'Sinning daily and not repenting, the fear of death disturbs me. Because there is no redemption in hell, have mercy on me, O God, and save me.'

But it seemed as though God was not listening to her; it was as though her spirit had died and her soul was lying frozen in a forsaken tomb. Perhaps her soul was only sleeping and Warwick could awaken it. He was, she realized, her only hope. He must never know how completely she had failed him.

BURGUNDIAN COURT OCTOBER 1470

Jack ran his hand over his bruised cheek. His jaw and lip hurt too, but he could not help smiling, even though it made him wince; the man who had punched him was now missing several teeth and was probably nursing cracked ribs too and at least one of his accomplices was a victim of Jack's swift knife.

Raucous laughing sounded outside his cell.

Jack walked stiffly towards the door and looked out through the bars. Two guards were drinking and playing cards. Jack shook his head; that would never happen in the Earl of Warwick's household, he thought, but these were Burgundians, not Englishmen he reminded himself.

He sighed and moved back to the pile of straw that was to be his bed. It stank of stale urine and was evidently home to several rats, but it was either that or the filthy stone floor.

In spite of the smell he sank down onto the straw like a poleaxed ox; he needed to pull his scattered wits together and try to work out why he was here.

He had only been contemplating his predicament for a matter minutes when he heard the rasp of the bolt on his cell door.

The door swung outwards painfully and a burly captain stepped in.

'On your feet!' he growled.

Jack eyed the man sullenly from his bed. Grey stubble peppered the man's chin above which black teeth glowered. By his grim expression his mood was going to be even worse than his teeth.

241

'Get up, English scum!' the captain roared, drawing his sword. 'It will not trouble me to finish you here.'

'But it will trouble your master,' Jack said smoothly, recognizing the badge of Duke Charles on the man's livery coat.

The man took a step towards him and Jack began to rise reluctantly.

The captain came close to him and pushed his face into Jack's. Jack recoiled at the stench of the man's breath.

'You think because you are a favourite with the duchess our duke will spare you?' the man sneered.

'The duchess?' Jack asked innocently. His stomach turned over – how could they know of his connection to the duchess?

The captain gave a humourless laugh. 'Ah, my pretty lad!' he said shaking his head. 'You will not be so pretty when we have finished with you!' He grabbed Jack's arm and pulled him towards the door. He threw Jack at the opening.

Jack lost his balance and landed on all fours in the dirt. He found his feet quickly and narrowly avoided feeling the captain's boot in his back.

When he reached the door the other guards were waiting for him. One gripped his collar and pushed him ahead into the darkness.

The smell of ordure stung Jack's nostrils as he walked unsteadily behind his captors; if there was one part of his body that did not ache he had yet to discover it. Dark slime dripped incessantly from the walls and it sounded like a strange and ghostly heartbeat.

Jack chewed on his swollen lip and tried to quieten his thumping heart. If they really had discovered the truth about the duchess, then perhaps the duke had ordered his capture, in which case he could expect nothing but a slow and painful death.

NINE

WESTMINSTER PALACE OCTOBER 1470

The night candle had all but burned out when Elizabeth heard the footsteps. She saw a shadow pass in front of the window.

Elizabeth gasped.

The shadow moved closer.

She let out her breath as the shadow met the candlelight.

The bed sighed as Warwick sat down beside her. Elizabeth looked into his eyes.

'Forgive me sweeting,' he said huskily. 'I could not sleep.'

He covered her hand with his. It was warm and offered the promise of comfort she craved so much.

'You should not have come,' she said softly. 'Alyson is loyal to Edward's queen.'

Warwick smiled. 'And she will think me your vile tormentor, no doubt?'

Elizabeth nodded.

He leant forward, putting an arm across her to support his weight. Then he lowered his face to hers. He held her eyes with his and then kissed her slowly. 'There is nothing we cannot face together, sweeting.' His words were a warm breath on her face. 'We still have time...' His voice sounded wistful, as if he did not truly believe what he had just said. He kissed her again, gently, soothingly, and Elizabeth brought an arm up about his neck, holding him there. He slipped his arms about her and pulled her to him, cradling her against his chest, plainly knowing that she needed to be held.

The warm pulse in his neck ticked against her cheek, and she smelled his familiar scent and for a few blissful moments, all was well in the world. She yearned to have him love her, comfort her, but she knew she could not let that happen. She lifted her head from his shoulder. 'You must go. Alyson must not find you here.' It was the last thing in the world that she wanted, to send him away, but she knew she had to be strong.

Warwick smiled at her. He wound a long strand of her hair round his finger and then untwisted it, watching the curl dance as it fell back into place. 'All will be well, Elizabeth. When Edward is defeated, then can we be together; there will be time for more sons.'

Elizabeth's heart stopped. For the first time she did not believe what he said to her. There was a melancholy tone to his words that sent a warning to her core. Part of her wanted to challenge him, to make him give voice to definite plans for them, but she knew in reality that would serve no purpose because they both knew the 'when' of Edward's defeat was still only an 'if'. And even if the 'if' happened – what future did they really have?

Elizabeth looked up at his face through her lashes. There were lines about his eyes she did not remember and at his temples was a touch of silver she could not recall.

'Do you find me much changed, Elizabeth?' Warwick asked her.

She blushed at his perception; he must have noticed her study of him. She had almost forgotten the way he could read her like one of Senor Gruuthuse's books.

'A little,' she lied.

Warwick smiled. 'It is because I have not had your company sweeting, that is all.'

'I think the taking of England also had much to do with it.' She did not add the other troubles he'd had to bear; they were too raw to think on and they mirrored her own.

He shrugged as if he had done nothing important. But she saw how the cares sat upon his shoulders like demons.

He turned and looked out of the window to where the moon slipped gracefully through the soft clouds; there was something he was keeping from her. The silence lengthened between them and Elizabeth wondered how they had become like strangers; both with secrets they could not give voice to.

Eventually Warwick turned to her. He gave a soft almost regretful sigh and then met her eyes. 'I would ask something of you, sweeting,' he said softly. 'I would not ask, not now of all times, but there is no on else who can do this. If you say no, I shall understand.' His voice was heavy and Elizabeth knew immediately that it was something important. Her breathing shortened.

'What is it, Richard? You know that you only have to ask.' She ran her fingers lightly over the velvet of his doublet. Elizabeth smiled but Warwick did not return it. She reached for his hand and drew it to her lips. She kissed it slowly and gave him a long look. He met that look, but still he did not smile.

He cleared his throat. 'Elizabeth,' he said.

Elizabeth seized upon the tremor in his voice. 'You are sending me away?'

Warwick clenched his jaw.

'I will not go,' she said indignantly. 'I almost drowned crossing the Narrow Sea to be with you, Richard. I shall not leave you again!' Yet how could she be with him with Alyson here and Jack in Bruges with Edward?

He let his breath out in a long slow sigh. He brought his hand up to touch her face gently. 'Hush, Elizabeth,' he said.

Elizabeth heard the worry in his voice. She met his eyes.

'I need your help, my love,' he said slowly. 'Will you not at least listen to my request?'

Elizabeth nodded; she could not trust her voice to give him a steady answer.

'You may know that Elizabeth Wydeville is with child?'

Elizabeth nodded. 'I learned it from Edward himself,' she said.

She saw Warwick's eyes darken at the mention of Edward's name.

'Indeed,' he said. 'She has now taken sanctuary at Westminster for her confinement.'

Elizabeth searched his face. What did Edward's queen matter?

'I need to be certain... I need to be certain what happens there, Elizabeth.'

'But Lady Scrope attends upon her does she not? What further use can I be?'

'Aye, she does sweeting.' He stroked her cheek again and Elizabeth closed her eyes at the soft pleasure of his touch. 'But I must be *certain*,' he continued.

'I am not sure I understand, Richard,' Elizabeth said.

He linked his fingers into hers. 'If she bears a son, my love, then it gives Edward more reason to fight on, for he has an heir of his blood. A girl would not be so important to him.' He paused. 'There is only your word I can trust.'

Elizabeth's heart thumped. God in heaven, if only he knew how faithless she had been! 'Do you really fear someone would switch the child?' she asked.

'Some would do anything to strengthen Edward's cause. Sons have been acknowledged by men other than their fathers before, have they not?'

She knew he meant Edward's own doubtful paternity, which even his mother had once denigrated.

'Are you in earnest, Richard?' She felt something of a fool for asking, but the thought of having to be in Elizabeth Wydeville's chambers; the solemnity, the formality and of course the birth itself, all filled her with fear.

Now Warwick smiled gently. 'Yes, I am in earnest,' he said quietly, 'though with our loss so close...' he caught his breath '...I should not ask you.'

Elizabeth untangled her fingers from his. 'You said we would never again be parted!' she reminded him.

His wide beautiful eyes met hers. 'It will not be for long, my love. Only you can I trust.'

She turned to face him. 'I don't know, Richard.' How could she face the birth of a child having discovered the loss of her own? The conflict raged in her heart; did she not owe him this after what she had done? The secret she had still not confessed to him. 'I thought I would not have to spy on anyone again,' she said quietly.

Warwick sighed. 'Ah, my love, we cannot be free of this until Edward is defeated. I think Jack told you that.'

Elizabeth shivered at the mention of Jack; the man to whom she was still bound!

Warwick stroked the hair back from her face. 'I know you can do this,' he said. 'Jack trusts you with his life. He said you make the perfect spy!'

Elizabeth's eyes flew up to his like startled birds flying from cover. God in heaven what exactly had Jack told him?

'Do not look so worried, my love,' Warwick smiled.

'Is he here?' she asked frantically, wondering if Warwick had discussed this plan with Jack in person.

'You know better than to ask after Jack, Mistress Thornton,' Warwick said teasingly.

God's blood, Jack *had* told him everything!

'And as Mistress Thornton there will be no objection to you entering the Wydeville household, will there?'

Elizabeth's head swam; there were more threads to her tale now than in a tapestry, how would she keep track of them all?

'Tell me, sweeting, will you do this for me? Do you think you can bear it?'

Elizabeth bit her lip, trying to gather her scattered thoughts. She didn't want to do what he asked, knew it was beyond her endurance; after all, she was not a Neville! But when she had failed him so completely, how could she refuse the chance to make amends?

They pushed Jack roughly into another dingy cell. It smelled no better than the previous cell had, though there was not even the comfort of dirty straw to be seen here. Instead, two things dominated the room: a strong-looking chair and a brazier, which glowed ominously and which Jack knew had nothing to do with giving warmth.

He was manhandled briskly into the chair and manacles fastened to his wrists and ankles. He looked at the grey stone walls and wondered what horrific tales they could tell and what part he was going to play in their story.

Behind him he heard the door open and strong boots thudded in.

His visitor's musky perfume smothered the air; a sword clanked at his hip.

'Sir John de Laverton!' a strong Burgundian accent hissed.

The hair at the nape of Jack's neck prickled; he had not used his real name since leaving France with Elizabeth. No, that wasn't true – he had been announced at Jehan's banquet! Could that have been his mistake? Hadn't Elizabeth warned him?

He turned his head as far as he could, but the man was standing infuriatingly out of sight.

'You have nothing to say?' the man said. His boots paced a line along the cell behind Jack. 'I thought you would at least be curious!'

Jack said nothing.

'We have waited a long time for this moment,' the man said sternly.

Jack wondered whom he meant by 'we'.

Suddenly a hand grasped at his hair and pulled his head back sharply. 'You think you are so clever Laverton,' he spat, 'but we shall laugh the last!'

Jack still could not see his face, though he could smell his wine-soaked breath; it made him want to retch. His mind flew in circles; who in the Burgundian court would be so interested in him? Who would want him dead?

The man pushed Jack's head forwards and sharp pain jagged down his neck.

Jack's breathing quickened as he raked his mind for answers. Who in God's name had waited a long time for this moment?

Suddenly the door opened again and Jack heard a sound that froze his blood. It was harsh laboured breathing, like the tumbling of gravel, like the grating of metal against stone.

A cold knot tightened in Jack's stomach.

A rough voice whispered to the Burgundian. 'Thank you, my friend. Once again, I owe you much.'

Jack closed his eyes. His heart thumped in his chest. He murmured a quiet prayer but he knew it would do no good: Higgins would kill him. Somehow he had known Higgins hadn't died that night at the harbour. Now Jack would pay for not finishing the job.

But how did Higgins come to be here? The Burgundians were not his friends - they had tortured him! But Jack could see what had happened; Higgins must have discovered Jack's visits here and had ingratiated himself within the Burgundian court. At the first opportunity he had betrayed Jack as one of Warwick's spies, even though he must know Jack was now working for Edward. That was the irony, Jack thought with an absurd curve of his swollen lip; coming here for Edward had been his undoing!

'Well sweet Jack,' Higgins lisped like a snake. 'I thought this moment would never come. Since that night at the harbour I have dreamed of this chance.'

'Higgins, you are making a terrible mistake,' Jack said quickly.

Higgins's hooked hand silenced Jack as he struck him hard across his face. Jack licked the wounded corner of his mouth and tasted blood again.

'The only mistake I ever made was to trust you!' Higgins snarled.

Jack turned to look at him.

Higgins's eyes were narrow strips of bright anger in his cruel face.

Jack shook his head. 'I am for Edward!' Jack whispered fiercely.

Higgins laughed dryly. 'Like hell you are!'

'It is true! You could ask Elizabeth were she here! You must know we are together,' Jack said, trying to deflect Higgins's attention away from hurting him.

'Elizabeth?' Something flickered across Higgins's face. 'You keep your filthy gypsy hands away from my child!' He leapt at Jack like a madman, his deformed hands tightening like a noose about Jack's throat.

Jack gagged; the pressure built behind his eyes as the hot twisted hands constricted his windpipe.

The Burgundian pulled Higgins away, but with little haste.

Jack coughed and spluttered as he fought for air. His throat burned. Evidently mentioning Elizabeth was not the right tactic, he thought. He realized that what Elizabeth had told him was true though, somewhere in Higgins's warped mind Elizabeth and his long-dead daughter had merged into one!

Jack wheezed, trying to fill up his lungs as he collected his thoughts. Perhaps Elizabeth was the answer after all! What father would hurt his own child?

Jack fixed his eyes on Higgins. 'She loves me, Higgins,' he said slowly.

'What!' Higgins leapt towards him again, but the Burgundian held him back.

'Elizabeth loves me and is that not better than her being in Warwick's bed?'

Higgins's eyes widened and his lips curled into a snarl. 'You lie! You will say anything to try and save your skin, Laverton!'

Jack shook his head. 'No Higgins. It's true. You know she was with me at the harbour. She even wears my ring!'

Higgins growled like an angry hound. 'You took her from me, you bastard!'

'You would not want to cause Elizabeth any pain, would you?' Jack asked.

Higgins screamed as he shook himself free of restraint.

He leapt towards to Jack and pulled his knife from its sheath. The red glow from the brazier glinted along its edge. He grabbed Jack's hair with one twisted hand, and slammed his head back, and with the other he held the knife up to Jack's cheek. 'You are a liar, Jack Laverton,' he hissed. 'I know what you did to her at Scarsdale. Matthew told me you almost raped her!'

'That was a long time ago,' Jack said in a husky voice. 'Elizabeth has forgiven me. We are married.'

Higgins laughed sourly. 'Another lie, Jack; another trick! You think I was born yester night?'

'We even changed our names so Warwick would not find us after we left you on the boat!' Jack continued quickly as the hard blade pressed into his cheek. 'Why else would I have come to Edward, but that I could have Elizabeth?' Jack asked breathlessly.

'You lying cur!' Higgins spat. 'You took her from me – you had no cause to do that but your own!'

'Higgins!' the Burgundian caught Higgins's arm and pulled him away. 'What if he speaks the truth? What if he really is King Edward's man?'

'Why else would I have stayed at Senor Gruuthuse's when King Edward arrived?' Jack said, taking the chance to push his cause further. 'Why else would I be here?'

'You came here to see the duchess!' Higgins snarled. 'Don't think I don't know where you like to sleep when you are here! How could you do that to Elizabeth if you are married?'

'The duchess is a powerful woman,' Jack said. 'But I haven't seen her of late, I swear it!' Jack restrained the ironic laugh that threatened to come: it *was* the truth.

Higgins snarled again. 'I don't believe you, gypsy! Not a word! You spy for Warwick, I know it and Duke Charles hates Warwick almost as much as I do – he will thank me for this!'

Higgins turned away and nodded to one of the guards. 'I shall have the truth from you, Jack! By God's bones I shall!'

On the edge of his vision Jack could see a man near the brazier. His heart quickened as the man began to pump the bellows, puffing sparks into the gloom and bringing an ominous red glow to everything.

Jack gulped. He heard a chinking sound like metal tools being emptied from a bag.

'Higgins,' Jack said through a tightening throat, 'Elizabeth will never forgive you if you hurt me, I swear it.'

Higgins laughed dryly. 'I owe you this,' he said bitterly, ignoring Jack's plea. 'Remember France!' he hissed.

Jack shook is head. 'Elizabeth will hate you. She loves me.'

The guard began to move the objects in the brazier.

Higgins stared at Jack, but remained unmoved.

Jack's head swam. God's blood, he needed to think of something quickly! He twisted his wrists against the manacles; they were tight and strong, no man could break them. Christ in heaven what could he do? Sweat beaded on his brow.

Higgins stared at him still, enjoying Jack's discomfort.

Jack held his gaze; perhaps there was some shred of humanity left that he could reach?

Higgins nodded to the guard.

'Elizabeth loves me, Higgins,' Jack repeated as firmly as he could, but his appeal was wearing thin.

It was as if he had never spoken. Higgins took an object from the guard. The tip of the knife glowed white and the blade was a sickening bloody red.

Jack pushed his back against the hard chair and the manacles bit into his wrists.

Higgins came closer. 'Are you going to beg me, Jack?' he hissed. 'Are you going to beg me not to ruin your handsome face?'

Jack said nothing. His heart screamed in his chest.

Higgins laughed as he brought the knife slowly towards Jack's face. His eyes were bright with hatred. 'Your face *first*, Jack,' he lisped.

Jack's breathing was shallow and quick. Sweat ran down his back and soaked into the curls on his brow. He gripped the arms of the chair, bracing himself for the inevitable pain. His nails splintered on the wood.

Higgins leant closer and Jack could smell his breath; could feel the heat emanating from the sharp knife in his hand.

With a sound like thunder the cell door crashed open.

Higgins jumped up quickly and dropped the knife.

Jack strained his neck, but could not see what had happened.

Suddenly Higgins dropped to his knees at Jack's side, his head lowered.

Jack heard shuffling behind him as though the Burgundian courtier had done the same.

Heavy boots came towards Jack and two men-at-arms came into view.

Higgins continued to stare at the floor.

There was a softer swish and Jack heard the gentle hush of a woman's footstep.

Red and gold velvet glided into his vision.

'Your Grace,' the Burgundian said.

'Your Grace,' Higgins echoed pathetically.

A smile twitched Jack's mouth. Relief caressed his body.

'Release him,' the woman's voice said sternly. 'How dare you lay a hand on my brother's messenger!' she hissed.

Higgins did not look up and plainly knew better than to try to defend himself.

A guard began to release Jack's hands and feet.

Jack looked up gratefully to where the Duchess of Burgundy stood; her chin lifted; her eyes fierce.

She turned and smiled at him.

Jack rose from the chair and then knelt at her feet. 'Your Grace,' he said as smoothly as his galloping heart would allow him to. 'Thank you.'

She thrust her hand towards him.

Jack took it shakily and pressed it to his lips. Her fingers were cold against them. Her perfume swamped his senses.

'I am sorry you have been treated thus, Master *Thornton*. Please tell my brother that I shall deal with these fools in a way that would please him.' Her eyes met Jack's in an eloquent look. 'And you,' she added softly.

Jack bowed his head.

Then she turned and left the cell.

Her men-at-arms escorted Jack past the still-kneeling Burgundian and his men.

As they moved along the dank passageway in a blaze of flickering lights, Jack heard the tortured cry of an animal. Then he realized it was not an animal; it was Higgins.

WESTMINSTER PALACE OCTOBER 1470

Suddenly Elizabeth was awake. The sheets were cold beside her. How she wished Warwick was here to warm her on the last night before she went to Elizabeth Wydeville! It was dark and the night candles flickered in the draught from the open casement. She listened, but there was no birdsong yet to announce the arrival of morning. A shadow moved across the room and Elizabeth watched from the bed as Warwick, wrapped only in a long velvet gown, walked to the small oak table and poured sweet, spiced wine into a gilded goblet. How long had he been here watching her? He swirled the cup in his hands and then studied the small crimson whirlpool he had created. Then he drank. Slowly he drank a deep draught and Elizabeth watched his smooth throat as he did so and imagined herself planting kisses there. She put her teeth over her bottom lip to stop herself from breaking the vision. Candlelight sparkled in his hair and highlighted the gentle creases about his eyes she so loved. He refilled his cup and then moved to a cushioned chair by the window. He slumped into it and slid his hips forward so that he could rest his head on the carved back of the chair. She heard him sigh and guilty tears burned at her eyes, for if she told him all as she wanted to, she could only add to the troubles so apparent in his furrowed brow. For a hundred heartbeats he sat thus, staring at the flickering shadows on the ceiling, the full goblet hanging dangerously at the tips of the fingers of his trailing hand. The breeze caught his hair, ruffling it about his neck as if Elizabeth had tangled her fingers there.

She could bear it no longer. She slid silently from the bed and like a ghost moved towards him. She knelt at his feet and rested her head on his knee. She breathed in the welcome scent of him. 'Richard you should not be here,' she whispered. 'You know we can trust none of the ladies here...' She trembled with both anticipation and fear. She did not want him to leave; she wanted him in her bed more than anything, but if Alyson reported they were lovers what would happen to Jack? Would they think that she had betrayed her husband or would they realize that Jack was a spy for Warwick's cause? She could not take that risk.

Warwick tore his gaze from the ceiling and smiled down at her. He brought his free hand up and stroked the curve of her shoulder, following it up along the line of her neck gently. But he said nothing. He brought the goblet up to his lips and drank again.

His eyes met hers. It seemed in the half-light of the bedchamber that they were completely black, their only light being from the image of the golden candle flames that flickered about them.

'Sweeting,' he breathed, 'that is why I did not wake you. I knew if I did - '

Elizabeth heard the longing in his voice, but he too had thought of the danger to others.

'Yet I could not let you go without seeing you alone one last time.' Warwick's eyes swept over her face, caressing her with his look before he pulled her closer to him.

She heard the clank as the golden cup fell to the floor and then he drew her up on her feet, his arms tightening about her. She slipped her hands inside the gown to find his warm body. She stroked the curve of his ribs, and then slid lower to the smoothness of his back.

He rocked her gently against him, breathing in her hair which hung loose like a summer mantle and Elizabeth wanted him to hold her forever. Tears stung her eyes; she did not want to be parted from him again, but knew that it was the only way she could help him and not loving him was the only way she could protect Jack. She had to be strong for all of them.

'Richard, you must go before they see you,' she said in a voice tightened with danger.

He met her teary look. 'You are right, sweeting,' he said softly and then, disregarding the warning, met her lips with his.

The world ceased to exist as he held her there and Elizabeth did not care.

Eventually he broke the kiss.

Elizabeth smiled into his eyes. 'You must go now, Richard.'

He pulled her to him again. In spite of the warmth of his body Elizabeth shivered as she thought on the enormity of the task ahead of her; she wondered if Warwick knew how much she feared being in Elizabeth Wydeville's company and it was not only the childbirth she was dreading. Elizabeth had seen Edward's queen's haughty demeanour at court, had seen how even William Hastings was wary in her presence. Doubt flickered within her. Would she be capable of the mission both Warwick and Jack believed she could carry out? If she failed...she caught her breath. She must not fail, for she knew Jack's life depended on her success. Reluctantly she withdrew her arms from Warwick's waist. 'Please Richard,' she said. 'They must not see you.' She took a step away from him.

Warwick held her in a long look before he smiled wistfully. 'Adieu sweeting,' he said. 'Pray God it will be over soon.'

'I shall,' she said trying to sound more confident than she felt. As he turned away from her she wondered if she would ever see him again; she tried to kill the thought quickly before it undid her completely.

With a click of the latch and a rush of scented candle-smoke he disappeared into the darkness and Elizabeth prayed that no one had seen him leave. At the side of the bed she dropped to her knees as the tears came to burn her eyes. She clasped her hands together in a despairing entreaty to God and wondered how she was going to get through the challenge Warwick had set her and wondered if Jack de Laverton was worth the sacrifice she had just made.

Jack followed the guards along a myriad of tangled passage-ways. As they walked the air grew less damp and began to taste a little sweeter, and with it Jack's own sense of relief began to grow.

Once beyond the prison, Jack noticed the familiar opulence of the court. Tapestries shimmered along the length of the corri-dors, so it seemed as though the walls were clothed in jewels. Everywhere smelled of honey and spices, sweet perfume and ambergris and the intensity of it made Jack's head swim.

As they moved closer to the duchess's apartments the light grew brighter still; golden cressets glittered at every second step and the tapestries were even more brilliant, rippling with gold.

They reached a pair of large doors with gilded handles and their party halted while passwords for entry into the duchess's house-hold were exchanged.

Jack's stomach turned over, partly because he was ravenous, but more so because he wondered what the duchess had in mind for him now, though from their previous encounters, he thought he could probably guess.

The room he was shown into was swathed in white silk and, as in the corridors, golden cressets sparkled along the walls.

Jack's eyes widened involuntarily at the magnificence of it all; this truly was the greatest court in Europe!

The steward and body servants came to greet him.

'My lord,' the steward bowed to him as though he were a prince. He beckoned Jack to follow him.

Jack almost felt guilty for putting his filthy boots on the sump-tuous Arabic carpet that ran the length of the apartments; he had never seen anything so wonderful. He ran his hand across his chin, feeling the prickle of his growing beard and he suddenly remembered a conversation he'd had with Elizabeth, when she had teased him for his stubble, and had jestingly offered to take a blade to it for him! He suddenly felt guilty for being here, for he knew how this would end. How far away Elizabeth seemed to him now, not because she was in England, but because he knew she would be with Warwick!

He was shown into a richly decorated ante-room. Perfumed steam caught his lungs. Sumptuous clothes adorned the dresser and a knot tightened in his stomach as he wondered if this was how Elizabeth had felt when she was dressed in the green damask gown for her meeting with King Edward in London.

Reluctantly Jack followed the steward into the bath chamber. Even though the room was hot Jack shivered as he realised what was to come.

* * *

Jack bowed elegantly.

'Master Thornton,' the duchess purred as she saw him.

The appetizing smell of rich spices wafted to him.

The duchess raised an eyebrow approvingly as though she was judging the conformation of a stallion.

'I must say you look so much better,' she breathed.

Jack had to agree with her and he felt better too, particularly after the restoration of his weapons. 'I am most grateful, Your Grace,' Jack began, but she raised a hand to silence him.

She smiled. 'I know you are, Jack.' Her eyes sparkled at him as she said his Christian name. 'And Thornton? How amusing! Plainly Master Higgins thought so too!' The look she gave him was incandescent. 'It has been some time, Jack. And yet I hear you have made several visits to my husband.'

Jack wanted to defend himself but her liquid eyes silenced him again.

'I shall forgive you, for have we not been friends for such a long time?'

'We have, Your Grace,' Jack said quietly. It was almost ten years since that first meeting, where she had held him speechless in the corridor with a molten look that had spoken if not to his heart, to his youthful lust. Only the intervention of William Hastings had prevented what would then have been a very unwise dalliance. Jack almost smiled; ever since she had been an unwise if irresistible dalliance! But now there was Elizabeth to think on.

'You must make amends, Jack!' she said silkily. 'And you of all people know how to do so.'

Jack gave her a half-smile; he definitely knew how this interview would end.

She spread her hand, indicating for him to sit beside her on the cushion-strewn settle.

A table was scattered with gold and silver dishes from which drifted the most tantalising aromas. There was a large gilded jug and two jewelled goblets, already filled with wine. Jack noticed the servants had been dismissed.

'Please,' she said.

Jack washed his hands in the bowl of fragrant rosewater and then placed some pieces of venison and some frumenty on a platter for her. He moved as slowly and gracefully as he could, never taking his eyes from the food until it was arranged perfectly.

As she took the platter from him she fixed his eyes and smiled. 'Thank you, Jack,' she murmured. She ran her tongue over her lips expectantly, but Jack knew from his previous experience of her that it was not the food she was anticipating so eagerly.

Jack looked away and began to serve food for himself.

When he looked up again she was still watching him. Her eyes were wide, the pupils dark pools within the deepest lapis blue. This was unfamiliar ground for him; usually he was the hunter not the hunted and he had forgotten how it felt to be in her presence! He wondered if this was how Elizabeth had felt when he had watched her at Scarsdale. He found that he was gripping the handle of his knife so tightly that the jewels had made fierce dimples in his palm. But why was he so uncertain now? It was not so unusual for him to have to make love to a courtier's wife in the line of duty, why did he feel so uneasy here? And here he was at least on familiar territory. He knew why he was so uneasy; what would Elizabeth think of him if she learned the truth of this now?

He ate slowly, trying to prolong this part of their meeting, trying to delay what he knew was inevitable; how else could he pay for his freedom; for his life?

He reached for his goblet. 'Your Grace,' he said and toasted her.

She smiled almost wistfully and watched as he drank. Then she toasted him in return; 'To gratitude,' she said with a vulpine smile.

Jack's stomach coiled.

The wine tasted good. Perhaps if he had more of it, he would be able to accomplish his task more easily. He drained the goblet and then refilled it. As he moved to pick it up, she lent forward quickly and placed her hand over the cup.

'Jack,' she murmured.

He met her gaze.

She shook her head gently. Then she reached forward and took hold of his hand.

Jack's heart quickened.

She tightened her grip and then began to stand, pulling Jack's arm so that he knew he must rise with her.

She drew him round the table towards her, all the while meeting his eyes; she looked like a she-wolf about to kill.

Once he was in front of her she raised her chin so that she still held his gaze. She ran a finger lightly over the bruise on his cheek and down to his swollen lips. Then she reached up and put her arms about his neck. Her perfume overwhelmed his senses.

She curled her fingers in his hair and drew him down to her.

Jack almost recoiled from the warmth of her lips, from her tongue questing in his mouth, from the pressure of her belly against his. But instead he gathered his strength and drew her closer to him. Even though his mouth was sore he pressed his lips down hard on hers and she gave a little moan of pleasure, which sent an involuntary shiver to his loins.

She pulled away from him. He saw her chest rise and fall rapidly, saw the jewels glitter seductively against her cleavage and another spasm of lust pulsed within him.

If only he didn't think about Elizabeth he would be all right, he told himself. He closed his eyes and pulled the breathless duchess closer, knowing that his life depended on what happened next.

WESTMINSTER ABBEY NOVEMBER 1470

The wind whipped the rain across the dark courtyard in savage gusts and as she followed Lady Scrope, Elizabeth huddled deeper into her cloak for comfort.

'Lord, this weather is worse than Yorkshire!' Lady Scrope grumbled.

Elizabeth smiled. She had not been to Lord Scrope's castle at Bolton, but she remembered seeing its impressive keep from the tower at Middleham. 'I think it is not driven by such a wind as buffets us in Wensleydale,' she said.

Lady Scrope gave her a rueful smile as they ducked into a doorway. 'You also miss the dales?' she asked.

Elizabeth nodded.

The door complained loudly as Lady Scrope pushed it open and for a moment they allowed the tempest into the sanctuary. She closed the door behind them and the roar of the wind was muffled by the thickness of the oak.

'Perhaps when this is over you could return with me?' Lady Scrope asked. 'I would have need of you.'

Elizabeth shook her head. 'I thank you my lady, but I cannot leave Warwick,' she said, though part of her doubted there was any future there.

Lady Scrope's lips tightened. 'I was thinking of that,' she said. 'I have known him for such a long time, Elizabeth, yet I have never seen him so content as when he is in your company. But you cannot think you will ever be together in London. But in the North...'

'Her Grace awaits you,' one of Elizabeth Wydeville's women announced from the top of the stairs.

Elizabeth was glad she did not have to answer Lady Scrope. It had been reckless to talk of Warwick here, especially when she had been so lately in Edward's company with Jack. She must be more careful; Jack was still in Bruges and she could not be certain what communication existed between the queen and her exiled husband, just as she could not be sure whether Alyson had sent word of her every move inside Westminster Palace.

'Lady Scrope,' Elizabeth whispered, 'there is something I should tell you, about my time in Bruges.'

'Your time with that rogue Laverton, you mean?' Lady Scrope said caustically.

Elizabeth sighed; someone else who judges Jack badly, she thought. Her face flushed. 'Jack is still there, Lady Scrope, working for Warwick,' Elizabeth whispered. 'I must not reveal him as Warwick's man.'

Lady Scrope nodded. 'I see,' she said.

They had reached the top of the stairs. Large double doors faced them. The woman went before them to announce them to Edward's waiting queen.

'But there is something else, Lady Scrope...I am married to him!'

Lady Scrope's eyes widened. 'Married to Jack de Laverton? God in heaven! I had heard a rumour that you were promised to him, but I never believed it! I thought Lady Catherine had refused! And I thought you and my lord of Warwick...'

'No, Lady Scrope you do not understand...' Elizabeth began.

The doors flung wide before them.

'Married to Jack Laverton indeed!' Lady Scrope whispered fiercely. 'Well at least your poor dead father will be pleased!'

Elizabeth had no time to answer as they ventured in together. Perhaps it was no bad thing if Lady Scrope believed she and Jack were married; the fewer people who knew the truth, the better!

The windows rattled in their casements, the wind threw rain against the panes like stones, and Elizabeth Wydeville's eyes were as dark as the brooding cloud. She did not attempt to quench her molten gaze as they bowed themselves closer to her.

Smoke from the chimney stung Elizabeth's eyes and she struggled to stifle a cough as they curtsied at the beleaguered queen's feet.

But Elizabeth Wydeville remained motionless, her hands folded over her rounded belly. Elizabeth shuddered at the thought that she would be almost as swollen by now, if she had not lost her babe at Ellerton... and if Jack's story in Bruges had been true.

'So Warwick has sent you to me?' Elizabeth Wydeville asked darkly.

'Yes, Your Grace,' Lady Scrope replied. 'Your time is close. My lord Warwick wished you to have every assistance possible.'

Elizabeth Wydeville sucked her breath in sharply through her teeth. 'Is that so? He thinks so much on my comfort that the witless Henry of Lancaster sits in the apartments I had prepared for my confinement, does he not?' she hissed.

Lady Scrope knew better than to answer.

'And you,' Elizabeth Wydeville addressed Elizabeth with a glacial voice. She paused and Elizabeth looked up at her tentatively.

'I know you,' she said, narrowing her eyes.

'Yes, Your Grace. I was briefly at court.'

Elizabeth Wydeville laughed without humour. 'I do remember. Lord Hastings was very impressed by your dancing!'

Elizabeth's cheeks burned and she heard Lady Scrope move uncomfortably beside her.

'Much has changed since that day, has it not?' Elizabeth Wydeville continued.

'Your Grace?' Elizabeth asked hesitantly. Much had changed for all of them, but how much did she know of Elizabeth's circumstances?

'Lady Scrope, leave us!' Elizabeth Wydeville commanded.

'But Your Grace.'

The appeal was denied fiercely. 'Leave us!'

Lady Scrope rose slowly and then bowed herself from the room.

Elizabeth could hear the hailstorm against the windows, the crackling of the smoky fire and the swish of Lady Scrope's skirts on the floor, but most of all she could hear the pounding of her own heart.

'Come here,' Elizabeth Wydeville said when the doors had separated Lady Scrope from them. 'Come and sit by me.' Elizabeth Wydeville's voice was softer now, her eyes more gentle. She patted the cushions next to her.

Elizabeth then joined the queen on the large carved settle.

Elizabeth Wydeville smiled. 'It is a comfort to me to have you here,' she said softly, 'knowing that you are part of Warwick's ruin.'

Elizabeth blinked slowly and her eyes stung again, though this time it was not only because of the smoke. 'Your Grace?' she asked.

Elizabeth Wydeville took her hand. 'We both know you have lately been in Bruges and that your husband is still in the king's service there. That is why I am surprised Warwick let you come to me.'

Elizabeth looked down.

Elizabeth Wydeville spoke softly. 'And I am sorry for the loss of your child, Elizabeth, truly. I think I am fortunate amongst women; I have carried every one of my babes to full term.'

Elizabeth looked at her. Her face was indeed full of compassion and she was certainly well informed. Elizabeth assumed Alyson must be communicating with her. She tried to focus on her tale; Jack was depending on her. 'It was the storm, Your Grace,' Elizabeth said. 'I almost drowned.'

'And does your husband know of your loss?'

Elizabeth shook her head. 'I cannot write to him. I have not told them anything of him.' She thought then of Jack and wondered how much longer he would stay in Edward's company. 'Please, Your Grace, say nothing to Lady Scrope, for she will tell Warwick and I will be undone!'

Elizabeth Wydeville patted her hand. 'You may be sure I will protect you, so far as I am able. You risked much in taking Edward's letters to his brother, and I know also of your father's sacrifice in our cause. It will not be forgotten.'

'Thank you,' Elizabeth said.

'And if you wish it, I can get a message to your husband.'

What a fool she had been to think she had left espionage behind with Jack in Bruges! She tried to focus her mind. 'I do not know how to tell him, Your Grace. It will break his heart,' Elizabeth said, playing her part as Jack had taught her. Tears stung her eyes as she thought of the pain on Warwick's face as he told her of the loss of their son. Desperately she tried to gather her thoughts. Should she try and uncover their messenger? What would Jack do in her place? All he had asked was that she still play the part of his wife and in spite of the sacrifice that had entailed, she had done so. She must do so still.

'I will tell Ned, and I know he will break the news gently,' Elizabeth Wydeville said.

'How can it be gentle?' Elizabeth asked tearfully. 'He has lost a son.' She felt a twinge of guilt, felt as though she were somehow betraying her own sex as she deceived Edward's queen, though it was true that *she* had lost a son!

'At least you are safe and that will be a comfort to him,' Elizabeth Wydeville continued. 'You are young and there will be time aplenty for you to be together when Ned returns.'

'Be together?' Elizabeth whispered. She went cold.

'Ned will see to it that you are both rewarded for your pains,' she said.

'You are very kind,' Elizabeth managed to stammer, but her mind was swirling like mist. If Edward defeated Warwick, she could never extricate herself from her counterfeit marriage to Jack! If the truth was revealed they would both be unmasked as traitors! She swallowed thickly: Elizabeth Hardacre and Jack de Laverton were no more!

WESTMINSTER ABBEY NOVEMBER 1470

It was still dark when Elizabeth became aware of a hand shaking her.

'Elizabeth,' Lady Scrope whispered, 'it will not be long now. She is asking for you. Lady Rivers is with the girls.' Elizabeth Wydeville's mother and her young daughters were also in sanctuary, but Elizabeth's attention had been focused on Edward's queen.

Elizabeth shook her head sleepily. She had not left Elizabeth Wydeville's side all day and it seemed only a few heartbeats since she had retired to bed.

Suddenly a woman's ragged cry pierced the darkness and Elizabeth's stomach turned over. Now she was awake.

She met Lady Scrope's eyes.

'You have not seen a birth before?' Lady Scrope asked gently, evidently recognizing Elizabeth's fear.

Elizabeth shook her head. 'No my lady, I was sent away when my brother was born. They thought it would be a difficult birth and so it proved to be.'

'I remember it. Lady Catherine never fully recovered, I think,' Lady Scrope said sadly. 'But it is what we are on God's earth for, Elizabeth, you must remember that. One day you too will have a husband...' Lady Scrope stopped as she remembered what Elizabeth had told her. She cleared her throat.

'Lady Scrope...' for a moment Elizabeth thought again about explaining about Jack but another savage cry swept over them.

'Come, Elizabeth, she will need you now.'

Elizabeth Wydeville was naked except for the long cloak of her golden hair. It was damp at her brow and it curled tightly where it had not been shaved, as it usually was when she was at court. She was panting now, the mound of her belly heaving with each breath. When she saw Elizabeth she smiled thinly and held out her hand.

Elizabeth dropped a little curtsey and then came to her side. Marjory Cobbe, the midwife, busied herself at the other end of the bed beneath the raised sheet and Elizabeth was grateful that she did not have to help deliver the baby. It made her think of Sarah and it made her think of Isabel. She shivered as Elizabeth Wydeville's clammy hand slipped into hers. Her fingers tightened and her nails bit into Elizabeth's palm as another fierce contraction took hold of her. Elizabeth returned the grip, conscious that these events were beyond politics and dynastic struggle – this was the struggle for life!

Elizabeth Wydeville roared like a wounded animal as, under the encouragement of the midwife, she pushed with all her strength. Her face creased with pain and her veins stood out in her neck with the effort. Suddenly her beauty was transformed, replaced by a fierce raw power drawn from somewhere else, perhaps from the Virgin or Elizabeth thought, perhaps from something much older.

Elizabeth winced from both her crushed hand and from the evident pain of childbirth; at this moment it definitely seemed like the punishment of sin!

'Your turn will come,' Elizabeth Wydeville said breathlessly, 'when Ned comes to see his son, so you shall have your husband!'

Inexplicably Elizabeth thought of Jack as he had been on the quayside at Bruges. She missed him more than she would have believed possible and she smiled. 'Yes, Your Grace,' she said softly.

The contractions were stronger now and there was little time for Elizabeth Wydeville to rest between them. Elizabeth found herself pushing with her, gripping her hand as tightly as she held hers.

Elizabeth Wydeville screamed with effort and pain. Sweat ran down her face and between each contraction she fell back, looking thin and pale, like a half-drowned kitten. It seemed as though she would not be able to lift her head from the pillow even if Warwick entered the room, never mind force a child into the world, but she summoned her strength again and pushed and roared and cried for what seemed like an age to Elizabeth. Then Edward's queen sank back with a groan.

Elizabeth turned to see the midwife pull a tiny wet bundle clear of the sheets.

Within a few heartbeats there was a strangled angry cry from the bottom of the bed.

Elizabeth held her breath as the child was bathed and wrapped in a warm blanket. All eyes fixed on Marjory Cobbe.

'A son, Your Grace!' the midwife cried. 'Praise be to God!'

Elizabeth turned to Elizabeth Wydeville. A smile claimed her tired face and her eyes glistened with tears. 'Edward,' she breathed happily. 'We shall call him Edward.'

Elizabeth's eyes stung too, but with a mixture of emotions. She was moved by the powerful experience of a new life entering the world, but she knew it was the worst outcome for Warwick. Edward had a son; his dynasty was at last on firmer ground and she knew there would be those amongst the Lancastrians who would not want this child to live. But she was certain that Warwick would ensure the baby's safety; he knew too well the grief of a child's death.

'I am the happiest woman alive,' Elizabeth Wydeville whispered as she turned to her. 'Write to Ned for me; tell him the wondrous news, Elizabeth. And promise me you will write to your husband also; say that when he returns with Ned you will give him a son too! You cannot dwell on your loss, Elizabeth.'

Elizabeth's cheeks flushed and she looked down to the counterpane. How could she write such a thing to Jack? She twisted Jack's ring on her finger. But as her letter might be read by someone other than Jack, how could she not do so?

Elizabeth Wydeville saw the gesture. 'You can make him as happy as I have made Ned. Elizabeth, promise me that you will write to him! Today you can deny me nothing!'

Elizabeth nodded meekly. 'I shall, Your Grace,' she said and wondered what Jack would say when he received her letter; a letter delivered through a network of spies who if they knew the truth, would kill them both.

BURGUNDIAN COURT NOVEMBER 1470

Jack was suddenly aware of voices. Instinctively, eyes still half-closed, he reached for his sword, pulled back the covers and leaped from the bed in one swift movement.

His sinuous action was greeted with shrieks and giggles and he realized with horror that the voices belonged to the duchess's women.

Naked, and with his face burning as hot as coals, he bowed to them, which only made them huddle together, babbling excitedly. Then they rushed from the room, still giggling, while Jack sought to regain his clothes and his dignity.

'Wait.' The duchess's voice was as soothing as warm honey. 'Do not leave so soon, Jack.'

Jack had already pulled his shirt and hose on and was searching for his boots.

'Your Grace,' he hoped the plaintive look in his eyes would suffice as an appeal. 'You are already late for Mass,' he admonished her gently.

She laughed. 'So I am, Jack! And it would not do for my husband to be kept waiting would it? He might come looking for me!'

She said it lightly, but Jack understood the threat. He was on dangerous ground and he needed a firmer foothold if he was not to fall. Too many people knew the truth; he could not wait for more to learn of it.

'And I must return to your brother,' Jack said, pulling hard on a boot. The effort made him wince; making love to the duchess had done nothing to heal his bruises.

'Must you, Jack?' she asked. She turned to face him, and liquid eyes sought his.

He smiled. 'Yes, Your Grace. You know I must.'

He heard her sigh.

'I am one of the richest women in the world and still I cannot have what I want!' she said petulantly.

In that moment she reminded him of her brother Clarence and Jack stifled the urge to say that she had certainly had what she wanted from him last night!

'Unfortunately God tests us all, Your Grace,' he said as evenly as he could, finishing his other boot.

He stood up. 'I must go, so that your women may attend you.'

She pushed herself up in the bed, unashamedly exposing her body to him. She held out her hand to him and Jack moved to take it. He pressed it to his swollen lips and she smiled into his eyes.

'I suppose I shall not see you again?' she asked huskily.

'Who can say, Your Grace? I am at your brother's command,' Jack said neutrally, knowing that if Edward's appeals to the duke were successful, he would have no choice but to accompany him here.

Undaunted, she pulled him down to her and kissed him hard on the mouth.

'Go then,' she said 'and this time take more care, Jack. You have made enemies here as well as friends.'

Jack slipped his doublet over his shoulders and then bowed. 'Your Grace, I am truly grateful,' he said and, picking up his sword, strode towards the door.

'If you come to court again, Jack, I shall be waiting,' she purred after him.

Jack gave her a broad grin, but inside he shivered; he had thought this was a game he would never tire of; indeed he had lost count of the nights he had spent with her over the years, but since his time in Bruges with Elizabeth this jewel had lost some of its lustre and the dangers of being caught had never been greater.

As he entered the anteroom the duchess's women eyed him coyly. He swept them an elegant bow, which they acknowledged with brief curtseys and knowing looks.

Jack gave them a wide smile, as they obviously seemed pleased with what they had seen.

They giggled again, but were willing enough to give him directions to the stables.

He needed to get away from here as fast as he could, before the duchess changed her mind about letting him return to Edward or Higgins had chance to speak to Duke Charles; he could not be certain that the duchess had taken care of him completely and cuckolding the Duke of Burgundy was not something for which Jack wished to be called to account.

BRUGES NOVEMBER 1470

The greasy smell of tallow candles seemed to clothe the tavern's largest room. Jack poured disinterestedly from the jug of ale and then sipped from the pewter mug. The pewter gave the ale a metallic flavour, which Jack thought made it taste more like an apothecary's brew than beer. He wrinkled his nose and placed the mug back down on the wooden trestle, being careful not to place it too near the sloping edge. From his place in the darkest corner of the tavern he could see the door clearly. He could also see the stairs, which curled up to the bedrooms above, a staircase which was certainly getting a lot of use tonight. Jack was confident he would see him, whichever entrance he used.

Jack's eyes explored every face that entered, many he vaguely recognized for there were plenty of Edward's adherents here; inwardly he cursed his choice of meeting place, perhaps a tavern nearer the port would have been better.

Suddenly wide hips blocked his view and the strong smell of perfume assaulted his senses. He looked up. A young woman smiled down at him.

'You should not be drinking alone, monsieur,' she breathed.

Jack ran expert eyes over her body.

She pouted full lips at him. Plump white breasts tempted him.

He swallowed down the lust. 'Not tonight, sweetheart,' he said. His body still ached from his encounter with the Burgundian guards and all the hard riding of one sort or another he had done since. Besides that, he was still feeling guilty about his bedsport

267

with the duchess and a further betrayal with this doxy was more than his conscience could take.

The girl however was not to be brushed aside so easily. She came and sat beside him and slipped a hand onto his thigh. 'Really, *cheri*, you should not drink alone,' she whispered.

Jack smiled. He had to admit this girl was pretty and it was a little heartening to have her at his side. But he knew that really he was missing Elizabeth and that playing the field once again would not bring him the comfort he craved. He had trodden that path before and he thought that now he at least knew the difference.

The girl snuggled closer to him. 'You are English?' she asked.

'I am,' Jack replied, trying not to let her wandering hand distract his attention from the door. He saw himself as English even though he had been born at Rouen, just as Edward did.

'There are many English here,' she said, 'but there are Englishmen who do not love Burgundy.'

'Is that so?' Jack asked, feigning interest while he still kept watch.

'*Oui*, I heard some of the English soldiers talking. Your Earl of Warwick hates us.'

'He doesn't hate you, sweetheart,' Jack smiled, 'he just hates your duke!' he said, pouring her a cup of ale. 'He would like you very well!' He laughed at her frown; she was indeed very pretty.

She pouted at him again.

A smile twitched Jack's lips; she really was very good. He could see she was trying to unravel his defences and he knew if he had longer, she might just succeed.

His eyes flicked to the door as it opened.

Small eyes as bright as jet sought him out and the thin face smiled lustily as he saw Jack's companion.

'Leave us,' Jack said to the girl as his man approached them.

She was about to protest, but when she looked at the hooked features of Jack's man, she clamped her lips shut and pulled her hand away from Jack.

'Another time, perhaps, *cheri*,' she said as she slipped away from him.

They both watched her drift across the room to greet an English soldier wearing the murrey and blue of York.

'Calais is for Warwick,' his companion said softly as he sat down. 'Everyone is wearing the ragged staff!' He grinned and then helped himself to Jack's ale. 'And King Louis has declared his support for Lancaster too, by signing a treaty with the young Prince Edouard.'

'What?' Jack's heart slammed into his ribs.

'He means to force Warwick into war with Burgundy sooner than Warwick would like. His ambassadors have gone to England to that end.'

'Are you certain?'

The jet eyes flashed indignantly. 'Of course.'

Jack scanned the tabletop while his mind thought on these new events. 'Warwick cannot do this,' he said. 'Not yet, not until England is secure.'

'Ah, but the spider-king is impatient for Burgundian lands.'

Jack shook his head. 'You must go to London. Warwick must know of this. He must realize that making war on Burgundy now is a grave mistake. Duke Charles is yet with Lancaster; such an attack will change his mind. Warwick must understand that!' Jack cast alert eyes round the room. Then he reached into his doublet and withdrew a letter. 'And give him this,' he said. 'To no one but Warwick himself, as before,' he added firmly.

TEN

WESTMINSTER ABBEY NOVEMBER 1470

A baby's angry protest woke Elizabeth from her sleep. Lady Scrope was standing in her room, the crying child draped over her shoulder.

'I am sorry Elizabeth,' she said, 'but no one can settle him and now the queen has woken and is in a mood which could send thunderbolts to heaven! Will you take him from me? At least in here she cannot hear him!'

Elizabeth sat up slowly and knuckled her tired eyes. 'Of course, if you wish it. Or would you rather I went to the queen?'

'God in heaven no!' Lady Scrope cried, 'I would rather face her, for I cannot quieten him!'

Elizabeth held out her hands. She took the warm bundle and pulled him into her chest. Lady Scrope left her. Almost immediately the baby's crying dwindled to a murmur and as Elizabeth gave him her finger to suck she was reminded of her brother Edmund and how he would always settle if she sang to him. She took a deep breath and then began to sing quietly:

This endris night I saw a sight
A star as bright as day;
And ever among a maiden sung,
'Lullay, by by, lullay.'
This lovely lady sat and sang,
And to her Child did say:
'My Son, my Brother, Father, dear,
Why liest Thou thus in hay?'
'My sweetest bird, thus 'tis required,
Though Thou be King veray;
But nevertheless I will not cease
To sing, By by, lullay.'
The Child then spake in His talking,
And to his mother said:
'Yea, I am known as Heaven-King,
In crib though I be laid.
'For angels bright down to Me light:
Thou knowest 'tis no nay:
And for that sight thou may'st delight

To sing, By by, lullay.'
'Now, sweet Son, since Thou art a king,
Why art Thou laid in stall?
Why dost not order thy bedding
In some great kingès hall?
'Methinks 'tis right that king or knight
Should lie in good array:
And then among, it were no wrong
To sing, By by, lullay.'

Before she had finished all the verses she saw that the baby had fallen asleep. But this was not simply a newborn babe she told herself; this was Edward's child and the future of his line. She gazed at the downy bloom of his skin and the faint sandy brows and she wondered how so much could rest on one innocent child. She ran a fingertip over his soft warm cheek. Her chest tightened suddenly as the magnitude of her own loss threatened to overwhelm her.

WESTMINSTER PALACE NOVEMBER 1470

'Sweet Jesu brother, do you think that I am mad?' Warwick demanded. 'Do you think I cannot see the problems that lie before us? Why do you think I have not yet left for Calais?'

Archbishop Neville did not flinch. He spread his hands in humility without moving from his seat opposite Warwick.

'Ah, George,' Warwick sighed, 'but that the winning of England was the end of it all!' He picked up the wine Thomas had poured for him and put it to his lips. He watched his brother from over the rim of the golden cup. Their eyes met and held for several heartbeats.

'Richard, I did not mean to imply that you were anything other than in possession of your faculties,' Archbishop Neville began.

'Ha!' Warwick cried, lowering the cup, 'I may be the older brother, George, but I am not yet in my dotage. Tell me who else could have carried a Lancastrian alliance and now a French one upon his back?'

'No one, Richard,' Archbishop Neville conceded with the quiet grace he could always muster, as he had done at the opening of parliament with his brilliant speech. 'But there is yet much to do,' he added softly.

Warwick laughed and threw the sharp wine into his throat as if it were water to flame. His brother was the master of the understatement, he thought.

'Must the assault on Burgundy take such precedence?' Archbishop Neville asked quietly. 'The merchants make much of their trade with Burgundy and will not happily look elsewhere for custom.'

'I know,' Warwick said with a sigh, 'but has Louis not extended free trade to all English merchants in France for two years? That is worth much more to them if they think on it. The cloth merchants especially will benefit, seeing as they cannot export to Burgundian territories!'

'But will they think?' Archbishop Neville asked. 'Do they ever think beyond next week?'

Warwick shook his head. Exasperation tightened the muscles of his neck and he flexed his shoulders trying to ease them. 'In faith, I do not know,' he sighed.

'You must make sure they realize the advantages, Richard, and you know they do not love France,' Archbishop Neville continued. 'You cannot accomplish much without their goodwill.'

'Without their money, you mean?' Warwick snorted. He was well aware how empty the Royal coffers were; Edward was certainly no miser! But George was right to be concerned, for without money and land to soften anxieties he was struggling to hold it all together. He had never been more popular with the common man, far more popular then Edward, but the lords were where he lacked backing, and if the merchants too turned against him, then all was lost.

'Besides, George,' he said evenly, 'I gave Louis my word, and with his ambassadors newly arrived from France I cannot be seen to waiver. Louis d'Harcourt, the Bishop of Bayeux, Tanguy du Chastel and the rest, they are not easy people to please, George. My agents warn me that any attack on Burgundy will push Duke Charles towards Edward, but truly, what choice do I have? I gave my word to Louis!'

Archbishop Neville gave an almost imperceptible sigh, but it was just enough to fuel Warwick's anger.

'By Christ's Holy blood!' Warwick swore as he rose, knocking the cup and several documents to the floor. 'Is there not enough for me to do? Marguerite and Edouard have gone to visit King René when they should have come with Louis's entourage and

Clarence looks on me like the Devil himself whenever I meet with him! And that after I managed to secure for him the duchy of York and to hold onto Richmond for him against the petition of Henry Tudor!' He spun round on his heels and thumped his fist into his hand. 'George, I can only do so much!' He wanted to say and with Elizabeth gone into sanctuary he had no safe harbour in which to think, but he managed not to.

Archbishop Neville moved uncomfortably in his chair. 'Richard, believe me I am here to help you, as is John.'

'John can help me best by holding the North,' Warwick said quietly. 'He was a Yorkist far too long.'

'But did he not apologize to parliament?' Archbishop Neville said. 'You know John is no statesman, but he gave a most assured speech. Everyone could see his contrition.'

'I know,' Warwick said softly. He looked back at his brother. 'And I am grateful for it, truly. It is just that when all is done I can still envisage our ruin, George. Especially now Edward has a son!'

Archbishop Neville raised his brows in surprise. 'A son?' he whispered.

Warwick nodded; and did this not wound him more than he could say to his brother? He had lost a son as well as a grandson while Edward had gained a boy – was it not a mark of God's favour?

'But we have Edouard of Lancaster; this child of Edward's is yet but a babe!'

Somehow Warwick did not share his brother's optimism. 'Even when Lancaster is crowned King of England, can you honestly see Marguerite honouring her promises as I have kept mine?'

Archbishop Neville plainly knew the question was rhetorical.

'And what of Exeter and Somerset? Now that Edward has gone skulking to Burgundy, they will soon be coming home. Will all these honour me as the saviour of the Lancastrian cause?'

Archbishop Neville sighed. 'We cannot be certain of anything except God,' he said philosophically. 'But you must admit your choices were getting thin, Richard. There was no way back to England that I could see other than the path you have chosen. And the marriage of Edouard to Anne must count for something.'

Warwick laughed ironically. 'Aye, brother, except that Louis has now had to send to Jerusalem for a dispensation, the original one named her Anne of Salisbury, for God's sake! They are yet still only betrothed, George!'

'Louis will see it done!'

Warwick drew himself together, gathering his resolve. 'I made a vow on the True Cross, George, and I will not be forsworn.'

Archbishop Neville gave a little cough.

'I mean it, George. They may shift and change as the sands in the wind, but I gave my oath at Angers and I shall keep it, whatever the cost to me or mine.'

'And when Edward returns?'

Warwick smiled at the certainty with which his brother now spoke; he remembered how once George had doubted it was possible.

'When he returns we must defeat him in battle,' Warwick said flatly, 'and having sworn the most holy of oaths, George, we must pray that God is on our side that day.'

WESTMINSTER ABBEY NOVEMBER 1470

The baby slept contentedly in the wooden cradle. Now fully swaddled, his princely face was a vibrant pink above the embroidered coverlet, his cheeks plump and round, his breathing gentle.

Elizabeth sat beside him, her book of hours in hand, a finger tracing distractedly along the gilded border of a page; how it reminded her of Senor Gruuthuse's books in Bruges. Bruges — where this baby's father was still in exile. How incongruous it seemed for her to be nursing Edward's child and how much it made her think of the son she had never seen. She wondered where at Ellerton they had buried him; wondered if Sister Johanna had said prayers for him and if they had given him a name, though she knew he could not have been christened. Her stomach knotted; she knew she would have called him Richard.

There was a sudden sharp rustle of silk and Elizabeth turned to see Lady Scrope enter the room.

Elizabeth stared at her and pressed her finger to her lips. 'Please, Lady Scrope,' she whispered, 'do not waken him!' Then she noticed the gravity of Lady Scrope's features. 'What is wrong?' she asked, rising. She put her book down on her chair. Elizabeth's heart flew to her throat.

Lady Scrope beckoned Elizabeth to her.

Elizabeth moved to join her by the window. Part of her did not want to know what her news was. Had something happened to Warwick? Or Jack? Her heart was beating wildly now.

A pale golden light gilded the courtyard and the pointed tips of the roofs beyond, giving an air of tranquillity to the Abbey that Elizabeth knew was about to be shattered.

'You have a visitor, Elizabeth,' Lady Scrope said in a heavy voice.

Elizabeth's heart leapt; she hoped it was Warwick. But in almost the same instant she thought how stupid a thought that was; neither could it be Jack for he had lately written to her from Bruges: a bawdy answer to her own incongruous missive. She searched Lady Scrope's face, but she said nothing further. Instead she took hold of her hand and led her out of the room.

'Come,' Lady Scrope said gravely.

Tentatively she followed Lady Scrope into the corridor.

Although the vaulted passageway was short, it seemed to take a thousand steps to reach the end of it, and Elizabeth's fears grew into a tight knot in her stomach as she walked.

The door to the anteroom creaked loudly.

A thick pale cloak huddled beside the meagre fire, long thin hands rubbing together furiously. A candle stub guttered in the sudden draught. The figure turned to face her.

Elizabeth gasped. 'Brother William!'

It seemed as though he was paler than ever. His ice-blue eyes fixed hers intently and Elizabeth shuddered at the gravity of his look. Then she remembered that this was the man who had saved Jack; no wonder he had read her guilt that day at Jervaulx: he had been nursing her victim!

'Brother William, what is wrong?' she asked, dismissing the past quickly and moving to take hold of his hands.

'Ah, Elizabeth, *benedictus*,' he sighed. 'It is good to see you, even though I wish it were under better circumstances.'

Elizabeth gripped his hands. Her heart hammered in her chest. 'Warwick?' she asked.

'No, mistress. It is not about Lord Warwick that I come.'

'What is it then?' she asked him through a tightening throat. 'Jack?' she stammered.

Brother William smiled and shook his head. 'No, not Jack either, though I must apologize for my part in that deception, Elizabeth. If only you had allowed me to hear your confession, I could have relieved you of some of your burden, I think. But I could not trust that Master Conyers knew anything and so I could say nothing more. Please forgive me.' He sucked in a deep breath. 'Elizabeth, I am sorry. It is your mother.'

His words fell like stones into a well.

'My mother?' Tears pricked at Elizabeth's eyes. 'Is she...is she...?'

'No, Elizabeth, she yet lives,' he said squeezing her hands reassuringly. 'But she does not have so long I think.'

'Oh!' Elizabeth gasped. She felt as though all her breath had been sucked from her body. Pink and blue pinpoints of light swam into her vision and she wilted onto the settle. She bit her lip to prevent a sob from coming.

Brother William sat beside her. 'I am sorry...there was no easy way to tell you.'

Elizabeth looked up at him through blurring vision. 'But she disowned me, Brother William,' she stammered. Elizabeth stopped herself from saying and that because of her mother, she had betrayed Warwick; Jack's lessons had been well learned!

'But she is asking for you now, Elizabeth,' Brother William said gently. 'And you have the power of forgiveness, my child. It is a great gift Elizabeth, as it is said in the book of Luke.' He paused and then said solemnly, 'Judge not, and you will not be judged. Condemn not, and you will not be condemned. Forgive, and you will be forgiven.'

'Forgiveness,' Elizabeth whispered, suddenly remembering Jack's words on the subject. She tried to recover her scattered wits. 'But how can I leave here, Brother William? And what about Warwick? I cannot desert him again!'

'I have spoken with the queen,' Brother William said, patting her hand. 'She was reluctant at first to let you go, but she has agreed.' He sighed. 'Elizabeth,' the blue eyes looked at her meaningfully, 'if you delay, you may not see her alive. As it is we may be too late...'

'Too late?' Elizabeth gasped. Hot tears ran onto her cheeks and she sniffed them back as best she could. 'And Edmund?' she cried, suddenly thinking of her little brother with only Alice, her nurse, to comfort him. If her mother died, who would look after him? What would happen to their home?

'You must do what you think best, Elizabeth,' Brother William said gently. 'But do not take too long to decide.'

Elizabeth's eyes studied the floor as though the rushes would give her an answer. If she wanted to make her peace with her mother, she would once again have to accept being parted from Warwick. But he had gone to Calais, Lady Scrope had said so; mayhap she would return before he did! And how could she let her mother go to her grave with enmity between them if she had the remedy of it? Forgiveness was what she craved from Warwick; how could she deny that to her mother?

She gave a deep sigh and fixed Brother William's face. 'Brother William,' she said softly, 'I have made my decision.'

BURGUNDIAN COURT DECEMBER 1470

As he rode into the familiar courtyard behind Lord Hastings, Jack tried to remind himself how he had ended up returning here. His thoughts after his last visit had been to return to England while he still could with his head still joined to his neck. But Hastings had been reluctant to let him leave and so now he found himself wrapped in his thickest furs against the icy wind, and heading once again for the lion's den that was Duke Charles's court.

It wasn't an encounter with the duchess that bothered him as much as the thought that Higgins might once again be at liberty. He only hoped the duchess had dealt with him as she said she would; the last thing he needed was his true identity being revealed to his Yorkist lords, for that would then put Elizabeth in danger also. He smiled as he thought on her recent letter promising him more sons when he returned home with the king! He didn't know which the more incongruous part was.

As he dismounted and followed Hastings into the brilliant perfumed warmth of the castle he could not help but question why he was still with Edward and Lord Hastings. He could simply have left, as Elizabeth had, that would have solved his dilemma for him; they would have realized that he was Warwick's man, but he would have been well beyond their reach. But he could not quench the feeling he had that there was something yet to be discovered, something that would be a reward for his endeavours that would aid Warwick's cause. He certainly hoped so, for the longer he served Will Hastings, the harder it was going to be to extricate himself from this web of his own weaving. He liked Hastings and thought it was a pity that they were on opposite

277

sides, for he could imagine himself settling happily into Hastings's retinue. But that, he told himself, was never going to happen, for if Warwick won the field, Hastings would surely become a casualty; he would never forswear his allegiance to Edward, no matter what the cost. And Jack was similarly sworn to Warwick.

Hastings drew his horse to a halt and grooms ran to tend to him. Some nodded to Jack, more comfortable now with his presence.

'You have done well, Jack,' Hastings said as they walked towards the impressive entrance. 'I had begun to wonder if Duke Charles would ever agree to see us.'

Jack smiled. He knew it was not only his work that had brought this about. 'Her Grace has also worked hard for this, my lord,' he said, knowing the duchess had thought on little else but the alliance of her husband and her brother.

Hastings arched his brows. 'You do have interesting friends, Jack,' he said. 'Take care when there is a woman involved; especially this woman.'

Jack knew exactly what he meant, but he could not resist a reply. 'I always take care, my lord,' he said neutrally.

Hastings laughed. 'You think you can handle her? A hundred marks says you cannot, Jack, though what Elizabeth would do if she found out would be a worse punishment than losing a hundred marks, I'll warrant!'

Jack lowered his eyes; he now thought he understood something of Elizabeth's feelings; loving one person and being in the company of another. He tried to put it from his mind; it would be the least of his troubles if Higgins was here.

Trumpets announced their arrival in Duke Charles's apartments. Glittering and golden, they were much as the duchess's were – room after room of incomparable luxury and Jack struggled not to give voice to his awe.

Duke Charles was seated on a velvet covered chair; jewels shimmered about his neck and body and a golden sword at his side.

Jack knelt beside Hastings. He flicked a glance around the room before he lowered his head in obeisance; there was no sign of Higgins here. But then would Duke Charles openly acknowledge that he was also using Edward's spymaster as his own?

After what seemed like an age Duke Charles acknowledged them.

'Lord Hastings, it is good to see you,' he said in a smooth yet neutral voice. 'You must forgive the delay in sending for you, but King Louis and some other Englishmen have kept me busy!'

Jack knew he meant the threat to Burgundy from the French king; but really was that a good enough excuse?

Hastings spoke skilfully. 'My lord it is forgotten now that I am here, but my liege would wish to speak to you himself, of course.'

They were shown to chairs beside Duke Charles and gilded cups and trenchers of sweetmeats were offered to them.

Duke Charles gave a wave of his hand. 'I have other guests, Lord Hastings, and of course I could not give them less than my full attention.'

Hastings smiled. 'I understand, Your Grace.'

So did Jack: the exiled Lancastrians.

'But you must acknowledge, Your Grace, that as your brother, my liege would claim a special place in your heart, surely?'

Now it was Duke Charles's turn to smile ingratiatingly. 'My wife has missed him sorely,' he said diplomatically. 'But you must see my difficulty? I cannot with ease dismiss my kin because Edward is here, you must see that such a situation is impossible?'

Jack saw Hastings's cheeks colour, but he imposed control on his voice. 'I think we both understand that they have now out-stayed their welcome, Your Grace.'

'Indeed they have arrived at the same conclusion!' Charles said impassively.

'And when they leave?' Hastings's asked hopefully.

'I hope to receive my brother before the month is out. My lord, you know what women are!'

Jack smiled inwardly; he certainly knew what the duchess was like and he knew how she would react if she knew he was here!

'And now you must excuse me. I promised my cousins some sport and the horses are waiting!'

Hastings and Jack bowed quickly as the duke rose. He turned in a cloud of thick white velvet and fur and then marched from the room.

When he had gone Hastings and Jack returned to their seats.

'So that's it!' Hastings hissed. 'That's all he has to say. Does he not care for the safe return of England?'

'No, my lord, he does not,' Jack said quietly. 'He has Lancastrian blood in his veins and Yorkist blood in his family by marriage.'

279

Hastings sighed. 'He waits to back the winning horse.'

Jack nodded. 'Though there is some hope, my lord.'

Hastings turned expectantly.

'If King Louis presses him too far he will certainly turn to the House of York!'

'Jack, you are right!' Hastings said, brightening. 'King Louis does not realize that his tactics could yet be to our benefit!'

'Yes, my lord,' Jack said in an uneasy voice; he hoped his urgent message stopped Warwick's attack before it was too late.

LAZENBY MANOR DECEMBER 1470

Elizabeth and Brother William rode on into the gloaming. The black naked branches of the winter trees stood like flaming firebrands against the deep and darkening sky. The shadows lay like tombstones across the track over which they had to ride. Their breath hung in white clouds about them as the temperature plummeted and the hoarfrost began to settle on the iron hard ground, edging every fallen leaf, every twig and blade of steel-coloured grass in glittering whiteness. As they came wearily to the foot of the hill they heard a wolf howl amongst the trees behind them and the cry was taken up by another and then another; the chances of them surviving a night out here in the frozen waste were few, so they pushed on, bathed in an ever deepening crimson light, until the sun sank remorsefully below the horizon, leaving Elizabeth to wonder if it would ever rise again.

She nudged her horse with her heels for encouragement, for with only a frost bright moon to light their progress it would be difficult to find their way, even though Elizabeth had ridden this track perhaps a thousand times before.

The horses' hooves crunched on the frozen earth as they came up the hill, their breath blowing plumes of white smoke into the chill; their harness jingling in the stillness, setting a soporific rhythm that lulled Elizabeth. With hardly any conscious thought she rode past cottages huddled together like sugar subtleties, past brittle woodland and fields in which the barbed grass stood like a forest of silver spears – places she had known as a child and loved, but which now seemed to hold no meaning; it was as though she rode alone in a wilderness of winter.

Lazenby Manor nestled snugly in the valley, blanketed by crisp folding hills. The stream was a silver ribbon, rippled with white where the water was succumbing to the cold. Yellow candlelight flickered out onto the sparkling cobblestones and Elizabeth could imagine nothing but warm fires and hot spiced wine; this did not look like a house of death.

She was aware of Brother William's eyes upon her. When she turned to face him they were wide with sympathy. She smiled. Perhaps if she had trusted those eyes and confessed her sin of murder she would have learned that Jack was not dead. How much easier her life would have been if she had done so, she thought.

'You have faced many difficult things, child,' he said softly, 'and this will be more difficult than most.' He reached across and put his hand on her arm. 'The Lord is with you, Elizabeth.'

Elizabeth shook her head; somehow she thought not. She would need a scroll to list all the sins she had yet to confess and she added to them daily; every lie, every deception, almost every thought seemed to take her further from the truth and add countless hours to her time in Purgatory!

She clenched her fingers inside her fur-lined mittens. She nudged her horse's flanks and moved away from the uncomfortable thoughts.

Hooves slithered on the icy ground as they made their descent and Elizabeth drew her cloak more tightly about her, but the chill she felt had nothing to do with the weather. She sucked in icy air as she tried to steady her nerves; she wondered if her mother was still alive.

* * *

Elizabeth stood at the foot of the stairs. They seemed somehow steeper than she remembered them. She placed one foot on the bottom step gingerly as though it would not take her weight. Then she placed a hand on the smooth wooden rail. It was unbelievably cold. She stared upwards as she climbed into the gloom slowly, deliberately. The fourth stair creaked as it always did, but Elizabeth was oblivious to everything but the sound of her blood thumping in her ears. Her candle flickered, sending thin wisps of smoke curling up beyond the light. When she reached the top she was gasping, as though she had climbed Dallow Gill rather than a simple wooden staircase! The familiar smell of beeswax drifted to her, breathed out by the oak of the dark hallway. Carefully she walked along the passageway as though she were treading on insects rather than sweet smelling rushes.

Elizabeth hesitated at the door. She could hear someone sobbing quietly from within and she guessed it would be Alice. The air seemed dark and heavy, like a weight pressing on her, making her head swim. She did not want to do this, but as Brother William had said, she could not let her mother depart this world without some attempt at reconciliation. Santa Maria, she had sacrificed much to do her mother's bidding!

She knocked gently at the door and without waiting for a reply she ventured in. The door swung obediently inwards uttering a small cry from its hinges.

A musty smell rushed out to her and she knew it was the smell of decay: the smell of death. A knot tightened in her stomach.

The room was smothered in an eerie red glow. Red cloth had been hung at the window and red fustian had been used to cover the bed. It hung down from the bed canopy like bloody rags. Elizabeth wondered if doing this would make any difference; could a colour really possess healing powers?

Alice was at Lady Catherine's side; her face blotched with much weeping. Elizabeth's reluctant eyes then drifted to her mother. Her face was bloodless against the deep red counterpane. Her breathing was erratic and shallow.

'Oh mistress!' Alice rose quickly and threw here arms around Elizabeth. 'I am so glad Brother William managed to reach you in time!'

Elizabeth nodded meekly; it had been so long since she was here that it hardly felt like home and even dear Alice seemed like a stranger to her. Santa Maria, if only I could tell her the things I have seen! Elizabeth thought, but reflected that all of it would have to remain hidden.

'Please mistress, sit down,' Alice gestured to the hard wooden chair she had just vacated. Then she whispered, 'She still hears us, mistress. Tell her you are here.'

Elizabeth bit her lip and stared at the pallid skeletal figure lying next to her; she barely recognized her as the haughty Lady Catherine who had admonished Jack like a naughty child. She sat down in Alice's chair and placed her hand over her mother's. It was deathly cold. 'Mama, I am come home,' she said gently.

She looked at the face on the pillow; beads of sweat stood out on her mother's brow like tears, and her hair was damp where it showed beneath her cap. But she made no response.

'Mama, it is Elizabeth!' she said more loudly, and this time her mother's hand twitched within hers. Dull eyes flickered open and searched the room to find her.

'So you have come home, child?' Lady Catherine's voice was a ghost of its former strength.

'Yes, Mama,' Elizabeth said tremulously. She struggled to force the words out.

Her mother's skin was almost translucent and had a peculiar yellow tinge to it which Elizabeth had never known her to possess in life. She took hold of her hand; it was as though she had picked up only bones.

'I am glad you have come,' Lady Catherine said hoarsely. 'I did not know if you would, but I prayed to the Blessed Lady that Brother William would persuade you and that I would last long enough to make amends.'

Elizabeth swallowed against her dry throat. 'Mama...'

Lady Catherine silenced her with hollow sunken eyes.

'Child,' she coughed. Her chest rattled. 'I should not call you that, Elizabeth, for you are a young woman now.' She coughed again harshly and it was some moments before she could continue.

Elizabeth bent forward and hesitantly kissed her mother's cheek.

Her mother smiled weakly at her touch, but her eyes were closed again as though she did not have the strength left to keep them open. 'I have given Matthew all the instructions. I shall be buried with your father, in the family chapel, and I am sorry, child,' she wheezed, 'sorry for everything.' Her eyes fluttered open.

Elizabeth squeezed her hand. 'Mama, I forgive you,' she whispered.

Lady Catherine shook her head. 'You do not know what you must forgive.'

'For sending me to Edward,' Elizabeth said quietly.

Lady Catherine smiled. 'That is part of it, yes.'

'Mama, what do you mean?' Elizabeth asked her tentatively.

Lady Catherine hesitated. 'There is something I must tell you, Elizabeth. Something you will perhaps not believe but which I hope you can forgive.'

Elizabeth's heart began to race. 'Mama?'

Lady Catherine breathed deeply, gathering her strength. She reached out a hand feebly and Elizabeth passed her a cup of wine from the cabinet. Lady Catherine drank slowly, each swallow rippling through her whole body. Then she settled back against the pillows. 'When your father died I confess I was much angered by you, by your liaison with damned Warwick; he who will never rest until he brings the kingdom of heaven down on his own head! I wanted him to fail and I wanted you to be part of his destruction! I wanted you to take your father's letters to Edward; revenge for his needless death!' she growled. There was a spark of fire in her dull eyes for a moment. Then she continued more softly; 'But that is only one thing for which I crave your forgiveness.'

Elizabeth was puzzled. 'Mama?'

Lady Catherine's chest rose and fell. She swallowed and then rasped another deep breath. 'You know that your father left a will?'

'Yes, Mama,' Elizabeth replied, wondering what was to come.

'Everything was clearly laid out as one would expect from him, including his wishes for yours and Edmund's futures.'

'My future, Mama?' Elizabeth's heart missed a beat and her eyes widened; surely he had not put that wish into writing!

Lady Catherine nodded. 'And for what I did I am truly sorry, Elizabeth. I did not want you to leave me; I wanted things to stay as they were. And I could not contemplate your future with *him*!'

'With – with whom, Mama?' Elizabeth's voice was shaking now. Although she knew perfectly well whom her mother meant, she needed to hear her say his name.

Lady Catherine fixed her gaze. 'With Jack de Laverton,' she whispered.

'Jack!' Elizabeth cried. Jack had told her the truth; she *had* been promised to him!

'I knew you would find it incredible, child, but I swear by all that's Holy, it is true!'

'But how could father have done this without speaking to me?'

Lady Catherine sighed. 'Your father left it to me to tell you, Elizabeth. I am the one to blame. I am the one who failed you.'

'And Jack?' she asked. 'What did he say?' The wounded look Jack gave her when he told her that she was promised to him came to her now and she fought to dismiss it before it unravelled her completely.

'When Jack de Laverton came for you I refused him, even though he carried a letter from your father. I knew your father thought well of him, for Jack saved your father's life at Towton, and those of many men, but I thought him too base a man for you for his mother was a gypsy and he was his father's bastard child, and...and I did not want you to go away!' Lady Catherine's voice tore as she spoke. 'And then when I saw it in your father's will, I knew I had wronged you, but by then it was too late, you had gone to London with Master Higgins!' Lady Catherine began to tremble. 'I have been so selfish; I have denied you your future...' She panted heavily and then said in a threadbare voice; 'You should have had a husband and a household of your own, Elizabeth and I should have been a grand dam by now!'

Elizabeth leaned forward and hugged her mother to her chest. 'Oh, Mama!' she cried. Elizabeth stroked her hand down her mother's back. She could feel her bones as though they were without flesh. 'Hush, Mama,' Elizabeth said. 'I do forgive you.'

Lady Catherine struggled to be free of her embrace. 'But Elizabeth, it is not too late,' Lady Catherine whispered. 'You may have him yet. We can still honour your father's promise to him.'

Elizabeth tried to quell the rising panic. 'No Mama,' she said quickly. 'It *is* too late. I love the Earl of Warwick and I am no longer the virgin bride Sir John de Laverton would expect!' Elizabeth knew exactly what Jack would say to that and she felt guilty for yet another deception, but she could not agree to this!

'You may be right, Elizabeth, but we must try!' Lady Catherine sobbed and it shook her frail body to its core. 'We must try!' She clutched at Elizabeth's gown desperately. 'I must do what your father wanted; I must!' The effort was too much and Lady Catherine wilted onto her pillows, her chest heaving with the sobs that still shook her.

Elizabeth said nothing. Inside she was a mêlée of emotions. Part of her agreed with her mother; they should try to fulfil her father's promise; that was the honourable thing to do, especially as her mother was on the edge of life in this world, but the reality of what that meant lay heavily on her like a wet winter cloak; it was close to madness! But if her mother demanded she marry Jack, how could she refuse her?

Tears squeezed through her lashes and involuntarily she twisted Jack's ring on her finger; what would her mother say if she knew the truth of what had passed between them? She shivered at her deceit.

The door creaked again and her cousin Matthew entered the room. He came to Elizabeth's side and put his thin hand on her shoulder. A shudder ran through Elizabeth's body as if he had touched her with ice.

'It will not be long, I think,' he said with a gentle nod to Lady Catherine's weakening body.

Elizabeth looked up at him sadly. She met his eyes; they seemed hollow in his pinched face.

'Come. Let her sleep,' Matthew said, tucking a lock of lank grey hair behind his ear. 'Alice will keep a watch on her. We have much to discuss.'

* * *

Elizabeth's heart had still not attained its normal rhythm as she followed Matthew into the solar. Jack would not leave her uneasy thoughts; dark and beautiful and dangerous, he was the man with whom her life seemed to be inevitably entwined.

Elizabeth sat beside Matthew at the table where a small supper had been laid out for them and it reminded her of her time at Scarsdale; she almost expected Jack to join them as he had when he watched her for Warwick. It seemed a lifetime ago.

'Did she tell you?' Matthew asked as he put some cold mutton onto a platter for her.

Elizabeth looked at him quizzically.

'About the marriage?' he added.

Elizabeth nodded.

'I can imagine no worse a husband for you than Laverton,' Matthew hissed. 'After Scarsdale...'

Elizabeth did not answer him. She could not tell Matthew that she knew Jack much better than that now, and that she had forgiven him. She had grown so used to his company in Bruges that she almost felt she was his wife already; it seemed incongruous to now deny him!

'So we are agreed we must do something about it then?' Matthew asked as he offered her some wine, oblivious to the turmoil in Elizabeth's mind.

Elizabeth took the cup from him and sipped at it. It tasted bitter. 'But you will be the executor of my mother's will,' she said, avoiding his question.

'I shall,' Matthew said flatly. 'And it will be on my conscience not yours if I do not fulfil that particular obligation.'

Elizabeth gasped. She had been certain Matthew would comply with Lady Catherine's wishes; she did not believe he had the spirit to resist, but maybe he had more strength to resist the dying than he did the living.

Matthew smiled broadly. 'You look puzzled, Elizabeth. Do not worry, all will be well.'

Elizabeth shuddered at the smoothness of his voice. 'How can it be?' she asked, knowing that Matthew had no idea what she would consider to be well.

'I think there is an arrangement which would suit us both and which would guarantee Edmund's future also.' His eyes searched for hers and widened as they met.

Elizabeth's blood ran cold as she read them.

BURGUNDIAN COURT DECEMBER 1470

Jack found the smell of the duchess's perfume intoxicating. She lay with her head against Jack's chest as if checking that the drumming of his heartbeat had slowed following their lovemaking.

Jack stared at the painted ceiling ruefully; she had promised him that if he ever came to court again she would be waiting and, like a cat stalking a bird, she had watched him throughout the Christmas celebrations, narrowing her eyes lasciviously whenever he met her gaze. And although Jack was serving Edward by being here, he felt guilty at the luxury of the surroundings, the decadent opulence of the court and the wantonness of Edward's sister which were all his to enjoy. He hoped it would all be worth the sacrifice he had made, for his soul screamed out that he should be in England and that being here was wrong.

'*Cheri,*' the duchess purred. Her hot breath tickled his skin and he stirred involuntarily. 'How long can you stay, *cheri*?' she asked him softly.

287

Jack stroked a hand over her naked shoulder. 'Tonight must be my last,' he whispered. 'I must return to your brother.'

She turned deep blue eyes up to his. 'Will you take something for me?'

Jack nodded. 'Of course.'

She kissed his stomach and then rolled away from him, slipping lightly from the bed.

He watched the curves of her body as she drifted to the other side of the room. She drew back a heavy curtain to reveal a large coffer. She took a silver key from a box and opened it. Jack could see it contained many letters; how he wished he'd had the time to look through them for himself.

Slipping long fingers between the papers, she drew one folded parchment out. She held it up to the candle flame and satisfied it was addressed correctly, brought it back to the bed.

She smiled as she handed it to him. 'You noticed I have many letters,' she said dryly.

'You are an important woman,' Jack said taking hold of her hand and kissing the inside of her wrist gently. He wondered if he had aroused her suspicion.

She laughed. 'My husband does not think me as important as you do, Jack, otherwise he would not leave me so!'

Jack ran a finger over the line of her chin. 'Thank God he does leave you!' he laughed. 'He has much on his mind. If he makes the wrong choice, he could lose everything.'

The duchess nodded. 'And so could I,' she said. 'Far more than he. That is why you must take this to Edward. He need not worry about George. It is done.'

Jack's throat tightened. He struggled not to let his surprise show. 'Blood is thicker than water,' he said indifferently, as though her words had not had any effect on him.

She smiled and brought her lips close to Jack's. 'As you said, Jack, I am a very important woman, why should I not receive letters from all my brothers? Why would I not want to see the House of York reunited and my husband be the architect of its restoration to the crown of England? And why should I not ensure that it happens?'

Before Jack could form any reply, her lips met his, her tongue searching, her mouth pressing hard to his. She brought her arms up around his neck, wound her fingers in his hair and drew him to her hungrily.

As he made love to her, part of Jack's mind strayed from the pleasure and that part of his mind knew that somehow Warwick must be warned.

LONDON CHRISTMAS 1470

The new moon was a sliver of opalescent white against the clear dark sky as the Duke and Duchess of Clarence's carriage drew up in the courtyard of The Erber.

Warwick watched from the window as Clarence held Isabel's hand while she stepped from the carriage. She seemed as slim as a girl, her gown no longer blooming over curves as it once had. His mind wandered back to last Christmas, when Elizabeth came for the season with Isabel. He heaved a sigh as he thought on their illicit dance; when he would see her again he did not know, but certainly it would not be this Yuletide.

Clarence's smile glittered almost as much as the jewelled belt which girded his waist as he was announced into Warwick's presence, but Warwick noted it was a smile that did not light his eyes.

Warwick acknowledged him briefly then strode quickly to his daughter and, putting etiquette aside, drew her to his chest.

Isabel gasped and stiffened, but as he held her she relaxed against him, as if she were a child again.

'Papa,' she murmured into the velvet of his doublet.

He took comfort in the sweet familiar smell of her hair and his throat tightened as he thought on those who were not able to join him.

'How was Anne?' he asked softly.

Isabel shivered. 'She is now wed to Lancaster, Papa.'

Liquid dark eyes met his, and he knew they shared the same thoughts.

Slowly he released his hold. 'That is good news,' he said, and indeed it gave him some relief to know that Marguerite had at least kept that part of her bargain, but there was a twinge of guilt in his stomach as he remembered his and Anne's last conversation in France, when she had buckled on her courage like the cold steel of a cuirass. She had done this for him, no, that was not true; she had done this for all of them.

'My lord!' Clarence barked his annoyance.

Warwick turned his attention to his son-in-law. 'Forgive me, George,' he said thickly. 'It has been so long...' He gestured for them to sit at his board and then he joined them.

'I would have thought, my lord that you would have been with the king this night,' Clarence said.

Warwick smiled ruefully, trying to discern the tone of Clarence's enquiry. 'I have been with the king and the French ambassadors all day, George. I wanted tonight to be for family and I wanted to be here.' He wanted to be at The Erber, for somehow the essence of Elizabeth remained here, especially in the garden.

Clarence raised an eyebrow and Isabel too seemed a little taken aback.

'Family?' Clarence repeated, and now he could not keep the sarcasm from his voice.

Warwick saw Isabel flash a ferocious look at her husband, but he either did not notice or did not heed her warning.

'Family, indeed,' Clarence said petulantly, 'there are not many here, my lord!'

Warwick's blood burned in his cheeks. 'Archbishop Neville will join us for Mass later,' he said, clenching his jaw. 'John is in the north, arraying men.'

Clarence shrugged. 'I see,' he said flatly. He did not meet Warwick's eyes, but looked towards the chaplain, as a hint to start Grace.

Warwick nodded his assent, and as the words cloaked the food in blessing he studied Clarence carefully.

The servants poured their wine and carved slices from the boar's head.

'I thought it would be pleasant to be together,' Warwick said, turning to Isabel, 'for we cannot see into the future. Who knows where we will spend our next Yuletide?'

'If this is not the last,' Clarence said under his breath.

Warwick ignored him.

'It is nice to be without the French ambassadors, Papa,' Isabel said softly, trying to mend fences. 'I too have had enough of their clamouring and I have been here but a short time. It is good that we are alone.'

Clarence growled in his throat. 'We will have to make love to the French before long, Isabel, and the Lancastrians too, just like your sister!'

'We are all Lancastrian now,' Warwick said flatly, trying to bridle his anger.

Isabel dropped her eyes momentarily. 'But at least we are home,' she said, 'dear Anne is with Queen Marguerite!'

'Aye, you are right, Isabel. We are home. I think mayhap you have forgotten how your position stood before we left England, George.'

Clarence studied the perfect folds of the starched table linen.

'You had nothing, George,' Warwick reminded him. 'You were a traitor, attainted, with all your lands gone to that ingrate brother of yours I once loved like a son!'

'I know what I was,' Clarence snapped, 'and I am little better now!'

'George!' Isabel gasped. She reached out and gripped her husband's arm.

Clarence shook her off. 'Tutbury is to go,' Clarence complained, 'and how long will I keep the others, my lord?'

'You agreed to hand over Tutbury at Angers,' Warwick said coldly. 'For anything else you will be recompensed.'

Clarence brayed mockingly. 'Will I? I have nothing to maintain my status, and my lands were those of Marguerite's dower; she will want them all returning, you know she will!'

'And you will be recompensed!' Warwick said again, trying not to let his anger rise from his belly into his voice. 'Were you not given the Honour of Richmond? Have you not obtained the dower lands of Elizabeth Wydeville?'

Clarence nodded grudgingly. 'But they are too poor and too few,' he muttered.

'And you have your duchy of York!'

'But the lands are in godforsaken Wales!' Clarence bleated.

'God's blood, George!' Warwick's heart leaped in anger. 'I have lost land too, but it is more important that we hold the alliance together! There is no going back, George, the die is cast.'

Clarence shifted uncomfortably on his chair and pricked the tablecloth with his jewelled knife.

'I have lost the Clifford estates in Cumberland and Westmoreland, how does that help me as the Warden of the West March? The Butler estates in Northamptonshire and Buckinghamshire are also gone and in 'godforsaken Wales', as you so eloquently put it, Jasper Tudor now holds sway; I share the Stafford lordships of Hay, Huntington and Brecon with him! And all John has as his reward is the return of the Wardenship of the East March – but not the Percy lands of Northumberland to furnish it with – all he has is Wressel! We have all made sacrifices, George.'

Clarence poked at a piece of meat sulkily. 'I know,' he said glumly, 'but 'tis me they hate; I am Edward's brother and they let me know it!'

Warwick shook his head in frustration. 'And Somerset hates me, George. And soon he will be on England's shores and Exeter with him.' Warwick sighed resignedly; this was another battle he yet had to face, perhaps a harder one to win than the one to come against Edward! For Somerset was Queen Marguerite's favourite and how much she would favour him once Edward was defeated, he could not tell. ''Tis certain he will not forgive me,' Warwick said to himself.

'George,' he said gently, returning to Clarence. 'You were the king's brother and it counted for nought, he even forbade you to marry where you loved.' He glanced at Isabel and she smiled encouragingly. 'His only reason for doing so was to set himself against me, at the Wydeville's behest. You know this is true. And with the Nevilles gone they would have turned their venom to you and Richard. Hastings too they have no love for. I could not see all I care about ruined; their bones picked clean by these scavengers. We have made our choice, George. It is past regret.' He said the last sentence softly, knowing they all had regrets, some of which he knew he could not give voice to here. Clarence turned dark eyes up to him at last and Warwick saw the turmoil of his soul through them, as if he looked through an open door. But in spite of his second sight, Warwick could not see which way Clarence would turn in the end. Would his love for Isabel make him a Neville, or would he heed the call of his Plantagenet blood? For now he was with him and Warwick had no choice but to trust him.

LAZENBY MANOR CHRISTMAS 1470

'Lisbet, Lisbet!' Edmund's voice was high with excitement as he greeted her. He now came up to her shoulder and his puppy fat had left him a sinuous and lively youth.

'Edmund!' Elizabeth smiled.

He flung gangly arms about her waist and she hugged him to her. She ruffled his tangled blond hair and tried not to let him see the tears welling in her eyes.

'How you have grown!' she said proudly.

'Cousin Matthew has bought me a new pony!' he declared.

Elizabeth looked up to where Matthew stood in the doorway. Her stomach tightened. 'Thank you,' she said to him, but there was no warmth in her voice.

'Think of it as a Christmas present, if you wish,' Matthew said, plainly catching her tone.

'You must watch me ride him,' Edmund continued, oblivious to their conversation.

'I shall,' Elizabeth said returning her eyes to Edmund, 'but you must promise not to make too much noise, Mama is unwell.' She knew it was an understatement, but somehow she knew she must begin to prepare Edmund for what was to come. Yes he was still a child, but she would do him no favours by protecting him from what was inevitable. As she knew all too well, the world was full of death, and how many more would die when Warwick met Edward in battle!

Edmund squirmed free of her arms. 'Come, Lisbet, watch me now!' he said taking her hand and pulling her towards the door.

Alice was just in time to throw Elizabeth's cloak over her shoulders as Edmund raced ahead into the yard.

Elizabeth smiled as he leapt into the saddle of a fine black pony and Edmund was right, this was not a pony like his little grey, this was well muscled, more like a small horse.

'What is his name?' she called as Edmund began to trot round the yard.

'Arrow, because he is as fast as one!' he shouted excitedly.

Elizabeth folded her arms across her body, hugging her cloak to her; the winter wind was like ice.

'He rides well,' Matthew said.

Elizabeth had not heard him approach and she shivered at his closeness.

'He does,' she replied indifferently.

'He longs to follow your father and become a knight.'

Elizabeth closed her eyes for a moment and breathed deeply, for she knew the only way that would happen was if she made the sacrifice Matthew wanted.

'You cannot deny him that future,' Matthew continued.

Elizabeth bit her lip. She wanted to scream that it was Matthew who would take it from him, that if he left them alone they would be all right. But she knew it was not entirely true. For when her mother died and Edmund had Lazenby where else could she go, but where Matthew wanted her to be? She could not return to Warwick unless he sent for her and that would not happen until Edward was defeated. She shuddered; what if Edward won...

BRUGES JANUARY 1471

'To England?' William Hastings was evidently surprised by the renewal of Jack's request. He looked up from his wine quickly. 'At this time of year?'

'Yes, my lord. I wish to return to Elizabeth,' Jack said. 'And there are men that will sail.'

'For a price!' Hastings said.

'Indeed my lord, but a price worth paying, for me at least.'

'And who would not wish to be in England if they had a wife such as you do?' Hastings said with a smile.

Jack returned it. 'As you know from the queen's letters, my lord, she did lose our child and now her mother is dying, only because of that did she leave the queen's company. The long winter nights are a dark time to be alone with grief. I would be with her.' Jack sipped his wine and stretched his legs out towards the fire, emphasizing the warmth and comfort of company. Thank God for Brother William's letter!

'Truly, I am sorry for it,' Hastings said with a nod. Then he added more softly, 'but I did warn you not to let her sail alone.'

Jack met his gaze. 'You did, my lord, but you also know enough of Elizabeth to know she would not be cosseted.'

Hastings smiled and looked towards the firelight.

'And, my lord I can still be of good service,' Jack continued, 'for I can assess the scale of Warwick's defences; perhaps advise on the best place to land your fleet.'

"Fleet' might be too grand a word for it, Jack! Duke Charles has agreed to meet Edward at Aire before Epiphany, thanks to you, but he has not yet agreed to provide anything else.'

Jack leant forward eagerly. 'But he will, my lord, I know it,' he said. The duchess had told him that the argument was being won. 'For the English raids have told Duke Charles one thing; he can never make peace with an England under Warwick! It is now only a matter of time.'

Hastings smiled. 'I hope to God you are right, Jack.'

Jack leant back in his chair and resisted the temptation to say that he always was, and had he not tried to warn Warwick of the danger of this? He cursed inwardly that Warwick had not heeded him; it was as though he craved a confrontation with Edward: a battle that would resolve all.

Hastings studied Jack intently and Jack wondered if he still harboured some suspicion. There had been doubts there in the early days; both he and Elizabeth had seen it. But Hastings had had plenty of time to investigate him and his story if he had wished to. Then a cold thought struck him: what if Higgins had made contact? Jack realized he still didn't know what had happened to Higgins. Hastings was too smooth a character to leap to accusations and anyway Jack had been too useful to dispense with easily. But what if his usefulness was waning? Jack drank his wine awkwardly. It was more important than ever that he left for England soon. But Hastings had not yet answered him.

'My lord?' Jack asked as evenly as his thumping heart would let him.

LONDON JANUARY 1471

Warwick's desk was littered with documents. His wrist ached from signing what seemed to be a never-ending stream of letters, warrants and edicts and he wondered ruefully how the scribes managed to write so perfectly for hour after hour without suffering permanently from cramp. But then perhaps they did, he thought, and perhaps they were equally astounded at how a man might wield a sword or battle-axe for hour after hour, but then, Warwick mused, one's life depended on it, and it was amazing how that gave strength to one's arm!

'His Grace, the Archbishop of York, my lord,' Thomas announced.

Archbishop Neville came into the room in a swirl of velvets and furs. His breath was short and he dispensed with courtesies.

'Richard,' he gasped. 'Have you heard?'

Warwick smiled at his brother's distress and signalled for Thomas to bring him wine.

'Whatever it is will wait until you are recovered,' he said calmly. Part of him did not want to hear the news his brother brought, for he knew it was another stick to lay across his back, whatever it was.

Archbishop Neville sat heavily on a cushioned chair. He gulped at the wine Thomas offered and gradually his breathing became less raw.

Warwick raised an eyebrow enquiringly.

'Somerset and Exeter are here,' he said shakily.

Warwick nodded. Thanks to Jack de Laverton he had known that Duke Charles had allowed them to leave his court. He knew also that the motive for doing so was that they would be a restless influence amongst the Lancastrians, hating Warwick as they did, and he knew also that it was dear Edward who had begged Charles to let them loose. He sighed. 'I have been expecting them,' he said impassively.

'Richard!' Archbishop Neville was incredulous. 'How can you remain so calm? They will bring nothing but trouble to already stormy waters. I had hoped they would journey to France and escort Marguerite.'

'Aye, brother that would have been a useful enterprise, for yet she tarries, though she has at least made it to the coast!' He smiled at the irony in his own voice. 'I wonder if she will reach us before Edward does.'

Archbishop Neville shook his head. 'What shall we do?' he asked.

Warwick leant back in his chair and pillowed his hands behind his head. 'We trust them,' he said flatly.

'Richard!'

'I mean it, George. We do not need to give in to their every demand, and I know there will be many, but we need to minimise their disruption and the only way to do that is to make concessions if we can.'

'Clarence will not like it,' Archbishop Neville said warningly.

'George, *I* do not like it, but there is little I can do. We cannot make war on our own band; we must fight Edward together. We share the same enemy, and that makes us if not friends, allies at least! They are fools if they do not see this.'

'But Somerset...'

Warwick slew his words. 'George!' The name was a plea for understanding, for support. 'We can trust in nought but God, you

296

tell me. I swore the most holy of oaths, George and I must trust in God to help me fulfil it!'

Archbishop Neville snorted.

Warwick laughed. 'Why do I sound like the Archbishop and you the doubter?'

'Richard I am just being realistic. We do not want to leave everything in God's hands!'

'What would you have me do with them? They are our allies!'

Archbishop Neville let out a deep slow breath. 'Keep out of their way, Richard. 'Tis you they hate most, you they blame for their exile, you they hold responsible for Lancaster's losses.'

Warwick laughed again. 'Because it's true; I *was* responsible, God knows it!'

'Richard, heed me, please,' Archbishop Neville said plaintively. 'It might be better if they do not see you.'

'You are right, brother, I know. But I will not hide from them. I will run from no one. Not from them and not from Edward. I must go to the Cinque Ports to recruit men for the ships parliament gave me to escort Marguerite and you know I must see the coastal defences too.'

Archbishop Neville nodded. 'No one knows the seas as you do, Richard.'

'Aye, and no one knows parliament like you do. Will you and Clarence be able to stand together?'

'Yes,' he said slowly.

'You hesitate about Clarence?'

Archbishop Neville met his look. He did not need to say anything.

'I know,' Warwick said sadly, 'I know more than he thinks I do, but so far he has not failed us, George. He may not keep his word to Edward; he may not keep faith with me. Who can say?'

LAZENBY MANOR FEBRUARY 1471

Elizabeth squinted through the red gloom; it was daylight outside, a glorious frost-bright day, but inside her mother's chamber it was as though someone had poured crimson smoke into the room.

'Elizabeth,' Lady Catherine's voice cracked. 'Elizabeth, bring me the cloth you see on the dresser.'

Elizabeth peered to where her mother's skeletal finger pointed.

The black damask was of the finest quality. It was silky and cold in her hands as she lifted it. It smelled a little musty and she wondered for how long her mother had kept it, knowing this hour would come.

'It is what was left from your father's bier cloth,' Lady Catherine whispered, 'I want to share that with him as I shared his things in life.'

Elizabeth's eyes began to sting, but she bit her lip to prevent herself from crying.

'I will see that it is done, Mama,' she whispered.

'And your father's will,' Lady Catherine said, 'I have had the same words written into mine. You know of what I speak.'

'Mama,' Elizabeth said hoarsely, 'Mama, I cannot promise you that. Much depends on Sir John de Laverton.' Somehow it was easier if she did not acknowledge that Jack was the same person. 'I do not even know where he is...and Mama, there is Warwick.'

Lady Catherine sucked in her breath sharply. 'Do not mention him, Elizabeth! He can never be yours nor you his. I forbid you to go to him. You must marry Jack de Laverton and take care of Edmund until he comes of age. That is what your father wanted. That is what I want. Can you not promise me that?' she asked tersely.

'I promise I shall see that Edmund is all right,' Elizabeth said.

Lady Catherine closed her eyes as fierce pain shook her.

Elizabeth reached for the drink the physician had left her, the one made from poppies, which eased the spasms and made her sleep.

Lady Catherine sucked it desperately between her dry lips. Her breathing was quick and shallow and then gradually settled as the pain eased.

'I cannot face your father knowing that I did not carry out his wishes. Elizabeth, if you love me, you will obey me in this. Speak with Cousin Matthew. He will help you.'

Guilt twisted Elizabeth's stomach; she could not admit to hers and Matthew's conspiracy, though the offer he had made was darker than the one her mother requested of her. 'I will speak to Matthew,' she said.

Lady Catherine melted into the pillows. Somehow they seemed much bigger today; seemed to suck her into them.

'Mama?' Elizabeth noted the change in her mother's breathing with alarm.

'Alice!' she called. 'Alice, fetch the priest, and send for Matthew!'

* * *

In the coldest darkest hour before dawn, Lady Catherine gave one last great shudder, as if a hand had reached within her body and plucked out her heart. Then all was silence save for the aching purity of the priest's ritual chanting.

The candles guttered, as if in a gentle breeze.

Swathed in cloying incense, Elizabeth gasped.

'Her struggle is over,' Alice said quietly as she touched her hand to Elizabeth's head in a soft caress.

Elizabeth looked up at her through blurring eyes. 'No, Alice,' she whispered, 'her struggle is just beginning.' And how much harder that struggle would be she thought, if she did not honour her mother's last wishes and marry Jack. For without their union her mother must face the consequences of failing to honour Sir Robert's promise to Jack; of failing to execute his will. Purgatory was indeed a cruel and frightening place. Elizabeth had not given any undertaking, had not eased her mother's troubled mind; how could she? She would have to live with the guilt of it.

'Master Hardacre must be told,' Alice said hesitantly.

'Now?' Elizabeth asked. She did not want Matthew to invade their privacy.

Alice nodded, plainly understanding Elizabeth's reluctance. 'He must pay his respects, Elizabeth, you must allow him that.'

Elizabeth shivered. She knew what this would herald; Matthew would execute his plan and she was powerless to stop him. 'Very well,' she whispered resignedly. 'But he must not stay too long, Alice. She must be washed and dressed before she grows cold. And Edmund must see her too.'

Alice smiled thinly, then curtseyed and left her. The priest followed her out after murmuring something Elizabeth did not quite hear, but assumed was meant to comfort her.

Elizabeth stared blankly at the hollow casket of human flesh and bone that once held her mother's life force. She leant forward very slowly and kissed her cheek. It was still faintly warm. 'Adieu,' she whispered. 'I am sorry, Mama. You must see I cannot do as you ask.'

Slowly she rose from the chair and went to the casement. Tugging fiercely, she pulled the blood red hangings from the windows. Then she forced the reluctant latch and allowed the night in. Cold air rushed into her lungs as she opened the window wider; it was a superstition she knew, but she did not want to trap her mother's soul within the chamber.

And then the tears came against her will, stinging, burning. They ran like rain onto her cheeks and she felt her energy being washed away with them, plundered by the grief and the dread of what was to come, but she knew Matthew could not be refused. Yet how could she face a future without Warwick? Santa Maria, she had failed him again! It had been an impossible choice and yet she had made it; she would not sacrifice Edmund's future for her own happiness, surely Warwick would understand that? And she could see no other way of protecting her little brother. She sighed bitterly; though he did not yet know it, Matthew had won.

~ELEVEN~

DOVER MARCH 1471

The wind howled over the sea like a dying soul. It found Warwick on the quay, staring out at the black water and listening to
the constant lapping of the waves against the harbour wall. He
had purposefully drawn away from his men. They were huddled
like hags over a large crimson brazier; its reflections dripped into
the sea and Warwick thought it looked like blood. His mind was
as dark as the water; his despair as deep as the unfathomable
ocean which tonight the new moon could not illuminate.

He moved further off. His feet crunched on the frozen ground
and his breath floated about him like smoke, yet his cloak hung
loosely; he did not feel the cold of the night. But inside was different; inside he was deepest winter. His heart was colder than
the wind at Wensleydale; his hope had frozen to silent despair.

God's blood, will there be no end to this waiting, he thought.

The men laughed again and the sound stung his ears like hail-
stones. He moved further away to where he could just pick out
the faint white wave crests as they dashed themselves to oblivion
on the rocks. Was that to be his fate too? For without Marguerite
and Edouard of Lancaster he had no teeth with which to grip the
country and rule as he wished. And with his beloved Elizabeth
held fast in the north by winter's icy hand, he had no one in
whom he could confide. 'Curse this season,' he thought. 'God it
were spring.'

'My lord.'

Jack's voice startled him.

Warwick turned to see Jack wrapped in a thick black fur-lined
cloak, his hands muffled in long gloves. Jack's teeth were chatter-
ing.

'Will you not come in, my lord?' he asked. 'Watching the sea
will not bring them any sooner. They surely will not come now
until the weather turns.'

Warwick sighed. 'I know Jack,' he said softly, 'but how long will
that be? You had to wait for how many weeks before the weather
turned? And you know I bear this idleness poorly. Like winter's
frozen grip, I wish to shake it off!'

'Aye my lord, so do I; this inactivity only breeds discontent,'
Jack said flatly.

Warwick smiled ruefully. 'I am the lord of discontent, Jack – the very harbinger of it!'

Jack returned his smile and began rubbing his hands together briskly. 'There will be discontent with or without you, my lord,' he said.

'Mayhap you are right,' Warwick said. 'But I know it would be easier if Lancaster were here.'

'And Marguerite?' Jack asked.

'You are right, Jack. She is a mixed blessing indeed.'

'Somerset cannot wait for her return, neither can Oxford.'

'Aye, Somerset thinks on revenge,' Warwick said darkly.

'And Marguerite does not?'

Warwick shrugged. 'It is a chance I must take, Jack. I have done all I swore to do in restoring Henry to the throne; now she must keep her side of the bargain. Remember, she swore on the True Cross as I did; that is a mighty oath to break!'

'You are right, my lord; even she might balk at that.'

Though he said nothing further, Warwick saw the doubt in Jack's eyes and it mirrored his own. Though he wished for Edouard of Lancaster and his mother, once here he might soon wish them returned to France!

'Jesu, it is cold my lord,' Jack shivered. 'May we not go in? I can vouch for the quality of the hippocras and there is something I must speak with you about.'

Warwick nodded.

As he followed Jack along the harbour wall he took one last look at the melancholy water and he prayed the wait would not be as long as Jack's.

LINCOLNSHIRE MARCH 1471

The sun was a pale yellow splash above the sleepy hills. Mist lay in the wooded valley like a cold damp cloak and tried to smother the irrepressible birdsong that wanted to greet the day.

Jack turned moodily towards the remains of last night's camp-fire and kicked at it sullenly with his boot, trying to force it into life, trying to milk some glimmer of warmth from the still-glowing, ash-covered embers. Faint silver smoke curled upwards like a thin snake and the smell twitched his nose. He groaned; his back ached, his knees ached; in fact it seemed as though the damp had crept into every joint of his body and rendered it as stiff as a rusty door-hinge. He threw off his blanket and rose reluctantly to a sitting position. He pushed his right hand through his tangled hair and then knuckled the sleep from his eyes. He ran his fingers over his chin and felt the raw stubble of his beard; no chance of a decent shave out here, he thought.

Comet whickered softly, evidently realizing Jack was awake, well half awake at least!

Jack forced himself upright. He reached into his bedroll and pulled out his sword. He buckled it on, adjusting the soft leather straps until it sat easily across his thigh. He surveyed the disarray of his campsite with some shame. Had he really been so tired last night that everything had slept where it fell? It was nigh on a week since he had left Warwick; much later than he had wanted to but it had taken that long to extricate himself from the tasks and errands Warwick had given him to do and though he had tried on several occasions, he still had not expressed his fears for Clarence's loyalty. Each time he had raised the subject, Warwick has changed it, as though he did not want to have the doubts let out into the open, but Jack thought he must share those doubts, surely! Eventually he gave up trying. He knew the reason why and it was the same reason that he had pushed both himself and Comet to reach this far north so quickly; perhaps he had pushed too hard. He gathered his things together and then reached into his pack. He pulled out some cold beef and began to chew on it. He made a face; it was stringy and tough, but he knew he needed this to sustain him if he was going to reach Yorkshire by nightfall. If Lady Catherine was indeed dead as Brother William had told him, then Elizabeth would be in need of his help. He hoped he was not too late!

Jack looked up at the darkening sky. Silver rain began to spear down to the damp earth. It cascaded from the bare branches and clung to the curls at his brow, dripping steadily into his eyes. It ran in cold trickles down his cheek and off his chin.

Comet shook his head, ruffling his mane and sending out a shower of icy droplets.

Jack sighed. He leant forward and stroked the damp neck of his courser soothingly. 'This is a Yorkshire welcome indeed,' he said ruefully. He cursed inwardly; this weather would slow them down; he had forgotten how long winter kept a hold in his home county.

He squeezed his legs to the horse's sides and Comet obeyed his command, willingly ploughing into the mud that had arisen where the track used to be.

As they continued on to higher ground, the rain eased off and Jack noticed the air turn suddenly colder. Even through his fur lined gloves his hands began to stiffen on the reins.

The sky became a crisp and lucid blue and Jack wondered if they would have snow before he reached Lazenby; certainly there would be a frost tonight at the least and he did not relish the thought of another night in the open, but a man travelling alone always took a risk when he sought shelter; not every town was as welcoming as Bruges and in Bruges he had almost died!

FLUSHING MARCH 1471

William Hastings watched the grey clouds scud across the horizon like great birds in flight and as he stared at the blur of sea and sky beyond which England lay, he wondered if they truly would be able to take the crown from Warwick. He had cloaked his own doubts in order to raise his king's spirits, but now they came unbidden to his conscious mind; could they really take back the country from the man adored by the commons as their Ulysses? In truth he did not know but knew he had to believe that they could, for if he did not who then would stand by Edward? As if summoned by thought his king appeared on the pier and Hastings bowed as Edward joined him. The hair at the back of his neck prickled as he saw that Anthony Wydeville had come to inspect their fleet too. He drew a veil over his thoughts, the last thing he needed was for Anthony Wydeville to see any weakness.

'Well done, Anthony, well done, Will!' Edward beamed as he cast his eyes critically over the flotilla of ships moored in the harbour.

Hastings looked across at Anthony Wydeville. They had worked well together, he had to admit, but he hoped once Edward was restored to the throne they would not have to work so closely together again; working with a Wydeville was almost more than he could take!

'How many ships?' Edward asked.

'Thirty-six, Your Grace!' Hastings and Anthony Wydeville replied in unison. Hastings turned quickly and Anthony Wydeville's' glare locked onto his.

Edward laughed softly. 'Lord Rivers, please see that all is ready at our lodgings,' he said.

Anthony Wydeville bowed, shot a scornful look towards Hastings, and then left them.

'Will, your face is as red as a sunset! Can you not put your differences aside?' Edward asked, still smiling.

'Ned, I assure you...'

'You can assure me that you dislike each other as much as ever, 'tis plain to see, Will. I only hope you both hate Warwick more than each other!'

Hastings bowed his head contritely. 'Of course, Ned,' he answered. 'We have recruited twelve hundred men,' he said trying to distract Edward away from his dislike of Anthony Wydeville. 'There are Flemish handgunners too and Henry Borselle, the admiral of Burgundy has given you his best ship!'

'His best ship?' Edward asked.

'Indeed,' Hastings answered.

'Remind me, Will, what is she called?' Edward grinned at his Chamberlain.

Hastings flushed again, knowing the jest Edward was playing. 'I forget, Ned,' he stammered, unwilling for once to play along.

Edward arched a brow and then laughed. 'So do I, Will. So do I!'

Hastings knew perfectly well what the ship in which they would invade England was called, but he wasn't going to say its name... the 'Antony'!

Edward walked down to the quayside and together they stared in silence at the pewter coloured sea. The wind whipped in from the east and sleet slapped in their faces, reminding them that spring was yet but a young season. Edward cast his eyes heavenwards.

'The seamen say there will be storms before we are ready to sail,' Hastings said flatly, looking at the darkening sky.

Edward nodded. 'I'd feared as much. Curse Charles for prevaricating!'

'But at least the storms that delay us will delay Lancaster also,' Hastings said hopefully, trying to salvage something from the miserable weather.

Edward smiled. 'We are so close, Will,' he said almost wistfully.

'I know, my lord, but we cannot risk all in this weather. As it is the odds are against us. What was it the Italian ambassador reportedly said? 'It is not easy to leave by the door and then to come in by the window!"

They both laughed ironically; there was more than a grain of truth in what the ambassador had said. If they did not recruit men as soon as they landed they would be swallowed up by the Lancastrian army, the size of which they could only speculate upon, but which for certain contained Warwick, Montagu and Oxford.

'It doesn't look good, Will, does it?' Edward asked, his eyes suddenly downcast.

'You must have faith, Ned,' Hastings said, feeling suddenly guilty for repeating the ambassador's words and for allowing his own doubts to surface. 'God has ever favoured your cause. Remember the sun in splendour and why you took it as your badge? Only God could have put three suns in the heavens.'

'Three suns,' Edward smiled. 'The sons of York you said, Will. But there are now only two.'

Hastings smiled. 'With or without Clarence you shall prevail, Ned,' he met Edward's eyes. 'You have offered him pardon. There is nothing more you can do for him.'

The wind grew suddenly stronger so that their faces began to sting.

'Come, my lord,' Hastings said with a wicked grin. 'Let us see what fine lodgings Lord Rivers has prepared for us!'

LAZENBY MANOR MARCH 1471

In the flickering light of the evening candle Elizabeth knelt at her prie-dieu and took out her rosary. The beads were cold in her hands, the floor was hard on her knees; Santa Maria, how many hours she had spent here already – why did she now think that prayer would help her? She closed her eyes tightly and breathed in and out slowly, trying to calm her grieving heart. She had to face the fact that she was now responsible for Edmund and responsible for Lazenby too, though she knew that even though Lazenby was her home she did not wish to be here; there was another part of this kingdom that held far greater affection for her and that was wherever Warwick was.

Her head told her it was impossible: she ached for Warwick yet how could she be with him? She wished she could return to the happy times they had spent together, when their love had been enough for both of them. 'Holy Mother of God, protect him,' she murmured, and almost added 'from me!' for the guilt of her betrayal was still a burning pain she could not assuage, and she knew the pain would never leave her until she had earned his forgiveness.

To stay here had been the most difficult decision she had ever made yet how could she fail Edmund? She had promised her mother she would look after him; it had been about the only thing she could promise her mother, for though her feelings for Jack were stronger than she would like to admit they certainly didn't run to marrying him, not that she knew where Jack was either!

Without Jack and without Warwick it seemed that her only option was to follow Matthew's wishes, even though they ran so contrary to her own. A shiver licked up her spine as she thought of a future with Matthew and she tightened the beads further, so that they bit into her wrist and hand as if feeling the pain would somehow negate her other feelings. She felt powerless and trapped, caught between her duty to Edmund and her love for Warwick, and like a songbird tangled in a limed hedge, she could see no way to escape.

LONDON MARCH 1471

Warwick's return from Dover was not as he'd hoped. He had thought it would be a triumphal procession of splendour as he escorted Queen Marguerite and Edouard of Lancaster and his own sweet Anne back into the capital. But Jack had been right; they would not come until the storms abated and he could not afford to be idle at the coast for so long.

As he strode into his apartments at the palace his brother was waiting for him. Archbishop Neville's brows were pleated with concern, though he did manage a brief smile of welcome.

'She did not come,' he said.

Warwick thought it was meant to be a question, but his brother said it so dispassionately that it was definitely a statement of fact.

A servant removed Warwick's heavy winter cloak from his shoulders, but he felt no lighter without it. He threw his gloves onto the table, ruffled the ears of a passing alaunt and then strode to the fire. 'The weather worsens by the day,' he said rubbing his hands together as near to the flames as he dared.

'You sailed through a storm,' Archbishop Neville said flatly.

Warwick smiled. 'I did, George, but I know when to risk all. Marguerite will not risk Lancaster until the sea is like a mirror. I can understand that. He is her future...' he fixed his brother 'and ours too, for from him comes the Neville crown!'

Archbishop Neville said nothing but Warwick could feel his uneasiness.

'At least let me sit down, George before you give me the worst of it!' Warwick said, seeing that even the promise of a crown had done nothing to brighten George's mood.

'I am sorry, Richard,' he said gently, taking a seat opposite Warwick's.

Warwick took a cup of hot wine and sipped at it slowly. He watched his brother over the rim of the cup, but George would not meet his eyes. 'Well, George. Let me hear it.'

'London is quiet,' Archbishop Neville said softly, 'too quiet, Richard. All wait upon Edward's arrival. Mayor Stockton has taken to his bed and several other aldermen are known to have begun packing their things. The French ambassadors too are nervous and request permission to return to France.'

'Like rats leaving a ship that flounders, eh?' Warwick said laconically.

Archbishop Neville shrugged. 'I suppose so, Richard.'

Warwick sighed. 'I will speak to the ambassadors tomorrow. It would be better if they waited for Marguerite. I do not want Louis distressed. Who knows what he might then do!'

Servants slipped into the room and silently set the board. They came to Warwick with rosewater to wash his hands. 'I have done all I can, George,' he said ruefully. 'We always knew Edward would come.'

'But the storms will delay him also, will they not, Richard?' Archbishop Neville asked.

Warwick shook his head. 'Not necessarily; and not for long if he has any courage in his veins. Edward is by nature a gambler, George; give him one chance and he will take it, whatever the odds. The greater the odds against him, the more illustrious the victory, that is how it will seem to him. One break in the weather and he will be here, George of that you can be certain.'

Warwick moved to the trestle, sat down and surveyed the array of dishes.

Archbishop Neville joined him, said a short Grace and was soon cutting a piece of barnacle goose. 'Will he really risk everything?' he asked.

Warwick laughed without humour. 'Of course!' He knew that this was the real difference between himself and Edward. Warwick liked to be sure, to be as certain as he could be, to have planned for everything. Edward had the blind courage of a younger man, one who had never had his fingers burned in battle.

'Is there nothing more we can do, Richard?' The strain showed in Archbishop Neville's voice.

Warwick sliced a piece of goose with his knife. 'Fauconberg has the seas. Scrope and Oxford are patrolling the east; Clarence is in the west with Isabel. Kent is as loyal as ever and the north...' he hesitated, 'the north we should not need to worry about for they are Lancastrian at heart thanks to Percy's restoration to Northumberland, but John is at Pontefract should Percy fail me.'

Warwick met his brother's eyes and he saw Archbishop Neville's doubts. 'Do not question John's loyalty, George,' he growled through clenched teeth. 'You will remember that it was you who counselled me to trust in his Neville blood!'

Archbishop Neville lowered his eyes. 'I am sorry Richard, but you yourself said he was a Yorkist too long!'

'Too long for many of our Lancastrian allies, George, not too long for me!' Anger tightened Warwick's throat. 'God's blood, George. How many times have I fought with John at my side? I will trust him with my life, but...' he tasted bile, 'but will the Lancastrians do so if you cannot?'

Archbishop Neville made a strange sound in his throat. 'I am sorry, Richard,' he stammered. 'It is Percy I doubt, Richard, and if he fails then will John make an end of it without you? Will John face Edward in battle alone?'

Warwick shook his head. 'We swore, George. We are brothers.' He reached for his wine and drank deeply, as if to wash the taste of the conversation away. John was the best soldier he knew, the bravest man, and his favourite brother. He had never really doubted he would eventually remember he was a Neville, never doubted he would be anything but true...never that is, until now.

Jack leaned against the warm flank of his grey courser, tightening the girth. The comforting smell of the stallion tickled his nose. The leather creaked as he pulled it up one hole against the stallion's bulging side.

'Too much bran, Comet,' he said as he forced the girth tighter. 'And we've a few more miles to go, boy,' he whispered to the dappled fur. But he knew both of them had benefited from resting here. He had relished the hot bath and warm pottage and Comet too seemed easy in his stall.

Comet blew out clouds of chaff by way of answer.

Jack patted the thick muscular neck and smiled; there really was nothing quite like the relationship between a man and his horse, he thought, whether it be his destrier to whom he might owe his life in battle, or his swift courser whom he hoped would get him to Lazenby before the weather froze Elizabeth beyond his reach.

Suddenly the hair on the back of Jack's neck prickled.

Comet stopped chewing and threw up his head, his ears twitching at something Jack had not heard, only sensed.

Quick as thought Jack spun round. His sword and basilard were in his hands before he had scarcely drawn another breath.

Two men faced him, just on the edge of the yellow pool of lantern light. They had faces that had lived. They were about his height and were well built. Their clothes were of good wool, not the best, he thought, but these men were well provisioned against the cold. And they were armed.

'We want no trouble, sir,' the older man said gruffly, holding up his hands. 'Just your purse, sir and then you can be on your way.' The men laughed.

Jack saw the younger man's eyes flick up for a second and turned just in time to see a third man. The man made a strong but clumsy lunge at him with his falcion. Jack deflected it upwards with his weapons crossed. Blade rasped against blade. Then Jack caught the man in the belly with a strong kick. The man gave a loud groan as the air rushed out of his lungs.

'Gibb!' one of the two men yelled as the man fell forwards under Comet's feet. The horse whinnied and swung his hindquarters round towards Jack, narrowly missing the prone man.

Jack turned quickly. He crouched low, centring his balance. He narrowed his eyes. He fixed each man in turn, waiting for him to make a move.

'Now that weren't very friendly, sir,' the older of the two men said. 'Gibb meant you no harm! It's just your money we want.'

'Well you can't have it,' Jack said. He sucked in a sharp breath through his teeth. His limbs tingled and he tightened his grip on his weapons.

There was a swish as both men drew their weapons.

Comet whickered nervously behind Jack and shifted his weight uneasily. He pawed at the ground.

The older man made a weak thrust towards Jack, but Jack saw it was a feint to try to draw him away from the protection of the stall and he ignored it.

The younger man had stepped away a little to Jack's right, trying to slip from his vision.

Gibb still lay groaning on the floor at Jack's feet. Jack kicked him again viciously, just to make sure he had no thoughts of joining the fight.

The two men came towards Jack simultaneously. They moved slowly, cautiously. He saw their eyes flick from him to each other and he realized that Gibb must have been their leader; these two were scared of him. That decided his next course of action.

Jack leaped forward, taking the older man's sword up with his and slashing at his ribs with his basilard. The man stepped back, narrowly avoiding the blow. Jack turned swiftly to counter the attack he knew would come at his back. The younger man was strong and Jack needed both weapons to prevent his strike reaching him. He pushed hard, knocking the man backwards and then he turned quickly again to meet the older man's charge. Jack stepped deftly to the side. The hilt of his basilard met the man's face. There was a sickening crunch of metal against bone. The man cried out, and then staggered backwards. He put his hands up to his face. His sword clattered to the floor. Blood rushed from his nose and mouth. He spat teeth out along with the crimson liquid.

'Tom! No!' the younger man shouted.

Jack whirled round and met the wild slash with the full force of his blade. There was a bright ringing sound as edge met edge. Jack's arm jarred with the force, but he pushed hard, his muscles spasming with the effort. He forced the man back towards

Comet. Then he brought his basilard through in a swift thrust that met the younger man's belly. His doublet began to turn red. He let out a strangled cry as much in horror as in pain. He sank to his knees. He dropped his sword and clutched at his guts. Blood began to pour through his fingers.

As the man slumped against Comet's legs, the stallion gave a piercing shriek and reared. He struck the wounded man with his front hooves, stamping down on his back, forcing him to the ground.

Jack turned again, expecting another attack from Tom, but he was nowhere in sight. The straw was stained with blood.

Jack's breath came in white gasps which made his chest ache. Sweat ran down his back. His blood pulsed in his ears. He gave Gibb another cursory kick and then cleaned his weapons before putting them away.

He moved to Comet's head. The animal twitched as Jack ran his hand down the animal's neck in long easy strokes. 'Steady, Comet,' he murmured.

As he calmed the stallion down Jack knew that he was in trouble. Of course he had been the victim in all this, but he doubted he would believed. He was sure that Tom, the injured robber, would return with the watch and he couldn't afford the delay.

Ignoring the two prone and moaning men, he untied Comet and led him from the stall.

As soon as he was clear of the stable, Jack swung lightly into the saddle. He gathered the reins in and pulled Comet round. The stallion fought him, plainly still unnerved by the fight, but Jack was equal to him. He clicked his tongue in encouragement and squeezed with his thighs. Then spur met flank as Jack urged him out of the yard and on towards the Great North Road.

Jack rode as though the watch were already after him. Hooves cut into the silent darkness, harness rang with a frenzied rhythm almost as fast as Jack's thumping heart: now he had to reach Lazenby tonight!

LAZENBY MANOR MARCH 1471

Hoarfrost glazed the night. In the strong moonlight Jack's breath swirled in front of him like mist. He shivered and pulled his heavy cloak about him. Comet's hooves crunched on the frozen ground and the rhythmical jingling of harness echoed about him as though it was the only sound on earth. Certainly no one else would be foolish enough to be abroad on a night as cold as this, Jack thought.

Through the twisted naked arms of the trees he saw the faint amber glow of candlelight and he smiled. He pulled gently on the reins and Comet drew to a halt in a cloud of snorted smoke. The horse twitched back an ear as he heard Jack murmur 'Elizabeth.'

The sight of Lazenby warmed his heart as if he had drunk spiced wine and as he looked down at the manor house he remembered the first time he had come here. A shiver slid down his spine as he remembered how full of hope he had been that day; hope which Lady Catherine had crushed as easily as glass and with as little thought. His stomach turned over and unconsciously he tugged at the reins causing Comet to throw up his head with a snort of annoyance. Now Lady Catherine was gone he wondered if Elizabeth would do the same. With apprehension churning within him he nudged Comet forward; there was only one way to find out his destiny and that was to meet it head on. Slithering on the icy path they headed towards the light. Whatever happened, he told himself, he would at least see Elizabeth again.

Jack entered the house. At the mention of his name by the steward Jack heard a woman's voice cry out 'God have mercy on us!' Then he heard her feet rushing away from him and he assumed she was running to Elizabeth.

He shook his head; this was the legacy he had left behind him, and no doubt the events at Scarsdale were also well recounted here too. He allowed his cloak to be taken from him. The servants kept their eyes lowered and he could have been forgiven for thinking it was out of deference, but Jack knew it was something else. How delighted they must have been when they thought he was dead.

Swiftly Jack followed the servant's announcement into the solar. He hadn't known who or what he was expecting, but he certainly wasn't expecting Matthew Hardacre and from the way Matthew's lip was trembling, he certainly hadn't been expecting Jack!

'Laverton,' Matthew stammered with a curt nod.

Jack's voice caught in his throat at Matthew's lack of respect. 'Hardacre,' he returned coldly.

Matthew's eyes were like the ice on the road as he forced them to meet Jack's.

Jack narrowed his gaze, but did not turn away.

Fire snapped in the grate and a red cascade of sparks danced up the chimney, but Jack felt no warmth.

Matthew motioned for him to sit down and a servant brought him a drink. The hot spiced wine was good, though he would have wished to be drinking it on a full rather than a half-empty stomach.

'I see you still have a fondness for drink,' Matthew hissed.

Jack took the blow. He expected nothing less than hostility from Matthew and how much worse it would be when he told him why he had come. He wondered, as he drank again, how much Elizabeth had told Matthew of their time together in Bruges. He suppressed the smile that came to his lips; how outraged Matthew would be at that! He put the goblet down and met Matthew's gaze evenly. 'I am changed,' he said softly.

Matthew snorted. 'Changed now that Warwick is the ruler of England?' he spat. 'We are all changed because of that!'

Jack raised an eyebrow warningly. 'I see things differently now...' What could he say about Elizabeth? But Matthew was quick to pick up his meaning.

'Leave her alone,' he snapped. 'Do you not think she has suffered enough?'

Jack opened his mouth to speak, but evidently the question was rhetorical for Matthew continued. 'She needs none of you. You men have ruined her life! Does great Warwick even notice she has come home?'

Jack leant forward in his chair. What would Matthew say if he knew Warwick didn't even know he was here? 'I am sorry for what happened,' he said smoothly. 'If I could undo what happened at Scarsdale then I would.'

'The only regret you have from that day is that I disturbed you!' Matthew snarled. His face was as red as a livery coat.

'No, Hardacre,' Jack said sternly. 'You are wrong. I regret the pain I caused, you must believe me.'

'You must think me stupid!' Matthew hissed.

Jack shook his head. 'I tell you the truth Hardacre,' Jack said flatly. He leant back in his chair, and fixed Matthew with wide eyes. 'It matters not. Elizabeth has forgiven me.'

'Has she indeed?' Matthew growled. 'Well I have not, and as head of the family...'

Jack trampled his words. 'But it is Elizabeth's choice as to whether she returns with me,' he said emphatically.

Matthew recoiled from his words as if from a blow. 'You cannot...she belongs here!'

'If she refuses then I shall leave her alone. I will not hurt her again. You have my word on it,' Jack said calmly.

'Pah!' Matthew snorted. 'Your word? It is worth nothing!'

Jack's cheeks began to burn. He breathed deeply, trying to control the swelling anger. 'Elizabeth must choose, Hardacre, not you.'

'She is so wracked with guilt and grief she scarcely knows the time of day!' Matthew cried.

Jack shuddered at his description and wondered if Matthew's new-found courage was purely linked to protecting Elizabeth; he suspected not.

'She has lost more than you could understand. Leave her be!' Matthew said. His knuckles showed white as he gripped the chair and Jack saw tears sparkle in the corners of Matthew's eyes. But how much of his anguish was for Elizabeth and how much was for the ruination of his own plans, Jack could not tell. Of course Matthew wanted her to stay here, Jack thought, Lazenby was a fine house with only a child for its heir and without her father Elizabeth was vulnerable.

Just then the door latch clicked and Elizabeth entered, escorted by Alice.

Jack's jumped up quickly. It took all his strength not to show his shock at her appearance. Her cheeks were hollow and blue circles lay beneath her eyes; the bright emeralds he had gazed into at Bruges were gone. Her lips smiled at him, but the fire he was used to in her eyes was elusive. Her skin was like white alabaster and he wondered if it was partly because of the harshness of her black mourning gown.

Jack moved towards her and, taking her hand, he drew it to his lips. He bowed over it. 'Elizabeth,' he whispered. Her hand was cold in his and he wanted so much to pull her to him and make everything all right. But Alice's fierce eyes had found him and he realized that this was to be a reunion of decorum and propriety; he could not be as bold as he had been in Bruges.

315

'Sir, it is good to see you,' Elizabeth said in a thin voice he barely recognized.

As she spoke there was no flicker of emotion in her face; her eyes did not brighten; and when had she ever called him 'sir' beyond their first meeting? Jack could see she was numbed by pain and loss and exhaustion.

'Please, be seated,' she said quietly. She withdrew her hand from his and waved towards his chair.

Jack's heart pounded in his chest, but he nodded politely and returned to his seat. Elizabeth sat near Matthew on the settle.

'A little wine, my dear?' Matthew simpered.

Elizabeth shook her head. Her beautiful hair was unbound beneath a short black veil and Jack marvelled at the stars of red and gold that moved within its silky curls and it stirred him as it had at Scarsdale.

Jack tried to gather his scattered thoughts.

'Laverton has come to take you away again.' Matthew sneered his disrespect, preventing Jack from easing into a conversation with her. 'I told him of course, that you are not fit to travel; that you have no wish to go with *him*.'

Jack caught his inflection and almost growled at the way Matthew spoke to Elizabeth – as if she were a child or a simpleton, when Jack knew her wit and courage was a match for most men, never mind a fool like Matthew Hardacre.

Elizabeth turned pale eyes to him. 'Is it true, Jack?'

Matthew gasped at her informality. 'Elizabeth!' he scolded.

Jack saw a flame flicker in Elizabeth's eyes at the rebuke. He smiled.

Elizabeth looked at Matthew. 'Matthew, would you kindly leave us please?' she said gently. There was nothing in her tone that could offend him, but it was the request itself that made him indignant.

'I shall do no such thing, Elizabeth!' Matthew said and Alice shrieked her agreement. 'You are still in mourning and...and after what happened at Scarsdale I...I cannot even...'

But Elizabeth's resolve had strengthened under the challenge. 'If I have to beg you then I shall, Matthew,' she said neutrally. 'I hope I would not have to do such a thing.'

'But sweet cousin...' Matthew whined. 'It is not proper. It is not right.'

'I need to speak with Jack alone,' Elizabeth said firmly. Her eyes flashed and Matthew evidently read the signal. Realizing that he had no hope of winning, Matthew lowered his eyes.

'You also, Alice,' Elizabeth said firmly. Her nurse looked horrified, but she said nothing further.

'Your word, Laverton,' Matthew said icily.

'You have it,' Jack replied.

Alice gave Jack a glare as she too left them.

The door clicked behind them but neither Elizabeth nor Jack moved. Silence lengthened into heartbeats. Jack looked at Elizabeth's thin face and his throat tightened at the change in her.

'So you have come to take me away?' she asked without emotion.

Jack could not answer her; his throat was too tight. He rose and walked to where she was sitting. He bowed onto one knee in front of her and took her hand in his.

He looked up at her and saw tears at the corners of her eyes and hoped that she was longing for him; longing for the closeness they had shared at Bruges.

'Sweetheart,' he said as he rose and drew her up onto her feet.

Her eyes darted over his face as though she was searching for something.

'I must thank you for not giving me away,' he said. 'It must have been hard for you in Elizabeth Wydeville's household, hard to keep faith with our plan when Warwick was so near.' He wanted to jest with her about the letter she had written promising him sons when he returned, but her lip began to tremble.

'Oh Jack,' she said. She brought a hand up to her face to wipe away sudden tears.

Instinctively Jack drew her to him. 'Hush, sweetheart, hush.' He tightened his arms about her. She did not resist him. He ran his hands over her back. He felt the prominence of her spine through the black velvet and if he had wanted to, he could have counted her ribs. She was shaking like a frightened hind and it squeezed Jack's heart to see her so. He did not know what to say to her. He knew something of the traumas she had faced, but had never imagined they could make her so ill; she had always been so strong. He held her fiercely against his chest. Fighting the tightness in his throat he whispered, 'I missed you, sweetheart. When I came to London you were gone.'

She looked up at him. Her face was blotched with red. She nodded. 'Brother William brought me home,' she said tearfully. 'My mother...' her voice tore with pain and she closed her eyes, blinking against the tears. 'I have lost so much, Jack.'

Jack stroked a curl from her damp cheek, but said nothing, giving her the chance to tell him whatever was on her mind. He widened his eyes, encouraging her. He saw her swallow hard, trying to gain some control over her emotions.

'Has Warwick asked for me?' she asked tentatively, changing the subject.

Christ's blood, he had forgotten how clever she was!

'You do not wish to go?' Jack asked, avoiding her question. He could not lie to her now.

She smiled thinly. 'I am surprised he noticed I had gone.' Her eyes flicked up again quickly. 'I do not blame him, Jack,' she said hurriedly. 'It is just there seemed no place for me there, though I would wish to be nowhere else than by his side, I see how impossible it is.'

'So you think your place is here with Hardacre?' Jack asked, lacing his fingers across her back.

She hung her head. 'I' faith, I do not know, Jack,' she said sadly. 'I can make no sense of anything anymore.'

'He is Edmund's guardian?' Jack asked.

'Yes, until he comes of age.'

Now Jack understood. 'And I suppose he will honour Edmund's title only if you marry him?'

She nodded.

It was like a sword thrust to Jack. His stomach tightened and blood pulsed into his cheeks. 'The bastard,' he cursed through his teeth.

'But I must, Jack!' Elizabeth's voice was shrill with sudden panic. 'Otherwise Matthew will not give him Lazenby. I cannot fight him in the courts. Who would listen to me? You know as well as anyone how hard that is, and for a woman and a child it would be impossible!'

Her eyes were frantic now. 'Please, Jack, say you understand.' Her fingers gripped the velvet of his doublet.

Jack's lip curled as he spoke. 'I will stop him Elizabeth,' he said coldly.

'How?' she asked. 'You cannot kill him!'

'No,' Jack said coldly. 'But there is another way.'

Elizabeth looked at him expectantly.

'You are married already,' Jack said quickly, 'and I shall claim it so in any court in the land if you want me to.'

Elizabeth gasped. 'No, Jack, please...'

Her body quivered like a shot bowstring.

'No one could gainsay it, least of all Hardacre,' he said solemnly.

He saw her hang her head, as if spending that time with him in Bruges was the most shameful thing she had done. Pain stabbed at his chest. 'My feelings have not changed, Elizabeth, nor will they,' he whispered.

She met his eyes. 'Warwick has not sent for me, has he?'

'I said I would never give up, sweetheart,' Jack breathed.

She shook her head. 'Jack, I am sorry.' Tears trembled on her lashes. 'All I ever wanted was to be with Warwick,' she said. 'Can none of you understand that? It is Warwick I love.'

She freed herself from Jack's arms and walked towards the fire. She folded her arms about her body and Jack could see she was fighting the tears. For a moment he gazed at her, mesmerized by the firelight that danced in her hair and highlighted the curve of her cheek and the turn of her throat. He chewed at his lip as he watched her and then he made the hardest decision of his life.

'I am sorry, sweetheart,' he said softly. 'If you wish it, I shall take you to Warwick.'

She turned to face him slowly, her eyes questioning him.

'I swear it,' Jack said and spread his hands to her.

'And what about Edmund?' she asked.

Jack thought for a moment. 'He can go to Middleham.'

'No!' she snapped.

The venom in her voice shocked him.

'Sir John Conyers killed my father; he will not have Edmund too!'

Jack came to her. 'Sweetheart, he will then make amends, will he not? He owes you this!'

Elizabeth shook her head. 'No!' she said fiercely.

'Please sweetheart, see the sense in what I say. How else can you go to Warwick?'

She looked up at him. 'I – I cannot think,' she said shakily.

'You know it is best,' Jack said.

'And you would do this for Edmund?'

'You saved my life,' Jack said softly. He wanted to say more – that he felt about her as she felt about Warwick; you didn't choose who you fell in love with! But he knew that would be unfair; she had never denied her love for Warwick to him. Instead he tried to reassure her. 'Edmund will be safe at Middleham. Warwick will protect his inheritance. Hardacre will not be able to hurt either of you.' It sounded so easy as he said it, but he saw from the frown on Elizabeth's face that it was going to take time to convince her.

He sighed, calling a truce between them. 'I am in no hurry to leave,' he said. He brushed her cheek with his hand. She shivered and it hurt him. He sucked in his breath, swallowing down his emotions. 'You have been through much, sweetheart. Time is the best medicine.' Part of him wanted to beg her to come with him now, but he could see he had already pushed her too far tonight.

'Come,' he said and offered her his hand. 'Take some wine.'

Her hand trembled in his as he led her to the settle. He held the goblet to her lips and watched her throat as she drank some of the liquid. It would be so easy to pull her into his arms again; but she had drawn a line for him tonight, and he knew if he was to retain her friendship, he dare not cross it. 'We will talk again tomorrow when you have rested,' he said gently.

Her eyes met his. 'Rested?' she asked. 'I do not sleep, Jack. Not since Bruges have I slept a night through.'

Jack smiled at her; he felt a small flame of satisfaction that she had not slept properly since she had left him.

'I see my mother's dying face, Jack; I see my father surrounded by Conyers's men and it is all accompanied by the incessant roar of the storm that nearly claimed me on the Narrow Sea. And I see Warwick...alone.'

He saw her lip tremble again; she was near exhaustion.

'Sweetheart, I can sit with you, if it would help. It would be like Bruges again,' he added hopefully.

Elizabeth gave him a tired smile. 'I think Cousin Matthew would not agree to that, Jack. He does not know of it. No one here does.' She looked deep into his eyes. 'I am sorry,' she whispered, 'somehow it seemed best. It was too...too complicated.'

Jack's heart fell; so she had told no one of their time alone. He could not blame her for that; how could Elizabeth tell her family that she was Warwick's spy or that her impropriety as Jack's counterfeit bride had saved their lives?

'And Alice would rather eat hot coals than allow you into my chamber,' she added.

Jack nodded. 'Aye and at one time so would you. But you know you can trust me.'

'I know,' Elizabeth said. 'But we are no longer in Bruges, Jack. We are no longer spies. We cannot be as we were then, surely you see that?'

Was there any regret in her voice? Jack couldn't tell, but he couldn't give up completely. 'What harm could it do, sweetheart?' he asked gently. 'And if you slept then you would feel so much better.' He did not add that as long as Edward lived their lives would be entwined, no matter what her wishes. There was time yet for the truth!

He saw her lip tighten and knew that she had made up her mind.

Although she had denied him, Elizabeth gave him a look that squeezed his heart. It was a look of longing, a look of pain as though part of her ached for the comfort of Bruges as he did.

'Just say the word and I will come,' he said.

She nodded. 'Thank you, Jack' she whispered. 'I knew...'

With only the briefest of knocks at the door, Matthew entered with Edmund.

Jack growled inwardly at Matthew's contrived interruption. He saw Elizabeth's face brighten and for a moment he was jealous of the effect her young brother had made upon her; if only she would delight in his appearance like that.

Edmund bowed.

'Sir,' he said ignoring his sister's arms. 'I would like to see your sword!'

'Edmund!' Elizabeth scolded him, but Jack shook his head.

'It's all right. Of course he may look.'

Jack rose from the settle and drew the polished blade smoothly from its black velvet covered scabbard.

Edmund's eyes widened as Jack held it out to him.

He nodded for Edmund to take it.

He saw the boy hesitate.

Jack saw that Matthew was glaring at him, and he realized this was an opportunity not to be missed.

Edmund grasped the weapon and it dropped in his hands as he took the weight of it from Jack.

'So, Edmund, you would like to be a knight?' Jack asked the boy.

'Oh, yes, sir!' Edmund said excitedly as he studied the gleaming blade.

Jack looked at Elizabeth. 'He is about the right age to commence his training,' he said.

Elizabeth shook her head; she obviously knew what was coming next.

'Would you like to go to a great castle and learn to be a knight?' Jack asked.

The boy turned wide hazel eyes up to him. 'I would love to, sir!'

'Then we shall have to see what can be done!' Jack laughed.

Edmund's mouth fell open. 'Could you, sir? Take me to your castle?'

'He has no castle!' Matthew spat.

Edmund's face fell.

'Master Hardacre is right,' Jack said evenly, 'but my lord does, and I have no doubt he would allow it.'

'What's this?' Matthew growled. 'You have an audacity that will see you in hell, Laverton! You have no right to say anything to the boy.'

But Edmund wasn't listening. His face was smiling up at Jack. 'Would you, sir, ask him?'

'I do not need to ask him,' Jack said tousling Edmund's blond hair. 'I can see you will make a fine squire in no time. I shall arrange for you to go to Middleham.'

Edmund squeaked with delight and almost dropped Jack's sword.

Jack reached out and took it from him. 'And you will learn never to drop your blade!' he laughed.

He caught Elizabeth's look. It was one of incredulity. He didn't think she was angry with him, but she was surprised he had sprung his plan so quickly.

'Mistress,' he said with a bow as he sheathed his sword.

Elizabeth began to smile, but before she could say anything they were called to supper.

As Jack entered the hall, glares flew like arrows in his direction and Matthew simpered with satisfaction.

Matthew took Sir Robert's seat at the table, and Jack understood the snub; as their guest and a knight he should have been accorded that honour, but Matthew was making his feelings plain to all. Not only was Jack removed from the centre of the table, he was seated at the opposite end to Elizabeth. It had one advantage in that he could watch her easily, but the disadvantage was he could not converse with her; could not ease into her company. Instead he was seated next to the priest, who insisted on telling him what grand funerals he had missed – those of Sir Robert and Lady Catherine. He looked to Elizabeth; she could evidently hear the old man's words of obits and black damask and her eyes had dulled again. Jack sighed; if only he could talk with her alone, he knew he could cheer her.

They were only part way through the third remove when Elizabeth excused herself.

Jack rose and offered her a courtly bow. He heard a murmur of approval from some of the servants and Edmund was evidently impressed too because he leapt from his place and tried to do the same.

Jack laughed and Elizabeth met his laugh with a thin smile.

'Good night, Jack,' she breathed as she passed him.

'Good night,' he answered her. He wanted to leave with her and take her to their chamber as he had in Bruges, but in a moment she was gone and he was left with only the hard stare of her bitter cousin and the ghost of her sweet perfume. He returned to his seat.

He saw Matthew nod to Alice to take Edmund out also, and Jack wondered what it was Matthew had to say to him.

CROMER POINT MARCH 1471

William Hastings peered out into the blackness. He could just make out two faint pinpricks of light on the headland, which he assumed must be from a fisherman's cottage. A rogue gull mewed in the spangled sky above him, fighting to fly against the strengthening wind and the waves rushed past him towards the shore in an incessant roar.

'Will?' Edward's voice was soft in his ear.

'As quiet as a graveyard, Your Grace,' he replied, anticipating Edward's question.

'Are you certain?'

'I've been watching the coast for nigh on half an hour by the track of the moon. I've seen nothing move. There is yet no sign of Chamberlain or Debenham.' He saw Edward's brows lower. 'This territory is as friendly as we shall see, Ned, I am sure they will be back soon,' he said more gently. 'The dukes of both Norfolk and Suffolk hold fast to the House of York, you know that.'

'Aye, Will you are right,' Edward said. 'And Anthony holds land here too, and has assured me his friends are prepared for our coming.'

Hastings drew in his breath sharply at the mention of Earl Rivers's name. 'Huzzah, for Anthony,' he said sarcastically under his breath.

But Edward had heard him. He cast him a dark look. 'Will,' he rebuked him, 'we need to stick together if we are to have any hope.'

Hastings lowered his eyes to the rail, but he couldn't bring himself to apologize. 'Ned...' he sought to explain, to make Edward understand why he thought as he did, but before he could say any more, he saw shapes moving along the beach towards them. 'Look!' he said and pointed them out to Edward.

Hastings's heart stopped beating and without thought his hand slipped to the hilt of his sword. His instinct told him the men approaching at speed bore them no malice, but until they came closer he could not be certain.

LAZENBY MANOR MARCH 1471

'So Laverton,' Matthew said coolly as he showed him to a seat in the solar. 'How long must you stay?'

Jack did not answer immediately but eyed Matthew coldly over his glass.

'Elizabeth needs time,' he said evenly, 'I will wait on her decision. And in the meantime I will arrange the boy's education at Middleham.'

Matthew spluttered. 'You have no right to interfere,' he growled.

Jack hardened his stare, knowing in truth that he had every right, though he dare not say so. 'Hardacre, you are fortunate given your Yorkist connections that my lord of Warwick is so lenient! That he would take Sir Robert's heir into his household is testament to the great friendship they once had, as well as his admiration and love for Elizabeth.'

He saw Matthew wince at his words.

'You think you are so clever,' Matthew said icily. 'But I tell you she will not go with you. She is worn thin by the adventures she has had, and you have been the worst part of them! Women are not made for such things. She will stay.'

But Jack knew a different Elizabeth. If only she could regain her strength he knew her spirit would return as strong as ever. He laughed at Matthew. 'I am sure you know all about such adventures,' Jack sneered.

Matthew flushed.

Jack raised his glass in a toast to Matthew. 'To adventures!' he said with a grin and then drained the goblet.

Matthew's eyes burned into him. 'She will stay with me,' Matthew said.

Jack shook his head. 'Not while I'm alive,' he growled. 'Hardacre, you disguise your lust as humanity,' he said sternly, 'but you will not win. Edmund will go to Middleham and Elizabeth will come with me.'

'But she wears my ring!' Matthew said.

Jack laughed at Matthew's feeble attempt at deception. 'Aye, I have seen it – your mourning ring!' How he wished Elizabeth had told them about the other ring she wore and about their time together in Bruges. Their counterfeit marriage would slay Matthew's opposition. But she had forbidden him to speak of it. He would have to think of something else.

Matthew sank into his chair as Jack glared at him.

But Matthew showed a surprising resilience and Jack knew what made him so bold. 'I remember what you were like at Scarsdale, Laverton, even if Elizabeth does not. Was there any girl in the village you had not tumbled?' he hissed.

Hot blood pulsed into Jack's cheeks. 'She has forgiven me for what happened, as I have forgiven her for wounding me.' He clenched his jaw and took a long deep breath. 'There is peace between us, Hardacre. A peace you will never understand!' He slammed his goblet down and then rose quickly. 'Good night, Hardacre,' he said with a curt nod. 'I think it best that I retire.'

'I have no whore to send you to warm your bed,' Matthew said.

Jack fixed dark eyes on him. 'You do not know me at all, Hardacre,' he said angrily.

325

The evening with Matthew had left a sour feeling in his gut, and though he would have liked nothing better than to destroy Matthew, it was better for Elizabeth if he retired now before he said any more and crushed what little civility remained.

* * *

Jack followed the servant along the gallery to his room. Candlelight gilded the walls and dancing shadows followed behind them.

He dismissed the man. He didn't want the attentions of any of the servants. He sat down on the bed and sighed wearily. What a return to Lazenby it had been, he thought. He was tired now; drained by the experience, but what had hurt him most was the change in Elizabeth. If only they could return to how they were! He remembered the night he had told her of her father's promise; the promise that made her his. For one blissful moment he had kissed her and she had kissed him back; they had shared both grief and love. His heart ached; would they ever do so again?

He had still not removed his boots when he heard a light tapping on the door.

He drew his slim jewelled knife from its sheath and holding it tightly he went to answer the door; he couldn't be sure how he would react if Hardacre pushed him further. The tap was so gentle though, that he was sure it must be Edmund wanting to hold the sword again. He pulled open the door and gasped.

CROMER POINT MARCH 1471

Hastings waited, but Edward did not answer him. Instead he stared at the empty wine flagon as if he would make it full again simply by thought.

The candle stub at its side guttered, sending pungent curls of smoke up beyond the diminishing light. The thick silence was punctuated only by the creaking of the ship's timbers as it rocked in the gale on an ever-increasing swell.

'My liege, where shall we go?' Hastings asked again. 'The men grow restless.' He knew if the storm hit them now they would be smashed to driftwood on this coast, they would be best trying to ride it out on the open sea.

326

Edward raised his head. The dying candle flame flickered in his eyes turning them to the deepest liquid lapis. 'I had gambled on receiving welcome here, Will and I lost,' he said sadly. 'You said it yourself; we would not get a better welcome anywhere in England.'

Hastings shrugged; he too felt the news like a blow to his guts.

'I cannot believe it,' Edward said, shaking his head. 'I underestimated Warwick. I never thought he would arrest Norfolk and our allies, never dreamed he would read my plans so easily.'

'Plans are Warwick's forte, Ned. He has returned like the prodigal son on two occasions now, if anyone would know where an exile would land it is he!'

'Aye Will, you are right and as Chamberlain reported, Oxford and his brothers have been arraying men for weeks! It would be folly to take him on as we are.'

'Then we must try elsewhere,' Hastings said flatly.

Edward sighed. 'But where, Will?

Hastings sighed; there was no better place in England than here, but it was now denied to them; he didn't like the option left open to them, but he knew they had no choice. 'In this wind we can do little but travel up the east coast,' he said resignedly.

Edward's eyes widened. 'No, Will. That would be madness indeed!'

'I think we have no choice, Ned.'

'We cannot land in Yorkshire!' Anthony Wydeville's voice came out of the shadows. 'Your Grace, you might be the rightful Duke of York, but that is the only comfort we would receive there. Percy is Lancastrian and has never forgiven you for Towton, and Montagu waits at Pontefract. We would soon be brought to bay.'

'It must be Yorkshire,' Hastings growled at him. He saw Anthony Wydeville's eyes harden into a glare. He ignored the challenge and turned to Edward. 'You restored Percy to his earldom, surely his place is more secure under you than it would be under Warwick. 'Tis no secret Montagu wishes Northumberland his again.'

Edward sighed. 'I have sent Percy letters to that end Will, but I cannot be certain of him,' he said wearily. He fingered the empty wine-cup on the table as if he could read his destiny in its bowl.

'Yorkshire is the answer, Your Grace, I know it is,' Hastings persisted; he had to get them back to sea, for come daylight Oxford would surely be upon them. He dredged his mind for something more. 'Did Bolingbrook not do the same when he took the crown, Your Grace? What do they call the place? Ah yes, Ravenspur!'

Edward's eyes met his. 'Ravenspur,' he whispered as if it was the echo of a distant memory.

'But my liege...' Anthony Wydeville began to protest.

But the smile that came to Edward's face silenced him. 'Thank you, Will. Once again when I have believed all is lost you've given me hope,' he said, brightening. His eyes flicked across the table as the thoughts stirred in his mind. 'We shall follow Bolingbroke's example and in saying that, Will, you have given me an idea, one I think Warwick will not have anticipated!'

LAZENBY MANOR MARCH 1471

'Sweetheart?' Jack said showing more surprise than he intended. 'What is wrong?'

Elizabeth swayed in the doorway, like bleached linen hung out to dry. 'Are you not going to invite me in?' she asked quietly. Her eyes were wide like a cat's and as she held his gaze Jack's heart quickened.

'Of course,' he said, feeling foolish. He stepped back and bowed her into the room. His heart crashed against his ribs; what did this mean?

She moved past him and he caught again the sensual smell of her perfume. How that scent had filled his nights in Bruges; it was strange how evocative a smell could be, he thought, and it brought fire to his loins.

She turned to face him. Firelight danced in her hair and her eyes glittered with something like their old lustre.

Jack closed the door and moved towards her. He slipped his knife back into its sheath and Elizabeth watched him silently.

Jack's mouth was dry; he could barely swallow.

She looked into his eyes again and he thought his heart had stopped beating.

'Jack,' she said tentatively, 'I...do not know how to ask you,' she stammered.

'You may ask me anything, sweetheart,' Jack said.

She chewed at her lip. 'I wondered if I might rest here tonight. Will you watch over me as you did in Bruges?'

Jack began to breathe again. 'Bruges?' he whispered.

She looked away from him. 'Yes, I am sorry if...' she said softly.

Hope left Jack's heart and he was suddenly cold. He tried to hide his disappointment. 'Of course...' he said hesitantly. 'If that is what you wish.'

Elizabeth nodded and gave him a weary smile. Then she walked towards his bed.

Somewhat dazed he watched her turn down the coverlet and still he did not move as she removed her cloak, slipped off her shoes and then swung her legs between the sheets.

After a few moments Jack brought the candle to the bedside. All his thoughts had sprung to his loins, but he knew it was hopeless; she loved only Warwick – had she not told him so? But did she not look beautiful, lying in his bed? He was torn; she had come to him for comfort, yet had forbidden him from loving her. Perhaps she still did not realize the depth of his passion or the effect she always had on him!

'Please, Jack. Do not blow out the candle,' she whispered.

He leant over her tentatively. 'Nothing will hurt you, sweetheart,' he whispered. 'I promise.'

She looked into his eyes. 'Thank you,' she murmured.

He wanted to lean forward and kiss her, but instead he lowered his eyes, knowing that however much she unwittingly tempted him, she did not want him as he wanted her.

He removed his boots and sword. His heart thumped in his chest like a blacksmith's hammer on an anvil.

'Jack? If I cry out, will you wake me?' Her eyelids fluttered as she fought to keep them open.

Jack nodded. 'Of course, sweetheart,' he said.

Just as in Bruges he slipped into bed beside her and watched the even rise and fall of her chest.

Smiling, Jack slipped an arm beneath her and drew her into his shoulder; she was already asleep.

* * *

The blackbirds were singing in the courtyard and suddenly Elizabeth was awake. Awake! That meant she had actually slept through the night.

She opened her eyes and breathed in the comforting scent of Jack. Her head was resting against his warm shoulder and his arms were wrapped about her protectively. She smiled. She could not remember when she had last been so at ease with the world. She owed him much, for he was the reason she had slept. And with that sleep had come the answer to her dilemma.

A woman's screaming shattered the bliss of the moment.

'Ah, sweetheart,' Jack breathed, 'they have discovered you are missing!'

Elizabeth laughed. It had taken Jack's arrival to bring her to her senses, to awaken her from her winter-long hibernation. Now she knew she would not give up either Warwick or Lazenby without a fight; Jack had given her the strength she needed.

Without warning the door crashed open. Matthew stood like a cuckolded husband in the doorway. His eyes blazed with anger and his chest worked rapidly as he fought for breath. 'You! You!' he blustered.

Alice stood behind him, maintaining a continuous howling that a professional mourner would have been proud of.

'Get out, Laverton!' Matthew bellowed. 'Get out of my house!'

Elizabeth looked at Jack.

He held her gaze.

She saw his lips were parted as though he held his breath for her answer.

She turned to Matthew. 'Jack may stay exactly where he is,' she said fiercely. 'It is you cousin who must leave!'

Jack needed nothing more. He flung the coverlet back and jumped from the bed.

'Jack!' Elizabeth saw what he was about to do. 'No!'

But it was too late.

Jack was face to face with Matthew, his unsheathed dagger in his hand and an angry curl on his lip.

'You heard the lady,' Jack growled.

Matthew's eyes widened in terror and his mouth formed a broad silent 'O'.

Alice commenced her shrieking again.

'Jack, please!' Elizabeth began to get up. 'Alice, be quiet!' Elizabeth's heart pounded at her throat. Santa Maria, what would Jack do to him?

'Move!' Jack barked and gave Matthew a shove backwards.

Matthew's mouth opened and closed like a landed fish as he staggered and began to lose his footing. As he did so he reached a hand to his belt and withdrew his knife.

Elizabeth knew he had made a terrible mistake. She knew she had to reach Jack.

Jack's eyes glittered darkly and his mouth twisted into a wry smile. 'So that is how you want it, eh?' he hissed. 'Believe me Hardacre, nothing would give me greater pleasure than to fillet you!'

Elizabeth lunged for Jack's arm, but he avoided her deftly.

Matthew took advantage of the distraction and thrust at Jack with his knife.

Jack deflected the blow with an easy twist of his arm and planted a swift kick in Matthew's chest. Matthew's knife clattered to the floor.

Matthew made a terrible sound as the air rushed from his lungs.

'Jack don't!' Elizabeth begged him as he moved closer to Matthew. She knew what would come next: a kick to Matthew's face!

Matthew was on all fours now, gasping and wheezing, trying to make his lungs work again.

'Jack!' Elizabeth cried in a desperate voice. 'Please!'

Jack flicked his eyes to her briefly and then heaved a deep sigh. He nodded reluctantly and then he slipped his dagger smoothly into its sheath. He reached forward. He grasped Matthew by the collar. 'Perhaps you did not hear the lady?' he hissed. 'She asked you to leave!'

He forced Matthew up onto his feet and then pulled him towards the door like a baker dragging a sack of flour.

Matthew continued to cough and splutter, but he put up no further resistance.

Alice began wailing again, but stopped when Elizabeth gave her a ferocious glare.

By the time Elizabeth reached the door, Jack had already hauled Matthew to the stables.

The stones were cold and sharp on her feet as Elizabeth hurried across the courtyard and the cold wind whipped her hair about her like an unfastened mantle.

A frightened groom led out Matthew's horse.

'Lisbet!' Edmund flew to Elizabeth's skirts and put his arms about her waist. 'Will Sir Jack kill him, Lisbet?' he asked as he hugged her tightly.

'No, Edmund, of course he will not kill him,' she said as she ruffled his hair reassuringly. She was fairly certain Jack would not kill him now anyway; but there was always doubt where Jack was concerned.

'Is Cousin Matthew a bad man?' Edmund asked her innocently.

'Yes, Edmund I suppose he is,' she said, 'for he would have parted you from Lazenby...' 'And me from Warwick,' she was about to add, but she thought better of it.

Jack had by now stuffed Matthew onto his horse. His eyes were black fire as he stared at her ashen-faced cousin and the look made Elizabeth shiver.

Elizabeth moved to stand by Jack's side, holding Edmund's hand.

'You know what awaits you if you come back,' Jack growled as he slapped the rump of Matthew's horse.

Matthew said nothing as the horse began to move. He glared at Jack and then turned incandescent eyes on Elizabeth.

She shuddered at the hatred burning in them. Jack slipped his around her shoulder and instinctively she leant against him. 'You should have let me kill him,' he whispered. 'He will be less trouble dead.'

Elizabeth looked up at Jack's wide eyes. She shook her head. 'Then you would be worse than he is Jack, and they already think badly of you around here!' She laughed dryly as she said it and she saw Jack smile too. But behind his smile there was a sense of uneasiness he did not cloak completely and she wondered if he really did think Matthew would return.

LONDON MARCH 1471

'Edward is in Yorkshire,' Warwick said flatly.

Archbishop Neville began to choke on his wine.

Warwick slapped him squarely between his shoulder blades.

'Are you certain, Richard?' he spluttered.

Warwick raised an eyebrow. 'I told you he would take the odds George, but I must admit I did not think he would choose Yorkshire! He has done as Bolingbroke did,' Warwick added. 'He even landed at Ravenspur!'

Archbishop Neville looked puzzled. 'Did no one stop him?'

'Hull refused him entry, Beverley allowed him in. He claimed he did not come for the crown, indeed his men did cry for King

332

Harry as they rode, wearing the ostrich plumes of Lancaster, if all is to be believed. When he reached York he even swore an oath at the high altar in *your* Minster that he came only for his duchy of York. He claimed that he never would have turned from Henry but for the stirrings of the Earl of Warwick!' Warwick laughed caustically.

'And where is he now?' Archbishop Neville asked, flushing, plainly piqued that Edward had been in his Minster of York.

'I was told he had sought sanctuary and that is what I have told King Louis,' Warwick said.

'But you do not believe that, Richard?'

Warwick shook his head. 'The gambler always throws the dice, George. He will come south.' They locked glances; both of them knew what that meant.

'John,' Archbishop Neville whispered.

'Aye, brother, we must rely on John.'

'Have you written to him?'

Warwick nodded. 'And to Clarence, though I suspect he knew of this plan long before we did!'

Archbishop Neville snorted his derision.

'I know, George,' Warwick said, 'but Clarence has given me no reason yet to doubt him.' He knew Jack had wanted to speak about Clarence, but just as now he did not want to discuss the subject. He had to believe he would not turn.

'Not yet,' Archbishop Neville agreed, 'but now that Edward is here...'

Warwick began to laugh at his brother's grim expression. 'God's blood, George! Edward has but put his toe on England's shore and you have us all defeated!'

Archbishop Neville looked down at his surplice.

'George, you know Yorkshire is Lancastrian! He has little chance.'

'Have...have you heard from Percy?' Archbishop Neville gave voice to Warwick's gravest concern.

Warwick shook his head. 'I fear he will do nothing. He probably expects that I would give Northumberland back to John at the first opportunity, either that or he cannot bring himself to fight alongside a Neville, I cannot decide.' Warwick knew what this meant. It was only a matter of time before Edward turned towards London. And then there really would be only one man in his path – John Neville, Marquis Montagu.

'What of Oxford?' Archbishop Neville asked.

'Oxford is heading northwards on the Newark road, but neither he nor Exeter will reach John in time.'

John was the bravest soldier and the best of men, Warwick thought, but would he strike the killing blow? Could he? Or would the Lancastrians think, as Archbishop Neville had said, that John had been a Yorkist too long? Warwick shook his head as if to shake the doubt from his mind. 'The French ambassadors have gone,' he said matter-of-factly, 'will their tales inspire or frighten Marguerite do you think?'

'She will not come before you meet Edward in battle,' Archbishop Neville said impassively. 'She wants you to have made an end of it.'

Warwick nodded. 'Mayhap John will do it all for me, eh?'

Archbishop Neville's eyes met his, held his gaze. 'Mayhap,' he said slowly.

TWELVE

LAZENBY MANOR MARCH 1471

Elizabeth glanced at her nurse; Alice's lips were drawn into a tight line. Her eyes were puffy and red from weeping and they burned with anger. She had said little to Elizabeth after Matthew's departure; had the lifetime of love and trust between them had been broken by the events of the last few hours?

She tugged now at Elizabeth's curls and Elizabeth fought not to snap at her, trying to build a bridge between them, though she thought it would be easier to bridge the River Swale in spate.

'There, mistress,' Alice said neutrally.

Elizabeth surveyed the coiled auburn plait in the mirror. She smiled. 'It is beautiful, Alice. Thank you,' she said genuinely. But Alice did not smile as she normally did.

'Mistress,' she said and bobbed a small curtsey.

She reached for the white linen headdress, but Elizabeth shook her head. 'Not here, Alice,' she smiled. 'Not at home.'

'As you wish, mistress,' Alice said curtly. 'But your mother would not approve. Not with *him* here.' She emphasized the word 'him' and nodded her head towards the window.

'No, Alice, mother never did approve of *him*, did she?' Elizabeth said dryly. No, Lady Catherine had never approved of Jack; not until she was breathing her last and realized she would have to face her husband and explain her denial of his wishes! Then it had been different. 'Even at the end, when she begged me to marry *him*, she didn't approve! Neither did she approve of Warwick...or of anything else I've done for that matter!'

'And she would not approve of you...of you going to... Oh, Elizabeth child, I cannot say what is in my heart!' Alice began to sob.

Elizabeth took her hand. 'Alice, I am that child no longer,' she said gently. 'I must choose for myself. You must see that.'

Alice nodded and sniffed. 'But after what *he* did...' Alice said, again inclining her head.

'And what I did to him!' Elizabeth reminded her. 'I almost killed him, Alice. If it had not been for Brother William ...' Her stomach turned over guiltily.

Alice shook her head. 'How can you bear to be in his company?'

Elizabeth smiled. 'I can assure you Alice that he is not the dishonourable rogue you think he is. He is...' How could she explain

335

about Jack? All she knew was that she had been so wrong about him and now he was the only way that Edmund would be settled at Middleham and she would return to Warwick. But it was more than that. He would do all this even though to escort her to Warwick went against his own desires. She shivered; she could not tell Alice all this.

Suddenly Edmund's laughter filled the air like birdsong.

Elizabeth turned from Alice, rose and went to the open window.

The cold night had given way to a crisp sunny morning and Edmund had evidently decided the weather was good enough to play outside.

'Oh, the boy will catch his death!' Alice said distractedly and hurried from the room.

Elizabeth looked down on him from the oriel.

He was running across the grass with his wooden practice sword held at the ready. His eyes glittered with happiness as he swung it.

Elizabeth watched him, her smile growing broader.

His opponent stood waiting for him. Jack looked every inch the soldier. His knees were bent, giving him perfect balance and he was leaning forward slightly, eyes wide and fixed as Edmund came at him.

They both laughed as Edmund attacked and Jack parried with ease. He turned quickly as Edmund passed him.

Edmund's shock of blond hair bobbed as he ran.

Jack called instructions to him, to keep his eyes focussed, and keep his sword level and under control, and Elizabeth's heart swelled with pride as she watched them.

Jack parried and thrust with him gently and Elizabeth marvelled at the sinuosity of his movement.

Suddenly there was a shriek as Alice found them. Jack looked round at her and was rewarded with a sharp crack on the forearm from Edmund's sword.

He growled and threw down his weapon. He ran at Edmund and wrestled him to the floor.

Edmund squealed in delight as Jack bowled him over and Alice shrieked again.

'No Master Laverton, he will get wet. He will catch a chill!'

Jack was laughing now as he rolled on the grass with Edmund and Alice danced around them like a dog after a bone. Finally she managed to grab Edmund's collar and haul him away.

Jack lay on his back on the wet grass, still laughing. He pillowed his hands behind his head and smiled up at the sky.

Elizabeth smiled too as she watched him; even though it wouldn't take long for him to take Edmund to Middleham, Lazenby wouldn't be the same without him.

TADCASTER MARCH 1471

William Hastings finished signing another letter to his retainers of Leicester: his stout men of Ashby de la Zouche and Kirby Muxloe. He also penned a short note to Katherine, his wife and Warwick's favourite sister. Though perhaps he did not love her as Jack Thornton loved Elizabeth, he cared about the mother of his children and he could only guess how she must be feeling, knowing that he was about to be part of her brother's demise. He smiled ruefully as he thought on Jack Thornton; he almost envied him being at home with his sweetheart and away from the bloody cares of this strife. What it must be to have the love of a woman like that, he thought. He sighed; in reality he would not wish himself anywhere else than by Edward's side, but he knew the worst was yet to come and he would be a fool not to acknowledge his fear.

He blotted deep red wax onto the paper and then pressed in his seal ring. He held it until the wax submitted to the impression of his manticore, the man-tiger, and then gave the letters to his messenger. Then he rose and went to meet his king.

'Good morrow, Will,' Edward called to him across the courtyard. The sun came from behind a cloud and bleached Edward's armour into pure white light. Hastings shielded his eyes from the glare as he bowed before Edward.

'My lord,' he said.

As Hastings he rose, he noticed Edward's gleaming smile fade to a tight line. 'Today we meet Montagu, Will,' he said gravely.

Hastings nodded. 'Aye,' he said. 'Of all the soldiers in Christendom I would not wish it to be him we have to give battle to.'

Edward nodded. 'I did not want to face John either, but he turned against me Will; deserted me for his brother. 'Tis John made us exiles, Will, if the tale be told, not Warwick.'

'You are right, Your Grace,' Hastings said with regret.

'Come, Will, you never did like John Neville!'

'I liked him well enough, my liege,' Hastings said, perhaps falling shy of the truth. 'I just never trusted him.'

Edward shook his head. 'Well today is his chance to crush us, for we cannot choose but ride close to Pontefract.'

Edward turned to his horse and mounted effortlessly. 'And the sooner we start, the sooner it will be finished.'

Hastings signalled for his squire to pass him his sallet and then he too mounted.

They rode together in silence, neither man wishing to voice anything more than he had said already. The only sound was the constant heartbeat of the army marching behind them. Hastings felt his heart beating within his chest and as they drew nearer to Pontefract he knew that it had quickened. If Edward felt the same he showed no outward sign of it, apart from an occasional quick glance behind him, as if he expected Montagu to appear from behind a tree.

There was no wind and it seemed to Hastings as if the world was holding its breath for Montagu.

The calm was shattered by the sudden thumping of hooves.

Hastings looked round quickly.

'My liege! My liege!' One of Edward's men charged towards them scattering dust and dirt from the road as he slithered to a halt in front of Edward.

Unease raked along Hastings's spine.

'My liege, Montagu's scouts have been seen ahead of us.'

'Just his scouts, man?' Edward asked vehemently.

'Yes, my liege, we loosed a few flights at them but they did not stay to fight.'

'Are you sure? It could not be...'

'My liege, they were only scouts, I swear it!'

Edward nodded curtly and the man to left them. 'He will know we are here, then,' he said in a tone as flat as shadow. He did not look at Hastings but stared unseeing at the road in front of them, his eyes flickering as the thoughts whirled in his head.

Hastings's heart beat more strongly. 'Yes Ned, he will know,' he said. He was surprised at how thin his voice sounded, at how dry his throat was. Christ on the cross, he wasn't a young squire! He had fought in many campaigns, he knew the field of battle, knew what to expect. And he also knew the nauseous feeling inside of him was fear.

338

Elizabeth watched Jack as they sat in the solar together. He was again chewing on his thumb, something she knew he only did when there was something troubling him. Edmund was now settled at Middleham; was it just that he must now honour his promise and take her to Warwick that made him so uneasy?

'We must leave soon, Elizabeth,' Jack said suddenly, as if he had read her thoughts.

'You have news?' she asked.

Slowly Jack raised grave eyes to hers and for a moment he did not speak.

'What is it?' she asked, her throat tightening.

'While I was at Middleham I heard that Edward is in Yorkshire, even now he heads towards the south.'

Elizabeth's heart quickened. The thing she had dreaded the most had happened: Edward had returned. There was now no hope of Warwick holding England unless he gave battle. She closed her eyes for a moment and tried to think how Warwick must feel. His protégé had come to teach his master a lesson!

'If we leave now we can make Warwick before Edward does,' Jack said.

Elizabeth stared at Jack, a thought burning her mind like flame. She hardly dared to give voice to it.

'What is it?' Jack asked, meeting her look.

'If Edward wins...' the words caught in her throat.

'Hush, sweetheart, we must not think on that!' Jack said. 'Edward has but a few thousand men and he is miles away from friendly territory. Montagu, Oxford, Exeter and Warwick all stand between him and London.' He smiled, but Elizabeth was not reassured. There was something else, something she did not want to contemplate. Jack fixed her gaze and she knew she must ask for the worst of it. 'And – and Clarence?' she asked tentatively.

'Clarence is recruiting for Warwick in the south-west,' Jack said. 'He could not be further away from Edward unless Edward was back in exile!'

Relief caressed her. Thank the blessed saints! Clarence would not matter then.

'So, what do you say?' Jack asked.

'My mother's Mass for Month's Mind is tomorrow, I cannot leave before then,' she said. 'With Edmund at Middleham I am the only one left.' She fingered the black velvet of her mourning gown.

'I shall be here,' Jack said gently. 'You are not alone.'

Elizabeth smiled thinly. Tomorrow would be a difficult day even with Jack's company and perhaps his presence would even make things worse, knowing what her mother had requested of her, and knowing that she was going to deny that request. Guilt twisted her stomach; should she tell Jack of it? He had always blamed her mother; hated Lady Catherine for refusing him. He had a right to know the truth didn't he? But it would serve no purpose, she told herself; it would only complicate things between them, for she had no intention of marrying him. Mentally she added it to her list of sins she must one day confess. She looked at him and he smiled. Then he pleated his brows questioningly.

'Is there something else?' he asked.

Santa Maria, he was so clever! Elizabeth shook her head and pulled her eyes away from his disarming look. The knot in her stomach tightened further. When she looked back he was still watching her, his eyes wide in the firelight. 'If there is anything you wish to say...'

She shook her head and tried to calm herself. By the saints how he could read her! 'Will you fight for Warwick?' she asked, trying to distract his attention.

Jack sighed. 'I hope it will all be over before I have to,' he said.

She smiled at his evasiveness. 'Will you, Jack? Fight?'

He ran his tongue over his lips and then pressed them together into a tight line will he considered her question. Then he met her gaze. 'Yes,' he said. 'I shall.'

In that brief moment Elizabeth saw his sadness, perhaps fear also and mayhap regret at having to take up arms against William Hastings, for she knew he liked him well. But she had seen the same look on her father's face when battle was spoken of and she knew where it came from: Towton. In a heartbeat the vision was gone and a smile twitched the corner of his mouth. 'Are you concerned for me, sweetheart?' he jested.

Elizabeth met his eyes, held his look. 'Yes,' she said. 'I am.' And she did not mean just on the battlefield; the tangled threads of their deception had loose ends, and like an unfinished tapestry, loose ends had a tendency to unravel.

LONDON MARCH 1471

Warwick looked proudly at the restless ocean of red and silver behind him. The sun shone briefly, punctuating the red and silver with spangled white for a moment before it retreated again.

His horse nodded its head, pulling eagerly against his hold.

'So, brother,' he said to Archbishop Neville who was standing alongside him. Their glances met and he knew he really didn't need to say any more, but he had to offer his brother something. 'You have Somerset and Devon, should Edward make it this far. And you have King Henry!'

Archbishop Neville breathed deeply. 'If Edward makes it this far that will not be enough to hold the city against him, Richard. And what will have happened to you and John if he does come?'

Warwick smiled. 'George, all will be well, you will see!'

Archbishop Neville turned his eyes up to him. 'Pray God you are right, Richard.'

Their eyes met again, held briefly and then Warwick gave spur to his stallion and rode towards the Great North Road.

Cries of 'A Warwick! A Warwick!' split the air and Warwick acknowledged the crowds that had gathered to watch him leave. When he next saw these streets Edward would be a dead man, he thought, and King Henry would be the undisputed King of England.

Briefly he glanced over his shoulder to where Archbishop Neville was a fast-disappearing glimmer of gold on the edge of the sea of red. His brother's worries had pricked him. Archbishop Neville was no soldier, he thought, if the defence of London was left to him he was right; there was no hope! His strength lay in his good and sensible arguments and Warwick hoped he would be able to persuade the aldermen to keep the gates locked to Edward for a while at least, if he did manage to come this far. For if they did not it would not only be London that was lost to him, but King Henry also.

Hastings watched as Edward's expression slid from frustration to anger.

'God's blood, where is he?' Edward said as they rode on. His eyes flicked to the surrounding woods as if he expected John Neville and his four thousand men to suddenly burst out at them in an ambush.

'Not in those woods, Your Grace,' Hastings said, 'you can be sure of that. Our scouts have been busy all day.'

'Then where, Will? Where will he hit us?'

Hastings shook his head. Sweat dripped into his eyes from the damp curls at his brow and it stung. He blinked it away. 'I do not know,' he answered truthfully.

'John is the best soldier there is, Will. Remember Hexham? Remember how he crossed the Tyne and then how he routed the Lancastrians? They knew he was coming for them, Will, like we know he is here, but it did not save them!'

Hastings smiled unwillingly at Edward's memories of John Neville's valour. 'Aye and how he executed thirty Lancastrians in the aftermath,' he said quietly. He wondered if any of the Lancastrians remembered that fact; he was sure they did. But still he wished John Neville was on their side. His stomach growled. Unlike Edward he had been unable to break his fast.

'I know he's there, but what is he planning, Will?' Edward's voice sounded ragged.

Hastings tried to concentrate on what Edward was saying rather than his stirring guts. He knew Edward was right; it would be better if they encountered Montagu arrayed across the road in front of them. Better to know the worst of it and meet it head on, he thought. The tension was making his head throb as though he'd had the heaviest night of drinking of his life. But still he did not come.

Slowly they travelled the road towards Wakefield, each mile feeling like ten. The shadows lengthened, making the trees seem as tall as giants across their path and yet the setting of the low sun brought with it a sense of relief; the day was almost over and John Neville had not come. Hastings shrugged his shoulders and rocked his head from side to side, trying desperately to release the cramp in his neck muscles. With each mile they covered he began to feel a little easier, the nausea now having been replaced with ravenous hunger.

'Where is he, Will? Why does he not come?' Edward asked. He gave Hastings a haunted look.

'Perhaps, Ned he still loves you,' Hastings ventured.

'What?' Edward turned quickly in his saddle, his eyes wide in incredulity. 'You cannot mean it, Will?'

'What other reason is there?' Hastings answered. 'He cannot be ignorant of our presence, we saw his scouts this morning.'

Edward looked down at his horse's mane as he contemplated Hastings's words.

'Warwick put him at Pontefract precisely to stop you heading south. He has not come. What other answer is there?' Hastings asked.

Edward smiled at him. 'If there is another reason I do not think I want to know it, Will, for it will taint him in my eyes. Let us say that he loves me still. And whatever the reason is, you can be sure that Warwick will not be pleased with him.'

'Aye, my liege.' Hastings smiled. 'Warwick will be furious.'

As they rode into the stout sanctuary of Sandal Castle it was plain that John Neville would not come now. Though Hastings had sent out extra patrols they were no closer to learning the reason he had not attacked them.

Sunset cloaked the walls in a rich ruby red and cressets were being lit against the fast approaching darkness. Word had been sent long ago that Edward wished to sleep in his late father's castle tonight and already the welcoming smell of roasting meat was scenting the air around them. Hastings's mouth began to water as it reached him and he realized he would probably pay a king's ransom for a drink too!

Edward dismounted silently, as one alone with his thoughts, and Hastings knew it was the deaths here of his father and younger brother Rutland that were haunting him now. John Neville was for the moment forgotten.

Hastings undid the strap of his sallet and handed it to his squire. He turned his head and his neck cracked loudly. God's blood, he thought, there was not a muscle in his body that did not ache. His head was throbbing still and he thought that never had he spent as tense a day as this. As he followed Edward inside he hoped that not only a hearty supper awaited them, but hot baths and soft beds also.

Hasting smiled as he recognized fresh captains in the hall. He followed Edward's lead and welcomed them cheerfully. The sight of them did something to lift the weariness from his heavy limbs and he saw that Edward too had brightened. With the promise of more men at Doncaster tomorrow under William Dudley, and his own retainers no more than three days' ride away, Edward's army was growing into a sizeable force. But he knew numbers alone were no guarantee of victory. As he called for wine and food to be brought, he knew their greatest test was yet to come.

WARWICK CASTLE MARCH 1471

Warwick stared blankly out of the window. Below him it seemed that every blacksmith and armourer in England had been gathered together and the noise of their hammers matched the pounding in his head.

'Ah John,' he whispered to himself, as if to say his brother's name would promote an understanding between them, but the fact was that he did not understand what had happened. Edward and his retainers should never have left Yorkshire alive. But now he had word they were safely at Nottingham and that John was shadowing his rear, Oxford moving on his flank. But still they did not attack him. Would all his allies be so reticent? Must he do everything himself?

'John,' he said again, still unable to believe what had happened. He knew what the rumours were amongst the Lancastrians; that John was still a Yorkist at heart, unwilling to crush Edward, for he loved him still. And though Warwick searched his soul for another explanation, for he was sure there was one, it didn't really matter what he thought. The men who would fight at John's side for Lancaster now doubted his loyalty; John had weakened them as if he had undermined castle walls at a siege. If they did not give battle soon, the Lancastrian cause was in danger of collapse.

'My lord?' Thomas's voice parted the fog of his thoughts.

Warwick flicked tired eyes to him.

'A messenger is without, my lord. He craves an audience urgently.'

'Whose messenger, Thomas?' Warwick asked wearily; his gut told him this was more unwelcome news.

'My lord of Oxford,' Thomas said.

Warwick brightened. Perhaps he had been wrong, perhaps Edward had been trapped between the armies of John and of Oxford after all; it was just that Oxford's messenger had reached him before John's had!

'Bid him enter,' he said.

The man strode quickly into the room and made breathless obeisance. 'My lord of Oxford does greet you well, my lord and...'

'The point, man,' Warwick cut in swiftly. 'Come to the point!' He did not like the way the man would not look up at him, the way his tabard was tattered and torn and his armour was streaked with dust. Dust – not blood!

'I beg your pardon, my lord, but my lord of Oxford has retreated to Stamford.'

'Retreated?' Warwick bellowed the word like an oath. 'Retreated from Edward?'

'Aye, my lord. Edward did turn upon him.'

'Edward did what?' Warwick roared.

The messenger was shaking now. 'He, that is the usurper, turned towards Newark and my lord feared himself outnumbered and out manoeuvred!'

Warwick came to the man in two strides. Hot blood pulsed in his cheeks. Without thought he lifted the messenger off his feet by his collar.

'*Feared* himself outnumbered?' Warwick repeated. 'He feared it, but it was not so, was it?'

'No – no my lord...it was ...only the vanguard!'

'Ah!' Warwick cried out as if the man had wounded him. 'Is it always to be so?' he shouted. 'It was but a gambler's bluff! If Oxford had held his ground he could have slaughtered them, what a blow that would have been to Edward, to lose his van! And then between Oxford's force and that of John's ...Edward should be dead!'

He dropped the man to the floor where he landed with a groan.

'Get out!' Warwick yelled at the messenger. 'I cannot construct a reply to this that would bear the writing down; it would be too full of oaths and blasphemies!'

The messenger half-staggered from the room.

Warwick returned to the window. He folded his arms across his chest while he tried to calm his hammering heart.

'My lord?' Thomas asked tentatively. 'Is there anything I may do for you?'

Warwick fixed him with stinging eyes. 'You once brought someone to me here that changed my life, Thomas. Would that you could bring Elizabeth to me now, for I have sore need of her!' He turned back to the window. Hot pain constricted his chest and he thought he knew how the armour felt as it was struck on the anvil.

He heard Thomas leave and he was once again alone with his thoughts.

What would Edward do now, he mused? He could not be far from Leicester! Warwick shook his head. Leicester meant only one thing: Hastings's retainers! Sweet Jesu, he would have by then nigh on ten thousand men!

'My lord.'

Warwick turned to see his scribe. 'The letter to Henry Vernon, my lord. You wish to sign it?'

Warwick breathed deeply, how many such letters had he brought him today! He pulled himself away from the window and settled on the chair at his desk.

Warwick took the pen from the black-stained fingers of his scribe. It took only a moment to read the brief history of Edward's journey so far that filled the body of the letter, and then came the request for aid to meet at Coventry in all haste, 'with as many people defensibly arrayed as you can readily make.'

Then he added his postscript 'Henry I pray you fail not now as ever I may do for you.' Then he signed it.

He leant back in his chair and ran his eyes unseeing over the beautiful ceiling of his private chamber. Vernon of Haddon was loyal to both himself and Clarence, owed them much, but would this be a tie of loyalty as fragile as the rest appeared to be – as insubstantial as mist; one that only held when Warwick was there to bind it tightly?

'All depends on Coventry,' he said under his breath. His town of Coventry would be in line with Edward's advance to London, for surely London was his goal. Coventry was certainly defendable, though not the best place to give battle. But if Clarence, John, Oxford and his own six thousand could come together at Coventry, then would Edward's fate be sealed!

He called again for his scribe; if he could just pull them all together perhaps the blunders of the past few days would no longer matter.

* * *

As she passed through the barbican of Warwick Castle, Elizabeth thought she had never seen so many people; it seemed as if the whole county had congregated around Warwick's stronghold and were preparing for battle.

Jack turned to her and raised his eyebrows in a gesture that said he too was impressed.

'All these people!' she exclaimed as she dismounted. She had to almost shout so that Jack could hear her above the noise.

Jack smiled. 'There will be yet more to come,' he said.

Elizabeth's eyes widened. 'More?'

'Aye, sweetheart. He still waits on Montagu and Oxford – they are shadowing Edward's march.'

'Shadowing it?' Elizabeth asked incredulously. 'Why do they not attack him?'

Jack looked away from her and patted Comet's strong neck.

'Jack, what has happened?'

Jack sighed. 'Edward had the temerity to ride between them. Percy of Northumberland did not move and neither did most of Yorkshire. Mayhap that is why neither Montagu or Oxford struck, perhaps they feared Percy would turn on them instead, or perhaps the men would not do so, who can say?'

Elizabeth thought on his words. 'They have left it all to Warwick?'

Jack nodded. 'He alone must face Edward.'

Elizabeth shivered. She could just imagine the swagger with which Edward now walked, buoyed by his own audacious success. He would be confident, glittering, believe himself incapable of defeat. His army would be sanguine, while Warwick...waited. The initiative was with Edward, but perhaps God was with Warwick after his solemn oath on the True Cross, she thought.

Jack touched her arm. 'Come, let us go in. At least your presence will lift his spirits, sweetheart.'

Elizabeth smiled, but inside her stomach rolled; Edward had the fortune of the Devil. But he couldn't win, mustn't win, the consequences were too awful to think on.

'My lord,' Elizabeth said.

Warwick came towards her slowly, as if he could not believe what his eyes were telling him. His face seemed pinched and drawn, lined at his cheeks. Elizabeth stared at him, unable to move. His hair had grown to beyond his collar and she noticed that it was streaked with silver and his chin wore at least two days' worth of dark stubble upon it. But what concerned her more was that his beautiful eyes were dull.

He smiled and she thought her heart would break. She hurried to him. He brought his arms about her, pulling her close and she pressed her head against him.

'Sweeting,' he murmured into her hair, 'I thought you would never come.'

She pulled back from him a little and looked into his face. 'Richard, how could you think so?' she asked in a voice tight with emotion. 'I would never desert you, even if all the kings in Christendom were fighting against you!'

He kissed her. His stubble prickled against her cheek and she knew more about the last few days than any words could tell her. And as she held him, she thought how thin he was. Elizabeth's eyelids began to sting. God – how can it have come to this? she thought. Warwick had always been indefatigable, courageous and resilient – he was never sick. Even when he had been wounded at Ferrybridge he had carried on and then fought at the bloodbath of Towton. She wondered if he could do that as he was now.

'Richard,' she whispered, reaching up to stroke the hair from his face.

Warwick smiled and she thought she saw tears in his eyes also. She held his look, trying to read what he cloaked from her.

Eventually Warwick spoke. 'Tomorrow I ride for Coventry,' he said flatly. 'Edward comes on apace.'

Elizabeth bit her lip. 'Richard, my love and prayers will be with you,' she said, 'I would fight alongside you if I could...'

He smiled at her. 'I know,' he said, 'but you cannot, my love and I do not wish the hell of battle upon you. You must stay here at Warwick where I know you will be safe. I will leave Jack to take care of you then if...' he stopped abruptly.

Elizabeth's heart leapt in her chest. 'I do not need to be taken care of, Richard, for you shall win!' she said emphatically.

348

Warwick smiled. 'I would like to think that you are right,' he said, 'but somehow...' his voice broke and he looked away from her quickly.

'Richard, do not say it. Do not even think it,' she said, her throat tightening against the thought. 'I cannot bear it!'

He turned back to her and gave a thin smile, but his eyes were glassy. 'The horrors of war are not for you, Elizabeth, whether I win or lose,' he said. 'I would spare you that, sweeting.'

Elizabeth shook her head. She struggled to speak against a dry throat. 'I would be with you,' she stammered.

Warwick pulled her to him and stroked her head gently. 'No, Elizabeth. I need to know that you are here; that you are safe. You cannot know what battle is like and I would to God that you never know it. Please, Elizabeth, obey me in this.'

Elizabeth could not answer. She was fighting the sob that wanted to come. But the last thing he needed now was a woman wailing over him! She tried to compose herself; she must be strong. 'Richard,' she murmured, 'I do love you.'

'I know,' he said gently, 'I know. And if only that were enough,' he said ruefully, 'then I would be the most powerful man on earth and would not doubt that I can defeat Edward.'

'But you do doubt it,' Elizabeth said huskily, 'and you are asking me to say goodbye.'

Warwick nodded, but did not speak.

'I cannot,' Elizabeth sighed.

'You must,' he said, 'for both of us. We must part on good terms.'

'Not now, Richard. We still have tonight, do we not?'

He smiled. 'I wish I could say that lovemaking was my uppermost thought, sweeting. But you will understand if I do not say so?'

'Richard, just to be with you is enough. That will satisfy me, for I have missed you so much.'

Warwick smiled. 'If you wish it. Though I warn you, somehow sleep eludes me at present.'

'You will sleep tonight,' Elizabeth promised, 'for I shall be with you.' She did not add that she had absolutely no intention of remaining behind at Warwick Castle. If he was going to Coventry then so was she, even if she had to walk all the way!

* * *

Elizabeth was awoken by the first pale light of dawn on her face. Slowly, dreamily she opened her eyes and immediately looked to Warwick. He slept peacefully beside her, the lines of worry gone at last from his face. He breathed deeply, contentedly and Elizabeth smiled. She did not wake him, though in that moment she wanted to tell him that she loved him more than ever. Instead she turned gently onto her side so that she could watch him more easily. If only their life could be like this moment, she thought, but now any future was cloaked in mist, let alone a future together! They had to live each moment as it came to them and thank God for it!

She did not know how long she had lain there, blissfully, when a loud knock came at the door and their peace was shattered: it was time to leave.

* * *

Warwick shook his head in exasperation.

'It is not an argument you can win, Richard,' Elizabeth said flatly. 'At Coventry there is a whole town full of women and children alongside your soldiers. Are you going to send all of them away too? Make all of them leave for Warwick?'

Warwick smiled at the indignant expression on her face as she sat stiffly on her courser, knuckles white as she gripped the reins. And was it not one of the qualities that endeared her to him, the fact that she did not obey anyone; was not swayed by convention or propriety but was ruled by deeper, stronger emotions? God's breath, she was even riding a courser instead of a lady's palfrey! He was reminded of France, when she had demanded to go with him to Barfleur; she had won that argument, but this was different: this was battle and he wanted her nowhere near it!

He put his hand on her knee. 'Sweeting...'

Her green eyes flashed at him. 'Do not even try,' she said warningly.

He laughed then and had to admit defeat. 'Very well, Elizabeth, you may come to Coventry.'

She rewarded him with a smile like sunshine.

He turned and mounted his own horse. The truth was he hadn't wanted to leave her; she gave him strength. Her unshakable belief in him showed him that the things he desired were yet possible. All he needed was but a little of Edward's good fortune. When Montagu, Oxford and Clarence joined him at Coventry then Edward would not be so bold!

BANBURY APRIL 1471

'Do you see them, Will?' Edward asked. It had been two hours since Edward had heard from his scouts that Clarence was approaching in battle array with perhaps four thousand men. Part of him could not imagine Clarence making a fight of it, but the scouts were clear – they were in battle array! So now they waited for Clarence, with the household guard at their side and the army drawn up close behind them.

Hastings stood in his stirrups, a hand shielding his eyes from the low sun. 'Not yet, Your Grace, but he cannot be far off. Certainly he does not march as fast as we did coming south!'

Edward smiled at Hastings's attempt at a jest, but the humour did nothing to uncoil the knot in his guts. Sweet Jesu, he had not seen his perfidious brother for nigh on a year. Who would have thought that they would ever meet like this – across a battlefield!

'There!' Hastings called, his right arm outstretched. 'I see his banners!'

Edward gulped. He strained his senses and convinced himself that he could hear the soft thunder of marching feet, could glimpse the ethereal wisps of pennants above the cloud of dust that was approaching. Suddenly he felt so very cold. But this was what being a king was all about, he thought, and if he had to kill his brother in order to maintain his hold on the crown, then so be it!

'He's coming!' Gloucester drew alongside, his face no less grim than Edward expected. Their eyes met briefly before Edward turned in the saddle and surveyed his army once again. Drawn up in battle order they looked magnificent, but somehow he still could not believe it had come to this.

'His herald, Your Grace!' Hastings was still keeping a keen eye on the Banbury road. 'He must want to parley.'

'Aye, probably wants to demand I surrender to him,' Edward growled. But if Edward would not yield to Warwick he certainly would not yield to Clarence; blood would be spilt this day.

They all stared as the lone horseman cantered closer, the dust pall thickening behind him. Edward could almost count his heartbeats for it seemed to take an age before the herald was kneeling at his side.

'Your Grace,' the man said breathlessly.

'How does my brother of Clarence?' Edward asked curtly, and then waited to hear Clarence's supercilious demand.

The Herald cleared the dust from his throat. 'He greets you well, Your Grace and humbly craves your pardon.'

'My...pardon?' Edward's heart kicked. What did this mean? He stared at the kneeling herald as if a ghost had spoken to him. What trick was this? What diversion to distract him from a battle he knew had to be fought?

'Your Grace?' Hastings's voice rescued him from indecision and the meaning of the words cleared in his whirling mind: Clarence had asked for pardon!

Edward turned to Gloucester. He was going to ask his opinion, but the wide smile that greeted him gave him an irrefutable answer.

'Let him come on.' Edward sounded calmer than he felt. God's blood, what a blow this would be to Warwick!

Edward nodded to Hastings and Gloucester and nudged his stallion forward, allowing Clarence the opportunity to speak to him without his entire household hearing their words. He dismounted, fumbled with his reins before handing them to Hastings and then looked up to see his brother dismounting in front of him. To his astonishment Clarence immediately knelt before him. He could scarcely believe his eyes; all those letters, from himself and Margaret, all the risk, all the planning, had it truly brought this about?

'Your Grace,' Clarence's voice was uncharacteristically hesitant. 'George!'

To Edward's amazement Gloucester had dismounted also and was striding towards their brother with open arms.

Clarence glanced quickly to Edward and then rose to meet Gloucester's embrace.

Edward then stepped forward too. 'You are most welcome...brother,' he said and received Clarence's hug stiffly. He suppressed the anger tightening his guts.

'You took your time!' Gloucester said, laughing.

Edward stared at his grinning brothers. How could Gloucester forgive Clarence so easily? Was it his youth that allowed him to sweep away Clarence's treachery with no more thought than if they had been cobwebs? Was it simply that he did not have the responsibilities of a king as he had? Or did he but cloak his true feelings for the sake of the crown, as Edward now must do?

'Were you trying to make us think you would make a fight of it?' Gloucester continued, punching Clarence on the shoulder in jest.

Clarence flushed, his lips trembled and then he bowed his head.

'There is something you wish to say?' Edward asked.

Clarence raised his head slowly, met Edward's eyes hesitantly. 'There is but one thing, sire,' he said, swallowing thickly. 'Warwick...'

Edward let out a long sigh. He knew what made Clarence speak so. 'You ask for what he will not accept, George. I have already tried. But there is no trust betwixt us. He does not believe that his life is secure.'

'May I not try, Your Grace?' Clarence asked. 'It is not too late.'

'God's blood!' Hastings cursed. 'I too have no wish to see Warwick mauled; but you cannot ask this...'

Edward heard the outrage in Hastings's voice: how could they trust Clarence to do this duty? In short how could they believe it was not a ruse to join Warwick and avoid battle today? Clarence turned fierce eyes on Hastings. 'He believed in me, my lord,' he said, 'and for Isabel's sake I must try.'

Edward saw Hastings look away, his cheeks colouring.

'We shall discuss this over supper,' Edward said firmly, 'but if we can avoid the bloodshed that will otherwise come, then I am for it.' As he walked back to his horse he wondered if Clarence realized what terms he could offer Warwick. He doubted they were conditions his cousin would ever accept.

COVENTRY APRIL 1471

A shiver of winter touched Warwick's face. Even though he had noted the new green of leaf buds on the hawthorn as they had ridden here; winter had not yet relinquished its hold.

He scarcely heard the hush of Elizabeth's footsteps as she joined him on the walls and silently they stared out together on the blackness of the plain beneath them.

'Edward cannot stay at Warwick much longer.' Warwick broke the silence reluctantly.

'Cannot?' Elizabeth asked.

'They are outside the walls; my castles do not yield so easily!'
He thought ruefully of the proud yellow-pink stone glaring down
on Edward's flickering campfires beneath. He shuddered. 'They
must have exhausted the land of resources by now; they must
either move or starve.'

'He will go to London?'

Warwick nodded. Just a little of Edward's good fortune was all
he'd wished for, but it seemed that the Lord did not hear him
despite his sacred oath.

'And you will follow?' Elizabeth asked, slipping her hand
through the crook of his arm.

'Yes, when all are come.' His throat tightened, feeling again the
pain of Clarence's betrayal.

Elizabeth must have felt him tense, for she pressed closer to
him. 'You are thinking on Clarence?'

He turned to look at her. Her wide eyes were beautiful. They
were almost black in the dancing light of the cressets and he
stood for a moment transfixed, wanting to remember her forever
as she was now.

'Clarence,' he sighed. 'Yes.'

Elizabeth gave a little cough as if she was going to say something, but what could she say about Clarence that he did not
know? Jack, Archbishop Neville and others had tried to warn
him that Clarence would turn away from him, but he had not
wanted to believe what had been obvious from the moment he
accepted Lancaster as his son!

'Richard, I...'

'What was worse, Elizabeth, was that he brought Edward's offer
of a pardon. If he is newborn Yorkist then good for him, but to
think I would perjure myself...' he paused, giving his next words
more gravity. 'I swore on the True Cross and that is an oath I will
not break, though God does not seem to favour it.' Anger tightened his throat. 'My life only, Elizabeth, that is what he offered
me, my life to rot in the Tower. Christ in heaven, I would rather
die on the field!'

The beautiful eyes turned to liquid before him and his own began to sting. He pulled Elizabeth to him.

'I am so sorry,' she whispered, her words a hot breath on his
neck. 'So sorry, Richard. I never meant...'

He hushed her with a deep kiss. What silly words. She could not
have prevented Clarence from making the choice he made, no

one could! But if God gave strength to his sword-arm then he would make him regret that choice!

The warmth of Elizabeth's lips pushed the thoughts of Clarence from his mind and sent heat to his loins. As soon as Montagu and Oxford came, he really would have to leave her, but until that time they still had each other.

THIRTEEN

COVENTRY APRIL 1471

'John, you are most welcome,' Warwick said as he embraced his brother.

Dark Neville eyes met and Warwick felt their united resolve. He did not mention John's hesitant past; his residual loyalty to Edward when Warwick had called to him previously. All this was irrelevant now. The Nevilles were now against the world.

John nodded yet said nothing as he withdrew from Warwick's arms, but Warwick knew what the gesture said – they were in this together. It made Warwick shiver; each realized that unity was now their only hope, for the ties with other lords, Warwick knew too well, were but gossamer threads.

Warwick's heart thumped with pride and love as he looked on his brother. John's absence had been like having only one hand with which to swing his sword. So many times they had fought together and so many times they had won.

'It is good that you have come,' Warwick said as he settled into his great chair. He gestured to John to sit also.

John hesitated a moment then took the wine a servant offered and sat down.

Although Warwick was relieved that John had joined him, his brother's uncharacteristically slow progress south was nagging him, like an old arrow wound. He watched John for a moment, trying to gauge his mood. 'I had expected you to arrive before Edward,' he said slowly. It was not an accusation, simply a statement of fact, but John's eyes flicked up to his and for a moment there was anger there. He locked his eyes onto Warwick's.

'Is that why you did not give battle, Richard?' John's tone was impassive, but yet Warwick wondered if there was an accusation lying just beneath the surface. He shrugged it aside.

'Aye, brother,' he answered honestly, 'I waited on you and Oxford both.'

'And Clarence,' John observed dryly.

Blood pulsed into Warwick's cheeks. 'Do not mention Clarence!' he hissed. The pain of Clarence's treachery was still too raw to deal with.

'And if you had not waited?' John's eyes narrowed shrewdly.

'Mayhap I still would have outnumbered Edward,' Warwick said, reading his thoughts.

'Aye,' John nodded.

'And all may have been decided by the time you arrived, John,' Warwick said sourly. Did he really believe John had delayed his arrival deliberately so that the outcome would have been known and he would not have had to choose between Warwick and Edward? The truth was, Warwick was not sure. He could not openly accuse John of diffidence, not now that he had made a choice, but there was still doubt in his mind. If the throne had been lost and won without John having to take up arms...But Warwick needed John now. This was no time for unpicking their love. He could ask John about Yorkshire, about Percy too, but he knew it would serve no purpose. John was still watching him, but he said nothing, and Warwick knew if he asked no more questions then he would not hear lies or perhaps worse, the truth from John.

John threw the wine into his throat. 'You know, Richard,' he said softly, 'I do not relish this battle, as I relished those we fought in ten or so years ago.'

Warwick sighed. 'Nor do I John, but it is unavoidable.'

'Aye,' John nodded, 'that is why I counselled you to accept Edward's authority, to make your peace with him and to forget France. This was what I wished to avoid,' he said sadly. 'But when Richard, did you ever heed my counsel?'

Warwick shrugged and then signalled for more wine. 'It is long past regret, John,' he said. 'We can wish things unsaid or undone, but they remain as they are. It is in God's hands now. We must have no regrets. This battle will decide all. Everything we have, everything we are is at stake. Whatever Edward's honey-mouthed words, there will be no pardon for you and I, John, of that I am certain.'

'Mayhap that is true,' John sighed, 'but I beg you, Richard to heed my counsel when it comes to war.'

There was a pleading insistence in John's voice Warwick had not heard before. He studied his brother; saw silver at his temples and lines about his eyes that he had not known.

'Richard?'

Warwick smiled. 'I promise you I shall listen to all you have to say, John.'

'But will you *heed* me? Take my advice?' John persisted.

Warwick sipped the sweetly spiced wine. How could he refuse John now? They had to stand together. 'Of course I shall, John,' he said softly. 'Together we can defeat him.'

John looked across at him. 'If they hold. Lancastrians and one-time Yorkists together, Richard; it is a heady brew. Will they stand for you, Richard when Edward comes on?'

'Will they stand for *us*, John?' Warwick said. John had hit the bull's-eye with his arrow. It was Warwick's greatest fear for the battle: that treason and mistrust would unravel his forces when he most needed them to be closely knit. 'If they fail us, John then we are all lost.'

John's eyes flicked to his and Warwick saw the worry there before John cloaked it with a smile. 'Still brother, you and I shall stand together, eh? *'Ne vile vellis'.'* He said the Neville family motto wistfully.

Warwick nodded. Never had it been more apt – 'think no bad thing'; for he was sure that the thoughts of treachery and betrayal would be their greatest foes. And if he was honest, he feared for John more than himself.

The silence between them lengthened as each thought on the dark battle to come and exorcised his ghosts.

When John spoke, he was brighter. 'What then do you suggest, Richard?' he asked. 'Where shall we meet the stoat?'

'Edward has turned for London,' Warwick said. 'Brother George holds the Tower and Somerset the gates. If we march quickly, we can catch Edward between the unyielding city walls and our force. We can then give battle more certainly than ever I could have at Coventry.'

John frowned. 'You are certain London will not admit him?'

'Somerset gave me his word.'

'Pah!' John scoffed, 'you would accept the word of a Lancastrian? And a Lancastrian that hates us at that! Your brain is soft as scrambled eggs, Richard. You know Somerset wanted command, and if you fail, he shall have it!'

Warwick's cheeks began to burn. 'John,' he said as calmly as he could manage, 'we are all Lancastrian now. You also swore your allegiance, gave your speech to parliament.'

John laughed ironically. 'You are right, Richard, so I did. But I think we make poor bedfellows.'

Warwick slammed his fist into the arm of the chair. 'John! We have to work together; otherwise all is lost. There *must* be trust between us!'

John's cheeks flushed too and he lowered his eyes. 'I am sorry, Richard,' he said, 'I cannot get used to it.'

'I know,' Warwick answered, 'I too have found these last few months the hardest of my life. It has been like walking on eggshells; the slightest look, the merest inflection in the voice; all go against me. And the lack of Queen Marguerite's presence has hindered me more than she will ever know. I could not reward returning Lancastrian exiles without offending the remnants of Edward's administration; I have tried my best, John, but at times I have been like the fool at the feast – juggling coloured balls at an incredible pace just to keep them from falling to the ground. And I think that without Elizabeth, I truly would have gone mad.'

'Elizabeth?' John's eyes flickered with interest. 'A woman, Richard?'

Warwick lowered his gaze for a moment, knowing he had said too much.

'Richard?' John pushed. ''Tis not like you. Who is she?'

Warwick shook his head.

'Richard!' John pushed.

Warwick sighed. 'She is Sir Robert Hardacre's daughter.'

'Hardacre? By Christ, Richard she is so young! And she was...is...' John curbed the sentence.

Warwick heard the disapproval in John's voice, and thought it somewhat hypocritical given that Isabella Ingoldsthorp had been only fifteen when John had wedded her! He gritted his teeth; but then John had been free to marry her, and that he knew, made all the difference.

'She is here?' John asked more quietly.

'Yes,' Warwick answered.

'Then you should let her return home, where she will be safe,' John continued.

'Do you think I have not asked her to leave?' Warwick said.

'You *ask* her?' John said, plainly astonished. 'Richard, you rule all England, yet you ask a woman what she wishes!'

'She will not go,' Warwick said flatly, 'and without her I think all would have been lost before now.' He did not know if John really understood what he was saying to him.

John shook his head.

'John!' Warwick growled. 'Do not play the Cardinal with me! I know you are not as pure as fresh snow. You were often in lewd Edward's company as I recall!'

John smiled at the memories. 'Aye, you are right, brother. But that was harmless fun; tavern wenches and bawdy houses, but this is a knight's daughter. You have taken from this maiden that which only her husband should have. What if you die on the field? What will happen to her then? She will not be wanted by anyone. Have you thought on that, Richard? Because of you, she is ruined.'

Warwick's heart lurched: John was right. God's blood he had been so selfish!

'Send her away, Richard,' John persisted. 'Send her home now, before it is too late.'

Tears stung at Warwick's eyes; Elizabeth had been his safe harbour as she had promised. She had sheltered him, loved him. How could he prepare for battle, perhaps even death without her by his side?

'Richard,' John said sternly, 'you must do it today.'

* * *

Jack thundered along the slick ribbon of road as if the devil was after him. In many ways he was glad to be away from the claustrophobia of Warwick Castle, though if he was honest, it was not the thronging mass of Warwick's adherents that were the problem; it was the sight of Elizabeth in Warwick's company that had galled him like a gadfly. It was his own fault; he knew that, for he had brought her here when he should have insisted that she stay in Yorkshire and marry him. That would have solved all their ills and brought him a rich inheritance, for he remembered his old captain, Will Kennerley, telling him that Elizabeth had been well provided for!

He kicked Comet on, oblivious to the mizzling rain stinging his eyes and streaking down his face and he tried to put Elizabeth out of his mind. He told himself that he could be more use to Warwick out here in the sodden darkness, shadowing his enemies than he could be counting arrows and harness as Thomas Conyers did. He would rather taste a little freedom before the inevitable call to battle, he thought, even if part of him had wanted to meet John Neville once again. Mayhap they would meet on the field and relive some of their memories of the North Country; but that thought only served to remind him of what he had lost. He dug in his spurs again; he must catch up with Edward tonight.

* * *

'My lady.'

At the sound of the deep soft voice Elizabeth turned, and for a moment she half expected to see Warwick. The dark eyes that met hers were similar, though they were a little closer together and sat under neat dark brows on which were written many tales of battle. The man's jaw was squarer than Warwick's and was darkened from a day's growth of stubble, which she thought rather complimented his weather-beaten skin. A thin white ragged scar on his left cheek told her this was the face of a soldier; this was the face of John Neville. 'My lord,' she said.

'I hear you have come from Yorkshire, my lady?'

Curious, Elizabeth turned to face him fully, her eyes searching his face for clues to his motives for being here. He averted his gaze, as if to hide an inner feeling he thought she might be able to read.

'I am, my lord,' Elizabeth answered with a curtsey.

John Neville nodded and Elizabeth saw that he was appraising her with his warrior's eyes. It was not as a courtier would; as Jack would, this was too blatant, an involuntary action from a man used to spending his time with other men, hard-bitten soldiers from whom he had no secrets.

'You are to fight with my lord of Warwick?' Elizabeth ventured uneasily.

He smiled, as if he had just seen an excellent horse or a new sword. He nodded again, but still he watched her.

'Against Edward.' The words stuck in her throat and she noticed that he sucked in his breath at the mention of Edward's name. His countenance changed and for a moment she saw a flash of pain in his eyes.

'I am a Neville, Mistress Hardacre,' he said gruffly by way of explanation. Elizabeth wanted him to say more.

Seeing the intensity of her look he said 'You do not understand. How can you? But be assured, lady, Edward will.' His voice trailed away like smoke. Elizabeth was puzzled. What was he trying to say to her? There was a distinct feeling of sadness about him, hopelessness even. She tried to tease more out of him.

'Richard will be glad you are here, my lord,' she said, 'he has been waiting for...'

John Neville cut in on her. 'Do not be in any doubt, lady,' he said harshly, 'that this is a sorry mess!' His eyes narrowed.

'But sir, you now will surely outnumber Edward!' Elizabeth's voice shook.

'Aye, if all stand!' John said. 'Do you not think some men hate my brother more than they hate Edward? They lay the blame for the downfall of the House of Lancaster squarely at my brother's door! Richard it was who declared Prince Edouard of Lancaster was a bastard and it was Richard who called Queen Marguerite 'The Bitch of Anjou'! And I, my lady, have slaughtered Lancastrians too in Edward's cause. Do you think they have forgotten that?'

Elizabeth saw that he was shaking as he spoke – and so was she. She was shaking with fear at John Neville's implications for Warwick. And she wondered why he was confiding his doubts about their cause in her.

'But you have to win, my lord!' It came out as a plea. 'Edward will never forgive you, any of you!'

'And you think 'The Bitch of Anjou' has really forgiven Richard, or half the men that will stand beside us? They are just as likely to turn on us for our Yorkist past as they are to attack Edward!'

Elizabeth's lip began to quiver. She bit into it, tasted blood. She did not want to contemplate Warwick's defeat – for defeat meant certain death, mayhap for all of them.

She turned her head away, hoping that John Neville would not see the tears she was trying to blink away.

He moved closer. His breath was warm on the back of her neck.

'Forgive me lady,' he said gently. 'I speak as a soldier. I did not mean to distress you. Only...'

Elizabeth turned back to face him.

'Only you are so young. You could yet make a life for yourself.' The words were a smooth whisper, almost like a prayer. 'Return to Yorkshire, lady, forget about my brother.'

She shook her head. 'I do not want...' she could not finish the sentence without giving in to a sob.

'We cannot always have what we want,' he said. 'Go home.'

Elizabeth was beyond speech and she swallowed hard, trying not to cry. She shook her head.

'I was in the North after bloody Towton,' John Neville said.

Elizabeth's eyes flew to his.

'There was a young man knighted on the field after the battle. A brave lad; a bastard son of a knight with gypsy blood in his veins.'

'No!' Elizabeth sobbed. She did not want to hear this.

John Neville locked his eyes onto hers. 'My brother was wounded in the battle, he did not hear the promise your father made to Jack de Laverton in humble gratitude, but I did. Do you want me to tell him what he does not need to know – that you are Jack de Laverton's betrothed?'

Elizabeth shook her head and tears burned onto her cheeks. 'Sir, I beg you do not do this,' she said. 'I knew nought of it until recent times,' she said. 'Why hurt him now when he has enough troubles to think on?'

'Your place is not here, my lady. Your place is at home.'

Elizabeth's chest tightened as she fought to maintain her self-control.

'He needs no distractions; a woman's place is not in war. You have a future in Yorkshire. Go home and wait for your husband. Wait for Jack. He is a good man. He deserves you.'

'No!' Elizabeth sobbed. 'Jack deserves much better than that!'

John Neville bowed his head momentarily and then looked back at her face. His eyes were dark seas of sadness. 'I am sorry,' he said. 'You know what the right course of action is, it was your father's wish; I implore you to do it. Go home Mistress Hardacre. I do not want to tell my brother what I know.'

Then he turned away from her and she heard his spurs jangling as he strode away. The door clicked behind him.

* * *

'But you cannot stay, Elizabeth. It will not be safe,' Warwick said.

'Richard, please do not do this.' Elizabeth's eyes were wide with pleading and he could see she fought back the first signs of tears.

Before he could say anything further she flew to his arms.

It was as he had feared – sending her away from him was almost impossible.

She pressed against his shoulder and he breathed in the perfume of her hair as he stroked her head gently. Even now, she stirred him; now when he knew he could not touch her, he needed her most.

'My lord, I would stay,' she murmured into the velvet of his doublet. 'There is nowhere I would rather be.'

'I know, my love...' he struggled for words. What could he say to her? John's words burned into his mind and he knew his brother was right. '...But if we fail, Elizabeth...' he broke off, his heart pounding at his throat.

Elizabeth looked up at him. There were pearls of tears on her cheeks.

'But you will not fail, Richard,' she said, 'I know it.'

He smiled at her belief in him and he wished he could share her confidence. He brushed her tears away with the ball of his thumb. 'It is not certain, Elizabeth and I could not bear the thought of what might happen to you without protection. A victorious army will cry havoc and, sweeting, I would wish you as far away from that as possible.'

'I can take care of myself!' Elizabeth snapped. 'I am not a child.'

Warwick wrapped his arms about her more tightly. 'You are certainly no child; you are all woman, and that is what worries me the most. Marauding soldiers do not only steal gold, Elizabeth...' He broke off; not wanting to frighten her more than was necessary. 'You must go home,' he tried to sound stern, as if it was an order to his army, but he knew his longing softened his voice.

'I want to be with you, Richard!' She paused; held his gaze. Her eyes pleaded her case; found a way to his heart.

'I know what you would wish, sweeting,' he said gently. 'But you cannot ride with the army; you cannot follow me into battle.'

'Please, Richard.' Her voice wrapped around him like a fur-lined cloak and he struggled to fight her. He steadied his voice, knowing that this time he had to be strong. This was not like Barfleur! 'I'm sorry, sweeting,' he said. The tone of finality he forced into the words had the effect he needed.

Elizabeth gave a soft sigh that almost broke his heart. She blinked tears through her lashes and he knew that this time he had won. He tried to soften the blow. 'I shall fight the better for knowing you are safe,' he said gently. He caressed a thumb across her cheek, blotting the tears. 'I have always thought I would die in battle, Elizabeth, and if it is to be in this one, sweeting, I would not have you see it.' His throat tightened and Elizabeth murmured something he did not hear. He drew her into a tight embrace, knowing that when he let her go again, it might be forever.

DAVENTRY APRIL 1471

Jack pulled hard on the reins. Comet fought for his head, whickered truculently and then submitted. Jack watched through the trees as the rearguard of Edward's army marched along Watling Street. Though he could not distinguish the words, he could hear that they were singing. He had to admit that they had kept up a good pace, one Warwick would find hard to match with his large artillery train. There was no doubt that Edward would soon be in London, for what could a few old men and a prelate do against the might of Edward's force?

Jack allowed some time for Edward's forces to clear the town and then he followed their path.

As he drew in to Daventry it seemed that the whole county had come to see Edward march through. Then Jack remembered it was Palm Sunday. He shivered, for Palm Sunday always brought chilling memories of bloody Towton. Without thought he touched his arm where the arrow had caught him that day. He took a composing breath and shook his head to clear his darkening thoughts. It must have been a thrilling sermon, he thought looking about him, for groups of townsfolk were in animated conversation, and he wondered if it was something Edward had done that had excited them so.

He drew up as close to the little church as he could. There was quite a gathering as people tried to force their way inside and Jack wondered what it was they wished to see.

'What news?' he asked a man standing nearby.

'Word has spread as far as St Albans, sir,' the man replied proudly. 'I always knew he was special and God has shown it today!'

'I do not understand,' Jack said genuinely.

'You have not heard then, that the king was here but a few hours ago?'

'The king?' Jack asked.

'Aye, Edward of York, only he proclaimed himself King of England again when he left Coventry!'

'Did he indeed?' Jack raised his brows. So the sword was at last unsheathed!

'Aye, mind you, there's only northerners who who'd have fallen for that as a ruse, eh?' The man laughed heartily.

Stealing himself not to come up with a quip about 'southrons' as they were known in Yorkshire, Jack continued. 'So what happened?' he asked, nodding to the writhing mass of bodies still trying to get into the church.

'In there we have a statue of Saint Anne,' the man said.

Jack nodded. There was nothing so special about that, though he knew she was a saint venerated by Edward.

'The king, hearing of it, decided to attend our service and make an offering to her.'

'Aye,' Jack said encouragingly. 'But she would be covered until Easter Sunday?'

'Aye, sir, she was. Boards were covering her as they have since Ash Wednesday, as is only right and proper.'

'Of course,' Jack agreed; so was the custom in all English churches.

'Anyway, as the king genuflected at the Rood, what do you think?'

Jack shook his head. 'I have no idea,' he said truthfully.

'She uncovered herself to him!'

'What?' Jack asked in disbelief.

''Tis true, I saw it with my own eyes! The boards flew off and crashed to the floor as if a hand was tearing at them!'

Jack raised his brows. 'Truly?' The man must think him an idiot!

'As surely as I'm standing here!'

Jack didn't know whether to laugh or not, the story was too ludicrous to be true! He'd heard of miracles, yes, but here, in Daventry of all places?

'So Saint Anne has him under her protection, so she does,' the man continued brightly. 'The Earl of Warwick had better watch out!'

Jack suppressed the twitch of his mouth that wanted to come. He could imagine the smile on Warwick's face when he told him of this later. But then a dark thought struck him; it didn't really matter what he and Warwick thought. The press of bodies at the doorway showed him what these people believed: that Edward was capable of miracles!

It was fine for Richard to send such messages, Archbishop Neville thought, but had he not warned him that he was an archbishop not a soldier? In theory, to hold Edward at bay for two days was easy; he just had to persuade the aldermen to keep the gates locked; Edward could not besiege London! But the aldermen had not wanted to hear him – Edward would arrive in two days' time at most and Warwick was ... well, not here to press his argument!

'Your Grace!'

His servant's voice dragged him from his thoughts. He pulled at the gold edging of his surplice testily and followed his servant to where the horses and King Henry were waiting.

'By all the saints!' he whispered as he saw King Henry. He turned to his men. 'Could you find him nothing better than that blue velvet gown? Was there nothing finer amongst Edward's clothes? Were there no jewels?'

'Nothing he would put on, Your Grace. He said he wanted to feel humble, as Easter approaches!'

'Humble!' Archbishop Neville cried. 'He certainly looks humble – he is supposed to look like a sovereign! We are trying to rally men to Lancaster's cause, not recruit for Edward!'

'There is no time to change it, Your Grace.'

'And where are Somerset and Devon?'

All eyes searched the floor. 'They have had word from Queen Marguerite, Your Grace.'

No one seemed to know precisely what the word was, but whatever it was it had prevented the lords from joining Henry's parade. Neither were any of their retinues present and Archbishop Neville had a sickening thought: they had left London! He sighed heavily; still he had to see this through so far as he was able.

All the while Henry sat still on his palfrey staring wide-eyed ahead of him, seeing nothing.

Archbishop Neville's stomach knotted. This had seemed such a good idea; a royal pageant, a rallying call at St Paul's cathedral to turn the hearts of the Londoners towards King Henry and Lancaster. But now he was not so sure. God's blood, what would Richard think? But it was too late to cancel it; people were already lining the streets.

He followed his squire round to his horse and mounted. At the sudden movement King Henry turned to face him. 'Good morrow, Archbishop Neville,' he said. 'Are we going hunting?'

Archbishop Neville looked heavenwards; this was going to be a disaster! Warwick would kill him; that is if Edward did not get to him first!

'No, my liege,' he said as calmly as he could, 'we go to rally your soldiers; to call the people of London to arms!'

'How so?' Henry asked him blankly. 'Are the French come?'

Archbishop Neville sighed again. 'No, majesty, the usurper Edward late Earl of March is come!'

'You speak truly my lord Archbishop; he is indeed late, for it is already April,' Henry said flatly.

Archbishop Neville strangled a cry in his throat. 'Let us go!' he said.

'One moment, Archbishop Neville,' Henry said, 'would you be so kind as to hold my hand? It has been a long time since I have ridden and I do not feel very safe!'

Archbishop Neville stared at Henry in incredulity, and then began to stammer that he would. His stomach rose to his throat. This could not get any worse, he thought, but he was wrong.

Grim faces and hateful jeers greeted their progress. Even those Londoners who had been feeling genuinely neutral saw Henry as Archbishop Neville had that morning: not someone worth risking their life for! Even the Lancastrian banner hung limply from its pole.

Only six hundred men were waiting for them at St Paul's churchyard. Mentally Archbishop Neville compared them to the three hundred or so knights and squires of Yorkist persuasion who had now deemed it the right time to come out of the London sanctuaries and reassert their allegiances! What a pity Warwick had been so adamant about upholding the inviolability of the sanctuaries!

When he returned to Westminster Palace he returned to the news that Somerset and Devon had headed for the coast to greet Queen Marguerite and the common council had met. Mayor Stockton was still in his bed and Sir Thomas Cook had also fled the capital, but nevertheless they had given due consideration to letters from both Warwick and Edward. Their pronouncement made Archbishop Neville realize that he too must make a decision, and as he entered his privy chamber he called out for his scribe; a letter must be sent immediately.

ST ALBANS APRIL 1471

Jack knelt at Warwick's feet, bowing his head. 'My lord,' he said.

'Jack, you are most welcome,' Warwick said as he rose stiffly from his chair. He stepped forward and raised Jack to his feet, gripping his hand tightly. 'Come, refresh yourself, Jack. You must have ridden hard to find me.'

Jack glanced quickly at his dust-covered clothing; he hadn't even wiped his boots before entering Warwick's tent. 'Yes, my lord, I have.'

He took the wine Warwick offered him.

'So, what news, Jack?' Warwick asked.

'Edward is in London as we speak, my lord,' Jack said tentatively as Warwick bade him sit.

Warwick sucked in a sharp breath. Then he drew his eyes up to Jack's. 'Archbishop Neville?' he asked hesitantly, as though he feared the worst of Edward for his brother.

'He sued for pardon, my lord and is resting now in the Tower.'

Warwick sighed. 'Thank the saints that he is well. I suppose he tried his best.'

'My lord, I think he had little chance when Somerset and Devon did not support him. He is no soldier, my lord.'

Warwick smiled ruefully. 'No he is not,' he said flatly. 'And he will not be an archbishop for much longer either, I'll warrant.'

Jack lowered his eyes. 'There is nothing else but to choose your ground, my lord.'

'You think Edward will not keep Easter in London?'

Jack met his anxious look. 'No my lord, he will not. He will come out with his host to give battle, I know he will.' Instinctively Jack knew Edward would not want to lose the initiative his fast march had given him. Warwick's men were tired and downcast; they knew they had missed an opportunity; several opportunities if the truth were told!

'You are probably right, Jack,' Warwick said.

Jack twitched a smile. 'I know I am, my lord.'

'So be it,' Warwick said sternly. 'We always knew this would be decided on the battlefield.'

Jack nodded. He had hoped to find Warwick more cheerful, more optimistic about their chances, had hoped to make him laugh with his tale of Edward's Palm Sunday miracle, but he knew now was not the right time. Perhaps when all this was over, they would share the jest over a cup of wine.

He had also wanted to ask him about Elizabeth. She was not with Warwick's army; he must have left her behind at Coventry. How hard that would be for her, to sit and wait, with no hope of seeing Warwick again until all was done and Edward was slain. He could imagine her annoyance, her frustration at being left behind; in fact he could almost imagine her defiantly coming to find them! He looked at Warwick again; it was not the time to mention Elizabeth either. 'Is there anything else, my lord?' he asked.

Warwick looked at him a little dazed. 'Ah Jack, what are kings?' Warwick asked glumly.

'My lord?'

'Was I not called 'the third king' by many?' Warwick asked.

'Indeed my lord, you were,' Jack answered, still unsure of where this was leading.

'But I never shall be a king, Jack and I do not think I will ever understand them.'

Jack furrowed his brow.

Warwick smiled sadly. 'You give your life, your heart in their service, Jack, but they feel they owe you nothing for it.' Warwick paused and then said: 'I have sent a letter to King Louis tonight, Jack.' His face tightened.

Jack wondered if this was Warwick's plan if all went wrong – to seek shelter once again in the court of France.

Warwick's eyes narrowed. 'As mendacious as Clarence!'

'My lord, I do not understand,' Jack said.

Warwick sighed. 'He has made a truce with Burgundy, Jack.'

Jack tried to control a gasp but failed; it was Louis's haste to crush Burgundy that had brought about Duke Charles's support of Edward! 'The traitorous bastard!' Jack cursed.

'Oh I did vent my spleen, Jack I can assure you,' Warwick said. 'There will be no refuge in France if we do not prevail.'

Jack looked at Warwick. How drawn his face now seemed in the candlelight. 'Then we must make sure we win, my lord,' Jack said as brightly as he could.

Warwick laughed without mirth. 'Aye Jack, the glory is there for us to take or to lose!'

Jack met his look and for a while they drank their wine in silence; they both realized the meaning of Louis's betrayal and they contemplated the finality of the battle to come. If Warwick had alienated Louis there would be no refuge if they did not prevail, no turning defeat into victory for a second time!

Eventually it was Warwick who broke the silence. 'You should find a bed Jack; you look like you could do with some rest.'

Jack wanted to say that Warwick too looked like he also needed a good night's sleep, but Jack doubted that any of them would know much sleep until the struggle for England was over. And how much harder that struggle had just become.

LONDON APRIL 1471

William Hastings lay back in the hot tub and savoured the wine as though it was the first wine he'd tasted in years. After the chaos of today, it was pure bliss to be at last alone in the tranquillity of the bath chamber, with only the sound of water to disturb his repose. He would have thought that after six months in exile he would never tire of hearing English voices again, but he had heard so many today; the cheering crowds, the endless questions of the aldermen and the shrill reconciliation of Edward and his queen as well as the first sight of Edward's new son and heir, that he thought he had heard enough to last him another six months! He sank lower in the water and relished its warm caress on his skin. He realized he had to make the most of these precious hours, for he knew Edward intended to finish all before Easter had passed.

He tipped his head back, closed his eyes and breathed in the fragrant steam within the bathing tent. His wet curls tickled the back of his neck and he thought that he was as close to heaven as a man might come to on earth. Perhaps if Elizabeth Thornton were here to massage his aching neck it would truly be perfect, but he was not complaining, for how nearly had it all ended in disaster? He could see why men thought Edward favoured, by either the saints or the Devil, depending whether you were a Yorkist or a Lancastrian. Who else would have gambled everything on an audacious march through Yorkshire between his enemies' lines and won? Who else would have bluffed an attack on Oxford with their vanguard and not had the bluff called? How many 'ifs' should have ended Edward's bid for the throne, the most puzzling being the inactivity of John Neville? He shook his head in astonishment; what an amazing journey it had been in this last month. He sighed. Only one thing remained to be done and though he knew it was the toughest test of all, somehow he no longer feared meeting Warwick in battle; he really did feel that Edward was blessed and the uncovering of the statue at Daventry had strengthened that feeling.

They had begun hesitantly, tentatively touching a toe to the shore of England and had finished with a triumphant ride into London; Edward most definitely had the upper hand. And once Warwick was gone, he saw no great difficulty in dealing with the rest of the Lancastrians; Warwick was certainly the best of them. He raised his glass in an unseen pledge of loyalty to Edward and his new young prince. Soon the nightmares of the past six months would be only that, nightmares. Life would once again be for agreeable living!

WARWICK'S CAMP APRIL 1471

Elizabeth pulled the hood of her travelling cloak over her head to hide her face, yet still she had to endure the jeers and whistles from the soldiers in the encampment.

A maze of campfires flickered like earthbound comets in the darkness. The smoky smell of roasting meat made her stomach growl with hunger and she was almost tempted to take up some of the less lewd offers made for her company. But she pressed on; he must be here – somewhere and she hoped he would honour their friendship still.

The hushed murmurings of voices blanketed the valley and Elizabeth cursed her own stupidity; how could she hope to find one man amongst the many thousands here? Had she really thought it would be that easy? The truth was, she had not really thought on it at all, had not realized just how many men followed her beloved Warwick. She tried to quell the panic rising within her. What if she did not find him? What would she do then?

She lifted her skirts to step through another muddy puddle and the sight of her ankles brought a bawdy cheer from some young soldiers beside her. Her cheeks flamed and she turned away from them quickly even though it seemed that each direction was as good as another.

Suddenly a large shape loomed out of the darkness. The smell of stale beer caught at her throat as a man's hand gripped her shoulder and he turned her where she stood. He leered into her face. 'And where are you going to, my pretty?' he asked.

Elizabeth looked at the swarthy face. Dark eyes peered at her intently and a tongue licked cracked lips. Her heart hammered at her throat. She took a deep breath, trying to calm it. 'My man is just over there,' she said as stoutly as she could.

'Your man, eh?' the man swayed on unsteady feet. 'Well he's a bloody fool for leaving you behind,' he sneered. 'He doesn't deserve you.'

Elizabeth tried to free herself from his grasp.

'Why so hasty, mistress?' he asked, tightening his grip. 'I can offer you good company and there's rabbit on the fire. And I promise, sweetheart, I will keep you warm!' He laughed a dirty laugh.

Elizabeth shivered. 'That is kind,' she said falteringly, trying to ignore his innuendo, 'but I must find him.'

She looked about her. How many men were watching from the shadows? Surely they could see what was about to happen, yet no one stepped forward to help her!

'It will be easier in the morning, my lovely,' the man said as he started to pull her closer. 'Come along, sweetheart, now don't make a fuss,' he whispered darkly.

His stinking breath was hot on her cheek and she tried to twist away from him. 'Perhaps you know him?' she asked, thinking on her feet. 'His name is Thomas Conyers.'

'Never heard of him, pretty.' The man shook his head, making a pretence of searching his mind for the name. 'Now, we don't want a scene. Come and take what is offered,' he said gruffly.

Elizabeth's stomach turned in knots.

His grip tightened enough to bruise her and his sword arm pulled her towards him. She wanted to scream, but her throat was too dry for that. She opened her mouth, but no sound came out. This was what Warwick had been afraid of, and the irony was that these were his soldiers, not marauding Yorkists!

'I know Thomas Conyers,' a thick voice said behind her.

'Stay out of this, old man!' the soldier growled.

'Leave the lady be!' the voice came again. 'You do not know who she is.'

Elizabeth tried to focus on the shape limping towards them.

'And you do, I suppose?' the man snarled. His hand slipped to his sword, but before he could draw it, the older man was at his side, his falchion already unsheathed.

'I do. I am his captain, Will Kennerley.'

For several heartbeats no one moved. Then the soldier's hand slipped from her shoulder. 'Sorry, captain,' he said softly, 'I meant no harm.' The man finally acknowledged Will Kennerley's superior rank.

'None done, eh?' Will Kennerley said sourly. He held out his free hand to Elizabeth and she took it eagerly. 'Come,' he said curtly.

'Thank you, Master Kennerley,' Elizabeth said as she followed him into the warren of soldiers.

He stopped suddenly and his grey eyes flicked over her. 'What in Christ's name are you doing here, Mistress Hardacre? Do you not know we are at war?' he asked her sharply.

Elizabeth did not know how to answer him. Where should she begin?

'I told Thomas you would bring him nothing but trouble!' he growled.

Elizabeth gasped. She had not thought of that. All she had been thinking of was being close to Warwick, of seeing him one last time before they gave battle. Will Kennerley was right; she had been selfish; she had not thought how her presence would affect Thomas. But now she was also puzzled; why would Will Kennerley and Thomas be discussing her?

'I am sorry...' she began. Tears stung her eyes and she hung her head to hide them. She was cold, she was hungry and exhausted and now she was being admonished like a naughty child.

Will Kennerley softened visibly. 'Now, mistress, don't cry,' he said more gently, 'I will take you to Thomas. Though what he will do with you, I've no idea.'

He set off again, picking his way through the camp as if he was following a town plan.

Elizabeth stayed as close to him as she could. She was completely lost, disorientated by the rows of shimmering blue and orange firelight and the lines of slumped bodies curled up against the damp night air, their cloudy breath the only visible sign of life.

Eventually Will stopped. Elizabeth looked ahead of him to where a group of men were sitting closely round a campfire. They were much like the hundreds of others she had seen that night; they were cooking rabbits and the smoke drifted upwards into the darkness with no wind to drive it away. They chatted quietly, their conversation solemn, their mood serious; they knew the gravity of their situation. She flicked her gaze over them and then saw, slightly off to one side, a man was cleaning his armour diligently. She smiled: it was Thomas.

The man looking after the steadily blackening rabbits looked up as they approached.

'Hey, Thomas!' he called. 'Stop making love to that harness! You have a visitor.'

Thomas looked up. His jaw slackened. He dropped the harness and then rose slowly. His face broke into a grin he could not restrain.

'Well, greet the lady, for God's sake!' Robert teased him.

Thomas came forward hesitantly.

Elizabeth wanted to run to him, but she could not move. She waited for him to come to her.

Thomas looked down into her eyes and she stared at him dumbly.

'What is it, Elizabeth?' he asked her softly. 'What is wrong?'

* * *

There was little privacy at the camp. Will had generously offered her his small tent, but she knew that the men sitting outside on the grass, whilst feigning disinterest, had their ears pricked for her every word. The thick canvas was painted with gold, red and blue and it was as taut as a sail. The only sounds were the crackling of flames and the muted conversations of men who knew that on the morrow they would march closer to battle.

Thomas watched her carefully. His eyes were wide in the half-light and she saw that he was eager to know her purpose, though he did not press her.

Her idea had seemed such a good one, but now as she saw the frightened eyes of the soldiers and felt the tension of conflict she realized that Warwick had been right: this was no place for a woman.

The silence in the tent lengthened as she thought on her selfish strategy for which she must enlist Thomas's help.

She turned to face him and he smiled.

'We are friends, you and I,' he said softly 'and this is no place for you Elizabeth. Tell me, why have you come? I thought you safely heading for Yorkshire. I thought Warwick had sent you home.'

Tears stung her eyes but she dashed them away with the back of her hand. 'I am here because I am a fool,' she said shakily, 'a silly naïve fool.'

Thomas frowned. 'No, Elizabeth, do not say so,' he said. He reached out an arm to comfort her, but he stopped just before he touched her.

'I thought – ' she faltered, swallowing hard. 'I thought I could see him one last time before the battle.' Tears blinked down her cheeks. 'I wanted to comfort him, for Thomas I do so fear he will not win and then I shall never see him again.'

'You were not to know what it would be like,' Thomas said gently.

Elizabeth sniffed back the tears. It was bad enough that she could get nowhere near Warwick, but what made it worse was that Thomas and his men must think her such a fool. 'Perhaps not,' she said, 'but I should have thought more on it.'

Thomas smiled. 'You never think anything impossible,' he said. 'You and my lord Warwick are alike in that.'

She smiled thinly. 'I think he is more of a realist than I am,' she said.

'Some would not agree.'

'I blunder in, Thomas,' Elizabeth said. 'I crash into people and I hurt them. I try to do the right thing but it never turns out as I expect.'

'As with your father?' Thomas asked.

Elizabeth nodded.

'My lord told me what happened and I am sorry for it.'

Elizabeth shook her head. 'It no longer matters; though for a while I cursed the name of Conyers! But that way will do no good, Jack showed me that.'

Thomas narrowed his eyes, but said nothing. The silence lengthened.

Elizabeth knew that was not the path to take; it was Warwick that mattered now. 'I have a request Thomas, a boon to ask you.'

He met her eyes evenly.

She cleared her throat. 'May I come with you tomorrow?' she asked. 'I shall be no trouble. I shall not complain on the march, I promise.'

He shook his head. 'I am sorry, Elizabeth, it is no place for a woman,' Thomas said quietly. 'I chose to be with these men because I know how hard it will be... I know I can trust them, Elizabeth...'

She contemplated his words and thought she understood, but now she had come so far, she could not give up. 'I must try to see him, Thomas,' she said.

Thomas sighed. 'Elizabeth it is impossible. There is so much to do, so many men, anything could happen. We might be ambushed, and then what would you do?'

She saw the anguish in his face, but she pushed him. 'Thomas you are my only hope. I am not sure I could make it on my own.'

'No, Elizabeth,' he said sternly, 'you must go back.'

Elizabeth drew herself up straight and flung her head high. 'I shall not leave him now when I am so close,' she said, forgetting about the eavesdroppers outside. 'If you will not help me Thomas then so be it. I shall go alone.'

'No Elizabeth. You must do my lord's bidding.'

'I will not go back, I will follow Warwick's army,' she said petulantly.

Thomas shook his head. 'Elizabeth, please see sense!'

'You said yourself that Warwick and I were alike, that neither of us acknowledges the impossible, so you know I will follow anyway!'

Thomas sighed again. He closed his eyes momentarily before casting them heavenwards in exasperation. He took a deep breath and then settled his gaze upon her again. 'Very well,' he said. 'But it is against my better judgement.'

Elizabeth sprang forward and threw her arms about his neck. 'Thank you, Thomas,' she said into his collar, 'thank you so much.'

Thomas gripped a hand on each of her arms and drew them to her sides. 'But still you may not see him, Elizabeth,' he warned. 'He keeps my lords of Montagu and Oxford close, no one else. No one that is except Jack de Laverton.' His tone was sour.

Elizabeth drew a short breath through her teeth; her cheeks flamed. 'Jack,' she murmured. She had not seen Jack since they had first arrived at Warwick Castle. Jack was here, somewhere among all these men. She saw the question on Thomas's face and wondered what he knew of her and Jack, but she did not want to say any more: Jack's lessons had been well learned.

Thomas looked away from her and for some moments there were only the sounds of the camp. Eventually Thomas sighed. 'Get some rest, Elizabeth. Tomorrow we march towards London,' he said flatly.

Elizabeth wanted to thank him again for his help, but he ducked through the tent flap quickly and she heard a chorus of whistles and jeers as he rejoined his men.

BARNET HEATH APRIL 1471

Jack peered into the dark valley. At first he hadn't been certain, but now he was sure that there was mist beginning to form on the heath. That was all they needed, he thought.

He gave the password to allow him into Warwick's tent and was surprised to find Warwick alone.

Jack bowed into his presence. 'My lord,' he said. 'You sent for me?'

'Jack!' Warwick greeted him brightly. 'Come, have some wine,' he said and offered Jack a seat at the trestle. 'Have you eaten?'

Jack shook his head. There had been plenty of mutton and rabbit on offer around the campfires, but somehow he did not trust his stomach to hold onto it.

'You must eat, Jack,' Warwick said. 'You will need all your strength tomorrow. I have seen men faint on the field for lack of sustenance.'

Jack smiled and helped himself to some bread.

'Good,' Warwick said, 'take some meat with you, for breakfast if not for now.'

'I shall, my lord,' Jack said.

Warwick poured him a cup of wine and Jack drank deeply. It sent fire into his empty belly, but it began to fortify him.

'There is something I would ask of you, Jack,' Warwick said fixing Jack's gaze.

'Name it, my lord and if I can, I shall do it,' Jack said. For one beautiful heartbeat Jack thought he was going to ask him to take care of Elizabeth, but he saw the gravity of Warwick's features and knew that it was not the task he had in mind.

'This is not easy,' Warwick said, 'and others may misinterpret what I ask of you.' He hesitated. 'Tomorrow, Jack, I would ask you to protect John for me.'

'My lord?' Jack did not understand. He had thought that he would fight alongside Warwick. Why did John Neville need protection? He was the best soldier on the field!

Warwick smiled thinly. 'I do not doubt him Jack,' he said widening his eyes, 'but many of the old Lancastrians feel that he clung to York for too long and his failure to intercept Edward at Pontefract... that did nothing to win him their trust.' He chewed on his lip for a moment. 'In short, Jack, I feel some will make sure John does not survive this battle, whether we win or lose!'

'Surely, my lord, all know of John's valour, of his courage at Hexham at least!'

'Aye, and many here remember it too well, for it was they he routed! If you remember he executed thirty of their number; thirty Lancastrians!'

Jack breathed deeply.

'What do you say Jack, will you do it?'

'I had thought to fight at your side, my lord.' Jack's heart thumped against his ribs; he could not believe that he would go into battle without Warwick; but, he told himself, it was Warwick to whom he had sworn allegiance and that meant he must do as he asked.

Warwick held his look. 'I can ask this of no one else, Jack,' he said softly. 'You have fought at John's side before.'

Jack saw the concern in Warwick's eyes for his brother. 'As you wish, my lord,' Jack said.

Warwick sighed. 'Thank you, Jack. I will do something for you when we return victorious! Name it, and if it is in my gift, it shall be yours.'

Jack smiled. There was only one thing Warwick had that he desired and that was the love of Elizabeth! But he thought then of something else; something which brought tightness to his throat. 'My lord, I would ask your indulgence,' he said quietly.

Warwick folded his arms across his chest.

'I would ask your permission to wear my father's livery tomorrow.'

Warwick hardly moved. 'Red with a black raven, as I recall,' he said.

'It is, my lord,' Jack replied. He wondered how he could express the emotions he was feeling. 'If I am to die tomorrow...' the words caught in his throat.

Warwick put a hand on his shoulder. 'Your father would be proud of you, Jack. May the colours carry you to glory.'

Jack's eyes began to sting and he cuffed them quickly. 'Thank you, my lord,' he said.

''Tis I must thank you, Jack,' Warwick said, 'for all you have done and what you shall do on the morrow. If only all our company were like you.' He reached for his glass and raised it to Jack.

Jack too picked up his cup.

'To victory!' Warwick said.

'To victory,' Jack echoed and then drained the glass.

As he walked out into the thickening darkness Jack tried to swallow the lump that had formed in his throat. Suddenly all the things he had left unsaid and unfinished came rushing to his mind; and many of them would remain so if he perished come the battle, he thought. But in all of these he had only one regret: that he had ever paid any heed to Lady Catherine Hardacre!

As he walked back to where Comet stood he noticed someone following him. He turned, the figure stopped. Instinctively his hand flew to the hilt of his falchion and for a heartbeat he thought of Higgins; but no, if Higgins were in this godforsaken place then he would be on the other side of the marsh, with Edward.

'You'd not use that on me, would you, Jack?' The shadow limped into view.

'Christ on the cross!' Jack exclaimed. 'By all that's Holy I'd not thought that you would be here, Will!'

Will Kennerley smiled. 'By the Rood, it's good to see you, Jack!'

They embraced as father and son and Jack's mind was dragged back to frozen Towton. Will had been his captain; Jack had been a baggage boy and it was Will who'd turned him into a man. He'd looked after him that day and it was Will who'd first brought Jack to the attention of the Earl of Warwick. Eventually they broke apart and Jack cuffed his stinging eyes. 'Christ, Will I thought you'd be enjoying retirement by now!'

Will laughed dryly. 'You know me, Jack; where the Earl of Warwick goes, so do I! He has always seen me right; he always will.'

Jack smiled. 'Aye, Will, I know.'

'But you, lad. I'd heard you were in Bruges with...'

Jack's eyes widened. 'With?' He had to know what stories were abroad about him.

Will cleared his throat. 'I heard you was married, Jack; that you finally had Hardacre's promise fulfilled.'

Jack shook his head. 'If only that were true, Will. It is complicated.'

'Things always were complicated with you, Jack,' Will said ruefully. 'Did you know she was here?'

Jack's heart thudded. 'Elizabeth? Here?' It shouldn't really have surprised him. He had to go to her, to see her before...

'Leave her be, Jack,' Will said softly, reading his thoughts. ''Tis the earl she loves. I heard it from her own lips.'

Jack sighed. 'I know, Will, believe me, I know.'

Will put his hand on Jack's shoulder. 'I'm sorry, lad. Maybe I should have left you in the baggage train at Towton, eh? Might have been easier on your heart!'

Jack smiled. 'No, Will, you shouldn't!'

They faced each other for some moments; they needed no words to express their emotions; not now, not the night before battle.

'I'd better get back to my company,' Will said suddenly. 'Don't want 'em thinking I've got cold feet!'

Jack forced a laugh. 'They would never think that, Will. Not of you.' He clasped Will's arm and held it tightly.

It was Will who broke the grip. He gave Jack a tight smile as he turned to leave.

'Adieu,' Jack whispered after him. His throat tightened; he doubted he would see Will Kennerley again.

* * *

Elizabeth lay at Thomas's side, the thin bedroll and blanket doing little to keep out the gnawing damp of the misty night. They had been amongst the last of Warwick's troops to arrive and there was no time to pitch tents. They had been allocated ground nearest to the guns for their camp. Each time a gun went off

Elizabeth jumped at the sound. Her ears hurt and her head began to throb from the barrage. She could see the gunners silhouetted in white and orange fire as they sent screaming missiles into the enemy camp. She saw the trace of burning splinters following each explosion, as the cannon spat hellfire into the night, each like a fiery comet coursing through the inky blackness. She shivered, not only because it was cold, but also at the thought of what the cannon fire could do to a man; and yet she could not hear any screams of injured or dying men and they did not return fire either. She was thankful for it, but wondered why it was so.

Thomas propped himself up on one elbow and looked down at her. 'Elizabeth?'

She turned to look at him. His face was serious.

'Yes?' she asked, but it was some moments before he forced a word through his throat.

'Tomorrow,' he said with difficulty, for the word seemed to almost choke him. 'You will go back to Barnet once the fighting starts in earnest?'

She looked at him blankly and chewed at her lip. She did not wish to think on the nightmare that would be tomorrow. 'I have no wish to see the battle, Thomas,' she said quietly, 'but I must see Warwick if I can.'

'Elizabeth?'

She met his eyes. What could she say? She wanted to see Warwick.

'Elizabeth please, promise me you will not stay,' he asked again. 'Go to 'The Green Man',' he advised her. 'You will be sure of an honest welcome there.'

She heard his anxiety. 'I promise,' she said.

With that Thomas's face relaxed a little, but there was something more. He fumbled in his kit and produced a piece of paper.

'Elizabeth, will you take this?' he asked tentatively.

Elizabeth struggled to sit up. 'What is it?'

'It is for my father,' he said. 'If – if I do not see the end of the day will you take it to him?'

Elizabeth sucked in a sharp breath. She did not want to think of Thomas dying in this horrible place, but she knew she must not refuse him this request. She held out her hand and he gave her the letter.

'I will, Thomas,' she murmured, 'I promise.' She tucked it inside her gown and then turned back to look at him. 'It will not come to that,' she said gently.

His answer was to lay down on his bedroll, though they both knew sleep would not come.

FOURTEEN

BARNET HEATH APRIL 1471

Elizabeth looked about her. There was a great fog rising, a melancholy mist so thick that it seemed to even circle shadows. She shook herself awake and in the half-light saw that Thomas was already up. He was adjusting the buckles on his armour nervously.

He turned to look at her and smiled thinly. His blue eyes seemed as though they had turned to ice in the night.

'I must go, Elizabeth,' he said, his voice sounding like an echo. 'Wish me luck.'

Elizabeth moved closer to him. She would have kissed him but for the flawless protection of his bevoir and sallet and the restraining metal of his cuirass. 'Dearest Thomas,' she said looking up into his frightened eyes, 'may all the saints in heaven protect you!'

She saw his mouth curve behind the steel. His eyes locked onto hers and for a moment they brightened.

'If I don't - '

She cut him off. 'No! Say nothing. Do not think so!'

He knew she had understood him. She had his letter. She would do as he asked.

'Thomas!' Will Kennerley's gruff voice growled through the murk.

'Tom?' Robert was there too.

'Adieu,' Thomas said and gave a wistful nod of his head to her. 'Don't forget, 'The Green Man',' he said.

'I won't,' Elizabeth replied. Her eyes prickled as she watched the fog surround and then engulf him. Like a spirit he was gone.

All about her was a cacophony of noise from hidden souls. Men and horses prepared for the oncoming battle; figures rushed out of the brumal whiteness like ghosts, seeking their companions and Elizabeth could smell their fear.

She moved through the hordes quickly, towards where Thomas had told her Warwick's tent would be. She hoped men would be too busy arming themselves and their lords to notice her or care about passwords. 'Please God, let me see him,' she murmured. 'I know I do not deserve such favour, but please Queen of Heaven grant me this blessing.'

And then, through the haze she saw Warwick. He was in full harness, which caught the first cold light of the dawn, making him shimmer like an apparition before her. He was astride his great destrier, its caparison a swirling sea of red and silver. She watched him as he spoke with his squire, as he gathered the reins and then began to ride slowly towards her.

She ran to his side.

Warwick's horse threw up its head, but Warwick remained motionless.

Elizabeth found her mouth suddenly dry. She looked up into his eyes, those eyes she loved so. She had wanted to relieve herself of her perfidious burden, but now she was here, looking into his wonderful eyes for perhaps the last time, how could she say such things? How could she absolve herself and lay her treachery upon him like a curse? It was impossible when he faced such an uncertain future; when all could be won or lost in the flight of an arrow or the thrust of a sword. For a moment they stayed thus, their eyes conveying wordless messages and neither of them had the strength to say what they felt. Eventually it was Warwick who broke the silence.

'I knew you would come,' he said with a wry smile. 'And I am glad of it, though you know I would wish you as far from this hell as possible, but to see you once again... Ah there is so much to say and so little time.'

'There is nothing to say,' Elizabeth said shakily. 'Words will not make a difference now.'

'You are right sweeting; we need words only for little things.' He paused, his eyes looking deeply into hers.

Elizabeth wanted the moment to last forever and for a hundred heartbeats it was as though they were completely alone, not in the middle of madness.

'But you should not be here, sweeting,' Warwick said, breaking the spell reluctantly. 'You should be spared this sorrow. John was right, what have I done to you?'

'You have done nothing, Richard. I chose this course for us,' she said. 'I gave myself freely to you. There is nothing for you to reproach yourself for.' But she knew she could not say the same of herself. How she wished she had never seen her father's damned letters!

385

Bright trumpets tore into the fog, breaking their incongruous peace.

'No!' Elizabeth called out despairingly and clutched at his armoured knee. How she wanted to be in his arms, to be comforted and to comfort him.

He leaned down to her and touched her cheek. He looked into her face. 'I must go my love,' he said in a tone of resignation.

'Richard, please. Wait!' she cried. Her heart thumped painfully, yet that pain made her realize how much she loved him and how much she did not want him to go.

Warwick shook his head sadly and Elizabeth gasped as she saw the determination in his eyes.

'No!' she sobbed, clawing at the cold steel of his harness as if she would tear it from him. 'No, please!'

Gently Warwick removed her hand from his leg. He flicked down his bevoir and bent forward so that his lips touched her skin. 'My love, 'tis God's will,' he breathed and suddenly Elizabeth knew exactly what he meant and it was as though he had struck her.

'Adieu, Elizabeth. Remember always, 'Seule une'.' He let her hand fall and Elizabeth's chest tightened as though in a vice. She reached for him again, but he was no longer close enough to touch. Hot tears coursed down her face. She strangled a sob in her tight throat; she wanted him to remember her as she would remember him: strong, composed, and facing the terrible future as a Neville would.

He held her gaze for several painful heartbeats and then he smiled as he wheeled his huge horse away from her with great skill. Slowly he headed into the gloom, to where the clamour of men and the pungent smell of terror hung in the mist like an echo from another world; a world into which Elizabeth could not follow him.

* * *

'They must not have had much rest last night, Richard,' John Neville said as Warwick drew alongside him.

'Indeed, John,' Warwick replied, his voice still thick in his throat from his meeting with Elizabeth. 'I did not hear them return fire; I wonder did we hit them at all?' He tried not to think of her teary green eyes; for he knew if he did he would be undone before he even drew steel.

John did not answer as they began to advance their horses down the slope to meet the Yorkists. Warwick took a long steadying breath and tried to focus his mind.

Shot whistled over their heads, but they could not see where it fell.

'Curse this fog!' Warwick said. 'It is as thick as witches' breath!'

'Aye, brother. I think it best we fight on foot,' John said. His hollow eyes betrayed his unspoken fear. 'The men like it better if we live and die by their side, Richard,' he added, a sad chill in his voice.

Warwick had only heard John's voice like that once before, when they had heard the news of their father's and brother's death at Wakefield fighting against Lancaster! 'They do, John; you speak true,' he said. He knew he must lift the mood or else they would be defeated before they had even begun. 'Do you remember at Ferrybridge I slew my great destrier to show them I was with them to the end? It was a grand gesture that cost me dear, but it held them together John, and I do not think anything else would have done so that day.'

'Yes, Richard I remember,' John said quietly.

Warwick looked at his brother thoughtfully and pondered his suggestion. He liked to stay mounted at the rear of his troops, surveying the battle and sending his reserve to where he could see weakness. But John had a valid point; if he stayed back too far he would be able to see nothing at all of the battle through this malevolent cloud.

He acquiesced. 'I think that you are right, brother,' he said, 'though I do not like it.'

They dismounted and sent their horses to the rear.

Warwick sighed, realising that he now had little chance of escape if the battle did not go well. They faced each other. For a long moment he held John's gaze before hugging him to him in a fierce grip of steel.

John's cheeks coloured, even his white scar darkened, and his eyes seemed suddenly glassy.

Warwick saw him swallow hard. 'Adieu Richard,' he said thickly as he broke their embrace.

387

'Adieu,' Warwick said, knowing that his tight throat would not let him say any more; but as Elizabeth had said to him, words would not make a difference now.

John turned away from him slowly and then, calling loudly for his banners, he was enveloped by the thick swirling white of the mist. Warwick tried not to think whether they would ever meet again in this world. God's blood, would he see any of his loved ones again? He tried to stop his resolve from wavering; tried to push the dark thoughts to the back of his mind. Had he not always known it would come to this? That he would have to face his destiny on the field. He had sworn an oath to this cause on the True Cross; surely God would favour him now!

Warwick dispatched Exeter and Oxford to their positions also and then drew his great sword. A loud cheer went up from his household men as they witnessed their lord striding to join them.

'To the last man!' Warwick cried and his men cheered his name. The battle cry was taken up along the line as a rallying call: 'A Warwick! A Warwick!'

* * *

Thomas stood in line. He heard the enemy shot screech overhead and saw a dark shower of arrows fall to his right. His heart hammered in his chest and his stomach twisted and knotted inside his metal covered body. He wanted to be sick. He heard the cry seething along their ranks and he took it up: 'A Warwick! A Warwick!' Robert stood by his side as he had at Edgecote, as he had at Dover, as he had through all things. His face too was pale. His eyes stared ahead of him, focussed on nothing, for there was nothing to see but the fog.

Their eyes met briefly; held and then they pulled their visors down as more arrows fell and the world was reduced to a narrow slit of tense grey. A man who had not been quick enough with his visor caught an arrow in the face and fell stone dead, the sudden movement causing a sea of silver heads to turn in unison.

Then Thomas heard something, faint at first. There were invisible drums to the right of them and then from the left also. Instinctively he turned to look in the direction of the noise, but the cruel wall of impenetrable fog kept them hidden from him. And all the while they banged on 'drum da drum, drum da drum', counting the pace at which the unseen enemy was marching, closing in with every beat. Louder now 'drum da drum, drum da drum' and now it was accompanied by the relentless rhythmical clanking of harness, buckler and sword as metal covered leg strode in front of metal covered leg. Thomas felt the men beside him shifting their positions and somewhere a frightened man muttered an Ave.

'Steady boys!' Will Kennerley growled.

Cold sweat ran down Thomas's back. It stung his eyes too, which were wide and unblinking, as he tried to see the enemy through his strip of vision. But they were still blanketed in grey, though now it was a throbbing, pulsing grey as the marching and the drums drew even closer. Thomas flexed and unflexed his hands on his sword hilt, trying to make sure of his grip for when the moment came. He couldn't feel his toes and his legs seemed too small to bear his weight. He tried to swallow but his mouth and throat were so dry that he couldn't. He tasted bile in his mouth.

Suddenly out of the gloom he caught sight of black shapes; their black banners barely fluttered in the still damp air; they seemed like an army of ghosts. The drums were vibrating the air; the noise entering Thomas's head and making it pound. He could hear their cries of 'For the king!' and 'A York! A York!' as well as more guttural animal sounds he had never heard from a man before. And it all echoed painfully in his imprisoned head.

'Look to your weapons!' Will Kennerley called.

Suddenly there was movement; a man stepped into Thomas's line of sight and a bill came hurtling towards him. Thomas did nothing; he did not duck or weave; his arms and legs refused to obey him as fear bound him fast in the soggy ground.

'Thomas!' he heard Robert's voice above the cacophony, saw a flash of steel as Robert's sword caught the man in his throat, his blood spraying into Thomas's face as he finally came to his senses. With the deafening noise ringing in his ears, Thomas followed his friend into the nightmare enfolding before him.

The Yorkists were directly in front of him; their forest of bills as menacing as dragon's teeth. Thomas fought his way blindly into the heart of them, heard himself crying out, screaming like an animal – no words could express the basic survival instincts which were all he could call to mind. Together with their company he and Robert pushed on steadily. They fought where the press was thickest; the billmen working together to pick off victims. But the screaming press of men became so thick that it became difficult to see who was alive and who was not, for some of the dead were held in their place, supported by the wedge of men around them. Thomas shivered at the thought of dead men still standing in line. Some had been unable to afford the visored sallet and their faces were rendered unrecognisable, others were missing limbs and others spilled their guts onto the sticky pungent earth. As they pushed forward the dead and the dying, limbs, bodies and harness were trampled underfoot. Friend and foe alike, once down, were simply an impediment to the ones who fought on.

'Hold the line!' Thomas heard Will Kennerley cry breathlessly and some of his comrades roared their allegiance 'A Warwick! A Warwick!' They would not give in.

But Thomas was now all but spent. His right arm was shaking, white pain cascading into his shoulder and neck like lightning. But he knew he had to keep going. The mud and gore were sucking his heavy unwilling legs down and every step became as demanding as ten; he wondered how Will Kennerley was managing to keep up with them.

'Take some water!' Robert's voice called to him and a hand dragged him backwards. A small boy dressed in Warwick's livery was distributing the precious liquid, men snatching at it as if it were gold. Thomas raised his visor and staggered with the coldness of the air that struck him. The water too was like ice as he gulped it down into his heaving stomach. He looked at Robert, wishing to thank him for almost certainly saving his life at the battle's start. But Robert wasn't looking at him He was standing breathlessly, his eyes searching the smoke for movement. There was a large dint in one of his pauldrons and dark blood was dripping from the fingers of his gauntlet. Thomas was about to point it out to him, but he stopped. This was no practice bout – he could not leave the field to have his wound dressed and then return later – that privilege was for the high nobility. And as he looked at Robert's blank expression he knew that he felt no pain – the alchemy of fear and adrenaline were keeping him going.

'Did you see Will?' Thomas gasped.

Robert shook his head. 'But I heard him; he's still in there!' Robert said with a nod towards the press.

'Then we'd better join him!' Thomas said as he shook his sword arm, trying to remove the cramp. Then he nodded to Robert that he was ready, pulled down the visor of his sallet and the two of them headed back into the writhing mêlée.

Thomas fought on, but his aching, stiffening muscles threatened to bring him to a standstill as he swung his sword. He had no choice but to use both hands now; he was unable to even hold it up with one anymore. There was no sight or sound of Will Kennerley, no rallying call and Thomas wondered if he was down.

But he couldn't waste energy on thinking about Will; he needed it all to ensure his own survival. He was panting. His hot breath filled his helmet and condensed on the inside of the visor, running down his chin and neck. Each blow brought out a deep rasping grunt, a noise he had never heard himself make before, but he knew it was because each sword thrust now took the effort of his whole body.

Sweat stung his eyes and he fought for his breath. God, if only he could breathe properly! All he craved was the delicious cool air in his hot lungs – but he did not dare raise his visor; there was still the sporadic threat of black rain from Edward's archers. 'Come on Thomas!' he called to himself and then to the world: 'A Warwick! A Warwick!'

He and Robert had now linked up with men in Montagu's livery. They too were using two hands to raise their weapons and some had taken the risk of raising their visors. Thomas's chest was hurting, a tight hot band constricting his every movement. It would be heaven itself to taste some cooler air. If only he could get some air! Thomas began to repeat it like a mantra and it clouded his thoughts. All he could smell was sweat and blood. All he could hear were the shouts of orders and the screams of the injured and dying; even the drums were silent now, as every man fought desperately for his life. His stinging eyes began to swim, losing their focus and his head began to spin. At last he could bear it no longer. He pulled frantically at his visor and without thought found himself doubled over, gulping in the cool yet tainted air. He heard his lungs wheezing and felt a strange euphoria as he began to regain control of his senses. He turned to rejoin the mêlée, but before he could lower his visor again blood and brains slapped into his face from the man who had been beside him. Thomas's stomach lurched. He heaved until he was sick as the man's contorted and mutilated body fell at his feet. Thomas stood for a moment, bewildered. Then he heard Warwick's clear voice calling out encouragement. Thomas clanked his visor shut. He must get to him. He must fight alongside his lord.

* * *

'Advance banners!' Lord Montagu's voice split the fog and sent a pulse of adrenaline through Jack's body.

As one voice, a loud roar went up from their battle. 'A Montagu! A Montagu!' and Jack knew murderous screaming would soon join the crescendo of noise as the perverse thrill of killing took a hold on the men. But for now it was a cheer of hope, of resilience and of courage.

Suddenly the fog lifted a little, allowing them a glimpse of the Yorkists. Jack had seen a line like this before at Towton, a line that believed itself infallible. They died.

Through the strip of sight his visor gave him, Jack looked towards Lord Montagu. He gave the slightest nod of approval and Jack knew that beneath the white steel of his sallet, John Neville was grinning. Then he raised his weapon high, ready to split as many skulls as his strength would allow him to.

Jack heard Montagu's voice taunting the Yorkists as they marched towards them.

'I will not die alone!' he roared. 'How many of you bastards are coming with me?'

There was the briefest of hesitations, as men comprehended what he had said, understood who the man was before them. Then they came on. The lines closed quickly, men suddenly rushing in to feel the embrace of steel.

Montagu met them head on. With a roar, Jack too drove into them. It was close and bloody work and Jack was glad he'd brought his falchion for there was no room to fight with the finesse of a greater sword. He hacked limbs, hewed bodies, and crushed skulls. Sweat stung his eyes, ran down his neck and back; already inside his harness he was so very hot. He pushed on at Montagu's side. Slash after impeccable slash raked the men in front of him and he strove to match John Neville's incredible pace. Jack screamed 'A Montagu!' It was a mixture of anger, fear and battle-fever that made him shout at the devils that faced him. Jack's limbs began to spasm and twitch, searing pain burned in his shoulder from Higgins's wound and he knew his strike rate was slowing. He bellowed again, 'A Montagu!' His voice cut the air as he crashed forward, plunging into the enemy like a madman: he would not let Warwick down.

He stepped over the mangled wreckage of a destrier. The dying horse half-lifted its blood-soaked head as if to rise. Then it screamed and fell back into the reeking mud and did not stir again. Jack barely saw it, there was no room for regret, remorse or compassion, those luxuries came only with victory, for now the battle-fever gripped him and he paused only to draw a deep breath before he dived after Montagu into the next breech.

BARNET APRIL 1471

Elizabeth walked into Barnet town in a daze. She could barely walk; her mind, numbed with fear, had no control over her feet. The mist was thinner here; wisps hung about street corners and floated through alleyways, which were graveyard silent.

She found 'The Green Man' without really looking for it, as though an innate sense had led her to her rendezvous point.

It was boarded up and the door was bolted as she had expected; no landlord would willingly expose his hostelry to the possibility of looting soldiers.

Barnet held its breath; it probably wished for Edward's victory so that the ensuing slaughter and rout of the defeated Lancastrians would be northwards as they sought refuge in their home counties of the midlands and the north. But if Edward were to lose then the remnants of his army would flee towards London. They would be pursued and cut down in these very streets.

When her hand was bruised with hammering on the door and her throat hoarse with shouting in vain for the landlord to let her in, she slumped onto the hard earth, her shoulders shaking with huge silent sobs; she was completely overwhelmed with sadness and fatigue, wanting to find this was a horrible nightmare from which she would soon wake. She knew it was not, and bewildered, she stared vacantly into the dirt.

And then they came. Just a few of them at first, mounted on wide-eyed sweating horses, their bloodied caparisons flapping wildly, their breathing harsh and heavy. Many of the men bore open wounds; mainly sword cuts to their faces or limbs, but some carried a protruding arrow shaft. They were desperate men and they spurred their horses mercilessly towards London.

Elizabeth jumped up for she recognized the livery of some of Gloucester's men. It was Gloucester's men who were flying from the field! Soon there were more of them, men-at-arms and archers, some limping badly but all of them looking back over their shoulders repeatedly for some as yet unseen enemy.

For a few moments Elizabeth was stunned into stillness as she watched, but suddenly their frantic backward glances registered with her senses and she ran for cover. Dim grey shapes thundered out of the mist, the de Vere star of Oxford dancing on their banners. Right in front of her they began to catch up with the stragglers from Edward's army, cutting them down from behind as they fled. Some turned around and put their arms up in supplication, but they were shown no mercy; they butchered them as if they were not men at all, but pieces in some barbaric and bloody sport. One archer fell screaming only a few feet from where Elizabeth stood in the shadows; his back pared open like a filleted fish, the bones protruding from a red and gory mess, frothy red blood gurgling from his mouth. His eyes rolled in his head so that only the whites were showing and Elizabeth knew that he was dead; she turned away and was sick.

Suddenly her own vulnerability struck her; Oxford's men were gripped with killing-fever, crying out like wolves as they roared into Barnet.

But so soon? Could Warwick really have defeated Edward so soon? Soon Barnet would be full of victorious Lancastrians and she would be prey to any enthusiastic soldier who saw her. She stepped deeper into the alleyway. She noticed a pair of dirty boots protruding from the darkness. One was excessively bloodied and she assumed that the owner carried a significant leg wound. She approached cautiously, her heartbeat protesting loudly at her recklessness. What if he was dead? What if he was not dead and was just resting up a while before heading off to London and safety? She must try and help him if she could, if it were Jack or Thomas lying here she would hope that someone would try to save them.

Tentatively she leaned round the corner post of the building. The soldier's face was in shadow, but she could tell from his expression that he was in considerable pain. When he saw her, he raised his arming sword feebly, the point wavering before her.

'Sir, are you in need of water?' she asked him.

'Go away, girl, before you betray me to my pursuers,' he said thinly.

Elizabeth pushed into the narrow passageway, holding out her water bottle, somehow convinced that he would not hurt her.

He snatched the water desperately and gulped down the liquid so fast that much of it ran down his chin. She saw that he wore the white boar badge of Gloucester on his left breast and saw too that his right thigh was red and wet with blood.

'I am no coward lady,' he said fixing her with wide eyes.

His sudden anger surprised her.

'But I am an easy target for Oxford's butchers; they would have cut me down.'

'I saw,' Elizabeth said, nodding her head in the direction from which she had come. She hesitated, and then said, 'what news of the battle, sir?'

'All is lost,' the soldier said sadly, 'our flank was completely overwhelmed by Oxford's men, and as you have seen they have come to Barnet to finish us off!'

'And what of the king?' Elizabeth was careful not to show him her allegiance.

'Truly, lady, I do not know. The fog was so thick that you could barely see your own foe, let alone see anything of the others, but some said the day belonged to the traitor Warwick, but I can't confirm it; though why else would Oxford leave the field? He would not have followed us unless he knew victory was theirs.' He winced with pain and Elizabeth could see the earth on which he lay was dark with the blood he had lost.

He was right she thought, and fought hard not to smile at the thought of Warwick's victory! No she must not yet allow herself to be overcome with joy, not until it was certain. She turned again to the soldier, but she saw now that his eyes were closed and heard him utter a soft exhalation; all his pain had been taken away: he was dead. She crossed herself and murmured a few words for him before gathering up what remained of her water and helping herself to his purse, sword and belt; she may yet need to defend herself, she thought, though she had to admit that against trained soldiers it would be only token resistance. She headed back towards 'The Green Man'.

Barnet was once again still and quiet. The main street was now littered with corpses; their blood lay in inky pools about them. Nausea rose in her throat again. She shuddered and closed her eyes to try to remove the sight of them. This would be nothing to the carnage Warwick would be in the middle of! She said a silent prayer to God to watch over him and wondered if God would answer it, coming as it did from such a sinner as she was!

Again she hammered on the inn door and this time the landlord opened it. He was convinced that they were in no immediate danger but that the battle could not be over because there would have been a continuous swarm of fleeing soldiers if it had. He therefore insisted that the shutters should be kept up and that they should feign that they had left Barnet with the rest of their neighbours. Elizabeth did not argue. She lay limply on a small wooden bed in a room upstairs, and tried to sleep; but the nightmares were just as vivid whether her eyes were open or closed. So she lay there feeling helpless and waited for news.

BARNET HEATH APRIL 1471

All too soon the enemy was upon them, crashing into the line like a storm surge breaking onto rocks.

Warwick's household men stood defiantly. They were experienced soldiers, hardened in war, and it showed in the carnage they wrought on the enemy, their red livery drowning them like an angry sea.

For some time it was difficult to see who had the upper hand. Warwick stood proudly with the reserve, encouraging his men to hold their ground, to fight bravely and with honour.

Warwick received triumphant word from Oxford who, having found himself misaligned with the enemy, had routed Gloucester's men. Finding themselves attacked from front, flank and rear they had broken and fled and Oxford had allowed his troops to follow after them, some of the deserters apparently running as far as London itself. Warwick was furious rather than elated by the news. The fool, he thought as he ordered Oxford to regroup and rejoin them. 'We need every man if we are to prevail!' he told the breathless messenger.

A sudden cry brought his thoughts back to the field.

They were outflanked. Hastings's men had wrapped around to Warwick's left and rear, out of the bog. Exeter was in trouble.

Warwick cursed, though he admired Hastings's determination in achieving the manoeuvre through the treacherous ground. But then Hastings was as much of a veteran as he was!

He committed some of his reserve and the whole line wheeled round. They began to push Hastings back slowly. The fighting was fierce, no man wishing to give any quarter to his enemy. They were evenly matched, neither side being able to gain the advantage.

Warwick now lowered his visor and stepped forward into the thick of the fighting, hoping to tip the balance in his favour. He swung his great sword, cutting a man in two from shoulder to hip. Reversing his strike another lost an arm and another took the steel in his guts. Each swing and thrust brought more screams from the dying, as he plundered their souls. Before him was a mass of men, steel and horses. Warwick fought on, like the bear on his badge, but it seemed as though ten men sprang up for every one he cut down and he wondered if Edward had thrown in his reserve. Edward – ah what he would give to meet him face to face.

Sweat stung his eyes and the muscles of his shoulders began to tighten and knot and he gritted his teeth against the pain. Still it felt as though he was swimming against the tide as more Yorkists swarmed towards him and died at his hands. But should he not have expected as much? – Many would wish to boast that they had killed the Earl of Warwick. And so far all of them lay at his feet.

* * *

Jack stared in horrified disbelief as he tried to wrench order from the chaos. Christ on the cross, it was Oxford! Desperately Jack tried to stop Montagu's archers, but it was no use, they had found their killing rhythm.

'No!' he screamed like a banshee, but his was just one voice among a multitude and no one paid him any heed.

Suddenly, as if they had realized their mistake, Oxford's men swerved away from the deadly black rain. But the archers did not yet understand who these men were. Jack realized all too well what had happened, though he could scarcely believe it. And then he heard something that froze his blood; the thing Warwick had most dreaded: the cry of 'Treason!' It flickered briefly on the lips of Oxford's men, before it spread through the ranks like flame to dry tinder.

'No!' Jack cried again, but this time the anguish of his cry was directed to Oxford. Oxford, who had so badly mauled Gloucester's flank, was retreating, still crying out 'treason'. He was deserting the field and in dismay Jack wondered if Warwick's hopes rode away with him.

Realizing there was nothing else he could do, Jack turned away from the disaster, seeking Montagu's banner. He found it in the midst of Yorkist foes. Jack ran screaming into them, slashing wildly, eviscerating, maiming, and killing.

But it was no use; though his frantic efforts succeeded in forcing the Yorkists away from Montagu's banner, Jack realized he had arrived too late.

In the brief space his courage had bought him, Jack stared down at John Neville's broken body in disbelief. Recklessly, he slammed back his sallet visor as though he could not trust the misty slit of vision to tell him the truth. But it was horribly true, brutally true: John Neville was dead.

Anger welled up inside Jack like fire inside a handgun and he exploded at the nearest Yorkists in a merciless rage that scattered men before him. Jack's breathing was ragged now and he panted heavily while he tried to gather his scattered wits. In this gasping, chest-aching reprieve, he realized what he had to do next and that not only his life would depend upon his action.

* * *

Warwick's muscles were aching now, that deep burning ache that told him he could not fight on much longer; somehow he needed to regain his strength.

Suddenly more men appeared behind him, coming out of the gloom like revenants. Warwick heard cries of 'treason!' and his blood turned to ice; something had gone terribly wrong. He tried to drag an explanation from his whirling mind. Was it Oxford finally returned, but to the wrong part of the line? Had Montagu's men attacked him? Worse still, had someone attacked his brother, as he had feared? Warwick could not be sure. He fought on, remorseless and fearless in the mêlée. He noticed that some men began to look out for themselves, seeking a means of escape. He heard the cries of treason again, only this time they were fading away; someone was leaving the field! He urged on the line and they responded with their battle cry 'A Warwick! A Warwick!' If only they could withstand this onslaught, surely the day would be theirs!

'My lord!'

Warwick recognized the red livery rather than the hoarse voice that spoke to him and it sent his heart into his stomach.

'My lord, Montagu is dead!'

Warwick's heart stopped as he looked at Jack, trying to take in what he had just said.

'It was Oxford my lord; he rode at us out of the mist and the archers mistook him for Edward!'

Warwick cried out; so that was what the cry of treason was for! 'And Oxford?' he managed to tear the words from his tightening throat.

'Fled,' Jack gasped.

Warwick tried to gather his thoughts; so in the end Oxford had not believed in John's loyalty, could not see that the archers had made a genuine mistake – in Oxford's eyes it had to be treachery! It seemed for a moment as if Warwick was completely alone. He heard nothing, not the screams of the injured, not the battle cries of those on the charge, nothing. He crossed himself. 'Ah John,' he murmured and he remembered his brother as he had last seen him that morning.

'My lord!' Jack shouted. 'They come on!'

Suddenly Warwick was animated again. 'To me! To me!' he called. 'Stand firm and the field will be ours!' He turned to Jack. 'John fought well?' he asked as men of the ragged staff flocked to his banner.

'Aye my lord, like a true knight!' Jack answered honestly.

That to Warwick was some faint comfort for the gripping pain that now tightened his chest. 'Jack,' he said. 'I would ask one last thing of you.'

Jack looked at him quickly. 'My lord?'

'Elizabeth,' Warwick breathed. 'Find Elizabeth, and if we do not prevail, meet me at Calais.'

'But my lord...' Jack protested.

'Jack!' Warwick seized his arm fiercely. 'Jack, there is no one else I can trust. And if Edward...' He fixed Jack's eyes.

Jack nodded and Warwick saw that he understood.

Briefly they clasped each other's arms in a hold of steel, glances locked, and then Jack left him. As he strode back to the battle Warwick swallowed down the choking sensation rising in his throat; he had always known that this battle would decide more than who wore the crown of England!

* * *

Robert de Assheton tasted blood. The sweet sticky blood ran into his mouth from a large gash on his right cheek. It had been so unbearably hot inside his sallet that he had taken the risk and raised his visor to suck in some cool air. And then the blow came; he had killed his assailant with a swift strike to his abdomen so that he had almost disembowelled him on the spot, but in the ensuing dreamlike dizziness that had engulfed him, he had lost sight of Thomas. He cursed himself, for he had taken an oath to stand by his friend and now he had let him down. As the fighting became even more frenetic and the odds started to stack up against them, he noticed that some of their company had begun to steal away. Cowards, he thought. He pressed on to where the fighting was fiercest, towards the Earl of Warwick.

He could hear cries of treason and treachery over to his right, but in the thick blanket of mist the cries were muffled and the combatants were only dim grey ghosts; he wondered what was happening. Above the noise he heard Warwick's voice thunder out, rallying his men, 'To me! To me!'

Robert followed Warwick's cry and saw Thomas at the heart of the mêlée, his sword flailing wildly against his many Yorkist foes. He rushed to help him, blocking a billman as he did so.

'Aye, Robert – what kept you?' Thomas panted. 'I thought you were lost!'

'You were enjoying yourself so much I didn't want to spoil it!' Robert jested.

Side by side they stood defending each other, striving to match their leader's courage and skill-at-arms. Robert could not help but admire Warwick, for he was twice Robert's age and yet his strength and stamina were unfaltering.

Then Robert heard something, quiet at first, like distant thunder, but it echoed around them, all the time getting louder and louder, until he realized with horror what it was: Edward's cavalry at full gallop and they were heading straight towards them.

* * *

Warwick stood resolutely against the explosion of cavalry; again and again he swung his sword, taking horse and rider indiscriminately, and wreaking havoc on the charge, which now faltered. Wounded horses careered sideways into their neighbours, disrupting the line. Dead men now rode with the living and the knights were no longer locked together, giving Warwick's men room to strike home. But, as he turned, Warwick saw that most of his best knights had been cut down like saplings by the onslaught, in as sad a scene of bloodshed as he had yet witnessed. His men were left reeling, their resolve plainly wavering. The cries of the wounded filled his ears and the air was thick with the smell of blood.

In the brief respite as the horsemen regrouped he thought of his family; his hopes for them now lay crushed in the blood-drenched mud beside him. And he thought too of Elizabeth, and his heart ached for her.

Then he heard the screaming of men as a fresh wave of attackers came upon him, shaking him from his reverie. The Yorkist reserves had been closer than he had supposed; Edward had deployed them with great effect.

Warwick heard their battle cry, 'A York! A York!' and his heart sank like a stone in a well. He knew his men could not resist this new assault and he now realised that the battle was lost. He must get to his horse. There was still hope. Defeat today was not failure; it could be turned around. There was always Marguerite; there was always Calais. If only he could get to his horse.

* * *

The survivors huddled together; their pink-rimmed eyes were dark and bulging. They kept their backs together as much as possible, as much for solidarity as for defence, their bills and swords bristling beyond the silent desperate band.

'Steady lads,' Will Kennerley growled hoarsely.

Around them lay their fallen comrades. Some were half-naked; twisted; frozen in death. Wounds like black mouths gaped toothless and sorrowful.

The cold wind blew in their faces. It carried the rotten smell of decaying flesh, the smell of blood, the fear of death and worst of all the low pitiful moans of those who could not stand with them but yet were not dead.

The sharp crack of gunfire echoed in the distance, but they knew there was no hope of relief or rescue. They were alone, but yet they did not run. These last few men of the ragged staff were too weary for flight.

The fog drifted with the breeze, giving them brief glimpses of the horrors that lay only yards away: stricken screaming horses struggling to stand, bloodied banners still held by dead hands, broken men and broken swords. Bodies lay emaciated in death; eyes closed on this world and now open to purgatory. God have mercy on their souls, Will Kennerley thought...all this lay beside them on Barnet Heath.

The bitter broken hedgerow loomed out of the greyness. If they could only follow this then perhaps...but as the mist lifted Will saw that Edward's soldiers blocked this way too and he knew there was no hope.

Through the clearing fog he saw Hadley church, but here too the Yorkists lingered and it seemed as though God had abandoned them.

A fistful of golden angels lay beside a broken lord. No one bothered to pick them up or even gave them a second glance.

And then the Yorkists came on.

* * *

When Robert came to he could barely move. A horse had fallen across his legs, pinning him to the ground. He looked about him helplessly; his sword was by his side, but just out of reach. He hoped no Yorkist saw him now, prone and defenceless. In fact he saw that none of his brave line remained standing, even Warwick had now given up on the day and was fighting a retreat towards the woods.

Then he saw Thomas and his heart heaved in his chest. He was face down in the reeking mud and his right arm was a soggy bloodied mess. His helmet too was covered in blood and as far as Robert could tell, he was not breathing.

* * *

Warwick broke away from the line and headed for the wood, calculating that he would make the trees before the fresh men could reach him. His heartbeat was loud in his ears and he was hot and breathing hard. Even with his bear-like strength every metal bound limb and sinew ached and every step now felt like a mile. Still he pushed on. He could not yet see his horse through the mist, but he knew it could not be far away because he could hear the harness bells jingling ahead of him, as it waited nervously. It gave him heart.

Suddenly the wood exploded with Yorkists. They were more lightly armoured than he and they were gaining on him. They cried out to him, taunting him, and Warwick knew that he had been recognized, singled out amongst the fleeing men. Closer and closer they came until Warwick eventually realized he could not escape them and that he must stand and fight. He turned to face them defiantly, sword in hand, and they hesitated at his courage. They hung back, unwilling to take him on. They circled him like hungry wolves, their eyes staring, their voices taunting.

Warwick was breathing hard; his chest ached with the effort of his flight, imprisoned within his fine harness, but he stepped forward quickly and swung his sword first right, then left and two men fell like dead wood, broken into pieces at his feet. Two more came at him and died. Then two more approached and then the others found their courage...there were too many of them and they surrounded him, jostling him, toying with him.

'Yield to the king's grace!' their captain yelled.

Warwick realized now that it was hopeless, yet as long as his lifeblood pulsed in his veins he would not give in to Edward.

'Yield, my lord!' the captain cried again. 'Get back, you bastards!' he called to his men.

The men stood round in a circle, like dogs baiting a chained bear and it was plain that they did not want to kill him, plain that they expected some sort of reward for taking him alive. Alive, he thought, but for how long?

The captain came towards him slowly, sword pointing downwards and his other arm spread wide.

Warwick watched him through narrowed eyes.

'Do not make me kill you, my lord,' he said. 'Enough men have perished on the field today. Yield, I beg you.'

Warwick knew he could not perpetuate this stalemate indefinitely, knew there was no real choice. He bowed his head.

'Give me your oath you will yield and I will give you safe conduct to the king,' the captain said.

* * *

Jack struggled to free his destrier from the horse park. The smell of fear and blood had unnerved the animal and it fought for its head. Jack raked back his spurs, pulled hard at its mouth and eventually brought the horse round.

The fog had cleared a little and he was able to glance back at the wreckage of Warwick's last stand. Jack could see that Warwick was surrounded; there would be no need for Calais. Part of him wanted to spur his horse into their midst; try for rescue. But Warwick's position was hopeless and he had sworn to find Elizabeth. Yet he couldn't take his eyes from the scene, as if it were a macabre mummers' play. As he watched he saw Warwick raise his visor and pierce Edward's captain with his stare.

The man cast a look downwards momentarily. Then he said something to Warwick that Jack could not hear. Then he took Warwick's sword.

Suddenly more men appeared from the trees and they did not lower their weapons. They came in rapidly, pushing into Edward's men and Jack saw that they wore Clarence's livery. With obscene speed Warwick was on the ground and Jack saw the glint of a thin war blade as it struck down towards Warwick's neck.

Jack turned away quickly, not wanting to witness the inevitable defiling of Warwick's body. With tears burning his eyes he kicked brutally at his horse and, as he rode away from the battle, he wondered how he was going to deal with Warwick's death and how in Christ's name would he tell Elizabeth? She must never know it was Clarence!

BARNET APRIL 1471

It had been almost two hours since Elizabeth had seen Oxford's men in the centre of Barnet and there was no more news. Her host was prepared to bet on a Lancastrian victory and was eagerly anticipating many celebrations at the inn that evening. In fact he had even tried to renege on his earlier agreement to rent out the large room to Elizabeth, trying to increase the price; 'It's all about supply and demand, my lady,' he had said, but Elizabeth had pointed out that the people for whom she waited would

404

be in no mood for his profiteering, knowing also that the only money she had had come from a dead man.

She returned to her chamber, sick of his constant chatter. The shutters were still up and it seemed as if they constrained her melancholia within the room. She lay on the bed, listless.

And suddenly she knew. Something deep in her soul told her that Warwick was dead. Tears filled her eyes and began to course uncontrollably down her cheeks, dripping off her chin. Her body shook with violent sobs, until her chest and throat ached so much that she had to cry silently. All she wanted in the world was Warwick, to see his handsome face, feel his warm breath upon her cheek and to know that he loved her. But he was gone; and however much she wailed and wept, nothing would bring him back to her; his great heart beat no more. She buried her face in the pillow and wanted to die.

* * *

Time was meaningless to Elizabeth; nothing mattered anymore. There was an emptiness inside her that would never again be filled, as if part of her body had been ripped out at the core. But after some time she became aware of tapping at the door. She wiped her tear-stained eyes on the back of her hand, then moved over to the door and opened it.

'Now, my lady, no need to cry for your sweetheart has arrived after all!' The landlord's beaming face greeted her. 'He is here in the courtyard, but he doesn't look too good. I shall send for the barber surgeon, for surely no physician will come!'

'Please hurry,' Elizabeth said in a tight voice and then followed him hurriedly down the stairs.

Robert de Assheton's blood-smeared face greeted her grimly. His colours were gone, as was half his harness.

Elizabeth almost smiled with relief; it was only Robert.

'You know?' Robert asked astounded, looking at Elizabeth's teary face. 'You know Warwick is dead?'

Elizabeth nodded, biting her lip to prevent another wave of grief bursting through.

Then she looked beyond Robert, to his horse. Even though it was not tied up, it did not move. Then her eyes flicked to its burden. A body was slung across its back.

Elizabeth's eyes widened in horror. 'Thomas!' she cried. 'Oh Santa Maria, not Thomas!'

BARNET HEATH APRIL 1471

William Hastings knelt at the side of Warwick's body. Tears stung his eyes and sadness weighed down his heart. Part of him wished it could have ended differently but the realist in him knew Warwick would never have borne a life of incarceration, if that was really what Edward had intended for him. He doubted that, for he knew how much the Wydevilles would have bayed for Warwick's blood and he suspected that they would probably have got it.

Warwick seemed much smaller now, stripped of his Milanese harness, stripped of everything but his braes and Hastings could not quite believe that this battered body had managed to contain all that Warwick had been. 'Adieu,' he whispered as he crossed himself. 'Cover him,' he said to the watching soldiers as he rose. 'The king has ordered that he be taken to St Paul's, along with his brother Montagu.'

Someone stepped forward with a blood stained red and silver livery coat and laid it over Warwick and Hastings felt as though a cloud had covered the sun.

Suddenly there was a commotion behind him.

'Where is he?' Gloucester's voice sounded frantic.

Hastings met his eyes warningly.

As Gloucester stepped forward to look Hastings put a restraining hand on his shoulder and shook his head. 'Not here, my lord,' he whispered. 'Pay your respects later at St Paul's. It will be more private.'

Tear-filled eyes met his and he saw Gloucester's throat working as he fought to contain his emotions. The silence lengthened. Then he nodded, glanced briefly at Warwick, crossed himself and then turned away.

Hastings followed him back towards Edward's camp. Sadness lay between them and Hastings wondered if the outcome had been different would Warwick have wept for Gloucester and he knew that he would.

'How is your shoulder?' Hastings asked, noticing the dressing on Gloucester's arm and trying to distract him from Warwick's corpse.

'Fine,' Gloucester said flatly. "'Tis nothing, I suppose,' he said sorrowfully and Hastings knew what he meant.

'It wasn't your fault,' Hastings said reassuringly. 'No one could have held that line against Oxford, never mind a man in his first command!'

Gloucester looked up at him. 'Do you mean that, Will?' he asked hesitantly.

'Of course,' Hastings said honestly. 'You did a fine job to hold them as long as you did. No one could have done more.'

Gloucester gave him a rueful smile. 'Thank you Will, it means a lot to know...' he hesitated.

Hastings slapped him on the back. 'Ned will be pleased with you, I know he will.'

When they reached Edward's tent he was half stripped of his harness. Hunched over in his chair, an untouched cup of wine in his hand, he stared unblinking at the ground in front of him as though he had no idea where he was.

'Your Grace,' Hastings and Gloucester spoke together and made united obeisance.

Edward looked at them slowly, as if waking from a dream. "'Tis over,' he said. 'I can scarce believe it.'

'Yes, my liege, 'tis over for now at least,' Hastings said. 'For there is still Marguerite to deal with.'

Edward nodded. 'I did not want them dead Will,' he said suddenly. 'You have to believe me.'

'I believe you, Ned,' Hastings answered softly, 'but I doubt it could have remained so.'

Edward nodded resignedly. 'You are right,' he said grimly. He threw the wine savagely into his throat and then rose. He looked towards Gloucester, who was still kneeling, head bowed. Edward went over to him and raised him to his feet, his hands on his brother's shoulders. Gloucester looked up at him and Edward suddenly embraced him, as Hastings knew he would.

Hastings heard someone clearing his throat and realized that Clarence was standing behind him. He turned, met the steely eyes with a hard glare and Clarence looked away. He could not trust himself to speak to Clarence, for he knew what the men were saying about Warwick's death; that it amounted to nothing better than cold-bloodied murder. He could not believe Clarence could stand there as if nothing had happened, but then there was not much he did understand about Clarence. Edward would be furious if he found out; when he found out.

BARNET APRIL 1471

Elizabeth sobbed against Thomas's bloodied neck, her tears falling into his sticky matted hair. He smelled of blood and smoke and battle; he smelled of death. She had thought she had no tears left, but the sight of Thomas's limp body had dragged them from her broken heart.

'No Elizabeth!' Robert cried. 'Look, he still breathes!'

Elizabeth stepped back for a moment and saw that Robert was right. It was very shallow and somewhat irregular, but Thomas was indeed breathing.

'I too thought the worst when I first saw him,' Robert said, 'but we need to get him a physician, soon.'

Elizabeth cuffed the tears from her eyes. 'The landlord has sent for the surgeon, I think there are no physicians in Barnet. Quickly, we must get him inside.'

* * *

Evading Edward's men was like trying to avoid insects on a summer's day, Jack thought: Barnet was crawling with them! He tugged hard on the reins and pulled his fractious horse into the shadows. Thankfully few knew his father's livery and shamefully he had removed his silver ragged staff badge that had adorned it this morning. Guilt pricked at him, but he knew Warwick would understand. His loyalty had ever been to Warwick not Lancaster; as far as Jack was concerned he had no quarrel with the Yorkists now and he had to admit he had never trusted damned Marguerite! He wished he'd kept the badge Will Hastings had given him in Bruges, but he had dropped it into the Narrow Sea, not believing he would ever have use of it again.

Sun slanted down into the streets and for the first time Jack felt there was some strength in its light. It outlined the stark twisted corpses of Gloucester's men and gilded the bloody trails in the dirt. He breathed deeply, trying to quell the queasiness of his stomach; it was too raw to think on. If he blocked out the thoughts he knew he could block out the pain of them, at least for now. There was one thought he could latch on to, one thought

408

that would sustain him; the reason he was risking his life by being here!

For some time he watched from the shadows, looking for anything or anyone who might give him the sign that he needed.

Men began to drag bodies away and haul them into carts with little more ceremony than if they had been sacks of grain. Still Jack watched and waited. His stomach growled, his mouth was dry, but he did not yet dare to seek the solace of an inn. Then he saw something that made him take notice. His eyes twitched with the glare of the sun as he stared across the square. He smiled at the sight of the man entering the hostelry; that was exactly what he had been waiting for.

* * *

The barber surgeon stood at the end of the bed. He ran a thoughtful hand over his chin. 'You are sure you will not let me bleed him, mistress? He feels very hot to me!'

'I think he has lost enough blood already,' Elizabeth answered, nodding to the newly dressed wound on Thomas's right shoulder. The surgeon sighed. 'As you wish, lady.'

With a shudder her mind was transported back to Bruges and to her encounter with Jack's physician. Jack! For a moment panic gripped her throat, Santa Maria, where on earth was Jack? She tried to swallow the panic down; for it was Thomas who needed her help now and the thought that Jack too could be lost would unravel her completely.

The surgeon began to examine Thomas's head. There was a large black-purple bruise on his temple, but there appeared to be no fracture. The blood had been mainly someone else's. Thomas however remained unresponsive to all.

The surgeon shook his head and turned to Elizabeth. 'This could take some time,' he said flatly, 'and you must not build up your hopes too high. I must warn you, I have seen cases like this where consciousness is never regained.'

Elizabeth looked at Robert who was standing in the corner, arms folded across his body. 'I know,' she said softly.

'Pray for him,' the surgeon said, 'God may listen to you.'

Elizabeth gave a thin smile. God might indeed pity the person who needed her to pray for them, she thought.

Elizabeth nodded to Robert and he showed the surgeon out.

When Robert returned he seemed suddenly older. Perhaps Elizabeth had just not noticed the lines carved into his cheeks and his wide and staring eyes. Silence lengthened into what seemed like years but even though she understood something of the shock he was feeling she knew she had to ask him. She sighed. 'I must know Robert, did you see Warwick? At the end I mean?'

Robert shook his head. He chewed his lip. 'We were cut down by cavalry, Elizabeth, it was ...awful...they were too many and at full gallop... one moment Warwick was there with us and the next... we were on the floor, Thomas and I, and my lord Warwick was nowhere to be seen.' Tears began to fill Robert's eyes; the horrors of the day were too close, too raw to share with anyone.

Elizabeth went over to him and hugged him and he sobbed into her shoulder just like her brother Edmund did when he was hurt.

For a long time they stayed together, sharing their grief wordlessly, both too stunned to really understand the magnitude of what had happened: Edward had won.

Slowly the realization came to Elizabeth precisely what that meant. As far as Edward knew she was his loyal subject and Jack Thornton's wife! But where in God's name was Jack? She had no way of knowing if he had even survived the battle, though something inside her told her that he had; Jack was the cat with more than nine lives! Slowly she untangled herself from Robert's embrace and went to sit at Thomas's side. She took his hand in hers and stroked the matted hair from his face. She owed him much; for without his help she would not have seen Warwick this morning and that had been a precious gift. Guilt knotted her stomach, for she knew that the man she needed now was not Thomas Conyers: it was Jack de Laverton.

* * *

'A gentleman?' Elizabeth asked.

'Aye, lady. He still wears most of a good harness, so he does,' the landlord said.

A smile came to Elizabeth's lips.

'Do you want me to come with you?' Robert asked, alarmed.

Elizabeth turned to him. 'No, Robert. I shall be all right! Stay with Thomas.'

She flew down the stairs two at a time. It was as if he had come directly from her thoughts. When she reached the bottom of the staircase she ran towards him.

He held out his arms and Elizabeth flung herself into them.

'Jack!' she breathed against his neck.

His arms tightened about her. 'Sweetheart,' he whispered.

Tears stung Elizabeth's eyes and for a long time she did not move, could not move. She did not want to relinquish the safety of Jack's embrace and he too did nothing to break it. He smelled of blood and sweat and his red livery coat was smeared with greasy dark stains she did not wish to contemplate. On his chest a black raven stared at her and Elizabeth realised it was the one she had seen flying on the castle banner in her dream.

Eventually she looked up at him. His face was flawed with blood and dirt and his beautiful eyes were dulled with pain.

'Warwick...' he began.

She put a finger to his lips. 'I know,' she said trying to swallow down the grief. The tears welled again. She had thought she wanted to know how he met his end, but if she did, it was not from Jack; that made it all too real. 'Please don't tell me, I could not bear it,' she whispered.

Jack nodded. He sniffed and cuffed his eyes. Then he took a deep breath. 'So sweetheart, what are we to do?' he asked.

Elizabeth took his hand and led him to the table by the fire. She held his look. 'What do you want to do?' she asked tentatively, barely able to comprehend the events of the day, let alone decide her future. But she knew that she must. The decisions they made now would determine the course of their lives.

Jack smiled. 'You know what I would wish for,' he said quietly, tightening his fingers around hers. He drew her hand to his lips and kissed it slowly.

His stubble rasped against her skin.

His eyes never left hers and in them Elizabeth read such longing and such pain.

Her heart fluttered. Part of her never wanted him to leave her again, but inside she had shattered like glass, how could anyone, even Jack repair that? She shook her head slowly.

Jack smiled ruefully. 'I thought you would not agree,' he said sadly. 'I understand.'

'No Jack,' Elizabeth said. 'You do not understand. No one does. No one can.' She held his gaze.

Jack looked down at the ring on her finger and he touched it gently. He looked back at her. 'I have thought long on this,' he said slowly. 'I always said to you that the truth comes out eventually...' he sighed. 'I think the time for the truth has come.'

Elizabeth heard the regret in his voice. 'Where will you go?' she asked him.

'I will seek a pardon and then I would like to remain with Lord Hastings.'

'A pardon?' she asked. 'Is that not a great risk to take?'

Jack laughed softly. 'I think there will be many seeking a pardon, sweetheart. Edward cannot kill them all.'

'Yes. I understand that,' she said. 'But they were not in Bruges.'

'And they were not in sanctuary with the queen either,' Jack added.

Elizabeth gasped. 'Me? Do I need a pardon?' She had never considered the possibility that she could need a pardon; that either of them would, she had believed in Warwick so completely! But how could she face Edward, or Lord Hastings? Or for that matter, how could Jack? Edward would have every right to kill them both!

Jack read her concern. 'It will be all right, sweetheart,' he said softly, 'I will deal with it.'

'No!' Elizabeth clutched his hand in hers; she could not face the possibility that she could be sending him to his death, for how did he know Edward would pardon them?

'It is too dangerous! What if...'

'I will speak to Lord Hastings,' Jack said.

Elizabeth shook her head and bit back the tears.

'He knows what I endured.'

'Endured?' Elizabeth turned her stinging eyes up to him.

Jack nodded. 'The Burgundians tried to torture me but fortunately the Duchess of Burgundy liked me the way I am.' Jack laughed mirthlessly.

Elizabeth widened her eyes. 'She? You?'

Jack nodded and looked down at their hands entwined. 'I am sorry,' he whispered. 'I had no choice.' Then he met her eyes. 'You are the stronger Elizabeth, for you refused her brother,' he said ruefully.

Elizabeth tightened her fingers in his. 'No,' she said, feeling anything but strong. 'I betrayed Warwick, you never did.' Panic gripped her throat. 'I do not want you to go, Jack. They may not pardon you, they may kill you and... I could not bear it.'

Jack smiled his beautiful half-smile. 'The only other option is to be Jack and Elizabeth Thornton of Yorkshire for always and...' he held her eyes, '...and to marry.'

Elizabeth looked away quickly; she could not contemplate it. Not now.

'But if we did that,' Jack continued, 'I could never be reconciled with my half-sisters and never see Laverton Grange again.' He paused, waiting for her to look at him. 'Jack de Laverton will have died at Barnet,' he said gravely.

Elizabeth took a steadying breath; so she had been wrong: there was a family waiting at a hearthside for news of Jack. 'Which do you choose, Jack?' she asked hesitantly. She looked at his handsome weary face.

'I...' Jack met her look. 'I choose the truth,' he said with a sigh.

Tears suddenly blurred Elizabeth's vision. She knew he had made that choice because it was the choice she wanted.

'Hush sweetheart,' Jack said, pulling her closer to him.

Elizabeth shivered. She had never wanted to marry Jack but somehow saying adieu to their counterfeit marriage felt wrong, especially when all around her was death and loss and pain; it seemed wrong to lose something else too. They had shared so much; she could not believe that it was over between them. She had lost Warwick and now she had lost Jack as well.

Jack wrapped his arms about her and rocked her gently. 'It is best, sweetheart,' he said. 'It is best for us both.'

Elizabeth heard his voice quiver.

'You...you will be wanting this then,' she said pulling back from him and twisting at the ring on her finger.

Jack covered her hands quickly with his. 'No, sweetheart, I want you to keep it. The sentiment is real enough,' he said and smiled wistfully.

Elizabeth saw the pain in his eyes and knew that the sentiment still burned within him. Her stomach churned guiltily within her; she had the capacity to help ease his pain, yet she was refusing him out of her own selfishness.

Jack cleared his throat. 'I must go now if I am to reach London before they lock the gates,' he said, rising. 'I will send word when it is done.'

She nodded. Her thoughts were like smoke; dissipated and intangible and the more she sought sense from them, the more their meaning swirled away from her. She rose too and held his look.

His eyes were as wide as the sea and the smile he gave her almost broke her resolve completely, but she knew he was right; this was best for both of them.

'Adieu, sweetheart,' he said.

Without thought Elizabeth clutched at him and then clung to him as if she would drown without him. She pressed her face against the dirty wool of his livery coat. Jack held her too and she knew they shared the same thought: they might not meet again.

After several moments Jack slackened his hold. 'It will be dark soon,' he said hoarsely, looking down into her face. He stroked her hair back gently.

Elizabeth looked up into his beautiful liquid eyes and then she kissed him. Softly at first, then she pressed her lips hard to his, as if she would press her whole self into his keeping.

'Take care, Jack,' she said breathlessly, not knowing how she could form any words let alone say them.

'I always do,' he said with a disarming smile.

In a heartbeat he was gone from her side. This time he did not look back, did not hang on the door latch as he always did, and in a few moments she heard hoofbeats galloping away. She slumped back onto the stool and stared at the floor through hazy vision; she could not believe Jack de Laverton was gone from her life.

* * *

Elizabeth hadn't slept for several days. She settled upon the bed and looked at Thomas's face. In spite of the horrors he had seen and the pain he had suffered, somehow it was still the face of the boy who had found her in Wensley Forest. Golden stubble marked his jaw and long blond lashes guarded his blue eyes from her and she wondered if he would ever open them again to look on this world. And how he would find it changed if he did, she thought. To Elizabeth it was now a grey world of shadows, and she wondered what she would have done if she had not had Thomas to attend to, for everything else seemed of no consequence. Her numb mind could think of nothing but her last vision of Warwick astride his warhorse; the perfect curve of his

414

smile and the flawless light in his eyes as he had looked at her for the last time. Her eyes stung; she had never managed to tell him her dreadful secret, never managed to obtain his forgiveness and she could never now be sure he would have given it. Jack had almost convinced her that confession was the right course, but in the end she had not had the courage, and on that final melancholy morning she dared not risk breaking Warwick's heart. She cuffed the tears from her cheeks. She told herself roundly that weeping would achieve nothing; it would not help Thomas and it would not bring direction to her meaningless life. And more importantly, it would not bring her Warwick or the forgiveness she craved.

She heard light footsteps bounding up the stairs and then Robert entered the room.

'How is he?' he asked with a quick nod towards Thomas.

Elizabeth shrugged. 'He seems settled enough. I tried to give him some of the chicken broth, but I think I almost drowned him. I do not know what else I can do until...until he wakes.' She did not want to contemplate what would happen if he did not wake.

Robert met her eyes, and then quickly looked down, plainly noticing that she had been crying. He cleared his throat. 'And how are you, Elizabeth?' he asked tentatively.

She looked away from him. She bit her lip to prevent more tears from coming. 'I am all right,' she murmured.

Robert came closer and as he sat down Elizabeth could smell a woman's scent on him. 'Martha?' she asked him, keen to divert his questioning. She had known from their time at The Erber that Robert had a sweetheart in the nearby tavern.

Robert smiled broadly, and then tried to stifle it, obviously feeling guilty at his own happiness in the midst of Elizabeth's misery. 'Yes,' he admitted. Then the smile broke into a wide grin he could not suppress. 'She is with child!' he exclaimed.

Pain stabbed Elizabeth's stomach. She stared at him dumbly. Then remembering herself, she smiled. 'Oh Robert,' she said, 'I am so pleased for you!' she said.

Without hesitation Robert hugged her. 'I've told her...if it's a boy...she must call him Richard,' he said into Elizabeth's hair.

Elizabeth fought not to recoil in surprise. 'Richard?' she whispered.

'Aye,' Robert answered in a choked voice.

He drew back from her and she saw the light in his grey eyes had faded a little.

'Elizabeth,' he said quietly, 'there is something I must do.'

Elizabeth kept her eyes on his face. She knew what he was going to say and she was dreading it.

'I have heard that Edward has placed his body at St Paul's Cathedral and...' he hesitated. 'I somehow cannot believe he is dead...'

Tears welled in Elizabeth's eyes as she thought of Warwick lying there in the cold church, stripped of his clothes and his dignity. She twisted Jack's ring on her finger anxiously.

'Elizabeth...if you would like to...'

She shook her head violently. 'No, Robert...I ...could not bear to see him thus. I – I would wish to remember him as I saw him on the morning of the battle. He was magnificent, Robert, sitting astride his destrier in gleaming harness!' Grief robbed her of any more words and she could hold the tears no longer. She buried her face in her hands and cried into them.

Robert pulled her to him instinctively. He was silent for a long moment. 'I am sorry, Elizabeth,' he whispered, 'but I must go.'

She nodded without removing her face from her hands as she strove for control. She understood Robert's need to see Warwick for himself. How could his life be finished with so little consequence to the world, as if the wind had snuffed out a candle?

And within her, her own need was growing, like a seed sown to damp ground. And she knew somehow she would have to assuage it.

FIFTEEN

LONDON APRIL 1471

'Where did you get it from?' Edward asked vehemently.

Clarence looked at his feet.

'By God's right hand George, I asked you a question!' Anger tightened Edward's voice and his cheeks grew hot.

Clarence lifted his eyes slowly.

Edward saw his brother's lip tremble as he attempted to dredge an answer from his throat. 'I...I cannot remember,' he stammered.

Edward slammed his fist onto the edge of the table and a filigreed wine glass shuddered to the floor.

'Honestly, Ned I can't!' Clarence protested wildly.

'You know nothing of honesty!' Edward growled. 'I want to know how you came by Warwick's ring if, as you say, your men had nothing to do with his death!'

Edward saw Clarence send an injurious look towards Will Hastings.

'God's blood, George I had given him safe conduct!' Edward gave a hiss of anger.

''Tis better this way,' Clarence said. 'He cannot rise again to cross you!'

'I wanted him *alive*!' Edward yelled. 'But that you did not, tells me more than you can ever say!' Edward saw his brother shiver. 'What tales could he have told me of you, eh, George? What things had you said that you would now wish unsaid? What deeds you would now wish undone?'

'It – it was not like that!' Clarence blustered.

'Oh, then what was it like?' Edward asked.

'It was a mistake!' Clarence cried. 'I never meant them to kill him, I swear it!'

'You're a liar!' Hastings said coldly. 'And a damned bad one at that.'

Edward looked round at him quickly, surprised by the venom in Hastings's voice. 'I am inclined to agree with my chamberlain, George!' he said evenly.

'No!' Clarence cried, tears welling in his eyes. 'It wasn't my fault!'

'It never is your fault is it, George?' Edward hissed. 'You never take responsibility for anything you do! The treachery was all Warwick's idea; the denigration of my birth was all Warwick's idea; marrying Isabel against my wishes was all Warwick's idea! Christ God, George, if he had told you to jump from a cliff into the sea would you have done so?'

'Would that he had,' Hasting hissed. 'It would save you much trouble, Ned.'

'Well, George?' Edward's pulse was hard in his cheek. He was not prepared for what happened next.

Clarence fell to his knees in front of him and wrapped his arms about Edward's legs, sobbing against them. 'Forgive me, Ned,' he wailed. 'I wanted to show you I'd changed, to prove that I was loyal to you!'

Edward knew he should have felt pity for his brother, but he felt nothing but disgust. 'I wonder how you will explain it to Isabel,' he said icily. 'How will you tell her that you had her father murdered?'

Clarence turned his pink and blotchy face up to his. 'You won't tell her will you, Ned? You can't!'

Edward raised his brows. 'Why should I not? Does she not have the right to know what sort of man you truly are?'

Clarence made a choking sound in his throat. 'Ned, please! It was a mistake, I swear it.'

Edward tasted bile. 'Get out of my sight,' he snarled. 'Before I change my mind!'

Clarence bowed his head and released his grip on Edward's legs. 'Thank you, Ned,' he whispered. He rose slowly and fumbled with his gown, his eyes fixed on the intricate embroidery.

'But if ever you cross me...'

'I swear I won't Ned. Never,' Clarence said frantically, looking up at him.

Edward gave a desultory wave of his hand and Clarence, looking relieved, bowed profusely as he retired.

The door clicked after him.

Edward closed his eyes and inhaled deeply. 'Remind me Will, why I took him back,' he said.

'Because you had no real choice,' Hastings said, coming closer.

Edward noted the acid edge to his voice.

'You needed his men, and needed to deprive Warwick of them, and besides, Ned, you made your sister Margaret happy!'

418

Edward smiled thinly. It was true, the Duchess of Burgundy had written to him effusing her thanks at his restoration of George into the heart of the family. 'Aye, he ever was her favourite, though I cannot think why.'

'Because he is vulnerable, Ned, like the runt of the litter. You know that women always think the weakest one is the sweetest; it needs their nurture,' Hastings said.

Edward shook his head. 'That is the first time I have ever thought of George as a puppy, but now I think on it, perhaps you are right!'

Hastings laughed. 'Perhaps the analogy only goes so far!'

Edward's mind darkened. 'I shall never trust him, Will. Never.'

'I should hope not,' Hastings replied. 'He has done nothing to earn it.'

'I swear,' Edward said under his breath, 'it will be only a matter of time...'

LONDON APRIL 1471

Even if Robert had not been to London before he would have had no trouble in finding the way. There were many who were intrigued to see the Earl of Warwick finally laid low. Some, like him, were lately his men-at-arms who still could not grasp that their leader was no more. Others were there to see the traitor whom they believed had finally got his reward for all his plotting and scheming.

Robert joined the long queue. Several of Edward's men-at-arms jostled the crowd, just to show that they would not accept any unruly behaviour, but then they laughed and joked with each other as though on holiday.

Slowly, very slowly the leaden-footed line shuffled towards the steps.

The sun was warm on Robert's back and he wondered if the good weather was in part responsible for the size of the crowd. His stomach began to curl as he edged forward and he wondered if he was doing the right thing. He had seen bodies before, of course he had, and seen too many men who had been killed in battle. But this was his lord; this was how he would remember him and he understood why Elizabeth had not wanted to sully her memories by seeing him like this.

As he drew closer several men and women began hurling insults at the plain wooden coffin.

'Traitor!' he heard them shout, and he fought with himself not to answer them. His cheeks burned, partly with anger and partly with shame at not defending Warwick's name. The anger burned in his gut and it fuelled his thoughts. Then Robert made a decision, one he knew Martha would not understand.

After a few moments the soldiers pushed into them with the staves of their bills, moving them on. The crowd jeered, but whether it was at the billmen or at Warwick lying in front of them, Robert could not tell. He passed painted columns, which swept towards heaven, snatching his gaze up beyond the light, and he wondered if that was where Warwick's soul would be; he could not stomach the alternative. He shivered in the gloom of the nave as finally he came to the front of the line. Red and blue light bled onto the floor tiles around the coffins from the high windows. Beneath their arrow-torn banners Warwick lay beside his brother Montagu. They were dressed only in loincloths, their skin pallid, mottled with ink-coloured bruises; the indelible marks of brutality Robert was glad he had not witnessed. The aromatic scent of rosemary assailed Robert's nostrils, and candles spluttered smoke up into the air, beyond his vision, but in spite of this the overwhelming smell of death lingered around the coffins. Robert stared in disbelief at his lord. Warwick's arms were folded across his once muscular stomach and his lips bore the blue-purple blush of death. Robert strained his eyes, but incredibly the deep chest remained motionless. Then he noticed the killing blow, the fatal violation of Warwick's neck, obviously delivered at close quarters. Warwick's face still bore the pained expression he had worn as he died, and Robert was glad Elizabeth had not come; this would have broken her. He glanced at Montagu, who also wore the expression of a man who had suffered. Robert chewed his lip hard. In spite of his efforts, his vision began to blur.

Suddenly he was being pushed and prodded by a large man-at-arms. 'Move on, lad!' he yelled in a harsh London accent that irritated Robert more than it should have done.

Wiping his sleeve over his eyes Robert moved away slowly, taking deep breaths to try to keep his aching body under control. He moved away from the church and the crowd and stood leaning against a wall, trying to take it all in, trying to control his grief.

Even though he was back in the sunshine his marrow was still frozen.

Around him men and women had gathered in small animated huddles.

'Of course you know it was Clarence's men what killed him?' a thin man close to him was saying to a younger man by his side.

'No, I didn't hear anything,' the younger man said.

'My son John was there when King Edward ordered Warwick to be spared, but Clarence didn't like it. He could tell by his face. I suppose he would be imagining all the things Warwick could say about him, if he was brought to trial.'

'I never thought of that!' the young man said.

'John says the king was furious when he found out Warwick had been murdered, disarmed and murdered – not a great reflection on him as king, eh?' the older man asked.

'No, that's as bad as the Lancastrians at Wakefield, when they killed young Rutland and old Salisbury!'

'Aye, it is. My John says the king wanted a trial, but Clarence well, he could only see himself as the heir to Warwick's estates.'

'Aye, he shall do well from it, to be sure.'

Robert shivered. He could scarcely comprehend what they were saying – that Clarence had murdered his father-in-law!

Robert knew then that he had made the right decision; he could never be a Yorkist with Clarence in their midst.

ST PAUL'S CATHEDRAL APRIL 1471

In the shivering gloom of the cathedral Edward stood at Warwick's feet, hands folded across his stomach, head bowed. It was almost as if the sight was too incomprehensible: Warwick was dead. Montagu was dead. It was over.

Edward glanced quickly at his brother Gloucester; he had said nothing since they had entered the close reverence of the church. Gloucester too had his head bowed. His cheeks were wet with tears and his throat was working hard as he evidently tried to choke down his grief. Edward shook his head and sighed.

'It's all your fault, Ned!' Gloucester's voice was high-pitched with anger.

Edward stared at his brother in disbelief, unable to respond to what he was certain his brother had just said.

Gloucester's eyes blazed. 'He saw himself as my father – as yours too Ned,' he hissed. 'He was my guardian; the guardian of the Yorkist cause! But you treated him as an ordinary subject, Ned – to be sent on a fool's errand to France for a bride for you, to be humiliated at court if the mood so took you or your queen...' Gloucester struggled for breath and his cheeks coloured as he realized he had perhaps said too much. 'You broke his heart, Ned...only lately did this white rose turn red,' he said quietly. Then he turned away from the watchful silent corpses. Edward heard him splutter as he tried to regain control.

'Richard,' Edward said softly, 'you know that isn't true!' His instinct was to comfort him; to put his arm round his younger brother's shoulder and say that he knew it was his fault; that he was wrong and that he was sorry Warwick and Montagu were dead. But the truth was he wasn't sorry and he didn't believe he was wrong. He was the king and they had stood against him; they had received nothing more than they deserved. Had they lived he would have had no choice but to punish them; they were traitors. Gloucester had to see that, surely? Their kinship counted for nothing, nor did Warwick's past deeds in York's cause.

After Warwick's refusal to accept his terms at Coventry he had known that either he or Warwick would pay with their lives. Had Gloucester known it too? Did he yet understand what Edward himself was only just learning – that to be the King of England demanded ruthless sacrifices – that even one's own kin were not safe? For a king, Edward thought with a shudder, was friendless. He could trust no one; not Hastings, not even his queen. But perhaps Gloucester did understand. He had lived in Warwick's household for long enough to know that everyone wanted something, and that everything had its price. Loyalty and patronage was the obscene symbiosis that ruled them all.

A shiver of guilt ran through him as he looked at Warwick's frozen face and the perfidious black wound that grinned at his neck. Perhaps Gloucester was right and it was all Edward's fault. But could he really have prevented Warwick's death? He doubted even Gloucester believed that he could. It was a long road that had brought them here and he was not sure of any other turns he might have taken instead. And if Gloucester felt so strongly what did that say for his own loyalty? He had thought Edward wrong yet he had stood by him. He must have been tempted – there must have been a time when Warwick had poured sweet words like wine. Gloucester had stood by him; perhaps he did have someone he could trust after all. He shook his head. God's blood but that was a dangerous thought for a king!

Boots clacking on stone roused him.

'My liege we must go.' Hastings's voice too was thick with emotion and Edward saw that he avoided looking at Warwick or Montagu. Edward met his eyes. 'A few moments more, Will,' he breathed, and then he looked at Gloucester. 'Alone,' he said.

He waited until he saw the white daylight flood in and then disappear again as they closed him off from the outside world.

Then it came. Like a spring torrent down a mountainside it flooded him. Without thought he knelt by Warwick's shoulder.

'Forgive me, Cousin Warwick,' he said quietly through his sudden tears. 'You knew it would always end with one of us lying here. Once we parted at Coventry there was no turning back from it.'

Edward started, as a cold draught brushed his face like a hand and the candles guttered wildly, sending smoke curling up into the empty nave. Icy fingers walked down Edward's spine. With difficulty he struggled to his feet and whispered a fleeting Ave for the Nevilles' souls. He swallowed thickly as if swallowing down sour wine. He wiped the back of his hand across his stinging eyes and then strode down the nave towards the door. It had to be forgotten, for there was still Lancaster to deal with; he still had to fight for his crown.

As he gripped the cold iron of the door handle he looked back at his cousins, and for a moment he saw Warwick as he had been, resplendent in his colours beside the Bear and Ragged Staff pennant, leading the Yorkist charge at Towton. That was how he wanted to remember him, when they had been of one mind.

With great effort Edward hauled at the door and a huge roar deafened him.

Hastings turned at the sound and smiled.

The sad chill began to lift from Edward's stomach at the warmth of the Londoners' reception.

'Long live King Edward!' they cried and Edward fought to keep the smile from his face, but they roared and cheered even more and Edward's lips stretched into a grin. Edward walked forward into the warmth of their love, leaving Warwick in the chill of St Paul's.

Jack watched from the shadows. A few of the men had nodded to him, plainly recognizing him from Bruges, one even acknowledging him as Master Thornton! He swallowed hard; he had hardly been able to look on Warwick as he was now; he wanted only memories of Warwick's greatness, not of his broken body. He sighed. That part of his life was gone and he turned his mind to Lord Hastings and his reason for being here, for without Lord Hastings he had no future to contemplate.

The courtly gathering began to break up and Jack saw his opportunity.

'My lord, I would speak with you,' he said as Hastings moved towards his horse. He remembered their last meeting, when they had talked of Elizabeth and home and Jack hoped they would be able to share such times again. Everything depended on this conversation.

Hastings turned slowly and Jack bowed.

'Christ on the cross!' Hastings said. 'Master Thornton, Jack, I thought you surely dead!'

'No my lord, I am not dead, as you see, but I crave your indulgence.' He drew Hastings aside. His heart thudded in his chest; if he could not convince Lord Hastings of his case then he would be a dead man before nightfall!

'What is it, Jack?' Hastings asked with widened eyes. 'Elizabeth? You found her? Is she well?'

Jack nodded. 'Yes, my lord, I thank you.'

Hastings smiled. 'Good, I am glad of it.' He studied Jack's face. 'What is it that troubles you, Jack? The battle?'

Jack paused; he had thought of a thousand ways he could start this conversation and each one of them was as bad as another.

'In a manner of speaking, my lord,' he said hesitantly.

Hastings gave him a puzzled look.

'Your pardon my lord, but my name is not Jack Thornton. It is Jack de Laverton.' Jack's heart threatened to escape from his chest.

'Laverton?' Hastings narrowed his eyes, knowing there was more to come.

'I was Warwick's man, my lord, but never Lancaster's, I swear it. I wish for pardon.' The words came out in an undignified rush.

Hastings's mouth opened silently and for several moments he stared at Jack with incredulity. 'But in Bruges?' he stammered. 'You helped our cause Jack, perhaps more than anyone.'

'I hope that will sway your judgement of me, my lord, for I fought for Warwick at Barnet.' Jack looked down.

The silence lengthened into painful heartbeats. Jack wondered what Hastings was thinking. Eventually he had to look at him.

William Hastings was unmoved; his face set, his mouth a tight line, his arms folded across his silk-clothed chest. 'This is grave news indeed Jack,' he said sternly. 'Though I must confess there was something in your tale that troubled me.'

'My lord?' Jack said.

'Aye, Jack: your marriage to Elizabeth; I could not help but wonder how that had occurred and why Master Higgins had remained silent, indeed why he remains silent still.'

'I have no knowledge of him, my lord,' Jack said truthfully; for what could he say about Higgins? That he *might* be dead? That he *might* be languishing at the Duchess of Burgundy's pleasure somewhere? No, the less he said on that score, the better.

'I see,' Hastings said gravely. Still there was no change in his countenance. What was he thinking? 'The charge of treason is a significant one, Jack,' he said at last. 'One that I cannot ignore.'

The word 'treason' brought Jack's situation into sharp focus. 'Yes, my lord, I know it is, but...'

Hastings held up his hand to silence him. 'And to implicate Elizabeth too, that I think is almost unpardonable. She was a good servant to the House of York, Jack. I do not know how you persuaded her to help you.'

Jack knew the answer: she had done it for Warwick. But what if Elizabeth suffered for this? He would never forgive himself for persuading her to stay with him in Bruges! He lowered his eyes; this was not going to plan.

After what seemed an eternity, Hastings sighed. 'There has been much blood spilt and I know our king would wish us to be conciliatory where we can.'

'My lord?' Jack asked hopefully.

'Ah, Jack, I cannot ignore your service in Bruges and you also have a powerful ally there, who I am certain would intercede for you, is that not so?'

Jack wondered whom he meant. Jehan? The duchess?

Incongruously, Hastings began to laugh. 'I would be a fool indeed to question the judgement of the Duchess of Burgundy! I know not how Warwick benefitted from you being in our company, but it did not help him on the field of battle, Jack.' He paused again, considering something else. 'And Elizabeth? Warwick's lover? Not your wife?'

Jack sucked in his breath as the truth of Hastings's words struck him. 'Yes, my lord.'

Hastings shook his head. 'That imprudent dance of theirs told me much, but I had forgotten its significance.' He laughed softly. 'How did you resist the temptation, Jack?' he asked admiringly. 'Christ, you deserve an honour for that alone!'

Jack stared at him and tried not to smile; at times it had been a close run thing! He cleared his throat. 'Would you speak to the king, my lord? I know he may yet wish to deal with us —'

'No Jack,' Hastings said firmly. 'I think you both did more good to our cause than harm, however you meant it and your deaths will be as pointless as others have been.' He nodded his head towards the church where Warwick and Montagu lay. 'Come to my chamber tonight, Jack. I will speak to the king.'

'Thank you, my lord,' Jack said as he bowed his head. 'I shall.' As he bowed himself from Hastings's presence he wondered just how much influence the lord chamberlain had over the newly triumphant king. Hadn't that been Warwick's undoing?

BARNET APRIL 1471

On the fourth day Thomas opened his eyes. Slowly at first, his blond lashes fluttering as though his eyes were not really sure if they should open or not; wondering what world he may open them to — maybe even heaven itself. The world was a glimmer of spinning colour as he tried to focus.

Someone smiled at him and whispered his name, and he realized with a jolt that it was Elizabeth.

She smoothed his hair back from his forehead and welcomed him back with a kiss on the cheek.

Thomas smiled; maybe this was heaven after all.

He struggled to sit up and his head swam. He found that his right arm refused to bear his weight so he sank back down onto the bed, dizziness engulfing him.

Thomas did not know for how long he had slept again, but when he again forced his eyes open sunlight slanted in from the small window and he could hear the sound of birdsong. Elizabeth was still there. She was sitting on his bed. She was staring straight ahead at the cracks on the lime-washed wall. He noticed her hands were moving as she twisted a ring on her finger distractedly.

As if by some second sight she suddenly turned to face him. Her eyes were puffed and red, her cheeks damp. When she realized he was looking at her, she sniffed and wiped her eyes quickly and he saw that her cheeks began to colour.

'Thomas?' she whispered.

Thomas smiled. It felt good to hear her say his name.

'You're back.' A smile came to her lips but Thomas saw that her eyes were still dull. 'Are you hungry?' she asked. 'Would you like to sit up?'

Thomas only half comprehended what she was asking him. His tongue was thick and dry in his mouth and he could smell his own pungent sweat and a sweet sickly smell of herbs he did not know. It seemed so strange to be here in a bright room with Elizabeth when the last thing he remembered... He shuddered at the brutal images that flashed into his mind.

Elizabeth leaned over and plumped up the pillows and helped Thomas to sit against them.

'There is some pottage in the kitchen if you would like some,' she murmured.

Thomas nodded and immediately wished he hadn't for a dull pain throbbed at his temple and then scorched down his neck.

Elizabeth must have noticed him wince. 'What is it?' she asked.

'Nothing...just a little stiff,' Thomas said thickly; his throat was as dry as if he'd drunk too much ale. As he began to rediscover his body he found that there were few parts of it that did not hurt.

'Robert has gone for the surgeon,' Elizabeth said.

Thomas widened his eyes.

'Don't worry,' she said with a smile, 'he will be very pleased with you.'

Thomas sighed and settled into the crisp softness of the pillows.

As if reading her thoughts there was the sudden sound of voices and boots thudded on the stairs, and in a few moments Robert opened the door.

'Tom!' he said excitedly as he saw Thomas. Thomas looked at Robert in disbelief. Though he was flushed with the healthy pink of life, his cheeks were hollow and his eyes were dulled: he

427

looked ten years older. Thomas wondered if he too wore the experience of Barnet in his face as Robert did.

An older man followed Robert into the room. Fluffy white hair billowed from beneath his cap and he had wide grey eyes that flicked over Thomas as if he was a horse for sale.

Elizabeth rose from the bed to allow him closer.

He smelled of the same strange herbs.

'I have seen cases where the victim simply fades away,' he declared to Thomas with a twitch of his lips as he peered into Thomas's eyes and pressed a plump finger against his temple. 'But you are stronger than I thought,' he said as Thomas flinched from the pain cascading down his neck.

The surgeon looked to Elizabeth. 'My poultices have done their work!' He laughed a little hysterical laugh.

Thomas glanced nervously at his wounded arm.

'That will heal too, in time,' the surgeon said, 'though it will always be weaker than it was.'

Thomas nodded solemnly; he would always have a memento of Barnet then, he thought.

'But it is the wounds of the mind that never heal,' the surgeon continued ominously.

Thomas shivered. He wondered if everyone saw things they did not wish to remember, even when they were awake.

'I think there is nothing more for me here,' he said with an almost regretful sigh. 'I shall check on you again in a day or so, but I think there is no further cause for concern. Now, if you will excuse me. I seem to be much in demand.' He gave the little laugh again and then left Thomas's side.

Robert showed him out.

Elizabeth came closer and then sat on his bed. She took hold of his hand and looked at him. She too carried grief in her eyes, Thomas thought. His heart shuddered.

'We should send word to your father, Thomas,' Elizabeth said softly. 'I did send a message to him to say that you were alive, and I know he will be most anxious to hear that you will make a full recovery.'

Thomas nodded, still feeling a little bewildered. He could remember very little and what he could recall disturbed him too much to dwell on. 'I would not have survived without you,' he said.

'It was Robert who rescued you from the field,' Elizabeth said. Her eyes left his modestly.

'Aye, I kept my oath eventually!' Robert joked, returning to them.

But Thomas did not laugh. The ghosts of that April morning were starting to appear in his mind again and he realized with horror that they had lost. His throat constricted. 'Warwick?' was all he could say.

The look on Elizabeth's face answered his question and he told himself how stupid he was for thinking her grief had been for anyone else other than Warwick.

'He is to be interred at Bisham Abbey with his brother Montagu,' Robert said and then hung his head, contemplating the counterpane.

Thomas shook his head in disbelief. 'How, Rob? What happened?'

Robert looked at Elizabeth uncertainly.

She nodded a silent assent but Thomas saw that she caught her lip with her teeth.

'I am still not certain, Tom,' Robert said. 'There was some confusion when Oxford returned to the field after driving Gloucester's men away, I think his and Montagu's men began to fight each other, both believing they had been betrayed!'

Thomas looked skywards and shook his head again.

'But it isn't over!' Robert said eagerly.

'It is for Thomas!' Elizabeth said tersely. 'He cannot even get out of bed!'

'Yes, but for me...' Robert continued. 'At St Paul's, when I stood before Warwick, I knew what I must do.'

Thomas frowned. He heard Elizabeth give a sharp hiss of breath.

'On the very day of Barnet, Queen Marguerite and Prince Edouard landed and were met by Somerset and Devon,' Robert said.

'Somerset and Devon?' Thomas queried. 'They should have been with us, Rob, we would never have lost if...'

'I know, Tom, I agree, but what is done is done, and they are mustering in the southwest even as I speak!' Robert's voice rose in excitement.

'And you wish to join them?' Thomas asked him.

'Yes, Tom I do. They are even saying that Warwick's defeat is a bonus to them, not a weakness, so little did they trust him!'

'If, as Thomas says, they had joined him as their honour demanded, it would all be over by now and Warwick... Warwick might still be alive!' Elizabeth said. Thomas heard her voice break and she turned away from them, wrapping her arms about her body as she did so.

'You do understand, Thomas, say you do?' Robert pleaded. The same bright eyes Thomas had seen when they sparred together flashed before him now. He smiled. 'Yes, Robert. Go if you must!'

Robert almost leapt on him, slapping his back with enthusiasm.

'If they will take a little boy like you!' Thomas jested.

Elizabeth said nothing, but her sad green gaze met Thomas's eyes over her shoulder and he knew she could not believe what she was hearing. The smile left his face. She looked heartsick of death and war and yet Robert was eager to join it all again. And Thomas wondered what he would have done if he had been fit enough. He could not say with certainty. In fact he couldn't say anything with certainty, for all he had been certain of had been swept away in the damp April mist at Barnet.

WINDSOR APRIL 1471

'It is Wales, my liege,' Jack said breathlessly as he bowed before Edward and Hastings.

'You are sure, Jack?' Hastings asked him bluntly. 'We cannot afford to be wrong.'

'I am certain, my lord,' Jack answered. He looked down at the dirt on his clothes, his heart still thundered in his chest. Knowing that despite his pardon, his loyalty was still on trial he had used all of his contacts and all of his strength in Edward's cause. He knew he was right.

'But the report from Salisbury?' Edward asked darkly.

'Is but a feint, Your Grace,' Jack said, 'as you did at Pontefract to such effect.'

Hastings nodded briefly and a servant offered Jack some wine.

Jack gulped it down, washing the dust from his throat. He saw Edward and Hastings exchange looks and he knew what Edward's look said.

'They have no design yet on London, Your Grace, I swear it. They go to meet Jasper Tudor,' Jack said quickly, determined to dispel Edward's doubts. If only Jasper Tudor had stirred himself a little with his mustering of men, mayhap he would have been able to fight with Warwick, Jack thought. But the Welsh had not seemed in much of a hurry and like Somerset and Devon, had failed to meet Warwick's call. Even now it was Marguerite who had to go to Wales to meet him and Jack wondered if that would be their undoing.

Hastings nodded. 'I think Jack is right, Ned.'

A smile twitched Jack's mouth, but he knew he didn't dare say it. Not here.

They moved to the table on which a map had been spread.

'God's blood, that is some march, Ned!' Hastings exclaimed.

'You must stop them joining together, Your Grace,' Jack said hurriedly, 'whatever the cost.'

Edward stroked a hand across his chin thoughtfully. His eyes darted across the parchment, flicking from London to Wales and back again.

'It cannot be done,' Hastings said. He paused and then met Edward's look.

Edward's eyes were as dark as lapis. 'It can,' he said flatly. 'And with God's grace it will be.' He swept his eyes to Jack. 'Refresh yourself, then come to me. I will have further messages to go tonight,' he said gravely.

Jack bowed and was about to leave the room when someone else was announced. The name froze his blood.

In a flourish of damask silk and velvet George Duke of Clarence whirled into the room. Jack's eyes narrowed to two slits of dark flame and he saw Hastings too stare at Edward's brother with loathing. Instinctively Jack's hand had slipped to the hilt of his sword and it was all he could do not to draw the weapon and plunge it into the unfaithful duke's throat.

Only Edward seemed unruffled. 'George!' he said brightly. 'I did not send for you, did I?'

Clarence rose, preened at his clothing for a moment and then strode over to them.

'Forgive the intrusion, Your Grace, but I had to come.'

'Had to, George?' Edward asked. 'Now? It is well past Compline!'

Clarence hesitated, looked quickly at Jack and Hastings, and suddenly seemed a little less certain of his purpose. '...erm, I needed to ask you something... Ned.'

'Yes?' Edward leaned closer to him, his eyes unflinching.

Clarence again looked to where Jack and Hastings stood.

'George?' Edward was plainly trying to keep the impatience from his voice.

Clarence picked at the gold threads of his clothing.

'George?'

'I want the vanguard!' Clarence demanded, suddenly meeting Edward's gaze.

Hastings spluttered and Jack bit his lip to stop himself from laughing out loud.

Edward's lips twitched, but he restrained himself. 'The van, George? But I have given it to Richard,' he said slowly.

'But he lost it didn't he? At Barnet they fled,' Clarence said smugly.

Hastings moved to intervene, but Edward held up his hand to stop him. Jack saw Edward's cheeks darken and his lips tighten into a thin line. He breathed deeply and then stared at Clarence with such fierce eyes that Clarence looked away briefly, but he did not give up.

'But I am older than he is Ned!' he whined. 'And he lost it at Barnet!'

'Enough!' Edward roared. 'The battles were misaligned George; he could not avoid being outflanked by Oxford. If you had been paying close attention to the battle instead of hiding behind me, you would have seen that, George. It was no fault of Richard's that they fled the field, God's blood he was wounded in the shoulder! I see no reason to change the command!' Edward's voice was now a low growl. 'When we fight with Lancaster, as I know we shall, we shall fight as we fought at Barnet.'

'But Ned!'

Edward strangled Clarence's voice with an incandescent look. 'Do you understand, George? You shall be with me. Richard will have the van, Will the rear.'

Clarence's cheeks coloured and his eyes searched the floor in front of him. Jack could not believe that he was even thinking of making another protest, but plainly he was, for still he did not move.

'Was there anything else, George?' Edward asked. His voice was measured, his control regained.

Clarence looked up and Jack saw the glint of tears at the corners of his eyes. He sniffed, and then inhaled deeply. 'No Your Grace,' he said stiffly.

'Then I bid you goodnight, George,' Edward said.

For a moment Clarence hesitated, his eyes sweeping over the map on the table.

'Goodnight, George,' Edward repeated.

'Goodnight Your Grace,' Clarence said sourly. Then he gave a less flamboyant bow than at his entrance and, ignoring Hastings and Jack completely, he flounced from the room.

When the door had closed behind him Edward let out a loud guffaw. 'Can you believe that, Will?' he asked, spluttering.

Jack saw that Hastings was not laughing. His eyes were still narrowed and were fixed on the doorway as if he could still sense Clarence's presence. 'Oh yes, Ned,' he said warningly. 'I can believe it.'

GLOUCESTER MAY 1471

Robert de Assheton slumped to the ground. The eastern sky was just beginning to brighten: they had marched nearly all night. It had taken them that long to reach Gloucester and now he heard that Beauchamp would not open the gates to them. He didn't care that the ground was damp, didn't care that his armour would rust; he needed to sleep, or at least get some rest. His feet were hot and aching and he thought with a wry smile of Thomas complaining of sore feet when they had marched with Warwick from London. That was when Warwick had taken Edward prisoner. Though it was only nigh on a year ago, how far away that all seemed now. As he lay there he tried to remind himself why exactly he had sought out this company, why precisely he had joined the Lancastrian army. In his muddled head he could no longer rationalize his choice, and he thought enviously of Thomas being cosseted by Elizabeth. Why on earth had he not stayed in Barnet with them, or gone to London and made a life with Martha and his firstborn child?

It seemed as though he had only closed his eyes for a moment when a heavy boot kicked him awake. The day was brighter, the sun higher in the sky and he realized he must have slept for a good two hours. He looked at his comrades. Their eyes were red-

433

rimmed and shadowed with dark circles and he wondered if he looked as tired as they did. His stomach growled and he realized that he had eaten nothing since yesterday morning.

'Come on, lads,' the captain called to them. 'On your feet!'

And now there was no time to eat. He gulped water quickly from his bottle and it made his empty stomach heave.

The groans of tired men rippled along the line as they struggled to their feet. Robert stood with his hands on his hips and he arched backwards and stared at the bright blue sky as he tried to get his back to work. It felt as though his hips had been nailed to his spine; he shouldn't have slept on the ground! He smiled as he suddenly thought of Thomas – he would probably have had a seizure if he had had to lie on the wet grass in his harness!

Robert fell into line and sank easily into the hypnotic rhythm of the march. This was when he missed Thomas and Will most. His heart caught at his throat as he realized it was not only Warwick they had lost, but probably Will Kennerley too.

'Must have covered twenty five miles yesterday,' the man next to him muttered. 'And now another fifteen miles to have a door slammed in your face.'

'Where to now, then?' Robert asked, glad of the distraction.

'Tewkesbury. That's the next crossing point on the Severn,' the man grumbled. 'And with the usurper's army shadowing us...'

Robert almost caused a collision as he missed his footing.

'Aye lad, did you not know?' the man smiled mirthlessly. 'He set out from Windsor when we left Bath. He's on the high road of course, but by God he's there. It will be a close run thing.'

* * *

Jack watched from the hill. The sun was hot on the back of his neck and he hoped his harness didn't catch the light too much; he didn't want to give away his position, though he guessed the Lancastrians knew they were being watched. The thin line of soldiers was strung out beneath him like an old rosary where the cord had been stretched thin with use, and one knew that at any moment it would break. He felt sorry for them, the Lancastrian soldiers. Not that his loyalties were torn they were not, but he knew how hard a march they'd had and they looked in no shape to give battle. They marched with heads bowed and feet slither-

434

ing unwillingly. And Jack knew what awaited them – Edward's keen and hungry army, buoyed by the news that Gloucester town had shut the Lancastrians out, and more than that, Beauchamp had attacked their rearguard and made off with some of the Lancastrians' hard-earned artillery.

Jack knew he was looking at an army under pressure, an army that had been pushed to the edge of endurance and the hot May sunshine was going to push them even harder, making these last ten miles to Tewkesbury seem like a hundred.

Having seen enough, Jack turned his horse away from them and spurred along the ridge towards the Yorkist van.

Up here on the plain Jack could see a shimmering haze of heat. The Yorkist vanguard was a dazzling blur of murrey and blue punctuated with the sparkling glint of silver from helmets, banners and weapons. Shielding his eyes with his hand, he had to admit they were an impressive sight.

As he closed on their ranks he saw Edward and his brother Richard of Gloucester side by side at the head of the column; the tall lithe Edward and the small slender Richard, and it was easy to see why men questioned that they were full brothers.

Jack kicked his mount on towards them. He slid to a halt and then turned the courser deftly to pull in at Edward's side.

'My liege,' he said as Edward met his eyes.

'What news?' Edward asked.

'They will reach Tewkesbury before Compline,' Jack said.

'And how seem they to you?' Edward asked.

Jack wiped sweat from his eyes with his hand. 'Like dead men walking, Your Grace,' he answered honestly. 'The calamity at Gloucester has hit their morale hard.'

'Will they cross the Severn?' Edward asked.

Jack shook his head. 'It is only fordable at low water and the tide is yet high. There is a ferry, but that would take them hours, and they would not be foolish enough to risk being caught with men on either side of the bank. They will wait 'til morning.'

Beneath the lifted visor of his sallet, Edward grinned, his teeth showing white and even against his dirty face. 'Richard, do you hear that? We have them!' he said excitedly.

Jack saw that Gloucester too was smiling.

'Ride on Jack,' Edward said brightly, 'find us lodgings at Cheltenham. There we shall rest and recuperate before we march towards Tewkesbury.'

'But Ned,' Gloucester protested. 'We cannot ask the men to move again. We must have covered nearly thirty miles already today.'

'I want to be within striking distance of the Lancastrians on the morrow,' Edward said firmly. 'What was the place called, Jack?'

'Tredington, Your Grace,' Jack answered. ''Tis but three miles from there into Tewkesbury.'

'I will not lose them again, Richard,' Edward said warningly. 'They gave us the slip at Sodbury; they will not do so again.'

BARNET MAY 1471

Elizabeth ran another rosary bead through her fingers blindly. Thomas was sleeping and she sought to comfort herself in the silence of prayer; but it gave her nothing. She had nothing; she was nothing. In truth what was there for her? Lazenby without Jack brought the threat of Matthew and there was no one else to whom she could appeal. Jack brought his own dangers, which she knew she could not face now, though she was more than grateful for his efforts on her behalf; how else would she have obtained a pardon from the king? Perhaps it was a good thing he had not come to tell her so in person. She knew there was no place for her at Middleham either for she knew she could never live under the same roof as Sir John Conyers, even if he was taking care of Edmund. In fact she thought, as a single woman there was no independent life, except as a rich widow and though she felt a widow's grief, she had none of the succour of respectability, for in the eyes of the world she had no legitimate claim to it; neither was she rich. She knew of women who had married men of good reputation to stave off the attentions of suitors, but she knew that was not for her either. Besides, she knew no man who would oblige her; Jack did not count, for he envisaged a consummated marriage. Lady Scrope had offered her a place in her household at Bolton, but how could she ever hope to reach there by herself, and anyway, there would lie a way to rekindling memories of Warwick she knew were too raw to think on.

She sighed deeply and slipped more beads through her fingers. She had long believed God and the Virgin had forsaken her and recent events had done nothing to convince her otherwise. God had certainly forsaken Warwick, she thought, in spite of his sacred oath. She paused. Perhaps the fact that God had taken him during the Easter Passion meant something else; that he was blessed. Edward may have won, Elizabeth reflected, but the only certainty of life was death and she wondered if Edward would face his own death with as much equanimity as Warwick had faced his. She realized now that Warwick had known that God was to call to him at Barnet, knew that his road had ended; that was why there had been that unfathomable light in his eyes as he had looked at her for the last time. Tears came heavily to her lashes and she chewed on her lip so as not to waken Thomas with her sobs. She twisted Jack's ring on her finger. Warwick had left her believing her to be more than she was, thinking on her as his safe harbour when her actions in France spoke so differently; Edward had pardoned her for her actions - didn't that say it all? She needed to tell Warwick the truth and she needed to deal with Edward's letter, the one Jack had returned to her when she left Bruges. What if it had been a pardon for Warwick and he had accepted it? Santa Maria he could yet be alive! She bit back the tears; she was not yet strong enough for that! Yet as she stared out at the dusty streets of Barnet there was something else she had to do, but how she would do it she did not yet know, but she knew that it was the only other place a broken woman could go.

TEWKESBURY MAY 1471

The sky had barely brightened in the east when Edward ordered them to break camp. The vanguard, led by Gloucester, was closely followed by the mainward under Edward's command with a petulant Clarence at his side and, as at Barnet, the rearward was lead by Hastings: the successful battle order was preserved. With his mind a mêlée of emotions, Jack watched from under his brows as they set off towards Tewkesbury. These were the men he had fought against that day at Barnet; these were the men who had defeated and killed Warwick. How on earth could he bring himself to stand at their side, make their cause his? He knew the inevitable answer: because he had no choice. Lancaster had never been his cause, only Warwick had. And with Warwick gone, how else could he hope to gain his inheritance? Certainly not from 'The Bitch of Anjou'! He swung his horse round and set off to follow Hastings.

Hastings had spoken up for him and Elizabeth to Edward. Edward had had no difficulty in forgiving Elizabeth; after all, Cla-

437

rence had returned to him hadn't he? But with Jack it had been a different matter. Hastings had reminded him of Jack's knighthood after Towton, his usefulness in Bruges with Duke Charles and the Burgundian court, and had pointed out that all Jack had really done was kept his allegiance to Warwick, as Hastings had kept his allegiance to Edward. That was what Jack liked most about Will Hastings, he understood. Edward had acquiesced and the pardon had been given. But Jack wasn't a fool; he knew how fragile Edward's pardons could be. He had heard of Lord Welles's pardon and that had ended with his execution at Loosecoat field in front of the Lincolnshire rebels!

'Jack, I will have need of that swift horse of yours,' Hastings said as he drew alongside. 'It is not the role you had imagined for yourself I suppose, for the position of messenger is not often wreathed in glory, but quick messages win battles, Jack.'

'Yes, my lord,' Jack said impassively. He didn't really know if he was disappointed or not. Being on horseback made him an easy target for archers, but if he survived the deadly black rain he had a good chance of making it through the battle, and if all went wrong he at least had a means of escape. His mind slipped back to Warwick's death; what Warwick would have given in that moment for a swift courser, he thought and how Jack wished it could have been so.

* * *

Robert heard the Yorkists before he saw them. The intimidating tocsin of sword on buckler echoed along the valley just before they appeared like the hellequin on the ridge. Their helmets glittered like jewels in the early morning sunshine and the white boar of Gloucester pitched and danced above them in the light breeze. Even though he had already been shriven, Robert crossed himself. He found that his heart was a hot kick at his throat, found there was a void in his guts where his courage should have been and found that the grey ghosts of Barnet were on the periphery of his vision. 'Sweet Mother of God,' he whispered in a tight voice. How he wished he wasn't here, or if he had to be here, how he wished it was under Warwick's banner and that Will and Thomas were with him. But wishes were not horses; he was here and they were not.

Though Edward deployed his battles quickly it seemed to Robert that it took an age. All the while his heart thumped in the prison of his body and his guts twisted in knots from his groin to his throat. He tensed and relaxed his grip on his sword without realizing he was doing it and inside his gauntlets his hands were hot and sweating.

The Duke of Somerset rode in front of them, steadying the line; plainly he too felt the tension rippling along his ranks. Robert hoped it was only the tension of waiting.

Suddenly, there was a sickening boom like thunder and a stone ball landed just feet away, then another and another. Smoke billowed across the plain below them, showing the advanced position of Edward's artillery. Realizing what would come next, Robert slammed down the visor of his sallet quickly as the black storm of arrows too came at them. Some stricken men screamed and fell, sending a twitch along the line that sent Robert's heart fluttering. Was Somerset going to make them stand here and be shot at? Again the guns growled, each sending a pulse of fear into Robert's stomach that made him want to be sick. Again the line convulsed under the shock of the hit. Wounded men cried to the saints or their mothers. Blood and entrails slapped against their neighbours, miring their livery. Robert's feet twitched; he took an involuntary step forwards. He even contemplated facing the prickers; the men of his own side meant to stop desertions, anything rather than stand here and let Edward pick them off. Mutinous babble shot through the ranks; this was not what they were trained for, they were trained to fight.

Suddenly there was an answering bellow from a Lancastrian gun, and then another. Robert looked on helplessly as the shots fell feebly short of the Yorkist lines. He cursed Richard Beauchamp and the men of Gloucester town: he had taken their best guns.

Horses flashed past as messengers sped between Edouard of Lancaster and Somerset. Robert knew what the argument would be. Lancaster had the high ground, let Edward come and take them if he could. But how long could they stand there and face his guns, when they had no comparable retort?

Shot whistled again all around them and Robert felt the line shudder again as men were hit. Again they were showered with arrows and again Somerset sent a rider to Edouard. Men were shrieking in agony, screaming like animals at the Martinmas slaughter and Barnet's ghosts filled Robert's mind. Again he stepped forward and this time others were moving, just a few feet, just enough to let Somerset know they were not willing to stand and be butchered, not here, not like this.

* * *

Smoke drifted to him on the wind. Jack looked beyond it, to where the massed ranks of the Lancastrians were arrayed. He pitied them; he knew the carnage guns could cause, had seen how they could wreck a division; if not physically then how they crushed its morale. Gathered on the hillside they had no hope of avoiding the pounding of Edward's artillery and Jack winced as he saw their lines ripple, for he knew each shudder of men was a hit. As he stared across the battlefield at Somerset's restless vanguard he could not believe what was now happening. For a moment his jaw slackened; he thought they would have held out for longer than this. He pricked his spurs to his stallion. The wind was cold in his face and the acrid smoke stung his eyes as he galloped down towards Edward's lines. It took only a few moments to reach Edward's command post.

Jack skidded to a halt beside Edward.

Edward's eyes were bright and piercing beneath his sallet, keen for Jack's news.

'My liege. Somerset is coming!' Jack gasped as his courser danced beneath him. His heart thundered at his throat, like the hooves of Somerset's horses on the unforgiving ground. Clarence was standing beside Edward, but Jack ignored him.

'Are you sure, Jack?' Edward asked, raising a hand to his eyes and peering towards the Lancastrian lines.

The way up the hill to the Lancastrian position had seemed closed to them, barred by hedges, ditches and a winding lane. But Somerset must have used the time he had had for reconnaissance, as he seemed to know secret paths that now brought his men towards them at speed.

'Yes, my lord. You can't see him for the hedges and trees, but believe me, sire, he is coming and quickly.'

Edward held his gaze for a moment, and Jack wondered if he doubted his word. Then Edward shouted the orders that saw his men snap into a tight block of resistance.

Still Somerset was invisible to them on the plain, but Jack knew he could not be far away.

'Somerset, pah!' Clarence snorted. 'He would not dare!'

Edward looked at Jack again.

Jack held his breath. Through the hammering of his heart he could now hear the resolute drumming of hooves. Then Jack saw Edward's ranks stiffen as they saw the horses tearing towards them, closely followed by Somerset's men-at-arms.

Edward grinned briefly at Jack and then slammed down his visor, and with Clarence at his side he strode forward to meet them.

Jack thought he saw Somerset's plan: to silence Edward's guns. But if that was his intention he was way off target, probably thrown by the lie of the land, and within heartbeats he came crashing into Gloucester's and Edward's battles as they stood side by side. Jack checked his stallion and checked the urge in himself to ride into the mêlée. All he could do was sit and watch and wait for orders.

* * *

Robert's lungs were bursting in his chest. The entire division was a screaming mass of anger as it hurtled towards Edward's line. They had certainly achieved one objective, they had neutralized the Yorkist guns, for now they were within striking distance of Edward's men, and at last they could come to grips.

Metal punched metal and the sound sang in Robert's ears. The force of the impact slewed up his arms, jolting his muscles. Soon he knew no fear, knew no pain as he fought for his life; fought for Lancaster.

After the shock of the initial onslaught the Yorkists had begun to rally. Gloucester's men closed ranks with Edward's, uniting the vanguard with the mainward and Robert realized they were not making any further headway, worse than that, they were being pushed back. He could no longer see Somerset's banner, nor hear anything approaching a command; he was locked in his own grim personal struggle for survival, which he perceived like a nightmare through the slit of vision his sallet gave him.

Behind and to his right Robert heard the screaming of horses and suddenly men were crashing into him, being forced in towards the centre of the van. He couldn't tell what had happened, who these new horsemen were or where they had come from, but he was sure that Somerset had not known that Edward had set a mounted ambush. Robert's comrades no longer stood together shoulder to shoulder, no longer screamed the name of Lancaster as their battle cry, a few tried to make a stand, but in truth the line's discipline was gone: Somerset's vanguard was broken.

* * *

Jack rode quickly between the Yorkist divisions, sending messages of encouragement from Edward and firm instructions to keep the line as level as they could. Hastings did not need to be told his duty and his division held together well, just as at Barnet, as Devon's battle met them head on, thus ensuring that Edward could not be outflanked. Jack could see that the breaking of the Lancastrian van would be the end of it, and he wondered why the mainward had not supported Somerset's charge. Whatever the reason, he could now see that the Lancastrians were beginning to disintegrate. Some of Prince Edouard's mainward now pulsed into Edward's battle. But it was too late; Edward's men had found a perverse rhythm to their killing, and spurred on by battle-fever they pushed the Lancastrians back and then hurled after them like devils, when the Lancastrians began to run. Jack saw too that Edward was at the head of the pursuers; his visor was raised and he was screaming for Lancastrian blood.

* * *

Robert gripped his sword tightly. How he had managed to keep hold of it for so long he didn't really know, for like the rest of Somerset's men he was running. His lungs and throat burned like lime and his breathing came in ragged gasps which daggered pain through his chest. Recklessly he lifted the visor of his sallet, desperate for fresh air. Every heartbeat was a punch. Sweat stung his eyes. He plunged towards the ford, hoping that once across the river he would be able to make an escape into Wales.

A terrified shout went up from the men around him. Robert glanced over his shoulder to see the Yorkist prickers; ghastly silhouettes against the brightness of the day. His heart crashed to his stomach; he would never outrun them. Instead Robert

442

stopped suddenly, weaved and ducked as the first man passed him, his blow missing by a good hand's breadth. He parried the second man's attack but the strength of the blow made him stagger backwards, almost putting him on the floor. The momentum of the two men carried them past him and he saw them wade pitilessly into the fleeing Lancastrians. Robert knew he had no time to view the carnage, no time to think of anything other than flight; he rushed towards the ford. Here the ground was slippery, churned up by fleeing feet and the Yorkists' pursuing horses. He slithered down the bank, pushing and jostling until he met the steel-grey water. His legs were suddenly cold and he gasped with the shock of it, dropping his sword. His limbs were suddenly heavy and he struggled to find any momentum at all. Cold seeped into his bones as the river tried to claim him; as it had claimed so many others. The stench of the water made him wretch. With horror Robert saw men stepping on others, trying frantically to find a way across, and he realized that to fall was to succumb. With supreme effort he forced his awkward limbs to obey him and he waded further in. His heart pounded in his ears and throbbed at his temples. Each breath seemed to take the effort of his whole body. Then he was reaching out, his fingers grasping for the bank, which was now nothing more than a mudslide. His gauntlets found a hold and somehow he managed to haul himself out of the water. Then he heard the terrible cry: 'A York! A York!' and he knew more of the Yorkists had found them. Desperately Robert looked about him for a way to escape. He knew he could not outrun the mounted men and without a sword he could not stand and fight. He clawed and grappled his way through the press of men and then, following the most primitive of his instincts, he staggered away from the bloody river.

Once beyond the narrow ford, men broke in all directions, scattered like rabbits before huntsmen. Blindly Robert ran too. Then he heard the thud of hoof beats getting closer. He stopped. He turned, hoping to dodge the inevitable strike. But he was exhausted and his movements slow. The axe bit deep into his shoulder, sinking down into his ribs. For a few heartbeats Robert felt no pain. Then it hit him: blinding, seething pain through which no rational thought would come. He fell to his knees. The metallic taste of blood filled his mouth as it bubbled in his throat. White pinpoints of light swam in his red and spinning vision. He slumped onto his side, gasping like a fish stranded on the bank, as he had seen men do at Barnet. Each breath frothed at his lips and with every heartbeat his lifeblood ebbed away. Slowly, painfully his sight began to diminish, his senses dulled, until everything was completely black.

* * *

Jack watched numbly as they slung the body of Prince Edouard over the back of a horse. The flower of Lancaster was dead, and with Henry in Edward's custody so was their cause, he thought.

Hastings looked at him grimly, his lips pressed into a thin line. Gloucester too seemed to acknowledge the gravity of the moment. And as they stood in heavy silence each man looked within himself and fought back the dark clouds of remorse that often followed a battle.

Suddenly Jack saw a horseman thundering towards them.

Hastings too looked up.

They looked momentarily at each other, wondering what the new calamity could be.

The horseman skidded to a halt before Hastings, covering them all with dust.

'My lords! My lords!' he cried breathlessly, ''Tis the abbey! 'Tis the king!'

Hastings glanced quickly at Gloucester and they both called for their horses.

'No,' Hastings said sharply, pressing a hand to Gloucester's shoulder. 'Stay with Lancaster. I will go.'

Jack saw Gloucester move to protest, but the determined look in Hastings's eyes stopped him and with a sigh he acquiesced.

'Jack,' Hastings said turning quickly, 'see that the heralds carry out their duties unmolested.'

For the first time that day Jack heard a quiver in Hastings's voice and he knew that it was fear.

'I will, my lord,' he answered with a bow of his head.

Hastings mounted swiftly.

The messenger swung his horse round and then he and Hastings raced towards Tewkesbury Abbey as if they were being chased by the devil.

SIXTEEN

BARNET MAY 1471

The woollen doublet was far too big for him, yet Elizabeth seemed pleased with it and Thomas did not want to hurt her feelings by pointing out the large discrepancy between his chest and that of the garment. It had taken her most of the day to alter it for him. She smiled as she helped him fasten the points, but he noticed that the smile was as fragile as ice in spring.

'Thank you,' he murmured.

Elizabeth stopped abruptly and met his eyes. She paused for a long moment looking at him. Then her eyes filled with tears and she turned quickly away.

Thomas sighed. He thought he knew what she was thinking, though she would never give voice to it: she was wishing Warwick was here with her now instead of him.

'I'm sorry,' he said softly. He moved towards her tentatively, his legs just about strong enough to carry him that far.

Her back was towards him, her arms wrapped tightly about her body. 'It's not your fault,' she stammered. 'It just catches me off guard. I still cannot believe it.' A sob shook her shoulders as she fought for mastery over her grief.

Thomas wanted to reach out and touch her, pull her into his arms and make her feel safe, but his hand froze in mid air. How could he do such a thing? He had seen on that frosty night at The Erber how much she had loved Warwick. How could he ever hope to be anything in her eyes after that? He swallowed thickly, feeling guilty for living when great Warwick was dead.

'We must go home soon,' he said, mostly just for something to break the horrible silence.

'No!'

Elizabeth's sudden venom shocked him. Fierce eyes met his.

'I mean... you are not yet well enough...' she stammered and then looked away.

'What is it?' he asked, feeling completely useless. He knew she was right, but there was something more to her refusal.

She shook her head and Thomas's heart squeezed. She would not tell him, would not trust him with whatever it was that troubled her beyond Warwick's death. He clenched his jaw as he wondered if she would confide in Jack de Laverton instead. Part

445

of his mind still wondered what had passed between them in Bruges, when Jack had called himself her husband. He scolded himself inwardly; jealousy, he thought, was a terrible thing.

TEWKESBURY ABBEY MAY 1471

William Hastings tasted blood in his mouth; he had bitten his tongue. He wiped his hand across his face and saw the dark crimson stain on his pale skin. He swore under his breath as he staggered to the edge of the green on which rested the magnificent abbey of Tewkesbury. Every joint and muscle screamed in agony as he pushed his body to the limit of its endurance. But he knew he had to find Edward.

He stared up at the square tower of the abbey. The gothic points were silhouetted against the darkening sky like giant spears. The tall and pointed windows which had glittered so beautifully in the sunshine now stared down at him like malevolent eyes; eyes that were weeping.

When he reached the abbey walls, Edward was nowhere in sight. Hastings fell against the grey edifice. He used the chiselled stonework, guiding himself like a blind man. His fingers were aching and stiff around the hilt of his sword and he was certain he would not be able to loosen his grip. His sword arm could barely support the weapon anymore and he carried it at hip level; any higher and his muscles began to spasm.

His fingers found the voluptuous fluting of the doorway and even in his distress he was impressed by its grandeur. The sound of his own heavy breathing echoed back to him from the cold stone and for a moment it seemed as if it was a living thing in its own right.

Then he heard other sounds, further off, muffled sounds that chilled the marrow in his bones. He sucked cool air into his straining lungs, forcing life into his taut and scorching limbs, demanding one final effort from his battered body. With one large breath he forced himself fully upright and pushed his unwilling flesh inside the church.

The noises he had heard were louder now, but somehow they did not sound human. It seemed as if there was an unearthly choir at work. With his heart punching in his throat he looked about him. Even in the shadowy light of the church he saw the splendour of the black and white patterned floor tiles and the painted arches; they seemed to glow in the gloom, illuminating the path to God and hopefully to Edward.

Then he saw something he had seen too much of already today, there was a thick trail of blood leading into the heart of the Abbey, to the place where he knew Edward must be. God's breath, was the king wounded?

He pushed on. He could hear the clamour of voices clearly now, they echoed in the high space above him, up beyond the candlelight. The sound of them made him shiver.

As he turned into the nave he stopped and what he saw ahead of him made him want to fall on his knees and pray, but that he knew would not help the victims.

'Ned!' he called as loudly as his seething lungs would allow him to. 'Ned, for God's sake!' Sweet Jesu, he had to stop him!

'Ned! My liege!' he called again, but his voice seemed to dissipate in the airy space so that it was no louder than the voice of a child. He staggered on; his spurs rang with alarm on the floor.

He could see Edward clearly now. He was at the front of a crowd of clamouring Yorkists, sword unsheathed, the silver blade glinting like a strip of moonlight in his hand; except the blade was no longer completely silver. A dark stain clung to the edge and point and Hastings realized with horror that Edward had drawn blood in this sacred place!

In front of Edward he saw the Abbott. He was holding a large crucifix before him. He held it up towards Edward's face, but Edward seemed blind to it as he railed at the prelate. Behind the Abbot were a dozen or so knights and some other ranks. Some were clearly wounded; others were as wide-eyed as children, plainly unable to believe what they had just witnessed. All of them shared one look; the hollow-eyed look of despair.

Hastings could see their weapons lay beneath the altar; they had trusted in the ancient right of sanctuary, believed that no man would flout the sacred law. But they had misjudged Edward's mood to their cost.

Hastings forced himself closer. Another shape loomed out of the darkness; a body was slumped at Edward's feet. Hastings sucked in his breath sharply as he saw a pool of dark liquid spreading across the beautiful tiles and realized that Edward had killed a man.

'Ned, no!' Hastings bellowed as he saw his king begin to move.

Edward, still raving with battle-fever, raised his sword again, as if to strike the Abbott from his path.

Hastings looked up to heaven. 'Please sweet Mother of God, help me!' he whispered. Then he took a deep breath that seemed to scorch his lungs. 'No!' he roared with unnatural strength and Edward stopped. His sword arm froze in mid-swing, and as Hastings reached him he sank to his knees, muscles trembling, and the blood-wet sword fell to the floor with a ring as resounding as the great bell.

The Abbott too fell to his knees in thanks.

Hastings moved to kneel by Edward's side. 'Ned,' he said softly. 'Ned 'tis over.'

Edward turned slowly. His eyes were glassy with tears of remorse.

There was a loud susurration as the Lancastrian knights joined the Abbott in prayer. All that is, except one. He leaned against a large tomb of marble and alabaster, his face a mask, every trace of emotion drained from him. He had been facing certain death from the raging king, a death for which he had plainly prepared himself, and it had not come. He stood in disbelief; a hand pressed to his forehead, unable to comprehend that he yet still lived.

'Come away, Ned,' Hastings said gently. He knew now was not the time for admonishing his king. The regret, the guilt, the sadness, that would all come later when the fever of battle had died. 'You have won, Ned. It is finished.'

Wide eyes drilled into Hastings from the shadows. He recognized several of the knights' shattered faces: the Duke of Somerset, Sir Gervais of Clifton, and the Lord of Saint John's. God's blood, would Ned have killed them all?

The Abbott was staring at Edward now and Hastings was only just beginning to comprehend what he had said. He looked at Edward who was nodding his agreement. 'Yes, I swear it,' he said and crossed himself.

But could Edward do what the Abbott demanded? Could he really pardon them all?

BARNET MAY 1471

Elizabeth watched as Thomas walked on ahead of her. As he began to grow in strength, she needed to help him less and less.

When the spring sunshine was warm enough, as today, she took him outside, walking with him to the edge of the town. They always headed southwards, for she did not want to relive her unhappy journey from the battlefield and it seemed that Thomas was simply glad to be in her company.

As they returned from their walk they heard of the disaster at Tewkesbury from the landlord.

Elizabeth saw Thomas's cheeks flush pink with anger and he only just managed to contain his words long enough for them to reach their chamber. 'What was Somerset thinking?' Thomas asked in disbelief. 'He should have stayed put; they should never have lost that battle!'

'Sshh!' Elizabeth said quickly. 'Everyone will be Yorkist now, Thomas,' she said. 'Speaking for Lancaster is a very dangerous thing to do!'

Thomas's anxious eyes met hers as they both thought of Robert.

Elizabeth sighed. 'That is now two battles that Edward was lucky to win!' she muttered. Grief began to tighten her chest; why had God favoured Edward and not Warwick? Oh, sweet Warwick! Tears burned her eyes.

Thomas drew closer to her. 'I am sorry, Elizabeth, I know your heart must be breaking...'

She cut him off. How could he know how she felt! 'You know nothing of it, Thomas!' she said angrily. 'He was trodden down in the mud and I never saw him, Thomas, I never had the chance to say...' She strangled the words in her throat. Only Jack knew her terrible secret, only Jack could possibly understand.

She swung away from Thomas and walked towards the window. She stared out at the meaningless sunshine dappling the dusty street and caught the incongruously cheerful song of a thrush in full voice; how could the world not know what had happened? She wiped her hand over her stinging eyes to stop the tears; suddenly it was important to know where Jack de Laverton was.

TEWKESBURY MAY 1471

William Hastings shivered. Today had been such a mêlée of emotions; he had been bursting with pride at Edward's knighting of his brothers Ralph and Richard for their part in the victory, along with others of their cause, then he had been struck cold

449

with horror, as Edward had ordered the taking from sanctuary of the fugitive Lancastrians.

They had trusted Edward's pardon. They could have fled under cover of darkness to save their lives, but they had believed what Edward had said to the Abbott in the aftermath of the battle and they had stayed.

'You will give them a trial, Ned?' Hastings forced the words through a dry throat.

Edward's eyes were like glass. 'A trial, Will? What need have they of a trial? They were caught in arms against me; there is no need of a trial.'

Hastings breathed deeply. 'Ned,' he said warningly, 'there is every need of a trial. I know Tewkesbury did not have a franchise as a sanctuary, but what happened there...' he paused, watching Edward's face, 'surely what happened there makes a trial necessary?'

Edward smiled a mirthless smile. 'Say what you mean, Will,' he said sullenly. 'That in battle fever we killed some of them!'

Hastings looked down. 'Yes, Ned. And on holy ground.'

He heard Edward suck in a sharp breath through his teeth.

But that wasn't what was worrying him. 'You also pardoned them,' he said softly. He looked up at Edward. His eyes were an icy flame.

'I meant only the soldiers, Will. Christ on the cross, did you think I could ever pardon Somerset?'

'I was not sure what you meant, Ned and neither will others be,' Hastings said hesitantly. 'Any man accused of treason must have a trial.'

Edward sighed. 'Even a man with a sword at my throat, Will?'

Hastings could see he was winning the argument so he pressed him further. 'Gloucester is Constable of England, Norfolk is Earl Marshal and they are both willing. There is no reason not to have a trial.'

Edward raised an eyebrow questioningly and then nodded slowly. 'I take your point Will,' he sighed. 'Men will say I forgave them and then reneged on the promise.'

Hastings nodded; men would remember Lord Welles and Lose-coat Field too, he thought. He saw Edward weaken and felt relief.

'Very well,' Edward said. 'Arrange it. But I tell you this, Will. I am not the king I was. The lessons I have learned here will not go unused. Anyone who crosses me will feel the bite of my sword.'

Hastings saw that something in Edward had changed. He had seemed somehow different ever since he had left him alone with Warwick's body in St Paul's and he wondered what ghosts Edward had seen there and what it meant for the future of England.

BARNET MAY 1471

Jack chewed on his thumb as he leaned against the wall. From the shadows he could see the light at the window of 'The Green Man'. A brief talk with the landlord had confirmed that Thomas was recovering and that Elizabeth was still with him, but he had resisted the urge to go straight up to see them, for he was the bearer of more bad news. And yet he did not have much time. Even now his horse was being fed and watered so that once he had delivered his message here he could ride on to deliver a more important one; one that might well cause Edward Plantagenet a few sleepless nights.

As the shadows lengthened Jack realized he had no choice, he had to tell them what he knew.

Jack encountered Thomas in the doorway. With one hand on the latch Thomas met his gaze with narrowed eyes.

Jack nodded to him and Thomas stepped back to allow him into the room.

Elizabeth was sitting by the window. She gave Thomas a quick glance as he closed the door and then her gaze met Jack's. He saw tears glitter at the corners of her eyes and within a few heartbeats she was in his arms. Puzzled yet delighted by her reaction he wrapped his arms about her and held her tightly to his chest.

'Jack, thank Christ you're safe,' she whispered against his neck as she clung to him.

'Sweetheart,' he murmured as the warmth of her body caressed him and he took in her familiar scent. Suddenly a tide of grief rose inside him and the guilty blessed relief of being alive almost overwhelmed him. Breathing deeply he tried to push the thoughts out of his mind, for he knew that survivors always carried this sort of guilt with them for living, and he knew he must not give in to it, in spite of the reason for his errand.

He heard Thomas's feet shuffle on the floor behind them.

Elizabeth gradually released her grip on his neck and drew back from him. Her cheeks were flushed and by the fluttering of her lashes he knew she was now feeling more than a little embarrassed by her show of emotion.

'Elizabeth. Thomas,' he said seriously, turning to acknowledge Thomas's presence.

He saw Elizabeth and Thomas exchange looks, knew they were expecting the worst.

'Jack please sit,' Elizabeth said, 'will you not take some wine?'

Jack shook his head. 'Regrettably I cannot. I am on my way to the king. I cannot stay longer than is necessary.' How could he say this when Elizabeth was so close and he wanted her so much?

'Necessary?' Thomas asked gruffly.

Jack ignored the intimation but noted the angry flash of Thomas's eyes and he presumed that was because of the warmth of Elizabeth's welcome for him. 'Yes, necessary, for I bring you grave news,' he said evenly. He paused, allowing the silence to prepare the way for his words. 'Robert de Assheton fell at Tewkesbury,' he said sadly.

The silence smothered the room like fog and for several achingly long heartbeats it seemed as though no one even breathed.

'How do *you* know?' Thomas snapped. 'Did you kill him?'

'Thomas!' Elizabeth rebuked him quickly.

'It's all right, sweetheart,' Jack said evenly. 'I expected as much. No, Thomas,' he said, meeting Thomas's angry eyes fully, 'I did not kill him. I did not fight, but I was with the heralds as they went about the fields.' He didn't add any more; they didn't need to hear what he had seen; he let the words sink in. He turned back to Elizabeth. Her eyes were silvered with tears.

'Poor Robert,' she said.

Jack nodded. 'Aye. He had no chance,' he said softly.

Thomas paced to the window and stared out into the gathering dusk. 'Poor Martha,' he whispered.

Elizabeth turned towards Jack and he wanted to hold her again, wanted to smother the pain he had brought her, but he knew he couldn't.

'I must go,' he said. 'Already I have stayed too long.'

'No!' Elizabeth said.

Jack met her eyes. God's blood – did she really want him to stay? He knew that whatever she said, he had to go. 'I must, sweetheart. I ride to the king.' He didn't try to keep the regret from his voice. 'Fauconberg is about to fall upon London with the men of Kent. The king must know of it.' He wanted to stay and comfort her but he knew he would have to leave that task to Thomas; the same Thomas who was glaring at him from the darkness.

Elizabeth moved closer. Her breath touched his cheek. 'Then I will see you out,' she said quietly.

Jack nodded his agreement. He wanted to tell her how he felt about her, not that she did not know already!

Thomas said nothing as he left but the hate in his eyes burned even brighter.

* * *

Elizabeth followed Jack down the stairs. What did she want from him? She hardly knew.

Jack's eyes caught the dancing flames of candle and firelight as he turned to meet her look. 'Sweetheart,' he breathed, 'it has been too long.' A smile flickered on his lips that made Elizabeth catch her breath. Her voice stayed in the dryness of her throat. She nodded hesitantly. It seemed the greatest understatement, she thought. Her world had changed from light to darkness; the brightness of Warwick's sun had been eclipsed forever and where her heart had once been, she was empty and hollow like a tree after being struck by summer lightning. But somehow, the rich melancholy of Jack's voice reached that empty place inside her and touched it.

'Jack,' she began, but her words were strangled by her rising grief. It tightened her throat and chest like the cold of a winter's night. White stars of light swirled in her vision.

Jack moved as lithely as a cat and reached her just before the tears came.

She leaned against him and the relief of feeling his arms about her was a pleasure she had only dreamed of. Instantly she was transported in her mind back to Bruges, to the illicit time they had spent together and suddenly she understood what had happened there.

'They have taken Warwick to Bisham Abbey,' she whispered into Jack's warm shoulder, trying to keep a grip on reality.

'I know, sweetheart...I saw him.' Jack's voice was a hoarse whisper against her cheek. 'I'm sorry.'

453

'You saw?' Elizabeth looked at him disbelievingly. 'At St Paul's?'

Jack nodded. Sorrow clouded his eyes like mist over a dark lake. 'I was with Lord Hastings...' he began. Grief choked him and he looked away.

Elizabeth gasped. She pulled back from him, but Jack's fingers laced together behind her back.

'You mustn't think I betrayed him,' Jack said huskily, turning to face her. 'My fealty remained, I swear it. Warwick was my cause not Lancaster!' His eyes darted for hers, plainly looking for a sign that she believed him.

A lump formed in Elizabeth's throat.

The fire crackled in the grate. Smoke stung at her eyes.

'Unlike me then Jack,' she said sadly. 'I betrayed him.'

Jack let out a slow breath and then laughed softly. It was like water caressing pebbles in a stream and in spite of herself a smile twitched her lips.

'You are too hard on yourself,' Jack said gently.

'But Clarence did betray him,' she insisted. 'He left him as he promised me he would! If I had not taken that letter...'

Jack shook his head. 'He would have done it anyway, sweetheart. His mother and his sisters also bombarded him with tokens and letters. Gloucester too. Your visit was only part of it.'

Elizabeth looked down ashamedly. She could not face the sympathy in Jack's eyes or the tenderness in his voice. 'But I spoke with him, Jack. He told me he would come to Edward! That must have played a bigger part?'

'You are wrong, sweetheart. Clarence was motivated by land, money and power, nothing else.' Jack tightened his arms, pulling her closer.

Elizabeth closed her eyes and drank him in, overwhelmed by the comfort he offered her. She relaxed in his arms, as though he was a sanctuary as safe as Ellerton.

'Forgive yourself Elizabeth, as Warwick would have done,' Jack said.

Elizabeth wondered how he could be so certain, when she had such doubts. Perhaps her transgression seemed nothing to him, but to her it was everything. And there was something else. Something she knew she could not deal with alone.

'There is yet this,' she stammered. Twisting in Jack's arms she pulled Edward's letter from her gown.

Jack's eyes widened. 'You have not opened it?'

She shook her head. 'What if it was a pardon, Jack? A pardon he would have taken. One which would have saved his life!' Her voice cracked.

Jack smiled softly and reached out a hand to caress her cheek. 'You had no choice, I think,' he said quietly.

'Oh, but I did, Jack! And I chose not to give him that chance. Not only did I betray him, I withheld this to conceal my own shame!' The words came out as a sob and tears blotted on her lashes. 'I could have saved him, Jack but I did not!'

Jack pulled her back to him. 'No sweetheart, he chose his own path. He would not have taken a pardon then, just as he did not at Coventry when Clarence brought the king's words. It is done. It is past regret.'

'I regret it daily,' she sobbed. 'How could I have done such a thing?'

Jack smoothed her hair from her face. Then deftly he slipped the parchment from her fingers. 'You must let it go,' he said.

Elizabeth stared into his face, wondering what he would do. She heard the thumping of her heart and the snapping of the fire in the grate.

Then Jack moved and before Elizabeth could even think what might happen, he had done it.

For a heartbeat the parchment flared white in the flames before succumbing to the heat.

Elizabeth let out a scream which Jack pulled into his shoulder and she let the soft wool of his cloak smother her torment.

Jack held her tightly. 'It is done,' he breathed. 'It is over.'

Elizabeth could not believe that it was. The letter was gone but her guilt was not.

After a long and comforting silence she noticed Jack's sudden restlessness. Selfishly she had kept him; had he not said he could stay no longer than was necessary? Yet for those few moments it was as if they were back in Bruges.

'What now, Jack?' she asked him in a taut voice that did not sound like her own.

'Now I ride to the king,' Jack said quietly as he stepped back from her.

She heard the regret in his voice. 'Take care then,' she said even though the last thing she wanted now was for him to leave her; yet it would be so unfair to ask for his help when what she had decided was so contrary to his wishes.

'Elizabeth,' he said. He reached out and touched her cheek gently as though he too was recalling their previous intimacy. 'You know what I would wish and you have made plain your answer.'

She looked down from his gaze for a moment. She swallowed guiltily; she had still not told him it was also her parents' wish for them to be together. This was like an unfinished tapestry with threads already woven and tied and others hanging loose and unfastened. Yet all must be stitched in eventually, including the one thing Jack did not know about her. She wondered if it would help him understand.

'I must go to him Jack,' she said softly, 'and then I must go to my son.'

Jack's eyes widened.

'They buried my son at Ellerton,' she said, barely maintaining her composure.

'Warwick's child?' Jack dragged the words from his throat. 'I never knew,' he stammered. Jack's eyes searched her face for answers. In all the time she had known him, from their first meeting at Lazenby, to answering their door to spies in Bruges, she had never seen him look so undone. 'Did Warwick know?' he asked after a long moment.

Elizabeth nodded. Her throat tightened as she remembered Warwick's pain. 'It was Higgins's revenge to tell him,' she said shakily.

Jack's eyes narrowed to flame at the mention of Higgins's name. 'If he ever crosses my path, I swear by the Rood I will kill him!'

This was the man Elizabeth recognized and she didn't doubt Jack's sentiment, but was it possible that Higgins would return? If he did, she knew that this time she would not save him.

They both considered the possibility in silence. They stayed as they were as if by alchemy. Eventually Jack moved, forcing them back to the dreadful reality of their current position. 'I'm, sorry, sweetheart, but I must go,' he said.

Elizabeth followed him, as close as she could be to him without actually touching him.

He stopped and turned; hesitated.

She slid her gaze up to his. Part of her wanted to stop him leaving, wanted him near. But she had no right to ask him, for she knew she could not fulfil her father's promise, knew she would break his heart.

456

'Adieu, sweetheart,' he whispered, his words a caress on her cheek.

'I meant what I said, Jack,' she said softly, 'take care.'

'I always do,' he said with a wry smile. '*Pensez de moi*,' he whispered against her ear. Then he turned in a cloud of black cloak and in three strides was at the door. He hung on the latch briefly as he let in the cooling air, just long enough to give her his crooked smile. Then he pulled the door between them and was gone.

Elizabeth's eyes burned with fresh tears. 'Santa Maria please protect him,' she whispered. She wondered if he had really understood what she had told him; what her course must be.

When the sound of Jack's horse died away into the distance, Elizabeth moved towards the stairs. As she put her foot on the first step she halted. A shiver scratched along her spine, as though she was being watched. She looked round but saw only the landlord, busy with a barrel. Yet the feeling was unmistakeable.

When she entered the upstairs chamber Thomas was at the window. He did not turn as she closed the door.

She moved to his side.

Outside the sky was turning to deep blood red as the sun sank below the horizon and a chill breeze ruffled Thomas's hair at his collar.

She touched his arm gently.

He shrank away from her as if she had touched him with ice.

'Thomas?' she asked.

'You said I had no idea how you felt,' he snapped. 'Do you think I do now?' Tears welled at the corners of his eyes.

'I only meant...'

'I know,' he said, his voice softening. 'Sweet Jesu, I know!'

Elizabeth pressed against him and he turned and she knew he was using all his strength not to break down and cry.

The sky darkened and stars appeared like tiny diamonds above them.

'It's so unfair isn't it?' he asked her at last.

Elizabeth nodded. ''Tis God's will, Thomas,' she said evenly, 'and we cannot understand it.'

'Rob will never see his child,' he said thickly. 'Martha will have to raise him by herself.'

'I know,' Elizabeth said sadly. By the Virgin, she knew about loss only too well!

'I must go to her,' Thomas said suddenly. 'Tomorrow.'

'Tomorrow?' Elizabeth echoed, as though it was a word she had not heard before.

'Yes,' Thomas said. 'I must.'

She knew he was right, knew that Martha had to know about Robert's death, but why so soon? Was it because of Jack?

She met his teary eyes. 'Of course,' she said.

Thomas held her look and suddenly she knew that he loved her. 'Oh, Thomas,' she whispered.

He shook his head. 'It was never meant to be,' he said huskily. His throat worked as he fought for control. 'Will Kennerley told me that, and he was right. He said you were promised to Jack...'

The air rushed from Elizabeth's lungs as if she had been punched. She had never realized Thomas had harboured such hopes, he had always been her friend...

'Do you love him?' Thomas asked.

Elizabeth closed her eyes. Tears squeezed through her lashes.

'Do you love Jack de Laverton?' he pushed.

'I loved Warwick,' she said softly, knowing that she had not really answered him. Part of her wanted to try and explain, but she knew she couldn't.

'Ah,' Thomas said with forced understanding. He moved away from her and began to look for his things for the morning.

Elizabeth watched him sadly. She wanted to lessen his pain, but knew she would only make things worse. Her stomach knotted itself; she seemed to hurt everyone she cared for! She took a steadying breath: she had made the right decision for her future.

TEWKESBURY MAY 1471

It seemed as though the Duke of Somerset's head had scarcely been struck off and his body sent away for burial when the messengers came.

Hastings waited, scarcely breathing.

Edward ran his fingers through his hair and then turned tired eyes towards him. 'The North *and* London, Will?'

'Yes, Your Grace.'

Edward sighed. 'Will it never be finished?' he asked wearily. 'And what do you suggest this time, Will? Do I go to London, or do I go north?'

Hastings looked at his shoes for a moment; he understood the jibe.

'Ah Will, I am sorry,' Edward said. 'God knows you have always given me honest words and I need them now as much as ever.'

Hastings looked back at him. 'Go north.'

Edward smiled ironically. 'And leave Rivers to guard London against Fauconberg's Bastard?'

Much as he disliked Anthony Wydeville, Hastings knew he would not panic at Fauconberg's attack. 'The Earls of Essex and Arundel are with him,' he said stiffly. 'And with the aldermen's help, London will hold.'

Edward laughed dryly. 'God's blood, Will!' he spluttered. 'That hurt your throat to say!'

Hastings tried to stop a smile from coming, but he failed. He made a disapproving sound in his throat. 'From what Jack said he has a goodly number, but they are not well trained, whereas the northerners have many knights among their company.'

'Tomorrow we head north then,' Edward said emphatically. 'Send Jack to Anthony to tell him of our decision and pray God our brother-in-law can stand firm.'

'I will Your Grace,' Hastings said. He bowed as he left Edward's presence.

'And let us hope that Fauconberg is the last Neville that will rise against me, Will, for by the Rood I tell you, I have had enough!' Edward called after him.

On his way out of the chamber a hurrying servant almost knocked into him. Hastings wondered what the urgency could be. He hesitated at the threshold.

'Your Grace, another messenger waits without,' the servant announced with an eccentric bow. 'He comes from Bruges.'

LONDON MAY 1471

'The Blue Boar' was as busy as ever, Thomas thought as he pushed his way through jostling revellers celebrating Edward's victory at Tewkesbury. Though many here thought Edward was a usurper, he owed so much money in London they were glad of his restoration as it meant his debts would be honoured, and that could only be good for London.

Oblivious of the threat of the Bastard of Fauconberg's ships in the Thames, the fiddler was in his customary corner. The music thrummed in Thomas's ears and he thought how out of place he was in this happy atmosphere. He scanned the beer-scented smoke for Martha, but it was Lucy's bright blue eyes that found him first.

He felt guilty at the smile he elicited from her and knew she would think he had come under a different banner.

'Thomas!' she called excitedly.

Before he could say or do anything she flung her arms about his neck and her warm lips met his.

Without thought he embraced her and as she pressed against his belly he felt a surge of guilt-ridden lust. Yes, he wished it was Elizabeth in his arms but it felt so good to be held and he responded to her kisses. He knew it was wrong, but knew too that he could not help himself and for tonight at least he would not be alone.

Eventually Lucy drew her mouth away and he met her sparkling eyes with a sad and guilty smile. He stroked her cheek gently with the back of his hand. Then he pulled his eyes away from hers. There was no easy way to tell her what he must.

'Where's Martha?' he asked gently, knowing there was no easy way to break this news.

'Martha?' Lucy asked and then gasped. 'Sweet Mother of God,' she said. 'Robert!'

TEWKESBURY MAY 1471

Higgins bowed low as William Hastings passed him. For a moment he was tempted to call to him, to tell him what he knew of his loyal servant Jack de Laverton. But something stopped him and Higgins knew what it was; it was his dark desire for revenge. For how much sweeter it would be for the King of England to know the truth and sweep Jack from existence as a man would swat a fly. And if Hastings knew of it first there was always the danger that he would perhaps intercede for Jack; would somehow see Jack's current service as payment for his Warwick debts. And Higgins knew that the king would harbour no such sentiments; he knew and understood the dark urge for revenge and would assuage it. His treatment of the late Lancastrians at Tewkesbury showed that.

Higgins bowed himself into Edward's presence, conscious of the mud still clinging to his boots and cloak. It was some months since he had seen his king and there was a hard symmetry to Edward's features that Higgins hadn't seen before. Edward sat with his head cocked to one side, his eyes staring as if at things unseen while he listened to Higgins's story of how Jack had abducted Elizabeth from him and had tried to kill him. He neglected to say that it was he who had struck out at Jack in the darkness of Bruges or that it was he who had arranged for Jack's visit to the Burgundian dungeons; Edward didn't need the details. When he had finished Edward nodded.

'I doubt not what you say Master Higgins,' Edward said evenly. 'But I am afraid you are too late.'

Pain seized Higgins's chest suddenly. 'Too late, Your Grace?' he asked.

'Aye, Higgins. I have already pardoned both Jack and Elizabeth,' Edward said slowly. Which was just as well, because Higgins was having difficulty in absorbing what he had said.

'Jack? Pardoned?' he stammered. The pain was like an iron band tightening around his neck, cutting into him, daggering into his chest.

Edward nodded. 'And we were grateful for his service, Higgins, of that be in no doubt.'

'But my liege...' The change in Edward's countenance silenced him.

'And your service too has not gone unnoticed. You both shall be rewarded, as shall Mistress Hardacre.'

Higgins nodded dumbly, not wishing to agree with what was taking place: Jack was in Edward's favour! This was not how he had planned things to be! 'As you wish, my liege,' he said mechanically.

'Even now Jack rides to London for us,' Edward continued, 'for yet there is Fauconberg's bastard to deal with!' Edward sighed wearily. 'And I cannot be seen to renege on a pardon, Higgins, especially one so well earned.'

Higgins stifled the choking splutter in his throat as he recalled the pardon given to Lord Welles before he died in front of the Lincolnshire rebels by the sword and the pardons Edward had

461

given so recently to the Lancastrians now removed from their hope of sanctuary in Tewkesbury Abbey and executed. What would the pardon of Jack de Laverton matter against these transgressions? But Edward's face was serious; he had pardoned Jack and Higgins could see there was no going back on it.

The pain still sank its teeth into Higgins's neck. Sweat began to form on his brow and trickled down his face. He could not speak, not even to ask for wine.

Edward noticed his discomfort and signalled for drink to be brought. Higgins knew no drink would cure him of this affliction. He threw the wine into his throat at Edward's command and for a few heartbeats the pain eased; but Higgins knew this agony would not leave him until either he or Jack de Laverton were dead.

BISHAM ABBEY MAY 1471

Sunlight dappled the road. The sky was the faultless blue of cornflowers with only a wisp of feathery white cloud here and there to mar its perfection. Elizabeth rode steadily, almost oblivious to the wonderful weather. Though the journey from Barnet was only some forty miles she had not enjoyed travelling alone, for it reminded her of her encounter with Gervase and rekindled unwelcome thoughts of her imprisonment at Ellerton Nunnery at the hands of the Countess of Warwick. She had been more than wary at her overnight stop, but the inn had been used to travellers and with enough money to ensure a privy room though people had watched her, she had not felt any malice, but she had slept with her knife under her pillow just in case.

Bisham Abbey was as handsome a place as she had seen. The white stone was almost silver in the sunshine and the large pointed windows glittered like diamonds. She raised her hand to stop the glare.

Once inside the quadrangle she noticed the entrance to the church itself. Large honey coloured oak doors beckoned her above sweeping steps. Her heart met her throat. Somehow she could not believe she was finally here.

She dismounted and a boy led her horse away with an inquisitive look. Some of the lay brothers stopped momentarily and then with a shrug returned to their chores.

She saw none of the brethren, and thought it unusual that no one had tried to stop her entering; it was certainly nothing like Jervaulx!

She walked slowly towards the steps. Lifting her gown slightly to avoid stepping on it, she did not see the figure approaching her until it was too late. First she saw his feet and then let her eyes wander up his fine legs in disbelief. Her stomach curled as she saw the finely embroidered black velvet of his doublet. Hardly daring to breathe she raised her eyes to his face.

'Sweetheart,' Jack said with a soft smile.

Elizabeth gasped and brought a hand up to cover her mouth. When he had ridden off to join Edward that evening in Barnet she wondered if she would ever see him again, wondered if he had understood, but she should have known better; Jack had been listening to what she said about seeking Warwick's forgiveness. Her eyes began to sting and she fought not to let him see how happy she was that he was here, for she knew it would only make her task harder.

'What brings you to Bisham, Jack?' she asked when she could finally breathe enough to speak.

'You,' he said smoothly.

Her cheeks coloured.

'And I come to pay my respects to my lord.'

Elizabeth watched the ripple of his throat as he spoke.

'Shall we go in?' Jack asked gently.

Elizabeth shook her head. 'No Jack, I need to see him alone,' she said. 'But afterwards...perhaps we could...talk.' She recalled how close they had been at Bruges and how their talks had nearly always ended in dispute.

Jack's familiar smile curved his mouth and he nodded his understanding. 'Of course,' he said.

Elizabeth smiled shyly. What on earth would she say to him? Her mind was such a mêlée of emotions she no longer knew how she felt about him, about Warwick, about anything. And how could she explain the decision she had made? Jack would perhaps never understand that.

The great stone steps of the abbey rose before them like a mountain range, a bridge between this world and the next. They began to climb. Elizabeth gripped Jack's arm tightly.

He smiled softly at her and patted her hand. She noticed his eyes fall to his ring still adorning her finger.

Grateful for his support, Elizabeth pressed her lips together determinedly.

As they reached the top of the stairs a monk stood waiting for them, dwarfed by the size of the abbey's great doors. He moved forward as if to question them, but upon seeing Elizabeth's face he stopped.

'Ah, it is you,' he said. 'You have come.' He bowed low and backed away from them, clearing their path.

Elizabeth gave Jack a quizzical look as she passed the monk. 'Why would he say that?' she asked.

'I do not know, sweetheart,' Jack answered with a shrug of his lean shoulders.

Elizabeth stared blankly ahead into the darkness of the great church, summoning her strength. She stopped. 'Please wait here Jack,' she said softly. 'I must do this alone.'

For once Jack did not question her.

Elizabeth moved inside slowly. Her breath was tight in her throat. She froze in the milky light, absorbing the church's tranquil atmosphere. Peace, she thought, that was what she craved also. Gilded painted columns spiralled up towards the sky, and they seemed to hold heaven above the earth. Each capital bore the devices of Warwick's ancestors and their pennants were mounted from the walls, hanging limply with grief. She shivered as she thought how they were once bright blazons of glory; flags for which men had fought and died, but now were just tattered wisps of faded history. The cloying scents of incense and rosemary hung in the cold air like mist and an indefinable musty smell sent a shudder down her spine, for it reminded her of her mother's funeral.

Elizabeth genuflected at the altar and, knowing this was the right moment to do so, made her vow. Then she turned towards the magnificent monuments ranging before her. Tentatively she walked towards them, surveying each one in turn. William, Thomas and John Montacute were the first she saw, carved in faultless stone. Then there was Warwick's father Richard and Warwick's brother Thomas, both murdered by the Lancastrians at Wakefield. Then her heart jumped as she recognised John Neville's banner. Fear clawed at her throat; the sight of John's tomb made the truth so very real. She remembered her conversation with him at Coventry, when he had told her to go home and wait for Jack. She remembered the passion in his voice. Now

464

there was only silence. She read the golden chiselled words that edged his obsidian plinth. 'As I am now, so shall ye be and thou knowest not the day or the hour'. She paused and tried to catch her breath. Warwick had known the hour, she thought. She began to tremble, yet she knew she must go on. While he lived she had tried to so many times tell him what she had done and each time something had prevented her from doing so. But she knew that this time she must not fail; this was the first step towards her future.

She moved further along, her footsteps a hushed whisper on the coloured floor tiles; her pulse drumming in her ears. Then she stopped dead. She steadied herself against the tomb with her hand; it was cold to her touch. Her head swam, overwhelmed by the intoxicating incense and the sight of the sepulchre before her, for here lay Warwick.

The velvet pall was drawn back for her. Warwick's effigy was fully armoured, his hands held up to his chest in prayer. She smiled irreverently as she thought on their illicit meetings in the chapels at Warwick and Calais and thought that she would not have laid him thus. Coloured light dappled the stone like rose petals and gilded angels kept diligent vigil above him. His head was cradled on a pillow of gold. Beautifully twisted gothic arches rose up from his jewelled bed in an ornate spire, stretching towards heaven itself and Elizabeth let her stinging eyes follow their glittering perfection before drawing them back to Warwick. For a moment Elizabeth held her breath; the painted alabaster effigy was so lifelike that it seemed as though he was breathing. Her pulse began to thump again at her throat. She clutched his praying hands in hers and kissed them, willing them to move. They did not. She touched his face gently and bent to kiss his lips, dripping warm tears onto his cold cheek as she did so.

'Richard,' she whispered, 'can you forgive me?'

There was no answer, save for the incomprehensible whistle of cold air in the nave and the flickering of the mourning candles. She pressed her cheek to his, desperate to feel the warmth of life instead of the heartless stone. She stayed with her face against his, sobbing quietly. Her chest tore with pain; her throat was a tight burn. She closed her eyes and breathed deeply, trying to remember him as he had been, more alive than other men; somehow more than could have been bounded by flesh and bone alone. Suddenly his familiar scent was all around her; she could

465

hear his smooth voice comforting her and she felt again his strong arms pulling her close against his deep chest. 'Richard,' she murmured and knew that he had heard her. For a lingering moment it was as if he lived again and he answered her.

A warm glow touched her core.

Her heart slowed to an evanescent murmur and she felt his hand stroke her head gently. Time hung like a gossamer veil and Elizabeth knew that it was all that separated them. She wanted the moment to last, wanted to stay with him forever, but she heard a cough from one of the monks and suddenly the spell was broken and she knew she would have to leave.

She heard footsteps on the stone.

Reluctantly, and with tears still heavy on her lashes, she rose. She stretched out her trembling hand so that she did not have to cease touching him until the very last moment. Then she turned and looked down at the gilded weepers carved beneath him. She recognized their grief-stricken faces: the countess and his daughters, Isabel and Anne. His father was there, his mother and his brothers, identifiable not only by their flawless likenesses but by their banners carved at their feet. But here, nearest to his noble heart, there was another figure, brighter than the rest, as though carved more recently. It had no banner. Her curiosity aroused, she knelt to examine it more closely. As she looked into its face she thrust a hand to her mouth to stop herself from calling out, for it was as if she looked into a mirror; it was her likeness. She fought back more tears as she stroked her hand down the distraught figure's robes to where something was written where the banner should be. Her fingers traced the letters carefully and a sad smile came to her face, for the words 'Seule une' were carved beneath it.

She closed her eyes and saw Warwick once again standing beside her as he watched her reading his love poem, heard his voice telling her she was his only one. She blinked away the tears and then moved back to the effigy. She bent close to him again.

'Adieu Richard,' she whispered.

Then she turned away and left him to his slumbers.

As she moved away from the tomb she saw Jack standing at Warwick's feet. His head was bowed in prayer. She moved to stand beside him and he turned to look at her. She saw the glint of tears in his eyes and the sight of them brought tightness to her throat again. She saw Jack's lips move and she wondered what he had promised him. She wondered if it was as demanding a vow as the one she had made silently to the Queen of Heaven at the altar.

'Adieu, my lord,' Jack said more loudly and then turned away from her.

She saw him cuff his eyes, as he began to walk towards the door and she knew that the carving had been his last deed for his lord.

Elizabeth didn't follow him immediately. She stood in the nave amongst the ghosts of Warwick's kin and tried to absorb the succour that they offered her. Then, when her mind was numb and her eyes began to sting again, she headed slowly for the light and the living.

When she reached the doorway Jack was already standing with the horses, one hand ruffling his courser's mane.

When she approached him he smiled thinly, and she saw it did nothing to lift the grief from his eyes.

'Sweetheart,' he said, offering her his hand.

Elizabeth took it gently and tightening her fingers around his, allowed him to lead her to her horse.

'Thank you, Jack,' she said huskily. 'I know what you did,' she said.

Jack's eyes met hers, but he said nothing. He watched her as she climbed into her saddle and then he too mounted. 'To Yorkshire then,' he said.

She nodded. Of course he had understood her completely; why had she doubted him?

'You should stay,' she said.

Jack raised his brows and then smiled at her and Elizabeth knew there was no use arguing with him this time and she was glad that she didn't have to make this last journey alone.

* * *

An uneasy silence haunted their chamber. After Bruges it had seemed ridiculous not to spend the nights of their journey together but now, as she watched Jack chewing his thumb she wondered if it had been a mistake to do so. Was it not so very wrong of her to keep him close when she had rejected him time after time? Did not every hour she spent in his company only torture him further? She should have been stronger; should have

467

made him leave her after Bisham, but she had not done so and it was now past regret.

'Jack?'

He looked up at her and his pensive face broke into a soft smile. That beautiful smile. She saw the hurt in his dark eyes and knew she was the architect of it.

'I am sorry, Jack.' She wanted to ease the pain, but how could she?

He shook his head. 'Speak no more of it,' he said quickly.

Elizabeth looked down and sighed. How she hated seeing him like this, knowing that she was the cause of his pain. And wasn't that part of the reasoning behind her decision? Yes, she would hopefully come to terms with her grief and perhaps, in time, find some peace in the world, but wasn't it also so that she would stop hurting Jack?

'You know he is out there,' Jack said. 'I will not let you go alone. Do not argue with me, sweetheart, it is pointless.'

She looked at him again and gave him a thin smile. She knew it was an argument she would not win and she knew he had only spoken a half-truth; she knew he still harboured a futile hope that she would change her mind.

He rose slowly and came to sit beside her. He smiled again and took her hand in his. 'I will wait forever, sweetheart,' he said. And Elizabeth knew it was true; he had waited ten years already, what was another week or so in that long sojourn?

'I am not worthy of such devotion, Jack,' she said, meeting his gaze. 'I only bring you pain.'

Jack shook his head. 'That is for me, not you, to judge,' he answered as he caressed the ring on her finger. He paused a moment and then smiled ruefully. 'And you know I am always right!'

YORKSHIRE JUNE 1471

The days of their journey were no more comfortable than the nights for Elizabeth. Jack said little and Elizabeth thought she would prefer it if he ranted at her rather than brood upon her decision in silence. Time after time she looked towards him, watched him as he rode beside her and he, unknowing, stared ahead at the road as though it were the most fascinating thing he had ever seen. She saw the grief in his eyes and knew for the most part she was the cause of it. But she had made a vow; a vow

468

she must uphold. Jack, she knew, had once made such a vow, to place his father's sword above his tomb even though it almost cost him his life to do so; surely he understood that this was a vow she must also keep?

He looked across at her and smiled thinly. 'It will be dark soon,' he said. 'There's a village through the trees. We should stay there tonight.' He glanced round quickly as if he expected to see someone behind them and Elizabeth shuddered. There could only be one man who would follow them so far.

The cottage they were given was small but clean enough and as there was no inn as such in the village it was the best they could do. A woman brought them food and ale and then bid them good night and Elizabeth let out a long sigh as the woman closed the door and left them in peace.

Jack sat quietly fingering the handle of his ale mug and staring into nothingness. Sadness flooded Elizabeth's heart; how she longed for the Jack she had known in Bruges; bright, confident, infuriating Jack!

'How much further?' she asked him.

He flicked his gaze to her. 'How much longer before you leave me?' he asked. 'Two days, three at the most.'

Elizabeth let out a long breath at the anger and hurt in his voice. 'Jack, you know I must do this.'

Jack sat up straight. 'I know why you must go there, yes,' he said, 'but why you would want to stay I cannot for one moment imagine!' His eyes were cold black flame. 'Life is for living, Elizabeth, if you remain there you may as well be dead!'

She met his fierce look and he looked away from her. 'Please Jack,' she said softly. It was a plea for understanding; it was a plea for peace between them, for in truth that was what she wanted most: peace.

The heavy silence fell between them again and Elizabeth knew the hardest part of this journey was yet to come. Jack returned his attention to his ale and Elizabeth continued to watch him as he did so, but just as when she had left Warwick on the morning of Barnet, she knew words would add nothing to what had already passed between them.

Jack looked up suddenly. Footsteps? He let go of his mug and then drew his knife smoothly.

'What is it?' Elizabeth asked, alarm in her voice.

Jack placed a finger to his lips.

The sound outside their lodging place had been almost imperceptible, but his senses, honed to perfection, caught it as if it were a thunderclap. He stepped away from Elizabeth, pushing her gently towards the farthest corner of the room. She did not argue with him and he was thankful for her trust. But he felt her fear and it heightened his own sense of purpose; if he failed, he failed them both.

His eyes were wide, the pupils dilated as if with lust, keen to catch the faintest movement. His lips pursed in concentration and his nostrils flared, controlling his breathing and hammering heart. He blew out the candle, plunging the room into a tense darkness; the ghostly trail of smoke and the pungent sniff of hot wax the only signs that it had ever been lit. He edged towards the doorway, stepping as if the floor was made of precious glass.

There was the sound again and this time there was a definite twitch at the latch. Jack slipped into the lea of the door and waited for it to open. He raised his knife and held out his other hand in front of him, ready to grasp the intruder.

Boots scuffed on the lintel outside and there was a soft click as the intruder tried to suppress the sound of the latch as he raised it.

Jack inhaled deeply, readying himself mentally for the strike that would end a life.

The door began to move. The hinges gave a soft moan of resistance as the door swung slowly inwards.

Jack heard a gasp; Elizabeth could see the intruder silhouetted in the doorway and with the bright moonlight flooding in, he could evidently see her. And from the look on her face, Jack knew he had been right.

Jack willed her not to panic, but he did not turn his eyes away from the place he knew the man stood. If he just moved a little further then he would be beyond the door's protection and Jack could use it to seal in the man's fate like a tombstone.

'Mistress Hardacre,' the intruder's voice lisped. 'You look surprised! You should have known I would come.' Higgins gave an unmistakeable throaty wheeze.

Jack prayed Elizabeth would not look at him; would not give him away.

'Laverton has grown careless since Bruges,' Higgins sneered.

There was a pause and Jack heard Elizabeth breathing quickly, trying to summon the strength to speak.

'Be careful, sweetheart,' he urged her under his breath.

'He will be back any moment,' Elizabeth said. Jack heard her voice quiver at the lie, but then he heard her draw herself up defiantly. 'And then you will be sorry you came!'

Higgins laughed. 'Laverton will do nothing to me, Elizabeth,' he lisped, 'for you will be my shield; he would not want to hurt you again.'

'He will kill you,' Elizabeth said evenly. 'You know that he will.'

Jack smiled at her confidence in him.

'He thought he had killed me once before,' Higgins said scathingly. 'But as others have found, I am not so easy to kill!'

'Go now,' Elizabeth said sternly. 'You can want nothing of me, Master Higgins. Warwick is dead as you wanted, your king has won his crown; I can be of no further use to you.'

'I have come to take you home, Elizabeth. You belong with Matthew not this whoreson gypsy, Laverton!' Higgins snarled.

Jack's blood burned in his cheeks at the insult and his grip tightened on his knife, making his wrist ache. But he fought his anger; controlled it. He had to be the master of his emotions if he was to strike cleanly. He adjusted his grip on his knife and willed Higgins to take one more step.

'You have no right to judge Jack!' Elizabeth snapped. 'And Matthew...' she made a disgusted sound in her throat.

Jack smiled at her courage.

'*Jack* is it now?' Higgins growled. 'I remember a time when you hated him more than anyone on God's earth, but you seem to have forgotten. Is that what happened in Bruges, Elizabeth? Were you his whore?'

Elizabeth gasped.

Jack fought not to give voice to his anger. Higgins would pay for that!

'You have no right to judge me either!' Elizabeth said indignantly.

'Don't I? When your father died I undertook to stand in his stead. That is what I'm doing now, for you evidently need a father's guidance!'

'No one asked for your intervention!' Elizabeth hissed.

'But if it was not for me you would still be at Ellerton Nunnery!' His voice was as harsh as a crow's.

'How dare you!' she cried, taking a step closer to Higgins. 'You had no right to keep my child's death from me! What kind of father would do that?'

Jack's heart punched at her distress.

Higgins shuffled uncomfortably. 'I sought to protect you from that pain, Elizabeth,' he said more gently. 'I know what it is to lose a child; that is why I will not lose you again. Come, Elizabeth, Matthew is waiting. You will go back to Scarsdale where you belong.'

'No!' Elizabeth snapped.

'I need to know you are safe and know that you are provided for.' Higgins sounded almost pleading.

'It has nothing to do with you,' Elizabeth hissed. 'Leave me alone! I will not come with you!'

'Then I will have to come and get you,' Higgins barked.

He took a step towards Elizabeth and that was all Jack needed.

Swift as prayer he kicked the door closed.

Higgins turned at the sound.

Jack grabbed the front of his cloak before flicking the blade savagely across his thin white throat. A narrow red line appeared and then hot liquid ran onto Jack's hand.

Behind him Elizabeth screamed, but Jack ignored her as he forced Higgins to his knees.

'You bastard!' Jack hissed through clenched teeth as he punched him with the dagger hilt. There was the sound of crunching bone.

Higgins reeled backwards and there was a clatter as his knife fell from his grasp. His hands clawed wildly at the ever-widening gap in his throat. His eyes bulged from his head.

Jack pushed Higgins down further. His lip curled into a snarl of hate. Christ how he wanted to hurt him for what he had said and done to Elizabeth and if she had not been here how much further would he have gone? For her sake he tightened his self-control. Breathing deeply, he looked down at the struggling man at his feet.

Higgins's throat lay open now, pumping his lifeblood into pools the colour of wine. His clothes were wet and his face was a pallid mask. He looked up at Jack, his thin lips quivering in a silent appeal for mercy; mercy Jack knew would never come; there was no remedy for the blow Jack had dealt him.

Pity suddenly gripped Jack; this was such a sad end to a human life, even one as twisted as Higgins's had been; for how many years had he hated Jack! But somehow that no longer mattered. Slowly Jack knelt beside Higgins; no one should die alone, he thought.

He could hear Elizabeth crying behind him.

He murmured a prayer, but he knew that Higgins was going to die unshriven and unloved and he shivered at the thought.

He heard the whisper of Elizabeth's feet on the floor as she came closer.

'Higgins, you fool. Why couldn't you leave us alone?' Jack whispered. 'It didn't have to be like this.'

Higgins spluttered.

Jack helped him to sit up.

'He blamed you for his torture,' Elizabeth said in a tremulous voice.

'He hated me long before that!' Jack said. 'Ever since we first met at Towton.'

'Towton?' Elizabeth asked.

Jack nodded. 'But it didn't need to end like this,' he said.

'He blamed you and he blamed Warwick for what happened to him,' Elizabeth said.

'Warwick knew nothing of France, nothing of his return, but I did. I thought he deserved something for all he'd suffered and Sir Robert understood...'

Higgins fixed his eyes on Elizabeth and struggled to sit up further, but he slumped back heavily against Jack. His eyes fluttered and Jack could see that he was close to losing consciousness.

Jack turned to look at Elizabeth. Her pale cheeks were wet with tears. She was fighting to hold in her emotions but she met Jack's look without judgement. 'She understands,' Jack said softly, 'and I promise I shall see her safe.'

Higgins eyes closed slowly and he gave a deep sigh.

Jack laid him down gently and said an Ave as he did so. He paused a moment by Higgins's side as he contemplated his passing into a better world. Then, shaking his head sadly, he stood up. He turned to face Elizabeth. She was shaking; one hand was raised to her mouth, trying to stifle the sobs. Jack held out his arms and she ran to him. He hugged her fiercely. He never wanted her to be hurt or frightened again.

'Jack!' she sobbed.

'Hush, sweetheart,' he whispered. 'It is over.'

'But he...it was so awful...there was so much blood!'

'He left me no choice, sweetheart...' He knew that was the truth: Higgins had always hated Jack because of his gypsy blood.

Jack felt the rise and fall of Elizabeth's shoulders as she cried and he rocked her gently.

'I told him to go Jack, but he wouldn't listen...I told him you would kill him, but he just laughed...' Elizabeth said into his shoulder.

'Hush,' he murmured. ''Tis over.'

'He wouldn't listen...'

'I know, I know,' Jack said. 'He chose this road, sweetheart, not you or I.'

Elizabeth drew teary eyes up to his. 'Did he really have to die?'

Jack held her look. 'Would he ever have left us alone?' he asked.

She closed her eyes. She knew the answer as well as Jack did.

* * *

Dusted with bright stars like a jewel-covered gown, the sky shone like damask above their heads. Elizabeth noted how many more stars she could see here, away from the crackling firelight; some as bright as diamonds, others nothing more than shimmering dust in the deepest blue of heaven.

Jack had thought they would reach their destination tonight, but in the end they hadn't and so they were to spend their last night together in the wildness of Yorkshire with the spangled starlight for their roof.

Jack stirred beside her and she turned her gaze towards him. The bright moonlight kissed his hair, turning the glossy black curls to silken tangles she yearned to touch. She bit her lip. How easy it would be to touch him now. How easy, but how dangerous! And how unfair, when she knew what she must do tomorrow.

She watched his chest rise and fall with each breath; saw his long lashes flutter as he dreamed. Her breath caught in her throat. Chewing her lip savagely she turned her look away from him, her eyes stinging with tears.

Jack murmured in his sleep as if he understood her anguish and he nuzzled closer to her.

Elizabeth closed her eyes as the weight of his arm pressed upon her; hot tears squeezed between her lashes and ran down her cheeks.

She knew she could not be with him; she had to make sense of what had happened in her life; had to find her son and confess her sins, if her soul was not to spend millennia in purgatory. She hoped in time Jack would understand.

She sighed. She both craved the morning and wished it would never come. She brought her arm up to meet Jack's and ran her fingers over the back of his hand lightly. She touched the soft hairs of his forearm and was tempted for a moment to tug them to waken him. But she knew that if they became lovers she would not be able to do what she must; what she had promised the Virgin she would do at Bisham.

* * *

Ellerton Nunnery had not changed. The harsh stone seemed somehow incongruous in the lush landscape surrounding it; a stark symbol of God's omnipotence.

Jack had said nothing since breakfast and as they drew rein at the head of the valley he still gave no voice to his feelings.

Elizabeth looked across at him. Liquid eyes looked up from beneath saturnine brows. The look melted the marrow in Elizabeth's bones, for her own longing was no less intense. 'Jack, please,' she said through a tightening throat.

He shook his head. 'If what has passed between us does not stop you, then how can mere words or looks?' he asked.

Elizabeth looked down, studying her horse's mane as if it were a tapestry of silk. She closed her eyes and the lids prickled. She dug her fingernails into her palms and took a steadying breath. 'I made a vow,' she whispered.

Jack moved his horse closer to hers. He put his hand on her arm. 'Do not try to explain it to me, sweetheart,' he said. 'You do not have to shut yourself away like this!'

She looked up at him through burning tears and saw that his eyes were glassy too.

'If it causes you such pain, you should not go,' he said. 'We should be together.'

'No, Jack,' Elizabeth said. 'It cannot be. I need tranquillity; I need to make sense of things. For once I must do what is right!'

475

She kicked at her mare fiercely so that he could not see the tears flood onto her cheeks.

Jack caught up with her just before the gatehouse. He reached out and grabbed her horse's reins, tugging the animal to a sharp undignified halt.

'Elizabeth, I beg you, do not do this!'

Elizabeth met his wounded look and it almost broke her heart. 'I am sorry, Jack,' she said. 'I need to find my son! I need to be at peace!' How could she explain that she was heartsick of loss, of pain, of death? How could he understand that she had to find her son and assuage the pain of his and Warwick's loss? But did it really matter what her reasons were? How could Jack ever understand? Jack was a fighter, a survivor; hadn't he told her that? He would never shut himself away from the world – he would always meet it head on!

Jack studied her face for a long moment and then let his hand fall away from her horse. 'If it is what you truly wish sweetheart,' he murmured, 'then go.'

Elizabeth held his gaze for several painful heartbeats and then urged her mare towards the gatehouse.

Jack did not follow.

Her chest tightened as she rode away and it was all she could do not to cry out at the pain of it. How could she leave Jack after all they had been through together? Didn't he know her better than anyone? Hadn't her happiest moments been spent in his company? What if one day she could not recall the timbre of his voice or the curl of his black hair at his collar? Or the scent of him or the darkness of his beautiful eyes?

Elizabeth looked back at him, trying to capture him in her memory and saw once again the handsome knight she had loved at Lazenby. And wasn't that the truth of it? That she had loved Jack from the very beginning! Didn't she need him as she needed air to breathe? She slowed the mare.

The hesitation was all the invitation Jack needed. He spurred towards her.

'What a fool you must think me!' she said as he reached her.

Jack shook his head. 'No sweetheart, not for a moment.'

He leaned forward and catching her hand, raised it to his lips. His eyes were a mêlée of emotions, his face alight. 'I understand, sweetheart,' he said softly.

476

Elizabeth gazed at him for a moment. 'I think you always did,' she answered.

'Perhaps not always,' he said and then gave her a smile that almost stopped her heart.

Elizabeth laughed softly at the honesty of his words.

'Come,' she said as she laced her fingers into his, 'let us go in together.'

* * *

The Burgundian Chronicler, Phillippe de Commynes tells us that 'a lady of quality passed by Calais into France with letters for the Duchess of Clarence from King Edward.' He goes on to say: 'the secret affair to be managed by the lady was to solicit the Duke of Clarence not to contribute to the subversion of his own family, by endeavouring to restore the House of Lancaster... This lady managed the task with so much cunning and dexterity that she prevailed with the Duke of Clarence to the King's party...This lady was no fool nor blab of her tongue and being allowed the liberty of visiting her mistress the Duchess of Clarence she for that reason was employed for this secret, rather than a man.' We do not know who this lady was, but I have appointed this task to the fictional Elizabeth Hardacre as she had links with both the Duchess of Clarence and the Earl of Warwick and a considerable motive for action following her father's death at Middleham.

There is only the testimony of another contemporary, Prospero di Camulio, the Milanese Ambassador to France reporting to the Duke of Milan which supports the idea that Edouard of Lancaster was illegitimate. He stated that Henry VI had remarked that Edouard 'must be the Son of the Holy Spirit', damning evidence indeed one might think, especially as it had taken Marguerite eight years to conceive and Henry was shortly to descend into a bout of apoplexy that would last until long after the child was born. However Camulio added a note of caution that 'these words may only be the words of common fanatics' and his report was sent in March 1461, shortly after Edward IV's bloody victory at Towton and seven years after Edouard's birth! This leaves us with the likely source being the Yorkists, perhaps even Warwick himself and certainly it is something for which I felt he would need to atone in his reconciliation with Marguerite.

Illegitimacy and sexual slander are not unusual weapons at this time and Edward IV was also accused of being illegitimate. The earliest surviving reference to Edward IV being illegitimate was made by Warwick in 1469, and repeated by Clarence in 1478. Doubts often surrounded births in foreign lands and the theme of a queen seduced by a commoner was common in medieval litera-ture. In his book 'Psychology of a battle - Bosworth 1485' Dr Michael Jones added some interesting facts to what had always been supposed to simply be another rumour: firstly he uncovered a document in Rouen Cathedral which stated that the monks were paid to pray for the safety of the Duke of York on campaign at Pointuse. He noted the duke would have been on campaign from 14th July 1441 to 21st August, 1441, crucially including the period during which Edward would need to have been conceived to be born at full-term in April 1442. Of course Edward could have been born prematurely but this was not noted, and it often was, though it might explain why Edward's baptism was conducted in a small chapel (i.e. hurriedly) while his younger brother Edmund's baptism the following year was a grand affair in the cathedral with all due honours. Though this could have been a grand affair because the duke had much more to celebrate! Of course the duke could have made the few days' journey back to his duchess Cecily at Rouen at any time, but he is known to have been well respected by his men for fighting alongside them; his absence during such an important campaign, while not impossible, would have been noticed. Of course there was nothing to stop the duchess visiting him at Pointuse and that most likely would not have been recorded.

Dominic Mancini, an Italian visitor to London in the summer of 1483, states that Cecily Neville, may herself have started the story that Edward was a bastard. In 1464 when she found out that Edward had secretly married Elizabeth Wydeville, she 'fell into a frenzy' and in her rage, threatened to expose him before a public inquiry as illegitimate – a step which would have destroyed her own reputation. Such a row would have been well remembered by members of the family and household and although he apparently spoke little English, Mancini was well-connected at court and knew John Argentine, physician to Edward V.

None of this proves Edward IV was illegitimate but Dr Jones's evidence elevates the possibility. The Duke of York accepted Edward as his own, although I think he had little choice but to do so: the scandal would have been unthinkable. It is also interesting to note that when exiled from England the duke took his younger son, Edmund with him to Ireland while Edward went with Warwick to Calais. Some have thought it unusual not to keep his heir with him, but it may have been prudent not to have both father and heir in the same place in troubled times.

If Edward IV was illegitimate and his brothers knew it then it would go a long way to explaining their behavior. Clarence would see himself as the rightful King of England and Richard too would have a greater claim to the throne than Edward's sons following Edward's death.

While there is no direct evidence that Edward's sister, Margaret of York the Duchess of Burgundy was unfaithful to her husband Charles the Bold, they spent more time apart than together. Even though Charles had three wives he had only one daughter. Vaughan states there is some evidence that he was homosexual and that at a generous estimate in 1469-1470 Margaret and Charles were together only a quarter of the time, and less than that in 1471, Charles being quoted as saying he would rather have the council and finances about him than women. He threw himself into all kinds of martial pursuits, and it was said that his pastime was 'to go in the morning from room to room to organize justice, war, finance and other affairs.' It was said of Charles that he would 'rather arm himself six times over than write one letter' whereas Margaret was not only literate but a great lover of books. Given these facts I have made him disinterested in Margaret, and who could possibly resist the alluring Jack de Laverton? There has been recent speculation that if Margaret was interested in another man then that man would have been Anthony Wydeville as both shared a love of books and both were patrons of William Caxton. Margaret stayed briefly with Anthony on a visit to England in 1480.

There are a number of reasons why John Neville did not attack Edward during his daring and improbable ride south. The loss of the Earldom of Northumberland had no doubt affected John Neville; it had been the culmination of all the feuding he had entered into during his youth and represented the triumph of the Nevilles over the Percys and Edward had undone it all; as Prof. Pollard says in his North-Eastern England during the Wars of the Roses: 'It is hardly surprising that the leaders of local society bore him no love. They had not done so since 1453...and as recently as 1469 he had, with his customary ruthlessness, suppressed pro-Percy rebellion in the district.' Too well they also remembered the rout and executions after Hexham - all at John Neville's hands. So understandably they would not rally to his call now; but more than that, if Percy's men were armed, John risked the possibility of their attacking him! If John attacked Edward, it was not beyond the realms of possibility that Percy would come at his back! In the end Northumberland's inaction - his sitting still - caused all those in the north parts to sit still, including those from Richmondshire who were of Neville persuasion - Northumberland's inaction was therefore a double service to Edward, for it prevented these men from joining Warwick on the field at Barnet!

There are many written interpretations for the Battle of Barnet - some have the armies aligned east-west and others north-south. Sources also vary as to the size of the forces present but Warwick probably commanded between 13,000 and 15,000 men while Edward had between 10,000 and 13,000 men. After all Warwick's machinations, it came down to a slugging match in the fog!

I have taken a controversial stance though it is the official view of the Barnet Museum. Fiona Jones writes that it isn't the experienced soldier and commander Will Hastings who loses his line to the rampaging Earl of Oxford and the mis-aligned battles, it's a young man in his first battle command - Richard Duke of Gloucester. As Jones says *The Great Chronicle of London states that Oxford routed Gloucester and the Arrivall says the Lancastrian right wing routed the Yorkist left wing. There is no other contemporary evidence for other Yorkist deployments."* This also fits with Edward then keeping the same successful battle order for Tewkesbury where we know Hastings was on the right and Gloucester on the left. Read almost any book on the Battle of Barnet and Tewkesbury and it has Hastings being routed on the left and then Edward switching the battles round for Tewkesbury, which never made sense to me. I think Edward stuck with the winning battle line-up from Barnet and so does Barnet Museum.

Warwick's death is recorded only briefly in 'The Arrivall' in which it states Warwick was: '...killed somewhat fleinge....' Warkworth has him 'lept a horse-backe and flede to a wode...where was no waye forthe'.

481

As Martin Reboul points out, later historians have embellished these words considerably: Hubert Cole states: 'He tried to get to his horse... was overtaken... turned and fought off his assailants... staggered on, wounded... overpowered as he reached his mount and killed...' And Paul Murray Kendall says: 'He grabbed the bridle, but ... was dragged down... visor levered up... knifed in the throat...' And P. W. Hammond: 'It seems he reached his horse, but became entangled in Wrotham Wood.... overtaken by pursuers and slain...'

But he wasn't.

In a private letter, to her mother-in-law, Margaret, Duchess of Burgundy states that Warwick was captured at the end of the battle, and was being taken to Edward when 'some men recognised him and killed him'. There would be no reason for her to fabricate this, nor for the Yorkists to admit to it if it didn't happen, for it does not show them in a good light - hence its omission from 'The Arrivall'.

It could be that Edward simply ordered Warwick's death, but I have given him the benefit of the doubt; just as with the death of Henry VI, though he must have wished for it, we do not know he ordered it ('The Arrivall' says he died of displeasure and melancholy; Warkworth that he was 'put to death') and he wasn't present for the sentencing of his brother Clarence's execution - conveniently being out of the chamber when the final decision was made!

So who else would want him dead?

Perhaps the most obvious candidate is George, Duke of Clarence, husband of Warwick's eldest daughter Isabel. What better way to confirm his rehabilitation than to solve this particular problem for his brother the king? There was of course the added bonus that if Warwick was dead then his estates would be forfeit and Clarence would be the main beneficiary (at the expense of the Countess of Warwick). A large gold finger ring, probably Warwick's signet ring allegedly taken from Warwick's body, is now in the Liverpool Museum. It is engraved with the bear and ragged staff, and Warwick's motto 'Soulement Une'. Of course it may not have been on his finger that day, but it certainly would not have been too far away. It's proposed journey to Liverpool via the Royal family suggests their involvement in Warwick's death and that the accepted version of Warwick's death is not the whole story. I have used the ring to link Clarence with the deed and tie up the story arc of Elizabeth's delivery of Edward's letters at the start of the book.

Warwick and his brother John were buried at the family mausoleum of Bisham Abbey. According to Michael Hicks Warwick wanted to be buried at St Mary's, Warwick, perhaps in a tomb similar to the one he saw created for his father-in-law, Richard Beauchamp. This is another indication of how much he identified with the Warwick legend. Although we know that there was a tomb effigy for his father Salisbury, it is unlikely that there was one for Warwick and as Bisham was demolished and the tombs desecrated during the dissolution of the monasteries it is unlikely that we shall ever know where his bones now lie. Let us hope he finally knows the peace he never knew in life.

The seeking of sanctuary was not uncommon throughout the Wars of the Roses and although the right had been introduced around 600AD the situation was often unclear, for whereas all churches could offer sanctuary to common felons, fewer were licensed to give sanctuary to political refugees and unfortunately for the routed Lancastrians, Tewkesbury Abbey was not one of them. Whereas Warwick had acted magnanimously towards Elizabeth Wydeville (and other refugees) when they entered sanctuary in 1470, Edward did not return the favour: the Lancastrians were removed and executed. The Tewkesbury Abbey Chronicle states that the church was closed and had to be rededicated, suggesting that sacrilege had taken place within its confines in the aftermath of the battle.

In a sense it was not the victories at Barnet and Tewkesbury that brought Edward peace, but the death of Warwick. It is difficult now to imagine the impact he had on the age; there is no modern equivalent. As Prof Pollard says: 'For twelve years he was the arbiter of English politics, not hesitating to set up and put down kings.' Had he escaped death at Barnet who knows what he might have achieved for the Lancastrians? It is unlikely that his peace with Marguerite could have lasted however; sooner or later there would have been something on which they could not agree and Warwick, never a team player unless he was team captain, would have felt the need to state his position more strongly than the Lancastrians would allow. And yet ultimately he got what he truly wished for, though it did not unfold as he had planned it, nor become the lasting dynasty he dreamed of: a crown for the Nevilles and a place in history as the greatest Earl of Warwick: 'the Kingmaker'.

Castor, H., Blood & Roses: The Paston Family and the Wars of the Roses (London, Faber and Faber, 2004).

Clark, D., Barnet 1471 - Death of a Kingmaker (Barnsley, Pen and Sword, 2007).

Dockray, K., Edward IV: A Sourcebook (Gloucester, Alan Sutton Publishing, 1999).

Dockray, K., Henry VI, Margaret of Anjou and the Wars of the Roses, (Gloucester, Alan Sutton Publishing, 1999)

Gravett, C., Tewkesbury 1471: The last Yorkist Victory, (Oxford, Osprey Campaign, 2003).

Hicks, M., The Wars of the Roses (London, Yale University Press, 2010).

Hicks, M., Warwick the Kingmaker (London, Blackwell Publishing, 1998).

Jones, M. K., Bosworth 1485: The Psychology of a Battle (Stroud, The History Press, 2003).

Laynesmith J.L., The Last Medieval Queens: English Queenship 1445-1503 (Oxford, Oxford University Press, 2004).

Jones, F., The Battle of Barnet (Barnet and District Local History Society, 2005).

Philips, K. M., Medieval Maidens: Young women and gender in England 1270-1540 (Manchester, Manchester University Press, 2003).

Pollard A.J., North-Eastern England during the Wars of the Roses: Lay Society, War and Politics 1450-1500 (Oxford, Clarendon Press, 1990).

Pollard A.J., The North of England in the age of Richard III

(New York, St Martin's Press, 1996).

Pollard A.J., Warwick the Kingmaker Politics, Power and Fame (London, Hambledown Continuum, 2007).

Reboul, M., The Battle of Barnet
http://www.r3.org/bookcase/texts/reboul_barnet.html

Vaughan, R., Charles the Bold (Woodbridge, The Boydell Press 2002).

Weightman, C., Margaret of York Duchess of Burgundy 1446-1503 (Gloucester, Alan Sutton Publishing 1989).

~ACKNOWLEDGEMENTS~

Grateful thanks as always to my family for sharing our lives with the characters of the Wars of the Roses and for their unwavering support and belief.

Thanks also to the members of Towton Battlefield Society and the Frei Compagnie and to members of the Wars of the Roses Federation for their knowledge, time and patience with my continual questioning.

And finally to the members of The Frivolous Quill writing group for their advice, encouragement and proofreading.

www.smharrisonwriter.com

Printed in Great Britain
by Amazon.co.uk, Ltd.,
Marston Gate.